The Current That Carries

The Current

FLANNERY
O'CONNOR
AWARD
FOR
SHORT
FICTION

Nancy Zafris,
Series Editor

That Carries

STORIES BY **LISA GRALEY**

THE UNIVERSITY OF GEORGIA PRESS ATHENS

© 2016 by the University of Georgia Press
Athens, Georgia 30602
www.ugapress.org
All rights reserved
Designed by Kaelin Chappell Broaddus
Set in 10.5/13 Arno Pro Regular by Kaelin Chappell Broaddus
Printed and bound by Sheridan Books, Inc.
The paper in this book meets the guidelines for permanence
and durability of the Committee on Production Guidelines
for Book Longevity of the Council on Library Resources.

Most University of Georgia Press titles are
available from popular e-book vendors.

Printed in the United States of America
20 19 18 17 16 C 5 4 3 2 1

Library of Congress Cataloging-in-Publication Data

Names: Graley, Lisa, author.
Title: The current that carries : stories / by Lisa Graley.
Description: First edition. | Athens : The University of Georgia Press, 2016.
Identifiers: LCCN 2015047529| ISBN 9780820349879 (hardcover : acid-free paper) |
    ISBN 9780820349886 (ebook)
Classification: LCC PS3607. R3495 A6 2016 | DDC 813/.6—dc23
LC record available at http://lccn.loc.gov/2015047529

For my mother and father and brother

and in memory of

Esther Eleanor Lovejoy

$(1924-2010)$

as form in sculpture is the prisoner
of the hard rock, so in everyday life
it is the plain facts and natural happenings
that conceal God and reveal him to us
little by little under the mind's tooling.

—R. S. THOMAS, "Emerging"

CONTENTS

ACKNOWLEDGMENTS

From my earliest years, I have loved stories. I'm grateful to my mother, Joyce, for wonder-filled library books in the summers of my youth and to my father, Paul; my cousin, Elaine; and a host of other relatives who have always been in the habit of telling and listening to stories on front porches. I recognize with love, as well, my brother, Michael, whose constant camaraderie lent itself to our rich, imaginative childhood together. I appreciate the love still kindled on the home place.

A special thanks goes to Harold Edwards from McCorkle Elementary, and Pauline Rymer (now deceased), Betty Prunty, and Julian Martin, from Duval High School, teachers who introduced me to literature and whose nonjudgmental acceptance of marginalized people still matters to me.

Additionally, I'd like to thank Marshall University professors Rainey and David Duke, who acquainted me with the likes of Ivan Ilych, Gregor Samsa, Anne Moody, and Julius and Ethel Rosenberg, characters and people to whom I still give considerable thought.

Beyond this, I'm indebted to graduate mentors Robert Olen Butler, John and Carol Wood, Darrell Bourque, Marcia Gaudet, and especially Mary Ann Wilson for their instruction and continuing guidance and friendship. As well, I cherish the friends who have been readers of my stories and tellers of stories themselves, among them Maryclaire, Joe, and Jeff from newspapering days; fellow writers from McNeese State Univer-

sity: Pam, Neil, Amy, Tacey, Ron, Kay, Dave, Nadine, Adam, Mike, Steve, and Celeste; and colleagues from the University of Louisiana at Lafayette: Christine, Elizabeth, Jennifer, Lydia, Monica, Randy, Yung-Hsing, Susan, Jenny, Kathy, Felicia, Ian, as well as other colorful souls in Griffin Hall and on the UL–Lafayette campus. For the fellowship of all these people, I am heartily grateful.

To my entire Lafayette family, Lisa and Mark, and most of all Taylor —whose big-sky love and big-sky faith hourly light my vision—I express my thanks for refuge, sustenance, and companionship, as well as my love for their *being*.

For giving me the time to write and shore up stories in this collection, I extend my gratitude to the Louisiana Board of Regents for an ATLAS (Awards to Louisiana Artists and Scholars) sabbatical. It made an inestimable difference. Here I make mention, too, of my abiding esteem for the Friends of the Humanities in Lafayette for their enthusiastic support of literature and the other arts.

Finally, I give a heartfelt nod of thanks to Nancy Zafris, series editor of the Flannery O'Connor Award; the folks at the University of Georgia Press for their professionalism and kindness; and Barbara Wojhoski for her meticulous copyediting.

Several stories here have appeared in literary journals including "Crossing with Sassafras" and "Vandalism" in *Glimmer Train Stories*, "Feeding Instructions" in the *McNeese Review*, and "The Sorrows You Can't Enter" in the *Georgia Review*. To the editors of these journals, I am certainly appreciative.

The Current That Carries

VANDALISM

They were at it again. You could hear them way up at Ray Marker's. First there was a loud, ear-splitting crack—sharp lightning to a tree—then the reverberation of aluminum, like someone slamming the lid of a washing machine. You could almost feel the bat vibrating in your hands.

Denzil sat in his underwear on the edge of the bed with his shotgun. He hadn't held it in years, and it was heavier than he remembered. Olive would not have approved—no matter how many mailboxes he'd had to replace. Up the road, he could hear the engine goosed, then slowed, then goosed again. He stepped to the window and parted the curtain. Through the brush and trees, he could see the headlights as the car picked its way from one house to the next.

From his bedroom he tiptoed to the front door. There was no reason to be quiet, but Denzil was quiet out of habit. He turned the deadbolt gently, opened the door, and slipped out onto the porch. Tiger Boots squeezed out behind him. There was a chill in the air he hadn't expected, and a large harvest moon waxed in the southwest sky. He kept forgetting it was October, past time to gather firewood for the porch. Lately, his impulse to stock up and maintain had lost its urgency. There comes a time when you want only to sit on your porch, he told Glenn Turley. You want to think over the things you've done or haven't done—not the things you're planning to do. The car sped closer and closer, and as it rounded the curve, it swerved toward Glenn's driveway.

Denzil was late with his shot—it was drowned out by the solid whack of the bat and Glenn's mailbox scuttling on the road—like someone dragging a muffler. Denzil aimed again, for the passenger window, and stayed the course as the driver gassed the car and lurched toward his own mailbox. If they could feel the spray, Glenn had said, maybe they would stop. Denzil let out his breath, eased the trigger, held the gun steady, and braced for the kick. He felt the cat going around his legs.

Luck was with him, and he heard the scattering of rice on the windshield and the side of the car, then a screech of locked rubber on the pavement. The car skidded into the post of his mailbox—he heard the splintering of wood and winced. Last time he'd just had to replace the box. Don't let them, don't let them—he was thinking—slide on over into the creek. But even as he wished against it, he watched it happen, the rear end of the car sliding around first, then going down, so that the front end, when it was over, pointed straight up the bank toward the sky.

"Daggone it," he said under his breath. "Daggone teenage drivers." It didn't take much to put them in a tailspin. He imagined three or four sweaty seventeen-year-olds on his couch later, wringing their hands, while he called their fathers—if there were fathers. The kids would make the kinds of vows you always make under pressure, the kind he himself had made in their shoes back when tipping outhouses was the mischief your father sat you down for.

Suddenly, the dome light came on in the vehicle, and Denzil heard the radio, something with a bass line that jarred the porch floor under his sock-footed feet.

He took his gun and went inside, Tiger following. He dialed Glenn's number.

"You all asleep?" Denzil asked.

"How do you sleep through that?" Glenn asked.

"They're down in my creek."

"Oh, brother," Glenn said. "Turned over?"

"No. Right side up. Probably busted something underneath though."

"I'd like to bust something," Glenn said.

Denzil heard Dorothy's voice in the background. "What's she saying?" he asked.

"She says I'm liable to bust something I don't want, if I'm not careful."

Denzil laughed. "She may be right."

"What we need?"

"Winch, I guess."

"I'll bring my jeep," Glenn said. "Hey?"

"What?"

"Try and scare them till I get there."

"I'll try." Denzil could hear Dorothy's voice in the background, and he put down the receiver gently. Tiger was on the couch now. She had worked her head under his hand, while he peeked out the window. No one had gotten out yet. He hoped the wreck had done the job of scaring them—and that he would be left only with the task of consoling.

He turned on a lamp in the living room to let them know someone was awake and then went back to the bedroom for his pants and boots. Tiger followed him room to room.

"It's not morning yet, kitty," he said. "I'm not feeding you." In the kitchen he turned on the light. His cereal bowl from the evening was still on the table. It wasn't that he couldn't cook, he'd told his daughter Missy, just that he didn't want to. Why make extra work?

From the cabinet over the refrigerator, he pulled out a couple of six-volt lanterns, nearly tripping over the cat. "You been up on the table?" he asked, but the cat went around his legs, avoiding the question. "I said I'm not feeding you."

When he stepped back onto the dark porch, the cat followed. "Stay and guard the place," he whispered, scratching once under her chin. He heard them down in the creek trying the engine. It sounded like the intermittent coughing of a sick goat, something wedged in its throat. Maybe the engine was flooded.

On the top step, Denzil paused, wondering if he should take his shotgun, but an empty gun, he knew, was worse than no gun. Climbing down the steps, he felt autumn in his knees and ankles. Out from under the roof, the air was crisp—crinkly. He filled his lungs and smelled the leaves on the lawn and then wood smoke, too, someone burning the first fire of the season. It was the first year he didn't have anyone to burn for.

Down through the yard, he let the moon guide him. It was bright enough to cast his shadow. They were just boys looking for fun, he knew. On Fridays, the week loosened, it unwound itself. That was just the way

of it. He remembered how it felt. You had an energy, looked around for a place to put it after bottled-up days of school or even work. It was why his father always started planting or plowing up potatoes on Friday evenings. House painting. Bridge building. Bringing in the hay. Ditch digging. Anything to keep him home.

Down on the road, Denzil felt more strongly the vibration of the car's radio. The bass got mixed in crazy with his heartbeat, made a kind of pulse in his head. With his thumb, he clicked on a flashlight mid-swing, shone it toward the car. It was a ninety-one or ninety-two Camaro. Would be hard to pull out without tearing something more, the way these cars hugged so close to the ground. Already, he was sure, Mr. Louisville Slugger was bobbing his way down the creek. And probably a case or two of beer had been thrown over, too.

The voices in the car were arguing. "Shut up and get out."

"I ain't getting wet," someone said. "It's your friggin' car."

The car was at a steep angle. Denzil shone the light in the driver's eyes. "You boys okay?" he asked. The driver's pupils were large—as he had known they would be—even with the light. But he was young, younger than Denzil expected. Denzil smelled beer, maybe something else in the air, he wasn't sure what. It was strong, though, and his mind flashed to the craft room at vacation Bible school. Maybe he'd helped some of these boys when they were little. Denzil saw there were four of them. Lying back in their seats, facing the sky, they looked like astronauts in the cockpit ready for blast-off.

"We're okay," the driver said. He was normal-looking enough. Clean-cut hair—kind of wet-glistening, light-colored, sticking straight up like new grass sprouts. Just one earring, a tiny one. The boy on the passenger side leaned over and turned off the radio. Denzil shone the light to all their faces. One boy in the back had blood on his face, probably from getting thrown against the seat when they crashed.

"You all right?" Denzil asked, holding the flashlight on him.

"I don't know. I think my nose is broken."

Denzil recognized his grandson's voice—even nasally—before Elliot's face registered through the blood. A zigzag tremor ran from Denzil's head to his heart, triggering a string of questions whose ends were cut off by the beginnings of other questions. He felt the kind of disorienta-

tion you feel when a dish from the kitchen winds up in the toolshed. He clenched the flashlight tighter, wondered what he ought to say. But Elliot covered his face with his hands and turned his eyes away.

"He's all right," the boy at the passenger door said. Denzil shone the light back to that boy. He was probably the bat boy but wasn't as big as Denzil had imagined. Maybe that was the cause of it all, that he was a squirt and needed to prove something. His hair was short except in the front where his long bangs came down and curled away from his eyes like a ski jump you'd see in the Olympics. He had the beginnings of a mustache and a little patch of felt under his bottom lip.

Denzil saw how it was. Elliot had been given the least desirable seat, back of the bat boy where he was most likely to get clobbered by the ricocheting bat. Maybe that was how he got his nose busted.

"Your parents know where you are?" Denzil asked again, directing the light back to Elliot, whose face was still in his hands. Missy had said there was some kind of trouble with Elliot. His grades had dropped. He was staying late at school for a lot of art projects.

"I got projects," Denzil told her. "Send him over."

"You come and get him," she said. "I can't twist his arm."

Denzil hadn't known what to say to that. No time before had anyone had to twist the arms of his grandsons for them to visit.

"He's tired of being in his brother's shadow," Missy continued. "He quit the football team."

"He's not one to push—not like Danny," Denzil remembered saying. "He's tenderhearted. Like his grandmother."

"Not just his grandmother," Missy had said.

For a moment, no one spoke. Then the driver said, "Maybe you can help us get out of the creek?"

"What? Now you go'll make an old man push?" the one in back with Elliot asked. His head was shaved bald.

Denzil stepped back from the car. He shone the flashlight all along the bottom of the car. "I dunno. Looks pretty bad. I guess you better go sit on my porch. Let me call a wrecker."

"No, man. No wrecker. Are you out of your mind?" The driver opened his door. He had to push hard against gravity and the weight of it. "We can get it out ourselves."

"You can try," Denzil said. He watched the driver squeeze out like he was releasing himself from a spring-lock trap.

The driver looked back inside. "Get out, you bunch of morons," he said.

"I told you my door's jammed," the bat boy said.

"Get out on my side," the driver said. He strained to hold the door open for them. There was a rocking of the car, and one by one, the boys climbed out and made their way up the bank onto the pavement. They had on baggy jeans. The boy in back with Elliot had green tattoos on his arms—snakes or something with long tails. All the boys were scrawny. Not the bruisers Denzil had imagined. In their too-big pants, they reminded him of cornstalk scarecrows, the kind Olive made for the porch at Halloween when the boys were little. Elliot, with his promising big feet, was the runt of them all. That was what happened when you took kids away from farming. No wrestling with heavy bales of hay, no buttermilk, no biscuits.

"Oh, wow," the bald one said. "That was some ride. Some ride. I mean friggin' Camden Park. My heart feels like it's going to come out of my chest."

"I think I'm going to be sick," Elliot said. He bent over and vomited on the pavement. Denzil felt sick, too, a heartburn that radiated out to his fingertips.

Elliot wiped his face on the sleeve of his T-shirt.

"Maybe you better come inside, let me see about your nose in good light," Denzil offered. "I used to drive for the VFD."

"I'm all right," Elliot said.

"I think you're supposed to put your head back to make the bleeding stop," Denzil said.

"What do you know about it?" Elliot asked.

And then Denzil saw how he was supposed to play it.

"Come on," the driver said. He led the boys down over the bank toward the rear of the car. Elliot went with them. Denzil heard a splash. "Shit," one of them said.

"Quit crying, candy-ass," someone else said.

When Denzil was their age, not many boys talked like that. You weren't raised that way. He guessed they did it to impress each other. It was hard to get used to, but maybe TV made it easier. He moved down

the bank sideways, getting his footing carefully, and held the flashlight for them. He had heard of people, in wrecks, having superhuman strength. He watched now to see if it would be true of these skinny boys. The bank was steep. The car was nearly straight up and down.

"Don't let it tip back over on you," he yelled down. He listened to their straining and groaning. Good for them to work out some adrenalin. He hadn't planned on them being so quarrelsome. He looked up into the woods for Glenn's headlights but saw no sign of him. It was too late for anyone else to be out.

Denzil held the lantern, flicking it occasionally from one boy to the next. Without better light, he couldn't tell if any of them, besides Elliot, was worth saving. It was hard to tell a boy gone bad from one who was just learning his way. If he could detect a preference for any one of them on Elliot's part, he decided in the darkness, he'd do his best to help them both.

"Don't you have a tractor or something?" the driver yelled up at him. "You could pull us out."

"Well, I dunno," Denzil said. "Looks like you're wedged in pretty tight."

The driver stepped out of the water and climbed part way up the bank. He opened the car door, squeezed himself in, fumbled around, then brought out a lit cigarette. "Let's take a break," he yelled to the others. He came up the bank to where Denzil was standing.

"Look here," Denzil said, leading him to the front of the car. "Looks like you're hooked on my mailbox post for one thing."

"Like a friggin' fish," the driver said. He sucked deep on his cigarette, held the smoke. Denzil shone the lantern for the boys climbing up the bank. Their wet shoes squished on the pavement. Elliot was not with them. Denzil heard him vomiting again, down in the creek. He wondered if he would remember catching minnows there with Daniel. Or floating wooden boats Denzil had helped them build when the water was high. The boys would chase them with sticks from one end of the creek to the other, freeing them whenever they snagged. Running with sticks made Denzil nervous. Be careful you don't put an eye out, he'd told them. One summer Denzil brought home a tractor inner tube, taller than himself, and blew it up with his air compressor for Daniel and Elliot to float on. It looked like a giant black donut. There was nowhere to float to—since

the inner tube took up all of the largest fishing hole. But Elliot would lie back for hours and let you spin him around and around, sometimes with his eyes closed and sometimes with them open to the swirling trees and clouds above him.

"Your friend down there may need a trip to the emergency room," Denzil said to the driver. "I wouldn't mind to take him."

"You were shooting at us," the driver said, taking another deep drag. "Why was that?"

Denzil had been working out an answer to this in the minutes while he held the light, in the minutes while he was remembering Lonzo Loftis and the spontaneous combustion of his outhouse just as he and Glenn and Romie Moore had crept up to it. Only time he ever saw Glenn Turley running scared, but later Glenn claimed he was just pretending.

"I was aiming to use dynamite," Denzil said. "I could string a fuse up to the porch, wait for you to get close enough, then blow the mailbox sky-high to heaven." The other boys stood listening. "And you all with it," he added, just for bragging points with Glenn.

Denzil felt their collective attention.

"I still might light a match, throw it back there at your gas tank," Denzil said. "I brought some just in case." He reached in his pocket, took out the little box of matches, shook it. "See?"

Denzil felt the driver's hand come around his wrist. The suddenness of it scared him. With the other hand, the driver snatched the matchbox. "Are you crazy?" he asked. "Ellie's still down there."

"I'm up," Elliot said, mounting the top. "What was he doing? Trying to kill us? Over a little old mailbox?"

"It's true it don't bring much these days," Denzil said. "Just duns."

"Just what?" the bald, tattooed one asked.

"Duns," Elliot said. "What old people call bills." Denzil felt the sting of the words and a second sting, knowing they'd been aimed to hurt him.

"He's just bluffing," the driver said, blowing out, long and slow, the way of characters in crime movies.

"Be one way of getting your car out," Denzil said. The cigarette smoke, what he had given up years ago for the sake of Olive and the children, was pleasing to him. He was taking chances he wouldn't have taken with Olive alive. But he didn't know how far he could go. Maybe the trick would lie in dividing them, separating the fearful from the brave.

"You say your parents are expecting you?" Denzil asked again.

"Listen, you fat bastard," the driver said, whipping down his cigarette to the pavement. "You're going to go get your tractor, and a chain, and pull us out." Denzil felt the cold, hard end of something—he guessed handgun—against his temple.

He swallowed. "It was just rice," he said. "I was just shooting rice."

"Well, I ain't just shooting rice," the driver said. "So you'd better do what I say."

What Denzil thought—*you think I'm afraid of some Mickey Mouse pistol, you'd better think again*—he didn't say. He pulled his lips together, concentrated on the half-smoked cigarette burning on the pavement at his feet. He would curb the tide of courage he'd been riding. He felt in the boys now what he had been hoping for—reverence and awe for the situation at hand. But he hadn't expected it to take so much. The shotgun would have raised the stakes considerably, and he was glad he hadn't brought it.

"I know a guy with a winch," Denzil said. "Lives right up there." He nodded his head the direction of the woods.

"Let's just get your tractor," the driver said, pushing on Denzil's head with the gun, "and not bring anyone else into it."

"I'll go get the key," Denzil said, but he didn't move, waiting for permission.

Elliot groaned. "I gotta lay down." He sat on the edge of the pavement, then leaned back.

"We better get him to the doctor," Denzil said.

"What do you care?" the driver asked.

"I care," Denzil said. He wanted Elliot to hear.

"The tractor," the driver said. "We're gonna go get your tractor."

Denzil didn't want to take the boys to the garage. He didn't want them to see what tools there were to steal. "Better just let me go alone," he said. "Don't want to wake up everybody."

"Who's in there?" the bat boy asked, stepping closer.

"Well, my wife, for one," Denzil said, trying to think of who else he might name.

"Is that right?" the driver asked. "Maybe she'd like to make our acquaintance."

"Bet we can give her some things you can't," the bat boy said.

"No, man," the bald one said under his breath.

"She's dead," Denzil said. "My wife's dead." He didn't like saying it, but he didn't like the direction things were going either. He didn't like Elliot hearing this talk. Elliot had stayed away when Olive was sick, even during the bouts of remission when the prognosis looked good. "He's just being a boy," Denzil had said to comfort her, but it was Elliot's absence that told them how hard he was taking it.

"You probably killed her," the bat boy said, "crazy old loon."

Denzil heard the crunching of gravel and saw Glenn's headlights high in the trees. He needed to get some kind of control back before Glenn showed up. But it was hard with the gun pointed at him.

"You don't need the gun," Denzil said. "I'll help whatever way I can."

"Maybe I like having the gun," the driver said. "It's like a security blanket." He took the gun from Denzil's head, pointed it at his own face, put the muzzle to his mouth, and kissed it. Denzil grimaced. He wondered what they were high on. He wondered how deep in Elliot was.

The gravel crunched louder up on Glenn's driveway, and Denzil felt the boys hearing it.

"Who's that?" the bat boy asked.

"That's Glenn," Denzil said. "The guy with the winch."

"Now we're talking," the driver said. "You mind you don't try anything funny."

At the bottom of his driveway, Glenn stopped, then got out of his truck. He walked into the headlights, kicked something, picked it up. Then he got back in, eased on down the road, and slowed at Denzil's bridge. When he pulled off the road, he caught them in his headlights. Then he switched on the rack of fog lights on top of the jeep. The whole creek lit up.

"Jeez," the driver said. "It's like Jeminy Christmas?" He put his gun in the back of his pants.

The jeep door swung open. Denzil held his breath. He saw Glenn carrying a rifle and something else. Always one to lead with a strong hand.

"What's going on here?" Glenn asked.

Denzil waited to see if the driver would reach back for his gun. But he didn't.

"They had an accident," Denzil said. "Need to borrow your winch."

"That right?" Glenn asked. "These wouldn't be the same ones clipped off my mailbox, would they?" Denzil saw the motion of Glenn's arm, hurling something toward the creek, saw the silver flash of mailbox in moonlight, saw Glenn, silhouetted in the headlights of his jeep, raise his rifle, heard the shot, saw the fire from the muzzle, heard the solidity of hit on the tin of the mailbox. He had to admit it was impressive.

There was an echo, then two or three more on the hills around them, as if Glenn had split the night itself and driven it, momentarily, into separate corners.

"Good grief," Elliot said from the pavement. "They're just friggin' mailboxes. Twenty bucks tops at Walmart."

Denzil swallowed. He felt sweat trickle down under his arms. Elliot didn't grasp the evident gravity of their situation. "I don't think it was them," Denzil yelled to Glenn. "Matter of fact, I know it wasn't. I hit your mailbox on my way home. Had a little too much to drink. I'll buy you a new one." Denzil didn't like the sound of his voice, but he knew the high-pitched tremble conveyed to Glenn what he needed to know.

Already he'd told more lies in front of Elliot than he'd told in his lifetime. He wondered now, what would have happened if, when seeing Elliot's face in the car, he had just said, "Hey. Don't I know you?" Now that it came to him, what he could have said, he marveled that he hadn't.

Glenn stood still. He was deciphering and making adjustments.

"Look, mister," the driver said. "I want to use your friggin' winch. I want my friggin' car out of this friggin' creek. I want my boys and me on the friggin' road in fifteen friggin' minutes."

Denzil felt the driver's arm against his own as the driver moved his hand behind his back. Denzil held no illusions about grappling with him. He was too old to fight—and had never been much of a scrapper. He didn't want the gun to go off. He didn't want it to hit anyone. And he didn't want Elliot back in the car where the gun and the gun-holder would be.

"You won't need that," Denzil said low. "He'll do what you say."

"Tell him to put his gun down," the driver said.

"Glenn, go put your gun away and come help these boys get back on the road."

Glenn began walking backwards, toward his jeep. Denzil saw him

put the rifle inside. Then he got in, took his time shutting the door, then started the engine. Finally, he inched it toward them.

The driver stepped away from Denzil and went to stand over Elliot. Denzil swallowed, his pulse pounding in his ears. By the light from Glenn's jeep, he saw the driver bending over Elliot. Denzil was afraid of any funny business with the gun. He stepped closer.

"Get up so you don't get run over," the driver said. "Come on." He reached down for Elliot's hand.

"I just wanna lay here."

"No. Get up, man. I don't wantcha to get run over." The driver bent further, extending his reach, and Elliot held up his hand, allowed himself to be lifted.

The driver ducked under Elliot's arm and helped him stand.

"I got a porch swing he can lay on," Denzil said. "Be outta the way."

"You wanna lay on this fella's porch swing?" the driver asked.

"No," Elliot said.

"Just for now," the driver said. "Till we get the car out."

"I wanna help push," Elliot said.

From somewhere, the driver pulled out a white handkerchief and started wiping blood off Elliot's face. He spat on it to rub off the dried blood, and when that didn't work, went to the car and brought back some kind of water bottle that he squirted on the handkerchief. Denzil didn't know why care was so long in coming, but he hadn't expected it at all. Amazing, too, that any boy these days carried a handkerchief. His grandsons didn't. But then their father had failed them in every way.

Glenn positioned his jeep so the lights shone on the Camaro and got out. Denzil wondered if Glenn was wearing his flak jacket under his heavy coat. When their eyes met, Denzil looked away. He didn't know what kind of signal to give and didn't want to give the wrong one or one that might be misinterpreted. A lot rested in the balance.

"First thing is we need to chop down the rest of the mailbox post," Glenn said. "I got an ax in my jeep."

"Don't you think we can jack up the front, shove the car off?" Denzil asked. The boys stood listening.

"The car's already high on the post," Glenn said. "I don't think the jack will go that high. We could try."

"No, you're right," Denzil said. "Go ahead and start chopping."

"What about a chainsaw?" the bald, tattooed one said.

"That's good," Glenn said. "I got one of those, too."

"He's like friggin' Rambo," the bat boy said. "Prepared for everything."

"Not everything," Glenn said, pleased.

He jerked the starter a few times, revved up. Then stopped it. "You boys will have to hold up the front of the car, keep the weight off the post so it doesn't kick back on me."

Without questioning, the boys gathered round, got their hands under the front of the car. "Don't get in a strain," Glenn said. "It'll take some time."

Denzil looked for Elliot and saw him lying on the pavement again. He wanted to go to him but needed to hold the lantern while Glenn sawed. The chainsaw whined in the night, and Denzil inspected the scrawny boys, doing their best to keep the car from weighing down on the post. In the sagging waistband of the driver's pants, he saw the gun, a wonder it didn't just slide on down. Denzil considered going after it but didn't know if the other boys had guns. He didn't want them to feel threatened. Every now and then Glenn gassed the chainsaw hard. The heady scent of oil and gasoline rose. The chainsaw spat out streams of confetti. Finally, Denzil saw the post wobble. He knew Glenn was through, but the post didn't fall. Glenn shut off the chainsaw, grasped the post with both hands, worked it loose, and pulled it free. He handed the post to Denzil. "There's your first piece of firewood," he said.

"Thanks, buddy," Denzil said. "Always looking out for me."

The driver reached down to pick up Glenn's chainsaw. He had to take an extra step forward to help with the weight of it. "Could do some real damage with this," he said.

Denzil saw Glenn cinch his mouth into a quick smile. "Hand me one of those lanterns," Glenn said, avoiding Denzil's eyes.

He took the flashlight down over the bank, shining it along the car's edges. He got down in the weeds, looked under it. Every now and then he flicked the light in the windows.

"What's he doing?" the driver asked.

"Deciding which direction to pull," Denzil said.

"I don't like him snooping around."

"What you got in there you're so worried about?" Denzil asked.

"None of your business."

"Don't worry," Denzil said. "He's not the cops."

"I never been in a wreck before," the bald, tattooed one said. "It's some kind of rush."

The bat boy spat. "That's nothing," he said. "One time I flipped three times. Was like being in a rock tumbler."

By their slurred words, Denzil could tell the boys were wearing down. But the long night would go on. He didn't know which ones of them would last. He didn't know if he would. He hadn't been sleeping well. The bed was colder than he was used to, and in the late hours, he fretted about vandals on the loose.

"You need to keep your friend awake," Denzil said to the driver. "In case he's got a concussion. You don't want him slipping into a coma."

"He ain't got a friggin' concussion," the driver said. "Trust me."

"What's he got then?" Denzil asked.

"Too much of a good thing."

"What good thing?" Denzil asked.

"None of your damn business."

Denzil felt the meter running. He reached in deep, tried to find another coin. It had to be sound. Finally, he said, "He seems to trust you."

"Why shouldn't he?"

"No reason not to, as far as I can see," Denzil said.

"Would you trust me?"

Denzil took a deep breath. *'Bout as far as I could throw you*, he was thinking. "Sure. Why wouldn't I trust you?"

"Because I pulled a gun on you," the driver said. "You shouldn't trust somebody who pulls a gun on you. Because," the driver drew his words out with seeming pleasure, "you never know when he'll do it again." He turned from Denzil and walked back over to Elliot, knelt down beside him. Denzil watched, heard their voices, but did not press closer.

"You all right?" Glenn asked, beside him now. Glenn trained his lantern on the back of the driver. Denzil thought he probably caught a glimpse of the gun.

"We just need to finish this," Denzil said. "Get them back on the road." He didn't mention Elliot, how he needed to keep one of them with him.

He would say that later. He hoped Glenn wouldn't get close enough to recognize Elliot till they had a plan under way.

"You think this'll run when we get it up?" Glenn asked. "Smells like it might go at any moment. What's that smell? Mineral spirits or something?"

"I don't know," Denzil said. "But it's strong."

"We can blow it up if you want," Glenn said quietly. "It wouldn't be hard. It's leaking gas."

Denzil looked in Glenn's eyes. He was serious.

"Think about it," Glenn said. "You give the signal, and we'll torch her. Be one way of putting a stop to it."

After all his years knowing Glenn, Glenn still surprised him. He'd never lost his edge, the thing about him that made him take action—instinctively—and seemingly without thought.

The driver came back. "Okay, Cinderella, what's the plan?" He looked at Denzil.

"Glenn's gonna give it some preliminary turns, see what's going to happen," Denzil said. "We don't want to tear anything up, right, Glenn?"

"The whole bottom's probably busted out," the driver said, his voice rising.

"They make things a lot tougher than you think," Denzil said. "Let's just wait and see."

Glenn backed up his jeep and chained it to a large poplar on the other side of the road. The plan was to pull the car diagonally—so they wouldn't scrape so much of the belly on the pavement at the top of the bank. Denzil knew that Glenn would be looking for a sign, for the okay to detonate it.

"Everybody ready?" Glenn stood at the winch, looked from one face to the next. He flipped the switch, and the winch began its slow whine, taking up slack. Then Denzil heard metal scraping against rock. The winch's whine pitched higher as it began the real work. More scraping. Sure to be sparks, Denzil knew. And with the grass so dry, it wouldn't take much to get it going. He thought of what the bat boy had said about Olive. He thought of the matches the driver had taken from him, like he was a child. If he had them now, he wondered would he light one and throw it over the bank.

The car rose up, scraped more. On the passenger side, leafless willows that had been lain over sprang back up. The farther up the car moved, the more hope Denzil felt in the boys. They were entranced by the slow progress of the winch and the apparent strength of the poplar that anchored the whole enterprise. *That's why we build houses out of two-by-fours*, he wanted to tell them, but he didn't think they'd hear him over the noise Glenn was making.

With the Camaro's front wheels in view, Denzil saw the chance he'd been looking for with Elliot. To the driver, he said, "Watch that it don't start to roll when he gets it to the top. Yell loud at Glenn. Make sure he hears you if it starts to roll. Don't let anyone get close."

Denzil went over to Elliot on the pavement. "You okay?" he asked, kneeling down. Even this far from the car, there was the faint scent of gasoline.

"Just looking at the stars," Elliot said. "They're spinning. The whole world is."

Denzil sat on the pavement beside him, glanced up at the sky. The light from the moon drowned out most of the stars.

"You think your nose is really broke?"

"Might be. You never can tell."

"You let me feel it?"

"No."

"You wanna sleep here tonight?"

"No."

"I want you to."

"No."

"Think about it."

"No."

Denzil didn't know when he had run out of credit. If someone had warned him, he would have been saving up. Elliot hadn't spent the night since Olive's death. Daniel hadn't either, but Daniel was away at college. He worried there was a bad seed. Their father had gone bad. Had left them and gone to another state, wouldn't even pay for school clothes.

In the darkness across the gritty asphalt, Denzil reached for Elliot's hand. It was warm but not clammy. Soft and uncalloused. Denzil lifted it—it was limp—and Elliot didn't resist. Denzil held his hand, and with his other fingers, found Elliot's pulse. Systolic, diastolic, systolic, diastolic.

How often, absentmindedly, he had found Olive's pulse, her hand in his. Or better, heard at his ear the drumming of her heart with his cheek resting on the round of her breast. No other place like that on Friday evenings. Or Saturday mornings. Eventually, most boys learned that.

Silently, he counted off seconds, and his fingers gauged the pulse against his counting. Elliot's ran in the eighties or nineties, about a beat and a half per second, high for resting but not dangerously alarming. Even after calculating, Denzil held on like he was still measuring.

By Glenn's fog lights, he saw the Camaro perched at the top of the creek bank, in the position he had hoped they could avoid, the car near horizontal, its front end on the pavement but its rear end flying out high over the creek. They had done what they could to prevent it, and Denzil didn't understand how they had failed. The car teetered on the edge. Three choices, Denzil knew. Drag it on up, scraping its underside more. Let it down to try another angle. Or Glenn's way. Denzil imagined the fireball that would light the night, the explosion sure to rock the hollow, the impression it'd make on the boys, and the pervasive heat that would blister all their faces. No way Elliot could go with them after that. It would cause quite a stir. The boys would all remember it the rest of their lives. It might even be the thing they'd tell their grandsons. But it'd scare them tonight, maybe make them think twice before going out to tear up jack. It would harden some of them, soften others. Denzil thought of Tiger Boots and the numbing fear she'd feel with the creek afire—even as far away as the porch where she waited. He thought of her, hunkered stiff in her tracks, eyes bright with blaze, not knowing which way to run. The driver, the bat boy, they would harden. Maybe enough to retaliate. What Glenn had wanted all those years ago, Denzil remembered, was to get even with Lonzo Loftis by burning his barn down.

"Listen," Denzil said softly. "This old man won't ever shoot at you again. Not for a friggin' mailbox. Not for a friggin' anything." Elliot didn't respond. "You hear me? Just squeeze my hand if you hear me." Elliot sighed, then Denzil felt his grip tighten.

He was about to go, but Elliot still held his hand. "You could have put an eye out," Elliot said.

"You're right," Denzil agreed, relieved. "It's true. Don't tell your mother."

When he got back to the group, Glenn was explaining why they didn't

want to keep dragging and scraping, dragging and scraping, why they needed to start over.

"I want my car now," the driver said.

"Let's get out of here," the bat boy said. "Let's just take his jeep."

Glenn looked at Denzil. Denzil looked at the car. It made his belly hurt. He knew the longer they went at it, the more tempted Glenn would be to end it once and for all.

"One of the boys injured?" Glenn asked. "I got a first-aid kit in my jeep."

"He's sleepy," Denzil said, glancing at the driver. He felt he was in on a secret with the driver but didn't know what the secret was.

"Why don't we try one more time at a different angle?" Denzil suggested, "and if it doesn't work, we can drag it on up, scraping as little as we can."

"This is your fault," the driver said. "You shouldn't have been shooting at us."

Glenn raised his eyebrows.

Denzil swallowed, looked away. "I know," he said. "I don't know what got into me. I'll help you fix it."

"If it *can* be fixed," the driver said. Bravado had faded to pouting, but Denzil figured him still a wild card. Though he had just met him, he felt he'd been knowing him a long time.

"I'm gonna let it down slow," Glenn said. "Then I'm gonna pull it from the other direction."

By the time they got the car up and towed into Denzil's driveway, the sky along the east ridge had lightened. A few cars passed, the ones on early weekend shift. They slowed to see what morning activity another Friday night had brought. Elliot was asleep on Denzil's porch swing, and the other backseat boy was curled up on a rug. He had rolled the edge of the rug over the top of his bald head. Denzil and the driver took turns going to Elliot, making sure he was okay. Elliot grumbled each time Denzil woke him.

With the gray light, a tranquility set in—the way it will do when you are sick through the night, or sitting with someone who is sick. Denzil and Glenn and the driver and the bat boy were all moving around the car, taking turns dipping under the hood like minnows around a slice of ba-

con. The car, as in the night, wouldn't start. It was clear early on the boys didn't know anything. Finally, Denzil stationed the driver at the wheel and the bat boy at the driver's window so he could signal when it was time to turn over the engine. He and Glenn had their heads under the hood.

"You going to let them just walk away from this?" Glenn asked. "This might be your last chance."

"One of them is Elliot," Denzil said. "The one on the swing."

"Our Elliot?"

"Mm-hmm."

"Oh," Glenn said, readjusting a battery cable. "Tell them to try it."

Denzil raised his head up. "Try it now."

The engine clicked and wound and wound but wouldn't take. Denzil's back ached. He wanted to sit on the porch. He was tired of being under the hood.

"There's some kind of switch," Glenn said. "Some kind of impact switch. Shuts off the fuel pump."

"The inertia switch," Denzil said. He had read about it in *Popular Mechanics.*

"Yeah. That's it. You have to reset it. Where you think it is?"

Denzil shrugged, shook his head. Late-model cars were mostly a mystery to him.

"How're we going to get him away from them?" Glenn asked.

"I don't know," Denzil said. "And then, where would he go?"

"Any place be better than this."

Denzil looked sideways at Glenn. Saw the night's gray and black stubble on his chin. Saw narrow, penetrating—but tired—eyes and the face most familiar to him at the end of long, tunneled nights. He could not count the nights. More recently than even long ago. "I don't know," Denzil mused. "Would it?"

In the gap under the bottom of the hood, Denzil could see the driver through the windshield, his forehead resting on the top of the steering wheel, his eyes closed, a half-smoked cigarette hanging from his lips. The bat boy had abandoned his post and sat on the porch steps, head against the railing.

"Look here," Glenn said, quietly, nudging Denzil. "You think that's it?"

Denzil grabbed Glenn's hand before he touched the toggle switch, pulled it back. Then he reached in himself and jerked loose both ends of the coil wire—as a backup plan. He handed the wire to Glenn. "Slip it in your pocket," he said. It was the simplest thing for now. Later, when they were gone, he would unhook the wire to the fuel pump.

"You sure?" Glenn asked. "You know what you're doing?" Denzil felt Glenn studying him, the way he had the night when the doctor asked if Olive should be put on a ventilator. That was the hardest. He remembered stepping back from it, feeling amazement that hard moments came so late when all you wanted was ease for the rest of your days. He didn't talk about it with Glenn. Glenn was just there.

Denzil nodded his head. "I know," he said.

Glenn considered. "Mr. Watts," he said, lifting the corners of his mouth in appreciation. "You're full of surprises."

The fumes were strong under the hood and around the car. Denzil stepped back to get his breath, then walked to the driver's side. He felt the kind of fatigue that sticks and hangs off you like cobwebs in the fall when spiders make their last-stitch effort for winter provisions.

"Get out," Denzil said. The driver looked up at him. "Go sit on the porch. You're gonna blow your car up."

"And all of us with it," the driver said, flicking the long ash off his cigarette.

"Go smoke on the porch," Denzil said. "Check on your friend while you're there."

The driver reached in the back of his pants and pulled out the gun, held it, inhaled his cigarette. It was a revolver, seemed real enough. Looked heavy. Denzil was tired. Nights always took him through things. The driver, too, maybe.

"Put it in the glove compartment," Denzil said.

The driver ran his finger along the smooth barrel. "My father's going to kill me."

Denzil felt relief that there was a father somewhere—and that the father inspired fear. But what kind of father let his son have a fast car—and then didn't tell him how to repair and maintain it?

"No," Denzil said. "No, he won't."

In the floor of the cockpit Denzil saw the cans of spray paint and bottles of glue. He thought of the art projects. Weapons for some other kind

of vandalism is what Glenn had said. Denzil said there was an awful lot of it. It was what they'd been smelling all night.

Finally, Glenn threw up his hands and slammed the hood. "I give up," he said. "I need a few hours to sleep on it."

The driver sighed and looked at Denzil. "My dad's going to sue your ass." He pulled his bloodstained handkerchief out of his pocket, began wrapping the revolver.

"I said I'd help you fix it," Denzil said. "No need to threaten me."

"You'll pay ever last dime," the driver said, relaxing as he exhaled. "I'll bleed you dry." He clicked open the glove compartment, slid the gun in, then snapped it shut.

"I won't pay a cent," Denzil said.

"You said you would." The driver opened the door, put his feet on the ground. "You're a liar," he said through the window. He looked like he might cry.

"I said I'd help fix it," Denzil said, opening the door more so the driver could stand. "Not pay to have some monkey wrench put his greasy hands all over it."

"You're not keeping my car," the driver said.

He was bound to be suspicious, Denzil knew, but he felt, too, some slack in him. "Think about it," he said. "I can fix it, maybe even throw in some extras. There's some body work needs done."

The driver shook his head, sucked on his cigarette, tossed it down.

Denzil stepped on the butt quickly, mashed it out. He turned toward the porch, left the driver beside his car. He squeezed past the bat boy and climbed the steps. Elliot and the bald, tattooed boy were sleeping sound. The bald one was rolled up completely in the rug now. Elliot lay on his side deep in the cushions of the swing. Recognizing him, Tiger Boots had curled against his belly to warm herself. The ball of the sun had just slipped full now over the east ridge, placing everything in high definition. Denzil could see dark rings of blood caked around Elliot's nostrils, but his eyes weren't bruised, his nose wasn't swollen. Denzil sat down on the edge of the swing at Elliot's head, put his hand across Elliot's brow. No temperature. With the back of his hand, he stroked the side of Elliot's face. There were hints of down, just hints still. Elliot's lips were dry and chapped. He smelled like vomit and gasoline. One of Olive's little men, as she always called them. One of their own little darlings.

Denzil felt the driver's eyes on him and looked to the driveway where he stood beside Glenn, watching. The driver knew. At some point between the swatches of light and dark and light, sometime between the winch's steady winding and the relaxing of the night, Elliot must have told him. Now he stood reading and making adjustments. Denzil waited. He would ask them all to stay. Olive had written out for him her recipe for biscuits. He leaned back in the porch swing to rest a minute and thought ahead to the breakfast he would fix them.

THE CURRENT THAT CARRIES

Dear Ron Howard, Director:

I have thought how you ought to begin with Caleb, his face the face we see onscreen, his voice the one we hear going in—if he is willing. You can judge for yourself after you watch him on *The Today Show*, what I've enclosed here, already forwarded to the first mention of the story—what Vera Lee says they call a teaser in Hollywood:

> And later on in the program, we have a story guaranteed to move your heart. Hear how one man's courage and sacrifice gave life to a young boy drowning in a river. We'll talk to the boy and his grandmother as well as the parents of the man who drowned while saving him. But before that, we have Dean Smith with the weather, and a few tips on summer barbecues.

Wade on through the weather and barbecuing tips—just old-fashion common sense, not to cook too fast or too hot—and finally, you'll see a close-up of Matt Lauer, then some footage of the shoals on Coal River, and wa-la, you are there. First, is the interview with me—nothing flashy in that—then the family of Guy Shamblin. We are, all of us, squenched into new clothes, with lots of makeup and polish, so much so that Vera Lee—that's my sister—said that I, at least, was beyond recognition. The Shamblins, for their part, look more like themselves. Picture, if you will,

a spruced-up Clint Eastwood alongside Meryl Streep—the one angular and chiseled, the other with skin smooth as porcelain. On TV, they both look as healthy and glamorous as when they drop by for their inspections, or visits, as they say. But that is another story.

On the program, Matt Lauer is especially good with Caleb, though Caleb, on his side, weighs every word coming and going like he's in a game of egg toss. He avoids meeting the eyes of Matt Lauer—though Matt is nothing but gentle in his line of questioning.

> MATT: Can you tell us what you and your little brother and sister were doing the weekend of July Fourth?
>
> CALEB: We were all playing in the river. I was riding the shoals.
>
> MATT: Now when you say "riding the shoals," what do you mean by that? Did you have a raft?
>
> CALEB: No sir, I just rode with my body.
>
> MATT: Sort of like body-surfing on the river. Were you wearing a life jacket?
>
> CALEB: Otcher and Misty were, but I wasn't.
>
> MATT: Can you tell us what happened? When you first felt you were in trouble?
>
> MATT: I was in the long shoals, riding through. I was holding my breath, waiting to come up downstream.
>
> MATT: When did you know you were in trouble?
>
> CALEB: When I felt Mr. Shamblin pulling on my arm.
>
> MATT: Now, he was able to deliver you safely to the bank. But then what happened?
>
> CALEB: (pause, hesitation) He just washed on by.

You'll never see a more perplexed look from Caleb. He opens his hands, palms up, as if to illustrate the way Guy Shamblin disappeared. Which I guess, from his perspective, might be how it happened. But his shrug, the way he finally looks at Matt, eyes wide and eyebrows raised, turning his hands up—like *that's all I know*, or *it beats me how it happened*, or *I wish I could tell you more*—is something I've watched a hundred times without knowing what interpretation to pin to it.

Ron, when you see Caleb there, don't be surprised if you see yourself—for at that age, he reminds me ounce for ounce of little Opie Tay-

THE CURRENT THAT CARRIES   25

lor—the reason I'm sending you the story. I know you'll identify with a country boy who loves fishing and swinging on old tires and who can't wait for summers so he can go barefoot. Like you, Caleb was smart for his age, a regular King Solomon, Vera Lee always said. He started memorizing the Golden Texts in Sunday school when he was just four. Seemed like he could reel in words and ideas, make them his own, then turn around, hand them right back to you. I can just picture him in front of the church commencing in on the Beatitudes, unfolding them one by one on his fingers: "Blessed are the poor in spirit, blessed are them that mourn, blessed are the meek." Some in the church thought maybe he'd go on to be a preacher as was his granddaddy—my husband, Harmon, who's gone on now. And maybe he will yet. I guess that's for Caleb and the Good Lord to decide.

He never did have the wide-eyed innocence of Opie. I tell you this from the start. I'm not trying to whitewash his life. His daddy, Layne— our son—was never associated with the sheriff, except to be running from him. And no parent, no matter how often it happens, ever gets used to a deputy's car in the driveway. This is not to say Layne was a rabble-rouser in the truest sense. But like Ritchie or Potsy or Ralph, he sometimes fell in with the wrong crowd. The difference was he didn't have a Fonzie to turn him back to the right path. Harmon and me, we done our best keeping him in the fold, but anymore it don't seem parents have the influence they once did.

There were three mouths to feed when his wife, Cindy, left, sent Layne to drinking and carrying on, then gardening things he oughtn't, and from there, it was just one thing, then another, him never in his right mind when it came to important decisions—so he made bad ones. I write this here and suppose, you being so smart, will understand what I mean. But this story—the one I'm giving you—is not so much about Layne as it is Caleb.

Caleb's been able to absorb more than his share of tribulation without visible damage. For sure, he's seen things no child ought. The worst, till the drowning, was coming across his mother with another man. Now tell me that wouldn't be enough to mark any child. It happened one Saturday when Layne had taken Caleb down to the river to fish. Cindy and this fellow climbed the ladder to Caleb's tree house and let theirselves in. When

Layne sent Caleb back to fetch a life jacket, Caleb caught them there. He was just a little bitty thing, six or seven, and of course couldn't, at that age, tell sex from violence. He thought it was a burglar had wrestled his mama to the tree-house floor. He made the awfullest racket ever was, yelling like he'd got into a yellow jackets' nest, just crying, "Help, Daddy. Help, Daddy, help," over and over like that.

When I got there—for their trailer was right next door—Cindy was on the ground trying to shush him, and Caleb stood, trembling, his hands crossed over the front of his pants where he'd peed himself. Layne come along then and was nothing for him to do but go on up and throw the fellow out of the tree house, which broke the man's leg and a couple of ribs—and a good thing not his neck.

I don't mention this as something ought to be included in the movie version, but going in, you should know the obstacles Caleb faced. He himself has not been prone to trouble—leastways not yet—though one time he stole a roll of Lifesavers from the B-Mart at Alum Creek. Just wormed them into his pocket, what the cashier said. I made him put them back, then give him the money to buy them. I've done the best I could to raise him—all three of them—and though there's always room for improvement, I don't think I was doing such a bad job before the Shamblins come along. But as I say, that is another story all together.

Ron, maybe you ought to begin with a scene or two *before* the accident—back when things were more or less as they should be. Open with a sunny day on the river. Use a blurring effect going in, so we will know it is memory, background, the foundation that the rest is built upon. You'll want to get to the point, I know—with something dramatic—but please be patient. The point will be missed if the past is ignored. Say, it's a sunny Fourth of July, back when Caleb and Misty are younger, and Layne isn't in jail. He and Cindy are making a go—she's pregnant with Otcher. They are happy, carefree. A young American family. They bring me along to fish and grill on the sandbar. At the water's edge, I help keep Misty corralled while she builds castles with her red bucket.

Meanwhile, Layne leads Caleb out to the shoals. Already, Caleb can swim, but Layne ties a life jacket around him anyway. Train the camera in close, and you'll see the kind of swimmer he is. Like an eel, Vera Lee said one time. He has a gliding ease and fearlessness. He's a natural—not

because of any strength but because he can read the current and move with it.

Riding the shoals is much the same as going down a slide at one of these newfangled water parks. You shoot down, rippling where the current takes you. It's just that in the river, there's a longer stretch—in deeper water. If you go under, you wait to pop back up. That's how Layne explained it. Let me be clear, Ron. It's not the white water you see on the New River where people ride rafts. It's not nearly so fast, nor so pounding, nor so swift to change. That's not to say bad things can't and won't happen, and sometimes they do.

Here, I make reference to a letter Layne sent from jail, not long after the newspaper article:

> I believe Caleb would have got out of the current himself. He was always a good swimmer. Of course, I wasn't there. But the last time I seen him swim, we was riding the shoals like that. What it means is giving yourself up, just seeing where the current carries you. Well, we know the river can haul you a pretty long ways. But Caleb could hold his breath a long time, too. Even if he'd gone further than he wanted, he would have washed down about Web Pauley's—what we had practiced—where Web had strung his trotline, and he would have caught himself and pulled up there.
>
> Whatever else is said or done, please don't let Caleb think he's to blame for this man's death. He don't need that on his shoulders on top of everything else. Just tell him it was this man's time to go.

It's only natural Layne would think Caleb an apt swimmer since he's the one taught him. You never like to think it's your own is deficient, but everybody else. As to Caleb's not feeling guilt over Guy Shamblin's death, it would be best to let Caleb answer for it. Which, I confess, Ron, has been part of the trouble. He won't answer. We get so far along in the conversation, then he corks up. I keep hoping you will arrange an interview, just a short one even, to see if you can break through to him.

Perhaps the beginning of the movie ought to be bigger than a scene from the recent past. Men on rafts used to move timber up and down the water—before people started tossing in their washing machines and old tires. You could show how it was the river what took you one place to an-

other. How it was the principal means of trade. Or go on further back. How it was the water what carved out the mountains and made paths, whittling away the soft layers and getting itself hemmed in by what was hard and impenetrable.

All I'm saying is I've had occasion to think about the water and its role, whether it shares in the guilt. And it's hard to blame the river, Ron, just flowing along as it's always done. You could open with the cosmic picture, the big scheme. Imagine rushing, roaring water, fast-moving streams—quick cuts, from one shot to another. Then here, slowly, is the bed the water makes, gradually meandering to the present, the Coal River, a narrow ribbon, easy-going for the most part, with shoals—like spangles—every couple of miles, and a few new waterfalls developing, signs the coal companies have been spooning in under the bed though it's illegal, and they claim never to do it.

At any rate, as you lead up to the accident, you could give a glancing shot to the day Caleb was baptized, the water hole, him wading out in his navy pants, his white shirt and a tie. Show how Harmon dunked him under, his arm around the small of Caleb's back. How Caleb bent his knees, was plunged in the watery grave, trusting he would be lifted again. No one I know of ever drowned during a baptism, and it's the same river. You'll show that the water, though menacing at times, can be life changing and purifying, too, and maybe Caleb will take it to heart when he sees the way it unfolds on the big screen.

But it's true, that on this day we speak of, the day Guy Shamblin drowned, the river was up. We'd had rain for three straight weeks—till every feature and creature that had breath was waterlogged. Everyone's seeds had rotted in the ground or washed away, that is, if you'd been able to get out and do any planting. Once the sun ventured back, we gave the river about a week, time for the mud to settle, before we set out on our picnic. Layne was in jail. Cindy was off somewhere—who knows where? A grandmother, you know, isn't the same as a parent. I knew I'd have to tighten the reins in the days to come. But on this day, I wanted them to know what fun we could have.

Guy Shamblin and his girlfriend had our sandbar. From the beginning this felt like a trespass. Every summer, we'd walked down there to picnic—just a couple stone throws from our place, see? No one else seemed

to know about it. But on this day, when we got there, Misty carrying the picnic basket, Caleb carrying the watermelon, and Otcher crying because there was nothing *big* left for him to carry, they was already on the sandbar with a tent and two fold-up canvas chairs—the kind you all use on your movie sets.

Seeing them, I hesitated. For one thing, I didn't want to expose the children to any R-rated behavior. Sometimes now I think about how different our lives would've been if I had turned back. I guess it would've been different for the Shamblins, too, though who's to say now. But at the time, the children were big-eyed and expectant, longing for the first dip of summer.

"Get in and wade up the river a ways," I said. "We'll find another place."

Caleb turned to look at me, as if to say, *But here's where the best shoals are, here's where we always swim.*

"Go on," I said, gesturing with my head. All along the banks, you could see a thick web of sticks and leaves, diapers and jugs, marking the high-water line.

The children went in first, anxious to get their shoes wet. Then I climbed down with the cooler. As we passed, I said hello to Guy Shamblin, though I didn't know his name at the time.

"Hello," he said, nodding. His girlfriend sat all bunched up in one of the director's chairs. I took this to mean the water was cold. Imagine my happy surprise when I stepped in and found it warm. I stood a moment and let the water seep through my shoes—you can't go barefoot in the river like you used to, Ron, not with so much broken glass. Anyway, it struck me—and perhaps this is hindsight talking—that there was strung between the young man and the young woman a kind of stretched silence. But maybe it was entirely that they were waiting for us to move. It's one of the mysteries of the day, something to consider when you commence filming.

I guess if it was left for me to choose an actor for Guy Shamblin, I'd draw a blank. He remains a blur—though he's the one actually spoke. Time and again, I've tried to conjure him in my mind. He was not so polished as his parents—or so it seemed—standing naked but for his blue bathing trunks and river shoes. He had a lean, taut body, a boyish face,

and brown curly hair. There was about him a ruggedness, but he was good-looking, too. He was young. I have marveled often just *how young* a life it was that was taken. He was in college, what I've learned since, studying to be a biologist. He'd had a short stint in the military. The girl would have been along the lines of Meg Ryan. She had a softness in her face like Meg that made you believe there was in her an essence of sweetness—even as she sat huddled and sullen in the chair.

When you choose actors for *our* parts, Ron, just show us as regular people, respectable people—though I'm inclined to think Caleb might could play himself. We don't have the shine of the Shamblin set. But we're not toothless and scraggly and lopsided neither. We have a little less, a little more, than folks around. Preachers don't have pensions—not on earth, leastways—but once I got custody of the children, the government started sending checks. Like our neighbors, we stretch every dollar till it's thin enough to see through. But we've got shelter and good heat. We grow a garden, do some canning, stock up when we can. We are never what you would call hungry.

Which is why the Shamblins' first appearance in our driveway was so startling. The four of us were sitting on the front porch, Caleb and Misty playing checkers, maybe two weeks after Guy Shamblin drowned. His father and mother pulled up in their white car—I knew it a Cadillac from the flag emblem on front. Recognizing them from the funeral, I have to admit, my first worry was they had come to collect from us—since their boy had died trying to save our Caleb.

"Good morning, Mrs. Kelly. Good morning, Caleb," Mr. Shamblin said, cresting the top of the porch steps. "Checkers, is it?"

"Yes, sir," Caleb said, not moving his eyes from the board. "I reckon it is."

"Won't you all take a seat?" I got up from the swing and shooed the cats off.

"Don't get up," Mr. Shamblin said. "We were just in the neighborhood."

"Taking a drive," Mrs. Shamblin said.

"This is the road that goes straight to the river, isn't it?" Mr. Shamblin asked.

I realized, then, what kind of drive they meant. The kind where you go visit the last place your son was alive. I said, "Yes, right to the river."

Mr. Shamblin firmed his lips, looked at his wife. "We were just on our way there." He paused, then said, "Have you been back yet?"

I shook my head. "We thought we'd wait a spell."

"You're welcome to come with us," Mrs. Shamblin said.

I read Caleb's sigh—just a wisp of a sigh—as saying he didn't want to. "We'll wait," I said. "You sure you all don't want to sit down?"

He looked at her, she looked at him, then he said, "Well, maybe we *could sit* a minute." He held the swing while she sat, then he eased down beside her. They was dressed real smart like they were going to another funeral, and sitting there on our swing, the paint peeling off, they made everything seem a little more dismal than it really was.

"What did you name your cats?" Mrs. Shamblin asked Misty.

"Callie and Boo-berry," Misty said, rolling her head the way little children do while locking their eyes on you.

"Blueberry? Is that because he's blue?"

"Boo-berry," Misty said again. "Like the ghost in the cereal."

"Oh, I see." Meryl's smile seemed sincere. "What grade are you in?"

"Third."

"That must mean Caleb is in the fourth—or fifth?"

"Fifth," Caleb said, jumping one of Misty's pieces and bringing Misty's attention back to the board.

Mrs. Shamblin asked them what were their favorite colors, what they liked to do, if they had bikes, this and that, and the children brought back short answers—like they knew something else was coming and this was just the preliminary act.

When there was a clearing in the Q and A, I offered, "Would you like something to drink?"

"No, no," Mr. Shamblin said. "Listen." He reached in his pocket, I thought, for a handkerchief or a mint. "We wanted to buy you a new roof—." He brought out a wad of money would choke a horse. I tried to remember did he run a roofing company.

"Or something," Mrs. Shamblin said. "We wanted to do something for you." I could tell she was used to cushioning for him.

Caleb lifted his eyes, kind of held them on a line between the checkerboard and the splayed cash in Mr. Shamblin's hand.

"It's kind of you," I said. "But we don't have any leaks. This roof's not that old."

"We want to do something," Mrs. Shamblin said again. "We want to help out."

"Help out?" I was searching.

"If Guy gave his life to save this boy, then this boy must be worth saving," Mr. Shamblin said, nodding toward Caleb. "We want to be part of it."

Caleb stared at the checkerboard. He had his fingers on a piece poised to slide forward to Misty's back row but was scanning for other moves he might have missed.

"You know," Mr. Shamblin said, gesturing widely across the yard, "we want to be involved."

"In Caleb's life," Mrs. Shamblin said. "And of course," she added, perhaps sensing the other pairs of ears listening, "that of his brother and sister."

Ron, I felt sorry for them. As a preacher's wife, I had seen the ways people shoulder grief. Losing someone, some folks tend to direct their energy toward someone else. Naturally, they might turn to the last connection their loved one had. In this case, it was Caleb. He'd been there. He'd seen their son die. I'd been there, too, but I wasn't the one trying to pump water from his chest.

Maybe they read in my face understanding and sensed softening on my part, for directly Clint Eastwood said, "If it's not too much of an imposition, we'd like you to consider our offer to send Caleb to a private school."

Imagine someone suggesting such a thing for Opie—and all that Andy Taylor would have felt! A wide splash of shock, for sure, like cold water in the face. But then mistrust and feeling looked down upon, then anger even, all rolled up like a rubber-band ball that bounced first one way, then another.

I had my mouth open to protest, but before I could, Meryl Streep held up her hand. "I know it sounds like a lot—*is* a lot to take in, Mrs. Kelly. But we'd really like to do something that would make a difference."

Caleb fidgeted in his chair, squinted at the checkerboard, tried hard not to look up. He was pretending not to have heard.

"I think he's pretty happy where he is," I said. "Aren't you, Caleb?"

He nodded, glanced quickly at me, I guess, to make sure I wasn't go-

ing to sell him out. "Yes, ma'am." Then to Mrs. Shamblin, "I'm happy where I am."

"Ah, happiness is fleeting," Mrs. Shamblin said. "Education—a good education—will be with you always."

"Just think about it," Mr. Shamblin said. "We don't want to push." He reached in his shirt pocket, took out a card, then reached it forward. Supposing he was handing it to me, I was in the motion of holding my hand out, but he lay it on the checkerboard in front of Caleb.

Caleb's eyes climbed slowly from the card to Mr. Shamblin, a testing glance. Then Caleb lowered his eyes, the way of a dog under its master's gaze.

"Just call if you need anything," Mr. Shamblin said. "Anything at all. As I understand it, you're the man of the family now."

When they left, they eased down the road, in the direction of the river—maybe looking back in their mirrors at our roof, or the windows, or something else on the property that might need attention. I tried to imagine the way they might see it. Certainly, Ron, it's not a big, two-story house like Opie lived in with Andy. Nor the double-decker where Howard and Marion Cunningham raised their children. It's just small and plain—faced with white cinderblock. By the same token, it's nothing like the shabby, ramshackle hut the Darlings lived in either.

But maybe they weren't looking back, the Shamblins, when they drove away. Maybe they were just slow approaching the place they were going to.

"That was a lot of money," Misty said. "I hope they don't get robbed."

The days of summer passed slower than usual. Dog days rolled in. The weeds along the road filled their tight parcels with colors that would signal fall, the deep purple of ironweed, the bright yellow of the buttercups. But the parcels held back, waiting. You could see the tips of the colors—but the blossoming, the rich fullness, was slow in coming. There wasn't a day went by I didn't think about mentioning the river, asking Caleb if he wanted to swim. But there was about him a brooding silence—like an electric fence strung round. You got too close and felt the energy from it—and feared its intensity—so you skulked around the perimeters. What, I asked God, was the right thing? Was it better to steer clear? Or should we go back to the river, try to salvage some of what we'd had be-

fore? Should I, for Caleb's sake, take him there, walk him through it all? Or should we let it lie sunken, hoping time and distance would erode it?

In the night hours, Caleb cried out, and I would find him asleep, clutching his tangled sheets tight around him. In the mornings, I'd ask about his dreams.

"I don't remember," he'd say, in a way that said he did.

He moved through his days like he was dreaming, too. He'd start off organizing his tackle box, then suddenly get up, leave the floats and lures and spoons in a jumble. He'd be patching the inner tube of Otcher's bicycle tire, then leave off, the patch unglued. Him and Otcher would set up their Tonka trucks to build a road, but Caleb would saunter away, leave the road a dead end. Him and Misty would be playing checkers, and he'd leave off in the middle. Would make her so mad, but she didn't quarrel. Maybe she sensed it would push him away further.

One day Caleb came in while I was mixing up my pie dough. "Is happiness really fleeting, Grandma?" he asked.

I saw then that the Shamblins had planted a seed. But I didn't know what kind of soil it had fallen to. I sprinkled more flour on my dough and mashed it in with my fork. Then I asked, "Do you know what 'fleeting' means?"

"Passing. Short-lived. Transitory." That showed he'd been in the dictionary.

Harmon's way was always to reference the Bible in the face of the dictionary, so I asked, "Do you remember the preacher in Ecclesiastes?"

"To everything there is a season," Caleb quoted, "and a time for every purpose."

"Do you remember what it was brought the preacher happiness?" I set out the clump of dough on the pie mat, commenced rolling it with the pin.

"Nothing," Caleb said. "He couldn't get enough of anything."

"Except?"

"To eat, drink, and enjoy the labor of his hands," Caleb said, pleased, I think, that he remembered so well. But you can see by this, Ron, how easily it comes to him.

Not knowing how to guide him to the rest, I just spelled it out. "And to remember your Creator in the days of your youth."

"But he tried everything," Caleb protested, "big houses, men singers and women singers, musical instruments—before he figured it out."

"Yes, it's true. He *tried* it all, then wrote about it so no one would have to go to all that trouble ever again." I lifted the edge of my crust, slid the glass pie dish under it, then began massaging the crust snug in the bottom with my fingertips, careful not to tear it. I glanced up at Caleb. He was watching my hands, but his look was far off. Finally, I said, "That's what got your daddy into trouble, you know. *Trying* everything."

"But he was trying things that were bad," Caleb said. "At least that's what the sheriff said."

I pinched the excess dough from the edge of the crust, put it in front of Caleb to mold. "Your daddy loves you very much. He just made some mistakes."

"I know." He kept his head down, rolling the dough between his hands. "Do you think you know when you're making a mistake, or it's only later you figure it out?"

"I'd imagine it depends sometimes. If your conscience bothers you at the time, that's a pretty good sign you're doing wrong."

Caleb didn't say anything, just squeezed and pressed the dough.

"What if your conscience says two things?"

I was afraid where he might be going, and then it just came to me, what Layne had said in his letter. I said, "But some things just happen—and they aren't anyone's fault. You can't blame yourself for something like Guy Shamblin's death. It was just his time to go."

The way he started, you'd thought I'd set off a firecracker. "I'd better go to the barn," he said. "I forgot to feed Boo-berry and Callie." He mashed his dough to the table and darted out before I could even say, "Go on then."

But I couldn't help replaying it, rolling it back and forth, as I flattened the next piecrust. How the thread of that day changed colors mid-spool, went from the gold and river green to the ash-gray face of Guy Shamblin, his gray torso, his gray-blue feet.

From the big rock upriver where we'd set up our picnic, I kept a pretty steady eye on Caleb with my binoculars. Though I couldn't see him in the shoals, I could pick out his orange swim trunks each time he waded back up along the edge of the sandbar to start again. I could observe, too, the

young man and woman nearby, so I knew he wasn't alone. They paced back and forth across the sand, sometimes knelt at the edge of the water, sometimes moved from the sun to the shade of their tent. But there was no R-rated material, at least none that I could see. Still there was a familiarity about them, slight touches every now and then. It's clear now I should have been down on the sandbar, too—or kept Caleb out of the shoals.

You can show me at fault here, Ron. I know you can't portray any of us picture perfect. But listen, I was doing my best, three children in tow, one of them fairly intent on going his own way. I guess if we went on back, I could list times I wish I'd been there for Layne, too. But would any of those times made a difference?

When the girl started screaming, there was no mistaking trouble. It was of a hair-raising pitch. Misty, Otcher, and me, we turned that direction, then left the rock, started wading down the river. Though it was just knee-deep most places, the water slowed you down considerably, even flowing as it was the same direction we were going. And Otcher—it was to his waist, poor thing. I kept turning to make sure he didn't fall, but finally, I just picked him up and carried him. I prayed it was just a snake or muskrat that this woman—Meg Ryan—had seen and that Caleb wasn't in any real danger.

When we reached the shoals, we splashed up onto the sandbar, and I swung Otcher down mid-stride. The water from my shoes sloshed out, the sand slipped in. I ran past the tent to the other end where the woman stood. I can tell you, I was scanning the river the whole time for Caleb's orange trunks. That's when I knew the shoals were running higher than I thought, for there was too much movement to discern a swimmer, even close as I was.

My heart gave a sinking. "Where's Caleb? Where's my grandson?" I yelled.

"Guy's in the water," she said, pointing. At the time it sounded like she meant there were guys in the water—which I'd already figured out.

I told Misty and Otcher to stay put, then I waded in. The woman followed. We stayed near the bank, skirting the shoals. I could feel the tug of the current, but we weren't in the froth of it. You could stand—as long as you stood strong. We went on around the bend, and I saw the flash of

orange of Caleb's trunks and this fellow's blue trunks way down at the river's edge, and I was thinking, at least they're both safe now, whatever's happened. But as we drew nearer, I saw Caleb pounding on the man's chest. How he learned to do that I never did find out. When we got there, the woman took over CPR, crying the whole time, "Oh, Guy, why'd you do it? Why? Oh, why? There was no reason," her voice trailed off in a slur. "You wake up now, Guy. Come back to me. Come back." She pushed on his chest while she yelled, and I saw her, more than once, wipe her eyes on her shoulder while she worked.

The rest is in the newspaper article, conveniently paper-clipped here for you:

Alum Creek Man Drowns, Saving Boy

Guy Shamblin, Jr., 22, of Alum Creek, drowned July 4 while saving a ten-year-old boy swimming in the Coal River. Paramedics pronounced him dead on the scene.

According to an unidentified woman at the scene, Shamblin jumped in to save a drowning boy, and after bringing the boy to safety was swept away in the current, which was running high after recent rains.

"He was a hero," the woman said, noting that Shamblin was as brave in death as in life. Shamblin was a U.S. Navy veteran.

The boy's name is not being released.

Curry Funeral Home, Alum Creek, is in charge of arrangements.

I never quite knew how the Shamblins got a hold of Caleb's name. Maybe it was the deputy. At any rate, not long after their first visit, they started stopping by regular-like. They usually brought some little something—a Frisbee, casserole, frozen steaks, some old pants and shirts of Guy Shamblin's they thought Caleb might grow into, Tinker-Toys, bubble-makers. Whenever I asked if they wanted Coke or water, they refused. They just sat on the porch and watched the children play. I guess maybe they needed a dose of children, none left to them now. To an extent, I identified. Losing a son to prison wasn't the same as losing one forever, but in the day-to-day of it, there were similarities. You couldn't pick up the phone to call. You didn't expect him pulling in your driveway. He wasn't around for holidays or birthdays—or for any gesture you wanted

to make to him. He wasn't there for you to hug, the boy you'd loved so much since you first held him in your arms. In my case, though, I could at least write and receive letters—even if the prison mail took longer than you'd think, especially the jail being so close and in the same state.

Each time the Shamblins left, Mr. Shamblin—Clint—made a point of shaking Caleb's hand, looking him in the eye, and reinforcing, "If you need anything at all, anything, just give us a call."

The offer to send Caleb to a private school was still on the table. It hung like one of those paintings of naked people in the museum at Charleston, embarrassing to look at—though the museum folks themselves wanted you to admire it. The Shamblins asked me to notice it, and I looked, then glanced away. But one day on the porch, when they made reference to it, I managed to ask, "Did you send Guy to a private school?"

Clint Eastwood shook his head.

"We tried," Meryl said. "He just wouldn't stay. He wanted to be with his friends back in the public school."

"If we had it to do over—" Clint said.

Meryl patted his hand, "But we will never have it to do over."

Not long after that we got the call from *The Today Show*. And later, once we'd watched the program in its entirety, Caleb remarked, "They didn't even show the front of our house—after all the mowing I done— and the flowers you and Misty and Aunt Vera planted. Why was that?"

"Could be the back has more personality," I ventured. "It looks lived-in." Which was true. We had garlic strung up drying under the porch roof, and on the back wall, license plates from bygone vehicles—Harmon always tried to preserve them. We had an old couch where we sat in the evenings when the sun was too hot out front, plus an old freezer Layne had fixed, kept the venison we'd frozen after hunting season.

"But they showed the front of the Shamblin house," Caleb said. "And not their back."

He had me there. "Maybe their back isn't lived in," I said. "When you think about it, the place they live most is *our* front porch."

Just before school was about to start, Vera Lee told me she'd seen in the newspaper an announcement that the Shamblins were establishing a scholarship and donating ten thousand dollars to the science department at Guy Shamblin's high school—that is, the county school. There was to be a special tree dedication.

"Ten thousand dollars," Misty said. "Can we go?"

"You ought to," Vera Lee said. "Just support them. They've been through a lot."

"Come on, Grandma," Misty said. "We've never even been to the football field. At least, we can see what it'll be like before we have to go there."

"What are we going to do at a tree ceremony?" I said. "We'll feel out of place."

"Just show your respects," Vera Lee said. "That's what I would do."

And that's how we wound up at the edge of the high school parking lot. "Isn't it wonderful," the principal began, "that the memory and name of a hero like Guy Shamblin will live on? The students who might not have been able to afford college can now join their peers. Our science department will join the ranks of the best in the state, in the nation."

The Shamblins saw us, and when Misty waved, Mrs. Shamblin waved back. But they did not leave their post near the podium.

Some of Guy's former teachers and coaches were called upon to say how they remembered him. Then his science teacher, Mrs. Reed, was introduced. I remember there was at my feet a line of ants, and I was in the motion of stepping back to avoid their freeway when I heard a voice I'd heard before. "I think we will all always remember Guy Shamblin as a student who had the natural curiosity of a scientist," she began.

It was her voice first told me told me she was the young woman from the river—Meg Ryan. Then I recognized the sweetness in her face. Of course, she looked different—in clothes now and blown up as she was, pregnant, though not in a glaring way.

"He would have become a brilliant marine biologist," she went on, "and this gift from his parents is extraordinary. All our young scientists from Lincoln High will thank his parents for decades to come."

She didn't fog up any while she spoke—just kept the blinders on and focused on the speech before her. You wouldn't have thought she was anything more to Guy Shamblin than his teacher. But then at the end, she happened to glance up and see Caleb. There rose a deep blush in her face, and she stumbled over her last line. When she went back to the crowd, she stood beside a man—let's say, Kevin Bacon—who put his arm around her like a husband, not a father. I saw that Caleb's eyes followed, and when I looked over at the Shamblins, their eyes were fixed on Caleb.

They delivered new bicycles the next day. Then they started send-

ing checks. Vera Lee said I had to cash them, would I want to insult the Shamblins? But I didn't, and the Shamblins called, insisting. Then they visited again. Still insisting.

"But you can't keep giving us things, Mr. Shamblin," I protested. "There's no reason for it. We may not have as much as you, but we're not poor."

"Now, now," Mr. Shamblin said. "We know this is what Guy would want."

"He was a good boy. He would want us to do this," Mrs. Shamblin said.

"We know we're doing the right thing," Mr. Shamblin said. "But are you doing right, withholding from the children what would make their lives better?"

I didn't know how to respond. You do your best, Ron, but when is your best not enough? When does your best fall short and turn to failure? Turn to a young man spending years in a jail cell? Eventually I gave in. At first, it seemed like we'd landed on the good side of the equation. The boy's life spared—plus extra money to maintain it. Then the strings began to show. They were thin as cobwebs at first. Mrs. Shamblin called to ask, Was Caleb getting enough to eat? What was it I cooked mainly? What all did I buy at the grocery store? Didn't we need more meat in the house? She hoped the children could have such and such, and such and such. Pineapples and star fruit was two of the things she named. Surely, they shouldn't be forced to eat so many sardines.

Now when I offered refreshment on their visits, the Shamblins accepted. Meryl followed me into the kitchen, looking things over. She didn't open drawers or cabinets, but just as soon as I got in the refrigerator, she twisted her neck to peer in.

One morning, not long after the Shamblins had taken the children to the circus in Charleston, I found Caleb in the yard stringing a long tow-rope from one sycamore to the other. All week the children had been juggling apples, swinging on grape vines, chasing the cats with chairs and belts. They had told me, big-eyed, they'd seen tigers and elephants and monkeys. Though the Shamblins had offered to take me, I hadn't gone. It was one less ticket to buy, one less thing to owe them—though as to that, I'd given up hope of repaying them for anything.

"You gonna walk that rope, Caleb?" I asked.

"Gonna try."

"Hadn't you better practice on the ground first?"

"Been practicing." He had the rope positioned about a foot from the ground, high enough to feel airborne, I figured, but low enough to avoid a broken arm.

"You ought to do that over the river," I said.

"You'd just like to see me get wet," he said.

"Maybe I would." For now we had commenced to mentioning it casually without the early heaviness.

"Caleb," I began. "There's something I've been meaning to ask."

"What is it, Grandma?" He kicked off his shoes, ran the bottom of his foot along the top of the rope, testing it.

"That day at the river, did you see anything unusual?" I watched his face, but he didn't look at me. He stepped up on the rope barefoot, grimacing as he wobbled first backward, then forward, then backward and finally, stepped back to the ground.

"Unusual?" he asked—almost to himself.

"Did you hear what they said, Guy Shamblin and Mrs. Reed? Did you see them—do anything," I faltered, "that concerned you, or bothered you?"

He walked over to the sycamore and held onto it while he stepped onto the rope again. He kept his hand on the tree, gaining balance.

"Because I worry," I said, "that maybe there was something going on that shouldn't have been."

"Like what, Grandma?"

I tested my thoughts the way you try the edges of an almond to find your sound tooth before chewing down. I decided to dial direct. "Maybe they were kissing," I said.

"It's no crime, is it, to kiss?" he asked. The rope stretched left then right with the swaying weight of him.

"Not with your husband or wife," I said, knowing full well I might unzip the memory of his mother and her boyfriend in the tree house. "But maybe with someone you're not married to—or not about to marry."

I couldn't tell if Caleb was considering this or just concentrating on the rope.

"Mrs. Reed gave you a funny look at the tree ceremony," I finally said. "Like you two were in on a secret together."

Caleb lifted his hand from the tree, held his arms out, and made a tentative step, grimacing as he did. He took a couple steps, the arches of his feet trying to curl around like bird claws. He jacked his arms up and down the way of chickens too young to fly.

"The Shamblins said—I might be—worth saving," Caleb punctuated each phrase with another shaky step across the rope. He struggled to stay up. I closed my eyes each time it looked like he would lose his balance and bobble off.

"Was you in such bad shape before?"

"Maybe it's God's way," Caleb said. He got back up on the rope, started again. "It's not hurting anybody—they've got the money—it makes them feel good—."

"It don't make *me* feel good," I said. "Whatever happened to 'blessed are the *poor*'?"

He was walking the rope pretty good now, moving with considerable more speed, which helped. When he reached the other sycamore, he held to it, turning himself around, never once stepping down. "*In spirit*," he said. "It's the poor *in spirit*. You can be poor in spirit, no matter how much money you have."

He had me there, trying to use Scripture to further my own ends. I watched him position himself again, his back to the tree.

"Caleb, did you see anything unusual between Guy Shamblin and Mrs. Reed?"

He stepped forward, his hand behind him still holding to the tree. "Grandma, I've seen you put stuff back on the shelf at the grocery store and known you wished for all the world you could keep it in your buggy."

"What stuff? Probably it was something I remembered we had already." I watched to see if this made an impression. "Did you hear me, Caleb? Something we already had." But Caleb kept his focus on the rope before him. He let loose of the tree and started back the other direction, his steps more assured than before.

I think of that day now and wish I could go back. I was close to asking if he'd made some kind of deal with Mr. Shamblin. I felt the words whirl in my head. But how did you ask a ten-year-old such a thing? Maybe I

knew the answer and didn't want to tempt him to lie. But maybe I should have pressed. You like to protect their innocence, Ron, but Caleb will soon run out of innocence—if he hasn't already. He's launched himself off on a path, but what kind of path? Will he be able to backtrack if he needs to? Or is there some detour ahead we could steer him toward? I'm appealing to you because I can trust you—and because I know you're acquainted with solutions for impossible problems—like what we saw in *Apollo*. (I should admit here that I considered asking Spielberg for his help, but didn't know enough about his upbringing or his life as a young man. And like as not, he would want to throw in something supernatural—which doesn't really belong in a story like this—though I know you dabbled with that, too, in your series on the Cocoons.)

When the paramedics loaded Guy Shamblin in the ambulance, we still had hope. He didn't have a pulse, we heard them say. But didn't they have equipment to bring him back? Wouldn't they know how to save him? All evening we prayed—even little Otcher—but then come to find out the next morning, the answer was no.

But to get back to Caleb. About the time school started, the wildflowers alongside the road had finally opened. And I thought maybe we were back on track—just because the normal cycles had kicked in. It was a beautiful time—the skies blue and clear, the light vivid, the air with a crispness that showed fall was on its way, the days of summer ending. The children caught the bus in the morning. Caleb was occupied with homework. Otcher was home from Head Start in time for lunch. I had mornings to myself. Time to do the deep cleaning it's hard to do with children undertow. Mopping and washing the curtains, things like that. The Shamblins visited on the weekends, when the children were home.

One morning, when I was there alone, a man in a suit came knocking on the door. Picture him as Robert De Niro. He said he represented the Shamblins' insurance company and wanted to ask me a few questions. I invited him to sit on the porch. Then he pulled out a tape recorder. He termed it a routine visit, but, Ron, there was nothing routine in the questions he asked. Everyone, I guess, even the dead, has a day in court. On *earth*, I mean, and not just in heaven. Did Guy Shamblin seem like a man who might try to drown himself? Was there any reckless behavior on his part?

"Did he seem especially depressed on this day, Mrs. Kelly?"

"Of course, I couldn't tell," I said, "even with binoculars."

Did I know how much alcohol Guy Shamblin consumed before the accident? Did I know he had a record of mental illness since serving in the military? Did he have a death wish? Was there anything to suggest emotional distress? Did I think the current was strong enough to tow him under? Why didn't I try to save the boy myself? Did Guy Shamblin push me aside? What was his relationship with the unidentified woman in the newspaper? Did I know who she was? Had there been an argument of any kind?

I could see what he was after, and my mind divided itself. The Shamblins had been good to us—but they had set their hook in Caleb, too, and I'd been praying for a way of escape. Was this divine intervention? But how could I be sure the man—this Robert De Niro—wasn't baiting me with his own intentions. He must have sensed my doubt, for directly, he slid out a long sheet of paper from his briefcase. Had I seen the police report? At least, Caleb's testimony—what he had scrawled out for the deputy that day:

I was swimming in the long shoals and felt something take a hold of me. It was pulling me down. I fought to get free, then saw it was a man. I thought at first I was tangled in a drowned body but then saw it was the man from the sandbar. I felt him grab at me again, and I broke free, then pushed him away. The current carried us down to a little pool where the water was calmer. I climbed out, expecting him to follow. But he just washed on past. I ran along the bank, then waded in where I could, but he was floating face down. I couldn't get to him no sooner than I did. I pulled him out, and his girlfriend come along and started doing CPR. Grandma stayed a while, then went back up to check on Otcher and Misty. She tried to get me to go, too, but I waited for the ambulance.

I can see Caleb there—maybe you can, too—in his orange swim trunks, his wet hair pasted to his head, chill bumps along his arms and shoulders—because the sun was on its way down and the evening shadows falling. Probably his chin quivered as he spoke to the deputy. Most likely, he remembered all the deputies who'd come to the house before. Maybe he even recognized this one.

"Mrs. Kelly," the insurance man began. "If there's anything you can say that would cast a doubt on the *accidental* death of Guy Shamblin, you would spare us a case of insurance fraud, something that could lead to jail time if discovered later on."

I thought of what the Shamblins stood to gain—and then of how much they had lost. I didn't see how I could go against them and not go against Caleb, too. But I thought about the truth, how the truth is supposed to set you free. I did want Caleb freed, there's no doubt as to that. But there was nothing, except what I've written you, that I knew with certainty, and even then, Ron, it's not something I would swear to in court. It's all based, as Andy says sometimes on *Matlock*, on conjecture.

I held the police report damp in my hands. I stared at Caleb's handwriting. What had made Guy Shamblin take hold of him? What did Caleb mean about pushing him away? Did Caleb think, in the end, he was the cause of Guy Shamblin's death? And if he did, what did it mean that he was accepting the Shamblins' charity?

Finally I looked at the man. Square in the eye, I looked at him. "It was just Guy Shamblin's time to go," I said. "Just his time."

Ron, I'm writing you as a friend—not someone you know personally but someone who watched you grow up. The story—our story—is tricky in places. Not so cut-and-dried as people imagine. What's so far been reported is how one man's life was lost, but no one ever mentions the boy's life that was lost, too.

I cannot rue Caleb's success at the new private school where he's just been enrolled. Vera Lee says we just have to let nature run its course. But I have to ask, "Is it all for the good of the boy?" The Shamblins say Caleb stands a better chance of going to college—I can tell you he had no college aspirations before. But now he has begun writing what they call admission essays. The one he just completed—what I found in his room yesterday—is entitled "Saving Others." I can get you a copy if you think it will help in the filming.

The ending, Ron, is in your hands. You hold sway here—as much as anybody. Imagine how it was when you were fishing with Andy, and you suddenly caught a fish on a tangled line. How did you untangle the line without losing the fish?

Just remember there's going to be a young man watching, and he's the one most in need of a lifeline if ever anyone was. I know you'll be

obligated to show other viewpoints, especially those of the Shamblins, maybe even Mrs. Reed's, if she will talk. I don't ask you to leave out their stories. Nor do I think ours is more important. All I ask is for equal playing time, that our story—our *loss*—be shown. When you meet Caleb, Ron, the spitting image of yourself a boy, I feel sure you'll want to save him, too.

—Your fan and supporter,
Mrs. Jewell Kelly

A WILD, TO THE RIM,
NET OR NOTHING,
OVEN-FIRED LADLING OF LOVE

No flash, no daring, no dash. That's what Grandmom said. Not the one scoring touchdowns or drag racing at the strip mine on Saturday nights. But the one sitting in the back corner, behind the scenes. The quiet, steady kind. That would be the boy you would want to marry, the boy to watch.

But I watched all the boys. Edgar with his bangs combed straight down to hide his startling green eyes; Perry with tousled hair like he'd just crawled out of bed; Nate with sleepy, droopy eyes like Rocky Balboa's; Colby with his downy sideburns; John with hair on his legs that grew thicker as your eyes moved up; Brent with a fine line of curly red hair down the middle of his abdomen to his waistband, maybe even past, you just didn't know. Buck with beautiful blue veins in his wrists that made the strap of his watch fit funny; Rod with the two halves of his chest carved nearly square—the way of my old Ken dolls; Jarrell with his Adam's apple that jogged when he talked; Archie with his tight, tight can, and the balance shifting from one side to the other when he veered left, then veered right, avoiding tackles down the field.

I watched for their shaven faces, the boyish faces of the ones weren't yet shaving, Old Spice, Mennen, Dial soap, their quizzical, glistening eyes, their fine taut arms in the motion of passing or receiving, the bulges in their uniforms which you couldn't help but notice. For all of them, for any one of them, for their curious parts and wholes, I was always on the

lookout. But mostly, I kept my eyes on Seth, the coach's son, who had the queer taste of bubble gum and wintergreen Skoal whenever he kissed you, but about whom, my grandmother told me, there were rumors circulating.

"Boys like that think they've got something coming to them," she said, driving me home after the game.

"What rumors?" I asked.

"One minute you're kissing, the next, you don't know what you're doing—or what they're doing either." She made it sound like you could lose your mind and act like a maniac, something that certainly hadn't happened to me.

"I was just kissing him," I said, for the third time. "What's wrong with kissing?"

But it was awful to talk about—as if you were dissecting the soft belly of a small animal—awful to turn the skin back and poke. Why couldn't she leave it be? It was just what you did, what all the girls did. You cuddled with the players in the dark behind the locker room, leaning against the cold cinderblock wall, for just the few minutes before your parents— or in my case, grandmother—rounded you up and carted you home.

I always wanted to say, "Be glad I'm not like Lorraine or Chrissie," but I didn't want to tip her off.

In the dark, I sneaked a glance and tried to read her expression by the pale green light of the dashboard. Her eyes were intent on the road. We drove in silence. Then I couldn't stand it. "What rumors?" I asked again.

"Never mind, Phoebe. Enough for you to know there's evidence against him."

I imagined her on the phone with Lorraine's mother, making lists of Seth's misdemeanors, the way they usually did, pooling their clues, deciding why one boy or another wasn't good enough. As far as I was concerned, he was innocent till proven guilty. And what could he be guilty of? Had he been with another girl? Not Amanda Kirby, surely. He'd sworn he didn't like her. But even if he did, would I, could I, through sheer focus and will, have *liked* him—*loved* him—any less?

"Just ask him where he was last weekend," Grandmom said, "when you wanted him to come sample your pumpkin pie."

"He was at his aunt Regina's house in Boone County."

"Yes, but who did he have with him?"

It wasn't like Grandmom to invent trouble where no trouble was. But I couldn't tell whether she believed everything other people said, or if she kept her own counsel. My mother had always remarked how hard it was to slip something by Grandmom, but I suspected her senses were dulled with age. It was easy, for instance, to talk on the phone with one person but say I was talking to another.

When we got home, Grandmom turned on the TV and poured herself a neat bourbon. Rupp Arena slowly materialized on the screen, and along with it, her beloved band of Kentucky Wildcats jogging backwards on the basketball court.

"Don't go to bed yet," she said, seeing me turn down the hallway. "Stay up and watch the game. There's a new guard, name of Kyle Macy." She sat with her legs folded under her in the recliner, her scissors and newspapers beside her on the table. It was her habit to cut out coupons, box scores, little newspaper articles for her files, but when Kentucky was on, she gave the team her full attention.

"I'm tired. I just want to go to sleep," I told her. Mostly I wanted to be alone so I could roll over in my mind how the evening had been, how the whole season had been.

In my bed, I started it post-game, imagining the boys in the locker room, showering, the water glistening on their skin. I'd seen pictures in magazines at Chrissie's house of players in the showers, their Loch Nesses loose and parading. I was sure our own players didn't dawdle like these, though, taking time to wash their ankles, for instance, or contorting themselves to wash their backs in a spirit of ease and leisure. For one thing, our boys slipped out the back of the locker room even before the lights were shut off over the field—like they'd run through the showers car-wash style—just enough to smell soapy. The ones who didn't have girls trickled out the front of the building slowly, then stood with the parents who were waiting for sons, looking for daughters. I'd come to think of those boys as the front line, blocking everyone else from the action behind the line of scrimmage. But like linemen, they could not block out everyone and left gaps that I came to think of as a kind of protection.

The boys were never more lovely than after a game, no matter if they'd won or lost. It was different, of course, either way. If they'd lost, they were sullen and pitiful, all their enthusiasm gone out, blaming themselves and each other, blaming the coach, blaming you. And you'd think of things

to console them, like cradling their warm necks with your hand, combing your fingers through their wet hair—just some slight touch—and then gradually they'd slough off their disappointment, like snakes shucking off old skin. If they'd won, as they'd done on this night, they showed themselves proud, cocky, strutting, and against you, would press hard and harder—as if they were still in the game, intent on showing who was boss. On these nights they had more daring, and you had to distract them, tame them, or you'd wind up having to rub their Nessies.

Lying there, I thought of the way Seth kissed me, the sweet salt of his lips, the inside of his mouth warm against the chill of late November. He had slipped me a sliver of peppermint—like a hot secret passed between us—that had set my heart to rocking. I don't mind saying I lived for moments like that—all that swirling you felt. He was inside my coat—for I'd worn a coat big enough to go around both of us. While we kissed, I felt his hands move behind to cup me, and I slid my hands around to hold his rear end, too. I anchored my hands in the tight corners of his blue jean pockets and pulled him to me. It seemed to satisfy him, being against me like that, and I rested in his arms.

Some girls went further, I knew, even with so little time, and it seemed like they didn't mind it. In the darkness I could hear a zipper, the rustle of fabrics, a kind of panting. "Mmmmm," someone said.

"Mmmm," I said, quietly, in my bedroom to see how it would sound.

I could still feel Seth against me. I hugged my pillow tighter, and eventually, after some time, went to sleep like that.

"If you can't pass the ball," Coach Lewis yelled, "then dribble it." As if that would be any better.

I bounced the ball and crab-walked backwards, using my body to shield the ball from Archie. Now and then, I felt Archie's hand on my back, then on my behind. I felt his thigh brush up against mine. I kept backing into him. Then I felt him take hold of my waistband. That was illegal, I knew, but you could get away with it if the coach wasn't looking. Easily, Archie could have darted around, stolen the ball, and gone to score at the other end, but he let me keep dribbling, backing into him. From time to time he swatted at the ball to make it look like he was trying.

I kept my eye on the ball so it wouldn't bounce off my shoes—but Archie's hands were a distraction. I felt them quick yet gentle—like falling leaves glancing off you.

When there was no place to back, when I was nearly under the basket, I stopped dribbling and looked for someone to pass to. Finding no one, I mustered the courage to shoot. Archie stood tall, arms vertical.

"Just an easy kiss off the backboard," the coach yelled. Why did he call it a kiss?

I closed my eyes and heaved the ball from my shoulder, lobbed it over Archie's fingertips. Opening my eyes, I saw the ball bounce on the rim. I prayed for a friendly bounce—just one single friendly bounce. The ball did bounce and bounced again, wobbled, rolled around the top of the rim, leaned in, leaned out, then dipped over—and finally rolled out.

"That's okay. Good try." Coach Tackett said it in a tone you might use with children. Coach Lewis blew the whistle, and Lorraine ran in to replace me.

Grandmom sat in the bleachers, but I didn't meet her eye. Instead, I went and stood beside Seth, who'd gotten himself sidelined for too much fouling.

"What was that about, Phoebe?" Seth asked.

"What?"

"You know what."

"What?"

He glared. His ears were red the way they got when he was angry. "You out there with Archie, that's what."

"What about it?"

"What were you doing?"

"Just playing," I said.

"Yeah, right. *Playing.*" He wheeled around and headed for the door.

I swallowed hard, watching him, then blinked a few times to ease the burn in my eyes. I gave a side-glance to the bleachers to make sure Grandmom was absorbed in scrimmage; then I took off down the sideline after him. There was a lot of maintenance to keeping a guy once you got him.

Outside, there was no sign of Seth, and in my T-shirt and shorts, I felt the sting of the December air. The door to the furnace room was unlocked, so I peeked in and sure enough found Seth sitting on the concrete

ledge, leaning against one of the units. He was staring straight ahead—he didn't even look toward the door. The room was even colder than outside, but I stepped in anyway and eased the door shut.

"What's wrong? What're you so sore about?" My voice cracked as I went to him. I touched his shoulder, hoping to soothe him.

He pulled back, folded his arms. "You know what."

I didn't say anything, just stood there, feeling the chill deepening.

"How can you say you're serious about me if you're flirting with every other guy who comes along?"

"That's crazy. You know how I feel about you."

"You think I don't see?"

"But, Seth, I love you."

"How do I know that?"

"Because I tell you all the time!"

"Then show me."

"Show you how?"

He reached for my hands, then pulled me toward him. I looked back at the door. The furnace room didn't have any windows.

"Kiss me," he said, smiling and pulling me near.

"Somebody'll come," I said. But I knew Grandmom's tendency to lose track of time once she got involved in practice.

"So?"

I leaned in and kissed him, and he pulled me between his legs. Maybe it was the shock of the warmth of his bare legs against my bare legs, maybe the difference between stiff denim jeans and the soft polyester fabric of gym shorts, but I felt a fast heat come to my face when I kissed him. The taste of his bubblegum and wintergreen washed over me. The scent and taste swirled through our kissing. But then I felt his hand sliding up under my shorts, and I took a step back.

"Someone'll come," I said, trying to stay him with my eyes.

"So?" he said, reaching for my hand and leading it to his waistband. "Here."

It seemed like all roads were bound to lead below the horizon. He pulled my hand in farther, farther and farther until my fingers brushed his Nessie under what I guessed was a jockstrap. He groaned and pushed into my hand. My face burned.

"I can't. Grandmom will come," I whispered.

"Grandmom, flandmom," he said. "Hang your grandmom."

He cupped my rear end and pulled me snug against him, leaving my hand inside his shorts. I nuzzled my head in his chest. He smelled of deodorant and sweat, laundry detergent, and of himself, just Seth. I loved him, didn't I? He was breathing hard, like panting. It was like an over-friendly dog, insistent on being rubbed, always nudging your hand even when you were ready to stop. Sometimes you just wanted the dog to lie there, wait for you to make up your mind to give it attention. You wanted to meet it on your own terms.

I slid my hand from his waistband around to the small of his back and massaged there in a spot I knew he liked.

But he pushed me away suddenly. "You can count on this," he said, standing. "I won't beg." He tore off toward the door, but over his shoulder yelled, "Maybe you'd rather I send Archie in!"

"The trouble with you," Grandmom said, on the way home, "is you don't know how to do a layup. It's fundamental. I can't believe one of the coaches hasn't taught you. Why don't you get Seth to teach you?"

The tears bunched in my eyes. "Seth thinks I like Archie."

"You and Archie *seem* awfully cozy. At least you let him guard you close."

"*Let* him? How am I supposed to stop him?"

"Throw an elbow." She glanced over, nodded her head, more serious than I'd imagined. "That'll make him keep his hands off."

I guess I wanted his hands off, but I wasn't sure. I couldn't imagine throwing an elbow into his sweet, chiseled face, or his washboard ribs, for that matter. I didn't want to hurt him. It was easier to imagine nuzzling against him as I'd nuzzled against Seth in the furnace room. Each time you started with a new one, you got all the sweet buildup, and you could go awhile, if you went slow enough, without getting backed into a corner. Somehow with Seth, things had gone fast. Maybe I'd been used to dating the ones who didn't expect as much, didn't expect anything, and so were delighted with whatever there was.

That night when I thought of Seth, I replayed how warm it was to be against him, skin to skin, how good it always was to kiss him. Lying in

the darkness, I felt my face heat up, the thought of my fingers around his neck. I hated myself for touching him, and I hated the way dogs could wear you down, wear you down until they got all the attention. At the same time, I hated myself for not doing more. Seth, after all, might turn out to be the *one*, the first. When my friends talked about it, they were always relieved to be done with it—like it'd been some yoke they were glad to get shed of. Lorraine had planned it all out, made Danny tote a sleeping bag. It was about as romantic as you could dream of, under the stars, the bed of his truck, out at the cemetery, the radio playing. When your friends told you, you didn't pass judgment. You wanted the details, without seeming to. The trick was to show enough interest to keep them talking, but not so much they'd think you were a virgin.

But Seth didn't call, and didn't, and didn't. Not that night, nor the next, nor the next. A week went by, him avoiding me at school, returning my notes unopened through the vent slots of my locker. It was like being tossed around in a rock tumbler, fractured, chipped, bruised, heaved round again. Where had it gone wrong? Was it just in the furnace room? The rest had been good, hadn't it? Cuddling together nights after games, holding hands in the hallway, sharing lunch, kissing on the bus, both of us hunched so low the driver couldn't see—though the window beside us steamed. Had I really been flirting with Archie on the court? Did I like him? I loved watching him walk, his wild swagger. Did he like me? Should I send out some feelers to Lorraine to find out?

"Don't you have a book to finish this weekend?" Grandmom said, catching me on the way to my room with a bag of pretzels.

"I haven't even started."

"If you start tonight, you can make a good dent."

I rolled my eyes. "No one does their homework on Friday night, Grandmom."

Her eyes brightened. "Then you can watch the game—*that's* what lots of people do on Friday nights."

When I moved in with Grandmom, I had known there'd be adjustments. I just hadn't known Kentucky would be one of them. Not that I had anything against Kentucky—or against anything Grandmom took a

fancy to. It was natural she would have her interests, and I would have mine. And it was sweet, really, the way she cared for her Wildcats. She'd grown up in Lexington, her father a Kentucky fan, and he'd raised her that way. At some point, she married a West Virginia man, my grand-daddy, and moved with him to Huntington. He died early, even before I was born. She had loved him, she always told me, heart and soul. Some-times, I had in mind to ask her, what part was *heart*? What part *soul*?

In the family, she had the reputation of being a little kooky—some-one who preferred flea markets to the Diamond department store, horse racing to NASCAR, *National Geographic* to *Good Housekeeping*. But her great passion—second to Kentucky basketball—was preserving endan-gered species. She spent hours writing letters to congressmen and sena-tors, even presidents of other countries, urging them to save leopards, al-ligators, kangaroos. To the Kentucky governor, she pleaded particularly for the cave shrimp, piping plover, and pearly mussel.

When I first moved in, I had thought it was poachers she was after, but Grandmom said it was the less obvious intrusions—like strip mining and dam building, timbering and spraying pesticides—that were most threatening. She fretted about natural habitats where there had been no human contact but now suddenly was. In almost every case, she said, hu-man contact brought disaster. In the bathroom she'd pinned up a poster, a Virginia big-eared bat hanging upside down that said, "Stay out of my hair, I'll stay out of yours." Until I got used to it, it scared the daylights out of me in the mornings.

Not that I cared. I much preferred a house wallpapered with bats and crocodiles to the shenanigans at either parent's house. My mother's boy-friend had had the habit of hugging me too often and too tight. And my father's new wife blamed me for every piddly thing gone wrong—plus wanted me 24/7 to babysit her two spoiled toddlers, both still in diapers. My parents had batted me back and forth until I didn't know whether I was coming or going. They both outwardly expressed regret that I'd come to live with Grandmom—maybe they were afraid I'd turn out loopy, too—but I think deep down they were glad to start fresh without me. Besides, I didn't see that Grandmom was any crazier than anybody else once you spent regular time with her.

On this night, she had popped herself some popcorn and sat with what she called a neat bourbon, untouched—waiting for tip-off.

With my book, I took a seat at the far end of the couch, furthest from the TV. I figured once I got deep enough in, thoughts of Seth and Archie and Lorraine and the pitiful, silent, lifeless phone would fade to background. So thinking, I tied my hopes to Pip, who was in trouble, turned upside down by a villain. I followed him home, where he had to tiptoe round things, stealing bread, dodging his older sister's darts. I stayed with him, right at his heels, shivered with him, fretted with him. Then the crowds roared. It was Rupp Arena, and I had to fight to dig back into the pages. Pip stirred the Christmas pudding. He learned about escaped convicts but went ahead and stole a file from his brother-in-law. He was dreadful under the sway of the man from the marsh. The crowd at Rupp Arena tried to drown out Pip on his errand. Glancing up, I saw Grandmom on the edge of her chair, gripping her armrests.

"Jack's open," she yelled. "Right under the basket."

I willed myself to stay with Pip and accompanied him, pork pie and all, back to the cemetery. The convict ate like an animal but treated Pip more kindly than before. Pip went home, worried about the pie. Then, just as he was fleeing the house, his heart burdened with guilt, the king's soldiers met him at the door, pointing their muskets at him. A solemn quiet entered the room—the absence of the crowd's roar. I surfaced momentarily to hear the solitary drumming of the basketball on the floor. Then I heard a swish. I can honestly say it was the sound of the ball rushing through the net that made me look up. The camera zoomed in on the white uniform of No. 4, a sweet-faced player, with wonderfully dark eyes. He dried his hands on his socks. Bounced the ball three times. Eyed the basket over the ball, then shot again. The ball made such a patient, graceful arch you could tell by its trajectory it would go in, even before its descent. It wasn't just a swish but was more the sound of the ball slapping the bottom of the net. It started as a *thread* then ended quickly, a snap, like -*et*, to sound like *threat*.

"That's the new guy," Grandmom said. "Kyle Macy."

Through the years stacked between that one and this, I don't remember whether Kentucky won or lost. I don't remember who they played. What I remember is that *threat* sound—those nothing-but-net shots of

Kyle Macy from the foul line. Everything else fell away. Pip and his ha-
ranguing sister. The convict of the marshes. The room. Seth. The silent phone. Grandmom. The crowd at Rupp Arena. There was a gentle
nudging in my heart—the way of a dog cracking the door open with his
nose—and instead of shutting the door, I left it open, and through the
crevice, I watched Kyle Macy.

I left my finger on the page of the book, pretending to read, but my
eyes kept darting back to the TV and to Kyle Macy dribbling the ball,
passing, and shooting. He had a spell on the ball and sent it where he
willed. No one I knew handled the ball like that—not Jarrell, not Brent,
nor Archie, certainly not Seth. The ball was a yo-yo attached to his hand
and he did tricks with it. It went out from him, then came back. He
pushed, pushed, pushed it, and all the while, it kept coming back. There
was something thrilling in it—like the first time you saw a trapeze artist
let go of one swing to fly to another. It had about it that kind of breathless
dazzle.

When I went to sleep that night, I dreamed of Kyle Macy. He was running and shoving the basketball. He pointed with his free hand, directing
traffic. In my dream, I was on the court. But he didn't point to me, didn't
look at me. Still, I had the feeling the ball was coming my way. It was such
an intense feeling that when I woke, my heart was racing, and I had to lie
there, reassuring myself it was only a dream.

But that didn't stop me from feeling it all day, that peculiar fear of the
ball coming to me. What would I do? Who would I pass to? But then at
the boys' practice, when the ball did come, I managed to send it off to Jarrell without having to bounce it.

"Good pass," Coach Tackett said.

Once, off to the side, I bounced one of the extra balls, trying to yo-yo
it like Kyle Macy. It was harder than it looked. Seeing me, Coach Lewis
said, "Not with your palm. But your fingertips. That way you have more
control."

The whole practice, Seth didn't give me a glance, and I kept my distance. A wedge had entered, and each day's silence drove it deeper until the gap was so wide, it couldn't be bridged with ease. Archie sensed
this—anyone with a finger on the string of the web work at school could
sense it. He hovered closer than before. More than casual brushes now,

his hands lingered. There was a solidity in the way he touched me, kept his hand on my behind. I thought maybe he did like me. I thought maybe he would ask me out.

But one evening in the locker room after practice, Stella said, "I wish Archie'd keep his hands to himself."

"Tell me about it," Darlene said.

The heat rushed to my face. Had they all been watching?

"What'd he do?" Lorraine asked.

"Felt me up when I went in for the layup." Stella cupped one of her breasts.

"Roughing the passer," Molly said.

"That's what they're there for, girls," Chrissy said.

"Not mine," Stella said. "I wish I had a way to protect them."

"You need a better bra," Lorraine said. "We all need better bras. Somebody ought to invent one. I jiggle all over the place."

"I just wrap this bandage around and around," Darlene said, unraveling herself like a spool of thread. "It works. You should try it."

"That wouldn't stop Archie," Stella said.

"No," Chrissie said. "Nothing stops Archie."

"They make straps to hold the guys in place," Darlene said.

"Oh, yeah," Chrissie said. "Good thing."

Some of the girls snickered.

I stuffed my sneakers in my duffle bag. "You could throw an elbow at Archie," I said, and for once, I wished I'd taken Grandmom's advice.

"Listen to Phoebe. Is that the way you handled Seth?"

"Maybe a knee would be better," Denise said.

"What happened between you and Seth?" Chrissy asked. "I thought he really liked you."

"Oh, I don't know." I calculated. "I guess he likes other girls besides."

"Who?" Lorraine asked.

"Who?" some of the others asked. Their attention turned to me in a way it usually didn't.

I shook my head. "I'm not one to spread rumors. It'll come out." I gauged to see if one of them flinched, but if someone did, I couldn't tell it.

Christmas was a sad time, I don't mind saying, to be without a boyfriend. I missed Seth—more than I might have missed him if I'd been at school, with other people around. But it was the holiday break, and I was home with Grandmom. I missed his voice, the warmth of his hands, the strong grip of his fingers, the slow winks he gave, the way his muscles—in his arms, in his thighs—felt under my hands when I clutched and rubbed him. I missed the hair on his forearms, his fluttering eyelids when he closed his eyes to kiss. The scent and taste of wintergreen and bubblegum mixed.

But what was the point of mistletoe or eggnog without a boyfriend? Of trading gifts when you didn't have someone special to give to and receive from? What was the point of caroling in the dark, of hot chocolate afterwards, of putting up and decorating a tree? You just had to hang back, go through the motions, try not to ruin everyone else's holiday.

But there were evenings when I'd shut my door and lock it quietly, then fold myself on the bed, my tears sogging my bedspread. The ache started deep inside—maybe there where my heart was—then radiated out to the tips of my fingers and to the tips of every part of me. I wanted and wanted and couldn't have told you for all the world what exactly I wanted. Yet it wrung me, on spin cycle. It was dreadful to be under the pull of such strong currents. I thought of Pip and the villain's power over him, driving him to steal files and pork pies. And what villain was it gripped me? Seth? Archie? Or something else all together? And what did I feel driven to do? At times, I'd be bursting with energy, wanting to tear through the world like the Tasmanian Devil, spinning and spinning my destruction, caught up in the whirlwind of it. But at other times I just felt quiet, wanting only to be held and comforted. And so I cried, under the radar of Grandmom, and then dried my eyes and tried, in her presence, to put on a good face so she wouldn't send me back to live with either of my parents.

"This is the proving ground for Kentucky," Grandmom said, pointing to the Notre Dame players just out on the court. "They haven't played a team this good yet."

It was New Year's Eve, and everyone else had gone to Lorraine's bonfire. I had turned down the invitation so as not to be the only one without

a date. Grandmom had volunteered to accompany me, as usual—having now taught herself to record games on the TV. But who, after all, wanted to be seen all the time with her grandmother?

"You want me to leave this bright light on so you can read?" Grandmom asked.

"I left my book in my room."

"It's just as well," Grandmom said. "You might get tomato sauce all over it."

She was baking a homemade pizza for halftime. There was no reason, she said, why we shouldn't celebrate like everybody else on New Year's Eve.

Of course, she had every reason to celebrate. Her Wildcats were on TV, for one thing. But beyond that, she had told me, there had been strides writing legislation to save a whole slew of endangered species. To top it off, one of her contacts had sent her a big photo of himself and a companion holding a baby brown pelican rescued from an oil spill. For Grandmom, all was well with the world—or at least moving in that direction. And as far as she could tell, everything was fine with me, too.

"He's just a sophomore," Grandmom said. "Look how he holds his own with all those juniors and seniors. It's because of his composure."

Kyle Macy did seem to bring a calm to the game. The announcer said he had ice in his veins, and while this didn't sound like a good thing, it was said as a compliment. Kyle didn't force the pass or shot either one. I didn't see how anybody could be so patient with the ball—or operate with such faith that things would eventually work out. But most of the time, things did. One of his teammates got free, or an opponent fell off balance, and there was an open shot to take.

There were nine other players on the court, but Kyle made it his game. Still, though he played every quarter, he wasn't a big scorer. He didn't hog the ball. He spent a lot of time feeding it to the forwards under the basket. For loose balls, he scrambled. He had a ruggedness you couldn't help being drawn to. His thighs were lean and muscular. That was in the day when players wore real shorts, not the baggy pajamas you see them in now. He had rounded muscles everywhere, but he didn't look like the Hulk or anything. In fact, compared to a lot of the other players, he looked small, though the announcer said he was six-foot-three.

Sometimes when he went to the foul line, the camera would train in, and you could see his deep, dark eyes under his full, dark eyebrows, peering over the rounded edge of the basketball like two black onyx stones rising up over the rim of the earth. He was something to see.

Back then, I imagine I wasn't the only one watching him. He was probably every coach's dream player, dribbling down the court, stopping suddenly and popping straight up like a jack-in-the-box. He'd shoot—talk about poetry—and the ball would arch through the air and—*t-h-r-e-a-t*—slap the bottom of the net on its way through.

"I believe they ought to give him more than two points for those long shots," Grandmom said. "It takes a lot of practice to do that. Not everyone can, you know."

"You should write and tell somebody. Get the rules changed."

"Maybe I should."

At halftime, with Kentucky leading, Grandmom brought out the pizza on a TV tray and set it down between us. It had about everything you could imagine—or want—pepperoni, sausage, mushrooms, green and black olives, pepper rings, red and green bell peppers, onions, a couple different kinds of cheeses. You'd have thought she'd been stocking up for such an occasion.

She slid two of the cheesiest slices onto a plate. "I've got another little surprise in the oven," she said, handing the plate to me. "Don't let me forget."

Though I didn't say, already I had caught the scent of her oatmeal cookies.

The cheese on the pizza was hot and stringy and looped down to my chin when I took my first bite. The hot tomato sauce burnt my skin, and I wiped my mouth quickly and just as quickly leaned in for a second bite.

Grandmom settled back in her chair with a paper plate in her lap and took her first bite. "Mmmm," she said. "We ought to do this more often."

"It's really good," I said. "Better than marshmallows and wieners."

"Well, they have their place, but this *is* better if I do have to say so."

Later when I loosened a third piece and dragged it over to my plate, Grandmom said, "I've been thinking, Phoebe. The coaches ought to let you play more in practice."

"Why?"

She shrugged. "You could improve that way."

"They don't care if we improve. We're just warm bodies—for when too many of the guys are out hunting."

I heard they're thinking of starting a team for girls next year."

"Maybe," I said, seeing then where she was headed. "But that would be for girls like Stella and Denise—the ones who can really play."

"You could play—if you had more practice."

I squenched up my face and frowned.

"I mean it." She reached for the pizza and worked loose another piece for herself.

"I know, Grandmom, but you must have missed something."

She was in the motion of taking a bite, but she stopped midair and looked at me.

I hurried and tried to soften it. "I'm sure last practice you probably saw me score for the other team."

"And that was a very good shot," she said, reclining back again as if I'd given more evidence for her side. "Just be glad you scored. Jenny Woodrum didn't score a point for anybody. You've got good height and speed. Those are the main things to start with." She nodded her head, took a bite, then rested her pizza in her plate while she chewed.

I was left trying to puzzle it out. The winter months gave her basketball fever, no doubt about that. But I knew she turned to horse racing in the spring. Would she want me to train as a jockey?

Just as the players lined up center court for the second half, Grandmom leapt from her seat. At first, I thought she was helping with the tip-off, but then, watching her dash for the kitchen, I caught the first scent of burn. I got there in time to see smoke pouring from the oven.

"Go open the back door," she said, stuffing her hands into oven mitts.

I held the door, and she ran out into the cold night, down the porch steps—quick and surefooted. She dropped the pan of smoking cookies in the snow.

"Mercy!" Grandmom said. "How's that for a bang-up New Year's Eve! We almost had our own bonfire!" She was laughing as she came back up the steps. But then in the light of the doorway, I saw her eyes rimming with water, and her nose red. "But I wanted it to be something you'd remember."

The look on her face made me want to cry, but I fought and didn't. In the next minute she was laughing again, her wet eyes sparkling. She said, "But I guess maybe now you *will* remember it. Ha-Ha."

That's when the smoke detector started squealing. We went around opening windows and setting up a cross-breeze with a fan. The air that rushed in was cold. It was really cold.

When we finally got back to the TV, Kentucky had fallen behind. As bad as Grandmom felt about the burnt cookies, you could tell she felt worse about the score.

"Come on, Phoebe," she said, patting the couch. "They need us."

We both sat on the edge of our seats, and through the ticking seconds, I felt my nerves straining. The lead went back and forth. But Kyle Macy stayed cool as the leader of the pack. The clock ran lower and lower, but when the ball came to him, he still welcomed it like an old friend.

"He's a good one in the clutch," Grandmom said. "You can't rattle him."

The house grew colder by the minute, and while we needed to close the windows, we couldn't leave Kyle Macy. Every time he took the outside shot, our hearts soared with the ball. Every time he went to the foul line, we planted our best hopes with him on that line. Slowly, the scoreboard tipped and stayed tipped in Kentucky's favor. In the end, we won. Probably the house was freezing by then, but we were too fired up to know it.

That January, a big snow came—a big, two-foot snow. It caught a lot of people off guard, and it took days and weeks to clear the roads. The further out you lived, the longer it took them to get to you. We were snowed in for a couple of weeks. The school buses couldn't run, leaving me homebound and restless. Through it all, Grandmom and I watched Kentucky. Most of the time, she fixed popcorn. And while she sipped her bourbon, I drank ginger ale—splashed with cherry juice to dress it up.

Gradually it came out, how she had played basketball in high school. "That was back when you divided your team into offense and defense," she explained. "Some girls stayed on one end of the court, some on the other. I guess they thought it was too much to ask the girls to run full court."

"It's pretty far, Grandmom. Especially when you have to run back and forth, over and over, the whole game. I don't know how they do it—without more subs."

"Look at these fellas," she said, pointing to the Wildcats. "They're not even out of breath. It's because they've trained their bodies. Back when I played, they thought a girl would mess up her female parts if she ran too much."

"Mess them up? How?"

"Just the jarring, I guess. The *exertion* is how they put it."

"Then what would happen?"

"Nothing," she said, taking a sip of bourbon. "Nothing would happen. They were wrong."

Sometimes the Kentucky games would be recorded and broadcast late at night when there was no other planned programming. On the evening news, the sports announcer would warn you the score was coming so you could, if you wanted, hold your ears and run into the kitchen to miss it. I guess Grandmom thought I was a convert. And maybe I was, but she didn't push. Every now and then, what she'd say was, "Now that was a textbook layup."

I had to admit sometimes I could see the beauty of the thing—like a ballet move the ice skaters made—a smooth leap with a graceful arm-lift that in this case happened to deliver a basketball *softly*—I could see now why the coach called it a *kiss*—off the backboard. Some small part of me wanted to try it. And I have to tell you, this was new. For though I'd been staying for basketball practice before the holidays, it was just an excuse to spend time with Seth and Archie and the other guys. I had never thought of myself as a player.

For a while, thinking about it was as far as I got. The snow kept everyone in. There was no school. There was no basketball practice. I slumped around from room to room. Grandmom probably got tired of hearing me sigh, tired of my long phone calls with Lorraine, where we compared scorecards, why Jarrell was hot, why David and Kenneth were not. Neither of us mentioned Seth anymore. I was trying to move on, and I guess Lorraine didn't want to open old wounds. A time or two, I started to mention Kyle Macy, but for some reason I didn't.

One day just as I got off the phone, Grandmom came to my room with a big box. "Look what came in the mail for you."

Inside, there was a deflated basketball. I turned it over and over in my hands, tracing my fingers over the Spalding.

"I had to save twenty box tops to get it," Grandmom said. "I had to choose between saving cows or rubber trees. But in the end I got the one I thought would last the longest." She clapped her hands together. You would have thought it was her basketball.

"Once the snow melts, you can take it to the court down at the elementary school. But for now, you can dribble in the basement, just to get a feel for it."

"It's cold down there."

Grandmom frowned. "Not that cold."

True enough, it wasn't *that* cold. I wore long johns under sweatpants, as she instructed. She got out the bicycle pump and put air in it for me. All I wanted was to dribble without looking at the ball. How did you get it to behave like a well-trained dog, or a yo-yo, going where you told it, as if it were on an invisible leash? I bounced the ball with my fingertips, as the coach had instructed. At first, I just walked around, my eyes to the ceiling while I dribbled. The ball bounced off my shoes more times than it didn't.

When the snows finally melted, I took the ball to the court at the elementary school and eventually got to where I could run the length of the court without looking at the ball and without losing it. I imagined Kyle nodding his head, clapping. Grandmom asked, didn't I get lonely practicing by myself? It was peaceful, I said—and it was. I didn't tell her Kyle kept me company—though I guess maybe it wouldn't have surprised her.

Beside the court there was a series of brick posts where once a wood fence had been strung. You could bounce the ball off one of the posts, and it would come back to you like a pass. I practiced getting the ball to ricochet from a post to meet me further down the court. I can't say how many loose balls I chased across the playground all the times I under-threw or overthrew the posts. But gradually it got to where I could run the whole court, passing to the brick posts—imagining it was Kyle running alongside me, passing the ball to me. Back and forth we'd go till we were under the basket.

That's where confusion and disappointment set in. I would throw the ball up any which way—off the backboard or just on top of the rim— hoping it would fall in. On TV, Kyle made it look easy. But it took a lot of strength, just getting it there. When I couldn't luck it in, I would throw

it hard, trying to force it off the backboard or lodge it in the rim so it wouldn't pop back out. But it popped out more often than it fell through.

I do not say I didn't think of Seth all this time. Or of Archie. Or of Jarrell. But I kept them at a distance. Their minds were already turning to baseball practice—which, till that year, would have been the place I wanted to be. From time to time, I thought about what Grandmom had said, that some people believed too much running would ruin your female parts. Maybe my parts were wilting, I thought, and that explained why I didn't care so much about sitting in the bleachers watching the boys.

When we shot, I talked to Kyle about the boys I knew—because Kyle and me, we could be just teammates, just friends. "Kyle," I would say. "I have a problem."

"What is it, Phoebe?" he'd say.

"I heard that Lorraine likes Seth."

"That's okay, isn't it? You're over him now, aren't you?"

"I guess. But I wonder who started it?"

"They're both free agents, right?"

"Yes, but what if it started before we broke up?"

"Don't let it get you down," Kyle would say. "You've got other things going on."

In secret places in my notebooks, I took to writing Kyle's name and No. 4. I clipped box scores and newspaper photos and put them inside my locker. There were photos of Jack Givens and Coach Joe Hall, and, of course, Kyle Macy. When I opened the locker, Kyle was there, his brow fierce in concentration, encouraging me to stay composed no matter what kind of day I was having.

One day Chrissie stopped at my locker. "Wow. Who's that?"

"Just one of the players from Kentucky," I said.

"Is he professional or college?"

"College."

"Do you know him?"

I shook my head. "I've just seen him on TV."

"No wonder you stopped hanging out with our boys. How long have you liked him?"

"It's not like that," I said, shutting my locker.

And it wasn't. Well, it was, but it wasn't. How could it be? Although he was the person I thought about all the time, it wasn't in the same way I'd thought about other guys before him. I could talk to him in ways I couldn't with regular boys—mostly because he listened and didn't hog attention.

By early spring, Kentucky was on the road to a national championship. Every game—Florida State, Miami-Ohio—there was more at stake. And Kyle was there every game, pulling it off at the foul line. Or feeding it to Jack or Rick Robey under the basket. There was a beauty in the games themselves, the way the players moved down the court like a herd of gazelles. My grandmother and I spent whole quarters standing in the middle of the floor, intent on every pass, every shot. Sometimes we clung to each other, hid our faces in the other's shoulder so as not to see. But in the end we found ourselves jumping up and down like it was as much our game, our victory, as theirs.

In the Mideast regional against Michigan State, everyone thought Kyle would meet his match against Earvin Johnson—a guard the announcers called "Magic." But all that showdown proved was that there was no one more magic than Kyle Macy. Down through the final stretch of the game, he scored enough from outside and on the foul line to give Kentucky the win that propelled them into the Final Four.

While the games heated up, so did my practices. All day at school, it would build in me. I felt a fullness, like little bolts of energy firing in my legs and in arms. My fingers grew restless, anxious for the first brush with the ball. Then after school, once I had the ball, my heart beat giddily on the walk down to the court.

There, I dribbled, and the first bounces of the ball sent a message to the basket—that I was coming, that I was on my way. No longer was it about forcing the ball but now was more about coaxing it. I understood better its rhythms and tendencies and adjusted myself accordingly. I tell you, I kept a dizzying pace. Round and round, I went, backwards and forwards, spinning first one way, then another, throwing would-be defenders off balance, moving closer and closer to the goal. Everything else fell away—papers I was writing for English, Seth and Lorraine holding hands, all the newspaper clips of whales and wolves Grandmom was trying to save.

I worked on my jump shots, setting up garbage cans in the middle of the court and learning to shoot from behind them without falling forward and knocking them over. Envisioning myself a rocket, I sprang straight up and only when I peaked, perfectly vertical, would I release the ball, launching it—arching it, ever so gently—toward the goal. The follow-through was key. My eyes, my hands stayed with the ball even as it left me. At such times, I felt connected with the net. I would send out the ball, and the net would welcome it, embracing it once it entered the rim. The net would hold it momentarily, swaying back and forth, then let it drop softly to the ground.

So close were we in those moments, I didn't know where I ended and the basket began. We were tangled up together, the basket, the ball, and me. Winding around and around in the zone, I lost myself, shooting and rebounding and shooting again, full throttle, all in a heady circle of give and take. An hour or two later, I was utterly spent. And when it was ended, I was panting, my legs aquiver, my face hot as an oven. I would go back to the house, and Grandmom would say, "Goodness. You better get a drink of cold water." In those evenings, my heart was light and happy.

The layup alone remained elusive. I would lie awake trying to negotiate its intricate movements. In my mind, I replayed Kyle's layups, or Jack's, and my own miserable attempts at it.

One evening home from shooting, I admitted it flat out. "I still can't do a layup, Grandmom."

"It's got to be one fluid motion," she said, "like you're taking a running jump to touch the backboard, but on the way up, you drop off the ball."

"I know. But you have to dribble till you jump, then catch the ball while you're jumping. Then lift it up, nearly one-handed," I said. "Kyle makes it look easy."

"He's been at it a long time, I expect. You know when he was in diapers, his folks had him dropping the ball in a basket."

The next evening, sporting a pink sweat suit, Grandmom accompanied me to the playground. She jogged in place on the court. Then moved somewhere else and jogged. It was such an unusual sight I had to turn my head to keep from laughing. I tried to imagine her a young girl in uniform.

"It's been a long time since I had my hands on a basketball. I probably can't even dribble."

"Here," I said, catching her attention, then bounce-passing it. "See if you can."

She wrinkled up her mouth and squinted her eyes and pushed the ball down, then caught it with both hands. Down again and up and caught. Down and up and caught. Then she sent it down, and patted it down, and patted it down again, without catching, and there she was, dribbling. "It'll come back," she said, watching the ball as she dribbled. Back to me she passed it. Solid.

"Now, let's work on the layup," she said. "Show me what you can do."

I started at half court and dribbled at a slow jog. When I got to the basket, I managed to catch the ball and jump at the same time. Then I hoisted the ball from my hip and felt it slip from my fingers. It spun out into the playground, and I chased away after it.

When I got back, Grandmom said, "You're doing much better at not looking at it. That's the main thing."

"What am I supposed to do after I jump?"

"Let's see." She went to half-court and bounced the ball, revving up. For half a minute, I expected her to break into a run like Kyle Macy. But instead, she walked, bouncing the ball, turning the problem over in her mind. When she got near the basket, she seemed to ladle up the ball—it reminded me of ladling anyhow—and sent the ball upwards. It hit the bottom of the rim and came back down fast—so fast I had to run over and knock it away to keep it from hitting her in the head.

"Goodness," she said. "It's faster than it used to be." She was laughing, so I laughed, too.

"Anyway, Phoebe, I think you need to scoop up the ball with one hand, and use your other to protect it from the top or side—so no one can strip it from you. The Kentucky players have football dummies standing in their way when they go up for a layup—so they have to concentrate and hold the ball tight. When you've got it good and balanced, pull the top hand away and lift the ball up with one hand. Just tap it into that little square—like you're tossing a rock at a window you don't want to break."

She went back to half-court and tried again. This time she brought more energy and skipped a little off the ground. She made the same ladling motion with her arm, going up, and she delivered the ball off the backboard into the basket.

"Wow," I said. "You really can play."

She winked at me. "It's coming back. It's in the blood, you know."

Over and over, I tried to ladle it as she'd done. Sometimes she'd say, "You jumped too late," or "You jumped too soon." Or she'd caution, "Don't put it up so hard—just lay it up easy." We practiced it that day, then the next, then the next.

Eventually, I felt in my body the shape of the layup emerging. I dribbled, caught the ball, got my right hand under it like a ladle and scooped it up. Then my left hand assisted to keep it from spilling. When the ball was balanced on the tips of my fingers, I pulled my left hand away, and made a faint springing motion with my right hand. The ball rose toward the backboard.

I did it over and over. The mastering of it was gradual, culminating in days with more hits than misses—though still a fair share of misses.

"You've got it," Grandmom said. "Once it gets in you, your body will remember it forever."

The layup was the single riskiest thing I learned in basketball. For while it brought you closer to the basket, it also put you in danger. You opened yourself up and made your body vulnerable. You couldn't jump backwards because you were jumping forward, flinging your body through space. You charged into it full steam, and once airborne, your body extended outwards. You surrendered control. I thought of all the players I'd seen on the floor after an opponent had taken their feet out from under them. On TV, the guys ended up in the crowds, on top of cameramen even! For me, it took a courage I'd never had before. But admittedly, too, there was a certain freedom in flying yourself at such a speed—and in knowing you could make the landing.

The satisfaction was tremendous. While the jump shot brought connection with the basket, the layup brought a different kind of communion. It was the difference between *sending* the shot from far out and *being* the shot from deep within. Time after time, I would move in, straining, reaching. Even more than with the jump shot, I felt a part of myself go upwards with it. And then I lifted the ball as something of an offering to the basket. It got to be where I was rewarded most of the time with the kiss off the backboard and the swoosh of the ball down through the net.

Kentucky won the national championship that year. For me, it was a

bittersweet victory—meaning an end to a season that in no small way had sustained me. A famine would follow, I knew, and it would be a long time before the first game of the next season.

But one day that summer, just after I came in sweaty from the court, Grandmom looked up from behind the newspaper she was reading. "Guess who's coming to Huntington on Saturday?"

The smile on her face told me.

"Kyle Macy?" I said, my eyes stretching wide.

"He's signing autographs at the Ford dealership."

All week I lost sleep. Over and over, I played it in my mind. Would he recognize me as a kindred spirit? Would there be a court where we could play? Would he maybe give me his jersey—like you saw athletes do on Coca-Cola commercials?

The line for autographs was about twenty people deep when Grandmom and I pulled in the parking lot. Immediately we were beset by car salesmen, but Grandmom waved them off. "We're not here for cars," she said. "We just came for Kyle."

In line were old and young fans alike and quite a few girls my age standing with their mothers. I don't mind saying I felt a tinge of jealousy. But I thought, too, if someone put all of us on the court at once, I could hold my own against any of them. I don't know if that's true or not, but I had a brief, momentary surge of confidence.

While we stood there, I fingered the paper that had my questions on it. They were pretty specific—about the backwards layup, the behind-the-back pass, occasional moves I'd seen Kyle pull off—not in the least showboating, Grandmom had said, but only when necessity called for it. Occasionally, Kyle stretched, looked back in the line, probably wondering how many more times he'd have to sign his name. Each time he looked, I tried to build my courage to look back, but always my strength failed me.

Every now and then Grandmom stepped from the line to get a better view of him. I knew she was anxious to ask him how recruitment was going. And there was a part of me, I guess, hoped she would brag to him. I could just hear her saying, "You should see Phoebe do a layup." This would be the only way, I figured, for me to earn his respect.

Finally, with just one person in front of us, my heart pounded like

it would shatter my ribcage. I held the basketball under one arm so my sweaty hands wouldn't dampen it and create a smudge where Kyle was going to sign his name. Finally, when the body standing between us moved away, and I found myself face-to-face with him, all my thoughts turned to mush. I couldn't think of the first question. He smiled at me, and I smiled back. At that moment, I knew that was as far as I could take it. It had been silly to think of asking him any questions at all.

Grandmom lifted the basketball out from under my arm and placed it on the table in front of him. "Hello, Mr. Macy. I'm glad we finally got to meet you. We were up all hours watching you play. We followed every game. My granddaughter Phoebe here is your biggest fan. I think she wants to marry you."

It took me a minute to understand what she had said, and when I did, my face flashed even hotter. It was such a shock—even from my Grandmom.

Kyle must have registered the surprise on my face. What had been a friendly smile now broadened to a full grin that pulled his dark eyes into it.

I was too surprised to say anything at all.

Suddenly, he moved around the corner of the table with my basketball in his hands and dropped to his knees. From there, he took my hand, and placed it on the basketball.

"Will you marry me?" He was still grinning, and it occurred to me he was trying to turn it all into a joke between him and me—to show my grandmother. But it only made me blush more. I felt the silence in the room where before there had been busy chatter. I felt everyone's eyes on me. A camera flashed. Then flashed again. From somewhere, a photographer had emerged.

I took a deep breath and let it out slow—just as if I'd been about to shoot a free throw, then I said, smiling, "I'm sorry, Kyle Macy. It's not like that."

I met his deep-set eyes over the basketball, long enough for him to realize—and for me to realize, too—that it really *was*. All he'd expressed on the court—playing his heart out every game—had made an impression on me, and I'd expressed it back—even without him there to know it. We'd felt the same aches—driving to connect with the basket, straining to move closer to the rim, flinging ourselves in the air toward that goal.

We'd felt the same exhilaration, the same pleasure when the basketball swayed snug in the net, or when it threaded through, then dropped back down to fill our hands anew. There was love in it for sure, no one could deny it, a wild, to the rim, net or nothing, oven-fired ladling of love.

The next day there was a picture of the proposal in the newspaper—him on his knees, holding the basketball between us. Had I been the newspaper editor, it's the picture I would have chosen, too—far more dramatic than a regular signature shot. But my favorite photo—of the handful the photographer mailed us—is the one I keep framed on the wall now. Not Kyle Macy proposing or even dribbling in front of me, motioning for me to steal from him, or the one where I'm dribbling and he's defending, but it's the one where we're posing: him standing between me and Grandmom, all three of us resting our hands on the basketball, and she's sneaking a glance over at me, so much certain joy in her eyes.

It was funny, really. For a long time, before his daughter married, Russell was afraid she would turn up pregnant. He braced for it each time Marlie came back to visit, especially when she'd gone a long time without seeing them. Pregnancy out of wedlock wasn't so uncommon as it used to be, and it seemed like it could happen to anyone. One man he knew had three daughters who came back that way. Each time it happened, Russell felt sorry for him. At least he and Evelyn had avoided that kind of scandal. But now whenever he saw the man in the yard on his riding mower, a young boy in his lap driving, Russell felt behind his sternum a hollow place.

This time, when Marlie said she needed to see them, Russell had hoped it was to tell them she was pregnant. That way he'd at least be able to spend time with a grandchild before he died. Or maybe, knowing a grandchild was on its way, something inside him would fight to stick around longer to watch the little one grow up. He'd always had a lot of love, but now, as he caught sight of the finish line, he felt he had even more—and couldn't help wishing for someone new with whom to share it. But when Marlie had swung down out of her jeep a few days ago, there was no bulge under her blue-jean jacket, and no pregnant woman would have worked as she had done since she'd been home—unless she was trying to lose a baby.

Now from the window of his bedroom, he watched her splitting wood.

She was making the maul work for her. It was different than with his son, Frank, who had big shoulders and arms and could bully his way through the wood. Marlie held the maul at the tip of the handle and swung with a long, high arch and with such a light touch that Russell worried the maul would fly out of her hands and injure her—or some innocent bystander.

Her rhythm was consistent, even machinelike. Clomp. Pause. Clomp. Pause. Clomp. Clomp. Pause. They were clean splits, too. Right through the heartwood. None of that splintering of the edges he had no patience for. Had he taught her to chop like that, or had it come by instinct?

When she was down to nine or ten logs in the oak pile, Russell left the window and went to the closet for his jacket.

"See if you can get her to stop after this," Evelyn said.

He shrugged. "I don't think I can stop her. She must be working through something."

Clomp. Pause. Clomp. Pause. Clomp. Clomp. By the sound of the split logs falling on the ground and on top of each other—like the high-pitched scattering of bowling pins—he could tell the oak was well seasoned.

He went back to the window. What did the neighbors think, driving by, seeing her doing his chores? By now they'd probably heard. A quadruple bypass, not wholly successful. He'd been given lists of instructions on everything from eating to avoiding stress to doing gentle warm-ups and stretching before loving his wife. And the kicker: enjoy your life because you might go at any time. Which, when you thought about it, was really the truth for everyone. But hearing the doctor say it brought it out from whatever drawer you'd been storing it in and made you turn it over in the light.

"Alan hasn't called the whole time she's been here," Evelyn said. "I guess they're not talking again." She was leaning over the bed, lining up old photos of the children, different rows for each decade.

"Maybe they just need a vacation now and then," Russell said.

"We never needed a vacation." Evelyn straightened up, put her hands on her hips, and arched her body backwards till it took the shape of a strung bow.

Russell crossed the room and gently commenced rubbing her shoulders. "Maybe you ought to work on the kitchen table," he said. "You

wouldn't have to bend over so far." He felt her muscles loosen under his fingers.

She leaned back into him. "There's just more room here," she said. "I've been meaning for years to get these in albums."

There were gray pictures of the baby years, some lightly touched with paint. Then came the fading colors of the toddler years when Kodak must have been working out a new chemical formula. All the early photos had white borders with scalloped edges. In the next row, a group of orange-tinted photos showed the kids in junior high with braces and big glasses and their hair parted straight. Finally, there was a set of momentous occasions—proms, graduations, and most recently, though already five years past, Marlie's wedding. The special haze of the formal shots blurred Marlie and Frank through their adolescence and early years of adulthood. Off to the side, Evelyn had piled a few Christmas photos taken since the wedding, but these seemed more an appendix. Of what was to come, there was little trace.

"She'll work herself to death," Evelyn said. "Didn't you see how tired she looked?"

He put his arms around her, and they stood together, the whole lengths of their bodies touching. Russell took comfort in it.

"I thought she looked okay," Russell said, but he knew what Evelyn meant. There was some new worry etched in Marlie—she wore it on her face and carried it in the line of her stance. He couldn't quite pinpoint it, but he'd noticed it the evening before in the kitchen when she was stuffing peppers and cabbage rolls with ground turkey—all healthy for his heart, she told him.

"She's a good cook," Russell said, remembering, too, the mashed turnips seasoned with cinnamon and nutmeg.

"And a good eater," Evelyn said, easing from his embrace and bending over the photos.

"And eater," Russell agreed.

But who wouldn't eat a lot after all the work she'd done? Since coming home, Marlie had cleaned the gutters and chimney, raked the yard, bagged the leaves, even dug a drainage ditch out at the side of the yard where water had been collecting. Russell had seen her eyeing the sun-cracked cedar siding on the northeast wall of the house and knew she was

thinking of replacing it. She had never been one to sit still. He supposed that was what kept her out of trouble. Frank had sown his oats, but Marlie had been a model daughter, what people called All-American, with good grades, after-school jobs, a stint as pitcher on the softball team, volunteer work at the nursing home and Habitat for Humanity.

Evelyn pulled a photo from the deck and placed it at the end of one of the rows. It was of Marlie and Frank on a camping trip. They had on their fishing vests, and their faces were rosy from sunburn. It'd been decades since Russell had seen smiles as big as that.

"I'll see what I can do," he said.

He called Josie the dog, and together, they went out. The sour scent of sap and drying leaves hit him, along with the hint of wood smoke from somebody's chimney. Russell took a deep breath and savored. It put him in mind of other autumns, other years, when he was out doing the things Marlie was doing. Clomp, pause, clomp. The splitting went on. Down through the yard he strolled, pausing to examine the large trunks of maples he'd planted when the kids were small. Their old wounds, from when the children had tried to tap maple syrup, were healed now, and the trees looked healthy with only a smattering of red leaves left in their bare tops. The trees would probably outlast him. But the day would come when they, too, would lose their strength, maybe rot from the inside out, or succumb to disease.

He steered himself again the way toward the barn, toward Marlie. By now she would have seen him in the yard. He was giving her time to collect herself, if anything needed collecting. At the barrel incinerator, he stopped again, peering in to make sure the last of the letters had burned completely. He'd lately taken to some housekeeping that involved rereading and destroying letters he and Evelyn had sent when he was in the Navy. It brought back their early years and plied his nostalgia for young love. But he didn't want anyone else—not even the children—reading them. There'd been a romantic side to him he wasn't keen on sharing with anyone but the one who'd inspired it. He and Evelyn had talked it over first. They were having conversations they wouldn't have had three months ago before his surgery.

The clomping and pausing at the woodpile drew him on, but still he did not hurry. He gazed curiously in the little creek, studying a spark plug

and a piece of old plate—might have been his grandmother's—what all the recent rain had uncovered, odds and ends just thrown away, no use to anyone now. Josie stayed with him, both of them circling and doubling, like hounds that couldn't puzzle out the scent of the trail.

When he finally got to Marlie, she had finished the pile of oak but was getting ready to start in on the hickory.

"That old tree was back there on the corner of the property a couple of years," he said. "I hated to see it go to waste. I wouldn't have bothered if it'd been poplar."

"I know," she said. "On account of the popping."

He nodded, then threaded his way through the strewn logs to one of the unsawed tree trunks he and Frank had dragged from the woods at the end of summer. That was the week of his heart attack. "Why don't you rest a spell?" Russell suggested, sitting back on the log. "You've been working since you got here."

Marlie's eyes and nose were red—and Russell understood she would start splitting the hickory to hide that she'd been crying. He marveled at the mix of softness and ruggedness in her. When the children were little and got hurt, they came crying to you, and you knew to put on salve and a Band-Aid to make it better. But when they were older, they hid their tears. And who could begin to know how to mend their wounds if they suddenly chose to reveal them?

But he was running out of time. That's what the doctor had said. And it was funny and absurd. Because he didn't feel bad. Nothing hurt him. He felt tired, but that was all. And anyone, at seventy, could feel tired. He felt fine really. He had been strong through the surgery and recovery. So far, nothing had been able to sink him. But then, none of it had done the trick to repair him either. He supposed it was how people in coastal areas felt when a hurricane approached. That there was some dark treachery lying in wait beyond the clear, blue horizon was just about more than you could believe.

Josie looked up at him, wagging her tail. He picked up a stick and threw it deep in the yard for her. She bolted. Marlie watched her.

"She won't overdo it, will she?"

"Nah," Russell said. "It's been two weeks since she had her stitches out. Dogs, they just get back up, go back to themselves. It's people who take a while to bounce back."

With her boot, Marlie shoved over one of the hickory logs, then bent over and rolled it a few feet toward the short walnut stump where they did their chopping.

"I wish I could help," Russell said.

"I can get it." She commenced rolling it again and wrestled it up, end over end, onto the chopping block. Not once did she have to take its full weight.

She wiped her forehead and stood back, eyeing the log and gathering her strength. In her short hair and on the sleeves of her flannel shirt—one of his that Evelyn had put in the rag pile—Marlie was sprinkled with sawdust and wood chips.

Josie came back dragging the stick. Russell took it and held it, watching her and trying to gauge her need for rest. She sat down and looked up at him, wagging her tail. She was a mix of collie and retriever, and maybe some other breeds, too, that hadn't yet manifested.

Marlie stood resting with the heel of her hand on the maul handle as though leaning on a cane. She was more angular than he remembered, and it seemed to him that since she'd married, she had toughened up. The word *hardened* came to mind, but he didn't like thinking marriage would do that to you. Still he could tell she probably went to the gym a lot.

"You work like this at your house?" he asked.

"I wish," she said. "I wish there was woods—and firewood to bring in—and a fireplace."

"You all could move back here," he said. "Plenty of room to build. Whatever piece of the property you wanted."

He watched her face, but she pulled up the shoulder of her shirt to wipe her forehead. It was funny to him, that either one of them could slice straight through a log, but when it came to speech, they were blocked up as a beagle that had swallowed a sock. On TV, people talked. Everyone talked naturally about everything. He didn't see how it was possible in real life. If you had the script before you, that'd be another thing.

"Pretty day for chopping wood," he said. "Not too hot."

"No," she said. "Nor too cold either." She had rolled up her flannel sleeves, leaving only her long-john sleeves to keep her wrists warm.

He tried again. "You think Alan would ever move back here?"

Again, she wiped her forehead—but maybe it was her eyes, he couldn't tell. "I don't know. He might."

"Does he help around the house?"

"Some."

"He probably wishes you would sit still."

"I try to stay busy."

"I was busy my whole life," Russell said, wagging the stick at Josie. "Now I wonder if it would have gone slower if I hadn't been so busy." Josie rose and faced him, fanning the air with her tail. He swung hard, sent the stick to the edge of the woods. Josie ran fast, so fast that when she got near the stick, her rear end seemed to overtake her front end when she tried to stop. She nearly went over in a somersault.

Russell grinned and looked at Marlie. She was grinning, too, and when she met his gaze, he sent his love, and she, perhaps feeling its intensity, ducked and shied away. She stepped up to the chopping block, then lifted the maul to let it rest on top the log as a batter might do before swinging. Then she stepped back and lifted the maul high and brought it down hard. The maul bounced back up as if it were a rubber hammer— and she caught and managed it from far back on the handle.

"Whoa," she said. "I wasn't expecting that."

"Good thing you didn't get hit in the head. Hickory's hard, you know. This tree was gnarled besides. You might have to use the wedges."

Marlie sized up the log. "I'll give it another try first." His daughter had a determination that Evelyn likened to his own. But what was strength in a man, he reasoned, might be viewed as stubbornness in a woman.

Marlie squinted her eyes at the top of the log, then gave the log a half turn as if a new angle might make all the difference.

"Your mother thinks you're working through something." He tried to dive in without thinking. "Is anything wrong?"

Marlie lifted the maul over her head, then brought it down considerably harder. The maul went deep, deep into the log and stuck there.

She pried up and down, but the maul was lodged tight. Russell scanned the ground for the wedges, and when he saw them, went over and picked them up. The weight of the tiny irons was startlingly heavy. He brushed the sawdust off and carried them to her. It gave him a chance to inspect the log.

"That dark wood in the middle, the heartwood," he said, pointing, "is dead, you know."

"Well, it's all dead now."

"I mean even when the tree's living, the dark part is dead—or dying."

"Funny they would call it heartwood then—and not deadwood," she said.

Russell smiled. "It's the sapwood, the white part, that lives. The outside part. I saw a TV show on it last week. But the heartwood—what's dead—weathers better than anything. It's full of tannin that makes it resilient, for outdoor furniture and things like that."

Sensing her interest, Russell continued. "I know you know about the rings?"

"Summer and winter?" she said.

"If I'm not mistaken, they said *spring* and summer. But anyway, it's the same thing. Fast growth as opposed to slow. The bark's a big deal. It's more important than I ever realized."

She nodded. "All the nourishment?"

"Yep. Water and minerals move up through it."

Marlie nodded. It was easy to talk about trees and animals—any natural occurrence. That was what they listened for, out in the world, to tell each other. It was just difficult for either of them to say a soft thing to each other.

"Probably you ought to lay the log on its side," Russell said, "and pound the wedges in that way."

She rolled the log to the ground, positioning it on its side. The maul handle jutted straight up. Then she inserted the first wedge, and with the sledgehammer, pounded it in as far as it would go. She tried prying the maul loose, but still it wouldn't budge.

Russell moved back to his place on the tree trunk, out of her way, and took the stick from Josie. "This is the last time," he said. "Then you'll have to rest." He threw the stick hard, and as he did, he felt a tightness in his chest where his stitches had been. The stick went up, end over end, and whizzed over the barn to the other side. Josie followed it with her eyes, half-jogging, half-dancing the same direction. Russell expected it would take her a few minutes to understand where the stick had gone.

Marlie pounded the second wedge twice, three times, then four, and freed the maul and the first wedge. She turned the log upright again and split it in half, careful not to hit the second wedge, which fell out as the

wood separated. Then she turned one of the half logs back up on its end, took up the maul again.

"Well?" he said.

"Well, what?" she said.

"What's wrong? Is there trouble in paradise?"

"I guess there's trouble in paradise," she said, lifting the maul high behind her and bringing it down to split the half into quarter pieces.

He steadied himself to prepare for the possibilities. Whatever it was, it might hurt him. Divorce would hurt him. But he would try not to take it too hard. He couldn't afford to. There was his own heart to protect now, his own life at stake.

"Are you dying?" he asked. Because to him, this seemed a yardstick now by which everything else could be measured.

"No," she said. "*I'm* not. But the marriage is. Alan and I have separated."

There. It was out. Now they could deal with it. It wasn't so bad as a terminal illness, he told himself. He would still have his daughter. But there was no guarantee in that either. Sometimes, with trouble in a marriage— at least on TV—depression seeped in. Then there was always suicide to worry about.

"I know how you feel about divorce," Marlie said. She swung high again, then guided the maul deep into the new log, where it stuck. She turned the log on its side, inserted a wedge near the maul. "But that's what we're going to do." She didn't look at him, just reached for the sledgehammer and started pounding the wedge. The ringing echoed off the hills around them.

Josie came back marching with the stick, pleased to have found it. She held her head high so the stick wouldn't drag the ground—giving the impression of a dog swimming. When he reached down, she brought it right to his hand, obedient in every step. The stick was slimy where she'd been chewing.

To Marlie, he wanted to say, "It's your life." But he held back, knowing she would take it as the jab he meant it to be. There were new rules now. You tried not to say things that would be hurtful—in case it was the last thing you wound up saying. You didn't leave anyone on bad terms. You didn't walk away harboring guilt or hatred or anger. You finished every-

thing like it was the last time, like there would be no other chance. In case there wasn't.

The maul was free again, and he watched her lift it, saw her steady herself. Her eyes scanned for the invisible vein she would aim for.

She sliced all the way through, quartering another half. It had the note of finality to it.

"Nothing can be done to fix it?" Russell posited.

"No."

She gathered up the quarter logs and loaded them onto the trailer behind the tractor. Then she wrestled another log up to the chopping block. She was moving from the smallest logs to the largest—the top of the tree down—and was still in the knotty region where the limbs had been.

"I'm sorry," she said. "I know it's not what you wanted."

It was old-fashioned, what he felt about marriage. But there were things he knew—how you learned the blueprint of someone, how they learned the blueprint of you, what it was to open the doors, walk through each other's rooms, the lovely pleasant ones but the grief-filled ones, too. And even the ones where the other person was too scared to tread alone. How a person could suddenly go around shutting all those doors to someone you'd opened them to, he didn't know. And then there were people who would open the house to lots of people, lots of lovers. How easy it must be, he imagined, to say the wrong person's name in a moment of honesty, just the way they did on TV shows. Or you might think you were waking up beside one person when it was really another. He thought of the divorced people he knew. The world was changing. Not much stayed constant. Divorce these days was more the norm than full-term marriage. Even if you lived in a place where there was a semblance of constancy, the TV might give you other ideas.

"Well," he said, feeling it his turn to speak and wanting to say a true thing, "I'm sorry it's not working out."

She went on clomping and pausing, clomping and pausing, every now and then ringing the wedges with the sledgehammer. He envied her, for he knew how it felt to work like that. He knew the heft of the maul, the back stretched to near breaking, the scrunched abdomen, the way your hands were jarred with every blow—the way that jarring vibrated in every part of you. Marlie struck so hard sometimes her feet came off the

ground. It was hard for him to sit still and watch her. He was used to sparing Frank whenever he needed it. And vice versa. That was the way to keep fatigue at bay.

Out in the woods he heard Ray Stoddard's hounds howling and running, probably on the trail of a rabbit. Josie heard them, too, and stood up. She looked from the woods to him, back to the woods and back to him, expectantly. Easy to read.

He was about to say, "Go on," but then remembered her recent incision and the brush and briars she would be apt to tear through in the woods. "You better *stay*," he said.

She barked, as if in protest. Then she lay down, he thought, pouting. She kept her ears up, though, monitoring the turns, coming and going, near and far, in the woods.

Marlie chopped. He wondered if he and Evelyn had done something wrong, somehow created a restless daughter. After college, she'd been one of those who couldn't find her niche. Couldn't, for some reason, take hold, though she was good at most things she attempted. Before settling down with Alan, she'd moved from job to job, state to state. A man like that was called a drifter. A woman was just called flighty.

Josie lifted her nose in the air like she was scenting out the rabbit the hounds were chasing. Russell reached down, patted her head. "It's for your own good," he said. But he hated making her stay when what she wanted was to run with the other dogs.

"We're not in love," Marlie said, between swings. "I guess we never were."

"Love," Russell said. It was not something he talked about—though he thought about it probably more than most would expect. He'd been, he supposed, one of the lucky ones.

Marlie rested, holding the maul diagonally across her body, at ease. She waited for what he would say on the subject.

He shrugged. "It's a mystery. How some people find it and others don't. You work hard at it. You work to stay together. But there's something there, too—not just familiarity—something I guess you can't create if there isn't some spark or some seed there in the first place." He was thinking of the early letters from Evelyn. She had written, "Clear across

the ocean I feel the tug of the line that connects us." Hadn't he, too—no matter what he went through—felt that strong line out to her, even before they were married?

He looked at his daughter. "It's more than a feeling," he said. "People have to work at it."

"I shouldn't have married him," Marlie said. "I did it for you and Mama. I wanted to make you happy." She swung the maul and chopped. "And me, too. I thought I could be happy." She chopped. "I thought I could make it work." She chopped. "If I tried hard enough." She chopped. "Stayed busy enough." She chopped.

A funny way to talk about marriage, Russell thought. Most people tried to carve out quiet hours to be together.

He asked, "Was he going out on you?"

"No, Daddy."

He wanted to ask if she was going out on him but couldn't bring himself to it. He didn't want her to have to lie. He hoped she had been faithful, but these days you could never tell. She had waited a long time to marry—and they figured she had chosen the one she wanted. They felt relief. They could pack whatever other fears they'd had in a trunk. She had finally found someone who suited her and maybe grandkids would be on the way.

"Did you all see a counselor?" Nowadays that's what people did.

"We tried that," she said.

What Russell heard were notes of the past tense. He firmed his lips and sighed and waited for whatever else might follow. He waited the way you wait to hear from a president who's taking you to war. He wanted reasons. He wanted convincing. But because it was his daughter—and not a military leader—he figured his heart would kick in and tilt him to side with her.

And didn't he want her to have love, too? Not just security but love. He wanted that for both his children—Frank hadn't found it yet either. But it was not always easy, love. He thought of the times when he and Evelyn had quarreled. Or when he had stayed late at work—with a restlessness. He had wanted to be alone, but she worried he was with someone else. Yet for all that, most of the years were years when they'd collapsed

into each other's arms, with the outside world, their parents, their children, all the burdens too heavy for them to bear alone easier to carry together.

Marlie was rolling one of the logs toward the chopping block with her foot. "There'll be some changes, you know," she said.

"I would expect." He was glad he'd taught her to change flat tires and fix leaky faucets. Out in the country, that was how you raised daughters. There was no telling which husbands might take a wild hair and abandon them, maybe with kids to boot.

"What if I told you I caught him wearing my clothes?" Marlie said, just before she swung the maul.

It took him a minute to understand what she'd said.

After her swing, she repeated it. "What if I said he was wearing my clothes? That he's decided he's a woman trapped in a man's body? That he's going to have a sex change."

"Alan?"

She swung again. "I know it must sound ridiculous to you."

He let out a low whistle. It was the kind of thing you saw on Oprah.

"People don't really do that, do they?" he found himself saying. But what he meant was, people *we know*. Sure, people in other places got caught up in snares like that. But not anyone in his realm of acquaintances. Alan, while he wasn't what you'd call a cowboy, wasn't really a sissy either.

"He's been good to me," Marlie said. "I love him. But not in a marriageable way."

Russell thought of what Alan had put her through, five years in a sham marriage. Wasting her time. No wonder there were no children. He felt a flash of anger that he tamped, tamped, tamped down to frustration. Then he went to thinking about Alan, whom he'd taken a sincere liking to. How could a young man let himself get derailed like that? Who put such ideas in their heads? Evelyn, he knew, would say it was the devil. Probably it came from TV, the sitcoms and movies, all the crazies in Hollywood. Things were all the time getting worse, you couldn't deny it. Still, he could remember way on back, in his youth, he'd seen Bob Hope and Milton Berle, from time to time, wearing dresses. But wasn't that all for the sake of a joke?

"Where did he get a notion like that?" Russell asked.

"He—just—figured it out," Marlie said, clomping. Pausing. Clomping.

"Been better if he'd figured it out sooner," Russell said. "Would have saved you some trouble."

"Maybe he suspected it, but fought it," she said. "Maybe he was in denial."

"Probably been best to keep on denying it," Russell said.

"It's no crime, Daddy." She said this in a pleading sort of way, and he couldn't understand why she was bent on defending someone who'd so clearly wronged her. He imagined her life with him. Him wearing her clothes. Them pulling from the same underwear drawer. That was too much.

"He's been awfully unhappy," she said. "He's gone a lifetime wishing he was in a different body."

It was a crime against nature, Russell thought, but he didn't say it. Surely, Marlie would come to see it as she gained distance. You didn't raise your children to do those kinds of things—or *feel* that way. How could you begin to conceive of yourself as separate from your body? What explained that? You put your children in Sunday school, brought them up in church, taught them the Bible, but when they got out loose, tossed to and fro, they lost sight of the way things were meant to be. When they were little, it was stray kittens and pups they brought home. But when they got older, it was stray ideas that were hardest to get shed of, like poisonous snakes in their pockets.

"Do Bob and Mavis know?"

"Not yet," Marlie said.

"It will break their hearts," Russell said.

"I guess that's why he hasn't told them," Marlie said.

"He ought to rethink it more. It might even kill them." Russell tried to imagine their reaction. At first, they wouldn't—couldn't—believe it. How could you? But later, as the seriousness dawned on them, they might think it was worse than death. And it *was* a death, really, when you considered. The loss of your son. And maybe—and this was the kind of spin Oprah would put on it—maybe you could think of it as a birth, too. A new daughter. But just a regular person couldn't be expected to come around to that himself.

"Can't you see how strong he must feel about it," Marlie said, chop-

ping, "to be willing to risk so much? He feels dead—that's what he says—and just wants the chance to live, as he feels inside." She wiped her brow and kicked the split logs out of her way.

Russell was sweating, too. He pulled off his jacket and lay it on the log beside him. He said what he was thinking: "But God wouldn't make a mistake and put you in the wrong body. How could that happen?"

Marlie's face was red from the work. "He doesn't see it as a mistake. But as a trial—and—a mission. Something he's been given to go through, something he can help others with." She put her foot on the log in front of her and gently rocked it back and forth. Then she looked up, and just for a moment, met his eye. "Besides, isn't it supposed to be the soul God's interested in? Isn't it the inside that counts?"

It was too much to absorb. Evelyn wouldn't buy it, Russell knew, convinced as she was that God didn't create homosexuals either. Though in that regard, at least, you had to admit there were examples of them in nature. It was true, too, in his lifetime, he'd owned a few she-dogs who always lifted their hind legs and peed like boys—that was the way Josie did. He was sure Marlie would explain it to Evelyn as she was explaining it to him, and he would try to help if he could, as much for Evelyn's sake as for Marlie's. Evelyn and Marlie had their confidences, he knew, just as he and Frank did. He wasn't called on much as a middleman between them. He thought of Evelyn back in the house now with the photos spread out on the bed. Probably they would do away with the ones of Alan. It would be something they'd want to forget. But Alan's parents wouldn't have that option.

"When's he going to tell them?"

Marlie shrugged, then took a half-hearted swing at the log before her. The maul wobbled when it struck the wood, and barely went in. By that, Russell knew Marlie's arms were turning to rubber. It would make the job more dangerous.

"He's afraid," she said. "Afraid they won't love him anymore."

"It'd be hard," Russell agreed and tried to imagine it.

Marlie lifted the maul, then lowered it again to rest. "You mean it'd be hard to tell them? Or it'd be hard for them to love him?"

Russell thought a minute. "Both, I guess."

Marlie raised the maul and took aim. Clomp. Clomp. Pause. Clomp.

Clomp. Pause. Though the log was one of the largest, Marlie didn't use the wedges this time but halved and quartered—and even split it into eighths—through sheer doggedness. He had figured her wrong with her tired arms. But surely, if not her arms, then her back must be strained to breaking. It made his back hurt, thinking of it.

At his feet, Josie sighed and stretched and rolled. Russell rubbed her shaved belly with the sole of his boot. Her scar was pink and healthy. He thought of Alan. The young man's body would probably be mutilated. It wasn't the same thing, of course. You did it to your pets to control the population and maybe to save them some agony in the long run. But by limiting them, maybe you took from them pleasure, too, what they might have had if left alone to nature. One way or another, people found ways to play God.

Marlie cleared the ground around the chopping block, piling the split logs in the back of the trailer. There was only one log left from the gnarled hickory; it was the base of the trunk. Surely she'd have to use the wedges for it.

"Why don't you rest a spell?" he said. "You can tackle the last one in a few minutes."

"I'm gonna try and finish," she said. "If I stop, I might not be able to start again." She took a deep breath, then bent over and commenced rolling the log with her hands. When she got to the chopping block, she stood up, looked Russell's direction, then rubbed her chin with her hand. She smiled weakly. "Daddy, it's not true," she said. "Alan's not wearing my clothes. He's not having a sex change. But it *is* true we're getting a divorce."

Russell grappled to sort out the truth from the lie. It was like isolating and capping the hot wire when you changed a light fixture—having about it all the urgency and trepidation that went along with that.

"Is he *gay* at least?" Russell asked. He'd never said the word before.

"No," Marlie said. "He's about as straight as they come."

"But why—?" He didn't even know the words to ask about the ordeal she'd just put him through. Was it to make the truth of the divorce easier to bear? He felt some relief and started to smile, but he knew he couldn't rid the puzzlement from his face. He felt cheated, like Marlie had stretched him unnecessarily. And him with a bad heart, on top of it. It

wasn't like her. For whatever she was, she had always been a kind person, a compassionate person, the most sympathetic he knew.

"I just wanted to see what you'd say," she said. "See if you'd understand—and if you could find a way to love him through something like that."

She bent down and half-wrestled, half-heaved the last log up toward the chopping block. She took some of its weight, and just as he was about to protest, he caught sight, the corner of his eye, some glint, some light that might have hit the edge of the maul and ricocheted toward him. There was something in her gesture, something about the way her arms, in a familiar motion, took and handled the weight of the log, that struck him as a move his son, Frank, would make, and suddenly he recognized what she'd been getting at. He'd been making his way through a dense pine grove and had stepped, unexpectedly, into a clearing where the light was so bright and the air so sharp that it burned his eyes and stung his lungs and splintered his heart where the stitching had been. The burn and the sting and the splintering radiated outwards from his core and filled him with heat and nausea.

He started to ascend and hover. Old navy buddies had reported it, when they'd seen sudden action. How you would rise above yourself to adjust to the horror around you. He felt paralyzed. He could no more have reached down to pick up Josie's stick than he could have tossed it a couple of feet in front of her. He wanted to believe Marlie was joking. In a few years it would be funny to tell at the dinner table. Then it dawned on him he might not be there to laugh about it. And probably she would have forgotten, would have moved on to something else. He started to smile. But the look on her face—while she wielded the maul high in the air above her head—said she wasn't joking. The seriousness crept in. How could he stop her? Why need she cause them such grief? He felt a sagging weight in his shoulders. She was his daughter. He didn't need, or want, another son. Surely she had swung too far one way and would swing back again. He could see ahead rooms of heartbreak and confusion. The neighbors would view them with pity. His heart would not be able to bear it—Evelyn's heart would not be able to bear it. This would be the thing, the very thing, that put them in their graves.

The maul trembled in the air above Marlie's head. How long could she hold it vertical? He saw the strain in the way her arms shook, the pale terror that flashed across her face. For a moment, he was afraid she would drop it straight down, ripping her skull in two, ending it there, with the sawdust and woodchips hungry to soak up blood. Then he envisioned the split—that what it came down to was saving himself and Evelyn or saving her. She shifted her eyes from the log to him. She waited for an answer. The maul stayed suspended above her head.

"I wouldn't understand," Russell said. "I couldn't." How could anyone? His eyes stayed fixed on Marlie's face, and he felt a surge of heat run through his chest, stirring him. "But I would try to love," he said. "I would try to—love."

FEEDING INSTRUCTIONS

You'll have to adjust, maybe even make some sacrifices—depending on the life you've lived before—but soon you'll slip into a pattern the way a cow or goat, on her way home for milking, furrows a hillside by taking the same route again and again. I've been nine years trying to find a formula, going by instinct mainly, just doing what needs to be done. You may find yourself better suited for it than I am. But don't worry if that's not so in the beginning.

You won't have trouble with her. She sleeps eighteen, maybe twenty, hours a day, and even awake, she lies motionless in bed—curled up the way of beans left long on the vine. Through the rails sometimes, she'll watch—say if you're folding towels and sheets in the living room beside her. But she can't see well. Look at her eyes. I always thought them the color of orange pekoe tea—after you dunk the teabag a few times. Now the color is fading behind clouds of cataract. Probably she will make out your shape. She knows me—inasmuch as she knows anyone—in a dim way, by my movements and voice.

You might talk to her, tell her about the weather. We have three dogs— Scamp, Fritz, and Lady—but she may know earlier ones better: Speck, Tanner, Duke, Rover, Buddy, and Foxie. Tell her funny things they've done. Make up things if you need to. Tell her they caught a rabbit or treed a coon. Repeat, over and over, to her, "Them's good pups." That's what Martin's daddy always said, and it will be familiar. We don't have a cat, but occasionally she sees one and enjoys stories about it—call it Kasey, Sam,

or Tiger-Boots. You might get her to grin—if she thinks you're tickled. To be honest, it's one of the few rewards. She may not know what you're saying, but a humorous tone stirs amusement in her.

She won't raise up. Look at her. She hasn't moved since you got here. She stays balled up like this most of the time. We keep the pillow between her knees so she won't get a bedsore. And you can see how thin her skin is—like the flesh of an overripe peach. A hand around her wrist will bruise her, and any kind of friction will peel back skin. Gentleness is a must.

Come back this way to the kitchen, and I'll show you where everything is. Her ears are still sharp. Maybe she doesn't grasp what we say, but I do my best not to alarm her. One day last week one of her sisters stood over her, saying, "Poor, pitiful thing. Wonder why she don't just go on, June?" Though I judged Mommaw—that's what our children call her—to be asleep, I asked Myrtle if she'd heard the dogs in the night, and while she was answering, I ushered us to the front porch. People don't realize, I guess, that some part of her may understand. She never wanted to burden anybody, and even now we don't want her to feel unwanted. Who knows why she hangs on?

If you watch her long enough, you'll see she can't lift her hand to scratch her nose, much less feed herself. She won't turn over—she can't. She won't try to scoot down to the foot of the bed and get out, like I've heard some will do. She's just not able. You'll have to turn her every two hours or so. Just pull up on the sheet and roll her. She's not heavy. I believe she'd stay in one place till kingdom come if we let her. She doesn't have strength to move anymore. We never used restraints, though no doubt in the beginning these might have helped. What we've done is just let her run out of steam. She had more steam—and still does—than any of us thought. It wouldn't surprise me if she outlived us all, but you can tell she's going down.

Gone are the days when she would appear on our back porch, rap on the door, and yell through the rusty screen that a strange man was eating stewed cabbage at her table. Well do I remember her quavering voice, the ribbon of fear she tried to modulate. Gone, too, are the days, after Martin's daddy died, when she was forever setting out on the road, a basket of cornbread in her arms, heading toward some home only she could see. A scarf tied around her head, she resembled those villagers you watch on

TV, the ones filing into exile from some unstable country. In those days, she was driven, let me tell you. I don't mean we drove her—oh, sometimes we did. Sometimes we had to. She would hound us till we gave in and tucked her in the car, steered up the road, and showed her all the houses, two belonging to sisters. One of them died last year—but that's nothing we will tell her now.

"Show us where you live," I'd say.

"Why, I'd talk about it. You know where I live, June. Why won't you take me home?"

"We just left your home."

"You fellas is crazy. After all I done for you, you play tricks on me. You just want the house. But I'll tell you something—." She shook her finger. "You're not gonna get it. You won't get it if it's the last thing I see to."

"Do you want to visit Myrtle or Zelma?"

"Is Zelmie home?"

"She's at *her* house. Right here." The thick planks clacked and rattled as we rolled over the bridge.

"No, no. I want to go home, June. Quit this nonsense and take me home."

Sometimes we'd coax her out to visit, hoping something would click. In no time, though, we were in the car, strapping a seatbelt around her with Zelma waving from the porch and her little cat, Ralph, going round her legs. Both were widows and might have kept each other company, but neither would have been satisfied living in the other's home.

On the way back down the road, she'd spy her house—this house. I don't think it was the white cinderblock—or our red brick beside it—as much as it was the location, the house stretched out longways, sloping itself gradually upward along the toe of a hill that began to rise sharply behind it. This wasn't the old house she visualized, yet it was the same hill, the same foot, where she'd been born and grown up.

"There, there. Let me off there. I hope Mommy and Poppy didn't leave for church yet. Did you tell them to wait?"

She was always wanting Mommy and Poppy. They'd been dead, fifty and sixty years, respectively. I memorized the dates. I'd have to tell her: "They're dead. It's written in your Bible. George Turner died January 16, 1935."

"Did Poppy die?" Her eyes would tear up and her nose blush red. "I can't seem to get it straight." Always this pained me, her blurred knowledge.

"He's dead," I'd say it more gently. "You won't see him no more on this side."

"No. But I miss him. Let me out at the house so I can talk to him."

"He's dead."

"Well, I *know* that!" she'd say. Easily today I hear her words and see her, angry, shaking her head: "Well"—shaking her head—"I"—shaking her head—"*know*"—shaking her head—"that!" A huff of air punctuated the sentence. Then, more softly, "But I want to see him. Let me off here at the house."

Martin would pull up the driveway, and we'd let her out. She'd walk across the worn path, in a hurry, like someone a long time hungry, just in from the fields. There was no relief in this for us—because we knew there'd be no relief for her. It would start up again, give her five or ten minutes to get inside, sit in her rocker, and then the longing would creak back in.

What was happening? Can you tell me? It was a failing of sight— but not eyesight—not then. There was a veil—the world, as if, through gauze. And with every day, every passing month—oh, there is a discernible pattern now—another layer of gauze and another and another, each layer tighter and more constricting than the last, less and less seen, less and less recognizable, less and less that was *her*.

Maybe, after Martin's daddy died, when she took a turn for the worse—snapping off like a light going out—we should have taken her to a doctor, a specialist, I mean. She told Dr. Weber she was fine. Said we were trying to take her money, money hidden in the hollow of an apple tree. Shouldn't that have told him something? She was getting forgetful, he said, tucking his clipboard under his arm. And old people simply get paranoid. He made no referrals. But today we hear about doctors who specialize in such things. Maybe we should have tried to find one. Now I can see this, for her abyss grows, day by day, separate from ours, but for the time—in the beginning—we were taken down with her, swirled around and under, skirting some kind of whirlpool, all of us struggling to stay afloat, and I could not see—there was no riverbank, no tugboat, not

even a trotline strung in sight. Just daily rations—not enough to count on, not enough ever for any one of us, not for her, for me, for Martin, for our children. We were just dragged along in a merciless current.

Only now have I begun to think about it. There are breaks—lapses—the current eases. An hour might go by when I'm not changing her, washing her, laundering her bedsheets and gowns, fixing her dinner, or feeding her. Imagine a river slowing, a river with occasional hiccups—time becoming again, though not with speed, your own.

In the beginning, the labor was not so much physical as mental. You will not face this. You just need to feed her, change her, keep her clean. For us, then, there was the matter of matching wits, and, I'll be honest, she whittled us down. We never had time to grieve for Martin's daddy. Maybe that's a good thing. She kept us hopping. You wonder why I tremble? I guess you might say it's grated on my nerves. Most evenings—and it was worse in the evenings—I had to plant myself on the driveway and go head-to-head with her like a sheepdog trying to steer her around.

"When will Martin be home?"

"Not till five, Mommaw."

"I want him to take me home."

"You just left your home."

"I know that, but I want to go *home*," she said. "If I set in to walking, will you watch me? Make sure I get there?" Her pleading softened me.

"You don't need to get on the road this time of day. There's too much traffic. We don't want you getting run over or picked up by a crank." I spoke her language.

Her brow wrinkled, and frustration clouded her face the way a gray film of rain slides over the mountains and into the hollows.

"I don't know why nobody will help me," she said. "After all I've done for you fellers. All the nights I spend taking care of Grandma and the baby. Why can't somebody do me just one favor?"

More than anything this triggered something in me. I didn't know then all I would do, all she'd require of me. I only knew how much I'd already done. "Who do you think we're taking care of?" I'd ask. "Are you blind? Can't you see everything we do is for you? Looks like you're the one ought to be grateful."

I don't know why I said it. We all have our limits. But it was nothing she could absorb. In her mind, she was perfectly healthy. There was no

sense in quarreling. I had to strategize, buy time. I was in the middle of fixing supper. The children were at basketball practice or 4-H. We wanted them to have fun, to have full lives still. I was there alone. I needed Martin to get home to help.

I'd say something like, "Well, if you're taking a trip, you'd better go next door and lock the doors." I could count on her being responsible— that was always in my favor. She *wanted* to do the right thing.

She'd shuffle in her house shoes back down the trail of tamped earth to her house, while I hid her basket of cornbread up at my house. When she'd come back looking for it, I'd say I hadn't seen it. Yes, it was cruel. But I ask you, what were my options? Of course, I returned it first chance— maybe I sent her back again to check on the "baby" and then followed behind. While she was in the bedroom, I'd put the cornbread on a plate here in the kitchen. All afternoon, she'd been at it—baking a pone of cornbread to take *home*, not wanting to go empty-handed, adamant about doing her share.

Beside the cornbread, I'd set out a glass of milk, water beading on it in the humidity. I'd lay out the dish of whatever we were having besides— chicken and dumplings or pinto beans or some kind of roast. Always there were potatoes—mashed, boiled, fried, baked. That was—and is— the staple. Remember that. Even today when you fix her plate, you'll need potatoes. These days I rely on the instant kind—it's just easier:

1 pkg. of Idaho instant potatoes
½ cup of water
½ cup of milk
margarine/butter optional (I always add lots of butter)

You'll find she eats good—it will amaze you. She's got a hearty appetite—and doesn't mind being fed. Back then, in the beginning, she couldn't, or wouldn't, pass up a meal either. Every day she said the same phrases, "I'm not hungry but I might set in and eat a big bait." Seeing the plate heaped—and thinking she had done the heaping—she'd say, "Looks like my eyes was bigger than my belly."

I did all that cooking six, maybe seven years, while she could still string together sentences. Or could she? They were more like recordings, played back over and over. Always she said, "It's good to eat someone else's cooking"—like she had a different chef every day. She was po-

lite. "Thank you, June," she'd say. "You're better paid," which was short for, "You're better paid in heaven than here on earth."

I'd fill her plate, sit her here at the table—you had to *put* her here. I'd scoot the chair close so she couldn't stand without effort. Then I'd slip out the door, edge my way up against the house, peek in the window. Sometimes she would stick the whole plate in the refrigerator—or the oven— and I'd have to come back in, start all over. But once she commenced, she rarely left halfway through—I'd have time to run back and feed Martin and the children, who were home by then. We tried having her eat with us, or us with her, but that didn't satisfy her either. Most evenings, I ate apart from everyone—standing at our kitchen window, watching her house. When I started the dishes, I'd be looking out the window, waiting for her to come out, searching again for home. When she appeared, I'd send one of the children out to distract her.

Sometimes we just let her go. There was nothing else to do. We'd corralled her five, maybe ten times, and we just couldn't keep doing it. Not without losing our minds. We'd watch her go. We'd hold our breaths. When she was in motion, it was hard to stop her. Folks got used to seeing her. Everyone knew, sooner or later, what we were going through. I don't know what they said, passing her—the road is so narrow in the curve there. Maybe it was along the lines of, "It's a shame they can't keep her off the road," or, "Too bad it's come to this for them."

We're a small community; you can probably tell. People are good-hearted. Lots of us take care of parents and grandparents, aunts and uncles. It's the way we were raised. Sometimes a neighbor would pick her up, bring her back. But most of the time, no one could stop her. She was just bent on going. Her body took on this mechanical determination— it was uncanny. Robotic. Like she was in a daze, brainwashed. She was eighty-five then. Have I already told you this?

That she was leaving home, what'd been her home for forty years, was something she could not fathom. But there was a home somewhere. In her heart she knew it. Does she see it now? It's a good question. But you can't really ask. Or expect an answer from her. The other day she said, "This is a pretty house," like she'd never seen it before. It *is* a pretty house. She and Martin's daddy built it, both of them carrying cinderblocks. She used to tell me about the work—before she got like this. I love the wide,

beveled trim around the windows and doors, this reddish-brown stain. And the hardwood floor. Martin remembers helping his daddy lay the floor—he would have been in high school then. Of course, you can see it needs to be refinished. The years with the walker and the wheelchair and the bed, the potty chair, and now the lift, all these have chafed off the color. Not to mention the puddles she made. I'd get her to the bathroom, wash her and change her clothes, while Martin went around with the blue-handled mop and a bucket of Murphy's Oil Soap. That was in the evenings. During the daytime I did it all myself. But I don't know why I'm telling you this. You won't have to worry about it. The hard part is done.

She will sleep in there under the tent I've fashioned with a sheet across the bed rails. Even in the summers I keep her covered—but cool. She can't tell you if she's hot or cold. You just have to sense it—like with a child. Sometimes she rubs her fingers together—I think she's string-ing beans. Sometimes she gently swirls her hand around like she's stir-ring some pot on the stove. When Martin's daddy died, we could see him planting beans, pinching one or two between his forefinger and thumb, dropping each into the soil, reaching to pick up the next one. When you see something so familiar, so ingrained in them, surfacing like that at the end, it breaks your heart.

This isn't the place to start, and I apologize. You need to know what to feed her. Really, it's not so complicated. You boil chicken—any meat will do. She's anemic, so it's essential to put red meat on her plate some-times—though you'll still have to give her iron, in liquid form, either an hour before meals, or two hours after:

2 tablespoons of iron
¾ cup of cranberry juice

The iron stains everything. Wipe the rim and bottom of the bottle—or you'll get a red ring on the counter. It's not a good idea to substitute or-ange juice for cranberry—the acid is too hard on her. You wouldn't want prune juice either. You don't want to upset an equilibrium it's taken months, years even, to establish. Cranberry juice doesn't affect her either way, and you need balance. That's what the Imodium's for. You go a few days handling about all you can handle—and her, too, handling what she can handle—everything goes right through her, comes out liquid like a

newborn's mess. Maybe it's because everything's pureed to start with, I don't know. But there's a limit. Too many times a day, too many days in a row, and her bottom starts turning red, and there's the risk of bedsores.

Janice, the aide from the medical group, said it was all right to control her bowels, stop the flow for a day or so, with Imodium. Just remember, you're the one in charge—you and God, I guess. Mix the Imodium—not too much and not too often—with pudding:

1 teaspoon of Imodium
2 tablespoons of pudding, vanilla or butterscotch

Martin is the one told me you might be interested. Says you've always had a good heart, that you like helping people in a bind. All along I've said we could do it ourselves—we don't really have the money to pay anybody—and in a few months after the surgery, I'll be able to relieve you. I don't think it'll take as long to recover as they say. It's true I could use a vacation—but what kind of vacation is it when you're laid up? Martin says I'll get some much-needed rest, and he's probably right. It will feel good to sleep later in the mornings, knowing she's in able hands. Knowing I don't have to wake up to clean her, that I can stay in my own house.

But you shouldn't be afraid to ask for help. All the buttons on the phone ring in at our house. Martin wired it that way when she was calling everyone—calling strangers even—to take her home. I'll be able to tell you where things are—though most everything you need is here in the kitchen. Don't be afraid to call. You have to take care of yourself. I've known plenty of people who've gotten down trying to do for someone else. Your health's important, too.

You will worry. There'll be plenty of nights you'll lie awake fretting about her bowels or about a bedsore on her hip or shoulder or knee. Don't be alarmed at her body. Maybe you will be at first. She reminds me of the photos of people in starving countries. You can make out her skeleton, the knobby elbows, the knobby knees, the shape of her skull, the eyes set deep in. We feed and feed her—but I guess this is just the way of it. You mustn't think she's losing weight on your account. All you can do is feed her—and maybe pray that God takes her. I don't know if I'm supposed to say that. Don't know if I'm supposed to *think* it even. Probably it's selfish talk—and will you forgive me for saying so? It's been a hard nine years—almost a decade of my life. But why should my last nine

years have been any better than her last nine years? I guess my question is: why didn't either of us have nine years better than what we had?

Feeding her, you will want to plan ahead:

7 or 8 skinless, boneless chicken breasts
1 can Campbell's low-sodium chicken broth
Boil the chicken breasts in the broth
Tear the chicken in small pieces
Puree in a food processor
Add broth as needed

She will eat about two tablespoons of pureed chicken with her potatoes. Wrap, in little foil packages, a week's worth of pureed chicken. Freeze, in these convenient sizes, everything but what you need the first week. Do beef the same way. Don't try fish—you don't want to risk bones. Whatever meat you use, moisten it with gravy. Here in the refrigerator, I've already got a jar opened. Just warm a few dabs on the stove. Warm everything on the stove—or in it. We can't have a microwave because she's got a pacemaker.

Naturally, as I said, there are potatoes. Of her fondness for them, she used to explain, "It's the Irish-man in me," but you won't hear that now. It's something you might mention while you're feeding her—it will be familiar. Lately, I fix only instant. Can she tell the difference? They're high in sodium, and that's a mark against them. But she always salted everything, just shook the shaker around a whole plate of food: fried squash, potatoes, green beans, chicken and dumplings, creamed corn, you name it. I fix instant because there isn't time to peel real potatoes—and maybe not the energy it requires—not enough to stand around waiting for them to boil, or to mash them. I know it doesn't sound like much. Maybe it will be different for you. In case it's not, you can just read the package:

1 pkg. Idaho instant potatoes
½ cup water
½ cup milk
butter (it's optional but I always add a bit)

Now, you have meat and potatoes. I don't give her many green vegetables for reasons I've already explained. You'll see what I mean. Risk it if you want. You're the one in charge now. I'm just telling you how I've

done, what's worked for me. You might try mashing green beans or green peas—but I wouldn't chance broccoli or spinach. For sure, give her a big helping of applesauce with a slice of white bread crumbled up tiny. Sprinkle sugar over it like it's a cobbler. This is for bulk. Give her as much as you like. Give her anything you like—or that you think she will eat and be able to swallow. It should not be too dry or too runny. Are her meals bland? Repetitive? She gets chicken and beef a lot. For us, there is variety: McDonald's or Arby's or Long John Silver's or Taco Bell, food Martin picks up on his way from work. Sometimes on Sundays I try to fix a big meal—but lately it's been too much trouble. Like her, I guess I'm relishing someone else's cooking.

Everything must be fine—pureed and somewhat liquid. Here on the counter is the food processor. Be careful washing it because the blades are sharp. It's been years since her teeth fit. Be glad you don't have to worry with them. She used to dunk them in a cup of water and hide them in the kitchen cabinets or once up here in the freezer. They might have froze and broke if we hadn't found them.

Even with her teeth, we had routines. Are you tired of hearing about it? Probably there are things you need to do. Maybe you'd like to unpack? We hate to ask you. I wish we didn't have to. But we don't have anybody else. The children help in the summers when they're home from college. But my doctor says this surgery shouldn't wait till summer, and we don't want them to have to leave mid-semester. If you can help for just a couple of weeks, till I've recovered, I'm sure we'll get back on even footing.

But let me explain about her teeth. I don't get to talk about it much. At church they ask, "How's Grace?" And I always say, "She's just the same." Is there time to tell them all about it? And where would I start?

Do you know how many visitors she gets? Four regular ones—every Christmas. There's a man who comes and plays the banjo. Then there's one dresses as Santa Claus. The others drop off their fruit baskets at the door. The rest of the year, there's a man and his wife from church who visit, at least every other week. Mayward and Glennis are their names. They've always been ones to see to the shut-ins. There will be a crown for them in heaven. Religion pure and undefiled, you know, visiting the widows and orphans.

I guess people think we don't want company. Maybe we don't. We've

got this schedule. If someone interrupts it, everything's thrown off. There are certain hours when she eats, when she takes her iron. It's what she's used to. It's what we're used to. Probably it doesn't seem like a big deal, whether there's a schedule, whether there's company. It's been nine years. If I say that when something like this happens, you get abandoned, will you believe me? People stop calling. It's just as well—you are tied to the house. You can't go anywhere—and leave her lying? People go on with their weddings and baby showers. It's easy to forget about the dying when the dying take so many years dying.

I know I need to go over her diet with you. See, I used to give her eggs and bacon and toast. It's what she grew up eating, what she loved. And oats. She loved oatmeal. We'd get her out of bed, Martin and me, take her to the toilet. I'd stay and coax her to use the bathroom—she couldn't even remember what to do. I'd say things like, "Go ahead and use the bathroom, Mommaw," and "Don't you have to pee? Go on, then," and, "Let the water fly"—things she used to tell the children. "Make your kidneys work," and, "Go on, empty your bladder. Didn't you say you needed to use the privy? Well, here you are." I'd repeat these phrases in different sequences. My daughter said it was like trying to find the key—a code that would unlock her mind. She wouldn't keep the Depends on at night, so the bed was wet, too—that was before the hospital bed. Do you know how many times I changed the bed back in her bedroom? There were three or four solid years of that—times 365 days—when she couldn't get up but could still manage to take off her Depends. I mean, sure, you do that for a child, but with children, you know they'll grow out of it.

Anyway, in the bathroom, I'd wash her face, comb her hair, present her teeth—what we'd had to coax from her the night before. Please understand, Martin's mother, in her right mind, would never have thought of going a day without cleaning her teeth. It was unthinkable. She was one of those ladies kept Listerine in business. But you see what happens. I don't know why. It just does. I had the awfullest time getting her to put her teeth in.

"Them's not mine, June," she'd say.

"Of course, they're yours. Who else's would they be?"

Sometimes she'd whisper to me, "Them's not hers." For a while, that threw me. Then I figured she was talking about the woman in the mirror.

As long as I understood where she was coming from, I could work with her.

"They are hers," I'd say. "She wants to put her teeth in, doesn't she?"

"She says she doesn't know," she'd whisper. Eventually, if I begged long enough, she'd dip her fingers in the cup, bring out the top plate, put it under the running water. She'd rub her fingers all over, cleaning the gums, the fronts and backs of all the teeth. She'd do it, over and over and over, while I stood by, holding the cup with the bottom plate.

"Put them in your mouth, Mommaw. Put them in your mouth."

Sometimes she'd slip the dentures back in the cup, and we'd have to start all over. Sometimes she'd stick the top plate in the bottom of her mouth. So many days I couldn't make her understand. Pitiful thing. I don't know why anybody has to go through it. God has his reasons, I guess. It was nothing she deserved. I used to say maybe it was sent my way so I'd learn to be more patient. But I don't think that anymore. I'm no more patient than before. If anything, I'm less so. I get aggravated easy. I cry. I fuss at her: "Why won't you pay attention? Swallow your food. Swallow. Swallow. Swallow. Swallow."

How hard can it be to swallow?

For breakfast you can give her Cream O' Wheat with tiny, tiny, tiny, pieces of buttered toast crumbled in:

1 pkg. of Instant Cream O' Wheat
1 cup of boiling water
one piece of toast, buttered and crumbled

When you feed her, put a bib on her—we use a dishcloth—with a paper towel. The paper towel takes care of little spills and keeps the dishcloth clean. But the dishcloth is for anything major. Call it a napkin. Don't say "bib" in front of her.

Before you give her breakfast, you must clean her from the night before. Would you eat your breakfast in dirty drawers? Even on the days Janice is coming to bathe her, you still need to clean her. Sometimes it takes a strong stomach. I never thought I had a strong stomach—but you do what you have to. Tell her you're changing her clothes. There's no use telling her she wet herself or that she soiled herself. Why remind her? If she doesn't remember—if she doesn't know—why bring it up, only to

cause her momentary shame? She would not wet the bed if she could help it. She wouldn't soil herself. None of it is willful.

For a while, when she could walk, I would march her, walker and all, into the shower stall. Always there were the same arguments: "Don't get my hair wet. I wasn't dirty. I just took a bath last night. It's cold. Turn up the heat. Shut the door. Don't let him—unspecified—in. Wash my back. Did you wash my back? While you're at it, June, wash my back. Hurry up. She don't see no sense in this. She wasn't dirty. She just took a bath this morning." Sometimes she said "she" when there was no mirror.

And my words: "You've got to wash your hair. We haven't washed it for a week. It's dirty, Mommaw. Tell me about when you and Zelma were growing up. Did you help hang the tobacco? Who climbed to the highest logs? Here's a washcloth. Tell her to wash good. She doesn't want to stink now, does she? I'm not looking. What would I see that I haven't seen before?"

But I was telling you about breakfast. After she's clean and you put a fresh housedress on her—these are slit up the back like hospital gowns—use the lift to move her to the chair. The lift is a lifesaver, you will see. We used to grasp her, Martin and me, under the arms, raise her to sitting, then raise her to standing. We dragged her upright—you cannot say "walked"—to her chair. I still haven't recovered from all that lifting. But you'll see. The lift will save you a lot of trouble.

Scoot your chair up beside her. If you want to watch TV, you can. *Good Morning, America* and *The Today Show* are my favorites. You get the news for the day, and you see familiar faces. People laughing. They start to feel like old friends. Over time, you learn about their families, their hobbies. And like I say, they laugh. They smile. It helps.

Most days she will eat well. You raise the spoon to her face. She opens her mouth. She works on swallowing while you lift another spoonful. I think she likes the warmth of Cream O' Wheat. It must be comforting. She likes to eat. It's the only activity of her day where she's a full participant. And while you're feeding her, you can tell her about the weather and the dogs and cat. You can tell this pleases her.

If you get her on a bad day, you'll have to coax her to eat. Sometimes she's groggy or preoccupied. You say: "Open your mouth. Open your mouth. Here's your food, Mommaw. Open your mouth. Good. Swallow.

Swallow. Here's some more. Swallow. Did you swallow? Swallow your food." On these days, you'll have to turn off the TV. It will take everything you have—and more. Some days you just have to walk away, try later. Pray for patience. Fussing will not help. I know this but sometimes forget. Or maybe I don't forget—I just fuss anyway: "Why won't you eat? Your food's getting cold. If you don't care, why should I? Some people would be grateful to have food. Looks like you'd be more grateful."

Sometimes, fussing, you might strike the right chord. You'll see her mouth open—it's like a shy baby bird's mouth—innocent, trying its best, trying to please you. It'll make you feel low. She opens her mouth because you're upset, and some part of her is moved by that. Can you see the effort it takes? In those moments, you know, deep in your heart, she's doing her best. But so are you. Forgive yourself and go on.

For lunch, mash a banana and crumble some bread or cake in it. She loves bananas. Used to be, you'd offer her one, and she'd say, "Not just one. Bring me a bushel." She's crazy about them. The way I figure, she's got only a handful of pleasures. Bananas are one of them. Even so, it's getting to where she has a hard time swallowing them—swallowing anything. I don't know if it's in her mind—like she's forgetting *how* to swallow—or if it's a physical problem with the esophagus.

Surely you'll see, though, it's one of her last strongholds in the world. She tries desperately to swallow. Watch the way her chin quivers. When her mouth's full, it's all she can do to hold her lips closed. Her lips tremble from the strain. And sometimes, she loses it, and food dribbles out. Or she balances it in her mouth, then works up her energy at the back of her throat, poises herself, finally swallows. It's a relief to her—and to you— every time. Praise her for it. Tell her what a good job she's done. I think, for her, it may very well be the feat of the day.

When the children were small, they'd laugh when she drank water and sometimes there was a noise in her throat—like with anybody— but she'd comment on it, say, "My swallower is a-squeegling," and the children thought it was funny. I guess *squeegling* was like a squeak and a screech and a jiggle all in one. I don't know where she got the word or if she made it up. She was always saying things to make us laugh. But giving her liquids is where you'll have the most trouble. Sometimes these go down her windpipe—and it leads to respiratory infections. Prop her

straight up—as straight as she'll go, whether it's in the hospital bed or chair. Do not, whatever you do, tip her head back. Keep her in a position where her chin is close to her chest. It got to the point where she was getting strangled with every sip. We had to start using Thick-It, this cellulose powder. Janice brought us a big can. You mix it in a cup of water or cranberry juice. Use it with every liquid, even the juice that's the vehicle for iron:

1 teaspoon Thick-It per cup = thin Cream O' Wheat consistency
2 teaspoons Thick-It per cup = thick Cream O' Wheat consistency

At bedtime, we give her orange sherbet laced with medicine—you have to use a pill crusher for this—it's over here on the counter beside the Thick-It. Kind of a grooved mortar and pestle. The pill grains get caked in the grooves, and you have to scrape out the grooves with a toothpick. She doesn't take much medicine—just a heart pill and Lanoxin. I've always wondered if Lanoxin contributed to her forgetfulness. Years ago, I read an article in the newspaper suggesting memory loss was a side effect. She started taking it when she had passing-out spells in her seventies—right before they put the pacemaker in. But why would a doctor prescribe a pill to get oxygen to your brain if it contributes to your brain's decay? Sometimes, I wonder, too, if the pacemaker, the constant rhythm it sets, keeps her alive maybe long after she was ready to go.

Martin has been the one to stay with her at night these last years, but he'll be taking care of me for a week or so after the surgery—I don't think it'll take much longer than that to recover. I feel fine. I don't see why it can't wait till summer, to tell the truth. It's hard to imagine not being down here, seeing to her, feeding her. But you'll be sleeping back in the guest bedroom where you can hear her if she calls. We prop her on her side with pillows to keep her off her back—but she thinks someone's sleeping too close, and Martin says she'll occasionally quarrel: "Why don't you turn over. Scoot over in the bed, Zelmie. Why do you have to sleep so close? I don't have no room. Well, I don't know why you have to sleep so close to a feller for."

I know some people don't have it as easy. Viney Pauley's mother tried to get out at night—even with someone staying with her—and they had to change the locks, so you could get in but not out. She was like a pris-

oner. But they're all prisoners when you think about it. I read now, in the papers, about a medicine to calm them, and I can think back to hundreds of evenings when a remedy like that would have been handy to us.

"Where are you going?"

"I'm going home."

"What you got in your basket?"

"I brought my things. Why don't you take me home?"

"You're going the wrong direction."

"I'd talk about it. I've lived here all my life. I've been here a lot longer than you. I know where my home is."

"Where is it?"

She'd point. It was always up the road.

"Maybe you'd better go check on the baby before you leave," I'd say.

"Is the baby still down there?"

"You said it was."

She'd turn to go. How many times? I don't know who the baby was—maybe one of our children. We never gave her a doll—though sometimes they do that in nursing homes. I guess we were trying to preserve some sense of dignity for her. But maybe it would have been soothing, having somebody to care for, a life to cherish, you never know. You look back. You don't know if you've done the right things. Maybe we should have taken her to our house—after she got bedridden. All along, though, we thought she'd be more comfortable here. I maintain there's some part of her recognizes things—maybe the wide, springing sound of the screen door opening, or the creaking of us walking across the furnace grate, the sound of the refrigerator door shutting, maybe the way the light comes in, a quality in the air.

We've done the best we could—in the moment. That's been the thing. It's always been in the moment—we've always felt cornered, like whatever we needed to do had to be done then, like there wasn't time to foresee the thing that was next approaching around the bend. There used to be video games the children played. You'd have your little figure on the screen, and different obstacles or enemies would appear, and you'd have to decide then and there what to do. It tested your reflexes. I guess that's how we've felt, like we're getting our reflexes tested.

People say they don't know how we've done it. I say, you just do what

you have to. We didn't have time for a plan. We've swung by the seat of our britches since the day Martin's father took sick and then died. Yes, there were times before that, times she didn't know him, but I'm glad he didn't live to see her like this. She didn't even recognize him dying in the hospital bed there where her own bed is now. Instead, she wept for her father dying, for how he'd shrunk down to nothing. She'd been married to him fifty-four years. We had them the big golden anniversary party with a two-tiered white cake. But she couldn't see him die—or wouldn't. I guess maybe these are the same.

I don't know when we did what. At some point, Martin turned off the gas to her stove. She'd stopped making cornbread and wasn't cooking anything—we encouraged her at first—but she was leaving the flames on, and sometimes the flames would go out, and the house would fill up with gas. She couldn't smell it. At some point we took the doorknobs off the bathroom door so she couldn't lock herself in.

Then we had to hide the basement door key, afraid she'd fall down the steps. I remember one time right before that, though, when I found her down there after bringing her supper. It'd been a while since I'd been in their basement, and the mustiness, the damp earth scent, brought back so much to me. She wasn't herself, but standing there in the basement with her, I could remember her, as she had been. I could remember the two of us there, admiring our canning—the rows and rows of green beans, of stewed tomatoes, of bread-and-butter pickles, of corn, all the things we had canned together, all the food we'd gathered from Martin's father's garden. Seems like I could picture it so clearly. If you've ever canned, you know how beautiful those gleaming jars of color are—you know the greens, the reds, the yellows. And she always lined them up so straight in their separate sections. Can you imagine seeing them? Say by the light of a couple of bare forty-watt bulbs? The beans were beans we had strung together, with the cold, metal, red-rimmed white dishpans on our knees, the paring knives flashing—that scent of green pervasive. The sounds of the children's voices in the yard. The corn was corn we had shucked together. I could hear the squeaking sounds as you pulled down those tight sheaves—you know, if you've done it. And the way the fine silk hair of the corn feels, the way it clings to your fingers and hands. Martin's daddy would lay it across his upper lip for a mustache, and the

children laughed—and I laughed. And occasionally, there'd be a big, fat green worm at the top of the cob—how I hated that. But I did like she did, jerking it once hard and flinging the worm to the ground, or taking one of the green sheaves, like a piece of paper, and pinching the worm off. Then, of course, we did all the chopping and cleaning, washing the jars here in her kitchen. I followed her the first few years and then, after that, knew the seasons of things.

On the day I found her in the basement, all the shelves had glass jars, but the jars were empty. A fine film of dust covered them. She was looking for something. Who knows what? The potato bins were empty. But though the potatoes were long gone, I could still smell them and remembered the early days of spring every year when we used the smallest ones, the only ones left, with their eyes sprouting.

"Are you hungry?" I asked.

"No, but I might set in and eat a big bait," she said.

"I believe supper's ready," I said. "It's on the table."

"Well, let's go and get us some." She led the way up the steep basement steps. At the top, she turned to make sure I was with her and then clicked off the light switch.

People should think of a plan. We didn't have time. Do this for a day or two, or for a couple of weeks, or months, do it for nine years and see when you have time for a plan. You do just what you need to. God helps you. Time passes quickly, as the saying is. At least, that's true when it's behind you.

And when you think about it, the future's not so far away either. It won't be long till summer—say, if I changed my mind and decided to wait and have my surgery then. Our children could help. Maybe we wouldn't have to ask you for anything. I could go on taking care of her. I think I'm going to talk to Martin about it. I feel fine really. I'm not having any trouble. None that I haven't learned to live with. I'll talk to him when he gets home from work this evening. You can wait till then, can't you? Just don't unpack anything. I'll talk to my doctor, arrange everything. I feel sure I'll be able to keep on feeding her and doing all the rest till summer comes.

As I said, nearly everything we need is here in the kitchen. There's milk and butter in the refrigerator. The pudding's in here, and in the freezer

there's ice cream and sherbet. If something goes wrong, if we have to call the paramedics, there's this DNR magnet on the refrigerator. You probably noticed. They'll know what it means: Do Not Resuscitate. The nurse brought it in. We did all the paperwork about three months ago after she took a bad spell. We'd seen her sister live a year on a feeding tube—like a vegetable—and we knew we didn't want that.

I don't like the magnet, really—oh, I know it's the right thing. I just don't understand why they asked us to put it *here* of all places. Every time I open the refrigerator to get out her cranberry juice or water, I see it, and I think, is this all it's come to? All these years, all this labor, this fretting, all the nursing I've done, and now just this: Do Not Resuscitate? I don't know what it is, it just strikes me as funny. You know what I mean? But here it is on the refrigerator if we need it.

THE SORROWS YOU CAN'T ENTER

"Can you keep an eye on my dogs today?" The voice is strange, and I have to think a minute who it is. Jack and me, we're not used to speaking by phone.

"They're not acting right," he says.

"How they acting?"

"Just funny. Sluggish. One's drinking a lot of water. The other won't raise his head to look at me."

"Not the coyotes, was it?"

"Nah," Jack says. "No wounds, no blood."

"Sure, I can look in on them."

On the other end of the phone there is wide quiet.

"Jack?" I say.

"I hate to go to work," he says. "And leave them." His voice cracks. "They're real sick, Lloyd."

"No," I say. "Go on. You got that load of pipe coming. I'll get up there soon as I can."

Jack has the kind of dogs we always kept around the house. Strays that just wandered in, what people always called Heinz 57s. Loyal, usually smart, leastways about knowing a good home. When the two spotted pups come to Jack's, he was building a house in the woods on the property I sold him. He had opted for a mountain view—though it meant extra grading for the road and house seat—a whole extra year toward con-

struction. Admittedly hard for a couple just starting out and with a baby on the way. The pups, motley as the coat of Joseph, showed up just after the wife took off with the baby.

The dogs are in a bad way. Soon as I see them I know they don't stand a chance. Ben is near gone—shuddering with spasms and taking his last breaths, deep, hard ones. His eyes are glassy and watery—looks like tears. It's not easy to watch. They are good, sweet dogs. Jack said they were sick, but somewhere deep down, he must have known they were dying. Jesse is panting hard beside Ben on the garage floor. His breath condenses on the concrete, forms a wetness on the gray.

I take Jack's extra key from the cinderblock stoop and let myself in to use the phone.

"Let me speak with Pat."

"Hold one minute, please."

On the tablet beside the phone, Jack has written the name Kathy Brumfield and a phone number. I remember this is the girl the apprentices are trying to fix him up with.

The house is clean—orderly anyway, not piled up like some houses get with only a man there. Things haven't gone well for Jack since he started building. He's a hard worker, but for some folks, that don't count for as much as it ought. I chose him—after doing my homework. With family land, you want to be careful. I had no one to inherit the property, my boy having been killed at a train crossing thirty-four years ago. I waited for the right man, one just starting out—with a good job. Someone from a respectable family and with a respectable wife. Someone not known to be a brawler or ne'er-do-well.

Jack had an earring, which I was naturally opposed to. But his hair was short, clean-cut. Won me with his conversation, deferring several times to his father, who'd recently passed away, died in his tobacco field, of a heart attack. I knew Jack's daddy—not well but knew of him. Word was, when he run out of insulation for his house in the fifties, he used burlap sacks stuffed with chicken feathers in his upstairs walls. I always wondered what some future unsuspecting occupant, maybe sawing through to put in a new light switch, would think when feathers flew out.

All in all, I don't think I made a bad choice. It wasn't long after Phyllis's funeral that I found him—but I still wish I'd had her vote on it. She had

good sense about people and maybe could have seen what was coming—
that Jack's wife would leave him for another man, saying the baby wasn't
his to start with, no matter that all along he'd been saving and scraping
together and working all those hours after his day job, well into the night,
trying to fix a house for them.

"He's back in surgery," the receptionist says. "Take a message?"

"This Sue?"

"Yes, who's this?"

"Lloyd. Lloyd Carper."

"Hey, Lloyd. What can we do for you?"

"I got a sick dog here. Want to bring him in. I think he's dying. Will Pat
be able to see him?"

"Well, he's got a lot of—"

"It's an emergency, Sue," I say. "Life and death. One dog's already
dead."

"Bring him in," she says. "We'll make time."

Jesse is dead weight. It pains me to take him from his brother, where
he's probably most at peace. But Ben's gone, not breathing now, the struggle over. And Jesse doesn't move his eyes while I carry him, doesn't care
what I do, is beyond fear—and so, I guess, past living. I haul him slowly
in the trailer of my tractor down to my barn, lay him up in my truck seat.
Jesse pants hard—the kind of race you can't run forever. His spotted belly
moves up and down.

"Just hang on, Jesse," I say. "Hang on."

The dogs come along just as Jack was nursing his wounds from his
wife leaving. Pharaoh's daughter couldn't have been happier with a babe
in the bulrushes. They give him love like only dogs could—without the
expectations humans have of one another. He named them after a team of
oxen or mules—I don't remember which—his granddaddy had owned
as a young man and reverenced later in life.

The dogs have never been mean—but curious, like to be in everybody's business. Jack hasn't been able to keep them up on the mountain. He locks them in the garage on garbage day, but that doesn't satisfy some folks. He gets calls, so-and-so, I will not say who, wanting him
to keep them penned up and off their property. Out here, though, so
many open acres to roam, you feel bad keeping a dog locked up. We've

tried hard to train them, teach them their boundaries, walking along the property line with them. Funny thing, when we're with them, they don't stray.

From the vet's office, I call Jack on his cell phone. "You got a minute?"

"Go ahead."

"I'm at Pat's, Jack. It doesn't look good."

"For both of them?"

"Doesn't look good for either one, Jack. Just prepare yourself."

"Is there any chance?"

I don't want to have to tell him on the phone. "Not much, Jack. Just be prepared."

When Jack pulls in, I'm sitting on my porch. For about a year now, he's stopped here every day on his way up the mountain, occasionally eating with me. The dogs usually wait right here to meet him, their tails fanning back and forth on the floor when they see his truck. Then while we sit, they lie on the porch, the way a dog will do, occasionally raising their eyebrows to entice you to throw them some little scrap. Today—them not here to greet him—Jack is reluctant to get out.

He's all balled up when he steps on the porch—tight-scrunched—face hard with worry. He's looking around the porch, making sure they aren't here, lying sick, some secret antidote discovered. Probably he reads my face. I've never been good at hiding things. Then everything leaves him, drops off like yellow leaves of a hickory in one of those hard October rains.

"Bennie died while I was up there," I say. "I rushed Jesse to the vet. There was nothing to be done."

He nods, sits down in the lawn chair.

"What was it?"

"Poison," I say. "It was antifreeze."

He takes a deep breath. Holds it hard. Then lets it go. He rubs his face. "Where'd they get it?"

I shrug my shoulders. "Don't know. Most people know not to leave it out."

He continues rubbing his face, as if he's trying to massage out his next words.

"I left them covered in your garage," I say. "Figured I'd help you bury them—if you want."

"Why?" he says. He leans his forehead against the porch post. "Why? Why? Why?" He bangs his head once for each why.

The Lord giveth, and the Lord taketh away. I heard it all my life. But I know enough not to say it to Jack. There's not much he will hear today.

"Come on," I say, standing. "I'll help you. There's a graveyard we've got—for pets and other animals. If you want—."

He nods.

"Let me go first," he says. "Give me about fifteen minutes."

"You sure?"

He nods again but doesn't meet my gaze.

I watch his truck struggle up the rutted mountain, hear it creak back and forth. When he's out of sight, I get on my tractor and start up the hill behind him. I want him to hear the sound of it coming. Not have time for the awful silence that comes in absence.

In my trailer are the two tarps I took off my roof when I got back from the vet's. I figured the dogs needed them worse than I do. On top of the mountain, Jack carries the dogs from his garage to the trailer—carries them like children, lays them gently on the sun-stiffened tarps. I start the engine and haul the dogs around through the woods to the cemetery. Jack walks along behind with a couple of shovels over his shoulder. The clearing is mostly in shadow now, but I park at the edge where the sun hasn't been cut off.

I shut down the engine, tell him, "The sun hits full here in the mornings. It faces east—the way cemeteries used to."

He takes a deep breath, lets it out. His eyes are full, but he's holding back.

"You want to pick the spot," I say.

"It don't matter," he says. "Wherever you say. I don't know what else is buried here."

"How 'bout over there—near the pines? They always liked to roll in the pine needles."

"Okay." He wipes his nose with the back of his hand. "I don't care really."

We both of us commence digging. Quietly. There's no need to talk.

What you hear is shoveling. The shovels scrape sandstone; they screech and grate on through. Sometimes pry up. Hit roots. Chop, chop, chop through the roots.

Jack digs hard and fast, working through it.

When he stops to get his breath, he says, "Everyone knows about anti-freeze. Any dog or cat loves it. Can't resist it." He examines a sweat bee on his forearm, then flicks it off. "You don't think someone done it on pur-pose, do you?"

I guess you suspect the ones complained the most. But that's not a fire I want to feed. You're bound to have quarrels with neighbors. Quarrels with God, too. But Jack's young, capable of—and blind to—things that might cripple him the rest of his life.

I hold my tongue. There's a lot I won't tell him. Won't say what hard, ugly deaths they suffered. How convulsion and anguish were wrung out till the last bitter breath. How they did not understand the suffering, poor things, and could not see the end till the end was right there and took them. A burning nausea had them by the throat, set fire to their stomachs. The vet said it shut down their kidneys—all their vitals. In their eyes was prayer for it, for everything, to cease. The vet gave Jesse a shot to help him along, but by then he'd already done most of his suffering.

"This land's been in your family a long time," Jack says. "You know any stories about it?"

"Stories? I've probably told you most of them. How my great-great granddaddy settled here before the Civil War? Only a wagon and kettle and goat and horse to his name."

"Haunted stories," Jack says. "I mean, do you think this place is haunted?"

"This place? The graveyard you mean?"

"This." He stretches out his hand, pans it slowly across everything. "I mean, is it haunted or something?"

"I don't reckon it's any more haunted than any other place," I say.

"Just that since I came here—." He sticks his shovel in the ground, rests his foot on it. "Maybe I'm the one that's haunted."

I catch his meaning. "Well," I say. "I lost my wife—my son, too."

"And dogs."

"And chickens and calves and goats. Once a horse I was partial to."

"What happened with him?"

"Her. She got the colic one spring. Died. I'd bought her for my boy but seemed like all of us took to her. She'd watch you—like she could read your mind. One time she got out, stuck her head in through the loose screen of the kitchen window where Phyllis was doing dishes. We ran in to look at her. Had suds on her nose. Phyllis was laughing. Was a sight to see."

But Jack isn't listening, his mind following its own back roads. I say, "I don't know that I've lost more than any other man my age. But I can see how you might feel, Jack. Seems like it's come early to you."

"Some things is natural and some ain't. What was done to my dogs— that seems like—"

"Meanness," I say. "*Seems like* meanness and *might be* meanness. But no way to prove it."

"And nothing to do about it." He says this as a statement, simple. But behind it there's a question. He waits for some response, to see if I agree. Probably the way his daddy has taught him to listen.

Folks just protecting what is theirs, I want to say. Maybe that's one way to look at it. Might've been an accident, someone flushing out a radiator. But I don't know what to say to Jack. Sometimes you can sit back and watch it all unfold, and it will unfold beautifully. But sometimes you watch it, and it will be sheer tragedy—and then you wonder what is the one thing, the very thing, you could have said or done to prevent it?

Finally, Jack asks outright, "What should I do?"

"My boy never asked me that," I say. "He never wanted me to interfere."

"He might've," Jack says, "if'n he got pushed into a corner."

I swallow. Jack isn't keeping secrets; he's telling me where he is. I think of Rickie, the last night—how one night's words and scenes are imprinted after so many years of rerunning them. He tried to slip out the front door, gliding quietly past me in my recliner. "Why don't you stay home tonight?" I asked. It startled him. But what father wouldn't ask it of any child—no matter his age? Maybe I could have said, "Leave the beer in the bag tonight." Or, "I don't want you drinking but at least drink at the barn where you won't be on the roads." Any number of things I could have said, done. Maybe grabbed my coat, said, "Wherever you're going, I'm going with you."

I had not given up—you don't do that with your children. But I was resigned to him having to learn his own lessons. A heart bent on something is hard persuaded from it. I locked the doors at midnight, knowing his mother slipped and opened his bedroom window.

You don't know when to step in and when not to. People nowadays talk about tough love. But I tell you, if I saw a train coming down the tracks and my boy in the path of it, I'd rush out and push him off—no matter the cost to me. No one tells you the train is coming, though, till it's already gone through.

I done a little carrying on myself when I was a young man—not much—tipping outhouses, letting the air out of tires, and the like. Sampling Harry Yeager's moonshine occasionally. I don't know if times now is any worse than then—though they seem to be. Each generation's capacity for meanness seems to grow larger. And the generation before— those of us left—are kept here to witness, in amazement. My boy was unhappy. Rickie was. He kept unfolding and refolding the map, trying new routes, never finding the place he was looking for.

"No one ever done nothing like this to me before," Jack says.

"What about that fella lured away your wife?" I ask. "That was ornery, wasn't it?"

"It was," he says. "But maybe I had it coming. JoAnn's lawyer told me I was negligent. Working on the house, not spending enough time with her. Maybe I was. I don't know. I don't see how I could have done different."

Out in the woods, there is a sudden crashing, running and plowing through dead leaves. Then it stops. Both of us turn our eyes that direction. Up on the hill behind us a coyote howls.

"Someone's go'll have to kill them," I say. "They're overrunning the place."

"I hate to hear them," Jack says. "Seems like it goes right up my spine. Ben and Jesse hated them, too, always barked when one was near, raised their hackles."

"For a long time they wasn't here," I say. "DNR brought 'em in to control the deer. Of course they won't admit it. But everybody knows it."

Jack commences shoveling again. "Guess we better dig deep to keep them out."

The sun settles behind the trees, filters through the tree trunks, leaves

us in pinstriped shadows. Jack keeps digging until he's dug out the dirt between the two holes and made one large grave. "They were never far apart," he says. "I reckon they'll rest better like this."

Around us rise the scents of the dark broken earth and pinesap from the roots we've busted. Jack stretches out one tarp in the bottom of the grave, then carries the dogs and places them back-to-back, against each other. No matter how many times you've seen it, the stillness in a body that's prone to motion surprises you. Bewildering, the way a living, moving being suddenly turns to object and shell, the husk that you throw away.

Jack gets down in the grave, kneels down beside them, kisses their heads. He puts a hand on each of their foreheads, like he might be checking for fever. He lifts one of Ben's front paws, rubs it like he would rub life back into it. I know the roughness he feels on the dog's padded feet. He does the same with Jesse. These are his good-byes. With a preacher, people all around, you don't feel so free. You feel boxed in, everyone keeping you in check. When I see Jack down in the hole, covering them with the other tarp like they're his babies, I can't stop the tears gathered in my eyes.

"The Lord giveth and the Lord taketh away," Jack says, stepping out of the grave. His face is all wet.

"Blessed be the name of the Lord," I choke out.

"I'm going to the house a minute," Jack says. He's about to break. "Go ahead and start covering them. Seems like I just can't."

I'm close enough that I could catch his arm, turn him to me, and hold him. But I don't. I keep my distance, respect his privacy. I've never been one to trespass on another's grief.

When he's out of sight, I start laying the earth down gentle on the dogs, saving the biggest rocks to place around on top. If there were a wife and son waiting at his house, Jack would do his best to comfort them. Losing the dogs would hurt but be bearable. He would be strong for the child, for the wife.

I wipe my eyes on my shirtsleeve, work fast so they'll be covered when he gets back. If he owned a gun, it would be harder to let him walk off. But there are other ways, I know, to dull the pain. I look up, and through the woods I see the lights come on in his house. I keep covering. I can

give him time. You have to—men do that for each other. You give lee-way, a wide berth. But he's too young, still new to the world's blows, these what have come all at once in a heap, to give him too much space.

Evenings after this, Jack continues stopping at my place. He's smoking again and uses one of my Folger's cans for an ashtray. We miss the dogs being with us, and Jack plays it back over and over.

"I guess I should have kept them penned up," he says. "But I've always hated to see a dog in a pen. Course, I guess, it's better than a dead dog.

"If it was just the garbage, I would have picked it up every day myself if they'd called me. Or if they'd said, this is your last chance—after this we're going to kill your dogs. I guess I would have done different."

I say, "Maybe I shouldn't have been saving scraps for them, encourag-ing them to go pillaging."

"Nah," he says. "They liked coming down here. It was their second home."

"Yeah," I say. "They was good company—even through the day after they'd made their rounds. They'd stay here with me, help in whatever way they could."

"Whatever they done," Jack says, "they didn't deserve this."

He stands up, goes to the corner where a moth has got itself trapped in a spider web. If he's done it once, he's done it a dozen times. He closes his hands around the moth, careful not to clamp its wings, then draws the moth out in the cup of his hands. He sits back down, opens his hands on his lap. The moth flutters free, out into the evening.

"What makes folks want to kick a man when he's down?" he asks.

"You got to quit thinking it was aimed at you—deliberately," I say. "Even if it was, there's nothing you can do about it. You go'll have to sleep through it. Just sleep. Even when you're awake, just sleep through your routine, till you wake up on the other side of it."

"But I ain't sleeping," he says. "I'm awake, all hours. I'm holding Ben and Jesse, and they're slobbering on my hand and licking the tops of RC cans and rolling on their backs wanting their bellies rubbed and smelling like dog. And you know," he says, "that's all I had left.

"When I finally go to sleep, the coyotes wake me up howling. I guess Ben and Jesse kept them at bay. The coyotes come in close now. And for

all the insulation, six-inches of it, and all those double-paned windows, all that effort I made to seal up the house tight, I hear them like they was right beside my bed."

Rain or shine, the porch is where Jack and me sit. It's the most comfortable room, partway in, partway out. I cook extra and always save leftovers for him. I stash the scraps in the garbage so he don't have to see them, don't have to think of the keen pleasure Ben and Jesse would derive from them.

One evening we sit through a downpour. Around us, the Folger's cans fill up, drip by drip, some drips pretty steady.

"That's a new one, ain't it?" Jack says, pointing.

"Just a bigger one," I say. "A louder one."

"You not ready to put on a new roof yet?"

"Nah," I say. "It's not more than I can bear."

"I could help you," he says.

"It's okay," I say. "This one will last me."

"What about the next person?"

"That's for him to decide."

"Kind of shortsighted, ain't it?" he looks at me. "I don't mean no disrespect."

"I'm used to the dripping—the sound," I say. "It's like music."

Jack flicks the ash of his cigarette into the water of the nearest can.

"I see you're smoking again," I say. It's the first time I've mentioned it.

"Yeah. I was down to two a day, morning and night, when Ben and Jesse died. Now I'm back up to two packs."

Killing yourself won't help, I want to tell him, but I don't want to put the idea in his head.

"Sometimes," I say, weighing my words, "you get started in on something and can't stop. Or it's hard to. Seems like one leads to one more. The first don't satisfy, and so there's a second, and so on."

"It keeps me calm," he says. "There's a storm underneath." He pats his chest.

I think of lava, volcanoes, cracks in the earth that let things seep through.

"With the dogs, see—" he blows out. "With the dogs, they had a calm about them. Soothing. In the evenings, so glad to see me. Anxious for

whatever we were going to do—in the yard or in the woods—even if we just walked. Was just a peace they had—and it would rub off on me."

The rain slackens off just as suddenly as it came, and around us, we hear the slowing drips in the Folger's cans, the drops from the leaves of the trees as they shake themselves off. The birds make last-minute calls before settling to roost. The lightning bugs start to raise up around us, one or two at first, then more. The frogs set in to singing. We sit quiet. It's near dark. There's just the glow of Jack's cigarette.

Then Jack raises his arm, points. There's a stray dog slinking just into the edge of the yard, up from the creek. It hunkers down, cautious. I can hardly see its coloring, but by its walk, I know it's not a dog I recognize. Then, as it draws closer to the house, it dawns on me: a coyote. For all the time I've been hearing them, this is the first I've seen. It looks like a dog, but is not exactly a dog.

Jack makes like he has a rifle, takes aim in the air, puts his finger on the trigger, his cigarette where the trigger would be. He hunted as a boy with his father, he's told me, but gave it up early, without the stomach or heart to follow through.

Jack keeps aim on the coyote with his invisible rifle. Then, "Ppulkhs-ksk," he makes the loud noise of a gun. The coyote raises its ears, looks to the porch, then tucks its tail, darts for the cover of the woods.

Next evening, Jack doesn't stop. And after that, doesn't stop. He smiles, waves out the open window when he goes by on his way up the mountain. I keep cooking. I cook loud things—with scents that will pass through the screen doors and saturate the yard, scents that might catch in his gut when he drives past. Fried fish. Always cornbread from Phyllis's recipe. French fries. Fried hamburgers. I cook for two. Every evening. He doesn't stop. He waves. I wave back, then watch him go, the dust whirling up behind his truck as he tackles the hill, the truck rocking in the ruts. I let him go. Maybe he's talking to Kathy Brumfield. What can I do? Can't run out and flag him down every day. He has his own life. Some sorrows you can't enter, not when the owner says off-limits. So I tell myself. There are boundaries to respect.

Eventually, though, it gets the best of me. I lose sleep myself. I lie awake. Any hour of the night I might hear the high-pitched, eerie howls of the coyotes. What if Jack has bought himself a gun? Will he remember

how to use it? Remember what to do and what not to? What if he sits up there at night, waiting for a coyote to stalk across his yard, waiting, the gun coddled in his arms, the trigger warmed by his finger, waiting, waiting, thinking what use is it anyway, why even go on trying?

One evening after he's gone through, I give him time to settle, then drive my tractor back, knock on the door. He opens the door, squinting at the light.

"Jack, here's some cornbread," I say. "I made too much this evening."

"Thanks, Lloyd," he says, reaching for the warm package wrapped in aluminum foil. "But I just don't have an appetite."

He seems to have lost weight in just this short time, and there are dark circles around his eyes.

"You got to eat," I say. I try to look through the door behind him, see the shape of his house.

"I'm still sick over it, Lloyd." he says. "Just sick. I want to do something. Take action."

I wait to be invited in. But he stands in place, blocking the door, holding the cornbread. "Maybe you give yourself an ulcer," I say. "Worrying so much over it. I had one once. Seem like your whole stomach is on fire, every time you eat."

He shakes his head, then concedes, "I guess it could be."

We're quiet on the porch. Him waiting for me, me waiting for him.

"How's the new site?" I ask. "You got the underground laid yet?"

"Mostly," he says. "We're testing for leaks."

I nod. "That, uhm, Reynolds fella. He still struttin' around?"

"Nah. He got transferred. Put on a job in Huntington." Jack doesn't volunteer anything more, just doesn't open up any other paths.

"You called that Brumfield girl yet?" Soon as I say it, I know I've barged in.

"Nah. What do I got to say?"

I shrug my shoulders. "Maybe she'd do all the talking," I offer.

"Maybe," he says.

I figure Jack knows what I'm up to, and there's no sense making a fool of myself, losing his respect. "Well," I say, "stop by sometime when you get the chance." I turn away as if to leave. And when he doesn't tell me to stay put, I follow through. I walk down the steps, then swing myself up onto the tractor.

"Lloyd," he says, coming out onto the porch and leaving the door wide open. "You know, I was just sitting down there till bedtime and only coming home to sleep. I feel restless," he says. "Just need to get into something."

I nod my head.

"It's hard coming home to an empty house," he says. "You of all people know that. But I got to learn to. You got your life. Don't think you have to babysit me."

I laugh. Around here, I'm still surprised when people say what they're thinking. Generally when people speak, they leave the shadows behind their words for you to read.

"Whether you're there or not, Jack, I sit on the porch till bedtime myself. But me and the lightning bugs, seem like we don't speak the same language."

Within the week, Jack is stopping again. I have stocked up on milk—in case he has an ulcer. And I'm learning to bake instead of fry. I cut back on tomatoes.

You don't know how much you yourself can stand. And as much as you measure a man, you don't know how much he can stand either.

"I got a big house on the hill and no one to live in it," Jack says.

"You live in it."

"I got nowhere to go." He inhales. Blows out smoke. "I feel lost."

His talk scares me—but not as much as his silence did.

"What do you do when everything's been taken from you?" he asks.

I think of Job in the Bible and say, "You look for the thing that's going to come along next."

"And what if nothing does?"

"You have to wait."

"How long?"

"Sometimes a long time. Sometimes not so long."

"You sound like a politician," he says. "Or a preacher."

"I'm only saying what I know."

"I know."

One Friday evening late summer we hear a cry come out of the woods— like a child. Then it comes again and again, and the closer it gets, the more

shape the sound takes until finally it resembles the bleating of a kid goat or a lamb. We hear crashing in the woods, leaves kicked up, sticks broken. Jack jumps up, runs off the porch to the back of the house, up the hill to the edge of the woods. The cry comes louder and louder.

Jack runs back down.

"You got a gun, don't you?"

"What is it?"

"Coyote after a fawn," he says.

I fetch the loaded rifle from the house, some extra shells, hand them to Jack.

"I'll go, too," I say.

His face lifts in surprise. Maybe thinks I'll slow him.

We enter the woods quiet except for breathing hard. You learn a lot about a man's character when he's carrying a gun. No matter where I walk, behind or in front, I take notice of the gun—and see that Jack always has it directed away from me. Another thing his daddy's done well teaching him.

Not far in, we step over the fawn's body. Its eyelid flutters, but there are flies already around it—like it's been hounded and running a long time. I don't expect us to find the coyote that chased it here.

Nothing but a shock, then, when we spot one so quickly. Down in a little forked hollow where three or four creeks merge and big rocks jut out in the air. Dead trees have fallen, making log bridges where the mosses can grow across the hollows. The coyote stands just out from under one of the overhanging rocks.

I feel Jack's forearm against my ribs. Stay.

He lines up the bead.

I close my eyes and want to cover my ears—but I don't move. You want for someone—that he not be killed. By cancer, by a train, by a drunk driver, or by his own hand. You pray for that. But you want, too, that he not have to kill. That he not have to step into that room—different from the one where he habitually lives, that dark cave he might be better off not entering—and from which he will have to come back stamping the blood from his boots.

Maybe Jack feels my hesitation. He considers. He covers the trigger with his finger. There's no sympathy for the coyote. I heard the fawn's cry

like Jack did. Both of us, we stepped over its still-warm body. The coyotes didn't kill Ben and Jesse. Killing the coyote won't bring them back. But the coyote—or one like him—killed the fawn, and will go on killing fawns forever. Or till there's peace in the valley, and the coyotes and fawns lie down together.

When I sense Jack stalling, I pray the coyote will move out of sight.

And amazingly it does. Jack lowers the rifle. Waits. Then the coyote emerges again, something in its jaws. Rabbit? Squirrel? But no, not those. Its own pup instead.

Jack raises the rifle again.

I want to touch his sleeve, but my arms feel lifeless. Like in a dream when you want to move and can't. Want to speak and can't. But, oh, how threadbare is that jacket you wear, the one that shelters your love.

"God's place," Jack whispers. "What do you do?" He's breathing, slowly, forcing himself to breathe, the way you have to, to keep your arms and shoulders loose.

The coyote senses us because she turns to face Jack, the pup still clutched in her jaw. She's considering her options, you can tell, the way her eyes dart to and fro.

If this is to be the ram in the bushes, I pray to see it, to accept it. I throw a quick glance at Jack's face, trying to get a read on him. His eyes are wet, not even trained on the coyote, but looking inside, backwards, at how things stand. There's a lot bottled, so much bottled he don't know what to do with it.

"Let me do it," I say, reaching for his shoulder. "Or we can come back another day."

The first shot drops the coyote, maybe kills her. The second allows for no doubt. The third shot rolls the pup away from her. The shots echo through the hollow and high above us, through the trees and to the tops of the hills and beyond. The scent of gunpowder hangs in the air and sickens my heart.

"There won't be another day," Jack says, handing me the rifle. "This is it." He has his teeth clenched, his chin tight. He tucks his shaking hands in his pockets. He scrunches his eyes, nods at me, then turns away from the coyotes toward the house.

BURYING GROUND

Brammer left the undertaker sitting in the hearse and climbed the hill, feeling the steepness of the incline in his legs. The men at the top were gathered around the backhoe and stood with their backs to the road. Funny how you could recognize them after so many years. There was Wetzel and Billy, Big Chew, Carl, Squirmy, Royce, Vinton. Was it that they wore the same old coats and caps? Or was it the build of their bodies, the habit of their stances that gave them away? Brammer didn't know who was on the backhoe—one of a newer generation—maybe one of Pete's sons.

Seeing Brammer, Pete waved from the top, but then turned around to supervise the digging. Most likely it was Pete who'd let news of his daddy's death slip. Pete, who'd encouraged the men to come. In small towns, people expected a funeral, a graveside service, at the least. Probably that's what he should have scheduled. But he hadn't thought he could go through with it, having to face them all and talk about his father's last months. That spiraling down until he didn't know where he was, who Brammer was, or why there wasn't an outhouse in the backyard where there needed to be one. Though he lived with Darla and Brammer his last two years, his father couldn't forget the West Virginia farm where he'd spent the rest of his life. By then, it was too late, Brammer imagined, for his father to learn about letting go. In the end, he was like a child wanting to go home. He cried for his own mother and father, wishing they would

come for him, and for that perceived abandonment, so far as Brammer could tell, there was no consolation.

Still, no one could say he hadn't done right by his daddy. He had always wondered if, when the time came, he would be able to follow through. But he and Darla had cared for his daddy up to the end. Darla, really, had treated him as if he were her own father. There was nothing to feel guilty about. No regrets. He could lay his father to rest, and they could all sleep in peace this evening when the shade crawled over the Griffith family burying ground.

At the top of the hill, Brammer paused to catch his breath. There was a loud scraping in the grave, and some of the men hunched their shoulders and winced. Rock was always a problem, Brammer knew. So much so that sometimes it took dynamite to break through. But surely, they would have tried dynamite yesterday or the day before—not now with the hearse idling in the driveway.

Brammer saw Pete shaking his head and waving his arms at the backhoe driver.

"You hit rock?" Brammer yelled toward him.

"What?" Pete yelled back.

Brammer cupped his mouth and yelled louder over the machine, "I SAID DID YOU HIT ROCK?"

"WORSE," Pete yelled, then said something Brammer couldn't make out.

Pete made a short slicing motion under his throat, and the driver backed away from the grave and shut down the engine.

"It's a tractor," Pete said, a little breathless.

Brammer looked from the partially dug hole to the backhoe, trying to attach some meaning. You could call it a tractor, but technically, it was a backhoe. He felt someone's hands on his arm, turning him. It was Wetzel, shriveled up into a little old man with big ears. He nodded toward the grave, pointed to the large mound of earth still left in the wide hole.

"There's a tractor buried there," Pete said. "We been digging around it, trying to bust through the rock on the outside edges without tearing up the tractor. "But it'll take shovels to uncover it the rest of the way."

Brammer peered over the edge, straining to see into the mound of earth.

"See the top of the steering wheel?" Wetzel pointed. "And one of the fenders?"

"Whose is it?" Brammer asked.

"Whose do you think?" Big Chew asked.

Brammer glanced around at the men. He was playing catch-up—as you had to with old-timers who were always a step ahead of you. But from the tone of Big Chew's words, he knew whose tractor they thought it was.

"Dad's?"

Pete shrugged. "All my years digging graves, I never seen nothing like it."

"What makes you think it's his?"

"Don't you recognize the steering wheel?" Royce asked. Again Brammer squinted, trying to adjust his eyes to the varying degrees of earth and shadow. Had he been able to see the steering wheel, he surely would have recognized it. His father had worn the original out—worn it down to nothing—till it broke in its narrowest place, with just a hard turn one day. His father took one from an old blue Dodge they had up in the hollow, just for temporary. And then had never seen reason to replace it.

"Vinton said you reported the tractor missing a while back."

"Yeah, about a year ago," Brammer said. "I was going to have it hauled over to my place so he'd have it to tinker with." It was the truth, but Brammer said it now to win points. "Someone had already got to it," he added, then looked back down into the hole. "I don't understand why they'd bury it though."

The undertaker strode up, breathless after the climb. "What seems to be the trouble, gents?"

Pete eyed the stranger. "No trouble really. There's a tractor buried in the grave."

"Yeah, I can see it," the undertaker said.

Brammer watched him squinting his eyes, studying the earth. He wondered if he really saw it or just said he did. "They say it's my father's tractor," Brammer told him. "But I don't see how."

"Well, I'll be," the undertaker said. "That's kind of curious, ain't it? How long'll it take to dig it out?" His question fell to Wetzel, the oldest among them.

"Not long," Brammer said, cutting Wetzel off. He looked to Pete hopefully.

"There was a lot of rock around the edges," Pete said. "But we couldn't use dynamite. We had to chomp and bust it up with the backhoe. We'll have to get in there with shovels now. It's just dirt from here on."

"How'd they get the tractor down there?" Brammer asked.

"They who?" Big Chew asked.

"Whoever did it."

"Don't you know who done it?"

"How would I know?"

"You lived with him a good part of your life."

Brammer looked around at the men, their arms folded.

Brammer squinted his eyes at Pete. "Do they mean Dad?"

Pete nodded. "That's what they're claiming."

"He couldn't have done it—he wasn't able," Brammer said. "Besides, he was staying with me." By their looks, he could feel the feebleness of his protest. The jury had decided, and with them convinced against him, Brammer felt like a teenager again.

"It's been here a long time," Billy said softly. "It's all rusted out."

"So you're saying you think he buried it sometime *before* he came to live with me?" Brammer questioned. "He wasn't strong enough. It would have killed him."

"All we know, there's a tractor buried now in your daddy's plot. Been there for some time," Wetzel said. "None of us did it—or even knew about it."

"But he used that tractor for everything," Brammer said. "He didn't know he wasn't coming back—*we* didn't know. We just took him till he could get back on his feet." He felt their eyes on him. Of course, his father might have known, the way people knew things they didn't put words to. The men here might have known, too. And maybe they held it against him. In the end, when it was clear his father was going downhill, Brammer had chosen to uproot his father instead of moving himself and his wife back to the farm to care for him. He could feel the protest of the men around him. That he had a job, a life elsewhere, did not matter much. There were ways of doing things, beliefs about what things ought and ought not to be done.

Following their ears, the men turned their eyes down the drive, where the backhoe driver and another young man were already dragging shovels like sleds along the graveled ruts of the road. The shovels screeched across the quartz pebbles till the men veered off into the grass to climb the hill. When they reached the edge of the pit, they paused, looking for the best way to descend. Then they scrambled down, what seemed to Brammer, the steepest part—just what you did when you were young. They walked around the mound of dirt, studying where to start. Then one, then the other began shoveling, like they were spooning ice cream, slowly as if they meant to savor it.

Brammer tried to picture his father digging such a big hole. It would have taken him weeks—steady work at that. And how could he break through the rock? In his youth, or even in his middle years, he surely could have—he would have gotten his hands on dynamite. But at eighty-two, he wasn't able—surely he wouldn't have tried to set off an explosion—and then he would've had to do all that shoveling and lifting the rock out. When Brammer picked him up that final day, he was down to skin and bones. He trembled on the way to the car, leaning on Brammer's arm. He groaned as Brammer had never heard him groan, joints and limbs rusty in pain. At the time, Brammer wondered how his father had managed so long on his own. He regretted that he hadn't taken him sooner. And maybe he would have, if his father could have found a heart to love Darla more. But that was a sad thing that no one could do anything about.

"He couldn't have dug this hole," Brammer said. "He must have had help." He gauged the men. They met his look, then turned their gaze back to the hole.

"Brammer's probably right," Vinton said. "He must have rented a backhoe or something. A little Ditch Witch wouldn't've done it."

"Could he even operate a big backhoe?" Brammer asked.

"Clive Griffith could operate any kind of machinery," Royce said. "You oughta know that."

"One time my old man rented a bulldozer to grade around the house," Billy said. "With Daddy on it, it was hit and miss, scrape the driveway, knock down the clothesline pole, the cats flying every which way getting

out of his path. Got right up near the house—the blade stuck in mid-air—so that any move up or down was going to bust out the wall and my mother standing beside the mashed clothesline pole shaking her head and my daddy in such a sweat. Him debating over moving the dozer right to left or left to right, and getting more and more confused about which way the switches worked—'cause, you know, some of them work backwards—and it just got too much for him, the pressure, so he just shuts her off, sends me out to find your daddy. I remember Clive was out cutting hay, and your mother radioed him on the walky-talky. So I come back home, and he nearly beats me there, bouncing along on his tractor in high gear down the road, sitting up high and pretty. Then takes the seat in the dozer, just nudges it in reverse, pretty as you please, backs the thing away from the house. Then after he'd fiddled with the knobs a bit, goes ahead and grades the section up near the foundation—careful not to get too close—he wasn't showing off none—just looked like he'd found a new toy."

"He loved machines," Squirmy said. "He understood them."

"He liked to try out new ones," Vinton said, "but his favorite was his tractor."

"His favorite was his tractor," Brammer repeated. "I can't see him burying it."

Down in the hole, the shovelers had uncovered both big rear fenders—so that the tractor looked like a crouching cat, its hind legs poised, ready to pounce.

"It was a good tractor," Squirmy said. "Wish mine was half that good."

The undertaker seemed amused. He ran his hand over the crooked wing of his hair. "Well, now, boys, just what kind of horsepower are we talking about?"

Brammer wished he could have warned the undertaker not to get them started. No telling how long they'd be here if the men got started.

"It had a mighty force," Vinton said. "I can't count the times that ol' tractor pulled my old jeep out of that creek in front of Jim McCallister's. One time Clive give me such a jerk, the jeep went lurching forward, and I had to mash on the brakes to keep from flying into Clive."

"Sure was a good tractor," Squirmy said again, with clear nostalgia.

"Was fast, too," Royce said. "So fast he had to rig a string around his hat to keep it from blowing off. I teased him, said why didn't he get himself a bonnet."

"Yeah, it was like he was from the Old West, that hat strapped to his chin."

"Never mind the pistols."

"Oh, I forgot about them pistols," Wetzel said. "Bet you remember them, Bram?"

Brammer smiled. They were his pistols, tucked into the handholds his father had welded on the back for him to hang onto when he was little. Eventually, he found other places to hang onto and kept his toy pistols in the handholds while they bounced along. They'd go all over the farm, from one chore to the next, or to the back door for supper. They'd ride up to his cousin Denzil's, or down to Wetzel's or over to Walton's. The men would just sit around, talking from their tractors, never get down off them. Brammer remembered going through the various yards, chasing cats and dogs with his pistols.

"Stay out of Lois's flowers," his daddy would warn him. And he'd just go on as before, maybe tiptoeing through the flowers instead of tearing through them. When he heard the tractor start, he knew it was time to go. That was the end of the visit. He'd run back and get on it.

"He sure took good care of that tractor," Billy said.

"Boy, did he."

"And that tractor took care of him," Vinton said.

It was hard to tell if the men more fondly remembered his father or the tractor.

"My old man used to say if ever there was an engine charmer, he bet Clive Griffith writ the book," Pete volunteered.

"That's saying something coming from Walton," Wetzel said. "He had his way with machinery, too. And it runs in the family—you and your boy." Wetzel nodded to the backhoe operator shoveling now in the grave.

"Don't know about that." Pete looked back at the tractor. "But my daddy was good as they come." He looked like he might say more but then simply firmed his lips.

Brammer remembered the death of Pete's father. It had been an early death, a violent death—the wind felling a dead tree, just the right place,

the right angle, to kill him. The randomness of the act amazed them. It happened quickly with no warning, no time to say good-bye, and Pete's daddy was young, in his prime. Pete and Brammer were just out of high school. Brammer was home on spring break, his first year of college. He remembered the way word had come, house to house, Wetzel stopping by on his tractor, getting down off his tractor—which, in a way, maybe prepared Brammer's father. He came up the porch steps, where they were sitting. Brammer was in the rocker, his father on the swing. Brammer remembered his father's face, disbelief first, then the slow settling of re-strained agony—they were good friends and wouldn't he have been out there helping Walton in the woods had he not stayed home to be with Brammer? That death had come as the Bible said, like a thief in the night, took just one, left the rest standing. But it stole their peace and security.

"They sure he's dead?" Brammer's father had asked, like it was a detail someone forgot to check.

After that, Brammer's daddy took Pete under his wing—and that made Brammer and Pete more like brothers than ever. But once Bram-mer started spending summers away, in between his college years, that about ended it—the camaraderie. And now that they hadn't seen each other in five years, Brammer felt shy around Pete. When you left, people assumed you thought yourself better than them. But that wasn't it at all. If anything, you felt lesser. You didn't call, you didn't visit—because you had the feeling of never making the cut, of being judged by people who didn't understand why you went off in the first place—you had property here, after all, why wouldn't you stay? At some point, it was hard to bear up under that kind of censure.

"Walt's been gone a long time," Wetzel said. "I reckon him and Clive'll have some catching up to do."

"Ain't that the truth," Squirmy said.

The men grew quiet, maybe thinking of others they knew who'd gone on. When you moved away, Brammer realized, you missed this grave-side talk. But you learned to live without it, the way you learned to live without many things. And it was true, too, living away, that you began to lose touch with death. You didn't know it as intimately as you once had. It wasn't part of the weekly fabric of your life. Sure, people died all around you. But you didn't know them—or hadn't known them all your life—

and so death lost some of its sting. It was then you had to prod it periodically with your toe—the way you might check the pressure in your tires.
But you went even further. You tipped it up and looked under—as if for
lizards or fish worms—to keep it from mushrooming on you. In this way,
it didn't swell, or envelop you in its surge.

"I can just picture Clive sitting on that tractor, out cutting hay or plowing or mowing—always mowing," Vinton said. "You'd see him from the
road. Would wonder what he was going to mow next. Would mow great
big patterns in his yard—checkerboards, big daisies, words even. You remember the time he mowed 'Hello' on the big hill in front of his house?
Liked to never got him to mow it out."

"Not till someone come along one night, mowed out the 'o.'"

"He always thought that was the McComas boy."

"I figure it was. He never did amount to much."

"Where's he now?"

"Last I heard, camping down't McCorkle, collecting workers comp."

"Well, it wasn't for his daddy's lack of trying."

The men grew quiet, and Brammer imagined them thinking of their
own sons and daughters, the best and worst of them, the ways they didn't
measure up. For how could you measure up when the men carried such
high standards?

"What I picture is ol' Clive pulling that old dog of his—what was his
name?

"Eeensie-Weensie," Wetzel said.

"Pulling him around on that trailer. That dog went everywhere he
did."

"I bet he's buried somewhere around here—I remember Clive chisel-
ing a stone for him." Royce turned his head, searching.

"Where'd he get that name?"

"Was you, wasn't it, Brammer?" Billy asked.

Brammer nodded his head. He'd given the name when a boy. The dog
had fine lines along the ridge of his back radiating out like a spider web.

Lots of the old dogs were buried here. Pets, sure, but work dogs, too,
or dogs that thought they were working, always padding along behind
the tractor whether it was the hoe, the rake, fence posts, or buckets of water you were hauling on the trailer. His father would be happy to see them

all again—and Brammer hoped he would, hoped that Saint Francis had been right about that, and the people of other faiths and others who believed in the souls of animals. For how could you look into their eyes and *not* see a soul?

Down in the hole, the hood of the tractor was visible. Brammer could make out the steering wheel now and the shape of the round seat—like a misshapen dishpan. The tractor appeared to be emerging from an ocean, the waves dropping lower and lower around it.

"Why do we have to dig it out?" Brammer asked suddenly. "Can't we just bury Dad on the other side of Mom? And leave the tractor where it is? If he put it there, he must have done it for a reason."

"The headstone would be wrong then," Pete said. He pointed to the monument that had been dragged off to the side so the backhoe could do its work. Brammer looked at the names and dates of his parents. He forced himself to stare at the stone. It was hard to see, hard to believe. It would be up to him to have the date added to his father's side. That would be one of the final things.

"See," Pete continued. "He would be where the stone says she is, and she would be where it says he is. Unless you put it at their feet, facing the other direction. Then it would go against the direction of all the others.

Brammer couldn't see that it made much difference in the long run, but maybe it did to everyone here. He wondered what Darla would have said. She seemed distant to him now, somehow out of this orbit. He had told her it would be a short trip.

"You remember that time he was sitting on his tractor in the middle of the hay field? One of Carl Lucas's boys was coming home from Buckeye—" Vinton said.

"Was Carl's grandson, I believe," Wetzel interrupted.

"I believe you're right. Was his grandson, little bitty thing—all those boys was tiny till they got to high school and busted out. Well, Clive was sitting in the field he'd been mowing, just sitting on his tractor, engine cut off. 'What you watching?' the boy asks Clive.

"Clive puts his finger to his lips, points. He'd jumped a rabbit and her young'uns, and the rabbit and all the little ones was hopping this way and that. She was hopping ahead, trying to get them to follow, but the little

ones was just hopping ever which way. When Clive sees this ole boy of
Carl Lucas's—"

"His grandson—"

"—this grandson—Clive hops off his tractor to help the boy catch
one. They was tiny, no bigger than your fist. So the two of them was running around and around the tractor, and Carl himself comes along, says,
'Is it hide and seek, boys?' And Clive, pretty as you please, stands up with
his hat in his hand, sort of bows like, then pulls a rabbit out. Carl said in
that moment, the light came on in that ol' boy's face, said you could have
lit a baseball field by his face."

"Course you couldn't help getting them rabbits sometimes when you
was cutting hay. That was hard on old Clive then."

"Hard on any of us—especially if they had young ones. Was like
you were the grim reaper," Billy said, then turning to the undertaker, he
added, "No offense."

"None taken," the undertaker said. "I done my share of mowing. Hit
terrapins and ground-chucks and things like that. Makes you sick to your
stomach."

"I believe that ol' rabbit lived to be fifteen or sixteen, and when he died,
that ol' boy broke down and cried. You'd thought he'd lost a brother."

"Used to ride him around in a milk crate attached to the handlebars of
his bicycle, didn't he?"

Brammer remembered Russell Lucas's rabbit mainly because his father had caught one for him from the same batch. Brought it home to
him in the pocket of his jacket that afternoon. They'd put it in the empty
hamster cage—was a tiny thing. It didn't live long, though. Died the next
day. Brammer was holding it in his hand. It was squirming and struggling
so much that he thought it was getting stronger, but then it just went stiff
in his hand. He felt the life go out of it. He never forgot. The way the rabbit turned dead—the way its breath left it and didn't come back. Was no
question. And Brammer knew it. But still begged to take it to the hospital—how ridiculous it seemed now—but his father wouldn't. He blamed
his father then, and had asked didn't he love him. For years afterward, he
wished he hadn't said that. It was the kind of early heartbreak you gave
your father. And it left a sore spot in Brammer and in his father—something that got nettled—for Brammer could read it on his father's face, every time somebody mentioned Russell Lucas's rabbit.

"Well, look here," Brammer said before the men could start in on something else. "What're we going to do? Instead of digging the tractor out the rest of the way, why don't we just bury him on the other side of it. There's enough room. We wouldn't have to dig anymore."

"Then the tractor'll be laying between him and your mother," Pete said.

"They can reach across it," Brammer said. He felt himself in the undertow of their talk. "They was always reaching across it anyway—when he was working. Her offering him something for energy, a bottle of RC or a spoon of peanut butter."

"He sure liked his RC," Big Chew said.

The young men were shoveling dirt now that had been packed in tight around the tractor. There were flakes of red paint in the shovelfuls landing at Brammer's feet, and he was glad his father wasn't here to witness it.

"I just don't see the point of going to all this trouble to dig the tractor out—if he wanted it buried," Brammer said.

"I don't know. I don't know," Big Chew was shaking his head. "I suspect he don't care what we do with the tractor so long as we found it. I believe he buried it so we'd find it."

"Be kind of hard to miss, wouldn't it?" Squirmy said.

"It's like a proxy," Royce said.

"What d'you mean, a proxy?"

"You know, the person who can stand in to vote for you—something that stands in your place—in case you're not going to be there. A sub."

Brammer felt his face growing warm. There'd never been any question about where his father would be buried. It was nothing they had talked about, but was just a given. But maybe it had been something his father feared when he left the farm to come stay with him.

"It's more like a bookmark," Billy said, looking at Brammer. "Something to mark his place till he could get back."

"Well, this'll be something to tell back in Belton," the undertaker said. "It beats all I ever saw. You still hear on occasion someone taking a tractor apart, building it back in the loft or on the roof of a barn—some place unusual," the undertaker said. "But no one thinks to bury one in his grave." The undertaker seemed to be enjoying himself.

"What we could do," Pete said, "is clear out a place over on the far side of the hole like you said, Brammer, but then scoot the tractor over—all of

us together—scoot it over so Clive could rest easy between your mother and the tractor."

"That all right with you, Brammer?" Wetzel asked.

"I guess," Brammer said. But he wished his father had been there to ask. What had he intended? Why hadn't he said something?

The men were down to throwing out half shovelfuls, the soil in the crevices and fine lines of the tractor. Despite the rust and so many loose paint flecks, the tractor retained some of its red color.

"That's the tractor I remember," Big Chew said. "He was always touching up the rusty spots."

"He'd sure have a job if he did it today," Wetzel said. "Would have to sand everything down to the bare metal, start from scratch."

"He didn't take much to a green tractor," Royce said.

"No, he didn't approve of John Deere. Was nothing again' the engine—but was the color that bothered him. Was like he didn't understand a green tractor."

Brammer thought of his riding lawn mower. Maybe that was his father's complaint about it. "It's not a real tractor," his father was fond of saying, in the same tone he complained that Darla's Yorkies were not real dogs. With the lawn mower, though, his father had mowed Brammer's yard every other day for nearly two years—even in the winter when snow wasn't on.

"That can't be good for the grass," Brammer had said, but his father shrugged him off. One day, Brammer found him in the neighborhood baseball field, mowing.

"How'd you get here?"

"Drove."

"On the road?" But Brammer knew the answer. That was the point when he decided to fetch his father's tractor from home. At least it would sit higher and be more visible to folks driving on the street. It had all kinds of reflective gear and flashing lights his father had rigged. But he didn't tell his father—he didn't want to get his hopes up. And it was a good thing, for when they went back to the farm and found it missing, Brammer's father had taken it hard. His father shuffled out to the barn to see for himself, then went around touching everything, putting his hands on the old logs of the barn, running his hands along the weathered planks. It was nearly more than Brammer could stand. His father stared

at the rutted ground where the tractor used to sit. But he didn't say anything, just firmed his lips. Brammer thought he was blaming him, and he
saw, by the light through the open door, his father's wet eyes.

But that was life, Brammer told himself at the time. You moved on—
you had to. It was this ability to adapt that helped human beings survive
loss—losses more awful than most of the people he knew went through.
The problem with his father's generation was that they held on to everything. They couldn't let go. His mother had stored away enough leftover tin foil to cover the dome of the West Virginia capitol. And his father saved little bitty slivers of soap that were smaller than sucked candy.
They had trouble throwing anything away. And it was also true, Brammer knew, with the connection they felt for each other. He understood
how his father had held on and sheltered the bond with his mother for
the five uneasy years after her death. Of course, that made more sense.
You couldn't help but cling, the biblical word was *cleave*, to the one who
shared with you your hopes and losses.

But here, in a wild—the word *ecstasy* came to Brammer—in a wild ecstasy, an uncharacteristic turn, his father had buried an old but perfectly
functioning tractor. It had seen better days, sure. But what on earth would
make his father do it?

"Say, what model would you say that tractor is?" the undertaker asked.

"He got it back in the sixties," Wetzel said. "How old are you, Brammer?"

"I'll be forty-eight in March."

"That's how old the tractor is," Wetzel said. "Libby was pregnant with
Brammer when they bought it. Was a big deal at the time. Could they afford the payments, and the baby on the way? Was all he talked about for
a while. But Clive wanted it so bad. It was Libby finally went and put a
down payment on it."

"I remember him telling about that. He was scared they would lose it.
Or the house one," Billy said.

"I believe it was hard for them the first years."

"Was hard for everybody."

"Always hard on anybody just getting started."

"Look," the undertaker pointed. "The big old headlights. Like frog
eyes."

Even with one of the headlights broken out, the tractor had a face, and

it seemed to gaze at them through its one good eye. The face was as famil-iar to Brammer as anyone he had ever loved.

"One time I tried to buy him a new one," Brammer said. He felt the at-tention of the men shift his direction. "He wouldn't hear of it. Then I was for going on and buying it behind his back. And finally Mom said, 'Even if you get him a new one, it's the old one he's going to use.' So I didn't."

"Like as not he would have warmed up to the new one," Wetzel said. "If it was from you. He'd found use for both of them. Wouldn't have wanted to hurt your feelings none. Or your mother's."

"I doubt it, boys," Big Chew said. "I give him the chance to buy my tractor at a real good price—after we quit raising a garden. He wouldn't have nothing to do with it."

"Yeah, but look at what you're talking about there," Vinton said.

Some of the men laughed. Even Brammer knew Big Chew's tractor, though bought new, was lopsided for some reason—and had a peculiar sound, when it was running, like a tea kettle. Every one of them had pro-posed some solution to get the whistle out—but no one, not Walt nor even Brammer's daddy could ever fix it. When Big Chew was coming to visit, everyone knew a long ways off.

"Don't much blame him myself," the undertaker said. "This is the first hearse I ever had." He pointed down the drive to where Brammer's fa-ther was lying. Brammer saw the undertaker had rolled down all the win-dows, and he imagined his father recognizing the breezes of home. He wondered if he minded being kept waiting. But then remembered it was by his own devising. Was that why he had done it? To keep them waiting?

"You got a son who'll take it over for you?"

"Nope. I'll be the last one. My daddy was an undertaker and his before him. But I'll be the last one. I had a boy, he got killed in a car wreck."

"That's rough," Billy said.

Brammer heard some of the men take a deep breath. He thought they were probably imagining it. For a minute, the only sounds were the slic-ing of the shovels, the bare metal of the shovels scraping the metal of the tractor, and the thudding of the dirt landing at their feet.

"Ain't you ever afraid of it breaking down, and you on your way to the cemetery?" Vinton asked, breaking the silence.

"Whew," Big Chew said, "and what if you were in the heat of summer? You probably ain't got no air condition."

The men recovered and laughed a little. But then, seeming to remember that one of them was lying now in the hearse, stopped short. They turned their attention to the gravediggers. The tractor had taken its old shape. The men had cleared most of the dirt away. Pete's boy brushed off a swath from the top with his forearm. It was something to see, the tractor sitting down there in the grave and, for the most part, composed. Brammer wished he had a picture of it, something to show Darla, for how could he describe to her all about it—and all that the men said, too?

"Looks like you all could use some brooms," Royce said. "Want me to get one from my truck?"

"I've got one in the back of my truck, too," Squirmy said. "Bring it, too."

With the brooms, the men made gentle sweeping motions over the tractor like they were archaeologists uncovering an ancient artifact. Brammer thought of King Tut, buried with all his treasures. So the tractor was what his father had intended to take with him? It had not been easy, he imagined, for his father to say good-bye to it. But perhaps he thought he'd be reunited with it. If his father had been on a desert island and told he could take only one thing, Brammer guessed the tractor would have been it. And why not? You used it to put out your crop and to bring in your crop. You cut your hay with it to feed your stock. On a farm, without one, you were nothing. You needed it from beginning to end.

He remembered that in the springtime, when they broke the ground, he had ridden on top of the disk behind the tractor to give it weight, so it would cut deeper. It had been, then, like a carnival ride. Around and around they'd go, the tractor pulling the disk, and Brammer laughing, his father smiling back on him, sometimes just speeding up or cutting the wheel hard, Brammer knew, to make it more fun—but not so much as to throw him off. From behind the tractor and disk would spring huge coils of earth, and out of them came fish worms hopping up, some cut in two, all of them hopping and wiggling to get back under the earth, for they were never more alive than when they'd just been uncovered. And he and his father would go along afterward, collecting them in coffee cans of dirt, saving them to go fishing.

With the tractor, his father had pulled out tree stumps, rocking back and forth, wiggling the stump, tugging it like it was a giant tooth. In the fall, they'd timbered in the woods for firewood that would serve

in emergencies or on special days when you felt like having a fire. They took fallen trees mostly, ones that were seasoned—so they didn't have to cut the live ones. His father would trim off the limbs, then hook a chain around the logs and pull them down the path coming off the mountain, the logs rolling and zigzagging through the woods, ricocheting off the trunks of standing trees, jarring the leaves out of them, all the way down, and Brammer ran out in front of the tractor, in utter abandon, headlong down the hillside, heralding their coming.

On the trailer, his father had hauled buckets of water, tubs of potatoes, bales of hay. He had hauled all the dogs with all the old names—Old Skip and Rover and Billy and Tanner and Bob-Randy and Bear and Eensie-Weensie, and together with them, Brammer.

His father had taught him to drive on the tractor, then later how to plow straight rows. After he learned, his father expected it of him—even on days when Brammer wanted to be out running with Pete in the old El Camino Pete's father had fixed up. One time Brammer was supposed to plow but sneaked off with Pete. That was the time they tried smoking pot with Butch McComas under one of the big hilltop rocks up Ely, which might have made for a pleasant memory if not for what always trailed it.

When he got back to the farm, his father had lain off all the field himself, plowed it, and even sown the corn. He didn't say anything to Brammer. That was his way. He didn't say anything to him for days, just kept him locked out of his conversation. It was one of those disappointments in you your father was bound to have. And you didn't know how to make up for it. There was no way to make it up. Your father kept stubborn and locked you out. There were so many things a father would hold against you when you were just making your way in the world, when you were just seeking joy and then later, too, when you had found your own steadfast sustenance.

"Say, guess what?" one of the young men yelled from the grave of the tractor. "He left the key in it."

"Give it a try," Vinton said.

"Nah." The man frowned. "There's probably not even gas in the tank."

"Like that'd be the main concern," Squirmy said.

"Let Brammer try it."

"Yeah, Brammer. You go try it."

Brammer shook his head. "It won't start," he said. "After all this time—and out in the weather, rain seeping down, rusting away." He glanced at the men to make sure they were joking, but they looked serious. That was just how they would look, leading you along. He had never really acquired the ability to read them, and he wondered if Pete had. He looked at Pete now for some sign.

"Go on," Pete said. "You may's well try before we cover her back up next to your daddy."

So Pete was one of them now. Brammer didn't like being put on the spot, but he wanted to do right by his father. He looked at the men again. Wetzel nodded toward the grave. "Go on down there," he said.

Brammer swallowed. His heart was beating hard, and he felt himself breaking into a sweat.

"It's all right," Billy encouraged him. "For old time's sake."

Sometimes the right thing was going along with them even when you knew what they were up to. Brammer started down the side of the hole and felt the loose earth slipping into the tops of his shoes. He knew very well that the tractor wouldn't start. Maybe they would laugh at his gullibility. Maybe that's what they would tell stories about at the next funeral, how he got down in the pit to start his father's tractor that had been seizing up and rusting more than two years in the grave. He knew it wouldn't start, but he didn't mind getting a closer look anyway.

He approached the tractor as if it were a strange horse, slowly, holding his hand out to it, in friendship. He could see the rusty brake pedals—pads long worn off, the clutch pedal—what was nothing but a rod, the paint worn off decades ago. All the pedals were rusty now—no boot soles to keep the rust at bay. And here was the big dent, the bent fender where Brammer had one time backed his father's truck into it because he had backed without looking in the rearview mirror. His father had been disappointed that day, too. And Brammer had cried—even though he was too old to cry—but he had felt the too-great weight of the violation.

On the tractor he saw the handholds his father had welded for him, and just barely he could make out the rust-swollen pistols—welded now, whether by his father or by time, as permanent fixtures. Brammer switched his gaze to the steering wheel, for it was too much to look at the pistols. But he would remember them and tell Darla.

When he touched the blue-vinyl steering wheel, he felt the first wave topple the flood wall. He sensed what was coming and knew there was nothing now left to stop it—it had been set in motion by the pistols and by the tractor and by the memories of the men, and now it spun closer. Most likely, the men had set him up. They had herded him into a chute where there was no place to go but straight through. He reached for the key with his right hand. The key ring was corroded and snapped in two at the touch of his fingers. But the brass key itself was firm between his forefinger and thumb. Leaning his wrist clockwise, he turned the key in the ignition and was surprised at its turning at all.

There was a click and then nothing. Nothing took hold. Nothing registered. There was no spark. No turn over. No intake. No anything. But in the silence, Brammer heard the familiar chug-chug-chug and chortle of the tractor starting. It turned over in his heart, and he felt it saturate him, the sound of the day starting, the goats waiting to be let out of the barn, the tractor puttering forward, the dogs all bounding toward it determined to go wherever it was going, the throttle increasing, and you were late to it and had to get running—ground to break, rows to plow, corn to sow, all of it starting without you, but starting, and you could run to catch it if you were fast enough.

It started in his abdomen and worked its way upward—not nausea nor faintness but heat, rushing heat, and he felt it rushing and overtaking him. He swallowed and clutched the steering wheel and blinked, trying to push it back but felt a hard sob escape, and others, lined up behind like waves on a shoreline. He knew the men were watching him, but he couldn't stop. He gripped the steering wheel tighter and leaned his head down on his arm. He longed for the comfort of Darla, the way she cradled his head, the consolation of her hand on his neck, her silent but strong presence when silence and strength was what he needed. What had they been thinking, when they decided she wouldn't come?

He heard the men mumbling and moving about. Would they leave him in the grave alone with his grief? When he looked up, he saw them climbing down, some sliding, one or two jumping into the pit. The undertaker was helping Wetzel. For just a second, Brammer thought it was the tractor they were coming for, but then he felt the solid grasps and pats of their hands on his shoulders and the circle of their arms around him.

CROSSING WITH SASSAFRAS

A goat that a fellow can see through is better than no goat at all. That's how I've come to think of it. With Emma and the children gone, Sassafras will be good company—even though her flying unnerves me. She jigs through the autumn air this morning, lighter than a cloud, her pink udder swaying side to side, flapping against her spindly legs, which jerk and propel her past me, sometimes within a hair's breadth. Her hot, grassy breath comes quickly, like she's anxious even, making me believe that if I leaned in close, didn't try to dodge her, she'd tell me a secret, something I want to know. But I haven't found the courage to stand my ground as a man ought, to not flinch when she gallops by so near. The times when I've gathered up my strength, tried to coax her to me, she keeps her distance.

Ever since she showed up, I've been mending her fence, and today, I'm at it again. It's not that I think she'll stay put. I mean, if the fence didn't hold her while she was alive, I can't expect it to keep her ghost. Then why get out and labor and sweat for a lost cause? you will ask. The answer is simple: I want her to know that a goat's ghost is welcome here, can stay as long as there's weeds to trim, bark to gnaw on, tender redbud leaves to chew and swallow and belch up later.

But putting a fence back together is a job for a young man. I'm not as stout as in the days when I chased her and the others back to the fence every time Emma found them in the garden. With my fingers, I trace the braided, rusty wire between barbs and remember the coarse white hair

I used to find snagged here—evidence of Sassafras passing through. I reach for my handkerchief to soak up the sweat on my head, a trickle under my nose. My fingers streak the handkerchief with gritty rust. I wave this, an orange-and-white truce flag, at the nanny goat ghost, and for a minute she makes like she will bolt but stays put over by the water well, wagging her head.

From my shirt pocket, I pull out a long peppermint piece, peel off the sticky wrapper, and try to draw her to me. Sassafras doesn't budge. But at least she's got her hooves on the ground for now. She stares at me like the pasture isn't green enough for her, and it puts me in the notion to just walk away and be done with all her blurry whiteness. But it's that habit she has of looking back over her shoulder, to some distant point in the field, that grips me. It's not the first time she has held me so, spellbound.

"Stop her! Obert—Obert," Emma yells for me. "Stop her. Obert! Where are you?" I've been two hours in the sun-striped stall of the barn, dung to my knees, shoveling flaky manure onto the trailer of my tractor, hearing clump after clump thud in the trailer bed. Despite the handkerchief Emma makes me wear over my face, dust still clots in my nostrils. But even so, I'm happy to take manure dust any day over the soot I breathed in the Buckeye Hollow Mine that one summer working for Emma's father. I choked down that fine coal powder only a month, but I never forgot the gritty dust that laid cover to everything, that burrowed its way under the elastic of your clothes like chiggers and rubbed you raw, that burned in your throat, grated in your teeth, hours after you'd left the hole in the earth.

"Stop her! Stop her, Obert!"

I step around the heaped trailer, and the warm, moist March air soothes my throat. The fullness of the sun takes away my vision a moment before I catch sight of Sassafras coming toward me, her mouth full of dishrag. Her neck cranes far around, looking back at Emma. All the while the goat walks stiff-legged, defiantly, jerking her legs like she's marching. Coming straight for me.

"Obert," Emma says and stops and stamps her feet. Emma. Catch your breath, this, seeing her again. Catch your breath. "Obert! You take this goat on over to Delano Burton's. I don't ever want to see her again. Do you hear me? Do you understand? It's not enough she eats my garden all

summer long, but now she's made a meal of my clean wash, too. It's more than a body can stand."

Sassafras hides behind me. I feel her there, warm flank against the back of my legs. Hear her loud breathing too. Emma drops her hands. "I'm too old to have to be chasing a goat all over creation," she says. "It was different when we were young. Can't you keep her penned in that fence you're always working on?"

Emma swings a poplar switch at her side, and I guess this proves too much for the white nanny. I hear her gagging, feel the ground jar behind me, feel scraping against the back of my boots. I turn to find her lying in the grass, spinning, her head rocking to and fro, eyes large, bright, a choking deep in her throat. The dishrag has vanished. Forcing her jaws, I reach for it, but it's too far gone for me to get a good hold.

"Get my pliers from the garage, from the bucket on the bench, blue-handled ones, long-snouted ones," I yell to Emma. I hold the quivering goat head in my lap, watch her glassy eyes roving to sky to grass to me and around again. How I have hated witnessing it, impending panic, each and every time. Her milky body stirs, then does not stir, life, still, but escaping out her fragile edges. "It's okay, girl," I tell Sassafras. "It's okay. Don't worry."

"Emma, hurry with the pliers," I whisper under my breath. "I'm losing her. Emma, hurry, hurry, hurry, hurry. Emma, here to me. Here to me, hurry. As fast as you can. Hurry now."

"Don't worry about supper," I tell Emma. "Just turn off the fire under the beans. The curtains are fine. It's almost dark. Hurry. I *did* lock the doors."

Emma. That month gone from you was a long time, not knowing when I would be back, if ever I would be. On Buckeye, they told me those deep, black tunnels have a way of burying a man's own deep things, of making him forget, deny what's most important to him. You give it all up every time you go down. But I remembered you. I never forgot. Hurry. Your neck, sweet, sweet neck, the delicate nape. Let me touch your neck there, where your hair trails off, swirls, barely wisps. Let me hold my face flush against your face. Do you hear me not breathing? Did you hear the air leave? I'm nearly afraid to touch you. But I do touch you. And cradle your neck in my hand. My face here, Emma, and the soft scent of your

skin. I dreamed of your neck in the camps at night. And remembered it and remembered it, remembering it against my face and under my lips, crawling in the tunnels every morning where I could not breathe for the dust. This, all of you. And don't hurry now. Home, to this length of you, against me. Fabric going away, your bare skin. I'm not breathing. Stifled beside you. My face hard pressed against your warm shoulder, I cannot even form my lips to kiss, my mouth, limp, open, against the flesh of your neck. Do you groan? Emma. Emma. I have known you forever. I have never not known you. Emma.

I narrow my eyes to the misty image before me, the nanny goat ghost in the tall, crisp horse weeds that've grown all around and up through the old wooden trailer of my tractor. She sighs, a delicate "mmeheh," and continues chewing her cud. She scrapes her hoof on the lowered end of the trailer like she's trying to get my attention, like she wants maybe to go for a ride—or like maybe she wishes the children were here, wants to pull them in the trailer the way the other goats did when the children were little. She's about ten feet away, keeping herself out of range of the short-handled hatchet I've been hammering and prying on the fence with. I see the brisk swats of her short tail, batting flies, and hear her steady, slow munching in the quiet of this place. I look around, take a slow sweep of the land, see the horizon wobble a little, move away and come back to me. I wipe my eyes and put the handkerchief back in my pocket.

The earth wobbles again and my head swims. I flip over the tin bucket that hauls my mending tools and sit down. In my deep pockets, the steeple nails scratch my thighs, and I shift my britches so they won't hurt. There's crimson crust on my arm where barbs have caught my skin.

I feel my heart beating fast and hard and close to my throat and wonder if I've overdone it. It's those pills that make me dizzy, the ones the doctor prescribes, pills the children make me promise to take, day in, day out, week after week after week. Before them, I was strong, but now I'm not. They're the same heart pills that took Emma. She told me they made her heart jitter and quake. But I said, "It's something you've been eating, Emma." She said they made her forget things and imagine things that never happened. I said, "Take them. They're for your own good. Take them if they keep you here with me longer." She wanted that, I know as sure as I'm sitting here. But it's been ten years since the pills ate

up her heart. Had I been in my right mind, had it not been such a jolt then, maybe I would have started taking them the day she died, the day she stumbled in the garden, panting for air, after we'd picked bushel baskets and buckets of beans and scooted them onto the plywood trailer, its onion-smooth tires sinking deeper in the dirt with each full basket. I remember how she wanted me to take the beans to the house and come back for her with the trailer. She didn't think she could walk. But I knew not to wait and made room for her between the baskets. She wouldn't let me leave any of the beans behind for fear Sassafras would gobble them down. And maybe she would have.

I pull out the handkerchief again and wipe my eyes. Why is Sassafras here—back from the grave? I treated her right. All of us did, even Emma. Did she just get lonesome? Fixing her fence, I haven't made it fifty feet from the barn, and from my bucket seat I survey the line ahead of me, the wire that's been wrenched from termite-whittled posts, some strands now burdened under the weight of a twisted, uprooted willow. It seems an impossible task.

Suddenly Sassafras lifts herself off the ground—like she's a giant bird, yet without wings. She sighs her familiar "mmeheh" and goes back to chewing, suspended there between earth and sky. The grass squeaks in her mouth, and periodically, she stops chewing and looks behind her, away over the eerie field like she's expecting someone. I look behind her, too.

Emma rushes, the blue-handled pliers in one hand, the other clutching her blouse at the top to keep it from flying open while she runs. "Here, hurry," she says, crouching beside me.

"You pull the dishrag out," I say. "I'll hold her jaws apart. You pull it out."

"I'm afraid," Emma says. "Maybe I should call Michael. It wouldn't take him long to get here."

"Don't be afraid. Just grab a hold when I open her jaws. Pull gently, not fast."

Sassafras is motionless now, without struggle. The goat's eyes are wide and rolling. I pry, careful not to disjoint her jaws, saliva on my hands, opening, holding open with all my strength. I am shaking. Emma moves her hand, pliers clasped, into the sticky muzzle, further now, and with

a good hold, she pulls gently. She pulls slowly, more and more red and white checkers appearing, wet, grassy even. We smell the inside of the goat, a bitter, rotting scent from one of her cavernous stomachs. She gags deep in her throat. They gag, both of them now gagging, and Sassafras coughs, kicks, with the dishrag out, kicks around and whirls herself up, no prisoner, stands coughing, her head down very low and each long, deep cough lifting her off the ground.

"I was afraid we lost her," Emma says and leans against me, and my nose brushes hers, hot tears on her face. Emma. I couldn't have risked missing this, not being here. I couldn't have gone back to the mine. It was harder on us this way, with your father's disappointment, and not the money we could have had, the nice cars other men had, the machines that would have made things easier for you in the beginning. I couldn't risk not seeing you again, my eyes filling with the night, the earth swallowing me. I never regretted buying my ticket home, even when I couldn't meet the eyes—eyes so white—of the other miners.

I look at the goat ghost, floating now, about two feet above the ground, above the upended trailer, staring past me to the house. I wonder if she's going to fly at me again.

When I hear Emma call that lunch is ready, I swivel on my bucket, my legs stiffening as I try to straighten up. Standing makes my heart beat faster again. She'll probably worry that I'm getting another goat since I've been working on the fence. Will I tell her Sassafras has come back? I picture her watching from the kitchen, scouring dried egg from dishes, muttering to herself, muttering about me out here pouring honey in the pasture. Of course, Sassafras would have nothing to do with the golden, oozing stream—though it used to be a treat for her. When I saw it was so, I wiped the rim of the jar with my forefinger and licked it, screwing on the cap. It takes patience to win a goat. I've always known that.

Inside the house I wash up. The kitchen is empty, and I remember Emma is not here, hasn't been here in a long time. I open a couple of cabinets stocked with the corn, tomatoes, pickles, and peach preserves that Katie's been canning. On the counter she's left a jar of green beans, though she knows I don't eat them now. Emma could grow them anywhere. Here on the kitchen floor if she wanted. She had a way with them. Slaved to save as many as she could, weeding, and picking, stringing and

snapping, washing, her hands in the cool water, fingers sifting, straining them, packing them in quart jars. Thump, thump, thump, the jar on a towel-softened counter, she made them settle tight.

Straight from Buckeye, off the train, with my bag of sooty clothes slung over my shoulder, I've scrubbed myself as much as I could. From outside the screen door on the porch, I watch her. Her elbows bend at right angles over the counter. There's deliberation in all her movements, all of it from memory, having done it so many times before, and the back of her neck, arched now, catches light as she reaches for another jar. The light stays there, a sign. I wasn't made for the dark as some men. I couldn't risk losing this, leaving her, not for any amount of money or her father's good opinion. I wanted every night of my life to be beside her. There wasn't time to waste, not even in the beginning.

How long I watch I don't know. I knock. I'm weak in the knees, all my joints watery. She dries her hands, throwing the dish towel over her shoulder. Backing from the kitchen counter, reluctant to leave, she turns to the door like she doesn't want to be disturbed. But then she says, "You, Obert!" The door swings out far, she fills my arms, just fits there, bouncing up and down, rocking me. Emma, you are lovely. I am not breathing, you are tight around me, tight inside my arms, every muscle straining to be closer, my face brushing your neck. I am not breathing. I am holding you inside my lungs and not breathing. Smile at me. Emma. What? You say, "We have so many green beans this year."

I warm some leftover potatoes and cream corn from the refrigerator and scoop them onto a plate. The jar of green beans I put on the table too. While I eat, I run a finger along the cold glass of the jar, the "Ball" lettering. I pick it up to feel the weight. I haven't eaten green beans in ten years. She could make them grow anywhere. But when she died, I tried growing a patch in the garden, just a small one, because I loved them so. Not a single split-seeded vine broke through the earth, and I knew I would never eat them again.

"Obert, will you be having any green beans this evening? There are so many," Emma says. "Did anyone have green beans, where you were, at the camp? When you came out of the mine in the evenings? I put lots of bacon in them, just the way you like them." Her hair is up because I keep going on about how happy I am to look at her lovely neck, to bury

my face against her neck. I've been asleep, and my clothes are scattered on the floor. The sheets are full of her scents, and above that, on another level, I smell the green beans cooking in the kitchen. My stomach growls. I watch her move around the room in her slip, unpacking my bag, holding my gritty shirt close to her face where the black mixes with her tears.

"Will you go back?" she asks.

"They can't pay me enough, Emma," I say. "I know they're others who like the money, especially when there's none to go around. But I'll see that we get by, I promise. Tell your daddy thanks and all, and not to worry. We'll get by."

I wait for her to say something, but she only smiles, looks at me.

"I've thought about it a lot," I say. "Do you think we could raise goats, Emma?" She squints her eyes like she's trying to better understand me.

"We could sell the milk, butter, cheese," I say. "Probably not much in it but a little something." I prop myself up on my elbows. "Emma, when I was down there, eating lunch on my back, no such thing as light, I could see them, all white goats, on our hillside, against the green of our hillside. We had them when I was a boy, Emma. Would you like that?" She comes to me across the bed, nestles in my arms, lowering her head on my chest so I can nestle my face against her shoulder. I think of her, my princess in the pasture, with white goats all around her flowery skirt.

I've eaten without savoring, have lifted my fork twenty, maybe thirty times without realizing or remembering. The pills make me forget so easily. When I stand, I take the head-swim again, blood gushing up there around my brain to the front of my eyes. Suddenly I feel overcome, having the goat ghost on my hands, zinging by my head occasionally, in and out of the house, Emma not around to help me chase her back to the pasture. I move to the bedroom, crumple on my bed, atop the covers. My body unfolds easily, smooths itself out.

I dream but find I am awake with Sassafras sailing about in the room, legs kicking this way and that, her pink udder swinging. Slowly I rise so as not to spook her. She moves like she's not flying but rather running in the air, leaning in as she cuts corners in the room. Come here, girl. Come down from there. We've got to go outside. I reach for her, thinking my hand will go through her, but I catch hold of her slim hind leg, the crook where her skin is thin. She yanks, but I don't let go and sense that she is

lifting me from the floor, and I am flying too. She pulls me higher, and when it looks like she will go through the ceiling, I turn loose and fall flat on the bed, almost in a daze.

"Mmeheh," she says, and goes dashing through the wall. I see her then out under the sugar maple, on the ground, looking behind her. Maybe I could call Michael to help me lock her in the barn tonight. But what will he say?

When I finally go back out to catch her again, the evening air is chilly, and the shadows of the hills are long. I pick my way out to the pasture, the goat a few steps ahead of me. I have a cinnamon roll and peppermint pieces for her, and at the pasture I offer them, but she won't come close to me now.

Emma's chased her from the bean vines, where she feasted all morning and now she won't forgive me. Neither of them will forgive me.

"She probably consumed fourteen quarts," Emma tells me. "That's fourteen meals when we could have eaten beans this winter, but your goat got them," she says. My eyes follow the direction of her finger, upper end of the garden, the white goat peering through the cornstalks.

"What will you do?" Emma asks. She picks up dirt clods and runs at Sassafras. Yelling, she throws them, and clouds of dust burst all around the goat. Sassafras waits until the very last minute, getting every bite she can, then turns on her heels and runs, cutting in and out of the rows of the garden so tenderly cared for, heading away and then back until she tricks Emma off balance, gets past her and runs to me, like I will save her. But she sees I'm braced to catch her, and when I dive, finding the hard, dry earth smoking in my teeth, she slips through my arms. Emma is over me.

"Get up, get her, Obert. Get that goat."

"Don't run, Emma, you'll scare her, walk slowly." I stalk the goat then, matter-of-factly, with her doing that stiff-legged trot she does, the pink of her behind shining under her raised tail, her looking over her shoulder, back at Emma. "Here, Sassafras, come here, girl. I won't hurt you," I say. "Come here, girl."

Sassafras leads me up the overgrown path. The horseweeds slap my face, and I feel their coarse edges, brown from frost. The air is cool. She

stays only a few feet ahead, like she knows I move slower these days. Soon enough, the going gets easier. Through the pine forest where the needles are orange, fiery orange this evening with the sun so low, we go. Around us are the twisted, crackling bushes, twined with dying catbriers. She mounts the hill, a youthful goat. I see her legs pushing off the ground, each strong step to take her higher. And now she leaps over the pushed-down fence, with the same ease she had when it was a good fence. She leads me over the crest to the family cemetery.

"You can't bury her there, Dad," Katie says to me. "What will people say?"

"But she's part of the family," I say. "She's been a friend to me."

"Bury her somewhere else—behind the barn maybe," Michael says.

"It's a private cemetery," I say. "No one comes here, no one will ever know there's a goat buried here. It's not like I'm going to buy a monument for her or anything. I'll just carve her name on a rock. She's been with me so long and given me reason to get up in the mornings after your mother died, after I got her home in the trailer that day and before I could even lift her from it, when she could not catch her breath."

"Breathe slowly," I said, "please, hold on, breathe slowly now." Her eyes were wide. "I don't want to leave you, I don't want you to leave, please, breathe slowly, in and out, in and out." My hand is under her head, cradling her neck, wet and hot. "Hold on, I'll call the children, hold on, they'll hurry, they will be here, we'll get you to the hospital, hold on, Emma, breathe, I am with you, don't be afraid, please, breathe, breathe, please, please, please."

Her eyes are far brighter than in life, wide open, taking in everything, or maybe nothing. "Emma, please, you're not breathing. You're not trying. Please breathe."

"Let me stay with her," I tell the ambulance driver. "She's scared, please save her, give her back to me, please. Emma. Let me hold her hand."

"Take my hand, Dad, while we walk there," Katie says. "Mom will rest there. She'll be okay, happy on this hill, near the pasture, not too far from the garden she loved."

"It's not an easy walk," I say. I've walked it hundreds of times, check-ing the fence, mending the gaps, but it seems like today I can't bring my-self to walk it. They carry her slowly, steadily. Sometimes they slide in the red mud. Their arms are tense. They don't want to drop her. Seems like

my feet are going without my moving them. At the graveside, they would leave the coffin on top like that, wait for me to leave, to turn my head. It doesn't make sense to me. Seeing a thing done means seeing it done.

"I'm not leaving," I tell them. "Be done with it, boys."

"Dad, walk back with me."

"You don't understand," I say. "Let me be." It doesn't take long, not long at all, once they've lowered her into the earth. Their shoulders and elbows bending, they send the red dirt through the air. It thuds below at first but then just falls softly and silently, and finally they're ready to leave. They think I'm going to be a hard case. But I'm not. I just want to be left alone with her. "Go on home," I say. "I want to be alone. Come back for me if it makes you feel better, just leave me here a while. I'll be ready when you come back."

I don't want to be alone, please, Emma. After that first month away, I never left again. I could not. You know that. We were never apart again.

"I will not leave you," I tell her, the bean juice sticky on my chin. "You never leave me either, you hear, Emma."

"Why would I?" she says, snuggling close. "You're my world."

The shoveling done, men gone, I can't wait for anyone to come back and I leave the mound, the place they've put Emma. At the fence, on her side for once, Sassafras—she knows. Through the fence I touch her pink nose.

"Mmeheh," she says.

"Mmeheh," I repeat. I walk up a ways to the gate and enter the pasture to be with her. We walk back together. Not wanting to go home but not wanting to go anywhere else either. She picks at a leaf here and there, but that's all. Like me, she's not hungry.

She leads me past the cemetery, high up on Mark's Knob, to that steep place. I know she's going to fly. I know it. I want to catch her at that moment, to stop her before she leaps up. I want to bring her home with me, tie her to the poplar in the yard till I get the fence fixed, keep her from going away from me again. I crawl on my hands and knees now and feel the earth under my palms. I scoot toward the edge where she pauses to look back over her shoulder—but not at me, past me.

"Mmeheh," she says. Her cry is urgent. She stares past me but I see nothing unusual. I reach for her as far as—reach—all of me stretching—another inch or—all my—this—is all—to grab hold of her, to clutch her

to myself. My fingers find her coarse hair, joint of her hind leg, almost within my grip. All the way. Emma, I have her. She's lifting off the ground. I have her, I will, I have her this time. But my hand is slipping, I can't hold on much longer, she is, I am, slipping, and I lose hold, fall, am rolling, down the hill. I go down, sliding and rolling, with the earth and leaves blurry fast in front of my face. Until it all stops, and my body curls inward to the burning pain.

I look up at the sky, see the ghost goat hovering above the persimmon trees. Can't she see I want her to stay, that there's room here for her? I stand up, my head reeling. Sassafras floats out of sight, leaving me behind. I brush off my clothes and head toward home. Emma will be worried, will have supper on the table waiting for me, maybe even her green beans this evening.

"Emma," I say, entering. "I'm home." But there's no answer and I guess she's running late. I don't know when she'll be home, and I figure I'll have to cook the beans for us. I wash my hands and pop open the lid of the jar with a can opener. Dump them into a pot on the stove and turn the fire on. I wash the day's dirty dishes while they heat up. I'm tired and I wish Emma would get home soon to eat supper. It's not like her to be gone anywhere this late.

Through the window I see Sassafras perched in the sugar maple—aglow. I can't tell if she's standing on a branch or just floating at the moment. It's too much for an old man like me, having a crazy goat who doesn't know whether she's beast or bird. I keep my eye on her, and when the beans are ready, I lift about five tablespoons into a dish for me and three into a dish for Sassafras. I set hers on the floor, trying to lure her into the house while Emma isn't here. I put the lid on the pot so the beans will stay warm till Emma gets back.

Back through the dark house I go with my beans. In the bedroom, Sassafras surprises me, having come through the wall. Her glow lights the room. Emma will not be happy about having a goat in the house, but Sassafras needs a place to stay until I finish the fence. I'll just have to explain it. On the bed, I pull the blankets over me and lie back. With my fingers, I eat the beans. They're fine in the way they're always fine, and I keep nibbling at them, trying to savor each one, figuring they'll tide me over till Emma's home for supper.

The dish is warm, is heaped high, green beans and a strand or two of bacon threading through, on my bare chest, warm, the dish, when you feed them to me, one at a time, with your fingers, picking one and putting it in my mouth, watching my face, waiting till I swallow before reaching for another, every green bean on the plate this way, and occasionally, one wrapped with a shred of limp bacon, until the dish is empty and there's just the juice then, which you drain into my mouth, down my chin, across my chest, that you kiss clean.

Sassafras never eats them hot because they burn her mouth. But she likes them cold, cooked or raw. When she takes sick, I bring some candy to the stall where she lies, thinking it might help her. She eats it all from my hand, careful, as she always has been, not to bite my fingers. She eats everything I bring today but tomorrow she won't. She doesn't stand now. There are no more bowel movements. She coughs. When she begins the loud, gut-wrenching bellows, I know what will have to happen.

"Maybe we can call a doctor," Katie says. "Or Delano Burton. He'll know what to do."

"She's very old," I say. "She's suffering. I'll hitch up the trailer, carry her back on the hill, and we'll put an end to it." Emma's been gone four years, so it's the children, Michael and Katie, who help me lift her, mmehehing, mmehehing, to the trailer.

"You ride back here with her," I tell them. But they don't want to. They are grown now.

"I can't do it, Dad," Katie says. "I can't."

"I can't either," Michael says. "Shouldn't we call the vet? Get him to give her a shot?"

"One of you will have to drive the tractor then," I say, "and I'll ride with her. You can leave before I do it." Emma would have stayed with me, would have known what it required—and would have been my help.

Beside the grave, just at the boundary of the cemetery, a place where no one else would want to be buried, I give her peppermint. The children leave, don't even look back over their shoulders. I watch them as long as I can and turn back to Sassafras, who drops the peppermint from her mouth. My jaws are so tight they hurt, my throat knotted like I might vomit. I pet her head, run my hand gently on her floppy ears. "Mmeheh." She is swollen and cannot stand. She cries out at all hours. She is four-

teen, a ripe age for a goat, one we thought would die a day old. When the mother died, Emma fed her formula with a nippled RC bottle, named her Sassafras, and the tiny kid ate, punching her nose at the nipple, milk bubbles foaming at the sides of her mouth, her tail spinning, spinning. You cradle her as one of your own, Emma, as me even, soothing her head, your fingers soft and strong, scent of green beans on them, taste of them, passing over my lips, the edges of my teeth.

The gun is nothing but weight and cold. It has always seemed so to me. You never asked me to do it, would never have, no matter how many beans Sassafras ate. But there isn't a choice now. She won't get up again. I've seen it too many times with all the other goats. You have been gone from me four long years. You were my strength. Just to have you again, Emma. That last day, losing you.

I aim, but not I, someone else, at her head, not her head, there, just a target, I pretend, and squeeze. One shot. Then a second. They shouldn't let me do it. I'm no good with a gun, have never been, have made a mess of it. And am too old. I don't have the stomach. Didn't even as a young man. They haul that miner up, pulling him out on a rail cart, mangled. He's one of the lucky ones, someone says. At least they got his body. I don't know him, so it isn't that. You just never know when you go under if you'll see daylight again, or the other things that light your life. His wife is soaked in the rain, a scarf pasted to her head. When she sees his body, so pale and broken, she reaches, knees going, her head bowed, her neck, a flash of your head bent, the back of your neck catching light, while you string beans. I couldn't go down there again. I walked away the same hour and bought my ticket home. Some men get over it or get used to it, your daddy told me. But I thought my train to you would never come.

My skin is cool, damp from sweat tonight. The cold dish lies empty on my chest. It's dark all around. Momentarily, I close my eyes, stilling myself, quieting my heart, while I wait. When I open my eyes, Sassafras is on her way down again, bright as day, pulling a trailer out of the sky. She looks behind her, away off in the distance toward the bean patch where Emma stands, waving, yelling that it's supper time. Sassafras comes closer and closer, trotting her stiff-legged gait, finally swinging the trailer down within reach. When she halts in front of me, I hoist myself up and climb on board to go.

teen, a ripe age for a goat, one we thought would die a day old. When the mother died, Emma fed her formula with a nippled RC bottle, named her Sassafras, and the tiny kid ate, punching her nose at the nipple, milk bubbles foaming at the sides of her mouth, her tail spinning, spinning. You cradle her as one of your own, Emma, as me even, soothing her head, your fingers soft and strong, scent of green beans on them, taste of them, passing over my lips, the edges of my teeth.

The gun is nothing but weight and cold. It has always seemed so to me. You never asked me to do it, would never have, no matter how many beans Sassafras ate. But there isn't a choice now. She won't get up again. I've seen it too many times with all the other goats. You have been gone from me four long years. You were my strength. Just to have you again, Emma. That last day, losing you.

I aim, but not I, someone else, at her head, not her head, there, just a target, I pretend, and squeeze. One shot. Then a second. They shouldn't let me do it. I'm no good with a gun, have never been, have made a mess of it. And am too old. I don't have the stomach. Didn't even as a young man. They haul that miner up, pulling him out on a rail cart, mangled. He's one of the lucky ones, someone says. At least they got his body. I don't know him, so it isn't that. You just never know when you go under if you'll see daylight again, or the other things that light your life. His wife is soaked in the rain, a scarf pasted to her head. When she sees his body, so pale and broken, she reaches, knees going, her head bowed, her neck, a flash of your head bent, the back of your neck catching light, while you string beans. I couldn't go down there again. I walked away the same hour and bought my ticket home. Some men get over it or get used to it, your daddy told me. But I thought my train to you would never come.

My skin is cool, damp from sweat tonight. The cold dish lies empty on my chest. It's dark all around. Momentarily, I close my eyes, stilling myself, quieting my heart, while I wait. When I open my eyes, Sassafras is on her way down again, bright as day, pulling a trailer out of the sky. She looks behind her, away off in the distance toward the bean patch where Emma stands, waving, yelling that it's supper time. Sassafras comes closer and closer, trotting her stiff-legged gait, finally swinging the trailer down within reach. When she halts in front of me, I hoist myself up and climb on board to go.

The dish is warm, is heaped high, green beans and a strand or two of bacon threading through, on my bare chest, warm, the dish, when you feed them to me, one at a time, with your fingers, picking one and putting it in my mouth, watching my face, waiting till I swallow before reaching for another, every green bean on the plate this way, and occasionally, one wrapped with a shred of limp bacon, until the dish is empty and there's just the juice then, which you drain into my mouth, down my chin, across my chest, that you kiss clean.

Sassafras never eats them hot because they burn her mouth. But she likes them cold, cooked or raw. When she takes sick, I bring some candy to the stall where she lies, thinking it might help her. She eats it all from my hand, careful, as she always has been, not to bite my fingers. She eats everything I bring today but tomorrow she won't. She doesn't stand now. There are no more bowel movements. She coughs. When she begins the loud, gut-wrenching bellows, I know what will have to happen.

"Maybe we can call a doctor," Katie says. "Or Delano Burton. He'll know what to do."

"She's very old," I say. "She's suffering. I'll hitch up the trailer, carry her back on the hill, and we'll put an end to it." Emma's been gone four years, so it's the children, Michael and Katie, who help me lift her, mmehehing, mmehehing, to the trailer.

"You ride back here with her," I tell them. But they don't want to. They are grown now.

"I can't do it, Dad," Katie says. "I can't."

"I can't either," Michael says. "Shouldn't we call the vet? Get him to give her a shot?"

"One of you will have to drive the tractor then," I say, "and I'll ride with her. You can leave before I do it." Emma would have stayed with me, would have known what it required—and would have been my help.

Beside the grave, just at the boundary of the cemetery, a place where no one else would want to be buried, I give her peppermint. The children leave, don't even look back over their shoulders. I watch them as long as I can and turn back to Sassafras, who drops the peppermint from her mouth. My jaws are so tight they hurt, my throat knotted like I might vomit. I pet her head, run my hand gently on her floppy ears. "Mmeheh." She is swollen and cannot stand. She cries out at all hours. She is four-

DIPLOMAT

By Charles W. Thayer

DIPLOMAT

THE UNQUIET GERMANS

HANDS ACROSS THE CAVIAR

BEARS IN THE CAVIAR

DIPLOMAT

BY CHARLES W. *heeler* THAYER

Foreword by Sir Harold Nicolson

HARPER & BROTHERS PUBLISHERS

NEW YORK

Library of Congress catalog card number: 59–6320

To

J. C. D.

whose diplomatic career is accomplished

and to his grandson

J. D. T.

whose career has yet to begin.

CONTENTS

CONTENTS

FOREWORD

Several books have been written in French, English and German about the art and practice of diplomacy, but Charles W. Thayer's *Diplomat* is, in so far as I am aware, the first comprehensive report written by a professional United States diplomatist and from the American point of view. It is to be hoped that it will be widely read by various sections of the American Administration and public. Hitherto American public opinion has been somewhat bewildered by several often contradictory views of a diplomatist's true function and importance. There are those who regard the Foreign Service as a kind of bird sanctuary for elegant young men, with the milk of Groton still wet upon their lips, arrayed in striped pants and spending most of their time handing sugar cookies to ladies of high society in Europe and Latin America. Conversely, there are those who regard diplomatists as an international gang of intriguers intent upon ensnaring the great white soul of the United States. I have often felt it strange that, whereas American business executives will come to Europe bursting with self-confidence and gullibility, diplomatists are diffident and almost pathologically suspicious. They are so determined not to be fooled that they scarcely enter into any connections at all. Another picture of the diplomatist is that he is little more than a clerk at the end of the telephone whose duty it is to interpret and carry out the often contradictory views of the White House, the State Department, the Pentagon, several Congressional Committees, and that vast and vague entity known as American opinion. There are those, again, who regard international politics as slightly disreputable and who condemn any undue interest in foreign languages, cultures or conditions, as not being in the spirit of the Founding Fathers and as specially obnoxious to men such as the late Senator Joe McCarthy (if there are any). Again, in contrast to those who regard the art of diplomacy as something intricate and even

dangerous, there are those who assume that it is, or should be, a comparatively simple task and one that can be performed by the facile application of sweet reasonableness. There is of course some historic justification for this theory, since the greatest of known diplomatic triumphs was when Benjamin Franklin arrived in Paris in December, 1776, and managed, owing to the mesmeric quality of his simple friendliness and his beaming smile, to induce the bankrupt French Government to advance large sums to the thirteen colonies and in the end to enter into an offensive and defensive alliance which proved of great advantage to the United States.

It is to be hoped that Charles Thayer's informative, sensible and witty book will serve to dispel these contradictory illusions and induce many millions of people to take a less distorted view of the diplomatist's true functions. After all, Charles Thayer has devoted to the Foreign Service of the United States many years of honorable and efficient service. He has derived from his experience, in many differing conditions and in many various lands, the conviction of several most important truths.

He knows, for instance, that the word "diplomacy" is in itself a misleading word since it is all too frequently applied both to foreign policy and to negotiation. The damaging term "secret diplomacy" is often applied to both although in fact they are distinct. Foreign policy should never be secret in the sense that the citizens of a free country should never be committed to treaties without their previous knowledge and consent. Negotiation, on the other hand, must always be confidential, as has been proved (if proof were ever needed) by the recent proceedings of the Foreign Ministers' Conference in Geneva. Even the committee of a country club would not consider the possibility of framing their own rules, or electing new members, in the presence of a tape recorder or in front of a microphone and television camera. Charles Thayer's book should enable people to make this important distinction and to use the term "foreign policy" when they mean foreign policy, and the term "negotiation" when they mean negotiation, without confusing the issue by employing the somewhat discredited word "diplomacy" to cover both.

Charles Thayer knows also that the practice of diplomacy is not in fact very different from the practice of sound business, in that it relies for its efficacy upon the establishment of confidence and credit. Ex-

perienced diplomats are traditionally suspicious of what is called "brilliant diplomacy" or "diplomatic triumphs," since they are well aware that these feats of ingenuity are apt to leave resentment and suspicion behind.

Thayer also knows that the aim of diplomats is the preservation of peace. The professional diplomat, to whatever country he belongs, is convinced that this is his main function and that if international differences lead to war he and his colleagues have failed in their main purpose. He is therefore conscious of world interests superior to immediate national interests, and the advice that he renders to his government will be conditioned by this ideal. The amateur diplomat, on the other hand, does not acquire these professional principles and is apt to imagine that some spectacular successes may win him applause in his own press and be viewed with pride and approbation in his own home town.

This excellent study of a diplomat's functions will also do much to counter the theory that the modern diplomat is little more than a clerk at the end of the telephone mechanically executing the instructions of his home government. People who hold such a view ignore the obvious fact that no large business and no responsible newspaper would employ as their agent or correspondent abroad representatives whose knowledge of local conditions was disregarded and whose advice they ignored.

Charles Thayer knows also that it is part of a diplomat's function to establish and maintain relations of confidence with those in power in the country to which he is accredited. In totalitarian states he must be very careful to avoid the suspicion of flirting with the opposition since he will then be denounced as interfering in the internal affairs of the country. One sometimes hears the criticism that professional diplomats only consort with the party in power and make few contacts outside, without realizing that the party in power is the one which is most useful for the efficient conduct of business, whereas to establish contacts with their party enemies would (except in the most liberal countries) expose an envoy to suspicion.

Apart from keeping his government informed of local conditions and advising them as to what policies on their part would be acceptable and what the reverse, it is, as Charles Thayer says, the duty of a diplomat to "represent his own country." This does not mean only that an American envoy is obliged to welcome visiting Congressmen and to

provide his countrymen with lavish garden parties on July 4, but it also means that he should convey to the people of the country to which he is accredited a picture of all that is best in the American Idea. He should be simple, straightforward, honest, truthful and benevolent. That is what we foreigners expect an American representative to be.

Charles Thayer, I am pleased to notice, tends to agree with me that diplomacy by conference is often a somewhat dangerous proceeding since it arouses wide public expectation and may cause disproportionate disappointment. It is obvious that occasions occur when it is essential for the heads of state to meet together and discuss their problems across a table. Yet such reunions should be preceded by careful and humdrum negotiations, between professional diplomatists and without publicity.

As one who was born and bred in the Diplomatic Service, and who has studied and even written books about diplomatic practice, I cannot recommend too highly Charles Thayer's admirable account. It is, as I have said, informative, well balanced, wise, witty and even at moments dramatic. It gives due prominence to important principles and diminishes the significance of unimportant incidentals. Above all, it is far more up to date than previous studies of this subject and includes from personal experience a most valuable analysis of the methods and prejudices of Russian diplomatists. I hope indeed that this book will be studied, not only by those young men who aspire to enter this excellent profession, but also by all politicians, newspapermen and other Americans who need to be reminded of the immutable principles that have governed the art of international negotiation from Palaeolithic days.

HAROLD NICOLSON

INTRODUCTION

IN the older countries of Europe diplomacy has long been accepted as an indispensable and respectable method of defending one's international interests. In the United States, however, despite oratorical references to "The First Line of Defense," it has more often been regarded as an expendable weapon like a hand grenade to be tossed among the enemy occasionally, chiefly to create confusion. Its indispensability has never been completely recognized and its respectability is still not fully acknowledged.

This attitude is not so odd as it may appear. Only in the generation since World War I has ordinary diplomacy been practiced by the United States, and then only spasmodically. European diplomacy has been associated in the public mind with Machiavellianism and cardsharping, the American version with striped pants and cooky pushing. It has been regarded by many as a necessary evil rather than a positive force. Wrapped in unnecessary mystery by its own practitioners, its purposes, functions and methods have seldom been fully grasped.

It is hoped that by removing the veil of mystery and examining its rules, both moral and technical, a little of this misunderstanding can be dispelled and the essential requirements of effective diplomacy made more clear.

C.W.T.

Unlike the military, the diplomat is not the spoilt child of historians.

—JULES CAMBON

DIPLOMAT

I

Embassy in Crisis: 1

YOU enter the American ambassador's residence in Beirut through two high gates, the first leading to an outer courtyard where the embassy cars are parked, and the second to a cool, green garden filled with jasmine, oleander and bougainvillea. Ordinarily the Lebanese policeman outside the first gate will not stop you, provided you are dressed in Western clothes and do not flourish a tommy gun.

The second gate is presided over by the embassy kavass, the ambassador's personal bodyguard, a relic of the days when embassies in the Ottoman Empire maintained their own police forces. Tewfik, the present kavass, is a dignified and usually cheerful old gentleman who has served the Americans for over thirty years. He wears a red Turkish fez with a black tassel, a richly embroidered gold and blue waistcoat across which hangs a heavy silver chain, and a red, white and blue silk sash. His trousers are cut from a dozen yards of white linen; they balloon around his waist and are wrapped tight around his ankles. On ceremonial occasions he also wears a long sword sheathed in an ivory scabbard.

Nowadays, when the ambassador is not entertaining, Tewfik leaves the tending of the gate to a junior footman but technically he is responsible for guarding it and when the ambassador goes out anywhere, to his office, to call on an official, or even on a picnic, Tewfik accompanies him riding in splendor beside the chauffeur.

Sunday morning, May 10, 1958, was bright and sunny. The tall

cypresses that reached above the shelter of the high wall surrounding the residence were swaying in a moderate breeze. Tewfik was lounging in a chair outside the front door when the ambassador appeared on the terrace.

Short and lean, with hazel eyes, black hair, and a trim, already graying mustache, the ambassador moved briskly with all the jauntiness of an undersized Irishman. Of his forty-nine years, twenty-seven had been spent knocking about the world in the Foreign Service and his tough, good-natured face had been weather-beaten by the wind and snow of Lapland and the sun and sand of the Sahara.

He exchanged a few words with the kavass, who responded without much animation. Then he went over to where his breakfast table had been set up in a shady part of the terrace and tuned his portable radio to the BBC relay from Cyprus. He would have preferred to listen to the Voice of America news from Washington but the VOA signal was not powerful enough to reach Beirut and so he relied—as do most diplomats in the Middle East—on the early-morning news from London.

Ordinarily on Sundays he took his wife and fifteen-year-old son David sailing on his little boat *Venture*. He was a passionate sailor and early in his career had published a learned paper on Naval Power and United States Diplomacy which had been published in the *U. S. Naval Institute Proceedings*. Few of his previous posts had provided the ideal sailing facilities that the Mediterranean outside of the Beirut harbor offered and he wanted to make the most of them.

But as he looked up at the swaying cypresses he had an uneasy feeling that there'd be no sailing today. The world news from London was relatively reassuring but the local situation in Beirut was troubled and had been for some days since an opposition journalist had been murdered on his way home from work. The opposition charged that President Chamoun's henchmen were responsible for the murder and were clamoring not only for their punishment but for the resignation of the President himself.

The ambassador had been in Beirut only five months but he had worked hard to dig himself into his new post and he already knew that the opposition's grudge went far deeper than the journalist's murder. It was, in fact, composed of two main elements, one purely local, the other deeply involving American relations with the entire

Middle East. Locally the opposition, consisting largely of the leaders of tribes and sects that fragmentize the Lebanon's body politic, felt that they had been cheated out of parliamentary positions, theirs by feudal right, by an unfair election and that furthermore President Chamoun was planning to alter the constitution to perpetuate his regime.

The other complaint was that Chamoun had aligned himself too closely with the West, i.e., the United States, when the State Department had dispatched an ex-congressman to "sell" the Eisenhower doctrine to the uncommitted nations of the Middle East. However, the salesman-congressman, a newcomer to the Middle East, had oversold his product in Beirut and not sold it at all elsewhere. While they were not Communists, many of the Moslem opposition wanted closer relations with Nasser's United Arab Republic and a more neutral attitude toward the United States.

For these two reasons the opposition was threatening to resort to force if necessary to oust President Chamoun. The night before at a dinner at the American Embassy, the President had assured the ambassador that the threats were empty bluffs and that his own position was entirely secure. But wisps of impressions had been building up a sense of uneasiness in the ambassador's mind that belied the President's apparent confidence.

When David, his son, appeared he told him to cancel the plans to go sailing. David was disappointed and resentful. "It's Sunday," he complained. "It's your day off." But the ambassador didn't even bother to tell him what he already knew as a Foreign Service son—presidents, cabinet ministers, and even the officials of the State Department in Washington could take Sunday off, but diplomats abroad are on duty the year round twenty-four hours a day. Even when he was traveling in the hinterland hundreds of miles from the capital he was still on post. Only when he had been granted leave, had formally relinquished command to his deputy, and had left the country was he off duty until he returned and sent the routine cable to Washington: "Have resumed charge."

Nor did the ambassador try to explain the causes for his uneasiness. The symptoms of impending crisis were difficult to describe: a tone of exasperation creeping into the normal vituperation of the opposition press; a certain tension among the guests at dinner the night before—

3

even Tewfik's gloom—sounded a small bell he had heard before and aroused what the Germans call his *fingerspitzengefuehl.*

In his many years of diplomatic work he had had plenty of occasions to test this almost intuitive political sixth sense: as a student in Buenos Aires during the Argentine revolution in 1930, as a vice-consul in the revolution in Panama two years later; as a third secretary of legation in the Haitian Massacres of 1937; as a second secretary in the Winter War between Russia and Finland in 1940, and later as chargé d'affaires during the German offensive in Finland in '42; as first secretary during the near revolution in Belgium, which led to the abdication of King Leopold; again as deputy chief of mission at Cairo, when Naguib and Nasser overthrew King Farouk; and finally as chargé d'affaires at Saigon during the Vietnamese crisis and the fall of Dienbienphu.

Now he was no longer a subordinate, but an ambassador. If a crisis came he would be the responsible chief of mission, responsible not only for American political interests but for the lives of the thousands of Americans in the Lebanon, including his son's. With a feeling of reassurance he thought of the Sixth Fleet now steaming about the Mediterranean. During the last crisis, at Dienbienphu, it had been the Seventh Fleet that had stood by. Perhaps he would someday write a supplement to his paper on Naval Power and United States Diplomacy —this time based on more personal experiences.

Breakfast over, he ordered the Cadillac and accompanied by Tewfik drove down the hill to his office in the embassy chancellery—a large, ugly converted apartment house on the waterfront.

In contrast to the ambassador, the counselor of the American Embassy was not an outdoor type at all. Usually he slept late on Sundays, breakfasted leisurely in his bathrobe, and sat about playing records on his hi-fi set to which he was just as attached as the ambassador was to his sailboat.

But after he had heard the BBC news and listened to his Arab maid's latest batch of rumors from the bazaar, he too felt a little concerned. The maid's brother, she told him, had heard machine-gun fire during the night in the Moslem section of town. Her friend, who worked for the *New York Times* correspondent in the next-door apartment, reported that the correspondent had left the house in a

hurry at eight o'clock. All was evidently not so quiet as the calm blue Mediterranean below his balcony indicated.

The counselor also had had his share of crises. He had been through the Winter War in Finland with his present ambassador. He had been in Trieste during the evacuation of that city when Tito threatened to take it in 1953. Since then there had been other tight spots. He turned off the hi-fi, dressed, and set off on foot for the embassy a few blocks away.

Barbara Spring, chief of the embassy files and code section, was entertaining a group of fellow clerks and secretaries for "brunch" in her small apartment. The code room was manned that Sunday morning by an experienced clerk and normally there would have been no reason for her to go down to the office.

Twenty-seven years old, an ex-schoolteacher from Rutland, Vermont, she had been a clerk in the Foreign Service for three years and her only other post had been Baghdad. The biggest excitements of her career had been the conferences leading to the Baghdad Pact and the more recent flap during the Suez Crisis, which had heavily strained the code room of Beirut, since Lebanon was the haven to which Americans evacuating Israel and Egypt had fled.

Barbara took more than a perfunctory interest in her work and carefully read the papers and cables that passed over her desk. In the past few days she had felt, less faintly and at second hand, the uneasiness emanating from the front office. Adding to the uneasiness was a large accumulation of air-mail pouches in the file room. From experience during the Suez Crisis she knew that airports have a disconcerting habit of closing down in an emergency. A U. S. Air Force plane, which could carry the pouches, was scheduled to leave for Washington early next morning.

Her guests seemed to be enjoying themselves over their brunch. So she quietly slipped out and walked over to her office to see what was up and to prepare the pouches for the Air Force plane. Not quite twenty-four hours later she returned home.

The Beirut Embassy at that time comprised about 220 Americans, seventy in the embassy proper and the rest distributed among the economic and military missions and the U. S. Information Service. Like

5

most new chiefs, the ambassador thought it was far too large and was planning to make drastic cuts. But he knew he faced a difficult fight with both the State Department and the dozens of other Washington agencies involved in foreign affairs, all anxious to keep their representatives abroad as numerous as possible. He also suspected that there were several weak spots in his immediate staff which he hoped to eliminate and in time to develop what he liked to call "a taut little ship." But all his key staff were experienced professionals and if they did not have all the mental vigor he would have liked, at least there were no bumbling amateurs about who might drop the ball in an emergency.

He was pleased, therefore, to find that by noon on that pleasant Sunday, in addition to his counselor and chief code clerk, all of his essential staff had come to the office, not summoned, but simply because they sensed that they might be needed. Only one of his Defense Department attachés, a newcomer both to Beirut and to diplomatic work, had gone off with his family to spend the day on the beach. When the attaché later complained a little bitterly "no one told me," his colleagues exchanged supercilious smiles.

The news and rumors that filtered into the embassy during the morning confirmed the fears of the staff. A clerk on the way to the office had seen some rioting in the heart of the Moslem section of town known as the Basta. The police, he said, seemed to be getting the worst of it and many of them were on the run. A veteran American correspondent dropped in and reported a rumor that Lebanese tribal leaders along the Syrian frontier had risen against government troops. A traveler from Tripoli reported that during the preceding day's rioting the American library in Tripoli had been burned down by what appeared to be Communist mobs.

Later in the day a missionary's wife telephoned from the American hospital in Tripoli with even more alarming reports. Mrs. Florence Boyes and her husband had for thirty-eight years been running the Kennedy Memorial Hospital but recently her husband had suffered a heart attack and was bedridden. Now Mrs. Boyes was managing the entire establishment as well as nursing her sick husband. She reported that government troops were fighting with rebel gangs who were evidently trying to get possession of the hospital. She also stated that, according to reports reaching her, the rebels were in control of the

6

old city which lay between the hospital on the sea and the new city farther inland. They were thus cut off from the mainland. Mrs. Boyes expressed little concern for herself but was worried about the safety of several American families farther in the interior who were cut off from both land and sea routes to Beirut. She promised to report any new developments as they occurred.

Shortly after noon the ambassador summoned a conference of his senior staff. From past experience he knew that one of the trickiest aspects of an emergency of this type is that at a certain point in the growing local tension a moment comes when any overt move to prepare for the worst can itself precipitate a panic.

During the Winter War in Finland, for example, the Finns, though exceedingly brave, had kept a sharp eye on every American reaction as if seeking reassurance in their desperate struggle with the Russians. At one point the danger of a Russian breakthrough to Helsinki had seemed sufficiently great to warrant the burning of the embassy's secret files. But by then the slightest wisp of smoke from the embassy chimneys might have caused panic among the townspeople. The moment for burning the files had passed, but fortunately the Finns held fast and the Russians never broke through.

Now the ambassador was determined to be ahead of events and to take precautions before they could cause panic. Accordingly, he ordered the embassy on "alert status." This was largely an administrative and internal measure. It meant only that all personnel were to be either at their posts or immediately available by telephone and should not leave the vicinity of the city without permission.

In announcing the alert he cautioned the staff not to mention the fact outside the embassy lest it cause alarm in the American community from which in turn it might spread throughout the city.

In times of emergency an ambassador has two essential duties: to protect the lives and property of American citizens and to protect his government's political interests. While retaining a general supervision over the first of these tasks, he turned over to his counselor chief responsibility for looking after American citizens and their property and devoted himself largely to the more delicate job of keeping in close touch with the local authorities and informing Washington of developments and recommending to it such diplomatic or military measures as might be necessary to safeguard its interests.

After ordering the alert the ambassador went to call on Dr. Charles Malik, the Lebanese foreign minister, whom he found in a considerable state of agitation. Malik claimed that Syria, already a partner of Nasser in the United Arab Republic, had the night before dispatched a "horde" of soldiers across the frontier to aid the rebels. Malik urgently requested that the Sixth Fleet be ordered to stand by ready to land in case the Lebanese government troops were overwhelmed.

From the Foreign Ministry the ambassador drove to the home of the commander of the Lebanese Army, General Fuad Chehab, who was apparently taking a much less serious view of the situation as he relaxed at his home fifteen miles from the capital. General Chehab, a descendant of one of the Lebanon's oldest and most venerable Christian families, was primarily a soldier interested in developing a strong army and anxious to keep himself and his Moslem and Christian subordinates aloof from internal political quarrels. He assured the ambassador that the current trouble was nothing to worry about. However, he added, it might be wise for the United States government to speed up deliveries of certain weapons it had promised the Lebanese Army.

From Chehab's home the ambassador motored back to the presidential palace and talked to Chamoun himself. The latter's tune had changed markedly since dinner the evening before. The report of the "Syrian invasion" had deeply disturbed him and he charged that Nasser was making a "massive" attempt to overthrow him and replace him with a man less tied to America and more friendly to Egypt. The United States, he argued, must either promise to support him or else watch his and every other pro-Western regime in the Middle East, including Iraq and Jordan, fall like ninepins to the Egyptian.

Back at his embassy office the ambassador quickly dictated telegrams reporting these views to Washington. To the reports he added his own comment that, while Malik and Chamoun's alarm was not fully justified, America's prestige in the Lebanon was deeply involved and that the State Department should be prepared either to support the current regime in resisting subversion or to cut its losses and learn to live with a great Arab nation presided over by Nasser.

The cables were promptly typed up and initialed by the ambassador. An articulate draftsman with a talent for writing, the ambassador prided himself on being able to dictate a finished cable requiring

8

little or no editing. His secretary then carried the cable down to the code room, with instructions it be marked NIACT. A contraction of "Night Action," this symbol at the beginning of the cable not only meant that it was to be coded and dispatched with top priority, but also it alerted the code room in Washington to decode it immediately on receipt and bring it to the attention of responsible officials at once whether day or night, workday or holiday. Usually the ambassador was reluctant to send NIACT messages as they conveyed to Washington an impression of breathlessness and panic on the part of the sender. But under the circumstances he felt speed to be essential.

Then he called in his counselor and went over with him the Emergency Plan for the protection of American lives and property in case a violent revolution developed.

Diplomats of two generations ago would have been utterly bewildered if asked about their embassy's Emergency Plan. Although wars and revolutions occurred, they were usually limited before World War I to actions by small professional armies, and embassies of those days could generally rely on the Old World chivalry and diplomatic courtesy of civilized states to protect them and their countrymen from the discomforts and dangers of less-than-total warfare.

But the total practices foreshadowed by World War I and perfected by the dictators in the thirties had often created such devastating destruction in both Europe and the Far East that the State Department had, shortly before World War II, instructed all its missions abroad to prepare and keep up to date a plan for the protection not only of the mission's archives and personnel but of the private American community in the event of a military calamity.

The early plans were prepared independently by each individual embassy. They contained measures for evacuating local American communities, the destruction of the files and codes, the cutting out of nonessential work and the reduction of the staff to a small nucleus, the assembly of emergency rations and transportation and air-raid and anti-mob protection. Since then they have been greatly elaborated and co-ordinated with the plans of neighboring embassies and consulates so that each could help the other in a time of crisis.

The Beirut plan provided for several stages of preparedness. The first was the "alert," which had now been declared. If the situation further deteriorated, Phase A would be put into operation. This called

for the voluntary evacuation at government expense of dependents of members of the staff. At the same time the embassy would discreetly recommend that dependents of the local American community also be sent out of the country. Phase B called for the mandatory evacuation of all nonessential government personnel and their dependents, with a similar recommendation for the private American community. Phase C contemplated the evacuation of all American citizens from the crisis area.

In Beirut the alert was also the signal for triggering the warden system which divided the crisis area into small districts, each with its own warden, usually a member of the embassy staff, to look after all American citizens and property within his district. The districts in turn were divided into subdistricts under subwardens. Each warden and subwarden was given a list of the Americans in his district registered at the Consular Section.

Since Beirut is a popular resort town to which Americans come from all over the Middle East for shopping and recreation, there is generally a large group of unregistered transients in each of the big hotels. To keep in touch with them, the concierges of the hotels were appointed subwardens to pass on to them information and warnings and to keep track of their movements.

By the time the counselor was summoned to the ambassador's office he and his staff had already appointed the wardens and subwardens and provided them with lists of their American neighbors. Emergency radiotelephone equipment had been distributed in case the municipal phones went out and instructions issued on how wardens were to act under any foreseeable emergency.

However, as in all such paper plans, defects became apparent as soon as the plan was put into operation. The chief defect now was that there was no central spot to which the wardens could report or from which they could be issued current instructions. The ambassador and the counselor were both fully occupied with special tasks. The other sections of the embassy, far from being relieved of their work, were facing increased burdens.

Fortunately the State Department operates an Arabic-language school in Beirut, where selected young Foreign Service officers study the various dialects of the Middle East. Late on Sunday evening the ambassador summoned the students to the embassy and told them to

set up what he characteristically dubbed a "command post." Within a few hours the young officers had taken over a set of offices, established their own switchboard and opened telephone and radio communications with all wardens in Beirut as well as with the American communities in other towns throughout the Lebanon.

Throughout the emergency the command post was manned day and night by one or more language students. Not only did they relay all instructions to the wardens but received, passed on to the ambassador through the counselor, and recorded in a "log" all reports telephoned in by wardens, subwardens, and other sources on developments in the growing crisis. Today the log of the Beirut command post provides an hour-by-hour chronicle of the Lebanese Crisis as seen from the American Embassy.

By Monday morning half the Lebanon was in open revolt. In Beirut the rebels had declared a general strike and armed bands prowled the streets tossing homemade bombs into the windows of shopkeepers who refused to close their stores. Others, armed with machine guns and rifles, attacked the homes of adherents of the Chamoun regime. In the Basta—the Moslem section—the rebels threw up barricades and tossed out the government police, taking over the entire section.

Outside Beirut things were even more serious. One of the first entries in the log was a report that 300 armed Syrians had been seen by German missionaries crossing the frontier into the Lebanon. A few minutes later another report of 400 more infiltrators was telephoned in. From the port of Beirut came word that the stevedores had gone on strike and that all port activities had been suspended.

In the midst of these alarms someone called to ask whether the Women's Club Tea would be held as usual at the ambassador's residence. The correspondent of the *Manchester Guardian* called to ask cheerfully whether it was true that fourteen Americans had just been murdered in the Basta.

The command post watch officer had hardly finished denying the rumor when an American named Cook telephoned in from his apartment in the Basta to say that he and his wife, three small children including a month-old baby, and two large dogs were blockaded in their apartment by rebels who refused to allow them to leave. Machine-gun fire directed at the apartment of a Chamoun adherent

above them was crashing through the windows and they were huddled in an inner passage.

A relief expedition was immediately organized. Taking an embassy truck, several language students drove to the police station nearest the Cooks' apartment and demanded an escort, but the officer in charge was afraid to enter the area which was now completely in rebel hands. They then went to the central police headquarters whence a jeep full of policemen reluctantly accompanied them toward the beleaguered American family.

All streets leading to the area were by now barricaded but they managed to slip through to within a few blocks of the apartment, where they suddenly found themselves trapped by a barricade of steel lampposts in front of which a large bonfire was blazing. Under cover of the jeep's machine gun the barricade was removed and the two vehicles raced safely through the blaze. But within a half block of their destination the police lost their nerve and refused to go any farther.

Gingerly the language students went on alone in their truck through the hostile area, expecting a burst of machine-gun fire or a bomb from a window at any moment. Fortunately they reached the Cook apartment building unscathed, hastily loaded the family, including the two dogs, into the truck and rejoined their escort. As they neared the burning barricade they found that it had been rebuilt and that an angry mob of rebels was standing guard over it.

The police officer in charge ordered them to remove the barrier. The mob refused. The officer drew his pistol and repeated the order.

"I thought we'd had it," one of the students told me later. He pushed the small child in his lap down onto the truck's floor and waited for the gunplay. But the officer kept his head and his nerve. The hostile mob, cowed by uniformed authority, subsided and sullenly pulled the barricade aside and the truck and its escort sped through it to safety.

The anti-American attitude of the rebel mobs was soon again demonstrated when an embassy chauffeur reported that his car had been stoned and the windshield smashed. But, though the crowds were hostile, many of the rebel leaders were anxious to show that they had nothing against the United States. From the beginning of the rebellion a stream of emissaries from the anti-government faction called on the

ambassador or his political subordinates or telephoned from their hideouts, explaining their grievances and their demands.

Before the rise of representative government it was a cardinal diplomatic sin for an ambassador to have any contact with the opposition. To this day, in countries where democratic institutions are not fully developed, governments look askance at contacts between foreign embassies and the opposition parties. Even in countries where parliamentary oppositions are tolerated, timid or inexperienced diplomats frequently shun the opposition rather than court disfavor with the party in power.

But the ambassador in Beirut not only had had many years of professional experience but had all the courage of his Irish ancestry. Despite his recent arrival, he had already established firm contacts and even friendships among the opposition and had ignored the occasional sour criticisms these contacts had evoked in government circles.

His forethought paid off when rebel emissaries slipped into his office or sent messages from their headquarters. Knowing most of them personally, he was in a far better position to judge the accuracy of their reports, the sincerity of their protestations, and the value of their advice. Later some of these friendships were to dissolve when the ambassador began to press, perhaps a little too enthusiastically, for a compromise solution of the conflict and the opposition accused him of meddling in Lebanese internal affairs. But now they were only too anxious that he interfere in their quarrels.

When an old Christian patriarch in Tripoli recommended that the United States intervene in the dispute or a fiery Druse leader in the south threatened holy war if it did, he could make a shrewd estimate of what stood behind the advice. As he sifted the messages, trying to cull the wisdom from the vituperation, and then cabled the distilled results to Washington, he recalled the dissuasive arguments of some of his friends many years earlier when he was contemplating a diplomatic career.

"Nowadays," they had told him, "diplomats are mere messengers delivering notes between governments. Modern communications have decapitated diplomacy." If only they had been a little right, he thought to himself as he closed his office exhausted at the end of a long day and night.

Washington's response to his cables was rapid. Within a few days

gigantic planes were landing small arms, machine guns, recoilless rifles, jeeps, and even small tanks at the Beirut airport to strengthen the government troops and police. Though these shipments were angrily denounced by the rebels, they contributed considerably to the self-confidence of the legitimate government.

The government and the rebels were not the only contacts the ambassador sought to maintain. The United States was a relative newcomer in the Middle East. For a century the British had been paramount in the area and had occupied the Lebanon during the early years of World War II to prevent an Axis invasion. They had also trained a half dozen first-class experts in their government service who from youth had lived among the Arabs, studying their language, learning their literature and history, their psychology and religion. Lawrence, Sykes, Glubb, and Spears are among those who had devoted their lives to gaining, and occasionally losing, the respect and confidence of the Middle Easterners.

The French too had had a long association with the area extending as far back as the Crusades. After World War I they had been the mandatory power over Syria and the Lebanon and had exercised at least nominal sovereignty until the independence of the Lebanon in 1944. In 1958 they still had many friends and supporters among the population who were able to advise and assist them in maintaining a measure of influence in the area.

The American government had, it is true, trained a handful of Foreign Service officers in Arabic languages and history during the thirties but no senior specialist was now in Beirut—or even in the Middle East Division of the State Department. The present ambassador was not an Arab specialist. He did not know Arabic and had never systematically studied either Arab history or Arab culture. He had served before in Cairo, where incidentally he had known Nasser intimately—after King Farouk was deposed on the day the ambassador (then counselor) arrived in Egypt. He had read as many books as he found time for though not, probably, as many as he might have had he been less devoted to his sailboat. But he had at least one advantage over the specialist—the same advantage a professional jockey who knows how to race has over an amateur rider who knows his horse. He was thoroughly trained in the techniques of diplomacy. He also had another advantage over the expert who had spent his life in the area:

he was not wedded to any single approach or philosophy nor was he the victim of any deep-seated personal loyalties or prejudices.

The ambassador, therefore, kept close contact with his diplomatic colleagues in Beirut—especially the French and British ambassadors. Almost daily during the first days of the emergency they met in one or another of their embassies, exchanging information, exploring possible solutions, debating possible actions.

They had never known each other before but they had all shared similar experiences, worked on similar problems, and lived at similar posts. They had many friends and acquaintances in common and, as in every other profession, they not only spoke in the same terms but assigned the same meanings and values to them. If, as Bismarck said, politics is the art of the possible, each was thoroughly familiar with the limits of possible diplomatic action by his own government and to a lesser extent by other governments. Finally, each had tucked away in his archives dossiers of his colleagues, prepared over the years by his fellow diplomats at posts where his colleagues had served. These contained a fairly full description of each of them: his major talents and weaknesses, his likes and dislikes, prejudices and hobbies, and above all estimates of his reliability. While personal animosities or antagonisms sometimes crept into these dossiers, they were, by and large, useful in evaluating the man's judgment.

Yet there were more than cables and conferences to keep the ambassador busy. From the first day of the rebellion old Mrs. Boyes, the missionary's wife in Tripoli, had been telephoning situation reports on the fighting around the city and more especially around the hospital where she and her husband were cut off.

At first Mrs. Boyes was cheerful and confident that things would work out all right in the end. But finally she telephoned to say that the rebels had all but surrounded the hospital, that the guards which the government had sent were about to surrender, and that the food supplies were running low.

Reluctantly she concluded that the time had come to bring her sick husband to a safer place. It was a bitter decision to leave the home they had established nearly forty years before. Long past retirement age, she knew that once they departed they would never return. There was no indication of alarm or panic in Mrs. Boyes' voice as she recited the reasons for her agonizing decision. Only when she men-

tioned the group of seven Americans, including some small children, cut off behind the town did she appear worried.

Checking with the Lebanese Army, the counselor was told that the road to Tripoli was threatened by rebel forces and that the Army could not guarantee safe passage for an embassy rescue convoy to Tripoli. At about the same time the naval attaché reported that two American seagoing tugs had arrived in Beirut harbor. Our nautically inclined ambassador lost no time in commandeering one of the tugs, the *Jackson Creek,* and ordering its captain to steam up the coast to Tripoli. He also requested the Lebanese authorities to send troops to escort the seven Americans stranded inland from Tripoli to the quayside at the port.

When he arrived at Tripoli, the *Jackson Creek*'s skipper radioed the embassy that he had taken the Boyeses and a dozen other foreigners aboard but that the seven Americans had not showed up. The ambassador ordered him to stand offshore for further instructions.

While they waited anxiously for news of the stranded seven, a fleet of taxis drove up to the embassy in Beirut and deposited them safely in the lobby. To the surprised ambassador they explained that Lebanese troops had escorted them to Tripoli at a moment when the road to Beirut was clear and had commandeered the taxis to get them to the embassy. The *Jackson Creek* was thereupon ordered to return to Beirut with its refugees, and the evacuation of Tripoli was completed.

That night an American correspondent got wind of the *Jackson Creek* saga, probably at the bar of the St. George Hotel, the unofficial headquarters of the foreign press. Exuberantly he called the embassy and got the watch officer on the telephone:

"What's all this about a damn tug evacuating Americans from Tripoli?" he asked. The officer said he didn't know.

"Who the hell ordered the tug up there?" the journalist persisted. The watch officer, who had just come on duty, did not know that either.

The correspondent's dander rose. "Well, who the hell does know?" he exploded. The watch officer was unable to suggest anyone.

Beside himself with frustration, the correspondent exploded into the telephone: "Well, God damn it, someone over in the embassy has pushed the panic button and my guess is it was the ambassador himself and what's more you can tell him so." With that he hung up.

When the message was delivered to the ambassador next morning

the strain of the past days and the tension under which he was working had put him in no mood to be called a panic-button pusher. His Irish temper flared and he sent word to the correspondent he need not show his face in the embassy in the future. But by then the correspondent's temperature was back to normal and when a common friend sought to mediate the squabble and suggested he apologize for swearing at the innocent watch officer the correspondent grumbled contritely: "For Christ's sake, Sam, you know I never swear at a damned soul." When this was repeated to the ambassador, whose humor is as Irish as his temper, the incident of the panic button was forgotten by all but the watch officer. He carefully sketched an electric button on a bit of cardboard, thumbtacked it to the wall by the watch desk and printed below it in heavy crayon: "Panic Button. Do NOT push!"

Despite the panic button episode, relations between the ambassador and the American correspondents were generally good. As a student Foreign Service officer he had been taught by old hands, not yet reconciled to the modern inquiring foreign correspondent, that press publicity was inherently bad for diplomacy. But since then he had learned that foreign correspondents, many of whom had much longer experience and wider contacts in the area, were an invaluable source not only of information but of advice and counsel.

Several of the Beirut journalists were intimate friends and had spent long hours with him in the quieter days before the rebellion, discussing the American dilemma in the Middle East.

Some of these "old Mid-East hands" were severely critical of Washington's policies in the area. One or two were so emotionally involved that they could not refrain from frequent outbursts of pent-up anger at what they considered the stupidities of American foreign policy.

The ambassador, too, held strong personal views on the subject— not all of them in accord with Washington policies. As a young officer he had often in private expressed his opinions in the most flowery and flamboyant terms and even today in talking to his friends he remained true to his convictions. However, he had accepted two important rules governing a diplomat's relations with his chiefs in Washington. First, it must ordinarily be presumed that with its broader point of view and fuller information the home office knows best. Secondly, even if an ambassador disagrees fundamentally with his government's policies he

must defend them with absolute loyalty so long, at least, as he wants to continue wearing his team's uniform.

Not afraid of personal publicity and confident of his own discretion, the ambassador frequently granted interviews and held conferences with press representatives at which he talked frankly but loyally. Less confident of the ability of his staff to draw the line between frankness and indiscretion, he tended to keep in his own hands the release of sensitive news, which placed his press officer in an awkward position and often provoked correspondents to complain of "gagging."

Because of the ambassador's relative inexperience in the area, correspondents who had devoted many years of their lives to studying the problems of the Middle East were naturally cautious in evaluating his judgments, slightly skeptical of his background knowledge, and occasionally irritated by his Irish self-assurance which they sometimes took for cockiness.

Such criticisms of diplomats by journalists (and vice versa) are not uncommon. Though they may sometimes be unjustified, they are understandable. The parallels and similarities between the two professions frequently lead to fundamental misunderstandings because of the basic but less obvious differences in their objectives. Both seek to find and identify truth, but it is the journalist's task to publicize facts and the diplomat's to reconcile conflicting ones. Since publicity is often a deterrent to the reconciliation of conflicts, the diplomat attempts to conceal what the journalist strives to reveal.

Furthermore, the average ego rebels at hiding knowledge. Most people can succeed only at the expense of appearing stupid or by making their interlocutors appear stupid. A rare few can do it without giving offense or losing face. On the other hand, only a naïve journalist believes that a diplomat can or will reveal to him the whole truth. However, correspondents are occasionally naïve.

II

Embassy in Crisis: 2

AFTER the first fortnight of excitement, Beirut and the surrounding countryside enjoyed a lull in the rebellion. Infrequently a bomb exploded in a shop window or a gang of rebels let go with a burst of machine-gun fire at a government patrol.

But in the Basta the rebels paused to collect their breath as well as arms, ammunition, and a radio transmitter. In the south the fanatical, feudal-Socialist Kamal Jumblatt, retired to his family castle to mobilize his Druse tribesmen and arm them with rifles acquired largely from Syria. In the north the rebel leader Karami concentrated on winning over the minor tribal leaders.

Then on June 14 the rebels in the Basta burst from behind their barricades and attempted to storm the government prison on the outskirts of town. After a furious skirmish their attack was repulsed. But the outbreak was the signal for renewed fighting throughout the country. The forces under General Chehab continued to avoid any pitched battles, intervening only when innocent lives or property were threatened. They patrolled the main roads, guarded government buildings and the Beirut airport, but unless attacked they left the rebels strictly alone in the areas under their control, which at times composed as much as one half of the entire country. But the adherents of Chamoun now organized their own private gangs and armed them with some of the equipment acquired from America. Clashes between the rival gangs took place not only in Beirut but in the provinces as well.

At this point President Chamoun, concerned that the American ambassador might himself be attacked, assigned a Lebanese bodyguard composed of two motorcycle outriders to escort the ambassador's Cadillac wherever it went. From then on the wailing sirens of the outriders' motorcycles provided a deafening chorus to the ambassador's excursions. Outsiders were inclined to make fun of this noisy display, accusing the Ambassador of being a little more flamboyant than was necessary. But he pointed out that, since the Lebanese government was in fact responsible for his safety, he could not reject whatever precautions they considered necessary to discharge this responsibility.

The day after the Basta outbreak the ambassador decided that it was time to declare Phase A of the Emergency Plan. This meant that the families of the staff could if they desired be evacuated to a safer place at government expense. Many families took advantage of the offer and soon between forty and fifty of them had taken refuge in Rome, Vienna, or Paris. Many families of private American businessmen also elected to leave Beirut at this time.

Almost immediately after the start of the revolt the embassy counselor had set up an informal committee composed of himself and leading members of the American business community. Meeting frequently, they exchanged information and discussed measures for the protection of their families and properties. Since a number of American institutions, including Tapline, the oil-pipe terminal on the Mediterranean, were located in the provinces, these were tied in by telephone to the command post so that they could be kept informed of what was going on in Beirut and could in turn inform the embassy of developments in their areas.

With the outbreak of renewed guerrilla fighting in Beirut a dusk-to-dawn curfew was imposed. After some confusion curfew passes were issued for personnel on night duty or detained in the embassy offices after the curfew sounded. However, for what had been one of the gayest and liveliest night-life spots in the Middle East social life came to an abrupt end. Nightclubs went out of business, restaurants closed, and entertaining dwindled to a minimum.

Because of the sporadic gun duels which occurred all over town, the embassy now advised all its personnel and all private Americans not to go out into the streets even in daytime unless it was absolutely necessary.

One earnest American thereupon called the command post and asked whether this restriction applied to going to church on Sunday. The watch officer explained to him that this was a matter to be settled between his conscience and his instinct for self-preservation. Two young American girls who had arrived in Beirut to perform at one of the closed nightclubs called up to ask if they might not go to the beach to swim. The watch officer said he couldn't stop them but he advised against it. The girls then announced that they would keep open house in their apartment for Americans seeking relief from the boredom of the curfew nights. The watch officer gratefully took down their telephone number and address and posted it on the bulletin board.

One morning in broad daylight a gang of rebels tossed a large bomb over the wall of the British Embassy garden, where it exploded with a loud crash but without injuring anyone. Next day a guard at the American Embassy spotted in the front doorway a suspicious-looking box which emitted a most ominous ticking sound. Gingerly the box was buried in a far corner of the garden. Sometime later an embassy chauffeur complained to the Marines that an alarm clock he had just bought for his wife had been stolen from the lobby. The box was retrieved from the garden and the incident was officially closed.

But if the evenings were dull, the workdays in the embassy were quite the opposite. While the language students worked sixteen to eighteen hours each day manning the command post and performing many other emergency jobs, the code room staggered under the load of cables pouring from the front office and from the State Department. In a normal month the code room handled between 100,000 and 150,000 words but after the rebellion broke out the traffic quintupled to 700,000 words. The eleven clerks in the section worked round the clock trying to keep up with the traffic. But operating coding machines is a meticulous job requiring a high degree of concentration. To relieve the pressure six additional code clerks were rushed to Beirut from neighboring posts.

The reinforcements—male and female—were warmly welcomed. Not only did they take over much of the coding but, as one code clerk later told me, the new faces provided a much-needed booster to the social life in the clerks' apartment building which had been severely dampened by the curfew. "No serious love affairs resulted," she said,

"but the newcomers gave our dreary evenings a hell of a shot in the arm."

The Consular Section too found itself flooded with clients. When the crisis started there were over three thousand Americans scattered throughout the Lebanon. Some of them were in business in Beirut or connected with the American University there but the great majority were Lebanese-Americans who had come to visit relatives or to spend the last years of their lives in their native villages. When the shooting began many swarmed down upon the Consular Section to get their long-forgotten passports in order or to arrange for passage to a safer haven in America. Many relatives of Americans also came to apply for visas to emigrate to their families.

Many of the wealthier Lebanese—of whom there are a surprising number—who considered themselves above the civil war abruptly decided that this was a good time to make the grand tour of the United States and came in to apply for visitors' visas. As a result of these crisis-inspired clients, the number of visitors in the Consular Section tripled.

In addition, the Consular Section had to cope with a flood of inquiries from anxious relatives in America about their kinfolk in the Lebanon. Not only the State Department but also congressmen and senators daily sent cables asking about important constituents' mothers, fathers, aunts and uncles. Since many of these lived in remote villages in the mountains, it often took days or even weeks to get word of their welfare through the harried Lebanese authorities, who naturally felt they had enough to do with a revolution without being burdened with someone's Aunt Sadie's whereabouts.

Subsequently, when the work of the command post settled into a routine, the young language officers took over the job of locating the Aunt Sadies tucked away in the villages in the hinterland. Dividing the country into eleven "tours" which included every village in which the Consular Section records listed an American, their motorized patrol scoured the entire country except for a few areas in the north where active fighting prevented them from crossing the lines between government and rebel territories.

In each listed village the patrol stopped in the market place and asked the brightest face present where they could find "Richard Speed," as he was listed in his American passport. No one, it would

become apparent, had ever heard of anyone with such an Anglo-Saxon name. Then the language students would use their ingenuity, imagination, and beginners' knowledge of Arabic to guess what the original name had been before the owner had Anglicized it. As they tried out possible variations a native eye would light up: "Oh, you mean old Ryad Spidan." Within minutes the scouts would be sitting on Ryad's front porch, reluctantly sipping a glass of an impossible potion tasting of mulberry juice and eau de cologne. From Ryad they would learn that half a dozen other Americans resided in or near the village. They would be called in or, if bedridden, visited, their names listed, and their passports checked.

Occasionally the routine varied. One patrol, for instance, was clambering up a steep hill off the main road toward the house of an alleged American when two rifle shots at close range came from a group of Arabs on a nearby hilltop. The Americans hastily took refuge in a peasant house, whose owner explained that there was nothing to fear as the shots came from partridge hunters. When they emerged from the hut three more shots sounded in rapid succession. There was a dull thud and a puff of dust rose a few yards ahead of them where a rifle bullet had struck the ground.

"When I get home," muttered one of the students, "I'm going to look up that word for 'partridge.' I bet it has a double meaning in Arabic."

Eventually the "hunters" got bored and went away and the patrol proceeded up the hill, where they found their American. He explained that a feud had developed between his village and a neighboring one involving a long and utterly unintelligible quarrel about three sheep and two oxen.

On another occasion the patrol was looking for a local rebel sheik to obtain an escort into a rebel area. They had been climbing a rocky trail for half an hour in the broiling sun when they rounded a bend to discover a Hollywood ranch house set in the midst of a daisy-filled garden. An expensive modern hammock straight out of the advertisements in *House and Garden* was set up beside a sky-blue kidney-shaped swimming pool. From it a pretty brunette rose and came forward: "What can I do fo' you all?" she asked in a rich Southern accent. She explained she was the sheik's wife and a native of Corpus Christi, Texas. Instead of mulberry juice she offered her guests bourbon.

The patrols, in addition to locating lost Americans, paid two extra dividends. News soon spread over the country that in the middle of the revolution the American Embassy was sending out parties to look after its citizens. A country which prized its citizens that highly, the Lebanese peasants concluded, could hardly be as bad as Nasser's radio was making out. In addition, the patrols were able to obtain information not only on local economic conditions, the state of the crops, the price of staples, and the extent of unemployment produced by the revolution but also on the political loyalties of the villagers from one end of the country to the other. When their eleven tours were completed the embassy had, if not a Gallup poll of Lebanese public opinion, at least a very good idea of how the population stood on the questions of Chamoun, Nasser, and the United States.

The renewed outburst of revolutionary activity in the middle of June had naturally greatly alarmed President Chamoun and his followers. Dr. Malik had already flown to New York to lodge a complaint in the United Nations against the alleged infiltration of Syrian soldiers under Nasser's orders. In response, a United Nations observer team was organized to watch the Syrian frontier and verify Malik's charges.

Though skeptical of the "massive infiltrations" claimed by Malik, the United States was not convinced that a United Nations observer team could either detect or prevent the smuggling of aid to the rebels across the frontier. Furthermore, Cairo broadcasts were actively inciting the Lebanese to revolt. Accordingly, Secretary Dulles announced that if the United Nations was unable to protect the legitimate government of the Lebanon, the United States would undertake to do so and, he added, by force if necessary. Just who was to define "necessary" was not clear but President Chamoun at least assumed that this was his prerogative.

This promise of support from Washington was soon receiving wide publicity as the "blank check" Chamoun held on the United States and speculation grew daily as to when he would submit it for payment. Though this was not publicized at the time, he came within an ace of cashing it on several occasions. Not long after the renewed rioting in June he sent word to the American ambassador through a special emissary that the time had come for American intervention. The ambassador was not convinced and refused to accept the emissary's message, insisting that so grave a communication must come personally from the President.

On a second occasion the President summoned the ambassador in considerable alarm and again demanded that the Sixth Fleet be ordered to Beirut at full steam. By this time Chamoun had been cooped up in his palace behind steel shutters for weeks lest snipers assassinate him. The smoke-filled gloom of his quarters was enough, the ambassador felt, to provoke delusions of disaster in the most stable statesman. He cautioned the President to think it over but Chamoun continued angrily to demand that the United States fulfill its pledge to support him.

Playing for time, the ambassador suggested that the request be put in writing. Immediately the President snatched a sheet of paper and began to draft his message. But as he wrote his alarm subsided and by the time he had appended his signature he slipped the paper into a desk drawer and agreed to wait a little longer.

While the ambassador was urging patience on the President, he himself was taking every precaution to get ready for the worst. At his own request and unknown even to Chamoun two destroyers were dispatched from the Sixth Fleet and were cruising about just over the horizon from Beirut, the head of steam in their boilers (the ambassador knew exactly what it was) sufficient to get them to the port within one hour. Furthermore, a special radiotelephone circuit kept him in constant touch not only with the destroyers but with the fleet's flagship farther west in the Mediterranean. Each morning the circuit was tested so that if necessary the ambassador could confer with the naval command.

About this time the watch officer at the command post was called one night around midnight by an irate and obviously somewhat drunken American who announced he had just been thrown out of a bar. He demanded that the consul come down immediately and defend his rights to be in any bar of his choosing. "And unless he's here in ten minutes," the drunk added, "you can tell him from me that he'll be an ex-consul by tomorrow morning." Since the curfew was on and the drunk obviously had no way of getting home, the watch officer persuaded the barkeeper to bed him down in a backroom till dawn.

A few nights later a much soberer voice called the watch officer. The caller said he was at the American hospital where his wife had just produced a baby. He had to get home to feed his other children but had no curfew pass. Resourcefully the watch officer suggested that

the hospital ambulance had a curfew pass and the problem was thus solved.

While the street fighting and bombing were reaching a crescendo, a cruise ship unaccountably put into Beirut harbor with a boatload of American sightseers. An officer from the command post hurried down to the ship and told the passengers that the ambassador urgently warned American citizens to stay off the streets of Beirut. Reluctantly the sightseers abandoned their tours. But one irascible old globetrotter who knew all the answers—a type familiar to every consul around the globe—spoke up and announced that what the "young man" had said was poppycock. He knew how to take care of himself and besides, he added, he had a letter of introduction from the Vice-President. Manfully the young officer refrained from telling him that a bullet-proof vest would be considerably more useful under the circumstances. The old man went ashore and some hours later the officer learned with mixed feeling that he had returned unscathed.

July 4 is ordinarily a day of tribulation for an American ambassador when he must entertain not only his foreign colleagues but the American community at a long, tedious, and expensive reception. But July 4, 1958, in Beirut was no time for celebrations. Instead the ambassador invited to his home only a few friends from the American press and those members of his staff who had shouldered the heaviest loads during the crisis—chiefly the code clerks and watch officers.

In his five short months the ambassador had won the respect of his junior staff. He was demanding and strict—sometimes almost a martinet—toward his subordinates but they realized that this was a common failing of younger Foreign Service officers newly appointed ambassador. With time his sharp edges would be smoothed down. But in their eyes his best trait was that he knew where responsibility lay and unlike the "politicos," as they call nonprofessional ambassadors, he never blamed one person for another's mistakes. Having grown up in the service, he knew most of their jobs as well as they did. As a junior vice-consul he had often been detailed to the code room during crises. And at one period or another he had occupied practically every position in a normal embassy from passport officer to economic reporter.

"If you do your job right," one of his clerks told me, "he won't give you any trouble."

Nevertheless, as the fighting dragged on and the curfew continued

in force, a serious morale problem arose not only among the clerks but also among the families of those who had elected to remain with their husbands in Beirut. Cooped up in their apartments, unable to go to school, the children created a particular problem. To keep them from under the feet of harassed parents, the ambassador arranged special movie performances in the afternoons in a nearby theater, using American films supplied through the U. S. Information Service.

But still the tension rose and nerves wore thin. At the beginning of the emergency the Lebanese government had sent a detachment of soldiers to guard the embassy and the buildings in which the staff were housed. But on July 4, the day of the ambassador's little party, four of the guards deserted to the rebels in the Basta. Not long after, one of the ambassador's Lebanese motorcycle escorts deserted. This seemed especially perfidious since only a few days earlier the ambassador had given him a wrist watch as a reward for his faithful services in accompanying the ambassador day and night—usually at a dizzy speed—through the hazardous narrow streets of the city. On at least one occasion a bomb had exploded so close to the car that the guard had been hurled from his motorcycle.

With the reliability of the Lebanese soldiers thus opened to question, the Marine guards took added precautions. A plan was devised for protecting the embassy office building against mobs. It envisaged a slow retreat to the sixth floor, where a last stand would be made to protect the codes and archives.

Simultaneously new precautions were taken to guard against sabotage and all visitors to the embassy were required to leave their cameras (but for some strange reason not their briefcases) at the Marine desk in the lobby.

To those unburdened by responsibilities, these melodramatic measures seemed at the time to verge on the absurd and provoked frequent references to Custer's Last Stand as well as many derisive smiles.

But the smiles abruptly disappeared when on Monday, July 14, the radio announced revolution in Iraq. There fanatical Moslem mobs had stormed the foreign missions, burning and looting the British Embassy and beating to death at least three innocent American businessmen.

The repercussions in Beirut were immediate. The rebels in the Basta shrilly announced over their radio that their day had come. The

strongly anti-Nasser government of Iraq had fallen and that of the Lebanon would be next. Those Lebanese who had heretofore remained aloof from the struggle began to wonder whether they had not better join the rebels before it was too late.

Between nine and eleven o'clock that morning, haunted by visions of the assassination of King Feisal and his pro-Western prime minister, Nuri as-Said, President Chamoun summoned separately the ambassadors of the United States, Britain and France to his office and demanded immediate intervention. Unless, he said, it was forthcoming within forty-eight hours, he was a dead man and the Lebanon would become a Nasser satellite. This time the American ambassador did not wait for any written request but hurried to his embassy to notify Washington. That Washington would order the Sixth Fleet into action was by no means certain. Many considerations far beyond the competence of the ambassador in Beirut to judge were involved. Among them was, of course, the question of the Soviet reaction. Would an American armed intervention in Beirut so close to Russia's southern borders provoke some sort of retaliation?

While he waited for an answer he took final steps to "batten down the hatches" on the embassy. Declaring Phase B of the emergency, he ordered all embassy dependents to leave immediately and urged families of the private American community to follow suit. To set an example, the ambassador arranged for his wife and son to board a plane for Paris early next morning. To a few key officers he distributed such small arms as the embassy had. Then he went home to wait.

III

Embassy in Crisis: 3

IN the early hours of Tuesday the ambassador was called from his bed. "Big news" was all his attaché on duty at the embassy could tell him over the telephone. Hurriedly he dressed and with Tewfik roared through the deserted streets, the motorcycle escort's sirens blaring, to the embassy office building.

President Eisenhower, the message read, had ordered the Sixth Fleet to land in the Lebanon. The message said the first ships would appear on the horizon off Beirut at about 2 P.M. and the Marines were scheduled to hit the beach at three—twenty-eight hours after Chamoun's appeal. Immediately the ambassador drove to the presidential palace. Chamoun was naturally delighted. Recent press dispatches had indicated that the Sixth Fleet was far off in the Western Mediterranean and he had seriously doubted that it could arrive in time to save him from the fate that had befallen King Feisal.

At President Chamoun's request the ambassador went to General Chehab, whose troops had dallied and procrastinated for two months, refusing to come to grips with the rebels. When told by the ambassador that American Marines were coming, Chehab was anything but happy.

An armed foreign intervention, he told the ambassador, might well provoke his troops to join the rebels and resist the landing with force. Perhaps, he suggested, the ambassador would hold the fleet offshore until he could make sure of his own forces. The ambassador agreed to forward the suggestion to the admiral commanding the fleet.

29

DIPLOMAT

He hurried back to the embassy and called one of the close-in destroyers on his special radiophone. But for the first time in two months the fleet did not respond to his signal—the link was dead. It was too late to send a warning via Washington and thence back to the fleet. Not having been informed of where the landings would take place, he selected the most likely spot—the harbor area—and dispatched his naval attaché to hail the first landing parties and transmit Chehab's message to the commanding officer. As it turned out it was a futile gesture.

Meantime in the embassy, where news of the impending landing was still a deep secret held by only a few top officials, the lobbies and corridors were a seething mass of milling children clutching their dolls and frantic parents clutching picnic baskets—all waiting to go to the airport for evacuation. Little by little the crowd thinned out but then came word that the airport was suddenly closed. There would be no further flights for the time being. Drearily the children and their alarmed parents trooped back to their apartments. Images of the massacre in Baghdad rose in their distraught minds as they sat down to wait.

Among the Lebanese in Beirut that July day the atmosphere was one of relaxed abandon. Something was going to happen soon— something big and far beyond their control. Many of them closed up their offices and apartments and took their families to the beach. Others went fishing off the rocks by the shore. For once the incessant honking of horns, the leitmotif of Beirut's street sounds, ceased.

A crown of Lebanese were swarming over the beach by the airport six miles south of Beirut early that afternoon. Some were swimming in the sea, others sunbathing or playing volley ball. Some were fishing. Among them pop vendors were carrying on a lively trade in Pepsi-Cola, Coca-Cola, and a dozen other soft drinks. Someone spotted a black cloud on the horizon. A few minutes later a half dozen large ships attracted the bathers' attention. The vessels were not following the normal sea lane along the coast but headed straight for land. Someone shouted, "Warships," and the whole crowd stood and watched, glumly silent.

Aboard the ships a battalion of young Marines were strapping on their last bits of equipment. Early that morning they had been assembled and briefed. They had all been through a dozen practice

30

landings but now, they were told, this was the real thing. They were issued live ammunition and told to be prepared for anything. Even their officers later admitted they had no idea what they would encounter. Some said they had expected to see the city in flames, the embassy wrecked, and the streets strewn with mutilated American corpses.

At the end of the briefing one officer explained to them carefully the purpose of their mission. It was necessarily a brief explanation and hence oversimplified but it was adequate for the purpose. They were, the briefing officer said, going ashore at the invitation of the Lebanese government to help protect that country's independence.

Precisely at 3 P.M. the first of the landing barges ground ashore. As its occupants struggled through the water to the beach they were greeted not by lead but by the eager pop vendors. The bathers on the beach watched silently and sullenly. A few perhaps realized that the Marines were landing to put an end to the revolution but the majority strongly suspected that they merely spelled trouble.

Within a few minutes the battalion was ashore. Then came swarms of jeeps and heavy tanks. Smoothly and quickly the huge ships disgorged their loads and with scarcely a hitch the powerful force rolled into position. The watching bathers were duly impressed. Never in their lives had they seen anything like it—and they were not likely to see it again.

While the landing operation proceeded with military precision, politically it left something to be desired. Though careful to brief the Marines, the Navy either carelessly or deliberately had failed to brief the ambassador. Apprehensive of a clash with the Lebanese forces which might not only cause fatal casualties but also spark a major conflict in the Middle East, he had already sent his attaché to where he suspected the Marines would land, to suggest a delay until the Lebanese troops could be brought under control.

Later, learning from journalists that the landing was taking place at the airport, he sent word to the senior officer present, a naval captain, suggesting he come to the embassy at once. He was sending his car to the airport, he added, to bring him into town. A polite but terse message came back that the captain would be glad to receive the ambassador on his ship and would send a helicopter for him.

Now, ambassadors not only outrank naval captains by many grades

but as representatives of the President they outrank every American in the country to which they are assigned except the President himself. The ambassador in Beirut did not wear his rank lightly. While he knew this was no moment to stand on matters of rank or protocol, it was also very clear to him that it was no time to go spinning out to sea in a helicopter leaving his staff in perhaps the tensest situation he had encountered in his long career.

He therefore repeated his invitation to the captain in somewhat more forceful terms, explaining that his business was not social but had the gravest political implications. The captain replied that his orders were clear and to the effect that the Marines would march into the city next morning. Until then he was staying on his ship.

When the ambassador finally turned in for some sleep that night he pondered the events of the day, particularly the subject of military-diplomatic relations. A graduate of the National War College in Washington, where senior professional diplomats and Army, Navy, and Air Force officers study the relationships between military and political power, he fully understood the necessity for co-operation between the armed forces and diplomacy.

In other nations which have been warring with each other for centuries longer than the United States, the military has long since learned that war is an extension of diplomacy by other means. Its object is political, from which it follows that military operations are guided primarily by political considerations.

As World War II demonstrated, however, the fallacious doctrine has grown up among American military leaders that the primary objective of war is military victory, preferably total military victory. After that has been accomplished the diplomats can pick up the pieces and do whatever they please with them. But while military operations are taking place diplomats should get out of the way lest they get run over by a soldier in a tank or a general in a staff car.

The events of July 15 demonstrated that, despite the lessons of the National War College, the fallacy had not yet been entirely eradicated from the American military mind. The failure of the Sixth Fleet to maintain its radiotelephone link with the embassy, the failure to keep the ambassador informed of the place of the landings, and finally the absurd spat about who was to call on whom certainly pointed in this direction. Later, when questioned about these lapses by

a journalist, the Navy's reaction was a frigid silence.

Early next morning a Marine brigadier general assumed command of the Marines on shore and eventually called at the embassy, where a Marine guard promptly ordered him to remove his sidearms before going upstairs to the ambassador's office. The general good-naturedly complied.

The ambassador explained the precarious state of mind of the Lebanese Army and suggested that any advance into the city be delayed until the local soldiery was more in hand. The general replied that he had rigid orders to advance into town immediately. He had in fact already instructed a battalion of Marines to form up on the airport road complete with six large tanks and twelve LVT's— amphibious personnel carriers which looked like enormous steel coffins. The commander of the column, Lieutenant Colonel Hadd, was only awaiting final orders to advance into the city. With some difficulty the ambassador persuaded the general to delay the advance for one hour.

At that moment an urgent summons arrived from the presidential palace for the ambassador. There President Chamoun told him that the Army and the rebels were plotting to seize him and then oppose the American Marines' advance. Chamoun had summoned Commanding General Chehab, and in a few moments Chehab arrived.

In no uncertain terms Chehab told the ambassador that, if the Marines advanced, Lebanese tanks, already deployed along the airport road, would open fire. If they did not advance, Chamoun told him equally emphatically, the rebels would debouch from the Basta and kidnap him leaving the United States in the embarrassing situation of maintaining troops in a foreign country to protect a government which did not exist.

It was an acutely awkward dilemma for the ambassador. But it occurred to him that two could play the kidnaping game. Later he admitted that it was a "truly desperate expedient" but there seemed no other alternative. With all the diplomatic suasion he could muster he gravely suggested to the Lebanese Army's hero, Chehab, that it was his and the ambassador's duty to inject themselves personally between the opposing troops.

Chehab, well known for his honor and courage, accepted. Accompanied by Tewfik, the kavass, and Golly, the ambassador's poodle,

the two set out in the Cadillac behind the screaming Lebanese motorcycle escort to the airport. On the way a dozen or more Lebanese tanks, recoilless rifles, and other weapons lining the road, their guns unlimbered and aimed directly at the spot where the Marine column was waiting, confirmed Chehab's warning that the Lebanese Army was ready to fight even if it meant suicide.

Just as they arrived at the point where Colonel Hadd stood at the head of his column, another car rolled up carrying Admiral James Holloway, the commanding officer of the entire landing operation, who had just arrived from his flagship by helicopter.

By now a half dozen journalists and photographers had assembled at the head of the Marine column and as the ambassador introduced the admiral to the Lebanese general there began what must have been one of the most open of all diplomatic conferences in modern history.

The admiral turned to Chehab. "General," he said sternly, "I am ordering this column of Marines forward at once. And if there is any resistance . . ." He did not need to finish the sentence and the ambassador interpreted for the French-speaking Chehab.

The general looked distressed. "Would the admiral consider breaking up his column into segments and placing Lebanese jeeps in the intervals so that it doesn't look quite so much like an invading army?"

The admiral and the ambassador exchanged glances. The latter nodded and the admiral agreed.

"And now, *mon général*" the admiral said in his Naval Academy French, "we advance *toot dee suitee.*" He waved a little swagger stick for emphasis and repeated, *"Toot dee suitee."*

The general shifted uneasily and glanced over his shoulder in the direction of his deployed tanks. "Would you allow me just fifteen minutes to tell my headquarters to pull back our troops?" The Americans exchanged glances again. "We'll go with you to the nearest phone," the ambassador suggested, determined that his prize hostage should not give him the slip. The cavalcade sped off to a police post a hundred yards down the road. The journalists waited with Colonel Hadd.

A crowd of urchins had by now joined the party at the head of the column and one of them, speaking halting English, shouted at one of the Marine sentries guarding the tanks. "What have you come here for anyway," he asked belligerently, "to start a war?" The sentry,

34

a gawky young Marine who looked as though his uniform and the equipment dangling about him were about to fall from his scrawny shoulders, glowered sternly at the young Lebanese.

"We are here at the invitation of the Lebanese government to help protect the country's independence," he recited, repeating word for word the briefing officer's formula. Then he added on his own, "And *not* to start a war." The journalists glanced at the Lebanese guns up ahead and exchanged skeptical smiles.

The fifteen minutes stretched to half an hour and then to an hour. General Chehab was clearly having difficulty persuading his staff to call off the resistance. But eventually he succeeded and the cavalcade returned to the head of the Marine column. Solemnly Admiral Holloway ordered Colonel Hadd to advance.

The ambassador with the most gracious of smiles took General Chehab firmly by the elbow. "Do me the honor," he said in flowery French and propelled him into the Cadillac.

The huge diesel motors of the LVT's started, the tracks dug deep into the hot asphalt, and the column started forward. At its head was the Cadillac, the Stars and Stripes and the ambassadorial flag fluttering from its fenders. In the front seat the kavass and the poodle sat erect beside the uniformed chauffeur. Behind them sat the Lebanese general flanked by the American ambassador and the admiral. If by any chance the Lebanese still wanted to make trouble, the ambassador thought with a smile, their first target would be their own beloved general.

But by now the Lebanese tanks had retired and the column entered the city without a shot being fired. Chehab then excused himself, left the convoy, and hurried off to his retreat outside Beirut. The ambassador continued to lead the noisy parade. As it passed the embassy chancellery it halted briefly. Golly, the poodle, who was becoming restless with all the excitement, was relieved and his place taken by a pretty embassy secretary, Nancy Boyle.

As the tanks rumbled along behind, the ambassador hastily dictated to her an urgent cable to Washington announcing the Marines' peaceful entry into the city. Then he instructed her to make arrangements for a formal call by the admiral on President Chamoun. Finally he ordered lunch postponed till four o'clock. Thereupon Nancy was transferred to a following car and hurried back to the embassy while

the ambassador, the admiral, and the marines clattered on noisily through the deserted, narrow streets.

The tanks took up positions around the harbor, beside the embassy chancellery, and at the ambassador's residence. One American tank, ostensibly guarding the embassy, covered the entrance to the presidential palace with its guns.

As soon as order was reassured in the city the Marines withdrew to the outskirts. After a little difficulty they accustomed themselves to their strange surroundings. One night soon after their arrival the commander of a detachment camped in an olive grove in the suburbs telephoned the embassy counselor. One of the olive trees, he said, interfered with the alignment of his pup tents and he wanted to cut it down. The owner, however, was having tantrums. Could the counselor explain the fuss about a mere tree?

Olive trees, the counselor told him, are a major source of income to Lebanese farmers. Since they grow very slowly and bear fruit only after many years, cutting them down is considered by the Lebanese a graver offense than cutting down cherry trees was by George Washington's father. There was a pause and then the officer answered, "O.K. I guess we'll just have to leave the tent line crooked."

Months of negotiation followed the landings. Robert Murphy, under-secretary of state, arrived soon after the Marines to help mediate a settlement between the rebels and the government, and the ambassador stepped temporarily into the background. The under-secretary's visit lent weight and prestige to the American effort to seek a peaceable solution and doubtless pleased the disputants by raising their own self-importance. The ambassador too, grateful for any help he could get in arranging a settlement, welcomed his arrival.

However, other students of modern diplomatic practice have pointed out that "personal diplomacy"—the practice of sending senior "trouble shooters" flying to trouble spots rather than letting the local ambassador handle the situation—has its disadvantages. Not only does it lower the prestige of the ambassador but seldom does the trouble shooter have adequate opportunity to study the essential background and personalities of a dispute and often he has even less time to devote to the protracted negotiations a sound settlement ordinarily requires.

In the case of the Lebanese Crisis a solution was soon found. Chamoun stepped down from the presidency and was replaced by General Chehab. However, it turned out to be a temporary lull rather than a settlement. After the under-secretary had returned to Washington the Chamoun faction staged what was known as the "Christian counterrevolution" which very nearly marked the end of an independent Lebanon. Only after weeks of patient mediation, hopping in a helicopter between Chamoun's headquarters and Chehab's was the ambassador able to assist in a more stable and permanent settlement—this time unaided by trouble shooters.

IV

The Origins of the Diplomatic Iron Curtain: 1

THE leading English authority on diplomacy, Sir Harold Nicolson, has suggested that the first diplomat was a hairy savage who, after convalescing from a fracas with his neighbors, laid aside his cudgel and returned to his adversaries' camp to offer a truce or perhaps to propose that, like wild animals, they delimit their respective hunting grounds. Provided, of course, that his neighbor did not take advantage of this unarmed emissary to slaughter him out of hand, the latter would probably qualify as the original diplomat or, as the British say, diplomatist.

Since that occasion, history indicates, the profession has not made the same progress as, for example, the scientists who, starting with the lever, have already reached the H-bomb and overtaken the moon. In fact, diplomacy in many respects has not yet emerged from its Stone Age, as is occasionally demonstrated by the rocks hurled by mobs of one government through the embassy windows of another. This lack of progress is not entirely due to the backwardness of under-privileged diplomats, as is often suggested. The communities of people with which diplomacy deals are more visible but less predictable than communities of electrons.

The first historic record of diplomacy found among the Greeks also demonstrates that the ills which it then had have not all been eliminated. Homer reported an early diplomatic mission to Troy. Its purpose was to obtain the release of Helen. Like the marathon Sino-

American diplomatic conference in 1956–1958 to obtain the release of Americans held captive in China, it failed.

The early Greek diplomats were chosen by the popular assemblies from the members of the various political parties. Often several parties insisted on each having representatives on a single embassy, so that a state was occasionally represented by several ambassadors—a practice that has always led to confusion. In the years immediately following World War II so many government agencies in Washington demanded representation abroad that there were at one time four American ambassadors stationed in Paris.

In most countries except the Soviet Union, where the Communist party selects its envoys, and in the United States, political parties have been almost entirely eliminated from the ambassador-appointing machinery. In the United States, though political parties continue to select ambassadors, the privilege is now confined to the party in power —and is further restricted by the partial use of professional diplomats.

In the days of the Greek states diplomacy was not a popular profession. The assemblies were extremely niggardly about pay and travel expenses and scrutinized the accounts of returning ambassadors as meticulously as a subcommittee of Congress or the General Accounting Office does today.

But the chief defect of Greek diplomacy and a major reason for its unpopularity was its failure to reconcile popular democratic control with effective prosecution of foreign policy. Ambassadors reported directly to the popular assembly which, if displeased with the conduct of the members of the mission, frequently confiscated their property, threw them in jail, or occasionally even sentenced them to death. The assemblies, ignorant of conditions beyond their own city walls and generally emotional in their reactions, were erratic and often fatally slow both in defining foreign policy and in implementing it.

On one occasion Demosthenes delivered a bitter denunciation of the Athenian assembly, accusing it not only of procrastinating but of causing interminable and occasionally disastrous delays in the ratification of treaties negotiated by its ambassadors.

Another severe handicap under which Greek diplomacy operated was the publicity which attended all negotiations. Without even the flimsy security of executive sessions, the assemblies heatedly debated every decision in full hearing of the populace, thus reducing Wood-

row Wilson's future dream of "open covenants openly arrived at" to an absurdity.

Largely because of their faulty diplomatic methods, the Greek city-states consumed their energies and their wealth in internal bickerings which eventually left them easy prey to the conquering foreigners. The problem of reconciling popular democratic control of foreign policy with effective diplomacy, which brought down Greek civilization two thousand years ago, has not been entirely solved.

The Romans, who carried on where the Greeks left off, made a number of contributions to diplomatic practice, but largely in legal and procedural matters. Because of the dominance of the Roman Empire, its ambassadors abroad enjoyed the rank of quasi governors, and ambassadors from areas outside the empire were treated more like colonial petitioners than representatives of sovereign states.

However, the system of law on which the Romans depended so heavily for the regulation of their internal life, including their commerce, was extended to their relations with foreigners. Thus, for the first time the sanctity of international treaties as an essential element in effective diplomacy was recognized.

The Romans also improved on the Greek method of selecting ambassadors. Realizing the importance of the office to the state, they generally chose as representatives only the most distinguished senators. There were, however, some exceptions. On one occasion they sent an athletic instructor as ambassador to Rhodes. The Rhodians objected bitterly and the ambassador was replaced. Two thousand years later, after playing host to a series of amateur American diplomats, the people of Luxembourg took a leaf from the Rhodian book with the same happy result.

The Romans also evolved an elaborate procedure for the recognition, reception, and dismissal of foreign envoys. Jealous of their paramount position, they were not prepared to receive ambassadors from every little tribe or community beyond their frontiers. Thus when a delegate from a foreign land appeared at Rome he was obliged to remain outside the city gates until his credentials could be carefully examined and his right to diplomatic status verified. Since the inns outside Rome's walls were anything but de luxe, it was often a grueling as well as a humiliating experience.

Today this system has generally been replaced by the practice of

requesting "agrèment": that is, the sending country asks the receiving government if it has any objection to the appointment of a specific person as ambassador. Until the receiving country signifies its assent, the actual appointment is, ordinarily, not announced.

With the decline of Rome as a world power and the rise of Byzantium, the fashions of diplomacy acquired a distinctly Oriental cut. Among the practices that developed in this period was that of permitting an ambassador to defray the expenses of his mission by bringing with his embassy merchandise from his native country which he might sell at his new post.

Nowadays, although diplomats are generally permitted to bring with them in their baggage anything they may need without paying custom duties, they are not allowed by diplomatic rules or custom to dispose of it for a profit. However, the temptation to profit from the customs-exempt status is frequently great.

In Russia, during the grim years of the thirties when luxuries were unobtainable in local shops, diplomatic admirers often kept actresses and ballerinas of the Moscow stage in Paris fashions with clothing brought into the Soviet Union in the embassy pouch. In fact, the trade in silk stockings became so brisk that the Soviet government objected and the State Department invoked stern measures to stop the innocent but nevertheless technically improper traffic. Nowadays, while the State Department strictly forbids the use of the pouch for personal use, the more poorly paid diplomats of smaller countries frequently supplement their incomes by importing through the pouch duty-free watches, liquor, and cigarettes which they then sell on the local black market.

A variation of this practice occurred in reverse during the twenties in the Soviet Union when diplomats used debased black-market rubles to purchase antiques, works of art, and other valuables from impoverished Russian aristocrats which they shipped out through the pouch for sale at considerable profit in their home countries. At least one prominent ambassador made enough money in this way to build himself an elaborate villa in which his widow is still living.

A third variant was developed by my own Chinese cook. Transferred from Afghanistan to England during the war, I flew from Karachi to London, leaving my baggage and my cook to follow by ship. When Yang eventually arrived in England my trunks were

admitted without customs inspection as diplomatic baggage. Some days later the first German V-1 bombs, landing close to my house, prompted Yang to ask me to store his valuables in the embassy safe. When he handed them to me I counted almost $2,000 in British currency. Knowing he had only $100 when I left him in Karachi, I asked where the rest came from.

"Master no askee, Yang no tellee lie" was all I could get out of him.

Though it was never judicially established what Yang had imported in my trunks, Scotland Yard insisted it was opium and demanded he leave the country. As it was wartime there was nowhere to send him but the United States. However, since he was on a list of suspected narcotic smugglers which Scotland Yard had given to the FBI, he was refused an American visa and spent the rest of the war in London, much to the annoyance of Scotland Yard and of Sir Anthony Eden, who protested periodically to my ambassador. Not till 1945 did Yang reach the United States, whence he was sent back to China as rapidly as postwar conditions permitted.

To return to Byzantine diplomatic methods, the Oriental traits of suspicion, sharp dealing, and chicanery combined to produce a form of diplomacy in which deception was the main element. The chief occupation of envoys dispatched by Constantinople was not to foster peace and friendship but to foment feuds and rivalries between the tribes on the outer borders of the empire.

Foreign envoys in Constantinople were regarded simply as spies, subjected to the strictest surveillance and treated with open contempt. To induce them to make exaggerated reports of the Eastern Empire's military might, they were obliged to watch parades of armed warriors marching through an arena out one gate and in again at the other in literally endless processions. To impress them with his exalted majesty, the Emperor received them seated on a throne mounted on an elevator which, after they had kissed his ring, would shoot up into the air where the sovereign towered above them while artificial lions beside the throne roared menacingly.

Hitler adopted a variation on the elevated-throne technique when he built his Eagle's Nest on a mountaintop to which foreign envoys were brought into his presence via a 300-foot elevator shaft cut through solid rock. The military parade technique is still an annual feature of the Soviet national holiday when powerful columns of

tanks rumble across Red Square while jet planes scream past overhead. The display, however, is sufficiently genuine and impressive in itself to permit elimination of the endless-chain maneuver

With the decay of the Eastern Empire, Byzantine diplomacy eventually left two offspring. One made its way to Medieval Europe by way of Venice. The other was brought to Russia by the missionaries who also brought Christianity to Muscovy.

The early rulers of Medieval Europe made good use of the treachery, deceit, and intrigue which characterized Byzantine diplomacy. In the dynastic quarrels, intercity rivalries, and family feuds that replaced the dying Holy Roman Empire princes clung precariously to their unstable thrones with a constantly shifting web of tenuous alliances and conspiracies. As agents of these machinations, diplomats were much in demand.

Perhaps the most notable of them, though by no means the worst, was Niccolò Machiavelli, whose treatise *The Prince,* on how to keep a prince on his throne, was for centuries the handbook of Italian diplomacy. Based on the assumption that all men and particularly all princes were evil, the diplomats at their courts were expected not only to bribe their host's servants, suborne his ministers, and seduce his wives but if necessary to assassinate the host himself. Diplomats were understandably considered highly dangerous persons and private citizens were forbidden by law to discuss affairs with them under penalty of going to jail.

Nor were the Italians the only practitioners of these arts. Long before Machiavelli, Louis XI of France instructed his ambassadors: "If they lie to you, see to it you lie much more to them." In England, too, diplomacy by murder was an accepted practice. The long procession of royal heads that rolled from royal shoulders in the Tower of London and the rivalries between their partisans kept a corps of diplomats busy negotiating and sabotaging secret pacts, alliances, and conspiracies. As late as the seventeenth century a member of Parliament found talking to a foreign diplomat might be deprived of his seat in the House of Commons.

It is understandable that under these conditions diplomacy was no more popular than it had been with the Greeks. While soldiers faced only the perils of open combat and priests the spiritual wrath of God, diplomats were exposed day and night to a stiletto in the back

or a pinch of ground glass in their wine.

Nor was travel in Medieval Europe an agreeable experience. By day highwaymen, cutthroats, and marauding bands threatened the traveler on the road and at night fleas, lice, rats, and other vermin infested his bed.

Because of these circumstances governments experienced serious difficulties recruiting personnel for their embassies. In fact, so great was the reluctance that in 1271 the Venetian government issued a decree imposing heavy fines on persons evading diplomatic service— probably the only diplomatic-draft-dodger legislation in recorded history.

Despite its basic acceptance of deception, Italian diplomacy made valuable contributions to diplomatic practice, some of which have survived to the present time. The Venetians, for example, were the first to recognize the importance of files and established the first archives for the preservation of treaties and diplomatic reports, many of which are extant.

The Italians also were the first to establish permanent embassies. Previously, diplomatic missions had been dispatched only on special occasions—to conclude a peace, to negotiate an alliance, or to sponsor a conspiracy. In 1455 Francesco Sforza, the Duke of Milan, sent the first ambassador to reside permanently at Genoa. The practice was not immediately adopted by other states and as late as the seventeenth century some states continued to send only temporary embassies. A survival of this practice is the present-day custom of sending special diplomatic missions on such ceremonial occasions as a coronation or a royal birthday.

The Italians, too were the first to require diplomats to write periodic reports of events in the capital in which they were stationed. A Venetian law of 1268 required ambassadors to file a final report within a fortnight of the completion of their missions.

Before the days of newspapers and news agencies, the diplomats were the principal sources of foreign news for governments. The rulers of that day were apparently avid scandalmongers, for the archives of Venice are replete with complaints to ambassadors that they were not sending in enough news. This insatiable appetite for reports has remained a dominant characteristic of foreign offices, including our State Department.

In order not to miss any tidbits of court gossip, ambassadors were obliged to snoop and spy in a way that would make a modern news reporter blush. They not only had to hang about the court day and night but also to follow the ruler to whom they were accredited on all his travels and even pursue him about the hunting field.

Also, the Italians were the first to recognize that if an ambassador was to worm secrets and scandals out of foreign courtiers he would have to have some spicy news to give in exchange. They therefore originated the practice of providing their envoys with news from home that could be traded for foreign information.

Occasionally this system broke down. One authority on diplomacy tells of a Venetian ambassador to France who was blasted for the paucity and staleness of his gossip. The indignant man retorted that it was all very well for the Venetian officials to complain but they never bothered to send him any local gossip to use in exchange. And what's more, he added, what about their failure to send him a couple of falcons that he had promised as a gift to a French cardinal?

The stabilization of political institutions and dynasties in the sixteenth and seventeenth centuries led to a gradual change in diplomatic practice. With the decline of the city-states and the replacement of petty principalities by larger states, diplomacy by deceit fell out of fashion. The more permanent regimes, such as that of France, began to recognize that in the long run honesty provided a more stable basis for international relations than deception. Machiavelli came to be regarded as the incarnation of evil. In England the expression "Old Nick" as a euphemism for the devil is said to be derived from Machiavelli's first name.

Historians have since rehabilitated Machiavelli, who is now hailed as the founder of modern political science. But the bad name he gave to European diplomacy persists, particularly in some American circles where diplomats in general and European diplomats in particular rank with cardsharps. Though this view has been a myth for three hundred years, its believers continue to exert a profound—and un-healthy—influence on American diplomatic practice.

Hugo Grotius, the seventeenth-century Dutch diplomat and legal philosopher, gave the diplomatic New Look its theoretical foundation. Machiavellian diplomacy had been fostered by the rivalries of the petty states which followed the breakdown of the moral and temporal

authority of the Holy Roman Empire, which had previously imposed certain standards of honesty and morality in international affairs. Grotius argued that the authority of the Holy Roman Emperor had been replaced by a law of nature which governed all human relations and took precedence over dynastic or national interests and aspirations. Unless this law of nature was obeyed, international relations would continue to decay into anarchy.

Grotius is considered the father of international law, and was the first to suggest that some sort of international body be organized to enforce it. Though his ideas had a powerful influence on seventeenth-century political science, his proposals for a League of Nations or a United Nations were about three centuries ahead of their time.

While Grotius was laying the theoretical foundations for the New Diplomacy, Cardinal Richelieu of France was perfecting its more practical application. According to Nicolson, Richelieu was the first statesman to recognize diplomacy as a continuing process and not just a way station where one stops for repairs when something breaks down. Today this sound principle is being assailed by a new form of "personal diplomacy," in which the permanent ambassador is pushed aside by a special envoy whenever a serious problem arises.

A realist, Richelieu also preached that national policies should be based on cold calculations of national interests and not on dynastic or sentimental considerations. A state, he said, should choose allies out of consideration of their power and permanence and not because it likes them. Although this lesson would seem to be self-evident, it has never been fully learned. The -phobias and -philes of the American public toward England, China, France and Germany, for example, have bedeviled our diplomacy for a century.

The autocratic Richelieu also was the first to appreciate the importance of public opinion in foreign policy. To popularize and explain his policies he even wrote and distributed pamphlets among the French public. Thus this cold-blooded little Frenchman is the spiritual father of the small army of public relations officials in the State Department, the U. S. Information Agency, and the numerous private councils on world affairs now scattered throughout America.

Possibly Richelieu's greatest contribution to diplomatic practice was

his insistence that an ambassador had the right to demand a single chief and a single policy. He demanded that France's foreign affairs be concentrated in one ministry and ruthlessly saw to it that other departments kept their fingers out of the pie. This logical and reasonable system, Nicolson has wryly but accurately remarked, "appears to be almost unrealized in modern times."

Another figure who left a permanent influence on diplomacy was the French diplomat François de Callières, whose book *On the Manner of Negotiating with Princes* Nicolson calls "the best manual of diplomatic method ever written." Callières's principal lesson in diplomacy is that "Honesty is here and everywhere the best policy."

From the days of Richelieu to modern times diplomatic practice has evolved slowly, its impulses altering with changing conditions and its techniques advancing with the application of modern inventions.

The gradual disappearance of dynastic rivalries and the rise of nationalism and of international commerce brought new problems to the green baize table. Colonies, markets, raw materials rather than genealogical tables became the desiderata of diplomatic negotiation.

Though older diplomats resented the changes and considered it beneath their dignity to deal with commercial matters, about which they knew very little, the later diplomats acquired new specialties and knowledge. Instead of dealing with the goings on about the royal courts, their reports were full of statistical tables and technical analyses. Instead of wrangling about whom the crown prince was to marry, they sparred about commercial concessions and bargained over tariffs and quotas.

The introduction of the telegraph and the airplane greatly changed the tempo of diplomatic life. Instead of waiting for weeks for a slow sailing ship to bring them instructions, diplomats received orders and transmitted recommendations by telephone or cable in a matter of hours.

One result of the new techniques was the plethora of paper that began to accumulate in embassy files. As Prussian ambassador to Paris, Bismarck used to dictate his dispatches simultaneously to two secretaries who wrote them down in full. He then compared the two copies, sending the neater and more legible to Berlin and keeping the other in his files. Today the duplicating machine floods the file

cabinets of every embassy with copies of reports from even the most insignificant of ambassadors.

But despite all these minor changes the basic principles of diplomacy remained the same: Honesty continued to be the best policy; and diplomats jealously guarded their reputations for integrity and probity.

V

The Origins of the Diplomatic
Iron Curtain: 2

WHILE Western diplomacy was thus developing and spreading throughout the world, the other offspring of Byzantium was undergoing an entirely different evolution, culminating in modern Soviet diplomacy. Some historians argue that Soviet diplomacy is not diplomacy at all. Nevertheless, as a method of negotiation—and in many instances a very effective one—it seems to fall within the definition of the diplomatic art if not within the ethical limitations imposed by Western diplomacy.

That it daily poses new problems for Western diplomats cannot be denied. To think it can be wished away by saying it is not diplomacy is, in my opinion, a fallacy. Furthermore, it seems to me that Soviet diplomacy is not an isolated phenomenon which burst full grown upon the unsuspecting chancelleries of the West after the Bolshevik Revolution and which, as Nicolson seems to suggest, will someday disappear just as dramatically.

Soviet diplomacy, I believe, has its roots deep in Russian and Byzantine history. When the emperors in Constantinople sent Cyril and Methodius to teach the Slavs Christianity and their scholars to teach them how to read and write, their painters to teach them art, and their architects to teach them how to build their onion-steepled churches, they also sent along their diplomats who, intentionally or not, taught them the deception, chicanery, and treachery which characterized the Byzantine diplomacy of that day.

At Kherson in the Crimea they established a subsidiary diplomatic bureau for the dispatch of embassies to the steppes and the conduct of diplomatic relations with Kiev, Muscovy, and the tribes along the Volga. Constantine VII in his *De Administrando Imperio* prescribes how the tribes should be embroiled with one another. For example, the Petchenegs, or Black Bulgars, should be incited against the Chazars and the Russians or Hungarians against the Petchenegs.

This strategy was used even in Western Europe. When Louis II's Frankish troops expelled the Saracens from southern Italy in 871 the Byzantines stood by until the fighting was over and then maneuvered the victorious Franks out of the province. Later they used the Crusaders to drive back the Seljuk Turks, just as the Soviets used the Chinese nearly a thousand years later in Korea.

Imperial princesses were frequently dispatched as wives to tame the barbarian leaders. Constantine's granddaughter Anna was married off to the Grand Duke Vladimir with the task of "civilizing" that extraordinary roughneck.

The Russians learned well and never forgot their lessons. Long after Grotius, Richelieu and Callières, the rules which Machiavelli inherited from Constantinople continued to be the guiding precepts of the court of the Czar.

A vivid diplomatic report from an ambassador of the Holy Roman Emperor at the court of the Eastern Empire, written in the tenth century, describes in some detail how the Byzantine emperors conducted their diplomacy in Constantinople. While its style perhaps lacks the polished reserve and restraint of a modern diplomatic dispatch, much of what it describes could as well come from a report of an ambassador in an Eastern capital a thousand years later.

The author Ambassador Liudprand, himself the son of a diplomat, was the distinguished Bishop of Cremona at the time of his mission. He had been brought up at the royal court at Pavia, then the seat of the King of Italy. Handsome, gifted, and with a keen eye for the ladies, he quickly attracted the attention (and because of his success with the ladies-in-waiting, the mild jealousy) of his master, the King. As his report indicates, he also had a delicate palate for good food and wine. Though wealthy, he seems to have had a keen sense for the value of money.

Liudprand eventually enlisted in the service of King, and later

Emperor, Otto I. Otto, having just conquered Italy, was seeking to placate his rival, the Byzantine Emperor in Constantinople, by marrying off his son, the future Otto II, to Theophano, the daughter of the current Eastern Emperor's predecessor. Liudprand, whose father and stepfather had both served on missions to Constantinople, had once previously headed an embassy there himself. He was therefore an obvious choice to arrange the marriage.

Arriving early one afternoon in the year 968 after an arduous journey with a staff of twenty-five, Liudprand recalled his previous visit and the many friends he had made and was looking forward eagerly to a pleasant reception. To his dismay and discomfort, the Emperor's officials kept him waiting in the pouring rain outside the city gates until almost midnight. "Insulting and abusive," he comments in his report. Eventually he was escorted to a house reserved for him in which he was to be kept virtually a prisoner for a hundred and twenty miserable days. It was, he says, a huge, barnlike structure which offered no protection from either the sun or the rain. Among its other inhabitants were five lions to which Liudprand took an immediate aversion.

The house was without water and there was nothing to drink except some local Greek wine which, he says, was adulterated with pitch, resin, and gypsum and was quite impotable. "Bathwater!" he observed contemptuously.

Three guards stationed at the front gate prevented visitors from entering and his staff from leaving this "horrible house," as he invariably thereafter referred to it. When old friends attempted to send him some decent food and wine, the guards tossed the food into the gutter and beat up the messengers. Only his Italian cook was allowed to leave the premises to buy provisions and, since he spoke no Greek and could bargain only with his hands, the food cost him four times the regular price. Inflation was raging in Constantinople, Liudprand reports, and it cost no less than three gold pieces to feed his staff and the guards a single meal. (One suspects that Liudprand reported these matters in such detail, as his successors do a thousand years later, so that his subsequent expense accounts would find readier approval.)

Two days after his arrival he was bidden by the marshal of the court, the Emperor's brother, to come to the royal palace, which was so far away that he was completely out of breath when he got there.

Immediately an altercation arose. The marshal charged that Otto had no right to style himself Roman emperor, since he was a mere king. Liudprand became incensed and the argument ended in a draw.

Two days later he was received by the Emperor Nicephorus himself, whom he describes as a fantastic creature with the body of a pygmy. His long, thick, matted hair made him look like a pig and his little beady eyes reminded the ambassador of a mole's. His skin was the color of an Ethiopian's. Though he was richly dressed in heavily embroidered robes, they were so old and worn that they smelled bad. He spoke impudently, was as sly as a fox, and a "veritable Ulysses" when it came to lying. "He is not," Liudprand summed up in his report to his master, "the type you would like to meet in the middle of the night."

The interview with Nicephorus was no better than had been the first with the marshal of the court. The Emperor began by stating that, though he would have liked to receive Liudprand in better style, the arrogant behavior of his master, Otto, precluded this. Nicephorus appeared to be particularly displeased that Otto had conquered Rome, which he claimed rightfully belonged to him, and had thrown out all his old and dear friends. Otto, according to the Emperor, was a godless murderer who had beheaded, hanged, exiled, and blinded the best people of Rome. Furthermore, he added ominously, he had sent Liudprand not as an emissary of peace but as a common spy.

Indignantly Liudprand defended his master, saying that when Otto had captured Rome it was ruled by whores. Otto had liberated the city from tyrants and had restored the Church to its dignity. "If you were the rightful Emperor of Rome," he asked Nicephorus, "why did you turn it over to harlots?"

Peevishly Nicephorus complained that all he wanted was peace with Otto but instead Otto had taken Italy from him. Liudprand retorted that Otto was the rightful ruler of Italy. Furthermore, Nicephorus' offer of a peace pact was a lie and a fraud. What Nicephorus really wanted, Liudprand said, was an armistice, a mere breathing spell in which to rally his military forces. If he honestly wanted peace all he need do to get it was to agree to the marriage of Otto's son to Theophano. After that, he hinted archly, Otto might be prepared to make "certain concessions." (Liudprand was too good a diplomat to show his cards at this early stage.)

This diplomatic exchange was interrupted by a church service. The service consisted chiefly of a choir singing the praises of Nicephorus, whom it called "The Morning Star," "Lucifer," "The Reflection of the Sun," "The Blight of the Saracen," "The Conqueror," and various other epithets which apparently infuriated Liudprand. He noted that the choirboys were barefoot and dressed in clothes so miserable that they must have been worn out when their grandfathers got them.

As he listened to this nauseating paean, Liudprand thought up some more appropriate words for the choir to sing: "You burnt-out cinder, creepy old woman, ugly old gnome. You boor! You mudlark! Pigheaded, surly, peasant barbarian! You impudent shaggy-haired shrew!" However, he was too discreet to pass on these variations to Nicephorus and included them only in his report to his master.

After the church service Liudprand was invited to lunch with the Emperor. Not only was the food "foul and loathsome" but he was seated number fifteen at the table, which was not only below the salt but below the end of the tablecloth.

During the meal the diplomatic exchange continued. Nicephorus asked how good Otto's soldiers were. When Liudprand said they were excellent. Nicephorus interjected: "You're lying! Your master's soldiers don't know how to ride or to fight." They wore such heavy armor, he claimed, and carried such long swords that they could fight neither on foot nor on horseback. What was more, he said, their stomachs were their god and they were such gluttons that they were too fat to mount a horse. They got their courage from the bottle and were brave only when they were drunk. Finally, Nicephorus taunted, Otto did not even possess a navy. "When I come to fix you," he threatened, "I'll destroy every town on the seacoast and invade every river."

By this time Liudprand was beside himself with rage. When he started to reply, Nicephorus ordered him to be silent but the incensed ambassador ignored the command. "You talk about your fine Romans," he said. "Everyone knows Romulus, the founder of Rome, collected a gang of insolvent bankrupts, runaway slaves, murderers, and other criminals whom he named Romans. When we from the north can't find a worse name for our enemies we call them Romans. And the next time we fight you'll soon find out who's the better, your Romans or we northerners!"

This outburst seems to have silenced Nicephorus for the moment and he ordered Liudprand to go back to his "horrible house." Their subsequent encounters were no happier. Once when the ambassador was again invited to dine with the Emperor he was seated below an "unwashed, unshaven Bulgarian who wore a brass belt." What was so offensive about the brass belt Liudprand did not explain, but he was so outraged that he refused to take his place, whereupon Nicephorus' guards escorted him to the servants' table.

On one occasion Nicephorus asked Liudprand whether Otto owned any "onagers." Not knowing what onagers were, Liudprand replied cautiously that Otto might not have any of them but he had a lot of other things. Nicephorus then invited him to visit the royal zoo where the onagers were kept. Next day Liudprand put on his hat, mounted his horse and set out for the zoo. He had gone some way through the park when a guard told him he was not allowed to wear a hat on the premises. Offended, he turned to leave but just then his local guide spotted one of the fabulous onagers. "And what do you think it was?" chortled Liudprand in his report. "Just a common ordinary jackass, the kind we have thousands of in Cremona!"

Liudprand soon concluded that his mission was a failure and asked leave to return home, but Nicephorus would not let him go. After four months of misery Nicephorus finally relented and gave permission. He also agreed that Liudprand could take as much merchandise with him as he wanted, apparently to defray the costs of the trip.

"But," Liudprand writes to his master, "now listen how that heathen treats his own promises! . . ." Liudprand's baggage was searched and several bolts of purple cloth were removed, the customs officials explaining that Liudprand's countrymen were not entitled to wear purple. Contemptuously, Liudprand told them he had not bought it for his countrymen, who wouldn't be seen in such effeminate stuff. The cloth, he explained, was for the women. Nevertheless, it was confiscated.

"What manners! What sexless creatures!" Liudprand commented sourly.

Finally, just as Liudprand was about to set forth, one of the Emperor's eunuchs refused to provide porters and he had to bribe some men with huge sums of money to carry his baggage.

"These men of no sex! These women!" he complained.

At last, just before departing, Liudprand took his revenge on his host by carving a long poem in Latin on a table in the "horrible house" in which he said exactly what he thought about the leaking roof, the lying Greeks, and their stupid emperor. Eventually after being placed on a rotten boat, getting shipwrecked, arrested and robbed, he made his way home and delivered the historic report. (It might be added that eventually Otto II did marry Theophano, but not thanks to Liudprand's mission.)

In 1934, nearly a thousand years after Liudprand angrily shook the dust of Constantinople from his shoes, Ambassador William Bullitt arrived in Moscow to set up the first American embassy in the Soviet Union. Recalling the warm reception he had had from Stalin and others on a visit the year before, when the Soviets were still concerned about recognition, he beamed happily from the train window as he saw a band and a delegation laden with bouquets waiting on the station platform. But as he stepped from the train his smile froze. From another car emerged a group of frowsy delegates to the Soviet Women's Day celebrations. The band blared forth, the women were showered with carnations, and the ambassador was whisked through the crowd by a minor official to his car.

His residence was sparsely furnished but it kept out the rain. However, the staff apartment building still had no roof. Eventually it, too, was completed but the water in the bathrooms ran spasmodically and seldom hot. When he complained, all the pipes were connected to the municipal steam system so that only steam emerged even when you flushed the toilets. The office ceilings soon showed ominous cracks but the government landlord refused to take cognizance until one night the ceiling collapsed and demolished the office furniture.

Bullitt was never again received by Stalin and for days after his arrival could not even get an appointment with the foreign minister. When he eventually ran down Litvinov in a hospital bed, Litvinov promptly began to repudiate all the prerecognition agreements reached in Washington.

On the whole, for the first months of his stay, Bullitt was far better treated than other ambassadors. He was allowed to see a few local friends and to tour the country freely, though guards in front of his gate turned away all visitors.

But gradually the atmosphere grew cooler. On visiting a china factory near Moscow he was presented with a pretty but undistinguished china dinner service. Some weeks later a bill arrived for $1,000 gold. Soon thereafter his closest Russian friend was arrested and shipped off north of the Arctic Circle, where he spent the better part of seven years. When Bullitt finally left the Soviet Union his mood was not far removed from that of Liudprand. But one of the latter's words he would not have used was "sexless."

The diplomacy by vituperation which Nicephorus demonstrated to Liudprand had by the sixteenth century spread throughout Russia. One of the most colorful and popular episodes of Russian history, venerated by every Russian schoolboy and commemorated in a well-known painting by Repin, is the reply of the Zaporozhie Cossacks to a demand for surrender from the Turkish Sultan Mahomet III. Omitting the unprintable words, this early Russian diplomatic note reads:

You, Sultan, Turkish Devil and brother and comrade of the accursed devil and secretary of Lucifer himself!

How in hell can you call yourself a warrior when you can't even ——— an ass's ———. Let the Devil take you away and gobble up your army. You son-of-a-bitch, you have no right to be the guardian of Christian sons; we aren't afraid of your army. We will lick you on land and sea, you hostile son-of-a-bitch. Go ——— your mother.

You Alexandrian goatherd, you Babylonian cook, you Macedonian wagonmaker, Jerusalem's traitor, Kamchatka cat, Podolian villain, swindler of the world and evildoer of the underworld.

Nephew of the asp himself, you are the ——— of our ———, a piece of pig ———, a little mare's ———, the snout of a dog, an unbaptized bastard. Go ——— your mother and go graze Christian swine.

Now we finish. We do not know the date as we have no calendar; we live by the moon. The year may be in the calendar but the day is the same as yours. Kiss our ———.

(signed) Ivan Sirko and his Zaporozhie Band

Some three hundred years after Sirko had penned this note, another Russian, Andrei Vyshinski, commended its style and frankness to his Western colleagues during a United Nations debate.

In the nineteenth century some of the outward forms of Western diplomacy were at least mimicked by the czarist regime. In part this may have been due to the Russian desire to become civilized and

cultured (a passion which is evident in Moscow today). In part it may have been due to the Western education to which members of the Russian nobility were subjected during that period. It may also have been due to the fact that the royal house, long since without a drop of Russian blood, and closely related to the other royal houses of Europe, found it awkward to be caught cheating at diplomatic cards by their uncles, aunts, and cousins.

There are, therefore, a number of instances in the latter phases of the czarist regime of negotiations with the Russian court at which all the rules of the game as played in the West were strictly observed. For example, throughout the long and tough negotiations preceding the Anglo-Russian Convention of 1907 (Persia) no indiscretions were committed nor confidences betrayed by the Russian diplomats.

But in this same period in their dealings with their Eastern neighbors, who shared the Byzantine heritage, straightforwardness, honesty, and discretion were notably absent. The Afghan Emir, Abdur Rahman (1880–1906), has written in his autobiography some candid comments on the Russian diplomatic method during the latter half of the nineteenth century. During that period Afghanistan was a bone of contention between the British, who looked upon it as an outpost on the mountain passes between Russian Central Asia and their Indian empire, and the Russians, who regarded it as a legitimate field for expansion.

"The Russian policy," Abdur Rahman wrote, "is to break their treaties and oaths at any moment that suits their purpose." (This observation on czarist methods came a generation before Lenin, the Bolshevik leader, expressed with unusual candor the opinion that "promises like piecrusts are made to be broken.") In an effort to be strictly objective and fair to his northern neighbor, the Emir hastened to add: "I do not go so far as to say that she breaks oaths and treaties without making some explanation and excuse. . . ." Then, as was his literary habit, he illustrated the practice with a little fable:

A hungry bear employed a small lamb to guide him to all the places where other animals were living, and made a promise that he would not eat this lamb, who was his guide and counselor. All the other animals of the jungle having been eaten by the bear, there remained nothing but the lamb. Thereupon the bear said in an angry voice:

"I must eat you because you have insulted me and broken your treaty." The poor lamb looked at him and said: "My lord, how should I dare to insult you?"

And the bear replied: "Your father insulted my father."

But the lamb said: "But there is no evidence about that, as both our fathers are dead."

The bear answered: "So-and-so told me."

The lamb replied: "He told you a lie."

The bear now got furious, and said: "Now you really have insulted me by calling my friend a liar before my face."

And he fell upon the poor lamb and ate him up.

There are other striking similarities between the Afghan Emir's experiences with the Russians and more recent Soviet diplomatic practices.

"The Russians," the Afghan complained, "believe they can go on breaking promises and treaties and advancing further and moving steadily onward." One diplomatic method which especially irritated Abdur Rahman was the Russian gambit which Machiavelli also had learned from the Byzantine Empire of stirring discontent beyond her frontiers between Afghanistan and her ally, Great Britain, while simultaneously professing "peace-loving friendship" (sic) with each. Fifty years later "peace-loving friendship" was again a favorite Russian word in the campaign to disrupt the North Atlantic Alliance.

Abdur Rahman puts those who believe in Russia's professions of peace-loving friendship into four categories which J. Edgar Hoover might well adopt today:

Firstly, those who are not politicians. These peoples are so simple that having before the eyes of their minds the dozens of treaties and vows broken by Russia still go on putting their confidence in Russian declarations of peace.

Secondly, those who directly or indirectly are "inspired" by Russian policy to plead her cause. [Here Abdur Rahman referred to Russian agents "inspired" by either ideological sympathies or money. C. W. T.]

Thirdly, those with ideas of their own greatness who imagine that it is impossible for Russia ever to think of opposing their mighty power.

Fourthly, the people who call themselves lovers of peace.

These last remind Abdur Rahman of "the pigeon who seeing a cat coming toward him closed his eyes thinking that if he did not see the

cat, the cat would not see him; but the cat did see him and caught him and ate him up."

In the matter of assassination and kidnaping, the Soviets have long since outstripped Machiavelli, who decried these practices as rarely necessary evils. Under the czarist regime conspiracy was confined chiefly to the revolutionary opposition and the czarist police and seldom if ever played a role in Russian diplomacy. However, after the Bolshevik conspirators had come to power they raised conspiracy to the status of a diplomatic procedure. The long arm of Soviet assassins has reached into every corner of the globe—Trotsky in Mexico, Krivitsky at the Drake Hotel in Washington, a dozen victims in Paris, London, and elsewhere.

Before World War II a mysterious black Soviet yacht, the S.S. *Dzerzhinski*, which cruised ominously from the Black Sea to Scandinavia, stopping at various Western ports, aroused the interest and curiosity of Western diplomats and police. A visit from the *Dzerzhinski* was often preceded by strange goings on in local Soviet embassies and consulates accompanied by rifle shots and screams. At night, long wooden boxes were slipped aboard the yacht and it would then cast off and slip out into the blue. The voyages of the *Dzerzhinski* during the height of the purges became of such interest that American consuls in all European seaports were instructed to report its appearances to Washington, but eventually it dropped out of sight and has since been forgotten.

During and following World War II the practice of assassination, which had previously been confined largely to émigrés groups and the Soviets' own officials, was expanded to include foreign government officials and diplomats, such as the representatives of the Polish government-in-exile who were slaughtered in Moscow in 1944, and Raoul Wallenberg, the Swedish diplomat who, the Soviets now confess, died during the war in a Russian prison. The most recent example of diplomacy by assassination was the murder of Imre Nagy, the Hungarian revolutionary leader, who was enticed from diplomatic sanctuary in the Yugoslav Embassy by false assurance of safe-conduct and was subsequently shot.

The devoted band of foreign agents in the Communist parties of other countries has proved a boon to Soviet diplomatic methods. Whereas Western diplomats must attempt to discover the intentions

of governments by discreet questioning or such prosaic devices as getting a bibulous minister drunk, the Soviets often maintain agents within a so-called friendly government to steal the secrets directly from the files.

In one respect the Soviets have made a concession to what they otherwise contemptuously term bourgeois morality. In commercial agreements with foreign firms and countries they have usually, though not always, lived up to the terms of their contracts. The reason for this concession can, I believe, be found in the realization of the necessity for good faith in short-term commercial agreements. Foreign firms would naturally be reluctant to make agreements if they believed, as Lenin did, that a contract with a Soviet trading agency was, like a piecrust, made to be broken.

Since the seventeenth century Western diplomats, by and large, have considered it their primary function to maintain the peace wherever possible. A diplomat, Callières said, is a man of peace not of war. "The function of the State Department," says a somewhat unctuous announcement of 1898, "is peace."

In contrast to this stressing of the peaceful functions of diplomacy, Soviet historians regard diplomacy as an extension of war by other means. In a three-volume work entitled *History of Diplomacy,* published in 1955 in Moscow, a Soviet Academician, E. V. Tarle, devotes a section to bourgeois diplomatic practices for the benefit of Soviet students of diplomacy.

In his introduction Tarle refers to "the ceaseless battle of diplomacy which precedes armed conflicts, follows armed conflicts, and at a somewhat reduced tempo does not even cease during armed conflicts."

Tarle advises "those who are preparing themselves to serve the fatherland in the diplomatic arena" to study its strategy carefully. Referring to Engels' advice to politicians to study the military arts, Tarle says that this refers not only to military affairs but to "diplomatic combat" as well. "It is necessary," he continues, "to be as familiar as possible with the methods and stratagems of the class enemy when confronted with them, not only on the field of battle but also in diplomatic controversy."

With this militant introduction Tarle then proceeds to outline the chief stratagems of "bourgeois diplomacy." He addresses his teachings to Soviet students of bourgeois diplomacy, but with only slight ampli-

fication the volume is an authoritative though incomplete catalogue of Soviet diplomatic stratagems and, as such, invaluable to the bourgeois diplomat as well.

Aggressors, Tarle points out, usually disguise their aggressions as self-defense. As examples he cites Frederick the Great's 'conquests, Germany's invasion of Belgium in 1914, and Hitler's attack on the Soviet Union. Historians will also recall that the Soviet Union declared war on Finland in 1940, despite a nonaggression treaty, on the ground that Finnish artillery had killed four Soviet soldiers in Karelia, thus menacing Russia's security.

Aggressors, Tarle warns, often hide their intentions behind fine phrases about liberty, truth, and humanity. As examples he cites Cromwell, the coalition against the French Revolution, and, of course, Hitler's attack on the Soviet Union. The bourgeois diplomat might add the Soviet "liberation" of Budapest after the 1956 revolution.

Pacifist propaganda, Tarle says, is often used by bourgeois states to mislead their enemies. As examples he mentions Napoleon III, Nicholas II at The Hague, and the British attempt to limit German naval rearmament after World War I. To this list one might also add the Stockholm Peace Offensive and the "Peace in the World" slogan today so widely propagated by Moscow.

Aggressors, according to Tarle, often conclude friendly agreements with prospective victims to lull their vigilance, as both Hitler and Napoleon did. One might also mention the friendly agreements Molotov concluded with the Baltic States shortly before the Soviets invaded those countries in 1940.

Propaganda about righteous war against the Soviet Union is often used to justify aggression, as Hitler used it. The Communist ideology, according to Lenin, similarly provides for "just wars" against capitalism.

Aggressors often demand the localization of conflicts in order to prevent others from interfering with their military operations, as Mussolini did when he invaded Abyssinia—and as Russia did when she invaded Finland in 1940, Hungary in 1956, and South Korea in 1950. Another version of this stratagem was Stalin's neutrality in the early phases of World War II, in which he devoutly but vainly hoped both sides would commit suicide.

Aggressors frequently attempt to sow discord among allies in the

enemy camp, as Machiavelli recommended and Louis XIV did so successfully against the English. Soviet efforts to provoke conflicts between capitalist states, as Lenin frequently recommended, and Khrushchev's attempts to undermine the North Atlantic Alliance might be added to the list.

Aggressors also exploit internal conflicts within enemy states. Tarle uses as examples Bismarck's activities against the Danes, the Bulgars' against the Serbs, and the Germans' in Belgium's Flemish minority. The basic activity of Communist parties in capitalist states is directed to the same end as demonstrated in the Spartakus Movement in Germany after World War I, the Spanish Civil War, and the Communist parties of Italy and France after World War II.

Aggressors, according to Tarle, hide their expansionist plans behind demagogic denunciations of peace treaties after a war as Italy did in the Balkans in 1928 and Hitler after 1933. He might also have cited the Soviet Union after Brest-Litovsk and Versailles.

Tarle adds that aggressors systematically use threats and terror to frighten their intended victims. Thus Napoleon threatened Russia, William II threatened England, Hitler threatened Poland. One might also cite the terrorization and indeed assassination of the Polish government-in-exile in Moscow, Vyshinski's threats againt King Michael of Rumania to force his abdication, and, more recently, Mr. Khrushchev's threats of atomic attack against the British at the time of the Suez Crisis.

Finally, aggressors often use the pretext of defending "weak" governments to disguise their own intentions, as Wilhelm II did in the Boer War and Germany and France at the time of the Morocco Crisis. Soviet sponsorship of Nasser of Egypt and the Iraqi government and even the nonexistent Kadar government of November 4, 1956, also are a part of the catalogue of twentieth-century Soviet diplomatic gambits.

These stratagems which Tarle denounces in the capitalist record and ignores in Communist history are strictly speaking not diplomatic practices but international policies. High policy is made not by diplomats but by rulers, elected representatives of governments and their senior advisers, and are put into practice by diplomats. Though the standard of morality which diplomats have evolved in the past three centuries have not always been matched by the governments in the

evolution of policy itself, this should not reflect, as unfortunately it often does, on the diplomats.

However, the degree of spiritual as well as material subservience that the Soviet regime demands of its servants is such that it is difficult to dissociate the Russian diplomat from the moral standards of his Kremlin chiefs.

VI

The American Era

FROM its earliest days American diplomacy has been subjected to influences peculiarly American which have stamped it with a character different from the classical diplomacy of the Old World.

The early revolutionary leaders, although forced to seek support and allies among the Continental powers, found the methods and forms of Old World diplomacy repugnant. Benjamin Franklin, on arriving in Paris, attempted to hold to the democratic forms of dress and conduct, appearing at court wigless, in a plain suit, and brandishing a knotty crabapple cane. But he soon found that if he was to be successful he must adapt himself to the elaborate customs and costumes of the court.

Other American diplomats came to the same conclusion and, despite their reluctance, learned to conform to European practice so long as the struggling Republic they represented could benefit from d' ' · exchanges with the European powers. But with few excep as John Quincy Adams, one detects in their corresponder conscious revulsion to the steps of the minuets they were r dance. Much more natural and honest to them was the att ferson assumed when he received the British minister, sitting chair in his bathrobe and tossing one slipper about on the e toe. This attitude toward the outward manifestations of I diplomacy was to persist until World War I wiped out man courts where it had thrived and the classes that it had personif

Another factor that was to influence American diplomacy until the present was the preoccupation of the founding fathers with the control of foreign relations. Although a period was to intervene when foreign affairs were a matter of almost complete indifference to the leading politicians and when diplomacy was to play little or no role in American affairs, the delegates to the First Continental Congress were so concerned with the unique importance of foreign relations that they jealously retained full powers in this field for the Congress as a whole. To assure the necessary secrecy, a Committee on Foreign Correspondence actually drafted communications to foreign powers and instructions to its diplomatic representatives, but the Congress kept a tight rein on its activities and eventually abolished it altogether.

When the delegates assembled at the Constitutional Convention to make a more reasonable distribution of powers among the three branches, foreign affairs still posed a major problem. While they were prepared to give almost all purely administrative functions to the executive, they balked at giving him a free hand in foreign affairs. A compromise was eventually worked out which like most compromises has since often caused confusion and occasionally disasters.

Envisaging the Senate as a small select forum of distinguished statesmen elected not by the mob but by state legislatures, the delegates agreed that it should share with the President the control of foreign affairs. Here, they believed, foreign relations could be discussed with sober deliberation and in strict confidence and valuable advice made available to the President.

Accordingly, in addition to the power to declare war, which was granted to the Congress as a whole, the power to make treaties was subject to ratification by a two-thirds vote of the Senate. The appointments of ambassadors, ministers, and consuls was likewise subject to Senate confirmation.

Even the drafters were not agreed on what this compromise meant. Jefferson maintained that the conduct of foreign affairs belonged "altogether to the executive." Hamilton argued that it belonged exclusively neither to the executive nor to the legislative branch. Many constitutional experts have since compromised on the formula that conduct of foreign affairs constitutes a "fourth branch."

But precisely where the executive's jurisdiction ends and the Senate's begins has never been clearly defined. Cynics have interpreted

the compromise as enunciating the right of a people in a democracy to go to hell in ways of their own choosing. Alexis de Tocqueville, otherwise a stanch admirer of the American system, was equally unimpressed by the compromise and concluded gloomily that the American form of democracy was incapable of successfully conducting foreign relations. He has since won many adherents on both sides of the Atlantic to this pessimistic view.

The inevitable tug of war between the President and Congress began promptly after Washington assumed office. Urged to appear before Congress to explain certain acts in the foreign field, he replied vigorously, "I'll be damned if I go to that place." One hundred thirty years later Woodrow Wilson was damned for precisely the same attitude when he refused to consult Congress during the Versailles peace negotiations.

Until the 1820's a series of strong executives, all of whom except Washington had previous foreign affairs experience either as a secretary of state or as a diplomatic envoy, kept a firm control of the conduct of foreign affairs. They selected American diplomats with great care and skillfully utilized their services to defend American interests against the old European powers.

But with the election of Andrew Jackson normal diplomacy ceased for almost a century to play a significant role in American foreign relations. Occasionally treaties were negotiated, but mostly between the Secretary of State and foreign envoys in Washington. From time to time, as critical situations arose, specially selected ministers were dispatched overseas to negotiate specific problems. But in the sense that its diplomats represented a permanent negotiating staff abroad the United States abandoned diplomacy almost completely.

Distrust of Old World institutions, which had prompted many settlers to come to America in the first place, moralistic objections to Machiavelli with whom European diplomacy was closely associated, especially in the Anglo-Saxon mind, and isolationist fears of entangling alliances, which Washington himself had warned against, as well as preoccupation with internal problems and westward expansion were among the causes of this development. The extension of the spoils system to include agreeable diplomatic sinecures and lucrative consular posts would have made the successful conduct of diplomatic relations a highly questionable undertaking, even if there had been a desire

to maintain permanent active relations with other countries.

Not until American trading ships had established our foreign commerce in all quarters of the globe was there a revival of interest in official representation abroad and then, naturally enough, not in the effete diplomats but in the consuls who protected shipping interests, merchants, and American seamen in foreign ports, and assisted exporters in finding new markets. In 1906 Theodore Roosevelt, always an opponent of the spoils system, put through legislation establishing a career consular service with fixed salaries and promotion by merit.

The diplomatic service, however, continued in the doldrums. Ignored by the general public and Congress, it appealed only to political officeholders, interested in comfortable posts where they might vegetate, and to a small rich, social elite chiefly on the East Coast, attracted to European court life and willing to make substantial contributions to the political parties to buy their way into it.

Occasionally men of both means and ability, interested either in foreign affairs or in some other aspect of activity overseas such as scientific research, archaeology, geography or exploration, managed to wangle a diplomatic appointment in which they made substantial and even distinguished contributions to American interests or American enlightenment. But there were few if any serious students of foreign affairs who could participate unless they had substantial fortunes.

Diplomatic staffs below the top rank were recruited largely from the sons of the rich who had a vague interest in foreign places or a specific interest in European social life. Some, but by no means all, were college graduates. Such screening as they were subjected to was to assure that they were well-born, well-bred, and well-heeled. In fact, as late as World War I, in applying for appointment they often had to submit documentary proof that they had private incomes above a stated minimum.

Congress could scarcely have cared less about them, and appropriated only token sums for their salaries. There is little evidence that the State Department even requested adequate salaries in its budget. A young man assigned as secretary in Tokyo, for example, might find his annual salary considerably less than the cost of his steamship fare to his post, which of course he was required to pay.

In other respects Congress was equally uninterested in the conduct

of foreign affairs. When important treaties came up for ratification, they were often dealt with on a strictly partisan basis. Faced with the formidable two-thirds Senate ratification requirement, the executive in the early nineteenth century resorted to the device of executive agreements which at most necessitated only a majority vote in both Houses. One of the first applications of this technique was the admission of Texas into the Union.

A number of secretaries of state during this era were men of unusual ability and foresight who skillfully negotiated with foreign envoys such historic agreements as the Alaska purchase. But their staffs in Washington were hardly better than those of their embassies abroad and such experts as they had were generally recruited from among friends who had business connections in Europe or a shipping line to the Malay Peninsula or who had been missionaries in China. Under these circumstances a consecutive policy or even a constant flow of information was manifestly out of the question.

In his book *American Diplomacy* 1900–1950 George Kennan has described how American policy with respect to Spain, which culminated in the Spanish-American War, was practically entirely independent of diplomatic channels and based largely on newspaper propaganda. The famous Open-Door Policy was drafted by a British subject in the Chinese customs service, and the manner in which this policy was later pursued had no relation to orthodox diplomatic principles.

This period of indifference to the nation's diplomatic defenses ended in 1919 with a severe jolt both to ourselves and to our neighbors. The American public was shocked by the way the Treaty of Versailles betrayed the high moral principles for which we had entered World War I. Our allies were shocked at the Americans' violation of the sacred diplomatic principle that a treaty signed by an authorized representative—on this occasion by the President himself— should as a matter of national honor be ratified.

President Wilson, who headed our delegation to Versailles despite the opposition of his friends and advisers, was himself a former professor of political science and history. The program that he brought with him had not only been accepted by the governments of the Western Allies but was regarded by the younger diplomats of London

and Paris as heralding a new era of international justice, morality, and even diplomacy. The defeated governments also had accepted his principles and the public throughout Europe looked on them almost as a new Emancipation Proclamation.

Wilson's staff was composed if not of career diplomats—there were no such things in the United States then—at least of very able and intelligent men. His principal adviser was Colonel House, whom Nicolson has described as "the best diplomatic brain that America has yet produced."

Yet, despite these trump cards, this first American venture into European diplomacy ended in dismal failure. When the diplomats eventually left Versailles and the dust had settled back on its cobble-stoned courtyard, the principles Wilson had brought with him had been twisted beyond recognition. The promise of no annexations had been replaced by the subterfuge of mandated states. International disarmament had become the unilateral disarmament of Germany. And the new frontiers of Central Europe bore little relation to the principle of self-determination. Finally, the dream of a universal League of Nations in which the United States was to participate was rejected by the Senate.

What were the causes of this failure? Many reasons for it can be found in the intricacies of European national politics, which have been analyzed by hundreds of writers and historians and need no amplification here. The rejection of the League by the Senate was the product of partisan American politics. However, it provided a valuable lesson for future American diplomacy: the conduct of foreign affairs without the participation of the Congress is illusory.

But much of the failure of the Versailles venture was due to American misunderstanding of the function of diplomacy. Despite his intellectual equipment and academic training, Wilson, like most of his compatriots, clung to the myth that Machiavellian diplomats had been responsible for the war. Mistaking diplomacy for policy-making, he put the blame not on the policies and their creators but on the men who had to carry them out. He was determined therefore that the post-war world was to be made safe for democracy by making it free of the old diplomacy.

Wilson's main charge against diplomacy was its secrecy. By opening the doors and raising the blinds of the chancelleries of the world, the

people themselves would henceforth supervise the making of the agreements that regulated international affairs.

But the misconception behind "open covenants openly arrived at" did not long survive the realities confronting Wilson on arrival in Paris. When the new messiah of popular diplomacy found himself faced not only by the wicked old European diplomats but by those heralds of democracy, the representatives of the world press, he promptly locked himself up in his study and put Marine guards outside the doors and even the windows to keep out not the wicked diplomats but the reporters.

Despite all that has been written about it, "open diplomacy" died a quick death. By the time the Allies came to preparing for a second Versailles after World War II, the diplomats on the European Advisory Council were instructed to shun all contact with the press, including even their personal friends, lest inadvertently the secrets of the new convenants be revealed.

Another cause for the diplomatic failure in 1919 was undoubtedly the very presence of the American President. Summit diplomacy, as the professional diplomats had known since the days of Louis XIV, was if not doomed to failure at least seriously handicapped by the additional burdens it imposed on a job already difficult enough.

Thirdly, one might cite Wilson's substitution of diplomacy by exhortation, the evangelistic and too often moralistic approach, for what he called *Realpolitik* and others called the trading of mutual benefits.

Finally, it seems to me, the American experiment in diplomacy at Versailles revealed that even the soundest and highest of moral principles are not substitutes for a continuing policy implemented by a permanent corps of professionals. When faced with the complexities of European national conflicts, the American position was based not on the continuous observations of trained diplomats but on hasty ad hoc investigations and missions which tried to fit the most involved racial and ethnographic situations into a set of principles that could not contain them. The facts being stronger than the principles, the principles gave way.

To the American public, however, the failure of Versailles was ascribed to quite other causes. Supporters of Wilson, like Ray Stannard Baker, reported back to America that the conference was a sort

of jousting tournament between the evil forces of European diplomacy and the brave idealism of the New World. The myth of Machiavellianism was further strengthened and the diplomats took the blame for what Wilson's own secretary of state called the President's slow-witted, humorless, chip-on-shoulder mysticism.

The Europeans, on the other hand, regarded the American diplomatic effort at Versailles as little short of sabotage. The United States had persuaded the Europeans to abandon balance of power diplomacy for a hodgepodge of conflicting national interests embodied in small states of dubious viability on the promise to help maintain stability through the League of Nations. But then, by refusing to ratify the treaty, it not only left the European Allies holding the bag but dangerously undermined one of the oldest tenets of diplomatic negotiation—namely, that ratification of a properly negotiated treaty practically automatically followed its signature.

What, the Europeans now asked themselves, was the point of negotiating with an accredited American diplomat if as likely as not the United States Senate was to repudiate him as they had repudiated President Wilson? Had not one prominent senator himself stated that "a treaty is a mere project of a treaty until the consent of the Senate has been given"? And with the two-thirds requirement for Senate ratification, a minority representing less than 3 per cent of the American population might torpedo the soundest of treaties.

While the Europeans struggled in vain to make the new system work, the United States, disillusioned and confirmed in its worst prejudices against European diplomacy, withdrew once more into a haughty holier-than-thou isolation.

But the weakness of the American performance at Versailles did not go entirely unobserved in Washington. Both in the administration and in Congress a few enlightened men realized that if the United States was ever to play a role in international affairs the rich young socialites who filled some but by no means all of our diplomatic posts must be replaced by carefully selected and trained professionals in a career service.

In 1924 the diplomatic service was combined with the already existing career consular service. Adequate salaries for embassy personnel were established so that thenceforth any young man of ability, regardless of his financial means, could apply for the service.

It would, however, be a mistake to assume that the Rogers Act of 1924 marked an abrupt turning point in the American attitude toward diplomacy. On the contrary, it would be more accurate to say that a professional diplomatic service was accepted with the most grudging reluctance. There remained among the public and Congress a warm suspicion that beneath the top hats and striped pants of these effete young cosmopolites there lurked a conspiracy, when they were not pushing cookies, to drag the United States into the deadly stranglehold of European politics. Every tiny appropriation by Congress was made with grim warnings against meddling in world affairs. For nearly two decades every young recruit had drilled into him that his function was to report on the other people's business but strictly to mind his own and avoid any associations that might involve him in world politics. To this day the Foreign Service Regulations contain relics of this attitude in provisions severely limiting participation in any foreign club or association that might conceivably be construed as having an international political aim. (It would be interesting to know the Soviet regulations on this point.)

The entry of the United States into world diplomacy after World War I was thus strongly influenced by the deep-seated American suspicion of diplomacy in general and by Congressional fears of entangling alliances in particular. Like a gawky overgrown youth, America shambled self-conscious and diffident onto the diplomatic stage, fearful that its big feet would knock over the tea table.

To foreigners this appearance was puzzling. Writing in this period Sir Harold Nicolson gives an Englishman's impression of the new American diplomats:

They enter a conference as Daniel entered the den of lions conscious that it is only their bright faith and innocence which will preserve them from the claws of the wild beasts by whom they are surrounded. It is in fact strange that whereas an American business man will negotiate with foreign business men in a spirit of almost reckless self-confidence an American diplomatist will in the presence of continental diplomatists become overwhelmed with diffidence and suspicion.

Like many other Europeans, Nicolson failed to realize that the diffidence sprang from a fear not of the claws of European diplomats but of stepping on an isolationist congressman's corns.

The age of Roosevelt marked a further step in the development of American diplomacy. Convinced of the need for a more active role in world affairs, Roosevelt began a cautious and skillful attack on the isolationists which ended with their rout after the Japanese attack on Pearl Harbor.

However, most of Roosevelt's diplomatic initiatives were carried out not by the professional diplomats already then available in the Foreign Service but by hand-picked special envoys and friends. An exception was Sumner Welles, a schoolmate of Roosevelt who had since become a skilled professional diplomat. Roosevelt's first excursion into world affairs was the Economic Conference at London in 1933, which Europeans heralded as the end of American isolationism and the beginning of a joint effort to overcome the world-wide depression. The American delegation, headed by Secretary of State Hull, contained several of Roosevelt's brain-trusters, each of whom believed he had the exclusive ear of the President.

The antics of these amateurs advancing contradictory proposals to the conference and pitted against each other in a wild scramble to win over the code clerks who controlled the communications link to the White House, initially amused the European delegates. However, when at the last moment Roosevelt, either for fear of the isolationists or for fear that the commitments envisaged by the conference might retard domestic recovery, retreated and torpedoed the conference, the amusement once more as after Versailles turned to bitter resentment.

Typical of Roosevelt's initial approach to diplomacy was his taking over of the later stages of the negotiations with Maxim Litvinov on Soviet recognition. In an atmosphere reminiscent of Boys' Day at City Hall, Litvinov was seated before the President while behind the commissar stood the President's private advisers signaling and coaching their chief as he pressed for further concessions. Having no other choice, Litvinov made the concessions but only long enough for an American embassy to be established in Moscow, whereupon Stalin promptly welshed on them. Machiavelli's maxims, as one diplomat later observed, were not written for amateurs.

Holding the permanent officials of the department and the Foreign Service responsible for the policies of his predecessors, Roosevelt fired some and wrote the rest off as fossilized bureaucrats. Similarly, mistaking the few holdovers from the old spoils system days as typical

of the new career Foreign Service he, originally at least, dismissed the latter as snobbish "Europeanized expatriates."

Indicative of his attitude was his insistence that the senior members of the service who had spent their lives at diplomatic posts be made to serve in consular capacities, presumably to learn how the other half lived. It was while doing his consular stint that Theodore Marriner, an able diplomat, was assassinated by a visa applicant at the Beirut Consulate in 1937. Another example was a presidential order issued early in Roosevelt's first administration threatening every professional diplomat with dismissal if he so much as asked permission to marry a foreigner. Based on the fears of certain of his advisers that American diplomats might be subverted or de-Americanized by connubial influences or that alien women were more indiscreet than Americans, the order was a godsend to footloose bachelors but a cause of deep personal and senseless unhappiness to others. Foreign diplomats, many of them married to American wives, while not oblivious to the veiled affront, dismissed the order with the comment that even Roosevelt had his isolationist moments.

Illustrative of the senselessness of this order was the case of a young Foreign Service officer serving in Switzerland during the war. Falling in love with a distinguished Swiss girl, he requested permission to marry her and was promptly dismissed. However, as Switzerland was then surrounded by the German forces, it was impossible for him to return home or for a replacement to be sent from Washington. He was therefore promptly rehired as a noncareer clerk at a considerably lower salary and continued to do precisely the same work as he had done before his marriage.

When the war ended the rules were relaxed and the young officer was asked to return to the service. However, embittered by his treatment, he went home to his father's business in Detroit and the service lost not only a well-trained but an unusually capable officer.

In his later administration, as the war pushed international issues to the fore, Roosevelt assumed almost complete charge of American foreign affairs, leaving only secondary questions to be handled by the State Department through established diplomatic channels. In fact, he conducted most of his diplomatic correspondence in Navy Department codes, thus bypassing the State Department completely. Following Wilson's precedent, he frequently indulged in personal diplomacy

at Ottawa, Casablanca, Tehran, and Yalta. At the Cairo Conference of 1943, for example, with the exception of interpreters, Roosevelt's entourage contained not a single professional diplomat and whenever it became necessary to draft an agreement the task was given to Sir Anthony Eden who, reasonably enough, took full advantage of the absence of an American professional to assure that the British point of view was fully provided for.

Nevertheless, Roosevelt's contributions to the professional diplomatic service outweighed the petty vindictive measures against it during his administration. It was Roosevelt who awakened the State Department to the dangers of the dictators' total diplomacy to its internal security in such matters as codes and couriers. After the initial economies of the New Deal, he came to recognize that even in a democratic diplomatic service patched blue jeans were not an adequate substitute for striped pants, and he supported measures not only to pay diplomats adequately but to reimburse them for expenses made for official purposes.

One of the results of World War II was the temporary domination of foreign policy by the military. Although Roosevelt acquiesced in this development, it would be unfair to hold him fully responsible. Throughout American history generals have been ignored in peacetime and glorified in war. Disregarding the precept that war is a deplorable means to a political end and mistaking military victory for political success, Roosevelt, like his predecessors, often permitted military advisors to subordinate his political aims to military expediency. As a result, during the war the counsel of professional diplomats was replaced by that of professional soldiers. When hostilities ended, the problems thus created, such as the occupation of Germany and especially of Berlin, were infinitely complicated.

A more far-reaching result of the war was that the American diplomat found himself catapulted from the passive role of an observer and reporter to that of an active negotiator and participant in "entangling alliances" from Canberra to Moscow. This abrupt change of roles was accomplished with varying success. Some Foreign Service officers adapted themselves quickly to the reversal of the old orders against involvement. Others were overcome with alarm at finding themselves thrust into negotiations involving the country's most vital interests, with the inevitable result that their collaborators both American and

foreign criticized them as unimaginative, timid, and downright incompetent.

The postwar period saw further progress in the development of a career service and its acceptance as an essential arm of government. Turning back the conduct of foreign affairs to his secretaries of state and relying heavily on the counsel of his professional diplomats, President Truman laid the ghost of the crooked Old World diplomacy and considerably raised the prestige of the American variety. He also redressed, at least in part, the balance between military and diplomatic influences in the formulation of foreign policy.

Another development of the Truman regime was the re-emergence of the Congress as a major factor in American diplomacy just as it had been after World War I. Not only because of its constitutional prerogatives in the field of foreign affairs but because policy in the ruined war areas meant money and money meant Congressional appropriations, both the Senate and the House suddenly found themselves wielding enormous powers far beyond the frontiers of the country.

Aware of their authority, power and prestige but not always imbued with the sense of responsibility that went with them, they set out to inspect their new domains with real gusto. In groups and committees or singly, accompanied by legislative assistants, secretaries or wives, they scoured the globe investigating, questioning, prying, and occasionally just plain junketing.

Scarcely an embassy, consulate or nightclub abroad escaped the attention of one or another party of congressmen. Foreign officials, from chiefs of states through foreign ministers and bureaucrats to taxi drivers, were interviewed and cross-examined on their need for American aid, loans, or other assistance.

The burden thus placed on diplomatic staffs was considerable and took many forms. The more responsible of the visitors required long and thorough briefings, introductions to foreign officials, interpreters and guides. The more frivolous demanded less intellectual stimulants: free drinks, cheap PX watches and perfumes. Almost all required cash from special funds set aside from United States credits abroad for which no public accounting was required.

Not all these early postwar expeditions were beneficial. Foreign officials begrudged the time spent in answering the questions not of one Congressional delegation but of half a dozen each month, often on

the same subjects. Many found the domineering attitude of the congressmen indulging in their new-found powers disagreeable if not offensive. Listening to the questions propounded, many of them superficial and revealing a dismal ignorance of their problems, they often wondered whether a country whose foreign policy was controlled by such men could be a dependable leader of an alliance against the Communists.

American diplomats likewise were not uniformly impressed by their legislators. Though glad to devote hours to briefing the intelligent and conscientious among them, the overworked embassy officers resented, and sometimes showed it, the time wasted in arranging for the creature comforts of those who obviously had little understanding of or interest in the problems they had ostensibly come to investigate. They also found small pleasure in entertaining in their homes congressmen who obviously considered the entertainment their due and the whiskey, to which they helped themselves freely, their own by virtue of the appropriations for entertainment that they had voted.

Some of the legislators, aware of their own inadequacies and not unmindful of the impression they were creating among the better-informed, earnest Foreign Service officers, allowed their own feelings of inferiority to provoke animosity toward their diplomatic representatives, and this was later to be reflected in their speeches and their voting in Congress.

Yet for all these deficiencies, the institution of the globe-trotting congressman was probably one of the most beneficial developments in the short history of American diplomacy. Even the most obtuse or indifferent legislator in the course of a foreign tour could not help but learn something of the political and economic problems of the countries he visited and of the difficulties facing the American diplomats who had to grapple with them.

Moreover, the many intelligent legislators who had entertained a somewhat parochial outlook on foreign affairs found themselves face to face with hard realities which were difficult to ignore when confronted by a roll call in the Senate or House. After they themselves had locked horns in debate with foreign officials on the need for aid, they could scarcely come home to support the myth that European politicians had cloven hoofs and forked tails and were too smart for the simple American plainsman. Finally, adverse newspaper reports com-

bined with the disdainful frowns of their Congressional colleagues began to restrain the carousers and junketeers.

To suggest that the Senate or the House had suddenly become the staid, wise and sober forum which the drafters of the Constitution had envisaged when they bestowed on the Upper House a share in the control of foreign affairs, would be an exaggeration. The deep-seated suspicion of the State Department and the Foreign Service lingered on and flamed into bitter hostility on the discovery that the department had harbored Communist sympathizers and possibly agents during the war years. Investigation followed on investigation and reorganization on reorganization with far-reaching results to the Foreign Service. In fact many of those professional diplomats who managed to endure the so-called McCarthy era became convinced that, though they had survived, the service they had helped build for thirty years had been destroyed.

Despite some reforms in the Congressional system for controlling foreign affairs, such as the engagement of able staffs of experts to assist the Foreign Affairs and Foreign Relations Committees, grave defects in the domestic machinery for the conduct of diplomacy still survive. In addition to these bodies, other committees enjoy overlapping jurisdiction in many aspects of international affairs. Foreign Commerce regulates international communications matters; Banking and Currency supervises the Export-Import Bank. Trade agreements fall within the jurisdiction of the Ways and Means Committee. The Appropriations Committees of both Houses have a dominant voice in the running of all aspects of foreign relations.

Each of these committees jealously guards its prerogatives. When the Marshall Plan was debated no less than eight separate bodies of Congress held hearings and conferences and made amendments. At least two committees went overseas to investigate the needs of the countries to be helped, followed by dozens of other inspection tours to keep an eye on the plan's implementation.

These time-consuming hearings and deliberations impose a further handicap in the conduct of diplomacy dealing with events that require speedy action. In his Memoirs, President Truman indicates how the Greek Civil War was very nearly lost to the Communists because of the time needed to get the necessary Congressional action.

The first warning that the British, then on the verge of bankruptcy, would have to withdraw from Greece not later than April 1, 1946, was telephoned to the President by the State Department on Friday, February 21. Four days later Congressional leaders were notified that some sort of action would be essential. But it was not until seventy-five days later, that the House on May 9, finally approved the measure. Meantime the Communist guerrillas had almost succeeded in overthrowing the Greek government.

The slowness of Congressional action is further complicated by the tendency to legislate the actual conduct of diplomacy in detail. In most other parliamentary regimes, members of the Parliament will not hesitate to address themselves to matters of policy, but even in England an opposition member will thrust himself into the actual conduct of diplomacy only on the rarest of occasions and then with great diffidence. The American Congress suffers no such compunctions. Not only does it occasionally pass resolutions directly contrary to administration policies but sometimes, as in bills providing special aid to China and Spain, it passes legislation forcing diplomatic action on the administration. Furthermore, no detail is too small to provoke Congressional criticism, whether it be the cost of the secretary of state's scrapbasket or the length of the dining-room table of the U. S. ambassador to the UN.

The result is not merely that the diplomats' time and energy is wastefully dissipated but, far more important, that diplomacy's field of maneuver is restricted and its suppleness greatly reduced. Thus when in 1956 Poland's loosening of her Soviet ties was largely dependent on foreign credits to replace Moscow's, it took the American diplomats almost a year to overcome the legislative obstacles to providing relatively minor sums to help tide over the Polish needs.

Legislative restrictions over administrative practices likewise often seriously hamper effective conduct of diplomacy, for example, restrictions on employment practices. On the rare occasions when a Westerner defects to the Soviet Union, the Communist authorities lose no time in making full use of such talents as he may have to further their interests, usually in the propaganda field. In the United States, on the other hand, the most able and useful Soviet defectors cannot be put to regular use often for many years because of legislative obstacles based on security considerations of doubtful validity.

But perhaps the gravest danger to the successful conduct of diplomacy imposed by the constitutional division of control over foreign affairs arises from a much more basic characteristic of Congress. Subject to frequent re-elections, the congressman must be keenly sensitive to current public opinion and is subject to strong pressures to respond to gusts of indignation, alarm, or other largely emotional waves of anxiety about some aspect of foreign affairs.

Because of its recently increased influence in foreign affairs, owing to its powers over the purse and the high cost of alliances in the cold war, the reactions of Congress to these gusts often directly influence the conduct of diplomacy. Thus the efforts of diplomats to carry out long-range policies are constantly being deflected not only by Congressional legislation or the lack of it but often by mere expressions of transitory opinion sweeping through the halls of the Capitol.

It was due largely to the erratic, occasionally irresponsible actions of the ancient Greek assemblies that the city-states' diplomacy was ineffective and defensive collaboration against the Eastern aggressors impossible. Despite growing recognition by Congress and the public of the purposes, methods and needs of an effective diplomacy, so long as the consistent pursuit of long-range interests and aspirations is periodically sacrificed to passing whims inspired by fleeting emotions in Washington, the danger persists of a twentieth-century repetition of the Greek debacle.

VII

Methods and Mechanics: 1

BEFORE the advent of the international postal service, the cable and the radiotelephone, the maintenance of diplomatic relations between countries by way of embassies was an obvious necessity. But today, when you can mail a letter to 10 Downing Street and get it there in twenty-four hours, or send a wire from the nearest cable office, or even telephone the German chancellor, what is the need for overseas diplomatic establishments and what do they accomplish?

Secretary Cordell Hull once said he required four things of his ambassadors: to report what was going on; to represent the United States before foreign governments and publics; to negotiate United States government business; and to look after American lives and property.

One significant task often associated with diplomacy—that of making foreign policy—was intentionally omitted from Hull's description. This is the sole responsibility of the government in Washington. Many a diplomat, surveying the ruins of a policy that failed, has taken refuge in the fact, often overlooked, that his job is not to make policy but to carry it out.

The rotten eggs and refuse that greeted Vice-President Nixon in Peru and Venezuela were the obvious fruits of a policy gone bad, but American diplomats in South America were not to blame. For a decade they had warned Washington that its indifference to South America's economic growing pains was arousing dangerous hostility.

But the harassed officials of the State Department, overwhelmed by more spectacular crises in Europe and elsewhere and running as fast as they could from conference to conference, like Alice in Wonderland just trying to stay in the same place, had no time for these warnings until the Vice-President returned with egg all over his coat to stir them to action.

George Kennan, a former career diplomat, has suggested that diplomacy is the business of communicating between governments. An American embassy is in a very real sense a switchboard for messages between Washington and a foreign government. It is duplicated by another switchboard in the host's embassy in Washington. Normally when Washington wants to raise a subject with London it puts the call through our London Embassy, and vice versa. Once a subject is under discussion it usually keeps to the channel or embassy through which it was initially raised but can be shifted, or both embassies can be used as, for example, when Khrushchev's letters are delivered by the Soviet Embassy in Washington and the replies by the United States Embassy in Moscow.

There are, however, a number of different forms of diplomacy by which the government can communicate with foreign states other than through the embassy. It can send delegations to special conferences, which is known as conference diplomacy. It can send its secretary of state to deal personally with governments, which is known as personal diplomacy. Or the President himself can participate in summit diplomacy. Finally, it can through the United Nations make use of so-called parliamentary diplomacy.

Sir Harold Nicolson in his classic work *Diplomacy* suggests that there are also different styles of diplomacy which vary from country to country, depending not only on differences in national character but also on the traditional policies of the European states.

For example, England isolated on an island with great overseas possessions is traditionally reluctant to arouse the antagonism or jealousy of the Continental powers. Hence she seeks to compromise difficulties and prevent great power aggression not by guaranteeing the smaller powers but by cajoling the larger ones. The British diplomat, Nicolson says, is often insular and even ignorant of foreign psychology. He is optimistic and loath to face unpleasant facts. He is

fair and tolerant, reliable and precise, poised and gentle but courageous. "He never boasts; he knows that impatience is as dangerous as ill-temper and that intellectual brilliance is not a diplomatic quality."

Nicolson maintains that the "heroic or warrior" conception of diplomacy differentiates the German diplomat from the commercially minded English. The German, he says, is given to "sudden diplomacy" to demonstrate strength and cause anxiety abroad. He adds that, though many of Germany's diplomats have been highly skilled and professional, their sense of discipline, the intrigues of the General Staff, and the bureaucracy have never really given them a chance.

Turning to the French, Nicolson states that theoretically they should have produced better diplomats than they have in practice. Their passion for logic, their quick intelligence, and their great culture blind them to the reactions of other countries, make them impatient of others less quick, and often give offense to their less polished colleagues.

The Italians, for their part, favor a diplomacy based on incessant maneuver, the purpose of which is to put the other fellow in the wrong and thus extract some concession from him. They are constantly bargaining between potential allies and too often in the end choose the wrong side.

Nicolson does not venture to characterize American diplomacy. The professional American diplomatic service, he pleads, was still too new to develop its particular style when he first wrote his classic work in 1939.

I am inclined to doubt whether today one can distinguish different styles of diplomacy among the great powers. Since 1939 their position, power, and politics have radically altered their diplomacy. Even as late as the thirties my own experience provided little evidence of national diplomatic styles. I have known and worked with English diplomats who were slow and insular and pretended to be intellectuals and others who pretended to be stupid and were brilliant.

At one of my first posts I met a newly arrived junior British diplomat who was well over six feet, with long dangling limbs and an unkempt, straggling red mustache that drooped mournfully at the corners of his mouth. His only interest he confided was " 'gels'—you know, nice American gels." Only after several encounters did one begin to suspect that he was an accomplished diplomat, an expert on

local affairs, spoke several languages fluently, and possessed a witty, penetrating mind. His ostensible interest in American girls was completely overshadowed by a passionate interest in Central Asia. Today Sir Fitzroy Maclean is a prominent member of Parliament and the author of several brilliant books.

Though I have dealt with arrogant Germans, others who have risen to the top of their service today are gentle, self-effacing, and completely free of the "warrior" concept—for example, the German ambassador in London, "Jonny" von Herwarth. I have known Italians who could never desist from minor *combinazioni* and others whose lighthearted pranks are sometimes embarrassing.

The Italian ambassador and his American wife were one day having a drink in the garden of my house when a loud voice boomed from the balcony above, "Who the hell are all those damned wops?" Horrified, I looked up to find the Italian counselor of embassy waving nonchalantly to his ambassador. Today the counselor, Bartolomeo Migone, is ambassador to the Holy See. As for the coldly logical, intellectual French, those I have known best and admired most suffered from almost emotional idealism.

Whether national styles exist or not, there are certainly well-definable personal styles of diplomacy. There is, for example, the "cold fish" type who plays his cards so close to his chest that he can scarcely read them himself. Negotiation with him is liable to be sticky. There is the gruff-tough diplomat who, provided you insult him vigorously enough before he insults you, tends to be friendly and co-operative and is generally scrupulously honest. There is the shock diplomat who tells you precisely what he thinks and before you can take offense chokes a Martini down you with a charming grin. And finally there is the ego diplomat who is generally self-centered, sensitive, and highly subjective. After six months' service in the Paris Embassy he will harangue you endlessly about ego-French relations.

There is, I confess, one national style of diplomacy—the Soviet. It is the product not of national characteristics but of traditional Byzantine practices coupled with long service in a police state. The prototype is Vyacheslav Molotov, generally considered the most ill-mannered, humorless diplomat alive. He once treated me to a dressing down for a mistake of his own language one would not use to one's delinquent child, let alone someone else's. Only when I made it clear

that his name did not appear in the American channels of command did he desist.

Soviet diplomats are almost always withdrawn and in my entire career I got to know only two well. One was an uninhibited young secretary on his first assignment in London during World War II. He was affable, had a keen sense of humor, and immensely enjoyed the company of foreigners. He has since disappeared.

The other I had known before the war in Berlin where he was a young Tass "correspondent." Ostracized by the Germans and unable to speak any language but Russian, he and his pretty wife became my good friends, dropping in at my apartment at all hours to chat and listen to recordings of Gypsy music, then forbidden in Russia. When, as an important ambassador, he turned up years later at a post where I was serving, he made it brutally clear that any previous acquaintance was completely of the past. My earlier hospitalities were neither acknowledged nor returned. One could only feel sorry that his original charm and pleasant personality had, together with his good manners, been eradicated by the system he served.

The Soviet type is taciturn, unscrupulous, and icily humorless in negotiation. He seldom utters a word that is not quoted from either his instructions or a *Pravda* editorial and when he concedes a point it is only with the minimum of good grace. As Liudprand said of Nicepheros, "He is not the sort you would like to meet in the middle of the night." At social functions, if the political climate requires it, he can in an awkward sort of way be civil or even affable. But spontaneous good-fellowship is ordinarily liquidated at an early date in his career. Of sincerity he knows little and expects none from his colleagues.

These traits are not characteristic of the average Russian nor are they necessarily the hallmarks of the new Soviet Man. In my travels through Russia and in my frequent contacts with Soviet Army officers during and after the war, I often found the ordinary civilian or non-diplomatic official to be polite, hospitable, well-mannered, and friendly. During the 1946 Korean negotiations I once asked a colonel on the Soviet delegation to dinner with a member of the former Russian royal family, then on the American Red Cross staff in Seoul. When I introduced the colonel to *Mr.* Chavchavadze, the colonel bowed low and said, "I think you mean *Prince* Chavchavadze." Till far beyond

midnight the two Russians chatted and gossiped about old times and old court personalities. The colonel sighed and bewailed the sad fate the Bolsheviks had meted out to the Romanovs, like a genteel old aristocratic refugee gossiping over tea in his shabby Paris apartment.

It is mystifying why the Kremlin leaders have adopted diplomacy by invective and deliberately deprived themselves of the obvious advantages in diplomatic negotiations of their innate Slav charm. In part it derives perhaps from the xenophobic suspicion of their Byzantine inheritance. It may also be the result of a lack of confidence in their own diplomats when up against the crafty Western European— a state of mind the American government and public has occasionally showed. But it reminds me most of an old-fashioned American football coach instilling "fight" in his team before a game. The only difficulty is that in the diplomatic game there are no referees to guard against fouls.

A further characteristic of Soviet diplomatic style is the indifference of a Soviet diplomatic representative to the background of the country to which he is assigned—especially the United States. Although Communist party officials of the Central Committee level make a point of being fully informed about conditions abroad, the Soviet diplomat is sometimes astonishingly ignorant. The American neophyte diplomat, on the other hand, spends months before a Moscow assignment, at one of the dozen institutes on Soviet affairs in the United States. Soviet officials have told me there is no such institute in all the Soviet Union. Instead, they rely on the scant references in their religious literature of Marx and Lenin to the politics, economy, and culture of "bourgeois" lands. Though Stenka Razin is a familiar character to every American diplomat in Moscow I wonder how many Soviet diplomats in Washington know who Robert E. Lee was.

Recently there have been signs, such as the activities of Ambassador Menshikov in Washington, that a degree of affability is being permitted to the Kremlin's representatives abroad; and Anastas Mikoyan has publicly deplored the lack of serious American studies in the Soviet Union. Perhaps the fall from grace of their prototype Molotov presages the emergence of a new style of Soviet diplomat. If so, no one will welcome it more than the Western diplomats who have had to endure the boredom of incessant Soviet vituperation across the green

baize ever since the Bolshevik delegates turned up for their first negotiations with the Germans at Brest-Litovsk over forty years ago.

Since Greek times, learned and less learned men have been preparing books, brochures, and monographs about how a diplomat should
carry on negotiations. Homer had something to say about it in the
Odyssey. Demosthenes in *De Falsa Legatione* wrote an indignant
account of how not to conduct negotiations.

Frequently today young Foreign Service officers, having just completed their probationary service, succumb to an irresistible impulse
to submit guides for even younger diplomats to the editors of the
Foreign Service Journal. These recall the comment of General Marshall to a junior general of MacArthur's staff during the war. The
young general had come to Washington to explain and defend Mac-
Arthur's strategic proposals for the war in the Pacific and on finishing
his exposition remarked, "I will stake my military reputation on the
soundness of these plans." General Marshall leaned across the table.
"General," he asked acidly, "just what is your military reputation?"

Thus cautioned I shall confine myself to citing a few of the more
important counsels of long-established authorities. Callières, the acknowledged master, says the first rule for an ambassador preparing
for negotiations is to inform himself precisely of the state of affairs
in the country with which he is to negotiate: the personalities of the
leaders, the local factions and rivalries; the character, interests and
weaknesses of the negotiators he will be facing, and of course, the
precedents and national interests involved in the subject of negotiation. In Callières's day, the diplomat's immediate range of knowledge
could be confined to the royal court. But today it spreads far wider
to include every provincial interest, every class and professional
prejudice, and every political party of significance.

When Maxim Litvinov arrived in the United States in 1933 to
negotiate recognition of his country by the United States, there had
been no American diplomats in Russia since the Bolshevik Revolution.
Nevertheless, a small group of specialists in the State Department,
under Robert F. Kelley, had for years been assembling materials and
background for just this occasion and when the negotiations opened
Litvinov was faced with a complete catalogue of every concession the
Soviet Union had ever granted another state, to support American

demands for like concessions. Even Litvinov confessed he was impressed.

When ten years later Roosevelt journeyed to Tehran and then Yalta to negotiate with Stalin the State Department again provided him with volumes of reports, special studies, and maps on the problems to be discussed. Though there is no record that Roosevelt had any time to study them, it is reported that Harry Hopkins stumbled across these thick files and read them with interest and amazement.

An intimate knowledge of the psychological processes of your diplomatic adversary is invaluable, especially if he is more powerful than you. During the thirties Maxim Litvinov one day called in the Turkish ambassador and complained bitterly that a number of Soviet "tourists" had recently disappeared while traveling through the remote villages of Turkish Anatolia. The Turkish ambassador, Vassif Bey, knew that the "tourists" were in fact Soviet espionage agents and that Litvinov expected him to deny their disappearance, hoping to embroil Turkey in a diplomatic wrangle.

Instead, Vassif Bey assumed a most contrite air: "You know, Mr. Commissar, what you say is quite true. But unfortunately the backward villagers of Anatolia believe that all Soviet tourists have cloven hoofs and forked tails. Whenever they see one they are so curious to examine these phenomena that they undress him and when they discover it is not true they are so angry that they stuff the poor fellow in a bag and throw him into the sea." Litvinov knew when he had met his match and the matter of the tailless and hoofless Soviet "tourists" was dropped.

If an ambassador is to negotiate successfully he should make himself agreeable to the officials with whom he must deal. Callières tells of a colleague who made it a practice to lose at cards to the monarch to whose court he was assigned. "Many a great enterprise," Callières says, "was conducted to success by the little pile of gold coins which passed from him to his royal opponent at the gaming table."

Nowadays few ambassadors can afford such forms of flattery and must limit themselves to agreeable speeches and compliments. The modern version of losing at cards is to make frequent flattering references to the similarities between one's country and one's host's. When Ambassador Bullitt first went to Russia in 1934 he was hard put to

find pleasant comparisons between the two countries. America had fine cars; Russia had few. Russia had fine ballet; we had almost none. We enjoyed democracy, they a "dictatorship of the proletariat." But finally he hit upon a common passion: trotters. Because of the great distances and appalling roads that existed before the railroad and the automobile, both countries had developed the light trotting horse instead of the heavy coach horse for speedy transportation. Since then trotting racing had been great national sports in both countries. From then on few of the ambassador's little speeches failed to mention the Orlov Trotter or the Hambletonian.

In making oneself charming, Callières warns that one should be careful to avoid getting overcharmed oneself. Shortly before the war ended, the military mission which I headed in Yugoslavia was replaced by an embassy. Before I left I drove the newly appointed ambassador—an ex-businessman with little foreign experience—to the White Palace to meet Marshal Tito. Slightly uneasy because of his inexperience, I had made sure that no interpreter other than myself would be present.

On the drive to the palace, the new ambassador kept muttering: "They say Tito has charm but he won't charm me."

When we sat down, Tito was in good form and sprayed his charm as though from a perfume flagon. Scarcely ten minutes had elapsed before the ambassador was leaning forward, hanging on every word as the little Balkan Communist vented his usual complaints about how he was misunderstood in the United States.

"Why, do you know, Mr. Ambassador, your newspaper people have even called me a dictator!"

The ambassador shook his head perplexed as I translated. "Tell the Marshal," he said to me, "there is only one thing to be done— for Tito to go to Washington and explain his position as he has to me. I know my government will welcome him warmly."

Aware that the ambassador had no authority to invite Tito and that scarcely anyone at that tense moment would be less welcome in Washington, I paraphrased the ambassador's words, expressing the hope that someday, after he had turned over the reins of government, Tito might find it interesting to come to America and see how we dealt with our problems.

Unfortunately, however, Tito had been taking English lessons and

had made considerably more progress than I suspected. He looked at me, smiled, and wagged his finger: "Colonel, you know very well the ambassador said no such thing."

A week later, back in Washington, I encountered the chief of the Balkan Division in the gloomy halls of the old State Department. "What's been going on in Belgrade?" he growled, waving a piece of paper in my face. "The Yugoslav mission here has just handed us a message from Tito accepting an invitation to visit Washington." While the unfortunate division chief was seeking a way out of his dilemma, President Roosevelt died and the Yugoslavs were informed that under the circumstances the visit had better be postponed. Tito, according to reliable reports, is still awaiting a renewal of the invitation.

It is an old rule of diplomacy to approach one's goal gradually and step by step. To unfold one's grand design all at once, Callières warns, may frighten or overwhelm lesser and more timid minds. The diplomats who in 1950 launched the European Defense Community which was to unite Western European defenses in a single army might well have heeded the warning. Though the treaty was negotiated, signed, and ratified by most European states, it was too grand a design for the French, who balked at amalgamating their defenses with their centuries' old enemy, the Germans. Eventually it was replaced by the more gradual unification plan embodied in the less precipitate Western European Union but only after five precious years had been wasted.

At the outbreak of World War II my chief gave me a lesson in the tiny-steps-for-tiny-tots approach, though the design was far less grand. After the British declaration of war, a British vice-consul in Hamburg where I was stationed had been thrown into jail while awaiting repatriation, in retaliation for the arrest of a German consul in Glasgow. The American consul general, Wilbur Keblinger, had taken charge of British interests. He was an old Foreign Service officer, strongly pro-British and not particularly fond of the Germans. Collecting a few of the vice-consul's belongings and adding a few items from his own supplies, he turned them over to me with precise instructions about their delivery.

The director of the Hamburg prison was a polite, old retired officer who welcomed me graciously, no doubt haunted, as so many Germans

then were, by the fear that if the Americans were offended they might join the British against them. He had the British vice-consul brought from his cell and one by one I handed over the items: pajamas, shirts, socks, and a toilet kit. When I brought out a phial of sleeping pills the prison director objected that they were forbidden lest the prisoners kill themselves deliberately with an overdose. The peppery little vice-consul retorted angrily that it took more than a stinking German prison to get an Englishman down. Taken aback by this outburst the director handed him the pills.

I then produced a bottle of sherry, explaining that the vice-consul should have it served before his luncheon. The director said nothing but took the bottle submissively. Next I produced a bottle of champagne which, I said, should be brought in properly iced with the vice-consul's dinner. The director shifted uneasily but remained silent. Next came a bottle of gin, another of vermouth, and a cocktail shaker. This, I explained, was for the vice-consul's evening Martini. "Now, you take one part of vermouth," I began, turning to the director, "and four parts of gin, add plenty of ice—" But I had reached the end of my tiny steps.

"*Verdammt!*" the director exploded, "I am willing to serve sherry and champagne and even gin to this prisoner, but he can damn well mix his own Martinis."

When I reported back to the consul general he agreed that his grand design had been substantially accomplished.

Threats as a means of negotiation are not generally recommended by experienced diplomats. They "always do harm to negotiations," Callières maintains. In fact, he says, the stronger the state the gentler must be its diplomats. Power should speak for itself, for when it is vaunted it is liable to arouse resentment. The Byzantine school does not subscribe to this teaching and occasionally even Western diplomats are forced to disregard it.

The same Consul General Keblinger of Hamburg was a most mild-mannered man who scarcely raised a finger in his well-run office and never raised his voice. The outbreak of war had left hundreds of Americans stranded in Hamburg with accommodations on Hamburg-Amerika Line ships which could no longer sail because of the British blockade. The line offered to transfer the tickets to Scandinavian lines

still sailing from neutral Copenhagen, but the cautious Scandinavians refused to honor the tickets until they were reimbursed in gold. The German Finance Office, however, refused to transfer the necessary gold.

When I reported this to Keblinger, the old man rose from his desk, clamped a stiff black Homburg on his white head, took a strong black Malacca cane, and nodding to me set off up the street to the Finance Office. A pompous uniformed doorman complete with swastika on his arm stepped up to him as he entered, but the point of the stick caught him in the pit of his stomach and he fell back. As the consul general marched into the director's outer office, a young man in a black coat and striped trousers stepped forward bowing. He caught the stick across his chest. Storming into the director's office, Keblinger marched up to the desk and brought the stick down across it with such a bang that the inkpot jumped and the director fell back in his chair.

"If those funds aren't transferred while I wait here," Keblinger growled, "there's going to be real trouble!" The director began to object but the stick came down again and Keblinger repeated, "I want no talk, I want action!" The director picked up the phone and called his head office in Berlin pleading for authority to transfer the funds. Occasionally, as Berlin objected, the pleas became less forceful and Keblinger's stick hit the desk again. Eventually the director hung up and rang for his assistant: "Transfer the Hamburg-Amerika funds at once," he told him.

As we left the building the old consul general murmured softly half to himself, "I hate scenes!" Then he turned into the next pub and ordered a grog for each of us.

VIII

Methods and Mechanics: 2

GENERALLY speaking, there are two methods by which nations exchange benefits: reciprocity and most-favored-nation treatment. The first calls for an equivalent exchange, the second for treatment equal to the best given any other nation. The second method is generally favored when a government is not prepared to give up some general discrimination against foreign states. For example, before the reciprocal trade program, the United States granted tariff concessions on the most-favored-nation principle. The Soviet Union generally insists on most-favored-nation agreements in all matters because of its special restrictions against all foreign interests.

Whereas diplomatic rights are prescribed by international law, the exchange of diplomatic privileges is on the basis of reciprocity. For example, diplomatic officials of Country X in Washington are granted the same privileges as American diplomats in Country X. The Soviet rejection of this principle in diplomatic matters has led to frequent conflicts and to the reverse of the reciprocity coin—retaliation.

At the time the United States recognized the Soviet Union it was agreed that diplomats might import and re-export their personal effects without restrictions. Subsequently the Soviet Union demanded to inspect the baggage of departing diplomats to ensure they were not exporting contraband. Reluctantly the American Embassy consented to customs inspectors being present during the packing operations at the embassy.

During the late thirties the Soviet authorities announced that personal baggage would no longer be inspected during packing at the embassy but would have to be reopened for inspection at the customhouse. When a departing American diplomat, the embassy public health surgeon, called for an inspector to be present at the embassy while he packed none showed up. Balking at this new restriction, the ambassador told the unfortunate public health surgeon to postpone his departure.

Some weeks later after lengthy exchanges between the embassy and Washington, the Soviet Foreign Office complained that two Soviet ships were being delayed in transit through the Panama Canal. The embassy expressed polite regrets and suggested it might be due to a shortage of public health surgeons to administer quarantine regulations in the Canal Zone. When told this the Foreign Office official nodded knowingly and a day or two later a customs inspector turned up to watch the public health surgeon pack. Subsequently the Foreign Office reported that its two ships had cleared the canal, and everyone apparently was happy.

This form of reciprocity or retaliation is a dangerous diplomatic maneuver which experienced diplomats are loath to employ. One disadvantage in using it with the Soviets is that their system is better adapted to raising the ante than are other less authoritarian forms of government.

A few months before the Germans attacked the Soviet Union in 1941, the Kremlin imposed severe travel restrictions on all foreign diplomats, requiring prior consent of the police before they might go beyond certain limits around Moscow. The American Embassy immediately applied for permission for several of the staff to travel to Tolstoi's home near Tula, a well-known sightseeing attraction. Permission was refused. Some days later the Foreign Office complained that it had word from its ambassador in Washington, Oumansky, that he had been forbidden to leave the capital without permission and that permission had been refused for him to go to New York. The embassy expressed its condolences for this sad state of affairs, the more poignant because Oumansky's mistress was believed to live in New York. At the same time it asked about the permit for Tula. It had not yet been granted and indeed never was.

The restrictions remained in force until after the Soviet Union and

the United States were allied in the war. Then the bans were lifted, but as soon as the war was over they were reimposed. In retaliation, Soviet officials were forbidden to travel in certain specified areas in the United States.

Restrictions on foreigners in the Soviet Union have never been revealed to the Soviet public. Traveling by air from Central Asia to Moscow in 1956, a Soviet traveler showed me an item in *Pravda* stating that a Russian writer had been forbidden to visit the home state of Eugene O'Neill.

"Why?" he asked indignantly.

"In retaliation for the Soviet rules which prevent me from visiting Alma-Ata," I replied.

"There are no such restrictions," the man answered, and to prove it summoned an airline official also in the plane who offered to sell me a ticket to any Central Asian town I wanted to visit. Since we were nearing Moscow, the offer was well timed. A violent discussion ensued, participated in by most of the passengers in the plane, until at last the pilot came back from the cockpit to complain that we were rocking his ship. But before the argument ended it had become all too clear how easy it is to be maneuvered by retaliatory actions into a position which appears to be not only contrary to Western concepts of freedom but downright unreasonable and childish—at least to world opinion. The Soviets, indifferent to public opinion, suffer from no such limitations in the game of retaliation.

Callières cautions that a diplomat must have "an equable humor, a tranquil and patient nature." He cites as an example Cardinal Mazarin on a mission to the Duke of Feria, then governor of Milan, to learn the latter's real intentions on a certain matter. "Mazarin had the cunning to inflame the duke's anger and thus to discover what he would never have known if the duke himself had held a wise hold over his feelings."

Nicolson states: "The occasions on which diplomatists have lost their tempers are remembered with horror by generations of their successors."

Particularly today when dealing with Byzantine diplomacy the ability to keep one's temper is the most difficult but valuable attribute of a negotiator. Vyacheslav Molotov is undoubtedly the greatest modern practitioner of the art of goat-getting. Among his victims

he can count the otherwise imperturbable General George Marshall, who was once goaded by Molotov beyond even his almost limitless imperturbability at a council of foreign ministers in London in 1947. Having listened to a particularly vituperative and insulting speech by Molotov, Marshall rose from his chair. "The remarks of the Soviet foreign minister," he said austerely, "do not enhance the reputation of the government he represents." Then he stalked out of the conference room never to return.

Patience during interminable, tedious negotiations is no less important than temper control. The records of the wartime and postwar allied conferences are replete with instances in which the weightiest questions were settled by hasty compromises in order to permit the delegates to return home for urgent appointments.

"The day you Americans are as patient as the Russians," the wise old Socialist, Kurt Schumacher, once told me, "you will stop losing the cold war. And the day you learn to outsit them by a single minute you will start winning it."

An unhappy instance of American impatience occurred at the Potsdam Conference. The American commissioner on the Reparations Commission was a Texas oil magnate. In the last hectic hours of the conference the Russians managed to slip a clause into the reparations agreement whereby certain Austrian properties were included under the heading of German assets from which the Russians might draw reparations.

When the commissioner was subsequently asked about this slip, he replied a little apologetically: "We seem to have overlooked that point in our hurry to wind up and go home."

For years the United States watched in bitter acquiescence while the Russians extracted millions in tribute from the Austrians, because of our commissioner's impatience to "wind up and go home."

Fortunately not all American delegates have shown impatience. It was due largely to the infinitely patient work of Ambassador Llewellyn E. Thompson in Vienna that Austria finally won her independence.

Thompson needed even more patience during the highly secret negotiations to settle the conflicting postwar claims of Italy and Yugoslavia to Trieste. London was chosen for the negotiations, as it seemed the place least likely to arouse the suspicions of the press. The day after his youngest child was born, Thompson was ordered there

for what was believed would be a brief conference of a few weeks. To explain away his presence Thompson told the few acquaintances he could not avoid that he was in London to buy some clothes. By the time the issue was successfully settled Thompson's fictitious wardrobe had assumed almost incredible proportions and his youngest daughter was eight months old. Later Thompson attributed the success of the conference largely to the fact that in its early phases at least the Italian and Yugoslav press did not have an inkling that the inflammable Trieste issue was even under discussion.

When in 1946 a Soviet delegation turned up in Seoul to negotiate with the Americans on Korean independence, the first question they asked was "How long are you Americans prepared to negotiate?"

The chief American delegate was Major General Archibald Arnold, a famous West Point football star, a distinguished combat soldier but without previous diplomatic experience. Arnold, however, had immense common sense and unlimited patience. In answer to the Russian's question he said unhesitatingly:

"Till hell freezes over." The Soviet delegates exchanged glances that were not particularly happy.

Within a few days it became apparent to the American delegates that the Soviets would permit Korean reunification and independence only under a "dictatorship of the proletariat" chosen in an election from which all but Communists and fellow travelers would be excluded as "Fascists." The Soviet delegates were wise enough to camouflage their instructions so as not to antagonize the Korean public, chafing under division and occupation. The Americans' problem therefore was to force them to reveal their real intentions before the conference stenographer so that when published the record would leave no doubt about Soviet aims.

At this point General Arnold recalled the tactics of Molotov. With infinite politeness he thrust a long delicate verbal needle into his adversary's flank and immediately drew blood. The Soviet chief delegate, General T. Shtikov (he refused to divulge his first name on security grounds), was a roly-poly little man of no great intelligence. (We later learned that the T. stood for Terentii. As this is written Shtigov has just been appointed Soviet ambassador to Hungary.) For several sessions Arnold drove his needles. As Shtikov's temper flared, he blurted out indiscretions. Beside him, tugging frantically

but vainly at his chief's tunic, was his diplomatic adviser, Simyon Tsarapkin, then on the threshold of a spectacular diplomatic career as a leading exponent of the rough-and-tumble Soviet school.

At last, goaded beyond endurance, Shtikov railed that in his government's view the Koreans were too primitive to be worthy of a free democratic government and that until they had grown up politically they needed an authoritarian regime over them. As he shouted, Arnold sat impassive, listening attentively and occasionally nodding approval.

"Well, General," Shtikov wound up in a purple passion, "what has the U. S. delegation to say to that?"

"Nothing," Arnold answered.

"Oh, yes, it has," Shtikov bellowed furiously. "I saw that note your staff passed to you. What does it say?"

"Must you know?" Arnold asked gently, and read from the note. "It says the delegates think you're sore enough for today." He paused for the interpreter to translate and then added softly, "Shall we adjourn?"

This time it was the Russians who a few days later wound up and went home. When they returned four years later it was with their armies.

The negotiations in Seoul illustrate an important innovation in diplomatic negotiation that has developed since the days of Metternich. It derives from the immense role played by public opinion even in the most secret negotiations. The negotiator must always be aware that whatever the outcome of a negotiation, whether it end in agreement or not, it will be subjected to the closest scrutiny in the press and in parliaments and by public opinion. Since he can never be certain, particularly in dealing with the Byzantine school, when or if the talks will end or whether the adversary will leak what is transpiring to the public, he must constantly take care to keep the record straight so that if revealed at any stage it will justify his position in the public eye. This innovation has made the tasks of the Metternichs of today infinitely more difficult than those of their predecessors.

The mechanics of normal negotiations have not changed greatly since the days of Callières nor do they differ basically from the mechanics of business negotiations though they are somewhat more formalized, even stylized. Normal diplomacy, as distinguished from

personal, conference or parliamentary diplomacy, can be carried out either by correspondence or orally or by a combination of both methods.

Correspondence between an embassy and a Foreign Office is of three types. The most official and formal is the *Note* addressed to the foreign minister and signed by the ambassador. Ordinarily it is in the first person though on the most formal occasions it can be in the third person.

The second category is the *Note Verbal,* which is addressed to the Foreign Ministry by the embassy, is never signed and is invariably in the third person. In American practice it usually begins: "The Embassy of the United States of America presents its compliments and has the honor to . . ."

The third category is the *Memoir* or *Aide-Mémoire.* It never bears a signature and is used chiefly to record certain facts already known to the recipient or to record statements already made orally.

Ordinary personal or private letters are permitted by diplomatic practice and may therefore be considered a fourth category. However, they are seldom used for the transaction of official business and are generally confined to thanking the foreign minister for a pleasant pheasant shoot, enclosing some rare stamps for his Majesty's private collection, or some similar personal matter.

Occasionally the embassies of several governments band together to sign a single communication to a foreign government, known as a *Collective Note.* Since this collusion is considered tantamount to bullying, it is rarely resorted to except when victorious allies are dictating to a defeated adversary, as for example when the Entente powers notified Vienna and Budapest after World War I that the Austro-Hungarian Empire had been liquidated. (Subsequently many statesmen and historians regretted that even this Collective Note had ever been dispatched.)

More frequently, several governments will collaborate in sending separate but practically identical communications to a single recipient. These are known as *Identic Notes* and, though somewhat less offensive than the Collective Note, nevertheless carry a connotation of ganging up.

Parallel Notes are the same as Identic Notes except that the wording may differ though not the basic reasoning. During World War II when the Western Allies sent very similar notes to Stalin he often

took offense on the ground that they were too parallel. His successors, however, have grown more accustomed to Western collaboration in facing up to Soviet offensives and no longer exhibit undue resentment at a certain degree of parallelism.

Notes, Notes Verbal, or Aide-Mémoires are never sent by mail. Routine messages are dispatched by embassy messengers who carry with them books in which the notes are registered and which the recipient's mail clerks sign for their receipt. Slightly more important notes are carried by an embassy secretary, a diplomatic official, and delivered in person to an official of equivalent rank in the Foreign Office. The most important communications are delivered in person by the ambassador to the foreign minister.

One frequently reads in the press that a diplomatic note has been "rejected" by a foreign government. The chances are that the report is incorrect and that the foreign government has merely rejected the arguments or allegations in the note.

In diplomatic practice to reject a note means to refuse its receipt or to return it physically to the sender after reading it. A true rejection is therefore a serious and somewhat rare slap. A celebrated contemporary example of a note's rejection was when Stalin sent an offensively worded telegram to Churchill complaining that a British convoy had failed to protect adequately certain shipments through the Arctic Ocean. Churchill promptly summoned the Soviet ambassador in London and handed the telegram back to him in an envelope. Ambassador Gusev, fearful of Stalin's wrath, complained he was under orders to deliver the message.

"But I am not prepared to receive it," Churchill replied austerely and indicated that the interview was over.

A more recent case occurred in 1959 when President Eisenhower refused to accept one of Khrushchev's more offensive letters concerning Quemoy.

Occasionally officials "reject" even oral communications but this is somewhat more difficult and less convincing. During the postwar negotiations for the joint occupation of Vienna, the American commander, General Mark Clark, became impatient with Soviet dilatory tactics and told his deputy, General Alfred M. Gruenther, to inform the Soviet High Command that unless they responded to his demands within twenty-four hours he would ask the White House to protest to the

Kremlin. Gruenther was in Salzburg, and since I was the only person then in Vienna who was familiar with the negotiations, I was ordered to deliver the message orally to Deputy Soviet Commander in Chief Zheltov.

The difficulty was that I was a lieutenant colonel and Zheltov was a colonel general. However, I managed to get into his office and after delivering a most military salute, repeated the message verbatim. Zheltov, as might have been expected, fissioned. His six-foot-six, 300-pound body rose like a mushroom cloud from his chair and hurtled about his big office for several seconds before he regained control over himself.

Slapping a pad and pencil before me he demanded that I write the message, in order, no doubt, to hand it back to me. I reiterated my instructions to deliver the message orally. Zheltov asked if American lieutenant colonels did not take orders from colonel generals. I replied meekly that I did when they were delivered through proper channels. After more vituperation, during which Zheltov said he refused to accept the message and I pointed out that it had been delivered, the irate general turned his back and indicated, with considerably less dignity or austerity than Churchill would have, that the interview was ended. I delivered myself of an even grander military salute and departed, infinitely grateful for the American uniform that had protected me from Siberia or some other fate worse than death.

The episode was, of course, a breach of diplomatic etiquette since diplomats are supposed to deal only with opposite numbers. However, we were all playing soldier in those days: Zheltov was a senior member of the Communist Central Committee and I was on temporary loan from the State Department.

Cautious or timid ambassadors prefer to conduct negotiations in writing to avoid misunderstandings or misinterpretations. However, the ablest diplomats have always preferred oral negotiations, which Callières himself recommended. Oral negotiation is not only speedier but is more flexible in finding solutions to conflicts of interest. Besides, an able diplomat can generally read more from the changes of expression in his colleague's face than a dozen formal notes would convey. Dwight Morrow, the American ambassador in Mexico during the oil disputes in the twenties, conducted practically all his negotiations orally and with great success.

DIPLOMAT

Occasionally a procedure known as *Mixed Relations* is adopted as a compromise between written and oral negotiations. This means that after the two sides have discussed a matter each will submit a written brief of its position. After a particularly intricate matter has been discussed orally, a cautious diplomat will make a memorandum of what was stated and submit it for verification to his opposite before reporting the conversation to his own Foreign Office.

Back in 1848 a British ambassador in Paris, after considerable wrangling, wrung a concession from French Foreign Minister Guizot and, without submitting to the latter a memorandum of the understanding for verification, notified his Foreign Office. Subsequently the French welshed on the agreement and when Guizot was reproached he argued that no agreement made orally was binding until committed to writing and submitted for verification. A recent example was the so-called Gentleman's Agreement on the occupation of Berlin between the Soviet and American High Commands. Subsequently the Soviet authorities, following Guizot's precedent, repudiated parts of the agreement, which led to the Berlin Blockade.

Before World War I the diplomatic language was French and every diplomat of every state was expected to be fluent in that language. In fact, the czarist Foreign Office carried on most of its communications with its own ambassadors in French. Since then, however, English has largely superseded French in most parts of the world. Furthermore, as a result of rising nationalism, most countries including the Soviet Union demand that all conversations, treaties, and agreements be in their own language as well as in that of the other party to the agreement.

Because of the absence of any formally recognized diplomatic language today, the use of interpreters has greatly increased. Interpreters serve a dual purpose of translating and acting as witnesses for what has been said. For example, Charles E. Bohlen, though fluent in Russion and frequently an interpreter for President Roosevelt during the war, when he became ambassador in Moscow invariably took a translator along with him to the Foreign Office or the Kremlin simply to record and witness what transpired.

Occasionally negotiators augment their staffs at a negotiation as psychological supporters like the rooters at a football game to overawe their opponents. In my first encounter with Simyon Tsarapkin

in Korea he appeared in the conference room flanked by a dozen aides whom he called assistants, experts, and translators. Confident that English would not become a dead language if we carried on in Russian, I suggested we dispense with interpreters for the sake of speed. Tsarapkin agreed to Russian but not to dismissing his interpreters and assistants. When after our first session I reported to my chief, a general, he promised to take care of the situation. On my return to the conference room I found a score of American officers flanking me at the table. When Tsarapkin asked who they were they replied that they were simply assistants, experts, and translators. After that Tsarapkin cut down his cheering section to a single assistant.

My little initial triumphs, however, proved my subsequent undoing. Some days later we agreed to exchange simultaneously estimates of the political strength of the various factions of North and South Korea. The simultaneous exchange was important lest one side, having seen the other's estimate, pad his own to compensate for it. When I appeared somewhat tardily with my estimate, I asked Tsarapkin if he had prepared his. He replied that his had been ready for some days and patted his briefcase in confirmation. I passed him my estimate and after he had read it asked for his.

"I left it at home," he said nonchalantly. Furious, I reproached him with being a damned liar but he simply laughed.

"I never said I had the paper with me, did I?" he said, turning to the single other witness—his own interpreter. From then on I never faced Tsarapkin without at least one witness.

The task of interpreting is not an easy one even for those thoroughly fluent in both languages. It frequently occurs that, unless the interpreter is fully familiar with the intricacies and nuances of the subject under discussion, a single slight misstep in interpreting will send the negotiators off on opposite tangents, arguing about entirely different points. Furthermore, if the principal negotiator is wordy or at all imprecise, it is difficult for the interpreter to translate his imprecisions accurately. Often negotiators unfamiliar with interpreted exchanges will resort to untranslatable slang or expressions utterly meaningless to the other side.

Once when I was translating for General Clark and Marshal Koniev in Vienna, Clark became annoyed with Soviet procrastinations and said angrily that unless they started playing ball no one would get to

first base. Switching to a metaphor more familiar to the Russians, I said that unless we started playing soccer no goals would be scored. Whereupon Koniev retorted innocently and his interpreter translated literally, that Clark should try kicking the ball. Incensed at having his baseball skill or his sportsmanship impugned, Clark exploded before I could explain away the misunderstanding.

Finally, when all ruses have been thwarted, misunderstandings cleared up, differences compromised, and mutual benefits weighed and exchanged, a treaty or agreement may be prepared for signature. However, in this age of nationalism each side will insist on having an original in its own language. Hence the interpreters must go to work once more and "agree" the texts in the languages involved.

The negotiation of the preliminary agreement for the joint occupation of Vienna by French, British, Russians, and Americans commenced one early morning in the outskirts of the Austrian capital and continued, with a single break for dinner, until two or three o'clock the following morning. By then three of the interpreters had collapsed, exhausted. However, a farsighted American medical officer had kept me supplied with Benzedrine until the last item was settled. Thereupon the Russian General presiding proposed: "It is time for the generals to sleep. The apparatus will have the documents ready for signature at dawn."

Half dead with exhaustion, I translated into English and French but then I added, "General, I don't mind working the rest of the night, but must you refer to me as an apparatus?" The general smiled, and amended his proposal: "The generals will sleep and the colonel will prepare the documents."

I roused my interpreter colleagues and hastily we edited, corrected, and agreed the texts. But the job was only half over. Nowadays every government insists that it not only have the treaty in its own language as well as the other languages employed but that each copy be signed first by its own representative. And no carbon copies! For several more hours a battery of stenographers sweated over their machines while the translators proofread twelve original copies of the agreement. This signature procedure is known as the principle of the *Alternat* by diplomats. Interpreters and stenographers have another word for it.

IX

Methods and Mechanics: 3

HERETOFORE I have discussed the techniques and mechanics of "normal" diplomacy. Perhaps the description is misleading. Before World War I international relations were normally carried on through ambassadors and embassies. Even multilateral agreements were negotiated by ambassadors of several countries and the host Foreign Office. Only rarely were great conferences like that of Vienna convened to settle world-wide issues. But beginning with World War I a new form of negotiation which might be called conference diplomacy gradually usurped many of the normal functions of established diplomatic channels.

The term "conference diplomacy" has been used by many authorities to include personal diplomacy or direct negotiations between chiefs of state, prime ministers, or foreign ministers. While personal and conference diplomacy have a common origin in the period of World War I and immediately thereafter, they should, I believe, be carefully distinguished.

Conference diplomacy is the procedure whereby special delegations, usually headed by special chief delegates, foregather to settle special problems. They may meet in a great capital, in which case the embassies are drawn into the procedure but usually only in a housekeeping capacity. The delegations are normally self-contained and independent of the embassy staff including the ambassador. Frequently conferences are held in small resort towns where the agreeable atmosphere is

deemed to have a mellowing effect on the negotiators and where the de luxe hotels can provide the sumptuous accommodations to which diplomats are supposed to be accustomed but seldom are.

Conference diplomacy owes its growth chiefly to the increasingly technical character of international relations. During World War I such technical problems as the financing of war purchases, the furnishing of shipping, and the collection and distribution of foodstuffs required the participation of specialists in these fields in international negotiations. International committees and boards of experts were established which negotiated these problems almost continuously. After the war the problems did not vanish but indeed became even more complex.

With World War II the need for international conferences became even more urgent and after the war, although the United Nations took over many technical functions, they mushroomed to the point where today scarcely a week passes without the convening of an international conference on any subject from child welfare to the standardization of the inch.

It is often argued that these conferences should be left in the hands exclusively of specialists and that old-fashioned diplomacy and diplomats are only a hindrance to them. Since, it is argued, the true scientists the world over are equally dedicated to the same goals, their discussions should not be hampered by diplomatic or political influences.

However, national interests, particularly national security, are often deeply involved and their negotiation in conferences requires the application of a different specialty than that which the physicist, geologist, or chemist has been trained for, namely, diplomacy.

In 1958 a conference was convened in Geneva to investigate methods of detecting nuclear explosions. It was billed as a purely scientific exploration from which all political considerations were to be resolutely excluded. When the Soviet delegation stepped from its plane it was headed by a shaggy-haired little man with an unprepossessing manner and a crooked smile. You could have searched in vain for his name in every register of Soviet scientific institutions. No American scientist had ever read one of his papers or heard him address a scientific gathering. But he was well known to many American diplomats as one of the Kremlin's toughest negotiators. The reader too will already be familiar with the name of Simyon Tsarapkin.

Conference diplomacy is even more formal and hence less productive than normal diplomacy carried on informally in some dim chancellery office. In the first place, if it is of any international importance, it is "covered" by the big newspapers, picture services, and wire agencies. To handle the press every delegation has a press or briefing officer or both whose duty it is to publicize as much as possible of the proceedings, even though these are held in so-called closed sessions. One of the press officer's first duties is to hold a preliminary briefing at which the aims of his delegation are explained, thus freezing its bargaining position before the sessions even begin.

The first formal session is generally attended by the flash of photographers' bulbs, the whirring of cameras, and the scribbling of reporters. Each chief delegate makes a formal statement hinting at the aims he hopes to achieve, thus solidifying his position still further and making profitable compromise even more difficult.

The press is then ejected and retires to the nearest bar to exchange rumors until the first closed session is over and the various briefing officers hold press conferences to publicize their delegations' initial triumphs and the unreasonableness of the other delegations' positions.

The first closed session begins with a discussion of the agenda—the subjects to be treated and the order in which they will be discussed. When both Western and Byzantine diplomacy is represented, this inevitably leads to a struggle as each side attempts to arrange the discussion so that its point of view is best presented. Ordinarily this means that the subjects in which each negotiator is seeking concessions be discussed first and those of the opponent last.

In 1951 the Palais Rose conference in Paris was called only to arrange an agenda for another conference of foreign ministers. After scores of meetings the conference broke up in disagreement.

The sessions themselves consist chiefly of statements, often interminably long, defining the position of each delegation, which any skilled diplomat present should have known before the conference opened. The statements are interspersed with proposals making cautious concessions designed to approach the delegation's minimum position as slowly as possible. If the delegation, as occasionally happens, has no concessions to make it simply repeats its original position in different language day after day. On the other hand, if the various delegations are seriously interested in compromise, the speeches are

reduced, the concessions move further and are introduced at shorter intervals until compromise has been achieved.

The proceedings are usually parliamentary and protocol is observed in inverse proportion to the diplomatic professionalism of the participants. Those who have attended a formal meeting of a journalists' association will have noted the interminable parliamentary formalities and rigid protocol over the most trivial questions inspired by the suppressed longing of the journalists to act like diplomats. (The diplomat frequently expresses his suppressed longing to act like a correspondent in the journalistic jargon of his telegrams.)

Every newspaper reader will recognize the formulas with which varying degrees of success are announced at the end of a conference. "Full agreement" but no published agreements means doubtful; "substantial agreement" means disagreement in at least some important fields; "full exchange of views resulted" means no agreement at all.

If unfriendly powers announce "full agreement," it may mean substantial success. No success is generally signaled by unilateral announcements that the conference adjourned *sine die,* meaning that the participants could not even agree on how to disagree.

Older diplomats generally deplore the rise of conference diplomacy because of its cumbersomeness and the obstacles to beneficial compromises that it creates. However, the continued advance of technology into the international field, the complexity of problems requiring specialists, and the increasing need for multilateral rather than bilateral agreements point to an ever-increasing reliance on conference diplomacy.

Personal diplomacy I have already defined as the participation in active negotiation of chiefs of state, prime ministers, or foreign ministers. Professional diplomats throughout the ages have frowned on this method of negotiation, principally because a sovereign or his immediate ministers cannot concede the adjustments and compromises necessary to successful negotiation without damaging their personal positions. An experienced fifteenth-century diplomat, Philippe de Comines, once said: "Two great princes who wish to establish good personal relations should never meet each other face to face but ought to communicate through good and wise ambassadors."

There are, of course, some advantages to personal diplomacy. A foreign minister can, especially in the age of jet planes, fly to a trouble

spot and, by using his prestige and authority, settle in a few hours problems that an ambassador following written instructions might take weeks to accomplish. By getting to know other foreign ministers personally and subsequently cultivating this friendship by personal correspondence, he can create a friendly atmosphere for the settlement of disputes and the prevention of misunderstandings.

There are, nevertheless, disadvantages to the practice. Sir Harold Nicolson, after returning disillusioned from the Versailles Conference, where his erstwhile hero, Woodrow Wilson, had by his presence revived personal diplomacy, had the following to say about the practice:

Nothing could be more fatal than the habit (the at present fatal and pernicious habit) of personal contact between the statesmen of the world. It is argued, in defense of this pastime, that the foreign secretaries of the nations "get to know each other." This is an extremely dangerous cognisance. Personal contact breeds, inevitably, personal acquaintance and that, in its turn, leads in many cases to friendliness: there is nothing more damaging to precision in international relations than friendliness between contracting parties. Locarno, not to mention Thoiry, should have convinced us of the desirability of keeping our statesmen segregated, immune and mutually detached. This is no mere paradox. Diplomacy is the art of negotiating *documents* in a ratifiable and therefore dependable form. It is by no means the art of conversation. The affability inseparable from any conversation between Foreign Ministers produces allusiveness, compromises, and high intentions.

Twenty years later he had not revised his views:

Repeated personal visits [he wrote in 1939] on the part of the Foreign Secretary of one country to the Foreign Secretary of the other should not be encouraged. Such visits arouse public expectation, lead to misunderstandings and create confusion. The time at the disposal of these visitors is not always sufficient to allow for patience and calm deliberation. The honors which are paid to a minister in a foreign capital may tire his physique, excite his vanity or bewilder his judgment. His desire not to offend his host may lead him with lamentable results to avoid raising unpalatable questions or to be imprecise regarding acute points of controversy.

There are other drawbacks to personal diplomacy. Personal acquaintance does not always lead to friendship but occasionally to quite the

opposite, and unfriendliness is no more conducive to successful diplomatic negotiation than excessive friendship.

When a foreign minister is absent from his capital, the decision-making process of his department must inevitably be impaired. Subordinates handling urgent matters in other areas of the globe must await the return of the chief to obtain his direction and counsel.

In the brief period a foreign minister can afford to devote to a single problem today there is scarcely time during his journey and necessarily brief visit to absorb either the facts or the essential atmosphere surrounding the problems to be negotiated—the personalities of the government and the opposition, the state of public opinion, and the local prejudices and aspirations of the country. He is therefore forced to rely largely on first impressions or the impressions of others acquired secondhand to guide him through the maze confronting him.

Finally, when the normal channels of diplomatic intercourse are for extended periods replaced by personal contacts between foreign ministers they tend inevitably to atrophy, leaving a dangerous vacuum in the machinery of foreign relations when the foreign minister, in whose person the contacts reside, is no longer in office.

It is not suggested that chiefs of state or their foreign ministers should never participate in negotiations. On rare occasions their presence at a major peace conference or settlement may be unavoidable. In such an event, with adequate deputies to make routine decisions at home, plenty of time to immerse themselves thoroughly in the problems to be negotiated, and no pressing engagements to harry them into hasty decisions or compromises, a personal conference or even its ultimate form, the summit conference, may prove profitable. The professional diplomat would stress, however, that such occasions are the exception and not the rule.

The League of Nations, and to an even greater extent the United Nations, has given birth to still another form of negotiation which has been called parliamentary diplomacy.

It would be superfluous both to the reader and to my theme to outline here even in the most summary form the machinery of the United Nations with its Security Council and its veto, the Assembly and its voting procedures, the Secretariat which provides the permanent machinery for many of the international conferences I have already described, and finally the subordinate international agencies with their

intriguing initials like WHO. There are, however, two features of the United Nations that have contributed something new and different to the diplomatic process. On the one hand, it has for the first time provided a neutral ground, complete with bars and lounges with comfortable overstuffed chairs, where diplomats representing most of the countries of the world are permanently available and where, protected from the prying eyes of the press by their very numbers, envoys can meet and exchange information as inconspicuously as housewives gossiping in the market place.

Here, too, occasional hints can be dropped or ideas discussed between representatives of different governments without the risk of sensational reactions or reverberations. It was, for example, in the lounge of the UN that Ambassador Philip Jessup dropped the first tiny suggestion to the Soviet ambassador that eventually led to the lifting of the Berlin Blockade.

The Council and the Assembly have added another dimension to diplomacy, namely, sound. The subdued murmur of diplomats' well-modulated French-speaking voices in the thick carpeted, high-ceilinged chancelleries of old has been replaced by the podium bristling with microphones, the acoustically designed hall, and the simultaneous translating system—all to assure that not a single snarl or gnash of teeth will be missed by world opinion. And lest a tear or a scowl go unseen, television cameras are constantly on the alert.

Here representatives of aggrieved nations can voice their complaints with the assurance that at least they will be heard at home, carried thither if not by the commercial news and wire services at any rate by the United Nations' own radio service. In a sense this is the ultimate in democratic diplomacy, putting to shame the ancient Greek ambassadors orating before their public assemblies.

"Forensic ability," Nicolson grumbles, "has again resumed its clumsy place among the arts of negotiation." As the delegates listen to the interminable speeches translated into a half dozen languages by the amazing but imprecise simultaneous translating system they are tempted to repeat the withering reply of the Spartans after hearing the ambassadors from Samos:

"We have forgotten the beginning of your harangue; we paid no heed to the middle of it, and nothing has given us pleasure in it but the end."

DIPLOMAT

The chief reason for the United Nations' becoming a debating society is, of course, the Soviet practice of appealing to public opinion over the heads of governments. Another result of this practice has been the debasement of the very language of diplomacy. Two generations ago if one government told another through its diplomats that "it failed to understand" the other's attitude observers would have considered the two on the brink of war. Today, due to the Soviet development of diplomatic invective, to call another government a liar has become standard operating procedure.

In addition to histrionics, the United Nations has added to diplomacy the oddly incongruous innovation of the vote, lobbying for which has become the major preoccupation of the diplomats at the UN. In a recent Senate appropriation hearing, Ambassador Henry Cabot Lodge, head of the United States delegation to the UN, pleaded for a dining-room table with forty seats because "that is where I try to line up the votes. Under United Nations rules, an important question must receive a two-thirds vote," he went on to explain to the senators, "and you know how hard that is.

"If you get a man up and give him a good dinner and get him into a good frame of mind, you can get a good deal more done," the ambassador added. Metternich might have applauded the techniques but he would certainly have deplored diplomacy by ballot.

"It's not diplomacy at all," said a former Italian ambassador to the UN to me recently, "it's just plain lobbying—and worse! Some African delegate proposes a resolution condemning colonies," he went on indignantly, "and how do England, France, and Portugal with all their colonies vote?—'Yes!' It's not hypocrisy, it's blackmail!"

Based on the double fiction that world opinion is sovereign, or at least wields a sanction, and that all states are equal, the UN's parliamentary diplomacy somehow lacks the quality of reality.

"It reminds me of slow-motion underwater ballet," an American diplomat commented to me after listening to a Security Council debate. "One can marvel at their ability to do without fresh air, but is it art?"

The answer is that it is a form of diplomacy no matter how odd. However, until world opinion acquires considerably greater sanctions, the parliamentary diplomacy of the UN must remain a distinctly secondary method of conducting foreign relations.

X

The Chancellery

MOST foreigners, including the British, would never dream of approaching their embassy unless they were international bankers who had just been swindled out of at least a million dollars by a foreign government or had roomed with the ambassador at Eton.

Americans, on the contrary, consider "their" embassy a combination complaint counter, loan office, and free cocktail lounge. If your hotel reservation was fouled up, the cover charge at the nightclub was too high, a policeman was surly or it's the Fourth of July, just drop in and see the ambassador.

Hugh Gibson, a well-known wit among professional American diplomats, once wrote to a friend at home:

Americans are fond of telling each other what a simple, easy-going, good-natured race we are. That doubtless holds good at home, but you would be surprised how many of your fellow citizens enter an American embassy with a chip on their shoulder.

As he crosses the threshold he undergoes the metamorphosis from a simple American to an American-citizen-taxpayer-and-don't-you-forget-it.

And the young diplomat or consular officer who has the privilege of receiving his fellow countryman has to draw daily on his stock of patience and sense of humor.

People who would wait uncomplainingly to see a dentist or a lawyer cannot brook delay in *their* embassy, even long enough for the visitors ahead of them to be served. Who has not heard in one of our offices "I

want service and make it snappy."

And the things they want service on would fill a book. They want to be taken around at once to see the King. They want to be invited to dine at the Embassy and demand it as a right. They want you to give a party—at your expense of course—so that they can play or sing or recite, preferably before some Royalties.

They bring warm letters of introduction from people you don't know—and who often don't know them—and then sound off with a list of their desiderata.

This kind comes in looking for trouble—and if it isn't there they invent it. They begin by being outraged that the man who opens the door speaks no English. If there isn't anybody actually waiting to receive them, they complain at having to wait, and usually place a staggering value on their time. They tell the officer who receives them not only what he has to do for them but also how he is to do it. If he is so misguided as to persist in doing it as experience has taught, they demand to see the Ambassador or Consul General. This is frequently accompanied by the phrase: "I made a mistake to talk to you in the first place. I always deal with principals."

If there is any delay in producing the chief, the servant of a simple and unassuming democracy can usually count on hearing at this stage that the caller is an intimate friend of one or more Senators and Congressmen—and in case of extreme annoyance of the PRESIDENT. This is recognized at once as the preamble to the statement that all of them, President, Senators, and Congressmen, are going to hear without delay how Americans are treated in this place.

Technically speaking, the embassy is where the ambassador lives and allegedly serves free drinks. Business is done at the chancellery. But in recent years the terms have been confused by government administrators, architects, and others equally unfamiliar with diplomacy. Today the ambassador's home is usually called the "residence" and the chancellery the "embassy."

So if you have a bone to pick, hail a cab and have him take you to the embassy. Most taxi drivers in foreign capitals nowadays know where it is—though they might not have thirty years ago.

You may well be puzzled by the building he takes you to which houses your government's representatives. It may turn out to be a converted apartment house like the one in Beirut or a run-down Oriental palace or a glass cigar box floating on pylons that appears to

have drifted from its moorings on Park Avenue. Occasionally you will find an embassy that actually looks like what you expected—solidly Gothic and monumental.

In the early days of American diplomacy embassies and offices were often combined in a building rented by the government for its envoys. It was often so small and dingy that wealthy ambassadors rented homes with their own funds. In 1823 the Sultan of Morocco, apparently feeling sorry for the poor Americans, gave them an embassy in Tangier. It is still in use but is somewhat dilapidated; the government would like to sell it but finds it awkward to sell a gift from the deceased Sultan.

Exactly a hundred years elapsed before another donor, the late J. P. Morgan, gave the government an embassy in London known as Prince's Gate. Apparently Washington had no qualms about offending bankers and sold the building after World War II.

In 1929 Congress began making small appropriations available to construct or buy embassies abroad. The embassies in Paris and Tokyo, both of which really look like embassies, were built in 1930. During World War II, while the palace we had lately bought at the Brandenburg Tor for our Berlin Embassy was being demolished by our own bombs, the State Department concentrated its construction efforts in South America, where a number of embassies and even consulates were built.

After the war counterpart funds and other credits generated in the war areas by the sale of American military equipment were used to build embassies. But, as often happens, Congress took exception to some of these buildings and held one of its periodic investigations of the State Department to inquire into its architectural talents.

As a result an Advisory Committee of prominent American architects was formed to pass on foreign building plans. Out of some eight hundred architectural firms who applied about a hundred were selected to build embassies abroad. Today when a new embassy is to be built one firm is selected from this list and its plans submitted to the Advisory Committee for its approval.

The results of this system have been varied. Several foreign cities have been embellished with handsome American buildings. In others charming Old World settings have had their ancient atmosphere rudely jarred by the erection of a glass box on stilts, eminently suited

to the New World of Manhattan.

But thus far no American architects have had the spectacular success of disfiguring an entire city that Stalin achieved when he presented Warsaw with a university building, built largely at Polish expense, which looks like a thirty-story birthday cake in a style known as Monumental Stalinesque.

On occasion local governments have objected to the New Look American diplomatic edifices. In Munich the lord mayor in 1952 disapproved the transplantation of American Modern to an area of Bavarian Baroque. However, when Bavarian architects were asked to do better, the glass-enclosed consulate general that resulted left the inmates stifling in sunlight and the passers-by equally breathless.

In some capitals such as Seoul and Bonn entire American communities were erected, complete with shopping centers, filling stations, schools, clubs and even churches. A plan to equip the church in Bonn with a revolving altar so that it could be quickly converted into a Catholic church, a Protestant chapel, or a Jewish synagogue, as need be, was scotched by the stories of American newspapermen tipped off to the plan by a God-fearing American diplomat.

These communities, called compounds by the State Department or ghettos by their inhabitants, are universally deplored because of the isolation they enforce upon the inmates and the envy and friction they provoke among the neighbors. However, occasionally they have had a salutary effect in selling the American way of life to foreigners.

Shortly after the American community was built in Bonn the embassy staff was temporarily reduced and some of the apartments were rented to other diplomats and German officials. One evening thereafter an American official was overtaken by a stout old German *Ministerialrat*, hustling down the street in the direction of the club. Asked why he was in such a hurry, the old man pulled a large gold watch from his vest pocket, glanced anxiously at it like the Rabbit in Alice in Wonderland, muttered "Bingo night" and hurried on.

Officials give economy as the reason for these much-disliked isolated communities of Americans huddled together and cut off from all but a minimal contact with their hosts. Economy is only part of the answer. In war-torn capitals and in primitive communities invaded by hordes of American officials and their secretaries and administrators, adequate housing was simply nonexistent. To build a community by

mass production methods was cheaper—and easier—than attempting to spread the staffs about town in separately constructed units. To Congressional appropriation committees, economy rather than effectiveness is often a primary consideration.

But another reason has been what one might call the ex-pioneer spirit. Though they have volunteered for service abroad, many Americans seem to believe that their forefathers did enough roughing it in the wilderness. From now on it is the descendants' turn to enjoy the luxuries of modern American living wherever they may find themselves. They expect not only all the comforts of home but also the cheap servants available in less advanced communities.

One reason for this new attitude was the example set by the military authorities in providing for U. S. troops overseas. But the troops had not volunteered for service abroad nor had they undertaken to live among foreigners in unfamiliar surroundings. Indeed, many were too young and inexperienced to do so. Furthermore, the restrictions of military life, the discipline and close quarters in which they were confined, justified every relaxation that USO and Coca-Cola could provide. When the military personnel were joined by civilians from the State Department they shared these facilities. Eventually, when the military went home, the civilians inherited both the facilities and the taste for a "home away from home."

Less than a generation ago a vice-consul reporting for duty in Berlin took a room at the Station Hotel, washed and shaved and then walked over to the embassy and reported to the officer in charge. After a brief interview he was referred to the telephone operator, who kept a list of boardinghouses in the neighborhood. If he could afford a car he might choose a place in the suburbs to live in, but if not he found a room within walking distance of the office.

Today a stenographer arriving for duty in Bonn is met at the airport by an embassy car, taken to a transient billet and thence to the office where he or she is "processed" through an assembly-line procedure of being checked in, briefed, and issued an identity card, a PX permit, and finally a furnished apartment. Thenceforth each morning a special bus service will take him from the street corner to his office. Unless he is inspired with special curiosity he need never see the inside of a German streetcar, shop, or even movie theater. Nor need he ever hear the German language spoken, even by the public telephone

operator, who has been taught to speak English for his convenience. The ex-pioneer spirit is not confined to Foreign Service personnel. The U. S. employees of private American business firms and engineers and constructors employed on foreign projects insist not only on American-style housing, including air conditioning, but even on substantial bonuses for the inconvenience of living abroad. In the Middle East or in Southeast Asia Point 4 specialists are housed in compounds complete with movies, clubs, and iceboxes, while Soviet engineers on neighboring projects content themselves with accommodations equivalent to those of the native officials with whom they maintain contact.

Economy is also an excuse for the modern style of architecture. Traditional monumental buildings with their high ceilings and wide corridors, their spacious halls and galleries, are, we are told, only 50 per cent efficient; that is, half the space is not, in the eyes of the architectural efficiency experts, fully utilized. Modern buildings, on the other hand, are 70 per cent efficient. If therefore a diplomat misses the nook where he can chat confidentially with his colleagues or the impressionable native leader is oppressed by the low ceilings, both can be comforted by the fact that, according to the architects, the new style is 20 per cent more efficient and incidentally saves the taxpayer considerable sums in heating.

A further reason for the new style is that few American architects today would undertake a job calling for traditional monumental edifices. A prominent American architect, when asked if he could not design a building that would fit more closely the neighboring Gothic structures, replied that neither he nor any other contemporary American architect was trained or competent to do so.

Some old professional diplomats brought up in the tradition that tactful flattery is an essential ingredient of diplomacy have suggested that the State Department call on local architects to design embassies in the local style. They point to the reconstruction of the handsome Old Market of Warsaw in Hanseatic style, in sharp contrast to the Stalin University, as an example of what might be accomplished.

At the other extreme is a school that argues that the opportunity of looking at an outstanding example of Modern American is or should be a flattery in itself. If the natives do not like it, it is the task of the diplomats to teach them to appreciate American tastes.

These opposing schools exemplify the conflicting concepts of diplo-

macy itself. Is it the primary function of diplomacy to reconcile conflicting interests and divergent tastes or is it to eliminate conflicting interests and tastes by imposing conformity to our own standards?

There is evidence of a further misunderstanding not only of the basic functions of diplomacy but of its methods. Thus some of the hundred firms chosen to build embassies seem to have confused diplomacy with hotelkeeping. The original plans for the new embassy in Madrid, for example, provided for a snack bar where, presumably, the ambassador could entertain the grandees of Spain sitting on high stools and munching hamburgers. Two lobbies on different floors also were planned for the embassy so that two staffs of doormen would be required during receptions. The architect did not apparently include in his plans a rumpus room where the overwrought ambassador and foreign minister could relieve their feelings without concern for the furniture whenever Hispano-American relations grew too tense.

It has often been suggested that before designing embassies architects would do well to familiarize themselves better with the functions of diplomatic life. In this age of diplomacy by flying inkwells and hurtled cobblestones, it might be more functional, for example, to abandon glass façades and revert to the architecture of Norman keeps complete with crenelated towers equipped with caldrons of boiling oil to be poured on rioting demonstrators.

The U. S. Marines would probably be the first to applaud this innovation, for it is they who are responsible for guarding most American embassies. In fact, the first person you are likely to encounter on entering the building is a U. S. Marine resplendent in red, white, and blue uniform. On seeing this familiar sight and the typically American clean-shaven face in a world of hostile bearded aliens, you may be tempted to greet him with a warm "hello" and even a friendly clap on the shoulder. You would be well advised not to. The Marine is strictly instructed to treat everyone as another alien until he has produced his passport. He takes his job seriously and hence is likely to turn a very cold shoulder to friendly advances.

Unlike most architects, Marines have been at home in embassies for generations. As their marching song boasts, they have been the spearheads of our sometimes pacifying, sometimes marauding diplomacy from the Halls of Montezuma to the shores of Tripoli. In Latin

America they have frequently landed to protect embassies and legations and restore order among rioting revolutionaries. They have run diplomatic despatches through fighting lines and rescued stranded diplomats from bandit gangs.

In Tripoli a squad of seven Marines under Lieutenant O'Bannon, at the instigation of the American consul, organized a conglomeration of Arabs and Greeks and set off across the desert to capture Fort Derne from the Barbary Pirates under the Pasha of Tripoli. In World War II Field Marshal Montgomery found it more difficult to capture the same fort from Nazi pirates under General Rommel. During the Boxer Rebellion it was again the Marines who drove the rebel Chinese troops from the American Legation compound.

But it was not until the rise of the total diplomacy of Hitler, Stalin, and Mussolini that the Marines were used to guard our European diplomatic missions. The first such Marine detachment accompanied Ambassador William C. Bullitt when he went to Moscow to establish the American Embassy there.

The sergeant in charge of that detachment was Bill Odeen, a tall, hard-bitten old Tennessee mountaineer. He had not been long in Moscow, living in a hotel, for the embassy apartment house was not yet finished, when he awoke one night to find someone filching his clothes.

Dressed only in a very scant undershirt, the sergeant chased the intruder and caught up with him just at the head of the broad staircase leading down to the busy lobby. Its occupants were somewhat startled to hear the dull thud of a fist on a jaw and see the burglar rolling unconscious down the marble flight. At the head of the stairs stood the Marine sergeant in his abbreviated undershirt rubbing his sore knuckles but with his suit as well as the situation, as befits Marines, well in hand.

"Geez, sir," he told the ambassador apologetically next morning, "I didn't mean to hurt the guy but they was my best set of civvies."

One of Sergeant Odeen's men posing as an embassy counselor escorted the late Mrs. Ned MacLean complete with Hope diamond through the nightclubs of Moscow. The disguise was so successful that even Mrs. MacLean did not penetrate it. The rest of the detachment soon became so useful as garage superintendents, store keepers, and general administrators that the diplomats took turns standing

guard and left the Marines to their more productive duties.

Today there are nearly a thousand Marines guarding more than ninety diplomatic posts in detachments varying in size from thirty-six men in Paris to little five-man units in minor posts.

Though a "diplomatic assignment" is popular with young Marines, they must first undergo a rigorous screening and training process. The standards set are understandably high, for the job is a delicate one involving not merely long hours of guard duty and inspecting embassy offices to see that the diplomats have locked up their papers properly but, occasionally, restraining rioting crowds or, even more difficult, irate American citizens who have lost their passports.

All detachments are commanded by noncoms which in itself provides a problem in discipline. Although their thorough screening and training assures excellent performance, occasionally life in an isolated community can strain nerves beyond the breaking point and when a Marine goes off the deep end it is liable to be a real occasion.

After you've passed the Marine guard at the embassy door the next person you will encounter is the receptionist. In London he is a distinguished gentleman known to all as Mr. Stewart. He wears a long black coat and stands behind a counter facing the entrance. Towering above the timid visitor, Mr. Stewart looks like a judge about to commit you to Wormwood Scrubs or even Dartmoor prison. But in fact he is a most amiable person who prides himself on remembering the names of the hundreds of officials who have served in the embassy since he started his job over thirty-one years ago.

In Rome the receptionist is a chatty young lady who knows your business almost before you open your mouth. Her desk is generally surrounded by a lively group of messengers, couriers, and clerks discussing the latest scandal which Rome society never fails to provide.

In Bonn the receptionist is a rather dour German ex-soldier in a policeman's uniform (uniforms are still fashionable in Germany despite two lost wars). No one but the charwomen pay much attention to him and provided you assume a haughty enough air he will cause no trouble.

But generally the receptionist is an elderly spinster who knows by sight everyone she considers worth knowing and hence has legitimate business in the embassy. If, therefore, she dismisses you highhandedly it is not a personal affront and there is no use complaining to the

ambassador. She has probably served at least a dozen ambassadors, a few of whom she was secretly in love with; some others she looked up to and the rest she has patiently put up with.

For her the world is neatly divided into two categories—diplomats and others. If you can prove you are the friend of a diplomat you may get by her. If you are a congressman she will show you on with strained politeness because she holds you responsible that she has not had a pay raise since twenty years ago when she was still quite pretty.

To help separate the sheep and goats she keeps on her desk the Diplomatic List, a printed catalogue put out by the chief of protocol of the local Foreign Office listing all foreign diplomats in the capital. It is usually her job to keep the list up to date, since foreign offices are notoriously tightfisted about issuing current lists.

Inclusion on the Diplomatic List is important to diplomats and particularly to their wives, for several reasons. First, it confirms the fact that you have diplomatic immunity; secondly, it entitles you to free import privileges; thirdly, it gets you on the invitation list for all the best parties.

Diplomatic titles have always been confusing and are becoming more so. The head of an embassy has the title of "ambassador extraordinary and plenipotentiary" but he is simply called "ambassador." The "extraordinary" was added many years ago by thrusting ambassadors in an effort to promote themselves above their colleagues. In self-protection the latter simply followed suit, thereby producing a stalemate. "Plenipotentiary" means the envoy has full powers to negotiate normal diplomatic problems. Should an ambassador be called upon to sign a treaty he must get special "full powers."

A legation is a second-class embassy. In its earliest days the United States maintained only legations but as it grew in importance began raising these to embassies. Today only in a few very small countries do we still have legations. The head of a legation has the title "envoy extraordinary and minister plenipotentiary." He is called "minister" for short. Just to complicate matters, an ambassador from the Vatican is a nuncio and a minister is an internuncio. The treaties the Vatican concludes are not treaties but concordats.

Americans usually address their own ambassador or minister as Mr. Ambassador or Mr. Minister but to a third person he is referred to as "the ambassador," *never* "the Mr. Ambassador." Foreigners addressing

American and Americans addressing foreign ambassadors or ministers usually say "Your Excellency" or to third persons, "His Excellency."

Traditionally the ambassador's deputy is called a counselor. When the ambassador is out of the country, the counselor becomes acting ambassador but his title is "chargé d'affaires, *ad interim*" meaning "temporarily in charge of affairs." He automatically loses the title as soon as the ambassador returns. With the twentieth-century inflation of titles, in some countries the second in command is a minister and in others a minister-counselor. In Foreign Service jargon he is called "D.C.M." or deputy chief of mission. Nowadays embassies may have several counselors: e.g., political, economic or even administrative counselor.

Under the counselors come the diplomatic secretaries, to be carefully distinguished from their secretaries. Their titles are first secretary, second secretary, or third secretary. Though there used to be fourth secretaries, they too have fallen victims to title inflations. Private secretary, though often a key position, is not generally recognized as a diplomatic rank and hence does not rate inclusion on the Diplomatic List.

Parallel to these diplomatic officers are the attachés, military, naval and air, and frequently agricultural, labor, treasury, and commercial, and more recently in a few posts scientific attaché. These seldom are regular career diplomats and almost invariably are career civil servants of the corresponding departments in Washington.

Ambassadors of some countries occasionally appoint their sons, nephews, or other outsiders to the post of attaché which is a diplomatic rank and is included on the list. The practice has in the past been forbidden by the State Department as a precaution against nepotism. An exception to the ban on attachés has recently been made for representatives of government agencies who prefer not to advertise their affiliations.

To confuse the uninitiated still further, these diplomatic ranks have little or no significance, except to protocol officers, receptionists and wives, beyond specifying where one sits at an official dinner or marches in a state funeral. To the career diplomat, but not always to his wife, what is important is his class in the Foreign Service, since this determines his salary. Presently there are ten career classes: career ambassador, career minister, and Classes No. 1 down to Class 8 for begin-

ners. It is curious that, whereas American Civil Service salaries increase with the number of your class, in the Foreign Service they diminish. There is no special significance to this phenomenon.

Assuming you have slipped past the receptionist into the chancellery proper, you will find that the ambassador's office is staffed by a private secretary and perhaps several stenographers. Frequently the immediate office will be headed by a personal assistant, a sort of aide-de-camp to the ambassador, almost invariably a junior Foreign Service officer. This is a key post, for it is the ambassador's main link not only with the public but also with most of the embassy staff. The personal assistant investigates the background and political leanings of would-be visitors, screens requests for personal appearances by the ambassador, and often helps prepare his speeches and addresses.

If the ambassador is not a professional, the assistant has the additional responsibility of preventing him from violating diplomatic etiquette, offending influential local leaders, or otherwise putting his foot in the quagmire of protocol that surrounds a senior diplomat.

The principal divisions of the chancellery are usually the political and economic sections. The political section is further divided into "internal affairs" and "external affairs." The internal affairs desk is responsible for following internal developments, both national and regional, and the head of it is usually a familiar figure around the Parliament (if there is one functioning). The external affairs desk deals with the host country's foreign relations. The head of it deals largely with the Foreign Affairs Ministry as well as with senior members of other embassies in the capital.

In addition to the internal and external sections there are often special desks concerned with particular aspects of the host country's problems. In many countries American embassies maintain well-staffed desks on Communist activities. Their task is not only to keep an eye on the local Communist party but to exchange information with the host's specialist on Soviet affairs.

The American Embassy in Bonn has a special desk on Berlin affairs as a separate German problem. Other embassies have "status of forces" desks to handle problems arising from the stationing of U. S. forces on the host's territory. There may be a NATO specialist or a desk dealing with the Common Market.

The economic division is likewise divided into sections dealing with specific aspects of the host country's internal and external economy: transportation, agriculture, mining, currency, and exchange. These questions are often dealt with by attachés from the appropriate bureau in Washington.

Whenever a problem between the United States and the host country arises in any of these spheres that requires the ambassador's intervention, he will ordinarily call on the desk officer to brief him, prepare the preliminary studies, and often accompany him to important negotiations.

There is a very good chance that the person you are calling on in the chancellery will be tied up at a meeting. This may, but should not, surprise you. The virus of decision by committee which has clogged the wheels of government in Washington for a decade has spread to every embassy of any size.

There are of course the regular morning meetings where everyone tells what he has learned in the past twenty-four hours. But there are also "ad hoc" meetings to deal with special situations as they arise. For example, if the price of tin in the United States has dropped, causing layoffs in local mines which in turn have produced unrest threatening the stability of the government, it is not sufficient for the economic officer to draft a report to Washington suggesting something be done about it. The matter concerns tin, which means that the Bureau of Mines attaché must be consulted. Naturally, since it involves unemployment, the labor attaché demands a hearing. Security involves the Army and therefore the military attaché. To avoid interservice jealousies the naval and air attachés also are brought into the picture.

Now we have at least seven or eight officials, which is ample for a meeting. The tin problem is fully discussed, each official expressing his views at length on all its aspects. Then they decide to hold off doing anything about the matter, as the tin price may recover and there is no need to disturb Washington, which is far too concerned with the Berlin problem or the Suez problem to do anything about it anyway. Wearily the economic officer goes back to his desk, having used up most of the morning and wondering whatever possessed him to raise the question in the first place.

If, by chance, it has been decided to send a cable on the situation to

Washington, the economic officer, after drafting the message, performs a ritual known as "clearing" during which every embassy official even remotely concerned with the problem must initial the cable before it is sent. To skip anyone in the clearing procedure not only is considered a breach of discipline but can lead to lifelong feuds.

Aside from attending meetings and "clearing" papers the principal functions of these desks are to keep the ambassador informed and write reports to Washington on developments in their fields. This they can do by either cable or pouch depending on the urgency of the matter. There will ordinarily be two quite different views on the urgency problem: that of the administrative officer, whose efficiency is determined by how closely the embassy sticks to its cable budget, and that of the reporting officer, whose rating depends on how well he keeps Washington posted.

Returning from lunch with a disconsolate Socialist member of Parliament, a political reporting officer may be alarmed that the M.P. is about to vote with the opposition, thus threatening the ruling coalition, the stability of the government, and hence the security of the United States. Unless Washington hears about this today, he reasons, it may be too late. The administrative officer, on the other hand, could not care less about a disgruntled politician. Besides, his security officer says Socialists are Marxists and should not be in the Parliament at all. Referred to the embassy counselor, the question is probably settled in favor of the reporting officer because the counselor, a career officer, cannot abide administrators.

During World War II, when everything was urgent and deficits normal, practically all reports from overseas went by cable or radio. To the harassed, overworked official in Washington anything reaching his desk not written on the colored departmental telegraph forms was automatically relegated to the pending basket for Sunday reading. Officers in the field soon realized that to send a report by courier pouch was like writing a letter to Santa Claus and burning it up the chimney.

The attitude long outlived the war, until Congress complained about the cable bills. Thereupon an ingenious administrative expert hit upon the idea of a form of report that looked like a cable, read like a cable, and almost smelled like a cable but was not a cable.

Colored forms were sent overseas on which reporting officers could type their messages just like a cable but then, instead of wiring them, they slipped them into the pouch. The receiving officers in Washington, misled by the colored paper, were thus induced to read them.

For a time this subterfuge cut the cable bills to reasonable proportions. But then the receiving officers noticed the new colored forms were called not "telegrams" but "airgrams." Thereupon they were dumped back in the pending basket. Quick to scent that their airgrams' covers had been blown, the reporting officers were forced back to the telegram, and once more the ether and the cables groaned until the Congress again growled.

Recently, short of new ideas and counting on the poor memories of officials, the administrators have resuscitated the counterfeit cable ruse and the airgram is once more out of the pending basket.

Cables are popular not only because of the attention they attract but also because they are easier to write than reports. Grammatical errors can be explained as the fault of the code clerk or the telegrapher. They are seldom scanned for syntax. A favored opening phrase of a cable, for example, is: "In a conversation with the foreign minister today he told me that . . ." Cables are also relatively short and if they contain no profound thought or thorough reasoning this can be attributed to the sender's laudable frugality with cable tolls.

Until recently the basic form of pouched report was the dispatch. This was a somewhat stylized official letter addressed:

> The Honorable
> The Secretary of State
> Washington, D.C.

and invariably began:

Sir:
I have the honor to report that . . .

It was always signed by the ambassador or his deputy but in the left-hand corner of the last page it carried the drafting officer's initials. When embassies were small and compact, it was no problem for the recipient in Washington to identify the writer.

Efficiency experts have recently replaced the dispatch by the simple report. This is addressed impersonally to the department, has no set

DIPLOMAT

style or opening, and bears the name of the writer blatantly clear for all to read on the first page.

Doubtless the report is a more up-to-date form than the dispatch, but one may wonder whether it serves its purpose any better or even as well, because of its streamlining. When one set about drafting a dispatch addressed to "The Honorable The Secretary of State" and beginning "I have the honor," the writer was at once in the proper mood of dignified respect for the recipient (who seldom, if ever, saw it) and at the same time filled with a sense of responsibility as the author of a state paper that one day might appear in the history books. The temptation to trifle with facts, express unconsidered opinions, or indulge in frivolous speculations was eliminated.

Since it was signed by the ambassador himself, it created a personal bond between the chief and the third secretary tucked away in the back of the chancellery. Finally the not-too-cryptic initials in the lower left-hand corner gave the drafter his pride of authorship without indulging in vulgar self-advertisement, just as a painter unobtrusively signs his masterpieces where none but the initiate can read it.

Furthermore, the dispatch was expected to have a literary quality. Grammar, style, and syntax were carefully scrutinized both by the ambassador when he signed the dispatch and by the official in Washing when he read it. Loy Henderson, my first mentor in dispatch writing, and now deputy under-secretary of state, invariably required his subordinates to review *Fowler's Modern English Usage* at least once a year and sometimes, if one's grammar slumped, more often.

Callières once write: "The best dispatches are those written in a clear and concise manner, unadorned by useless epithets or by anything that may becloud the clarity of the argument. Simplicity is the first essential and diplomats should take the greatest care to avoid all affectations such as a pretence of wit or the learned overweight of scientific disquisitions."

This advice has not always been followed. On the first day of my own diplomatic career my chief summoned me:

"Charles, I am preparing a dispatch on the Red Army. Since you are a West Pointer, find me some good quotations from Napoleon."

Though Callières frowned on humorous dispatches, the State Department did not forbid an occasional bit of wit. In fact, if one could acquire a reputation as a witty dispatch writer it was a guarantee that

one's reports would be read and, less frequently, one's views taken into consideration.

Today the dispatch is gone, replaced by the impersonal, often hastily written report. With it went a quality that made diplomacy a skill rather than an administrative procedure. Its form may have been dated, but so is good wine.

XI

Consuls, Codes, and Couriers: 1

TO the embassy receptionist only the sheep—the ambassador, counselor, diplomatic secretaries, and attachés—belong in the chancellery. However, parallel to the diplomatic staff there is another hierarchy which is perhaps of greater importance to most Americans—the consular establishment. Though in theory the ambassador is responsible for safeguarding the interests of American citizens, in practice it is the consul who looks after private interests while the ambassador devotes himself chiefly to intergovernmental problems.

As in most countries today, the U. S. consular service is combined with the diplomatic and an officer can serve interchangeably on either a consular or a diplomatic mission. While there is no difference in remuneration or general working conditions, the glamour of the embassy is considerably greater, at least to younger officers, than the drab consulate. Dealing with matters of a national or international scope also seems to have more attraction, though the consul often has a far more exciting life than the secretary buried in a chancellery.

Despite his position on the Diplomatic List and the honors and privileges to which he is entitled, the diplomat is a parvenu on the international scene compared to his lowly brother the consul. According to Herodotus, the Greeks maintained consuls in Egypt twenty-five hundred years ago. They were elected by the Greek colony and not only represented its interests before the Egyptians but also had legal jurisdiction over their compatriots. Ever since, nations have main-

tained consuls in foreign ports and trading centers and though they seldom exercise judicial functions, they have played an important role in the development of international trade.

Today American consular offices are divided into three categories: consulates general, consulates, and consular agencies. Between the first two there is little difference except size. There are no functions which a consul general may perform that a consul cannot. But, oddly enough, because of the wording of the laws of some of the states of the Union, there are a number of legal functions that a consul or even a vice-consul is authorized to perform that a consul general cannot. Consular agents, on the other hand, are generally businessmen, often foreigners, who are authorized to perform a limited number of consular services in return for the fees they collect thereby.

Until the establishment of a career consular service in 1906, consular officers always pocketed the fees they collected for issuing passports and visas and performing other consular services. For this reason many consular posts, such as that in London, were eagerly sought after, and the consuls at these posts often earned more than the President of the United States. Nathaniel Hawthorne got himself appointed consul to Liverpool in 1853 and served there four years, earning enough not only to live comfortably but to pay for a two-year vacation in Italy. Since 1906, however, all fees except consular agents' are turned back to the U. S. Treasury and consular personnel are paid regular salaries like their diplomatic colleagues.

In most capital cities the consular office is combined with the diplomatic mission and is called the Consular Section. Depending on its size, it is still presided over by a consul general or a consul, who usually holds a dual commission as "counselor of embassy and consul general" or "secretary of embassy and consul."

In other cities the consular establishment is independent. It is not, like an embassy, accredited to a national government but to a provincial or municipal authority. However, the central government issues an "exequatur" to the principal consular officer in each office, which is roughly equivalent to the operating license issued to doctors, lawyers, or hackers.

Consuls are undoubtedly the most maligned of Foreign Service officers. Musical comedies like *Call Me Madam* may be written about diplomats but tragic operas are written about consuls, who invariably

are cast in the role of the villain who delights in bullying beach-combers or preventing persecuted minorities from seeking asylum in the United States.

Despite the fact that they all belong to the same service and frequently exchange hats, one can sometimes distinguish the consular type who prefers the relative obscurity of a consular post to the hectic but perhaps more glamorous activity of an embassy. He is often an older man whose worldly ambitions have worn thin. He is apt to be bald and tubby and gregarious, reveling in Chamber of Commerce and Rotarian activities. Usually he is an excellent raconteur of ribald stories about his experiences in Tampico during the Mexican Revolutions or on the Marseilles waterfront. Because of constant association with stranded seamen, international bums, and mixed-up expatriates he has assumed a tough, hard-boiled manner which frequently hides the mildest of dispositions.

As in ancient times, trade promotion is still an important function of the consul. He is instructed to look out for new markets for American products or capital investments. He helps local American merchants to import and export goods and straighten out their financial transactions.

Occasionally the consul is called upon to protect the dignity of the nation from foreign merchants. As a junior vice-consul in Prague, "Chip" Bohlen, later ambassador to Moscow and Manila, was instructed to protest to a Czech dress manufacturer the use of the American flag which he had stamped on one of his products. "But I only use the Stars and Stripes on our top-grade brassières," the merchant explained.

For the local American colony the consul is a combination of spokesman and family lawyer. He registers the passports of new arrivals and issues replacements for those that have expired. Though he may not perform marriage ceremonies, he is often called upon to witness marriages and to issue a colorfully sealed certificate that he has done so. When babies are born he registers them and notarizes their certificates of birth.

He sometimes must go even further. Many years ago a young American called Edmund Stevens appeared before me to report the birth of a son. As I started to fill out the report of birth, it developed that he and his wife had not been able to agree on a name for his heir. She, being a Russian, wanted a Slavic name, he an American.

To break the deadlock I took down the Webster dictionary and combed the glossary of Christian names. Eventually I settled on the safe choice of William and thus the baby was registered. But in the end the mother seemed to have won out, for when I met the family fifteen years later on the Dalmatian coast the boy was known as Valodia. His father had meantime made a name for himself as a leading foreign correspondent.

Deaths among the colony are liable to be more complicated. If, as frequently happens, the deceased has no relatives on hand, the consul must collect and inventory his personal belongings, pay bills, and finally submit together with the remains of the estate a detailed report to Washington. Frequently he must also officiate at the burial. One of my earliest jobs as a vice-consul was to peer through a peephole of a crematorium furnace to witness the flames consuming an old and much-beloved member of the American colony.

One day in the early thirties the Soviet Foreign Office called the Consular Section of the American Embassy to state that a man claiming to be an American was being held in a hospital in Minsk. Eventually the man was brought to Moscow, where he was questioned by Consul Elbridge Durbrow. His name, he said, was Brother Matthew. (His last name I have forgotten.) In a deep Southern drawl he explained that he came from Alabama and that he had received a call to bring Christianity to the benighted Communist heathens. Having no funds, he had walked to New York, worked his way to Europe on a ship, and then set out for Moscow on foot without a passport or any other identification. He had crossed the German, Polish, and Soviet frontiers and got as far as Minsk where the local police questioned him and decided with some justification that he was not entirely balanced. So they put him in the mental ward of the hospital. After some weeks they called the embassy. Since the Soviets had long boasted that their barb-wired, heavily patrolled borders were impregnable to even the wiliest foreign spy, it was with acute embarrassment that they had to confess to us that a crazy Alabaman speaking no foreign language had strolled unconcernedly through their formidable barrier assisted by nothing more sinister than his religious fervor.

In the Minsk hospital Brother Matthew promptly fell in love with his nurse, who was a good Communist, with the result that he abandoned his mission and became an enthusiastic convert to Marx. He

still was a roaring Communist when he reached Moscow and did his best to convert the embassy staff, but his proselyting methods were more like those of Billy Sunday than of a party propagandist.

Months of cabling between Moscow, Washington, and his home county in Alabama followed. It was eventually established that Brother Matthew had indeed been missing for over a year. His identity established, he was shipped home from Leningrad on an American ship in the reluctant care of the captain.

Not all citizenship cases end so happily. When the embassy was established in Moscow, literally dozens of young Americans swarmed into the consular section asking for passports. They had, it turned out, been jobless in the United States during the depression and had been persuaded by Communist organizers to come to Russia. In their initial enthusiasm at finding work in the workers' paradise many had voluntarily renounced American citizenship, thus effectively debarring themselves from returning to the United States. On being told this at least one I knew went home and slashed his wrists.

Passport or citizenship law is not a simple subject. An American can acquire citizenship three ways: by being born in America, by being born abroad of American parents, or by naturalization. It was even possible under pre-World War II legislation for a grandchild to inherit citizenship provided his parent had gone to America with the intention of remaining. At least one old man I once knew owed his life to this strange loophole.

In November of 1936 Goebbels organized probably the most vicious pogrom of modern times. As a result the Jews of Berlin swarmed into the American Consulate General seeking visas or passports—anything to escape from the blood-crazed Nazis. The crowd in front of the office became so dense that the staff had to get in each morning through the fire escape at the rear of the building. All day and half the night the consuls, vice-consuls, and clerks tried to keep abreast of the flood of applications.

Early one morning the citizenship vice-consul, strained and nervous from incessant work and depressed by the crowds in the street outside, entered his office to find a wizened old man already seated before his desk.

Petulantly the young vice-consul told him to wait in the corridor until he was sent for. The day passed like every other with a constant

stream of pathetic applicants for passports. For lunch the vice-consul munched a sandwich brought by the office messenger. It was late in the evening when the last applications were typed and signed.

Locking his safe, the vice-consul left his office but in the corridor he recognized the little old man who had been sitting patiently awaiting his summons. Ashamed of his own callous forgetfulness, the vice-consul showed him in. His name, the old man said, was Kempinski. It was a famous Berlin name. A leading restaurant, a hotel, and even the Haus Vaterland were Kempinski's. The vice-consul asked whether he was related to the owner of these establishments.

"I am Kempinski," the old man answered quietly. Then he went on to say that his grandfather had emigrated to America during the Civil War and had eventually become a judge in Chicago, where Kempinski had once visited him with his father.

"Visited?" the vice-consul asked. "Or did you go there intending to stay permanently?" The old man got the hint. He had meant to stay, he said, but had been forced by circumstances subsequently to return to Germany.

He even offered some evidence of his "permanent" stay in Chicago but it was pretty flimsy. However, it was enough for the contrite vice-consul, and a day or two later Kempinski left Germany on an American passport. But he never got to the United States—he died in London during the war.

It was one of the last passports the vice-consul ever issued. When a report of the case reached Washington, an angry reprimand was sent by the head of the Passport Division, "Ma" Shipley, and the vice-consul was transferred to other work—not entirely reluctantly.

From time to time a consul can find less questionable ways of behaving humanely. An applicant for a passport faced the consul in Berlin. He too was a Jew in imminent danger of his life. His case seemed satisfactory except for one small point: proof that he had not disqualified himself by serving in the German Army. Vehemently the applicant insisted that he had been deferred because of physical disabilities, but he could offer no proof. The deferment papers, he explained, were with his police records and the Gestapo had repeatedly refused to let him take them out.

"After all," he kept repeating, spreading his hands before him, "I am just a Jew."

But the consul insisted. Since the man had been of military age in World War I and all able-bodied men had served, it must be assumed that he had too, unless the consul could see proof to the contrary.

Disconsolately the applicant left. That night a big blond German rang the consul's doorbell. He was dressed in a civilian hat and a civilian overcoat but beneath the coat the consul caught a glimpse of familiar black boots.

"You are handling the Abramovitch case?" the man asked. The consul said he was. "I can show you his draft deferment," the man went on, "if you come with me."

Together they walked through the dark streets to Alexanderplatz where the Berlin Police Headquarters were. They went to a side door which the man opened with a key. Up several flights of iron stairs they came to the police archives—row upon row of steel shelves reaching to the ceiling. With a flashlight the man found the Abramovitch file and took out the deferment paper. It bore the applicant's picture, and the seals and stamps on it were in order.

Next day when he handed Abramovitch his passport the consul, unable to restrain his curiosity, asked, "How much did that Gestapo officer demand for his little favor?"

"Plenty." The applicant smiled as he walked happily from the office.

Immigration law can be even more complicated than citizenship— and more tragic. During the same Goebbels pogrom two young couples of Jewish extraction walked from their home in Silesia to the consulate in Berlin. Placing a map before the vice-consul they pointed to a tiny dot in the Pacific Ocean marked "Johnston Island (U. S. possession)."

The two couples explained earnestly that they knew they could never get visas to the United States before the Gestapo caught up with them. Rather than wait for the police they were prepared to beat them to the job. One of them drew his fingers across the veins in his wrist. But there was one last chance.

"What about a visa to Johnston Island?" they pleaded. It might be desolate, they admitted, but it couldn't be surer death than a gas chamber in Germany.

The vice-consul shook his head gloomily. The island, he explained, was under U. S. Navy jurisdiction and *no one* was allowed to land there. They pleaded long and vehemently but at last the four young

Germans exchanged glances and hand in hand filed out of the office. From his window the vice-consul watched them leave the consulate and cross the street into the Tiergarten where their bodies were found next morning.

After the war an American GI came to the consulate general in Munich with his German bride to apply for a visa for her. Among the documents required was a certificate of good conduct from the police of the girl's village. Her certificate, however, revealed that during the bitter postwar winter of 1945–46 a forester had found the girl collecting fagots in the state forest. She was thereupon tried and convicted of theft. Prospective immigrants convicted of theft, the U. S. law said, could not receive visas. (The law has since been modified.)

Taking care of indigent Americans, particularly seamen at seaport consulates, is a regular consular function, especially in Central and South America, where sailors seem to make a point of getting drunk and missing their ships. Since funds are rarely provided for stranded Americans, the consul must either finance them himself or use his ingenuity to get them on a ship for home. This is especially difficult in countries where the jails provide no food for their prisoners.

Unlike some visitors to embassies and consulates, many seamen thoughtfully tank up before they pay a call. Any number of consuls can tell you about hasty trips round and round their desks with gigantic drunken sailors in hot pursuit. Consequently, the cautious consul will always keep a heavy dull instrument handy by his desk when a seaman staggers in to complain.

But sometimes welfare work, as it is technically called, can be more entertaining. A pretty young girl dressed in a man's slacks and shirt ambled gracefully into the Tehran Consulate's waiting room and, perching herself on the vice-consul's desk, asked him casually to cash a $200 check on a Washington bank.

She said she had recently been shipwrecked in the Caspian Sea and had lost all her clothing. A sailor had lent her the shirt and pants and she had hitchhiked over the mountains to Tehran.

The vice-consul knew his boss in the back room would never cash the check and his own finances were not strong enough to support any bouncing notes. The story sounded utterly implausible but the girl's face looked honest and was indisputably attractive. So he endorsed the check and cashed it and after she'd bought a dress he

took her to dinner. In fact he took her out frequently until funds arrived for her passage home. When she finally boarded the plane for Paris he was a very sad young vice-consul indeed. But he recovered and she eventually married another vice-consul.

The duties of a consul are so numerous and the ways of how to perform them, prescribed by domestic, maritime, international and foreign laws, not to mention consular regulations, are so varied that it would be impossible even to summarize them here. Graham H. Stuart in his *American Diplomatic and Consular Practice* says quite rightly that a consul must really be a master- as well as a Jack-of-all-trades. But perhaps the point could be illustrated with one final example:

After nearly twenty years away from consular work I became consul general in Munich in 1952. I had scarcely sat down, the first day, at the desk in my sumptuous office when the telephone rang. It was a distinguished American lady whom I knew slightly and she asked if I could not come to her hotel on an urgent matter. Self-conscious of my new duties as protector of American citizenry I hurried to the hotel to find her husband in bed and a German doctor standing anxiously beside him.

"As we speak no German," the lady said, "could you explain my husband's symptoms to the doctor?"

The consul general looked inquiringly at the helpless American.

"Diarrhea," the latter muttered.

XII

Consuls, Codes, and Couriers: 2

THERE are two ways for an embassy to send messages securely: by ordinary letter entrusted to a reliable courier and by a form unintelligible to anyone but the recipient—that is, by code or by such methods as secret ink. Today the great majority of diplomatic messages are sent in code by cable or radio.

However, before the cable, secret inks were extensively used. The United States' earliest instructions to its ministers on the Continent during the Revolution were frequently sent in secret inks, though there is reason to believe that British chemists revealed most if not all of them as fast as they were intercepted.

Even as late as World War I the Germans were adept at inventing secret inks for their spies. The British usually managed to find a solution to develop these inks but as quickly as they did the Germans invented new ones. On one occasion the British discovered an American in London whose socks were so impregnated that when soaked in water they produced a secret ink. The American, George Vaux Bacon, confessed he was working for the German secret service; he would probably have been hanged if Washington had not interceded. Eventually he was handed over to his countrymen, and they sent him to Atlanta for a year.

Subsequently ingenious German chemists invented a method of secret writing using simple tap water. This had the British stumped for weeks until someone discovered that an iodine-vapor bath revealed

where the paper fibers had been disturbed by the water on the pen. Hardly had they discovered this than the Germans produced a means of disturbing all the fibers on the page so that the iodine-vapor bath simply obliterated the writing. Eventually, toward the end of the war the British and Americans working together caught onto this new trick, but just how has not been revealed.

With the development of compact transmitters, codes have largely replaced secret inks but inks are still occasionally used in espionage work.

Strictly speaking there are two kinds of cryptographic messages: codes and ciphers. In the first, symbols, usually combinations of letters or numbers in groups of two or more (most usually five), are substituted for entire words or phrases. If you take an ordinary dictionary and paste next to each word a random group of letters you will have a crude code.

Ciphers are made by substituting symbols for each letter in a message or by transposing the order of letters. For example, if a message is written on a blocked pad and then the letters copied column by column instead of line by line you have a very simple transposition cipher. Frequently to make doubly sure messages will first be coded and the code then enciphered.

Prior to 1917 the State Department had several systems of codes and ciphers which, however, were so primitive that they were probably known to every major power. In 1913 a young, ambitious, and imaginative code clerk joined the department. He soon began to suspect that the code systems in use were unsafe. He set about studying cryptography in his spare time, beginning with Edgar Allan Poe's "Gold Bug." Poe, he soon concluded, was a rank amateur. Eventually he succeeded in breaking all the department's secret codes without reference to the key.

Like most innovators, the clerk, Herbert O. Yardley, had considerable difficulty in persuading his superiors that their methods were antiquated. One of the first secret cables he deciphered was a confidential message from Colonel House in London to President Wilson. Lest he be fired for snooping, he discreetly destroyed the text without telling his superiors. Later, as he became more expert, he wrote a memorandum to his immediate boss describing in detail the weaknesses of the State Department's codes. But nothing was done to remedy the

situation until the eve of America's entry into the war.

Convinced that his talents would never find recognition among the diplomats, Yardley approached the Military Intelligence Division of the War Department and, demonstrating his talents as a cryptographer, attempted to persuade it of the necessity of developing a cryptographic unit to break enemy codes and devise safe ones for themselves.

At first the War Department was reluctant. Though they commissioned Yardley and gave him a few facilities to work on foreign codes, they claimed that their own codes were entirely adequate and had proved themselves in the Spanish-American War.

But then the British government sent word through the State Department that the War Department's codes were so antique that they could not be trusted. About the same time Yardley discovered to his amazement that a copy of the military code had been stolen some time before in Mexico and could be presumed to be in German hands. This, however, had not disturbed the military unduly. Finally a young cryptographer trained by Yardley went to France with Pershing's staff. Much to Pershing's alarm the young man promptly broke every operating code of the U. S. troops at the front.

The accumulated evidence eventually had its effect even among the generals. Yardley was authorized to organize MI–8, the Intelligence Corps's first code-breaking unit and to recruit a number of amateurs who displayed what he called "cipher minds," as well as a large battery of clerks and stenographers to perform the tedious permutations and combinations necessary to break a code. He was also given the job of devising new codes and of delving into the alchemy of secret inks.

Realizing that he was only a beginner in these arts Yardley managed to persuade the British to send to Washington a leading secret-ink specialist and some of their cryptographic experts from the Admiralty, where they had been perfecting the science for generations. Soon he had an efficient operation going full speed.

One of his earliest successes came from monitoring a powerful German transmitting station near Berlin which was apparently exchanging messages with another near Mexico City. The intercepted coded messages were in a regular five-figure group, several of which were frequently repeated, indicating it was an ordinary code. Breaking

each group into two parts of three and two digits each, Yardley noted that the three digit numbers ran from 1 to 600 (about the number of pages in an ordinary dictionary). The last two digits gave numbers from 1 to 60 (about the number of lines in a fine-print dictionary). The first code group was 19716. Picking up the nearest dictionary he discovered the word "for," one of the most frequent words in the English language, on page 203—only 6 pages from 197. The second group in the message was 21206. Adding 6 to the page number (the difference between page 197 and page 203) he searched on page 218 for a likely word. On page 217 he found "German." By use of the same technique, the third group revealed close to the page he sought the word "minister": "For German Minister." With this clue he betook himself to the Library of Congress and hunted through every dictionary in the stacks till he discovered a little-known French-English dictionary, the second volume of which fitted his page and line numbers exactly. An hour later he had deciphered the long message from Berlin to its minister in Mexico City offering to pay Mexico ten million Spanish pesetas "if Mexico will remain neutral during war." Yardley's reputation was made.

His second triumph was more difficult, involving a cipher message picked up on a suspicious character caught crossing the Mexican border. Using a normal German-language frequency table he confirmed that the letters in the message appeared in almost exactly the same frequency as the letters in the table, thus suggesting that it was a straight transposition cipher in German. But how to place the letters in their correct order?

Knowing that the combination "ch" is frequent in German, he underlined all the c's in red and all the h's in blue. By counting he found most of the c's and h's were 108 letters apart. When he rearranged the letters of the text by various mathematical formulas several typical German-language combinations began to be revealed: *scha, iche, lich,* and *chen.* Once more he rearranged the letters according to the frequency of these combinations until finally the full text was revealed, stating in German that the bearer was a German secret agent and calling on all German authorities to co-operate with him. On the basis of this evidence the bearer was court-martialed and sentenced to be hanged by the neck until dead.

When the war ended the War Department lost interest in Yardley's

operation, but not the State Department. Though MI–8 continued under War Department auspices, it was financed largely by State. Preparing for the 1922 Washington Disarmament Conference, Yardley achieved his masterpiece—cracking the Japanese code, a language of which he knew not a word. The clue that gave it away was a message that Yardley suspected dealt with the Irish independence movement. Hence the phonetic analogues, or kanas, of the Japanese for "Ireland" and "independence" must somehow be in the message. On this basis he discovered certain key repetitions of Japanese kanas and within a matter of hours had broken the code.

This case illustrates an important element of code security. If the code breaker can match even a fragment of the clear, uncoded text of a single message against its coded text, half his work is accomplished. For this reason the true texts of diplomatic cables are as securely guarded as the codes themselves. If the text must be revealed to another government it is invariably paraphrased—put into equivalent but not identical language by using synonyms, rearranging the order of phrases, and similar devices. A text known to outsiders—a newspaper editorial, for example—therefore is generally put into a non-secret code or sent *en clair*—in clear.

Eventually Yardley and his little band of cryptographers were for security reasons moved to New York, where they continued to intercept and decode for the State Department messages transmitted to and from the foreign embassies in Washington. Having gone into operation in 1917 Yardley had by 1929 succeeded in cracking over 45,000 cryptograms and breaking at least some of the codes of twenty countries, including those of England, France, Russia (and the Soviet Union), and Japan.

But in 1929 a blow fell that put an end to Yardley's career. Henry L. Stimson had become secretary of state, and several days after his appointment an eager assistant put on his desk several of Yardley's deciphered intercepts from a diplomatic mission in Washington. Peremptorily Stimson asked where those messages had come from. When the eager subordinate proudly told him, Stimson at once gave orders that the State Department was to stop all code-cracking operations immediately. "Gentlemen," he later explained, "do not read each other's mail."

Yardley, his funds cut off, disbanded his staff and went off to write

a fascinating but embittered book, *The American Black Chamber,* but not before he had one final interview with a senior official in the State Department.

With his reputation as the leading American cryptographer established, Yardley had no hesitation now about saying what he thought of the State Department's codes—which was not much. Every one of them, he told the high official, could be and probably had been broken by foreign governments. "Our codes," he said, "are just as cumbersome, just as antiquated as sixteenth-century communications." The alarmed official asked what could be done.

Nothing, Yardley told him. Almost any code, he explained, could be broken because all involved repetitions of words or letters and hence frequencies. It was only a question of finding out how the code maker tried to hide the repetitions. There was only one possibility, he stated prophetically—machines. There were already on the market machines that could encode a message as fast as it could be typed. Another machine at the receiving end could decode it as quickly as the code groups could be fed into it. Properly converted by experts, such machines could eliminate all repetitions and hence all possibilities of cracking.

But, Yardley concluded, the State Department was too set in its ways to discard its antiquated systems. It was hopeless even to try. And on that bitter note he walked out.

A decade passed before Yardley was proved right. From time to time the State Department produced a new code book but the basic methods were the same and probably provided no problem for the foreign cryptographer. Under the prodding of President Roosevelt several new codes were composed. One of them was the Brown Code. It was popular with code clerks because it contained not only words but whole phrases dear to the hearts of those who drafted cables. "In a note dated today the Foreign Ministry states that" or "It would appear to be" or "It is suggested that" or "I am inclined to believe that," and similar expressions could all be handled by a single code group and at a considerable saving in telegraph bills.

But the Brown Code had a short life. Not long after it had been distributed a cable was flashed from Washington to every embassy and consulate. "The Brown Code," it said ruefully, "has been compromised." What had happened was that a gang of Ustachi bandits

had invaded the American Consulate in Zagreb and at the points of several machine guns had forced the vice-consul to open the safe, the contents of which they carried off into the forests of Croatia.

Other codes followed the Brown: the A, B, and C codes involved new cryptographic precautions but they greatly added to the time it took to code messages, especially since most telegrams had to be coded and then enciphered. Aside from the technical drawback Yardley had pointed out—the inevitability of repetitions—all codes in book form, like the Brown Code, are susceptible of filching.

During the first months of World War II I was visiting friends in neutral Stockholm. In the Grand Hotel, then the rendezvous for every eavesdropper, agent and spy in Scandinavia, I ran into a Yugoslav vice-consul with whom I had served at several posts. Enormously fat, a bon vivant and a great raconteur, he joined me at a table in the big central lounge and we ordered drinks.

A woman seated nearby was reading a newspaper which entirely hid her face, but as the Yugoslav started to recount the latest diplomatic gossip, the newspaper slowly descended revealing her listening intently to what he was saying. The vice-consul rose, walked over to her chair, bowed as deeply as his girth-line would permit, and said most politely:

"Madame, you speak English?"

"But of course," she said with a friendly smile, expecting to be invited to join us.

"Et vous parlez français, madame?"

"Mais oui, naturellement, monsieur."

"Und Deutsch auch?"

"Aber natuerlich."

"I po-russki?" he went on. But the woman's face went blank. With another deep bow he rejoined me and went on in Russian.

"And have you heard," he asked, "what happened to the Italian codes in Berlin?"

The code room of the Italian Embassy in Berlin, he said, was run by a dried-up spinster who had been in the embassy for thirty years and must have been well into her fifties. With few friends and a face not likely to make many more, she lived a very quiet life in a tiny apartment off the Tiergarten just around the corner from the Italian Chancellery. Occasionally she went to a nearby Italian restau-

rant for supper or a demi-tasse of espresso. One evening while she was sipping her coffee, a young man dressed in a Tyrolean jacket, whom she had seen once or twice before in the restaurant, joined her and asked to be allowed to finish his coffee in her company.

He was exceedingly good-looking, blond, tall, with an open cheerful smile and could scarcely have been more than twenty-three or -four. He explained that he was an Austrian and, he hinted, a member of an old aristocratic family. When they had finished their coffee the Italian clerk excused herself and went back to her rooms. But a few days later she met the Austrian count again and this time he asked her to dine with him. He was lonely in Berlin, he explained, because his only associates were "Prussian swine" whom he detested.

Soon the two were dining regularly together. Then he invited her to a concert and to a theater. A full-blown romance was now in progress between the handsome Austrian count and the deeply infatuated Italian. Eventually they took to spending the weekends at one of the converted *Schlösser* that before the war Berlin hotelkeepers maintained in the countryside around the capital for just such clients. Then abruptly the count disappeared. The code clerk was sad but bolstered her morale with the happy memories of those blissful months.

Some time later the count showed up in Zurich and let it be known to a few selected foreign governments that the Italian diplomatic codes could be had at a price. My Yugoslav friend had been sent to buy them for a large packet of unmarked dollars on behalf of his government. When the Italian government finally got wind of the affair and investigated, they charged that the code clerk in the Berlin Embassy had "loaned" the codes to her boy friend, who had promptly photographed them. Taken for trial to Rome, she readily confessed, but told the indignant judge she would gladly do it all over again if the count would too.

As totalitarian diplomacy of both Communists and Nazis developed, they became more refined in their operations. Since to blow a safe or leave other traces that a code had been tampered with would warn the user that his code was compromised, Croatian bandits were replaced by expert safecrackers who could open safes by manipulating the combinations.

How easy this was even with modern safes was demonstrated when, as security officer, I was one day required to alter the combinations

of the dozen or more safes in one of our embassies. Having done so and carefully written the new combinations on cards, I put the cards in my safe, slammed the door, twirled the combination and went home. Only next morning it occurred to me that the new combination of my own safe, which I had forgotten, was safely inside it together with all the other new combinations. For twenty-four hours the embassy was more or less out of business until one of the consuls admitted shyly that he made a hobby of opening safes. Applying a little sandpaper to his finger tips he went to work and simply by feeling the tumblers fall had it open in a few hours.

Since an ultra-powerful telescope in a window across the street might possibly be used to photograph the code books, code clerks are usually cautioned not to work near windows. The Hotel Crillon in Paris, for example, is directly across a narrow street from the American Embassy. From any of a score of rooms in it an agent could easily see the desks of the embassy's political section.

Microphones are a classic weapon of totalitarian diplomacy, not only to eavesdrop on diplomatic conversations but to record a diplomat's thought as he dictates his telegrams. Easily concealed in curtains or furniture—on one occasion under the connubial bed of an Italian ambassador whose wife was known to wear the ambassadorial pants—their only disadvantage is the wiring they require.

Once while I was inspecting the attic of one of our embassies my flashlight reflected a glint no brighter than a tiny star under the eaves. The wire that had reflected the light could scarcely be seen in normal light. Tracing it with the beam of the flashlight, I found that it led down a ventilation shaft in the wall. I squeezed down the shaft and found a small microphone hanging behind the plaster directly back of the ambassador's desk on the floor below.

To guard against microphones, specialists armed with powerful induction coils to reveal any suspicious live wire in the walls periodically "debug" our diplomatic missions. This method was considered adequate until one day a radio ham on the staff of an American embassy, while twisting the dials of his powerful set, was startled to hear the voice of his ambassador, apparently dictating to his secretary in a building many blocks away. Despite the most thorough debugging of his office no sign of a wire or a mike could be found. Eventually a plaster reproduction of the Great Seal of the United States, presented

by a local artist to the ambassador's predecessor to adorn his office, was torn apart and in the plaster backing was found a wireless microphone—a device previously unknown to our security experts. To this day our specialists are not saying what, if any, countermeasure they have devised for this latest contribution to the armory of totalitarian diplomacy.

The totalitarians found other ingenious devices to tap their enemies' communications. When Italy switched sides in 1942, the Italian minister in Kabul, who had up to then been on the enemy side, showed me a photostat of a handwritten message.

"Have you ever seen that?" he asked.

Reluctantly I admitted that it was a penciled draft of a top-secret telegram I had sent some months before, in my own handwriting. He then explained that the German minister in Kabul had given it to him, stating that it had been obtained by a devilish little instrument that could reveal the impression left on a pad through a dozen or more sheets below the original writing.

These products of the totalitarians' ingenuity gradually awakened the State Department to the necessity for greater security. One of the first steps was the Marine guard sent to Moscow in 1934. Slowly similar precautions were extended to other embassies and the Marines soon had replaced all the superannuated night watchmen who had heretofore been almost the only protection against espionage.

As new regulations were issued requiring the locking up first of secret documents, then of stenographers' notebooks, carbon paper and other working papers, and the Marine guards during their night rounds began to enforce them by formal reports of "security violations," the older diplomats complained indignantly that the restrictions were hampering their work. But the appearance of new espionage devices merely strengthened the security measures.

The weakness in the department's code systems received less attention until, as we approached World War II, it became abundantly clear that our neighbors were not all as gentlemanly as Secretary Stimson had assumed in 1929. Eleven years later, as Secretary of War, Stimson himself ordered the establishment of a new Black Chamber in the War Department beginning practically from scratch once more. The Japanese codes even before Pearl Harbor were once again cracked and gave us warning (which was not fully utilized) of the coming Japanese attack.

Simultaneously, the State Department's codes were tested, with alarming results. In the previous years new coding precautions had tended to add to their cumbersomeness but less to their security and during crises the coding effort in our larger embassies consumed the days and nights of much of the staff. During the Munich Crisis, for example, half the vice-consuls in Berlin were assigned to the code room.

But now, with war practically upon us, the department was finally forced to break with the traditions Yardley had inveighed against more than ten years before and to scrap the sixteenth-century code systems for the very solution he had recommended—machines.

Whether these new machines are as secure as Yardley suggested in this age of electronic computers to assist code crackers in the laborious computations they must make is, of course, a question that only the experts can answer, and needless to say they are not talking.

Even though machines save time and effort their operation requires tedious concentration and meticulous attention, which can soon exhaust the energies of the strongest operator. Furthermore, the code clerk, even with the machine, has many other duties to perform. In a recent complaint printed in the *Foreign Service Journal* a communications clerk bitterly described some of his duties: copying cables, logging or numbering each, distributing incoming messages by hand to officers who were not in their offices, indexing and binding the cables in the telegraph book, and finally the tedious business of paraphrasing. How carefully the last operation must be done was illustrated by Chancellor Bismarck who by deliberately mis-paraphrasing the famous Ems dispatch set off the Franco-German War.

Probably the most frustrating job of all, as the embittered code clerk pointed out, is unraveling the errors and slips that creep into the cables during the coding, transmitting, and receiving processes. Even if the machines are infallible, a copyist may strike a wrong letter, a telegrapher may omit an entire line of code groups in transmitting a message, or a receiver may transpose a couple of symbols. Such "garbles," as they are called, can render important sections meaningless or even make impossible the decoding of everything that follows.

Occasionally an expert clerk, by a combination of guessing, recording or transposing a letter or group or two, can find the error. Sometimes checking at the telegraph office will reveal a missing group or

line. If not, a "service message" must be sent to the originator and often valuable time is lost before the corrected text is received and decoded.

In the days of the simple colored codes—the Old Gray Code, for example, which preceded the Brown—experienced coding hands eventually memorized most of the more common five-letter symbols in the book. In the late twenties a senior consul who was about to retire was given a testimonial dinner by his staff at the Shanghai Consulate. Rising after the toasts, he made his farewell speech in gray, to the consternation of the uninitiated but to the delight of the old-timers who followed the address with ease.

During the thirties a young officer assigned to the embassy in Stockholm was having trouble finding his niche in the diplomatic profession. In every branch to which he was assigned he turned out to be misfit. In despair his chief finally assigned him to the code room. Almost at once the number of garbles in Stockholm's cable messages soared. The department code room complained and the ambassador asked the young man for an explanation.

"Everyone knows," the neophyte explained, "that good code clerks don't use the book and I'm just following their example. Since I'm only beginning, you can't blame me if I guess wrong once in a while."

All cables emanating from the department are automatically sent over the name of the secretary or in his absence the under-secretary, acting. Likewise messages from missions end with the name of the chief or of his acting deputy. While it is a useful way to find out who is on the job and who has gone on a vacation or a diplomatic excursion, it has often led to confusion.

It is said that when James Byrnes was appointed secretary of state, an assistant found him on his first morning in office laboriously reading and penciling answers to dozens of messages signed by important ambassadors overseas. The assistant explained that Byrnes' subordinates would draft the answers but Byrnes insisted that any personal message from an important ambassador deserved a personal answer. Only after the rules were made clear did the new secretary realize that the messages were not quite so personal as he had supposed from the signatures.

Novice ambassadors have been similarly misled. One of them, read-

ing a message signed "Hull" complaining about an error in the embassy's accounts, was found by a subordinate in the depths of despair. "To think," he said, "that with all the other troubles Mr. Hull has we have to burden him with this mistake."

However, occasionally the secretary or an ambassador will indeed draft a message himself. An experienced officer will detect it at once by the use of the word "I" instead of the usual editorial "we." To dispel any doubts of novices, the sender may begin his message: "From the Secretary."

The drafter of a telegram ordinarily indicates whether it is confidential, secret, top-secret, or of even a higher classification. Occasionally a message will begin "Eyes only for the ambassador," meaning that the code clerk who decodes it must hand it personally to the chief. Before the introduction of the machine it was not unusual for a cable to come in beginning "To be decoded only by the ambassador." The awe such messages inspired in the code room was generally mitigated by the delightful sight of the ambassador cursing and sweating over unfamiliar code books and intricate cipher tables.

But the complicated coding devices of today require skilled operators; the ambassador and the subordinate officers who in the old days were detailed to coding during crucial periods are no longer called upon. Though they are doubtless pleased with this development, it deprives them of what once was an important element in their training.

Nowhere was verbosity so conspicuous as in telegrams being enciphered by a weary code clerk. The more exhausted he was and the more hunger gnawed at his stomach the sharper his eye became in spotting unnecessary words and the quicker his mind in devising more concise ways of saying the same thing. Though he was not allowed to change a syllable of the text before him, he invariably left the code room vowing that when he rose to the eminence of a drafting officer no code clerk would be given the excuse of calling him "a verbose son-of-a-bitch."

Even before World War II, the air raids and upheavals of modern warfare raised the question of what happens to an embassy's communications when the cables are broken or the commercial radio facilities are knocked out. The obvious solution was for every embassy to have

its own radio transmitters. However, international lawyers generally agreed that the ether, like airways, belonged to the state beneath it and could not be utilized without permission. On security grounds as well as for practical reasons governments were reluctant to grant others the right to use the limited radio frequencies available within their territory.

However, the ease with which a transmitter could be concealed within an extraterritorial embassy and the difficulty of proving, if not detecting, that such a transmitter was operating provided too great a temptation to many governments. As early as 1917 Yardley had discovered the German Legation in Mexico using a clandestine transmitter to communicate with Berlin.

Furthermore, totalitarians resorted to illegal transmitting for espionage and other purposes, and eventually the less total democracies were forced to follow suit. Today it may be assumed, though the State Department will deny it, that every large American mission has its own transmitters for use in emergency. Whenever possible the permission or at least the tacit understanding of the local government is sought before the transmitters are operated, as in the case of the ambassador's communication system in Beirut during the 1958 disturbances.

XIII

Consuls, Codes, and Couriers: 3

DESPITE the coding machine, the basic means of diplomatic communications still remains the classic one of couriers. Since the earliest times one of the basic rights of an embassy has been that of sending couriers whose dispatch cases were immune from search or seizure. The right, however, was not always meticulously observed. Back in 1380 B.C. an Egyptian king, wishing to send a message by courier through an area in which his diplomatic status might not be recognized, had the courier's head shaved, wrote his message on the scalp and waited until the hair had grown over it before sending him. In those days diplomacy apparently operated in a more leisurely fashion than today.

One night over three thousand years later the Nord Express from Paris to Moscow was lumbering slowly across the steppes. The single sleeping car had only a few passengers: an American lady on a visit to her son in the American Embassy in Moscow, a couple of German engineers, and the Japanese diplomatic courier en route to Tokyo from Berlin where a German-Japanese alliance, the text of which was secret, had just been negotiated.

The passengers were all asleep when the train suddenly stopped and the conductor announced that the car had broken an axle. Fortunately, he added, another sleeping car was standing by quite by chance on the adjoining track. Equally fortuitously, a staff of porters also were available—apparently just standing about in the steppe in

the middle of the night waiting for a chance to earn an honest kopeck.

Lest the train be late in Moscow, the passengers were told simply to hustle across the track to the new car in their night clothes. Their baggage would be transferred by the waiting porters. After a mad scramble and the confusion that ordinarily accompanies any such operation in Russia, the passengers settled back in their new car. It was hitched to the train and the journey was resumed.

Next morning the Japanese courier joined the American lady at breakfast. Grinning broadly and hissing with mirth, he told her that his dispatch case had disappeared during the midnight transfer.

"But," he added gleefully, "it wasn't my real dispatch case at all. This is where I carry secret messages," he boasted and raised his left arm to which was firmly manacled what looked like a little toilet kit. "And all that 'wreck' for an empty bag!" the little Japanese giggled.

In 1641 the British established the first modern courier service. Known as the king's, or queen's, messengers, these couriers have since traveled around the globe carrying what is known in British diplomatic circles as the "bag." (In American jargon it is the "pouch" and in French the "valise.") Recruited largely from retired police officers, the king's messengers wear a small silver greyhound as a symbol of their proud profession. The symbol predates that of any busline by several centuries.

In his diaries John Quincy Adams, who was American minister to Russia from 1809 to 1814, indicates that most of his correspondence with Washington was carried by the imperial Russian couriers. In fact, on several occasions the Czar's ministers dispatched special couriers to carry the American minister's urgent mail—an undertaking which, in the age of post horses and sailing ships, was not to be compared in simplicity with arranging a transatlantic flight today. It never seems even to have occurred to Mr. Adams that his messages might be tampered with but this, of course, was in the days when gentlemen really did not read each other's mail.

During World War I the United States organized a courier system using Marines and soldiers as couriers, but with the end of the war it was disbanded and the pouch was once more sent by mail or entrusted to any American who happened to be going its way. During that chivalrous age even confidential dispatches were often sent through the ordinary mails. Locked and fastened with heavy wax seals, they

were not, one then presumed, inspected by customs officers or border police. More secret documents were usually turned over to American travelers known to the diplomatic mission, who were given letters appointed them "bearers of dispatches." It was considered quite an honor to be entrusted with diplomatic mail and it also entitled the bearers of dispatches to preferential treatment at frontier stations. They therefore did the work for nothing.

However, the age of totalitarian diplomacy was already forcing itself upon the attention of reluctant State Department officials. Though other governments, too, sent pouches by mail, these generally contained only newspapers, personal mail, and similar nonsecret correspondence. On one occasion in the early thirties the Polish minister in a Balkan country called on the foreign minister to complain about the tampering with his diplomatic mail. He did not, he explained, object to the local authorities' opening his mailbags, since they contained only nonconfidential material. However, he considered it an affront that they should have been so thoughtless as to reseal them with the official seal of Finland.

During the London Economic Conference in 1934, President Roosevelt learned for the first time that the State Department had disbanded its courier service years before. Astonished, he ordered that it be reestablished immediately. Small sums were allotted to the embassies in Paris and London to hire one courier apiece. But these single couriers were hardly able to take care of the pouch mail in totalitarian countries, where even personal correspondence could not be entrusted to the public mails because of the censorship.

To supplement them, the personnel of embassies in dictatorships took turns carrying the pouch. It was a somewhat slipshod performance, but somehow no pouches were ever lost—for long. At one Eastern post an elderly consul who was retiring was asked to carry the pouches to a neighboring country on his way home. His departure was celebrated wih a large farewell banquet but next day a telegram arrived from his destination reading: "We have the courier. Have you got the pouches?" Fortunately they were still in the pouch room where the consul had forgotten to pick them up after his banquet.

As war approached, the totalitarians' interest in diplomatic pouches grew warmer and their methods cruder. When the Soviets took over the Baltic States, the American diplomatic missions there were liqui-

dated and their archives sent to Tallinn across the Finnish Gulf from Helsinki.

After a considerable number of pouches had accumulated in Tallinn and the pressure from the invading Russians increased, Henry Antheil, a young code clerk in Helsinki, whom I had known well, volunteered to hop across the gulf in a commercial plane and fetch the pouches. On the return flight the plane was attacked by an unmarked fighter and crashed into the sea, with the loss of all aboard. Finnish fishermen who witnessed the attack reported that the plane had hardly struck the water before an unmarked submarine surfaced and began rummaging in the wreckage. Whether the submarine retrieved the pouches has never been officially established. However, at least one letter believed to have been in the lost pouches inexplicably reached its destination months after the incident.

About the time the plane was downed a British diplomat, Sir Gordon Vereker, bound for London from Riga on a Swedish ship and carrying several "bags," found himself in an awkward spot when a German warship drew alongside and seized the vessel. With considerable presence of mind the diplomat slipped into the galley, tied some fire irons to his pouches and hurled them through the porthole. Nevertheless, some nonsecret pouches were seized, together with the diplomat. He was temporarily interned and then exchanged. The pouches, which contained some personal correspondence including a number of pin-up photographs belonging to bachelor diplomats in the Baltic States, caused considerable ribald mirth among the German naval authorities stationed at Hamburg, where I was then serving. Efforts to protect the dignity of these British cousins, some of them close friends, by taking over the "art" objects as the custodian of British interests were rejected by the Germans on the ground that the pin-ups were war booty.

After these incidents the State Department for a time substituted pouches perforated with brass rings to facilitate sinking in emergencies at sea until it was pointed out that the mail inside the pouches was just about as buoyant as the sacks themselves.

During and after the war the U. S. Diplomatic Courier Service was greatly expanded and improved. Today sixty-six couriers cover the globe on courier routes emanating from three overseas courier centers—Frankfurt, Panama, and Manila. These three centers are

connected with Washington by military planes which feed the diplomatic mail to them. In a single year U. S. couriers cover over four million miles—mostly by air. The couriers call only at centrally located missions, from which local couriers distribute the pouches to neighboring posts.

The couriers themselves, unlike their more staid colleagues, the queen's messengers, are young bachelors. They must be college graduates and pass a severe screening, for applications for the positions greatly exceed vacancies. Normally a courier remains with the service for six or seven years, after which he can try for entry into the regular career Foreign Service or return to a less hectic civilian job.

At any large airport a traveler may encounter the tall, thin American with crewcut head and rumpled seersucker suit ambling off a plane behind an airline porter rolling a baggage truck filled with what looks like U. S. mailsacks marked "Dept. of State" and heavily padlocked. Ordering a cup of coffee, he will sit down in a corner surrounded by his pouches, an invoice spread before him, checking and rechecking the little linen bags he has removed from one of the large sacks. Presently another crewcut in a slightly better pressed suit accompanied by a chauffeur in the American Embassy uniform will appear. Together they will check more invoices, exchange little sacks and larger pouches, signing receipts and initialling lists while harassed airline officials cluster about them with warnings that they are delaying the plane. Finally, their paper work completed, they part shouting to each others: "Tell Smitty I'll see him in Lagos Thursday and don't forget to ask Jim about those empty pouches in Tabriz." Preceded by a porter with his pouches, the first courier hurries to his plane. The pouches are not taken to the hold but are stacked beside him on a reserved seat. The plane warms up and he is off on the next leg of his run.

A normal courier run may start from Frankfurt and end there twenty-nine days later. The first stop is Geneva, then Rome, Athens, Cairo, Addis Ababa, and Nairobi. Traveling day and night, pausing only for connections, he reaches Nairobi in two and a half days. There he "stages," that is, another courier, like a relay runner, picks up his pouches and goes on southward while he rests a day or two and flies up to Kampala in Uganda, then to Mogadiscio in Somaliland and north to Aden. Thence he flies back to Nairobi, where he in turn

picks up the baton from the courier who left Frankfurt a week after he did. He flies south to Salisbury, Rhodesia, and to Pretoria, in South Africa, and then strikes north up the west coast to Leopoldville and finally to Lagos in Nigeria where he stages again, this time for four or five days during which he makes a side trip to Abidjan on the French Ivory Coast and to Duala in the French Cameroons. Then he again relieves the next arrival at Lagos and proceeds to Monrovia, Dakar, Casablanca, Nice and Paris, and finally to Frankfurt. After a day or two of rest there he is off again for Geneva and points south.

Contrary to myth, couriers are seldom overtly attacked and they never carry guns. However, the planes they ride in are occasionally shot at—and down—for violating forbidden territory. One courier, Frank Irwin, was shot down in his plane by Tito's forces in northern Yugloslavia. Though badly wounded, he retrieved his pouches from the burning plane and stayed with them until properly relieved by U. S. officials. Then he was carted off to a hospital, where he remained for over a year recovering from his wounds.

Like the code room, the pouch room, usually next to it, is behind a steel door beyond which innumerable locked gates and iron grills keep out everyone, including embassy officials who are not directly concerned with its operation. In sensitive posts someone is on guard there twenty-four hours a day.

The other service branches of the embassy are ordinarily concentrated in the administrative section. Here is the personnel office, where leave records are kept, identity cards issued, and complaints of officers and their wives dealt with.

The accounting officer is a key member of the administrative staff. Embassy accounts, like all government accounts, are run on the principle that though a diplomat can be entrusted with the country's most vital interests he is not to be trusted with the disposition of a four-cent stamp. When during the War I was ordered to open a diplomatic mission in Afghanistan I was accompanied to Kabul by a single American clerk. The innumerable accounting forms and procedures, tables and statistics we were required to submit each month occupied the full time of the clerk and at least half my own, though the sums we were authorized to spend were considerably less than the clerk's salary.

Even so, I apparently neglected my duties to the United States General Accounting Office. Some years after leaving Kabul a stern message from the GAO notified me that I had overpaid the clerk one month by several dollars. As the war was still going on and my mind was fully occupied with other matters which seemed more important, I ignored the notice. It was followed up by perhaps a dozen reminders. When peace finally came I wrote out a check for the amount I had allegedly overpaid the unfortunate clerk. A half year later an apologetic letter from the accountant general returned the check explaining it had all been a dreadful mistake.

The equipment of an embassy is with few exceptions supplied from Washington. Local purchases of even scratch-paper and pencils are made under penalty of a disallowance in one's accounts. Before I left to open the mission in Afghanistan, the department had assured me that all necessary equipment would be awaiting my arrival. Nothing in fact was awaiting me and the only equipment we received in our first six months of operation was a water cooler which was badly smashed up en route and for which we had little use. The pads and pencils I eventually bought and donated to the government. A typewriter we borrowed; for an official seal I used my thumbprint; for the rest we did without.

This hasty tour of the diplomatic plant has not touched on a score of other government offices scattered throughout the building and very possibly in seven or eight other buildings in the foreign capital: the Defense Department's Army, Air Force and Navy attachés; the International Co-operation Administration; the United States Information Service; and a dozen other special agencies which together probably outnumber the embassy staff by three to one.

Though many of these agencies are temporary and their relationship to diplomacy is tenuous, they directly concern the ambassador and his immediate staff. Each of them has a keen interest in some aspect of our foreign relations. Each has its own particular point of view and its own specific goal. Whether regarding such minor questions as local wage scales or the more serious problem of a soft versus a hard policy toward the host country, each agency has its ax to grind.

After a period of semi-autonomy immediately following the war, all agencies overseas today at least nominally are under the supervision of the ambassador. Normally this authority is understood and com-

plied with. Occasionally it is resented. Frequently there are genuine differences of approach, and to enforce compliance with U. S. policies as worked out by the State Department requires all the tact an ambassador can muster.

"Co-ordinating and supervising other overseas agencies of the government," a senior career department official states, "has become the major task of an American ambassador. Reporting, negotiating, representing and defending our interests may be his primary responsibilities, but how well he accomplishes these depends on how well he co-ordinates his often highly individualistic team."

XIV

Diplomacy and Intelligence: 1

THE diplomat, Callières says, has two principal functions: to conduct the business of his master and to discover the business of others.

Today it is the latter function that probably occupies the diplomat most. It is often referred to as "intelligence," though it is neither a substitute for wisdom nor a cure for stupidity. In the broadest sense, intelligence is any kind of information, but it usually means the information a statesman would like to have in making decisions on policy or a general in planning his campaign. As such it is called "strategic intelligence."

The diplomat is chiefly interested in information bearing on political or diplomatic events, though he is expected to report on military matters as well. Two hundred years ago his principal concern was with prospective alliances involving royal marriages and the varying state of temperature of a monarch's feelings toward his neighbors, his wife, and even his mistress.

The diplomat, however, was expected to know a great deal more than the marital doings of his host. The state of the royal treasury, the prospects for further revenues, the state of manufactures, meager though they were, and agricultural conditions, even two centuries ago, were recognized as having an important bearing on the power potential of a ruler. The diplomat was expected to be familiar with the geography of the area—not only those provinces ruled by his host but such other parcels of real estate as those to which he laid claim or on

which he had designs. He also studied the legal system and the social customs of the common people.

According to Callières, the ideal diplomat included among his reports a portrait gallery not only of the King but of the influential personages around him and of such rivals and pretenders as threatened his regime. Each portrait described as intimately as possible the subject's personality, his talents and weaknesses, his likes and prejudices, his romances, and his politics.

Finally, the ambassador was expected to report on the state of military preparedness of his host. Two centuries ago this was not the problem it is today. Monarchs generally courted a reputation for military strength and were only too glad to show off their troops to foreigners. Since types of weapons were few and their design simple, a good military estimate needed to include scarcely more than the numbers of troops, their condition and morale, the state of their equipment, the state of repair of major fortresses, and the state of the treasury's ability to meet the military payroll.

National patterns of behavior were even then of concern to diplomats. Callières recommended that they acquire an intimate knowledge of the host's country's history, not only to be able to display their erudition but, more important, to learn from past events what a land and its ruler might do in a given set of circumstances in the future.

It was not sufficient, Callières warned, simply to study the dispatches of one's predecessors; it was necessary to keep an eye on new developments so that past reports, carefully preserved in the archives at home, could constantly be brought up to date.

The methods pursued by eighteenth-century diplomats in obtaining their information were varied. Their primary source was, of course, the monarch himself and his ministers, with each of whom a diplomat was expected to maintain the most intimate relations possible. Other diplomatic colleagues were prime sources and the diplomatic corps, then as now, kept up a lively trade in gossip, rumor, and occasionally hard facts.

Callières especially recommended as sources vain or disgruntled courtiers who might by their indiscretions give away important state secrets. Nor was he above bribery, and suggested that especially suitable for this type of information collecting were ballerinas and others who had private access on intimate terms with the ruling personalities.

Ballerinas have contrived ever since to play a role in intelligence. During World War II when the Moscow Ballet was evacuated to Kuibyshev with the diplomatic corps, many friendships between the dancers and the diplomats developed which did not go unnoticed by the secret police. On one occasion a young girl in the troupe who had been "going steady" with a clerk in our embassy was approached by the secret police with instructions to find out through her American friend what the United States' real attitude was toward the question of Indian independence. Unfortunately neither the girl nor her friend had the vaguest inkling of the subject. In their dilemma, the clerk discussed the matter with the ambassador and a report was worked up of what the latter thought it would be useful for the Soviets to know on this subject. The report was then passed on through the ballerina to the secret police, who never apparently suspected its source.

In parliamentary countries, such as Poland and England, Callières recommended that diplomats carefully cultivate the members of the Diet or Parliament as good information sources. For this purpose he suggested that Parliamentarians were especially impressed by a good cuisine and plenty of wine.

Objectivity in reporting was even then strongly emphasized by leading writers. Not only must a report be carefully considered and the information conveyed tested as to source and compared with other sources, but a diplomat worthy of his salt should never fear to tell the bad along with the good. Callières relates at length the sad predicament of a brilliant and honest Spanish diplomat, Don Estevan de Gamarra, who complained to his Foreign Office that he was never promoted whereas younger and less able diplomats were advanced over his head.

"You have only yourself to blame," the Foreign Office told him. His dispatches, they pointed out, always contained distasteful truths which "set the King's teeth on edge." To report what the State Department wants to hear is still a temptation to American diplomats. Especially in critical times, when both the public and the officials are prey to their emotions, it still requires courage to report unpopular truths which may set the State Department's teeth on edge.

A few well-chosen spies were essential to a well-run eighteenth-century embassy. Despite the relative lack of security regulations in a royal court, there were always a few rumors or plots incubating that

could be ferreted out only by the use of paid informers. In fact, the employment of a modest stable of spies was considered so essential that the diplomat was expected to pay them out of his own pocket—and very liberally at that. The ambassador seldom dealt directly with these figures but employed intermediaries or subordinates in order to be able to disavow them if double-crossed. Even in those days the double-agent was a familiar figure.

When, nearly a century later, America was introduced to diplomacy by Benjamin Franklin, neither the methods nor the goals of the diplomatic information gatherer had altered significantly. In seeking friends and allies for the American revolutionary regime, Franklin still found it useful to trade tidbits of gossip with his colleagues at the court of Louis XVI or to enlist supporters by an occasional flirtation with a lady in waiting or a prominent courtesan.

But during the nineteenth century a rapid change took place. With the growth of international trade, the commercial rivalries, and the race for colonies, economic and commercial questions began to over-shadow the petty personal rivalries of courts. Dynastic issues and genealogical charts gave way to statistical tables in the priorities of the diplomatic intelligence seekers. The technical advances of the industrial revolution raised the search for new machines and inventions to a primary concern.

The giant strides in the equipment of armies, improvements in the accuracy of firearms and new mechanisms for rapid firing, put a premium on spies capable of filching the design of a new breechloader or a machine gun. In 1894 the French Captain Alfred Dreyfus was accused of selling plans for a breech mechanism to the Germans.

Railroads greatly increased the speed with which armies could be mobilized and transported to one frontier or another. The rapid rise of Prussia as a military power under an integrated General Staff like-wise made troop movements and mobilization plans important intelligence targets. If France could put her armies into the field on M + 5 day and Germany on M + 4, it became imperative for each to have the earliest possible warning that the enemy was getting ready to press the mobilization button. Just before World War I, the Austrian chief of staff was convicted of selling Austria's mobilization plans to the Serbs.

To satisfy this mutual interest in one's neighbor's military estab-

lishment, governments eventually agreed to exchange military experts to reinforce the diplomatic staffs of embassies. These military attachés not only had the advantage of being able to appraise a new weapon or tactic better than the peaceful diplomat but they could be more easily controlled, and visits to military installations, maneuvers and inspections placed on a reciprocal basis.

Though not involved in these European rivalries, the Civil War taught the Americans the necessity of military intelligence. In a frantic search for an "expert" the Northern armies chose Allan Pinkerton, a famous private detective, to head military intelligence. Only after many months did it occur to the generals that military intelligence and gumshoe work had little in common and an experienced army officer eventually replaced Pinkerton.

World War I, a preview of the age of total warfare and total diplomacy, saw the appearance of experts in finance, transport, food and communications, who assisted the diplomats in negotiations and information gathering during both the fighting and the peacemaking However, the experience of America, a neutral for nearly three years and a combatant only in the last year and a half, was brief and the lessons learned, like that of Yardley and the Black Chamber, were soon forgotten.

In the periods between the wars, the principal intelligence continued to come from the embassy chancelleries and the military attachés. A few experts were trained in specific regions like Russia and the Far East where normal channels of information either did not exist or were blocked by police action and strict national security. But the average American career diplomat continued to be a general practitioner of the profession.

It is fashionable today to criticize the meagerness of the information our diplomats furnished prior to World War II. With the advantage of hindsight it is not difficult to find wide lacunae in the State Department's information archives accumulated during the prewar years. Almost completely lacking were such basic data as harbor capacities and characteristics, airfield construction, road and railway characteristics, population statistics, social structures and health facilities, mineral and mining figures, smelting capacities, and agricultural acreage. Such elementary intelligence as biographical information was spotty.

But one should bear two factors in mind before assessing the blame. In the first place, until the rise of the totalitarians international finance, shipping, communications, and commerce were in private hands, usually large corporations, trusts, cartels or banks which had maintained their own private information services adequate to their purposes. Morgan, Harjes et Cie in Paris, the National City Bank in Berlin, and the Matson Lines in the Far East each had its own representatives and seldom called for information from the government. Furthermore, who before Pearl Harbor had foreseen the need for data on dock facilities at Saigon or a description of the beaches of Normandy?

Secondly, one must recall that as late as the thirties the foreign policy of the United States was largely distinguished by its nonexistence. The diplomats and consuls were under the strictest instructions to observe but not to meddle. What they observed was what the State Department of an isolated country needed to know to be adequately posted on events abroad. It would be untrue to charge that the American Foreign Service kept the State Department less well informed than were the foreign offices of the other great powers on matters in which the latter were not specifically involved. In fact, foreign diplomats in the years immediately before World War II had come to consider the American Foreign Service one of the best informed in the world. When war finally came, the State Department knew as much on every important development as any other capital and better than most including Moscow.

Whether the same can be said for the intelligence furnished by the military attachés is doubtful, but the fault lay not with the attachés. Their job is an expensive and thankless one. Congress had never looked kindly on the attachés, and their pay and allowances were until just before the outbreak of the war so meager that only those with independent incomes could undertake the job. Furthermore, service in foreign capitals did not improve an army officer's promotion prospects. Nor did the attachés escape the problem of honest Don Estevan, whose frankness blocked his promotion. G-2 in Washington was no more immune to emotional prejudices than were other quarters not in daily contact with world politics and, like them, it was inclined to equate immorality with incompetence. Thus, because Hitler's regime was morally bad it could not, many officers in G-2 assumed, be militarily effective. The result was that any connection between military

intelligence and an intelligent military was largely coincidental—though not totally absent.

In the last years of peace the American military attaché in Berlin was both competent and courageous. Week after week Colonel Truman-Smith sent reports to G-2 that the Reichswehr was rapidly becoming the finest fighting force in Europe. But his reports were discounted and his warnings disregarded until the German armies swept across France, annihilating its forces in a couple of weeks and hurling the British back across the Channel minus their precious equipment. Then Truman-Smith's reports were hurriedly dug out of the files and reread and the colonel's subsequent advice more carefully heeded.

In Moscow another military attaché with strong political prejudices saw or thought he saw in the Soviet armies a force capable of containing the wicked Nazis and the, to him, even wickeder Japanese. With more passion than perspicacity he reported to Washington every boastful claim of the Stalin regime to military invincibility. While certain elements of the political world in the United States found comfort in his reports, the military who considered the Bolsheviks no less evil than the Nazis discounted his conclusions and in the end he was replaced.

When war broke out between the Germans and the Russians, the military attaché's office in Moscow was staffed by officers with no previous political or intelligence experience. As the Reichswehr surged across the steppes in the summer of 1941 one of the attachés, convinced that Stalin was all but defeated, was asked whether he had considered the implications of Napoleon's Russian campaign. "We military men make history," he replied. "We don't read it."

Under the circumstances, the confusion that prevailed in Washington military circles about the outcome of the war on the eastern front was understandable. Later, at Yalta, Stalin himself confessed that the rose-bespectacled attaché had been grievously misled by Soviet propaganda and that until long after his departure the Soviet armies had been woefully ill-led and ill-equipped. And General Winter, who had played so formidable a role in defeating Napoleon, this time proved ineffective in hurling back the Germans for three years, until the Russian armies had been re-equipped, retrained, and their old officers replaced.

But, despite reasons and excuses advanced for the inadequacy of

the intelligence-gathering agencies, the fact remained that the archives in Washington were ill-prepared to assist those who had to quarterback the total war which confronted them after Pearl Harbor. With one blow Pearl Harbor swept away many misconceptions, prejudices, and obsolete practices. On that day began a new era in the American diplomatic and military intelligence effort. The effects are still with us. Some of them represent a major advance in providing American statesmen and generals with the information they need to survive the struggle facing us. Others, like all measures designed to avoid the repetition of specific disasters of the past, seem to disregard the possibility that future disasters may take forms that the present system is not designed to cope with.

The first remedy to cure the ailing military patient was the formation early in 1942 of the Joint Intelligence Committee under the Joint Chiefs of Staff to operate a co-ordinated military intelligence system. In the civilian field General William Donovan was appointed co-ordinator of information with the duty of collecting and disseminating to appropriate officials all available strategic intelligence.

It quickly became apparent to Donovan that the problem was not merely one of assembling and disseminating available intelligence but of vastly increasing the intelligence available. For that purpose the Office of Strategic Services (OSS) was eventually organized under Donovan's energetic leadership. Soon the OSS was dispatching agents all over the globe under various forms of cover and with various degrees of training. Their reception by the diplomatic officers of the Foreign Service was not precisely warm.

In Kabul two young men appeared as teachers in the local English-language school. Both spoke Persian, the language of Afghanistan, both were students of Central Asia and above average in knowledge and intelligence. But neither had ever been out of the United States and neither had had any previous military or diplomatic experience.

Shortly after they arrived they officially confirmed to me what I and others had already surmised—they were secret agents of the OSS. Precisely what they were to do in Afghanistan was unclear, except that they were under instructions to increase the flow of information from Kabul to Washington. Since I considered that my own reports contained all available useful intelligence I was not a little miffed at the young men's audacity when they handed me a coded message

containing, they said, important secret information, with the request that it be sent through diplomatic channels to Washington.

Having been reared in the tradition that all messages from a diplomatic mission are read and approved by its chief I demanded to see the true text of their message. The inevitable argument ensued. After a few exchanges with Washington, it was agreed that the two men would in future collect and pass on to me any strategic intelligence they might succeed in unearthing.

Not many months elapsed before one of them was sent home with dysentery. Shortly thereafter the other international spy, incurably homesick and miserably unhappy in a primitive town which, he complained, did not even have sidewalks, also departed and ended up in the Army.

Apprehensive of the trouble the OSS agents might easily stir up in their inexperienced enthusiasm to gather information, the career diplomats' attitude toward them was not only understandable but often justified. For example, if one of the two young men in Kabul had been caught sketching a nineteenth-century fortress or a French 75 mm., with which the Afghan Army was equipped, the odds were that even if they were not blown from the mouth of a cannon, as spies had been in Afghanistan only a generation before, the American Legation would at the very least be put in a corner from which no valuable information whatever could be reported. The objection to the neophytes from OSS was not that spying was immoral or undiplomatic but that successful espionage was for experts not in Central Asian archaeology or history but in espionage.

The reaction of General Donovan's staff was equally understandable: how does a country which has shunned espionage throughout its history develop spies? The answer was, only by trials, often costly errors, and long experience. The old governments of Europe had been in the business for centuries and occasionally still made mistakes. Though the American neophyte is precocious and has learned fast, he still has much to learn. Fortunately he knows it.

Besides plunging bravely into the tricky world of international espionage, the OSS also tackled the equally delicate task of political warfare, dropping pamphlets designed to stir up political unrest in enemy territories, organizing and arming guerrilla forces, and acting as a political advance guard for the Allied armies both in Africa and

in Europe. In Washington imaginative inventors, engineers, and chemists developed a whole armory of devices to cause the enemy trouble in the areas they occupied. The chief and often fatal handicap of these home-grown and homebred troublemakers was their inability to envisage conditions behind enemy lines where passions were strong, risks enormous, and the costs of failure supreme.

Two years after my first unhappy encounter with the OSS I found myself a part of Donovan's organization as head of a mission to Tito's guerrillas. There my predecessor told me that a few months earlier a plane had parachuted to him a case of gadgets dreamed up by the OSS troublemakers in Washington, which he was instructed to demonstrate to Tito's troops in order to interest them in their use. But again the trouble was that the nasty-minded men in America were not nearly nasty-minded enough for conditions in enemy-held territories.

Reluctantly my predecessor took the case to Tito's headquarters where a group of hard-boiled guerrillas and saboteurs had been assembled to see the demonstration. The first item in the case—called a "Who-Me?"—was a tube of evil-looking substance. The instructions with it explained that the user should make his way into an enemy-held friendly city. Upon encountering an enemy officer about to enter a public restaurant or café, he should deftly and unobserved smear some of the contents of the tube on the officer's uniform. As soon as the officer sat down in the warm restaurant the stuff would give off such a foul odor that he would be forced to withdraw humiliated.

Tito's guerrillas were unimpressed and my predecessor turned to another gadget consisting of a piece of string attached to a rag impregnated with a special chemical. The instructions explained that if a guerrilla was being chased by enemy security police using blood-hounds, he should drag the rag behind him. The scent left by it would make the bloodhounds sick and end the pursuit.

Tito's officers began to look bored and the demonstrator took up a device called the "Hedy-Lamarr Panic Creator." The guerrilla agent, according to the instructions, was to make his way into an enemy city where a Nazi leader, preferably Hitler, was to make a public speech. After penetrating the auditorium, the agent was to fasten the Hedy-Lamarr under the rostrum and adjust the timing device to go off during the speech. Tito's men began to stir. Then, the instruction went on, if all went well, the gadget would explode with a deafening,

panic-creating roar but without harming anyone. "You mean after all that it wouldn't even hurt Hitler?" the officers asked, bewildered.

Hastily the American turned to his last gadget, a small pistol with a long barrel. Dramatically he shot it at a tree in the garden. It ripped a slash of bark from the trunk but the shot was completely silent.

"Now that," the officers said, their eyes glistening with excitement, "is something we could use. Give us five thousand." He was forced to explain ruefully that the silent pistol was in heavy demand and short supply. Only the one in his hand was available.

It would be most misleading to imply that all OSS agents were homesick neophytes or that their missions behind enemy lines were confined to demonstrating Hedy-Lamarrs and Who-Mes. In Switzerland, Allen W. Dulles, an experienced and sophisticated expert in foreign affairs, organized and operated one of the most effective espionage centers of any power during the war. Not only did he have agents within Hitler's key ministries in Berlin but it was he who persuaded the German commander on the Italian front to surrender weeks before V-E day.

Furthermore, the parachuted missions behind enemy lines performed daring and highly effective tasks blowing up bridges, tunnels and supply trains, harassing enemy troops, and collecting invaluable strategic and combat intelligence. One of them parachuted into a German air force garrison and elected himself a member of the Nazi officers' mess, where he gathered invaluable bits of information which he thereupon radioed back to headquarters from a transmitter concealed in an abandoned barn on the outskirts of town. Another OSS agent, a painter by profession, was in heavy demand on the Italian front, where every night or two he slipped through the lines and, on encountering a lone enemy soldier, put him out of action with a blackjack, stripped him of his identity documents and strolled back home to tell the local commander what troops were opposing him.

It was in Washington, however, that Donovan's OSS made its greatest and most lasting contribution to the science of developing diplomatic and military strategic intelligence. Starting with all but empty files, OSS was called upon to gather and collate an encyclopedic mass of information both for the military leaders and for the diplomatic policy makers. The range stretched from geographical studies on possible landing fields to the political convictions of obscure resist-

ance fighters.

To solve the problem Donovan recruited scores of professors, teachers, and specialists in every branch of knowledge from cartography to the social and political sciences. Applying the methods they had used in laboratories and workshops rather than those employed in chancelleries and ministries, they set about piecing together the parts of the puzzle that were at hand and searching through libraries, newspaper files, interviews with travelers, and finally the reports of their own agents for the pieces that were missing.

When pieces were still lacking with which to finish the picture they turned to sociological, psychological, and other scientific principles to find the needed information. Much of their work was for purely military purposes: encyclopedias of areas in which the troops were to operate and later to rule by military government. But much also concerned purely political problems: what was the true character of the partisan movement in Yugoslavia? Was Tito a Yugoslav nationalist as he often professed or a dyed-in-the-wool Stalinist as he subsequently, though temporarily, revealed himself to be? Was Mao Tse-tung an agrarian reformer or a Communist? To answer these questions, OSS sent special missions to observe and report from the source, while back at home every scrap of information about these men and their movements was gathered, evaluated, and collated.

These methods were to old diplomats a complete innovation, and the results were, as might be expected, not entirely trusted. Political decisions in foreign affairs, they had always believed, were made on the basis of reports from professional diplomats who culled them from conversations at the dinner table or during calls at the Foreign Office or even from press reports and editorials but never from the calculations, no matter how scientific, of sociologists.

XV

Diplomacy and Intelligence: 2

WITH the end of the war there arose the question of what to do with the OSS. Some, like President Truman, objected to its continuation for fear it might become another Gestapo. The military and the State Department opposed it as a rival intelligence agency. Yet its accomplishments during the war were sufficient to prove the value of a research and analysis staff, and each department wanted to take over this unit for itself. As for the central information clearinghouse, as far as this concerned foreign affairs it should, the State Department insisted, be returned to the department where it had always been since the Revolution.

The idea of an independent agency was vigorously defended by those who had helped build the OSS. If the diplomats were leery about OSS intelligence, some professors were downright contemptuous of the State Department's system based on diplomatic reports. Indeed, they implied that none but their own was entitled to be called an intelligence system. All old systems, including the centuries-old diplomatic method were dismissed as obsolete. Only those who had been trained during the war in OSS could be called intelligence experts and the diplomats who had for hundreds of years acted in that capacity had, they implied, been impersonators.

In the end a compromise was reached. Research and analysis were bodily transferred to the State Department. Military intelligence went back to the Pentagon and a Central Intelligence Authority, later the

Central Intelligence Agency, was created from the remains of OSS.

The specific functions of the CIA were to advise the President and the National Security Council on intelligence matters; to recommend co-ordinating measures, to correlate and evaluate intelligence and disseminate it; and to perform certain other functions including, one may assume, espionage and undercover political warfare measures.

The Central Intelligence Agency today supervises two important jobs which before the war were performed within the State Department or not done at all: the national intelligence survey and the national estimate. The first is a basic survey or superguidebook of other nations, the second an estimate of some specific problem by American intelligence experts. At present the intelligence surveys are being written by State Department personnel but with the assistance and supervision of CIA.

The national estimate is an effort to reach a consensus of the opinion held by the so-called "intelligence community" in the CIA, the armed services, the State Department, the Atomic Energy Commission, and occasionally experts from other interested government departments. The CIA is responsible for collecting the views of each agency, which are then assembled in a composite paper and discussed by the "community" until an accord is reached. If irreconcilable views still persist, minority opinions are set forth in footnotes. The estimate is then forwarded to the proper authorities.

There are several types of national estimates: the straight estimate, which attempts to assess another nation's future performance assuming no change in U. S. policy, and the general estimate, which attempts to weigh the consequences of a possible change in U. S. policy. For example, the President or another member of the National Security Council may request a national estimate on the reaction of the Soviet Union if the United States landed troops in the Lebanon. Or the Central Intelligence Agency itself may decide that a national estimate is currently needed to determine the threat to American security of a revolution in Venezuela. In both cases the estimate is confined to intelligence and tries to avoid as much as possible any suggestion for future U. S. policy.

In addition to these functions the CIA performs several others of almost equal concern; for example, it carries out espionage activities, which, as a result of Pearl Harbor and the war, are no longer beyond

the pale of American government activities. Although these operations are wrapped in the deepest secrecy, a few facts about modern espionage are available and worth noting. In the first place, it is not, as already suggested, a game for beginners. Espionage requires the most careful recruitment, training, preparation, and supervision—all by experts. In the second place, the information obtained by espionage is usually a small proportion of the total intelligence gathered. It may well be a vital part, but expressed in percentages it may not amount to more than 4 or 5 per cent of the whole picture, the rest of which is pieced together from diplomatic sources or materials published in the newspapers, trade journals, scientific papers, and from foreign government declarations and speeches.

Finally, not all secret information is obtained by espionage. Much is marked "secret" or even "top secret" not because it was obtained by violating a file cabinet but in order to protect some legitimate source or to prevent others from knowing what we know. For example, an indiscreet foreign official may tell the American ambassador of plans afoot by his country to invade a third country. If it became known that the official had divulged this fact or even that the United States was aware of the plans, it not only might be dangerous for the indiscreet source but might provoke his government into drastic and undesirable action. Also, if it is known that the United States has certain information, others can more easily deduce what course of action the United States will adopt.

An American ambassador is also inclined to classify his own views and recommendations as "secret," though they compromise no vulnerable source, in order to protect his own position. For example, if his opinions of persons at his post became known, his own relations with them might well become strained.

The label "secret" on a report entails certain risks. Human nature's craving for information that is not common knowledge almost automatically raises the value of any tidbit marked "secret" and lowers the importance of information not so classified. The result is that frequently an unreliable rumor, if labeled secret, may carry more weight than an established fact. Consequently information obtained through secret channels, such as espionage, though generally less reliable than more easily available knowledge, is likely to take precedence in the councils where policies are determined.

The compromise reached in the liquidation of OSS returned to the State Department primary, but not exclusive, responsibility for collecting overseas information on political, economic, cultural, and social matters obtainable through overt, or normal, diplomatic channels. This does not mean, however, that if a CIA representative, in the course of pursuing other objectives, learns something of political significance he must forget it. On the contrary, he is expected to pass it on to his ambassador or diplomatic representative.

All information obtained by diplomatic channels is made available in Washington to the CIA in accordance with its basic charter as the co-ordinator and evaluator of all intelligence. In a foreign capital, however, the ambassador, the senior American government representative, is, theoretically at least, entitled to know what other agencies are up to. This often places him in an awkward position if other U. S. agencies are engaged in undercover work. Even Callières warned that a diplomat should keep a discreet distance from the activities of undercover agents.

However, even in the best organized spy system it frequently happens that a valuable agent falls into the hands of the police of a friendly state. It then occasionally becomes necessary to request diplomatic intervention to spring him. Much of a diplomat's time has often been taken up persuading reluctant ministers of justice, police chiefs, and judges to release shady characters connected with other government agencies who had got caught in local counterespionage nets.

The normal resolution of this dilemma is for an ambassador to insist on being informed in general terms of the activities of his intelligence agents but to remain ignorant of the details of all specific operations. Thus the intelligence agent may tell the ambassador that he proposes to investigate the tie-up between a local opposition leader and the Kremlin. He will not, however, tell him that he intends to tap the man's telephone, seduce his secretary, or blow his safe.

In pursuing his major occupation as a reporter, the modern American ambassador and his staff have, with a few changes, stuck to the practices employed by diplomats for the past two hundred years. Their sources continue to be confidential talks with their host government's ministers and exchanges of gossip, speculation, and facts with their diplomatic colleagues at cocktail parties and dinners. Political officers continue to cultivate Foreign Officer officials, members of Parliament,

leading editors, and of course the American journalists who in the course of their search for news frequently pick up very useful reports.

A member of the staff is likely to be assigned to cover the opposition, reporting their disagreements, following closely their successes and failures at the polls for indications of a possible parliamentary upset, and carefully noting the programs they advocate in case they should come to power.

The methods of extracting information, too, have remained largely unchanged and, as Callières noted, parliamentarians continue to be attracted by good food and to become more communicative with fine wines. Some diplomats, however, have adapted their methods to the increasing tempo of modern life. Instead of the leisurely dinner party, they have favored the businessman's lunch from which wives are excluded and where less time is wasted on formalities.

In one respect a more profound change has taken place. The ambassador continues from time to time to compose a deep "think piece" or survey of relations in general, giving his views of the future and his recommendations on possible changes of policy. But the staff that two decades ago also was used to prepare lengthy dispatches, including their estimates and conclusions resulting from penetrating research, today confine themselves more to reporting simple facts, leaving the basic research and conclusion drawing to be done in the State Department, to which the research and analysis staff of the old OSS was transferred.

After its transfer this staff was promptly broken up into regional units and subordinated to the regional political divisions. Thus, for example, the researchers who had been specializing on Soviet affairs were amalgamated with the Eastern European Political Division.

Immediately the experts of the new intelligence method raised a hue and cry, arguing that intelligence should be strictly isolated from the policy makers. Too close association between the two, they insisted, would tend to destroy the objectivity of the intelligence experts. If subordinated to the policy originators, they would be under pressure to make intelligence estimates that favored the policies adopted. Besides, they said, the political personnel would inevitably call on the intelligence experts to do odd chores, taking them off their long-term research projects.

Both arguments are in part sound. Just after the war,

when OSS was still in existence, its field mission to Austria included a research and analysis unit composed of a number of very competent professors and specialists in Austrian affairs. When our troops entered Vienna we assumed responsibility for feeding the starved population of our sector of the city. The question then arose whether to refine the wheat we received from America and give them white bread or leave it brown. General Clark asked the OSS unit to conduct a survey to find out which the Viennese preferred. As I was in charge of the mission I turned the problem over to the learned professors. They objected violently. One of them explained he was doing a study on Austrian state-church relations. Another explained he was making a survey of Austria's long-term economic prospects. A third had an equally weighty and doubtless valuable subject under study. Somewhat peremptorily I explained that our immediate problem was to feed the Austrians, not to analyze their religion or economy. Reluctantly the professors gave in and reported back a few days later that the Austrians, deprived of white bread since Hitler's take-over, now wanted only the whitest possible. After a week of the diet, however, the luxury-loving Viennese changed their minds and begged for the more nourishing black.

As a result of the objections to breaking up the research staff, General Marshall, on becoming secretary of state, was prevailed upon to reverse the decision and once more research and analysis were taken off and isolated in their tower where they churned out their long-range estimates and studies. They are still in their tower at the time of writing. How much they are contributing to the formulation of sound policy remains to be seen. A brief survey of their output indicates they are chiefly engaged in gathering materials for high-level public speeches and re-analyzing foreign newspapers long since scrutinized in foreign capitals by our embassy staffs.

In one area the modern approach to strategic intelligence has produced an entirely new intelligence method variously known as Kremlinology, Sovietology, or Bolshevismology. Because of the secrecy which shrouds the Soviet Union's inner workings, Russian specialists have adopted an extreme variant of the research analysts' approach to learn the Kremlin's secrets. Reading every available newspaper or magazine, they carefully study the names of those reported present at congresses, the lists of recipients of awards which the Soviet Union

uses in place of material incentives, the signatures under published letters of condolence on the deaths of prominent leaders, the signatures of articles and letters of factory managers and technicians to editors, the promotions and demotions obscurely printed on the last page of *Pravda* and *Izvestiya* and, of course, the order of the pictures carried in parades on national holidays, to determine the relationship of the various individual members of the ruling hierarchy. For example, if Comrade Ignatiev was listed as county party secretary in the Ukraine during Khrushchev's tour of duty in Kiev and subsequently appears as a party official on a higher level in Moscow he is labeled a Khrushchev man. Should he at any future time be demoted, it might mean that Khrushchev's power is slipping. If a man bearing the Malenkov label is promoted, it can mean that Malenkov himself is staging a comeback.

Quite aside from the painstaking research this process demands, it has often been derided as based on faulty assumptions, abstruse reasoning, and farfetched conclusions. Occasionally the methods of the Kremlinologists recall the example often cited by General Hoyt Vandenberg to illustrate the difference between hard fact and speculation:

A Kentucky mountaineer went to call on his neighbor but found only his small son at home.

"Where's your paw?" he asked the boy.

"Gone fishin'."

"How d'ye know?"

"Had his boots on and 'tain't rainin'."

"Where's yer maw?"

"Outhouse."

"How d'ye know?"

"Went out with a Montgomery Ward catalogue and she can't read."

"Where's yer sister?"

"In the hayloft with the hired man."

"How d'ye know?"

"It's after mealtime and there's only one thing she'd rather do than eat."

Despite such criticism, if we accept research and analysis as the basis for intelligence we can hardly argue with those who pursue the

method to its logical conclusion. Furthermore, the Kremlinologists can claim a number of major successes in prediction. After all, it was they who noted the absence of Beria's name from a list of spectators at a state performance of the Moscow Ballet and predicted his downfall weeks before it was finally announced. Subsequently Khrushchev was generally listed in the press as "first Secretary" of the party, indicating he was the first among equals in the supreme Secretariat. One day a sharp-eyed Bolshevismologist noted in *Pravda* that he had been labeled "First Secretary." Immediately the expert concluded that he had in fact been raised to a new plateau of supreme power. Others, who had failed to detect the transformation of the lower-case *f* to a capital *F*, only much later came to the same conclusion.

The dearth of intelligence on Russia has attracted the curiosity of other branches of the social sciences. A psychologist, utilizing the public utterances of prominent Bolsheviks, has produced a study of the political behavior patterns of Communist leaders which, it is claimed, was used by the military negotiators of the Korean truce at Panmunjom to explain the odd behavior of their Soviet opposites.

As yet, however, the professional diplomats are not inclined to abandon Callières entirely in favor of the socio-anthropologists and the new scientific intelligence methods. In fact they question whether the new methods of intelligence gathering and evaluating are alone an adequate substitute for the older methods which have stood the test of generations of diplomacy.

Few would deny the valuable contributions that the intelligence experts of OSS and subsequently of the CIA have made to the science, if it be one, of collecting and evaluating information. Few would deny that a central archive of basic intelligence was greatly needed before the war, not simply as a convenience for ready reference but, more important, to spotlight the gaps in the picture puzzle that needed filling.

The effort to bring together and reconcile the views of experts from the diplomatic, the military, and the scientific worlds in one national estimate has certain advantages over leaving decisions to individuals who may be prejudiced or subject to blind spots. Such persons are not unknown in the State Department or other branches of the government: the devotee of Chiang Kai-shek or Adenauer, the man to whom de Gaulle is anathema, the Anglophile and the Anglophobe, all are

still with us and will probably be for generations to come.

Nor can the professional diplomat quarrel with the need for technical experts. The financial specialist, the mineralogist, and the automation expert must be consulted and their judgment given serious consideration if we are to have expert intelligence about the future intentions of our enemies and the prospects of our allies.

However, the problem lies in how these experts are used and what relative weight is given to their views.

One of the difficulties about "collective wisdom," as Churchill contemptuously called it, is that it does not so readily find acceptance in the minds of the policy makers. Its anonymity, its lack of personality, its cold, hard approach do not carry the same conviction as a report, no matter how superficial, from a man-who-has-been-there. Can the collective report, therefore, overcome the preconceived ideas, the pictures created by casual conversations with articulate but inexpert observers as well as does the report prepared by the qualified man on the spot—the diplomat?

After his one brief visit to Moscow, Chancellor Adenauer came home to announce that Russia was in grave difficulties because of a drop in the birth rate: during his entire visit he had not seen a single baby carriage. Furthermore, he had not seen a smiling face. Adenauer has at his disposal an unusually competent intelligence organization, but not one of its anonymous reports made the impression on him or had the powerful influence on his views that those allegedly nonexistent baby carriages and smiles did.

Perhaps a greater drawback to the "collective wisdom" is the danger it runs in the process of being "boiled down" and its differing opinions reconciled. Could not some significant truth be boiled away? Does not reconciling differences risk meaningless compromises in lowest common denominators? The defenders of the system insist that differing views are not compromised but argued out and the views of those who still do not agree are duly recorded. But does one always exhibit the necessary courage to refuse to conform to the majority opinion, especially when the clock in the conference room is approaching six?

Estimates and conclusions are the products of thought, and pure thought cannot but be individual. In fact is there such a thing as collective thinking? The weighing of infinitely complex relationships and the sorting out of hypotheses and selection of the one most applicable

to the circumstances must be the work of individual minds. Any attempt to synthesize the products of several minds must end by reflecting the product of none.

There is also a communications difficulty in endeavoring to reconcile the conclusions of the diplomat on the spot with the efforts of a researcher in Washington. The most detailed and complete report supporting an ambassador's reasoning cannot begin to enumerate the intangible but significant facts that entered into his decision. How does a scientific intelligence expert take into consideration and evaluate a subtle smile he never saw or a handshake he never felt? Can one evaluate the mass reactions of a crowd at a demonstration one has not witnessed?

Furthermore, there are the language nuances to overcome in translations. Suppose the ambassador in Moscow asks Khrushchev's opinion of a new plan for disengagement and Khrushchev replies "Nichevo." Suppose even that a tape recording of the interview were made available to the collective thinkers in Washington. The answer could be correctly interpreted as "nothing," which it literally means. But a slight shrug might give it the entirely different meaning of "so-so." Or a smile and gesture could give it the meaning it has when you see a pretty girl: "Not bad at all." Who but the interviewer can interpret the correct meaning and how is he to explain his reasoning?

I do not suggest that we can ever again dispense with the immensely valuable contributions of the scientific intelligence experts. However, I suspect that at least some of their methods were inspired by the gigantic mass of facts raised by modern problems to overwhelm the decision maker. And as is so often the case in the face of these massive assaults on the mind, numbers have been mobilized to substitute for the mental capacity to grapple with them.

It would seem probable that the new techniques of intelligence will remain a useful auxiliary of, but never a substitute for, the established methods of diplomatic intelligence gathering, reporting, and evaluating.

XVI

The Battle for Men's Minds: 1

REPRESENTATION is the term used to describe a diplomat's efforts to demonstrate through his personality, manners, hospitality, and erudition the admirable qualities of his country and thus the advantage of maintaining close friendly relations with it. While the wise diplomat seeks to win for his country the admiration and respect of others, he will not waste his time trying to inspire the deeper emotion of affection. International love is a fiction the search for which has frequently ended in embittered frustration, particularly among Americans whose passion for popularity is seldom understood and practically never requited by our neighbors.

In the era of absolute monarchs representation was almost exclusively directed to the small group around the king, whose opinions carried weight in the determination of national policy and with whom the diplomat sought to ingratiate himself by every means possible. When a British ambassador in Paris was asked by the French King to hold the candle lighting him to bed, it was generally acknowledged that the Englishman had achieved the pinnacle of success as a diplomat at the royal court. When another British ambassador, Sir James Harris, in St. Petersburg almost succeeded in establishing even more intimate relations in the imperial bed of the Empress Catherine II he was merely fulfilling his representational duties vis-à-vis his imperial hostess.

As the incidence of power within nations shifted away from the

absolute monarch to the parliament, to the market place, and eventually to the pub the need to broaden the scope of representation was not immediately recognized. Diplomats continued to prefer the luxurious atmosphere of the courts to the noisy mobs.

There was another basic obstacle to diplomats' pursuing the voters to the polling place. While host governments condoned a certain pressure by diplomats in international matters, they considered interference in domestic politics out of bounds to foreign ambassadors.

The French and American Revolutions had accelerated the shift in power from the palace but it was Karl Marx who first exploited it systematically and openly advocated flouting the diplomatic rule of noninterference to incite the proletariat of the world to rise against their governments. The Bolsheviks enthusiastically followed his advice. At their very first diplomatic negotiation, the Brest-Litovsk peace treaty with the Germans, in 1917, the Soviet diplomats headed by Trotsky hurled revolutionary pamphlets from the windows of their special train and delivered fiery harangues to the German troops to rise against their masters, while the German diplomats and generals looked on speechless with amazement at this gross violation of diplomatic protocol.

But the Russians had staked their fortune on world revolution and had no intention of being stopped by mere diplomatic rules. Though they failed everywhere in their initial attempt to stir up revolution, they kept right on trying. In 1927 a prominent Bolshevik, Rakovsky, serving as ambassador in Paris, had the audacity to advocate publicly that in the event of war the French proletariat join forces with the Red Army. The French government immediately demanded Rakovsky's recall but the rebuff was ignored by the Communists.

Using not only their Communist parties abroad but also such devices as Soviet Friendship societies to foment trouble and, if possible, insurrection, the Soviets continued to interfere openly in their neighbors' affairs. In 1933 when Roosevelt negotiated the recognition of Russia with Litvinov, the Soviet diplomat promised that his government would support no organization inciting the forcible overthrow of the American government. However, Litvinov had hardly arrived home in Moscow before the Communist International was again appealing to its affiliates in America to incite rebellion.

These pre-World War II Soviet efforts were for the most part

clumsy and ineffective. It took the genius of Hitler's propaganda minister, Goebbels, to raise "total diplomacy" to an art by exploiting the advanced techniques of radio broadcasting. With powerful transmitters which leaped unimpeded across national frontiers he hurled vilification and abuse at Hitler's enemies abroad and sought support among foreign populations for his master's totalitarian doctrines. The Germans, like the Russians, also organized cells, friendship societies, and "bunds" of Germans overseas to spread the Nazi cause with considerable effect.

Mussolini, the poor man's totalitarian, likewise used the radio to stir up trouble among his enemies. Even before World War II his Radio Bari, directed toward the Middle East and as far as India, preached revolt from British colonial rule, to the acute discomfort of the British who constantly protested the flagrant violation of diplomatic usage.

Shortly after the outbreak of war, Mussolini's minister in Kabul, Pietro Quaroni, succeeded in recruiting the Indian revolutionary, Chandra Bose, for the Italian propaganda service. Chandra Bose was at the time in a British prison in India, but the resourceful Italian arranged his escape and brought him as far as Kabul, together with his male secretary. At this time Soviet Russia, still neutral, had no compunctions about offering Chandra Bose safe passage via Moscow and Berlin to Rome. However, while they were waiting for their travel papers, hidden in a native inn in the Kabul bazaar, Bose's secretary fell in love with the innkeeper's son and contracted gonorrhea. He was shipped back to India and eventually a substitute secretary was spirited to Kabul.

After this awkward delay Bose and his new secretary traveled across Russia as far as Berlin. There Hitler, jealous of his fellow totalitarian's propaganda coup, kidnaped Chandra Bose and put him to work on the Nazi radio network. Toward the end of the war, while he was escaping by plane to Japan, Chandra Bose's spectacular career came to an end in a plane crash on a Pacific island.

Even prior to the war the Western democracies were not entirely idle in this radio diplomacy. Ever since the twenties the BBC in Britain had been building up an audience all over the world which listened faithfully to the cool, dispassionate voice from London giving the news as London saw it—or wanted it seen. The French government, too, attempted to thwart the Nazi campaign by radio. However,

at home its own people lent themselves all too readily to foreign propaganda. Even before the totalitarians it had long been a standard procedure of Paris newspapers to offer their services clandestinely to foreign powers. Prior to World War I the counselor of the Russian Embassy had been hauled into court, sued by a newspaper editor for not paying his agreed subsidy on behalf of the Russian government. He successfully pleaded diplomatic immunity. Subsequently a Russian, Arturo Raffalovich, became disbursing agent for the Russian government among French newspapers and, according to documents published after the Bolshevik Revolution, distributed millions of rubles not only to newspaper publishers but also to individual journalists.

During the twenties and thirties *L'Humanité* was avowedly financed by the Soviets. *La République* was considered German subsidized. The well-known columnist, Jules Sauerwein, was suspected of taking money from numerous sources including the Germans and the Turks. When M. Sauerwein in a column in *Le Matin* expressed doubts about the correctness of Turkish foreign policy, it was assumed that Constantinople was in arrears in its payments to him. Another famous commentator, Pertinax, who wrote in the *Echo de Paris,* was widely regarded as in British pay.

Only the United States among the great powers refused to participate in the propaganda war. When a Paris editor offered his paper for sale to the United States his proposition was indignantly rejected by the American Embassy on instructions from Washington. The American abstention was due in part to its isolationist policies which precluded any involvements in Europe. In part, however, it sprang from a moralistic repugnance to all "propaganda," which was associated in the public mind with anarchist and Bolshevik underground conspiracies to overthrow the Constitution with a combination of pamphlets and bombs. Just as Secretary of State Stimson had forbidden code breaking because gentlemen did not read each other's mail, his successors shrank from the dirty word "propaganda."

But with Pearl Harbor these inhibitions quickly vanished and the United States sprang enthusiastically into what was then called "psychological warfare." The Office of Facts and Figures, a creation of President Roosevelt, now became the Office of War Information. Eager to participate in the war effort, writers, publicists, journalists, editors, public relations experts and advertisers hurried to enlist

in the OWI to fight the Battle of Men's Minds.

The Voice of America was organized to broadcast around the globe and around the clock. Pamphlets, books, and even paper match boxes carrying the democratic message were smuggled or dropped into enemy countries and distributed more openly in the neutral and friendly areas. The Voice transmitters initially were weak and short-ranged and the pamphlet dropping was fraught with difficulties.

In the very first days of the phony war in 1939, the British had conducted a pamphlet-dropping operation on Germany. RAF planes swept over Hamburg and other West German towns dropping leaflets as they went. Unfortunately their navigation was poor or high winds carried off the pamphlets, for few found their way to the streets of Hamburg. Stationed in Hamburg at that time, I sometimes spent my Sundays shooting roebuck in a forest some thirty miles north of the city. There the forest floor was often white with British leaflets. They were clumsily written and poorly printed. Even the British Information Ministry was apparently not too proud of them, for it declared their contents to be "war secrets." When a few months later I brought some samples to London and showed them to newspaper friends, one was reproduced in a British newspaper. An investigation thereupon was instituted by Parliament to discover how the pamphlet had "leaked," so I cut short my visit and went on my way.

The American military, too, mounted a massive psychological warfare operation, using radio, leaflets, and various forms of "black" and "gray" information campaigns to confuse the enemy generals and subvert the troops and civilian populations.

When the war ended there was no turning back to the less noisy diplomacy of pretotalitarian days. Hardly had Germany and then Japan surrendered before the Soviets re-aimed their propaganda guns, turning them from their former enemies on to their former allies.

Initially there was considerable pressure, particularly from Congress, to dismantle the entire OWI organization and to abandon the propaganda effort which they still felt had an unsavory and un-American flavor. But the efforts of Radio Moscow, combined with the more brutal suasions of the Soviet armies in Eastern Europe, were convincing proof that the war had not ended. It had just become a shade cooler. Greatly reduced in size, the OWI staff was transferred to the State Department and with sharply cutback budgets continued to broad-

cast over the Voice of America and to turn out the movies, pamphlets, and news bulletins that OWI had originated.

In the early postwar years the fiction of friendly relations with Russia continued, and the Voice broadcasts pursued a policy known as the "full and fair picture." The picture was often self-deprecating and replete with confessions of our shortcomings but careful to avoid criticism or attacks on the Soviet system. Nor was any propaganda directed to Russia herself.

The reasons for this odd approach were several. A few known fellow travelers had during the war infiltrated into key positions whence they still advocated a friendly-to-Russia line. Others, accustomed to the wartime pro-Soviet line, found it difficult to change. Furthermore, the State Department, always cool to the OWI in wartime and unenthusiastic about the "psychological warriors" it had inherited when OWI was liquidated, either overlooked or ignored its responsibilities to bring their propaganda into line with the new cold war situation.

But in 1947, at the urgent insistence of the diplomats familiar with Russia, including Averell Harriman, recently ambassador in Moscow and then secretary of commerce, broadcasts directly to Russia were inaugurated and the tone of the other broadcasts changed to a much more vigorous anti-Communist approach. The fellow travelers were eliminated and the rest of the staff re-oriented to a more realistic line. At the same time a slick magazine in Russian was printed for distribution in Moscow.

The new line was welcomed in America but the competence of its dispensers was not so readily accepted by either Congress or the public. The touch of the red tarbrush was not easily eradicated and the potential effect of propaganda was doubted because of the inherent inability of the international broadcasters to demonstrate through listener ratings or sales figures, as commercial radio could, that they were being listened to. Nor were all career diplomats convinced of the effectiveness or the propriety of international propaganda. This was especially true of those who had not themselves experienced the massive and powerful Soviet propaganda apparatus in operation. Consequently such attention as they gave the Voice was halfhearted and often contemptuous.

The initiation of the Russian broadcasts was also attended by con-

siderable amateur bumbling. When I was dispatched to New York to recruit a staff and start the Russian broadcasts I had scarcely tuned in on a broadcast for years, let alone produced one. When, after several weeks of practice, the first program went on the air the *New York Times* asked to print the text in full. Scheduled for that day was a discussion on artificial manures. The purpose of the talk was to demonstrate subtly how American technology had made a surplus problem out of what in Russia remained a desperate shortage problem in agriculture. Only with difficulty did the public relations officials persuade me to substitute another program, which duly appeared in the *Times*.

For several weeks after the broadcasts began, the embassy in Moscow reported difficulty hearing it. The program was relayed from a transmitter in Munich which should have been powerful enough to put a good signal into European Russia. The radio engineers were baffled by the failure to get through until a batch of letters arrived from a colony of former Cossacks who had emigrated to Peru, expressing their appreciation of the Russian-language broadcasts which, they said, they were receiving very well. It turned out that the antennae in Munich had been accidentally reversed, so that the main signal was going backwards to South America. After the hookup had been rewired, Moscow reported the programs coming in strong and the Peruvian Cossacks stopped writing.

Though the wrong-way antenna was kept from its attention, Congress continued to be skeptical of the broadcasting effort and the budget was so low that unpaid volunteers including Averell Harriman's daughter, Kathleen, were recruited to help in the studios, in violation of government regulations.

An indirect result of Congressional suspicion was the polemical tone of early cold war broadcasting. Many diplomats familiar with Russian psychology advised the Voice to adopt a cool, dispassionate, almost impartial attitude in addressing its Soviet audience. However, anxious to prove to Congress and the public that the Voice was not soft or pro-Communist, we frequently fell to the temptation of broadcasting bitterly sarcastic, almost vitriolic, anti-Stalinist attacks and even for a time persuaded the BBC to do the same.

The result was that the programs lost much of their credibility while doing little to persuade the skeptics on Capitol Hill of our anti-Communist attitude. However, while the broadcasts themselves failed

to convince Congress of their effectiveness, *Pravda* succeeded dramatically when it bitterly denounced the new Russian broadcasts. From then on our appropriations gradually increased.

However, although *Pravda* had convinced the American press, public, and Congress that propaganda to the enslaved peoples behind the Iron Curtain was justified and perhaps worthwhile, public opinion continued to be suspicious of diplomacy by propaganda to other areas and skeptical of the ability of government bureaucrats to conduct it effectively.

Typical of this repugnance was the attitude of a powerful group of senators toward the broadcasts of the Voice to the free world. Persuaded that the Voice of America programs to Europe and South America were incompetently run and that professional networks could handle them better, these senators had directed that the programs be farmed out in large part to NBC and CBS. Some months later, after I had taken over the entire broadcasting operation, a script writer at one of the networks produced a show that referred to the state of Texas as having been "born in sin." Not only Texans but most of Congress erupted and I was ordered to Washington, where both the Senate and the House were to hold investigations.

The night preceding my appearance before the senators I rehearsed my testimony. With my hat hung on a bedpost in my hotel room to represent the senators, I hurled annihilating arguments at it. I pointed out that not only I but numerous superiors had personally warned the Senate that to farm out the broadcasting was courting precisely the trouble that had now occurred.

Next morning I took the witness stand before a dais from which twelve stern faces peered down. I launched into my explanation but only a few words were audible before a question interrupted me. I paused just long enough to deal with it and went back to my explanation, but a third and then a fourth question were already buzzing about my ears. After almost an hour of this procedure the hearing ended. I was never permitted to finish my explanation, but the senators seemed to know what I had in mind. At all events the committee eventually recommended that all private international broadcasting at government expense be abandoned. From then on international broadcasting became the exclusive responsibility of the Voice of America.

The Voice continued to struggle along on limited budgets until once again the Kremlin succeeded where the State Department had failed. In the course of a single day in the spring of 1949 more than a hundred powerful jamming transmitters went on the air all over Russia trying to drown us out.

From then on Congress was more generous. In 1950 it appropriated another ten million for radio facilities, in 1951 forty-one million and then another ten million. With these funds powerful new transmitters were set up in Munich, Salonica, Manila, and Tangier. A broadcasting relay ship, the *Courier,* was fitted out and dispatched to the Eastern Mediterranean to boost signals into the Middle East and southern Russia.

In addition to funds for construction, operating funds were greatly increased and by 1958 had reached the sum of almost a hundred million dollars. Meantime the Voice and other information activities had in 1953 once more been transferred from the State Department to the independent United States Information Agency.

XVII

The Battle for Men's Minds: 2

IN 1959 the USIA was operating the Voice of America and a global network of information centers in more than eighty countries. It published pamphlets and magazines, arranged exhibits of Americana, translated cheap editions of American classics, maintained a free news service for impecunious newspapers around the world, distributed press photographs, and even produced movies for illiterate audiences.

Although independent, the USIA worked closely with the State Department in Washington. Abroad its agents were even more closely integrated with American embassies and consular establishments. Public affairs officers, cultural officers, press officers, and their subordinates operated information centers and libraries, arranged lectures, distributed books and pamphlets, serviced editors with news files, photographs, texts of U. S. government declarations, and stood ready if called upon for editorial advice. They also arranged for their ambassador to address public gatherings, helped handle his press relations, and generally acted as an extension of his arm in spreading his representational activities, once limited to a handful of leaders in the capital, to the widest possible audience throughout the country.

In addition the State Department was administering the highly effective Fulbright Program whereby foreign students and political leaders were brought to the United States to see for themselves how American democracy operates.

The theory behind the information program is relatively simple.

As representative government has spread around the world and the power of ultimate decision has shifted from the absolute monarch to the masses, the diplomat has been forced to widen the stage on which he carries on his representational functions in order to persuade the decision makers of the desirability of friendly relations or alliances with the country he represents.

But the theory immediately runs into difficulties both in principle and in practice. True democracy exists in no country of the world. Even in the United States the ultimate decision maker, the voter, is often content to let a much smaller body of opinion make decisions in foreign affairs than he would be in domestic matters more directly affecting his daily life.

Even in the Soviet Union public opinion has certain ultimate sanctions, as is demonstrated by the fact that the Soviet government probably spends more money on trying to influence its own public opinion than on any other nonmilitary activity. However, in such countries public opinion operates only indirectly, limiting the power of the dictator to cut off all contacts with the outside world—which even Stalin found it impossible to do—or his freedom to undertake aggressive war against countries with whom the masses have no quarrels.

Furthermore, the propaganda output of the totalitarians during the past thirty years has been so great and so intense that it has numbed the senses and increased the resistance to all types of propaganda, whether it comes from a fuehrer, the first secretary of the party, or a democratic government.

The rise of nationalism during the past century, with its concomitant distrust of foreigners, also has increased the resistance of many countries to the diplomatic blandishments of a foreign information service. Furthermore, to reach the masses effectively one now has to speak their own languages. For this reason the Voice of America today broadcasts in forty different languages—in six to India alone.

Another practical difficulty is that of designing the approach to one's audience. The old-fashioned diplomat had a more or less single standard of tastes and erudition to cope with. The international information officer today has hundreds. A pamphlet on Communism designed for Germans would hardly be suitable for Laotians, to whom Moscow is a city four hundred days' march away.

In 1952 the information service sent a team of Hollywood writers

and producers to Germany to make films for German audiences on the Communist menace. The result was a film entitled *Streetcar Called Freedom*. It was a naïve fantasy about a streetcar which breaks loose in East Berlin and after dashing through its drab streets crosses into West Berlin, where the shops are full, the people gay, and life is free. It was possibly the sort of demonstration of the disadvantages of Communism that would appeal to a Hollywood audience that had produced its share of naïve fellow travelers. But when the film was tried out on a German audience, including a young student from Hamburg, the student walked out halfway through the showing. Asked his opinion, he replied with one word: "Thick." It was a relatively polite reply for a nation that has been cut in two, half of it enslaved, its men jailed and its women raped, and scarcely a family unharmed by Communism.

When the OWI first faced the problems involved in working out an effective propaganda approach, one might have supposed that it would have turned to the diplomats for help. However, for numerous reasons nothing of the sort occurred. Not recognizing that the OWI job was merely an extension of their own profession, the diplomats were delighted to let someone else cope with it. Like their predecessors, they were reluctant to leave the sedate, comfortable, and congenial atmosphere of the grand salon and go to work among those who had inherited authority from the feudal prince. When war broke out the Foreign Service also found itself saddled with enough problems and could scarcely have handled OWI's without extensive recruiting.

For their part, the OWI people saw little or no connection between their tasks and those of the stuffy diplomats. In consequence, each went his own way and when their paths crossed it was usually without warmth. The policies and goals that OWI followed were neither defined nor supervised by the State Department but came directly from the White House.

Ignored by and ignoring the State Department and the Foreign Service, OWI soon found a source of advice and guidance among the advertisers and public relations experts of Madison Avenue, who quickly put an all but indelible stamp on America's initial international propaganda effort. The superficial similarities between advertising and propaganda, like the superficial similarities between diplomacy and journalism, led inevitably to a confusion in both the methods and the aims of the propagandist which have persisted until the present.

The current director of the Information Service, George Venable Allen, has frequently referred to democracy, freedom, and human liberty as "products to sell." "Many of the United States Agency's techniques," he has said, "are borrowed from the tried and true tested methods of the [advertising] industry and many advertising men have joined in our work of convincing other peoples of this country's desire for a true and lasting peace."

Quite aside from the essential difference between marketing a pharmaceutical and convincing others of our desire for peace, the analogy between the two tasks breaks down in more fundamental aspects. If one must have an analogy between the information service and other activities, then perhaps the missionary provides a more apt and accurate one. His job, like that of the propagandist, is to "sell," if one must use the expression, not a soap or a toothpaste but an idea. He works in areas untouched by Gallup polls and other market-testing devices, where tastes, cultural levels, languages, and national aspirations have no parallel in the United States. Only after carefully studying the social and cultural background of his potential followers does he seek through whatever techniques seem suitable to persuade them of his beliefs.

The analogy has certainly not been lost on the Communists, who dispatch to foreign areas not supersalesmen but fanatical believers in and students of the Communist religion whose emphasis is not on the techniques of persuasion but on the persuasiveness of the theory they are propagating.

The Soviets, too, have appreciated as none others that the purpose of the propagandist is first and foremost to facilitate diplomacy. In fact, the real chief of a Soviet diplomatic mission is likely to be not the ambassador at all but a devoted party official who has made his life-work the study of Marx's doctrine, including his strictures on the weaknesses and vulnerabilities of capitalism.

Essentially the task of the American propagandist since the days of Franklin has been to demonstrate by whatever techniques are available the admirable qualities of the American system, political, social, cultural and economic, and thus to facilitate the conduct of foreign relations by smoothing the way for the policies the diplomat seeks to implement.

The advertiser, by the very nature of his profession, tends to empha-

size not the "product" but the technique. A propagandist, though he must learn the most effective way of writing a radioscript, running a library, or setting up an exhibit on the peaceful uses of atomic energy, has as his stock in trade American political, cultural, and social objectives and policies. Before he begins to "sell" them he must know not only these policies but also the political, cultural, and social objectives of others with which he is seeking to harmonize our own.

Frequently during my association with the Voice of America I was faced with the choice of filling a post with an expert in American broadcasting techniques or an expert in the politics of some area of the world to which we were broadcasting. Invariably it proved easier to teach the political specialist the basic techniques of script writing or broadcasting than to teach the skilled broadcaster the infinitely more complex and intricate differences and similarities between the American objectives and the foreign objectives he was harmonizing.

The detrimental influence of the public relations expert and the advertiser on the Information Service's recruitment and training program is illustrated by the proposal of the present director to establish a career service of information specialists, thus once more putting technique ahead of substance.

Today in many foreign cities one finds a large American information center staffed by cultural, information, press, film, and public relations "specialists." Across the street in a shabby office in the French Consulate sits an unprepossessing little man with a modest manner, a shabby suit, and a tie that seldom is straight, who knows intimately every personality and trend in Western painting, literature, and philosophy. When a congress of writers or philosophers gathers in the city, the behind-the-scenes services of the American "specialists" in furnishing a hall, printing a program, advertising the congress, and entertaining its guests will be greatly appreciated. But the little Frenchman will be on the platform expounding his French doctrines.

The press officer of one information center which I know well is an amiable woman thoroughly trained in the operations of a newspaper and the needs of an editor. Her only failing is that her comprehension of major political issues, aside from the "guidance" she receives from Washington, is nil. That she should follow current events in the local press or develop original thoughts on pressing political problems never occurs to her. Nor would it occur to a foreign affairs editor of

the local paper to consult her in preparing his news copy or his editorials.

That the successful propagandist must, first and foremost, be thoroughly familiar with his "product" was demonstrated during the war when Thornton Wilder was assigned by the Air Force to the American Military Mission in Belgrade as cultural officer. The Soviets had already flooded Belgrade with Russian films, ballet exhibits, libraries, and endless lecturers. But, singlehanded, Wilder, by circulating among the writers and journalists, the editors and critics of Belgrade, was able to re-establish the ascendancy of Western cultural standards and put the Russian effort to shame.

Wilders do not grow on trees nor do they crowd the government hiring halls in Washington. Only seldom do they volunteer for foreign lecture tours under Information Agency auspices. It is not therefore suggested that USIA attempt to staff its information centers with Wilders, Hemingways, or Faulkners but it is urged that in recruiting and training its representatives it stress not the technical skills of the salesman but in matters political, political skills and in matters cultural, cultural skills.

The problem of inducing adequately qualified people to participate in the information program has been further complicated by stringent security regulations of doubtful validity or effectiveness, militating against the employment of refugees and political exiles. When the rare political defector from the West seeks refuge in Moscow, the Kremlin loses little time in putting him to work for its cause—generally in the propaganda field where, because of the nature of the operation, even the most wily double-agent can do little harm under proper supervision. In the United States, however, security rules make it all but impossible to employ the most willing and useful defector for this innocuous task.

While recruiting a staff for the Russian radio program the writer was introduced to a phenomenal Russian refugee who, because of his size, his huge head covered with unruly gray curls, and his lumbering gait, was known as "the Bear who walks like a man." "The Bear" had been a Socialist under the czars and had frequently served time in Siberia. During one of his exiles he had been approached by a criminal exile called Zoza who was serving time for robbing a Tiflis bank and who, lacking the indispensable item of Siberian existence, a teakettle,

had borrowed the Bear's and failed to return it.

Subsequently the Bear and Zoza, now calling himself Stalin, had met again and the stolen teakettle had not helped to cement their relations. A deep political feud developed and in the end the Bear was forced into exile, first in Prague, then in Paris, and finally in New York, where he established a reputation as the first Sovietologist or Bolshevismologist, carefully following every twist and turn in Soviet developments.

Some days after I had hired the Bear, my administrative chief in the Voice of America, an ex-radio tenor, remonstrated that the man was hightly suspect by the security staff. "Not only is his English impossible," he told me, "but he writes for a Socialist weekly—*in Russian!*" No amount of argument dissuaded either the ex-tenor or the FBI that the Bear was not only an invaluable asset because of his familiarity with Kremlin affairs but that his anti-Communism was far more profound than either J. Edgar Hoover's or his agents'. Indeed, during the brief period I was allowed to use him his only shortcoming was the regularity with which his weekly radio talks suggested that the filcher of his teakettle be assassinated.

The misconception of the role of the propagandist is nowhere more apparent than in the thorny problem known as "policy guidance" in USIA. Policy is in essence the substance of a propagandist's task. United States policy toward a given development is its political attitude deriving from established principles, patterns of thought, and national interests, with all of which the diplomat is expected to be familiar. Granted that in the complex world relations today special efforts must be made in Washington to keep him informed, he should then be expected to know how his government will react to a given situation.

Since technical skills in the arts of advertising and public relations have too often in the past been the criteria in selecting information staffs rather than substantive experience in international politics and diplomacy, it has been necessary to devise an elaborate system for feeding "policy" into the information organization much as blood is transfused into the body of a person short of red corpuscles. Each morning the public relations staff of the State Department meets to determine what should be departmental opinion on the major events of the past day. Attending this meeting is a representative of USIA with the dashing title of "fast guidance co-ordinator." After the col-

lective mind has been made up, he hurries to his own office where "policy guidances" are prepared and cabled to information centers around the globe. These guidances not only give the daily line on events but instruct the centers what points should be emphasized and what played down. Supplementing these daily cables are special guidances on particular problems, giving the background of the event, what Washington is saying, and what points to stress.

One suspects that it is partly because of this arid and stultifying policy (or thought) control apparatus that it is difficult to lure top-quality people into the information service. To compensate for the lack of highly qualified propagandists, quantity is too often substituted. However, Parkinson's law is not a cure but a disease. Numbers beget numbers, which in turn stifle quality.

There is perhaps a still more serious drawback to the influence of the advertisers in propaganda. Salesmen have a tendency not only to oversell their wares but to oversell their capabilities. There is evidence that the salesmen of the Information Agency have overestimated the capacity of the weapon in their hands. Instead of regarding it as an auxiliary part of the machinery for conducting foreign policy they tend to look upon it as an independent force.

"Good foreign policy and good propaganda," says George Venable Allen, "go hand in hand." One might suggest instead that propaganda is the cowcatcher of diplomacy, attached integrally to it and designed essentially to sweep the impediments from the path of the man who is implementing policy—the diplomat.

Alone, propaganda has no creative force. It cannot forge alliances with our friends nor spark revolutions to annihilate our enemies. But as the handmaiden of diplomacy, as an extension of the diplomat's arm, it can and frequently has significantly furthered our international interests.

One of the dangers of considering propaganda an independent force is the temptation it arouses to acquiesce in a bad policy because it makes good propaganda. One need only recall the 1953 "liberation" policy which ended so tragically in Budapest three years later. Similarly it tends to raise false hopes at home and substitute them for less agreeable realities. A high-powered transmitter, it has been argued, costs less than a third as much as an intercontinental bomber. Let us, therefore, forgo the bomber and build the transmitter.

A thorough understanding of the limitations of the propaganda gun is as essential to its efficient operation as knowing the range of a piece of artillery is to its firing. While it can fan an existing flame it cannot light fires. The Hungarian revolutionaries were perhaps stimulated by Western broadcasts but the spark that started the revolution was made exclusively in Hungary. Propaganda can enhance the results of good policies and good diplomacy and can mitigate the effects of bad policies and poor diplomacy, but it cannot be a substitute for either policy or diplomacy or indeed exist without them.

The American propaganda weapon is still in its infancy. That it should have experienced growing pains and suffered from a few childhood diseases is hardly astonishing. That it is essential to our defense against totalitarian diplomacy is indisputable. That it will develop into a powerful auxiliary arm of American diplomacy depends on whether its leaders and Congress understand its proper role, its limitations, and its need not for numbers but for qualified personnel.

XVIII

Diplomatic Privileges and Immunities: 1

IN an earlier chapter it was suggested that the first diplomat was probably a caveman who visited his neighbor to arrange a truce and came home alive. The operative clause of this definition is the coming-home-alive one. A basic principle of diplomatic practice is that you may not kill, jail, or even poke the nose of a diplomat no matter how much he may seem to deserve it.

The rule of immunity is variously interpreted by the Byzantine and the Western school of diplomacy. In the West an entire body of law and custom has been built up to protect the diplomat, his family, and his aides and give them the greatest possible freedom. In the East, on the other hand, the tendency is to curtail an ambassador's movements as much as possible without actually taking his life. From the time when Liutprand was locked up in Constantinople in his "horrible house" with five lions and no running water, to the current American ambassador in Moscow, diplomats in Eastern countries have been frustrated and thwarted, sometimes with Oriental tact and courtesy, sometimes with brute force.

The difference does not derive from varying concepts of hospitality. In fact, the Byzantine is apt to be more lavish in his hospitality than the Westerner. Nor does the Western attitude stem from any superior native morality. Indeed, several centuries ago the courts of Western Europe had as low an opinion of foreign diplomats as Moscow has today. The Western code of immunities has been built up during those

centuries in the belief that diplomacy is useful in preserving peace. In the East diplomacy is, to paraphrase Clausewitz, an extension of war by other means.

The first recognition of diplomatic immunity in Anglo-Saxon law is known as the Act of 7 Anne. This act was promulgated in 1708 after the Russian ambassador in London had been arrested and badly mauled by several irate merchants to whom he owed money.

Today it is a basic rule that a diplomat not only may not be arrested but is entitled to an even greater degree of protection than the ordinary citizen. When Hugh Gibson, an American diplomat, was beaten up by a newspaper reporter in Havana in 1912, the reporter was first released by the judge, who said he did not care whether the victim was an American diplomat or a Cuban bum. After a strong protest from Washington, the reporter was finally given thirty months on the ground that Gibson, as a diplomat, was entitled to greater security than an ordinary citizen.

Assassination of ambassadors has been a favorite means among dissidents of getting even with unpopular governments. In the October Revolution enemies of the Bolsheviks assassinated the German ambassador in Moscow to stir up trouble between the Bolsheviks and Berlin. In 1923 a Soviet diplomat at the Lausanne Conference was murdered by White Russians. Four years later the Soviet minister in Poland was murdered by a Russian monarchist. In the Lausanne case the murderer was acquitted by a Swiss jury on the ground that his victim had not been invited to the conference. In the latter case the murderer got fifteen years.

Diplomatic immunity technically begins when the diplomat enters the country of his assignment and does not end until he leaves it, whether he leaves of his own accord or has been expelled. In fact, it continues to operate even if he dies at his post. In 1916 a French secretary of embassy was shot dead in a hotel bedroom in London. A local coroner started to hold an inquest but when the French ambassador objected the British government conceded that the diplomatic corpse still enjoyed immunity.

A diplomat is subject to neither civil nor criminal local law. In most Western countries diplomats even enjoy special protection from attacks in the press. Satow, the British authority on diplomatic practice, maintains that where a government controls the press it is its duty to prevent attacks on diplomats. The Soviet authorities of the

Byzantine school are of quite another opinion. They have frequently inspired personal attacks on diplomats and on one occasion at least have sponsored a book containing scurrilous attacks on the personal lives of American diplomats.

The book, entitled *The Truth about American Diplomats,* allegedly written by a disgruntled ex-American citizen who had been employed in the Moscow Embassy, was published in Moscow in 1949. It dwells at considerable length on the political and personal habits of the then principal American diplomats engaged in Soviet affairs. Since the supposed author was ignorant of many allegations contained in these juicy anecdotes, it is clear that they were taken from Soviet secret police dossiers. A curious fact about the book is that none of the personal details not published in any standard reference book predates 1941—the year the Germans attacked Russia and almost captured Moscow. There is thus reason to believe that when Moscow was hurriedly evacuated by the government in the fall of that year the secret police burned most of its dossiers on individual diplomats.

However, the loss should not prove too costly, since the Soviet government has long made a practice of framing or attempting to frame diplomats and manufacturing evidence against them whenever it finds this convenient. For example, a young married clerk in the Moscow Embassy sends his wife for a vacation in Switzerland. As he is sitting alone in his apartment a few evenings later, two young women ring the doorbell and enter. Speaking a foreign language, they begin making crude advances. Unless the young clerk is a cool, quick operator, the Soviet police may soon be in possession of a highly compromising photograph, together with two witnesses, with which to start blackmail operations, diplomatic immunity from which is not part of the Byzantine code.

Or, to take a more recent case, an officer of the embassy is asked to obtain some literary materials not available in Russia for a number of Soviet citizens. Acceding to the request, he reads some weeks later in the Soviet press that he has been attempting to buy and bribe honest Soviet workers with cheap gifts from America, just as the early English colonizers "bought Indian natives with glass beads and varicolored chintzes," as the Soviet press put it.

Diplomats may not be arrested for traffic violations. In some South

American countries diplomats are even tacitly permitted to go the wrong way down one-way streets. When a Belgian diplomat was caught speeding at 55 m.p.h. down Massachusetts Avenue in Washington, the only recourse of the traffic authorities was to complain to the State Department. When a Washington policeman remonstrated with an Ecuadorian diplomat for parking in the wrong place, the driver told him it was "none of his damn business" even if he parked his car in the middle of the street.

On one occasion an Elkton, Md., policeman stopped the minister of Iran and his wife on a charge of speeding. When the diplomat protested explaining that he was the Iranian minister, the policeman replied: "I've heard of Baptist ministers and Presbyterian ministers but never of Iranian ministers." Whereupon he hauled the unfortunate man to jail. Before the American government could make amends, the Shah had ordered the breaking off of diplomatic relations.

Diplomatic immunity extends not only to the ambassador and to his diplomatic (as distinguished from his clerical) staff but to his own family. The French and British authorities have even extended diplomatic immunity to estranged wives of diplomats living apart from their husbands.

There are, of course, exceptions to the immunity of diplomats' families. When the son of the American minister in Guatemala shot and killed another American in 1902, his father disclaimed diplomatic immunity for him on the ground that he was in business for himself and not connected in any way with the legation.

In times past friends of diplomats have frequently sought diplomatic immunity on the ground that they were allegedly employed as officials by an ambassador. In England, for example, a debtor claimed diplomatic immunity as the stableman of a foreign diplomat who kept no horses. Another claimed he was the cook of a diplomat who had no kitchen. A third said he was a gardener of a foreign envoy who had no garden. In 1823 in a famous court case a defendant claimed diplomatic immunity on the ground that he was a choirboy in the Portuguese ambassador's chapel. He lost the suit.

Diplomatic immunity extends even to the giving of testimony in court. Occasionally a diplomat may volunteer to give testimony, as the Venezuelan minister in Washington did when he appeared in court as a witness against the assassins of President Garfield. In such

cases, however, the diplomat's government must consent to his waiver of immunity, and American regulations specifically forbid American diplomats from testifying without first obtaining the consent of Washington.

The immunity a diplomat enjoys belongs not to himself but to his office and cannot personally be disposed of. In 1906 the son of the Chilean chargé d'affaires in Brussels was accused of murder. His father renounced immunity for his son, but the Belgian courts refused to accept it until the Chilean government had given its official approval. The Chilean government did so and the son was eventually acquitted.

Occasionally the prohibition against waiving one's immunity can prove embarrassing. In 1949 I flew into Sofia on Christmas morning, where I found a message from the American minister that I was expected at Christmas dinner immediately. However, the Bulgarian immigration authorities claimed that my entrance visa was not in order and insisted on fining me several thousand leva, which amounted to about $3. I pointed out that they could not fine me and I could not permit myself to be fined. However, their regulations made no exceptions for diplomats. While we discussed the problem I was reminded by my appetite that the minister's Christmas dinner was getting cold. The impasse was finally settled when I offered to make a charitable contribution of $3 to be used for the widows of Bulgarian policemen.

Fees for municipal services, such as garbage removal, telephones or light, are not considered either fines or taxes, and a diplomat is not exempt from paying them. However, this fine distinction is not always understood by unread diplomats. Before the war the German chief of protocol in Berlin once complained that half his time was occupied explaining to wives of certain South American diplomats that they were not exempt from paying streetcar fares.

Not only are the persons of diplomats immune from the law, but their offices and homes may not be entered by the police without formal permission. In 1827 the British and American governments had a prolonged dispute, arising when the London police arrested Minister Gallatin's coachman in the legation stable. Gallatin did not object to the arrest of the coachman, whom he had already fired, but he strongly objected to the violation of his stable's immunity. The British authorities refused to admit their error but took urgent steps

to see that the London police never did it again.

On one occasion in Berlin the irate landlord of the Rumanian Legation ordered the Rumanian minister to vacate his house. The minister refused. Thereupon the landlord sent for some masons and had them build a wall around the front entrance. The minister tore down the wall and simultaneously complained to the German Foreign Office. When the landlord attempted to rebuild it, the Foreign Office sent police to prevent him and to safeguard the diplomat's right of entrance. The frustrated landlord thereupon donated the building to the German government as a poorhouse, but still the Rumanian stayed on.

The immunity of the embassy is not always a blessing. In the thirties the embassy in Moscow housed, among others, three sisters who worked as scullery maids, known affectionately as "the Three Little Pigs." The youngest and prettiest eventually found a husband but the husband found no home. When she became pregnant it was suggested she move, but she had no place to go. As her time approached, the embassy arranged for a maternity hospital to take her in, but she still refused to move in the mistaken belief that if her child was born in the embassy it would be an American citizen. The police who stood guard outside the embassy were appealed to but they claimed they were forbidden to enter the premises. An appeal to the Soviet Foreign Office brought the reply that, since the embassy was extraterritorial, they could not intervene. Eventually the burly administrator of the embassy deposited the girl in an ambulance and took her to the maternity hospital. Soon afterward her two sisters disappeared, and nothing was ever again heard of the Three Little Pigs.

It might be pointed out that the Bolshevik government was not always so strict in its interpretation of diplomatic immunity. In 1918 it ordered Soviet troops to break into the British Embassy in Petrograd, where they destroyed the archives and a good deal of furniture.

The growing popularity of picketing in recent years has posed a problem for foreign embassies. The practice seems to have started in Washington during the Manchurian Crisis, when in 1937 local Chinese picketed the Japanese Embassy. Not long afterward American anti-Fascists rented a plane and trailed a huge sign reading "Quarantine the Aggressor" over the Italian Embassy. Later police confiscated a sign from a demonstrator in front of the Italian Embassy proclaiming

that "Mussolini Murders Babies." Eventually Congress passed a law making it illegal to demonstrate or picket within five hundred feet of a diplomatic mission.

Nevertheless, picketing continued, and with the establishment of the United Nations in New York it grew into a standard practice. The habit spread after the war to European countries, the victim usually being the Soviet Embassy. The Soviet government, unable to lick the craze, joined it, and on several occasions student groups were "spontaneously organized" to demonstrate in front of Western embassies in Moscow. The demonstrators once took their jobs a little too seriously and after smashing several hundred windows in the American Embassy laid out the Moscow policemen sent to restrain them.

These organized Moscow demonstrations call to mind an interesting aspect of international picketing illustrated during the Goebbels-organized anti-Jewish pogrom of November, 1938. For two days crowds roamed Berlin's streets, smashing windows of Jewish shops, looting the showcases, and often invading the homes of Jewish shopkeepers. On the second evening of that appalling episode I was walking through the streets accompanied by my Russian-trained police dog. A crowd of young hoodlums threatened me and in Russian I commanded the dog to stand guard. As the dog's hackles rose and he growled angrily, the mob backed off. But one of the leaders had recognized the Russian phrase and in answer to his question I said I was a Soviet journalist. The questioner then ordered the crowd off and took me on a stroll down the Canal Embankment explaining that he too was a Communist who had been instructed by the party to organize gangs of hoodlums to join the anti-Jewish riots. "It's the only way," he explained, "to show these lethargic Berlin workers what power they have if they would only use it against the right people." One wonders whether this may not apply to lethargic Moscow workers as well.

Since embassies are off limits to police, they have become favorite sanctuaries for fugitives. Diplomatic practice prohibits giving asylum to ordinary criminals or fugitives from justice. American Foreign Service regulations prohibit granting asylum except to protect persons in immediate mortal danger from mob violence.

However, in some countries where politics are occasionally conducted by means of mobs political asylum in embassies has become

a habit. In South America, for example, ousted politicians frequently seek safety in foreign embassies from the soldiers of their successors. Currently there are at least a half dozen politicians holed up in foreign missions in South America, one of them for the past eight years.

In Europe most authorities maintain that embassies do not have the right to grant political asylum. Nevertheless, even there it is occasionally resorted to. In 1958 the unsuccessful Portuguese presidential candidate opposing President Salazar took refuge in the Brazilian Embassy in Lisbon.

At the time of the Hungarian Revolution the Catholic Cardinal Mindszenty sought refuge from arrest by Soviet troops in the American Legation. He is still there. Other revolutionaries, searching for a more "neutral" asylum, fled to the Yugoslav Embassy, where they remained for several days until the Soviet-supported counterrevolutionary regime of Janos Kadar lured them out by promise of safeconduct to their homes. The promise was kept just long enough for them to be put into a bus, since when none of them has ever been seen again. The assassination of several who were on the bus was subsequently admitted by Moscow.

A happier ending for a case of asylum occurred in the Soviet Embassy in Paris in 1929. The counselor of the embassy had received peremptory orders to return to Moscow. Suspecting that this presaged his liquidation he promptly left the embassy but was unable to take his wife and child with him. He appealed to the police, explaining that his ambassador was on leave and he was in charge. As he was therefore entitled to waive immunity for the embassy, the police entered it and rescued his family.

In some Moslem countries a form of asylum known as "bast" has grown up, based on the principle that no gentleman refuses hospitality to callers. Sir Mortimer Durand, a British minister in Tehran, relates in his biography how this operated on occasion:

One day a eunuch from the royal palace galloped up and told the minister that the ladies of the Shah's harem were in open revolt against their lord's decision to marry the daughter of his gardener. Since she was the sister of one of his wives, this was against Persian custom. In protest the harem had decided to go on strike and seek "bast" in the British Legation. The minister sent back word he would be delighted and highly honored. When he discovered that the harem

numbered almost three hundred ladies he ordered a tent camp set up for them on the legation lawn.

After the camp had been established the eunuch reappeared to inspect the arrangements and declared them entirely satisfactory. Before galloping back to the palace to collect his three hundred ladies he confided to the minister that the Shah was furious but that the ladies were adamant and already climbing into their carriages.

But then, as Sir Mortimer waited for his guests, the eunuch appeared again like a whirlwind, wild with excitement, and shouted, "The Shah has yielded."

Following the Reformation, an important diplomatic immunity was the so-called "right of chapel" which allowed ambassadors to maintain churches of their own faith in countries where it would not otherwise be permitted. The right was often limited. For example, the ambassadorial chapels were sometimes forbidden to ring bells. Services had to be read in the language of the diplomat to discourage native heretics from attending them.

The right of chapel was revived after the establishment of the atheist Bolshevik regime in Russia. During the thirties the British ambassador, Lord Chilston, a Catholic, had his own private chaplain in the embassy. When the United States recognized the Soviet regime, Maxim Litvinov specifically acknowledged its right of chapel. However, like other Soviet concessions, the right was frequently nullified later by the simple device of refusing visas to foreign priests.

Perhaps the most prized of all diplomatic privileges is freedom from taxation. This privilege, legal authorities maintain, is not strictly speaking a legal diplomatic right, but is almost always conceded as a matter of international courtesy. The Russians circumscribe the privilege by setting quotas for embassies, limiting the amount of goods they may import.

Ordinarily a diplomat is not taxed by his host's country for his official or personal property. In many countries he is even exempt from taxation on any private business he may run on the side. However, this is not always so. American regulations prohibit U. S. diplomats from running businesses on the side, so the case seldom arises, though occasionally problems are posed involving royalties that diplomats may collect from books published in the country of their assignment.

A more important aspect of this immunity is the privilege of duty-free import. During the Prohibition period in the United States, foreign embassies in Washington were allowed to import liquor in unlimited quantities—a privilege prized equally by the diplomats and by their American guests and friends.

Diplomats, and particularly their wives, are so imbued with this privilege that they often go to the most extreme lengths to exercise it, buying their supplies and luxuries abroad rather than on the local market.

Before World War II, on setting out from Moscow for a vacation in Persia I was asked by colleagues from several foreign embassies to arrange for large shipments of a natural sparkling water known as Abali, produced at natural springs northeast of Tehran. "It is the best water for mixing Scotch and soda in the world," my colleagues insisted. The shipment was considerable and it took much of my vacation time arranging for it. When I was about to return to Moscow, diplomatic friends in Tehran asked me if I could not arrange a shipment of a natural sparkling water called Narzan, produced in Soviet Georgia. "It is the only decent water for mixing Scotch and soda," they assured me.

A year or two later, when I was transferred to Berlin, my Chinese servant, complaining about the kitchen equipment in my apartment, asked me to get him a good kitchen knife. I replied that I would immediately send to Sheffield, England, for one. A German friend, overhearing the remark, shook with national pride and asked indignantly what was wrong with German steel. Next day he sent me a knife from Solingen.

The privilege of free import is especially prized in the case of wines, liquor, and tobacco—luxuries which are usually not only highly taxed on import but subject to heavy excise taxes in the countries of their origin. Since liquors and wines can be produced excise-tax free in bond for export in most countries, the saving in both import and excise tax often reduces their cost, when imported under diplomatic privilege, to a small fraction of their open market value. Vintage champagnes which sell for $10 in New York can be imported by diplomats for less than a dollar. Tax-free American cigarettes cost about a quarter of the local price.

However, since some countries do not permit the sale of bonded

goods to local diplomats, curious anomalies arise. An American diplomat in London, for example, must pay several times more for his Scotch whisky than if he were stationed across the channel in Amsterdam.

The British, on the other hand, grant rebates for clothing purchased for export. A foreign diplomat in England may take advantage of this by having his London tailor send his suits to his port of departure when he goes on vacation. However, when he returns he must leave his London suits behind or else pay duty on them.

An important right of a diplomat is that of free communication. This does not mean that he does not have to pay his telegraph and telephone bills, but it does permit his couriers to carry his correspondence in sealed pouches across the frontier. This is a legal right and not a privilege. However, it can be and often is abused by using the pouch to import items—such as currency—that are contraband even for diplomats.

In the early thirties most foreign embassies in Moscow, for example, met their local expenses with rubles bought on the illegal open market abroad and imported by pouch. When the United States recognized the Soviet Union it objected to this subterfuge and demanded that the Soviet government supply its diplomats with sufficient currency at the black-market rate, legally, through the Soviet central bank. Under heavy pressure to obtain recognition, Maxim Litvinov acceded to this request. However, when the embassy was established in Moscow he welshed on his promise and privately told Ambassador Bullitt that he would have to get his rubles the same way other embassies did—that is, by importing them illegally in the pouch.

Since the Soviet frontiers were rigidly closed, the only way rubles could find their way to foreign black markets was with the connivance of the Soviet government itself. The standard source for purchasing rubles in the early thirties was Riga, Latvia. Later, when the Soviets took over Latvia, the black market by tacit agreement moved to Warsaw. Finally, when Hitler and Stalin destroyed Poland, the exchange place shifted to Tehran.

To each of these cities Soviet government agents would assiduously carry their sacks of rubles while foreign couriers would travel in another compartment carrying their empty courier pouches in which to bring the rubles back. The procedure, though cumbersome, had

the advantage of saving the Soviet government's face by maintaining the fiction that the ruble was worth its nominal value.

The couriers' pouches are often put to uses not originally contemplated. Diplomats of smaller countries are not above importing expensive foreign watches, nylon stockings, and cameras to sell on the black market. Though most countries forbid the export of national works of art, diplomats of even the greatest powers have been known to ship large pouchfuls of paintings, antiques, and other art treasures across frontiers.

One final prerogative of ambassadors is the right to be addressed as "Excellency." The right dates from the Treaty of Westphalia in 1648 and when strictly interpreted is limited to ambassadors. However, it has long since been extended to ministers and even junior diplomats. In fact, the head porters of most European hotels apply it to any guest who tips adequately.

The early American aversion to titles prohibits the use of "Excellency" for its own diplomats. These, if of ministerial rank or above, are addressed as "The Honorable." Foreign Service officers of career are addressed by the State Department as "Esquire," and all other employees simply as "Mr." However, in letters addressed to foreign envoys the State Department invariably begins "Your Excellency" and ends "Accept, Excellency, the assurances of my highest consideration. . . ." (Chargés d'affaires are offered only "high consideration.")

The British have a more elaborate formula. Though they begin "Excellency," "Sir," or "My Lord," depending on the recipient's title, the terminations are varied.

Ministers for foreign affairs rank the fullest treatment:

I have the honor to be, with the highest consideration,
Monsieur le Ministre,
Your Excellency's obedient Servant

Foreign ambassadors get the same treatment omitting the flight into French "Monsieur le Ministre."

Letters to a British ambassador abroad end:

I am, with great truth and respect,
Sir
Your Excellency's obedient Servant

Instead of "respect," a British minister gets "regard" and a British chargé d'affaires must content himself with the "great truth" alone.

Though these practices may appear stilted, especially when, as all too often, the body of the letter contains a scorching protest or a withering reprimand, at least they serve to tell the recipient he should not take it too personally.

XIX

Diplomatic Privileges
and Immunities: 2

CODDLED and pampered behind this formidable barrier of international law and custom, untouchable by the police, beyond the reach of the tax collector and the customs inspector, the diplomatic corps, one might suppose, would be the world's greatest breeding ground for adult delinquents. However, along with the immunities there has developed a diplomatic ethic based largely on custom which more or less adequately takes the place of the laws from which diplomats are exempt.

Since governments, on the whole, pick their diplomats with some regard for their ethical standards, crimes and even minor delinquencies are comparatively rare in embassies. Occasionally young foreign diplomatic secretaries who owe their positions to powerful relatives at home and are not seriously interested in diplomacy as a career make themselves objectionable by indulging in petty smuggling, fast driving, and by generally disturbing the peace. But these are not genuine diplomats—merely sons of the rich who would flout the law whether protected by diplomatic immunity or not.

The diplomatic ethic demands that diplomats observe local laws and regulations that are not abhorrent to their own beliefs or customs, especially in matters involving public security and health (quarantine regulations and the like). Occasionally, however, local custom is either contrary to the diplomat's creed or imposes undue restraints on him—for example, the religious practices imposed by local law in

Moslem countries. In such cases he is justified in disregarding them.

Up to a few years ago, if a driver ran over and killed a tribesman in the mountains of Afghanistan—not an unusual accident in the crowded bazaar streets or the narrow nomad-filled mountain roads—the driver's life was forfeited by local feudal law to the family of the victim, who might kill him on sight. However, if he expiated his crime by offering a sheep to the bereaved's relatives, and the gift was accepted, the blood feud was terminated. A young European with a penchant for wild driving who was living in Afghanistan while I served there boasted that he invariably carried a sheep in his car in case of emergency. Diplomats dispensed with the sheep and relied on their diplomatic immunity.

The diplomatic ethic possesses powerful sanctions. In the first place, a self-respecting government and its ambassadors are too jealous of their good name to permit it to be sullied by the misbehavior of the embassy staff. Theoretically, but rarely in practice, a diplomat may be tried in the courts of his own country for crimes committed on foreign service, provided the crimes are recognized by the home country, and punished according to its judicial standards.

In the past ambassadors have been known to assume the right to try subordinates guilty of crimes. In 1603 the Duc de Sully, on a mission from France to England, learning that a member of his retinue had killed an Englishman, promptly tried and condemned him to death and then requested the lord mayor of London to send around his executioner to carry out the sentence. Horrified at Sully's severity, the lord mayor persuaded him to turn the offender over to him for punishment. The murderer was subsequently pardoned by the English King.

Nowadays the most an ambassador can do to an offender on his staff is to demand that his government recall him. Some years ago a secretary of the American Embassy in Tokyo was arrested for gambling on a train—not an offense in the United States but a grave one in Japan. The offender pleaded diplomatic immunity and escaped punishment in Japan, but his chief promptly sent him home.

For an aspiring diplomat recall under such circumstances is ordinarily a severe if not fatal blow to his career. If the offender happens to be the ambassador himself, the normal practice is for the host country to suggest through its ambassador in the offender's country

that the latter has "outlived his usefulness" in this present post. Thereupon, if the facts appear to justify it, the ambassador is usually ordered home for consultation—and disciplined. In such cases, since neither government wants relations disturbed, the case is handled with great discretion and seldom appears either in the press or in the case books of international law.

When a government suspects that a foreign diplomat is gravely abusing diplomatic courtesy—as distinct from diplomatic right—it can withdraw the courtesy. For example, during the Hitler regime an American diplomat in Berlin was suspected by the German police of smuggling gold and other valuables out of Germany on behalf of German Jews. He was stopped at the Belgian frontier and his baggage searched. The goods were found and the diplomat was quietly withdrawn from Germany. This procedure has one drawback. If the search fails to reveal contraband, the host government lays itself open to the charge of abusing diplomatic courtesy.

In other cases of alleged violation of diplomatic ethics a host government has two recourses: it can declare a diplomat *persona non grata,* or no longer welcome, and request his recall or, in extreme cases, it can dismiss him without notice.

This latter procedure is referred to as "handing him his passports." The phrase is an anachronism, since no ambassador has more than one passport and ordinarily keeps it in his safe. However, in the old days host governments themselves issued passports to permit foreigners to enter or leave their territories; they were in fact simply exit visas. Hence to hand an ambassador his passports is a polite but firm invitation for him to go home. Similarly, if an ambassador is being withdrawn by his government because of displeasure with his host's government, he may in his turn "ask for his passports," which means he has been instructed to break relations as, for example, upon the declaration of war.

Occasionally a diplomat is declared *persona non grata* for personal reasons, such, for example, as repeated violations of traffic regulations or habitually disturbing the peace of his neighbors. However, lawlessness is a far less frequent cause for declaring a man *persona non grata* or handing him his passport than are political offenses.

There is considerable difference of opinion whether a government need make any explanations for dismissing or requesting the with-

drawal of a foreign diplomat. Most English authorities claim that a reasonable explanation must be provided. The American government has frequently requested a foreign ambassador's withdrawal without offering any explanation, contending that no explanation was necessary. However, it has occasionally refused to withdraw its own ambassador without adequate explanation.

Refusing to accept a request for withdrawal invariably puts the refuser in an awkward position. The host government simply ceases to do business with the ambassador and there is nothing much the sending government can do but retaliate by breaking relations.

During the 1848 revolution, which swept through Europe from Spain to Poland, the Spanish government adopted some very repressive measures against its liberal politicians. The British government then ordered its ambassador to suggest a little moderation to the Spaniards.

Showing somewhat more zeal than diplomats are traditionally expected to exhibit, the ambassador, Mr. Bulwer, wrote a formal note to the Spanish government advising it "to return to the ordinary form of government without delay." Incensed by this obvious intrusion into its internal affairs, Spain demanded Bulwer's recall but the British refused to comply. The Spanish foreign minister then wrote a personal letter to Bulwer suggesting with Old World courtesy and charm that he should "anticipate as much as possible the leave he was contemplating." Bulwer angrily replied he would not be hustled by anyone. The Spaniard then sent him his passports. After several ill-tempered exchanges of diplomatic notes the two governments broke off diplomatic relations.

When Franz von Papen, the German military attaché in Washington, was declared *persona non grata* during World War I for allegedly engaging in plots to blow up American ammunition plants, the German government withdrew him. However, they did not recognize his guilt or punish him in any way but allowed him to pursue his career, the high point of which came two decades later when he persuaded Hindenburg to appoint Adolph Hitler chancellor of Germany.

The most notorious case of demanding the withdrawal of a diplomat from Washington was that of Sir Lionel Sackville-West. During the presidential campaign of 1888 Republican supporters of President

Cleveland's opponent, anxious to prove that Cleveland was "pro-British," wrote a letter purporting to have come from a former British citizen asking the British minister for advice on how to vote. The British envoy wrote an innocuous reply indicating that Cleveland was a conciliatory President and enclosed a clipping from the *New York Times* supporting him.

The Republicans promptly published the letter, thus greatly embarrassing Cleveland among the anti-British Irish. He therefore demanded Sackville's immediate recall. When the British government hesitated, he handed him his passports.

The London *Times* observed with considerable justification that "a more ridiculous spectacle has rarely been witnessed in any civilized country than the flurried and unmannerly haste" with which Sackville-West was dismissed.

Times and circumstances have changed in the seventy years since Sackville-West departed from Washington. One need only recall the Italian elections of 1948, when not only private American citizens and organizations but the American ambassador himself campaigned vigorously and successfully for the democratic parties against the Communists. Nevertheless, interfering in politics still requires a certain amount of subtlety. When Mrs. Luce, subsequently ambassador to Rome, intimated to Italian voters that continued aid from America depended on a strong anti-Communist vote, the indignation she aroused was as helpful to the Communists as Sackville-West's innocent letter had been to the Republicans in 1888.

A recent case of the withdrawal of an American ambassador involved George F. Kennan, an experienced professional diplomat serving in Moscow. Arriving in Tempelhof Airport in Berlin on a vacation, Ambassador Kennan was besieged by journalists for his impressions of Moscow. Some of his questioners appeared to be so naïve that Mr. Kennan, in his anxiety to make the situation clear, momentarily forgot he was talking for publication and employed rather vivid language in his description of Soviet practices. The Soviet Union thereupon declared him *persona non grata* and the American government recalled him "for consultation."

The dismissal of an ambassador generally either follows an unheeded request for withdrawal or involves a very grave breach of diplomatic etiquette. When in 1584 the Spanish ambassador at London

was discovered in a plot to depose Queen Elizabeth in favor of Mary Queen of Scots he was handed his passports and told to get out of England without delay. Three years later the French ambassador in London was accused of attempting to assassinate the Queen. However, on this occasion the Queen did not dismiss him but simply read him a severe lecture on the role of an ambassador and admonished him not to try again to assassinate her.

In 1720 the newly appointed Russian ambassador in London, on instructions from Peter the Great, delivered a written bill of complaints to the British authorities and simultaneously arranged for it to be published in the London press. The complaint was so violent that the ambassador was handed his passports and given a week to get out of the country.

The United States has been a leader in dismissing or requesting the recall of ambassadors. In 1792 the French minister, Genêt, was declared *persona non grata* for using the United States to fit out privateers against the British. In 1809 E. J. Jackson, the British minister, was declared unwelcome for offending the secretary of state. In 1863 the United States demanded the recall of the Salvadorian minister for attempting to violate the neutrality laws. In 1871 the American minister in St. Petersburg was instructed to request the recall of the Russian minister in Washington because of lapses in his personal and official conduct. In 1898 the Spanish minister in Washington was declared *persona non grata* for writing disparaging remarks about the American President in a personal letter that was subsequently published in Havana during World War I. In 1915, the Austrian minister in Washington was asked to leave for allegedly attempting to instigate strikes in the United States.

The American Congress, well aware of the agreeable immunities and lucrative privileges of diplomats, for many years regarded them as adequate compensation for its representatives overseas. The first permanent official of the State Department was paid $500 a year and after one year quit for a better paying job, thus posing a problem for Foreign Service personnel and recruiting officers that has persisted almost to this day.

Not until the diplomatic service was amalgamated with the much better paying consular service in 1924 was any pretense made of pro-

viding a living for diplomats. Since then, as Congress has grown aware of the importance of the country's foreign affairs and of the necessity of maintaining a competent staff to manage these affairs, salaries have risen comparatively rapidly. Today salaries start at $4,000 and rise to $25,000 for ambassadors in the most expensive posts. Despite this liberality, the American diplomat is probably less adequately compensated than his colleagues from any other great power. The discrepancy arises not in the salary scale but in business expenses. These are a niggardly fraction of what the British, French, and Soviet governments grant their representatives and far below what any private concern maintaining overseas establishments must pay to attract competent employees.

Congress does not and probably should not provide the generous premiums private companies pay personnel required to live in strange conditions overseas. These are part of the diplomat's job and living abroad, sometimes with hardships, is implicit in his contract of employment.

However, the business expenses of a diplomat are often unusually high. Though he cannot expect to be compensated for the hardships of living in a tropical swamp or an arctic wilderness, it would seem reasonable and it is acknowledged by other governments that he should be reimbursed for the extra cash he must pay out in order to do his job properly. Congress, too, in authorizing legislation has recognized this obligation but all too often the amount appropriated is woefully inadequate.

Diplomatic privileges and immunities make up for only a small part of the surcharges on living a diplomat's life. Though his income is not taxed abroad, it is taxed by the United States. Surcharges begin when the diplomat and his family buy their wardrobe for their first post. Though the American Foreign Service has no uniform, the diplomat must have his dinner jacket, tails, and morning coat and his wife must have suitable dresses. These are even more essential in the small out-of-the-way post than in the greatest metropolis.

A family transferred from Norway to Malaya might as well feed its wardrobe of woolens and tweeds to the moths and start afresh with tropical clothes.

The government today generally provides living quarters or rent allowances for housing. However, initial installation costs, from

recutting the curtains to rewiring the television set, are all diplomatic "extras" that recur with budget-breaking frequency at every transfer. In addition to altering the clothing on his back, the frequency on his phonograph and the safety gadget on his car, he must budget for the change of schools, schoolbooks, and equipment for every child in the family.

The most heart-rending bleat that is sounded each year at the appropriation hearings is for entertainment allowances—"whiskey money," as some congressmen call it. It might be argued that diplomats should lead modest, retired lives, entertaining and being entertained only by their friends. Instead of elaborate banquets they should give business lunches at the local Schrafft's as everyone else does. It might also be argued that it is chic to be shabby and that they should occupy small apartments and wear slippers to supper while their wives prepare the meal in slacks or shorts.

The suggestion is not perhaps as absurd as it sounds. Probably the great majority of American diplomats would enthusiastically welcome such innovations. Foreign politicians, like most businessmen and Washington bureaucrats, overworked and surfeited with social engagements, would likewise shed few tears at the passing of the interminable diplomatic dinner.

In my own experience I have repeatedly found the small daily lunch meeting with local politicians, with the emphasis on brevity rather than on food and wine, far more conducive to accomplishing the business of diplomacy than the mixed gathering which meanders leisurely through five courses and as many types of drink.

Unfortunately, ancient customs, the traditions of diplomacy, and the human hankering to keep up with the Joneses are not so vulnerable to the tempo of modern life as are the habits of a business community. Like the ticker-tape parades of New York, the ceremonial visits to the Unknown Soldier's Tomb and the White House Easter-egg roll, diplomatic receptions, banquets, and balls are generally expected, if not demanded, in most capitals.

The traveling American public also expects to be entertained in the manner long associated with diplomatic tradition. Not only congressmen but businessmen, artists, writers, editors, ballet troupes, college bands and basketball teams, wrestlers, swimmers, and rope climbers, not to mention social climbers, consider it not a privilege but a right

to be entertained in the grand diplomatic manner at "their" embassy. Not a few career diplomats, eying their precious supply of whiskey, have listened tight-lipped as American visitors demanded a double Scotch from the butler explaining loudly, "What the hell, we taxpayers pay for it!"

Occasionally there is appointed an ambassador, usually from outside the career service, who deliberately shuns the social life of his colleagues and associates. Before very long his host government's officials, resenting his aloofness, will forget about him or subject him to slights which ultimately reflect not on him but on the sovereign state that he officially represents. His colleagues will omit him when entertaining foreign notables and even sometimes complain to their own governments of his indifference.

But even more inevitably gossip, rumors, complaints and even public denunciations will filter through to Congress from slighted American citizens to the effect that Ambassador X is not doing his job, is ignoring his obligations to the American community, and is deliberately standing aloof from the affairs he is charged with observing and reporting on.

Unlike the business community or even his friends in government at home, the diplomat knows no forty-hour week. Nor can he confine his entertaining to the "social season." His season for dispensing hospitality is the full twelve months of the year.

Though one might well deplore the waste of time, money, and refreshment, no informed or responsible authority can deny the obligations imposed upon an ambassador by custom. Yet frequently he is required to shoulder expenses that rightfully belong to his government. The most notorious instances are the embassies in London, Paris, Rome, and Madrid. In those posts the obligations exceed the allowance by as much as three and four times. The ambassador in Paris, for example, can expect to pay $60,000 or $70,000 a year for the privilege of representing his impecunious government.

Nor does the problem stop with the ambassador. Unable to cope with the hordes of visitors by himself, he must turn to his immediate subordinates to carry some of the burden. In recent years the deputy chiefs of mission in both Paris and London, career officials with only their salaries and meager allowances, have been forced to request transfers because they could not finance the difference between their income and their expenses.

If the privileges and immunities of diplomatic life appear enticing, it is, nevertheless, a fallacy to assume that the American Foreign Service is a way of making a fortune. No one ever got rich on the money he saved buying refreshments for his guests at a discount.

XX

Protocol

"PROTOCOL and striped pants," President Truman once wrote to me, "give me a pain in the neck." His sentiments would be virtually unanimously seconded by the American Foreign Service. Yet the fact is that American diplomats continue to observe the strictest protocol and don their striped pants to attend ceremonial affairs almost daily. Why?

Anthropologists claim that the more primitive the community the stricter are its conventions. Savage tribes are ruled largely by taboos and almost meaningless rituals. Nature's most primitive noblemen, whether in the trappers' camp or the trading post barroom, enforce their petty conventions at the point of a gun.

Most diplomats would perhaps resent being classified as anthropologically primitive, but in a sense their community is just that. Outside the local law, beyond the jurisdiction of the courts, the diplomatic corps would be a lawless community were it not for its self-imposed ethics and rules which together comprise protocol.

From its earliest origins, but especially after the emergence of national states in the Middle Ages, the diplomatic corps in every capital was a leaderless mob of inviolable representatives of sovereigns, each of whom considered himself at least the equal of his colleagues. Unlike barnyard fowl, they had no established pecking order. Occasionally the political or religious dominance of a Holy Roman emperor or a pope was universally acknowledged and his representative accorded

precedence over other diplomats. But with these exceptions, the rivalry of diplomats for the place of honor was just as keen as the rivalry between the sovereigns themselves. The seventeenth-century struggle between the French and Spanish kings for domination of Europe was, for example, reflected in miniature in every court where the Spanish and French ambassadors fought for precedence.

In 1661 the French and Spanish embassies in London both sent delegations, as was the custom at the time, to meet a newly arrived Swedish ambassador at London dock. As the cortege escorting the new arrival formed up for the return journey, the French contingent tried to squeeze into the place of honor behind the Swede's carriage. Thereupon the Spanish delegation, which had providentially brought an armed escort of about forty men, set upon the French delegates and hamstrung their horses, wounded the coachman, and generally raised havoc. When the smoke settled the French were out of action and the Spaniards were in the place of honor. When Louis XIV heard about the incident he was so incensed that he broke off diplomatic relations with Madrid.

A happier solution was found about the same time in The Hague when the Spanish and French ambassadors' carriages met in a narrow street and each solemnly refused to pull over for the other. After a long dispute it was finally decided to pull down a fence at the side of the road so that they might pass without either giving way to the other.

The Russians were no less assiduous in defense of their prerogatives. A century after the above incidents, at a court ball in London, the Russian ambassador, arriving early, sat down in the place of honor at the right of the Austrian ambassador of the Holy Roman Emperor. The Frenchman, arriving a few minutes later and finding what he considered his place taken by the Russian, leaped over the back of the bench on which the Austrian and the Russian were seated and managed to squeeze between them. The brawl that followed led eventually to a duel between the Frenchman and the Russian in which the Russian was wounded.

The great powers of the day were by no means alone in defending their seniority and place. The United States in its early history was constantly claiming that its dignity had been offended, and sent endless streams of protests to foreign governments.

Despite the efforts of Grotius and other authorities to establish order out of this chaos, nothing could be done until the Napoleonic Wars had so upset the hierarchical tables that some sort of international rule became essential. At the Congress of Vienna, therefore, a special convention was drawn up establishing precedence among diplomatic envoys. To overcome the pretensions of the various courts to first place the convention adopted the principle of "first come first served." Thus the ambassador who has served longest at a post is considered the senior and every other one takes precedence according to the date on which he presented his credentials. Ministers rank among themselves according to the same principle.

There are, of course, exceptions. For example, in Catholic countries the nuncio, the ambassador of the Vatican, is automatically the senior member of the diplomatic corps, known as doyen or dean. The Rules of Vienna, as the convention is called, cannot be considered international law and their observance is entirely a voluntary matter. However, most nations recognize it and enforce its practice in their capitals.

The dean of the diplomatic corps and his wife, the doyenne, or, if he is a bachelor, the wife of the next senior ambassador, have certain special rights and duties. At some royal courts the doyenne must present the ladies of the diplomatic corps to the sovereign. At most posts the dean can convoke meetings of the corps and organize joint action involving the community. He may never, however, take a political lead in other than purely local questions and may never invoke the names of his colleagues without their consent.

As spokesman for the diplomatic corps the dean is not without influence. Partly because of this many smaller powers, including the Scandinavian countries, often keep their ambassador at a post for ten or twelve years as against the normal three or four. Their ambassadors thus are often deans of the corps and enjoy a precedence over those of larger countries because of their length of service.

The Vienna Rules solved the problem of seniority between diplomats but this, in most capitals, is only half the problem. Where, for example, does an ambassador rank in Washington vis-à-vis the Vice-President or the Chief Justice? Local ground rules, established by the host government, generally regulate these touchy problems. For this purpose governments employ a chief of protocol or master of ceremonies as the arbiter of local custom. What does a frustrated diplo-

matic hostess do when confronted by an insoluble seating problem: the senior guest at her dinner party is a woman ambassador, her other guests include the Vice-President's wife, and the host, her husband, has just come down with the mumps? Instead of calling the whole show off, the hostess can submit the list of guests to the local chief of protocol and he is obliged to come up with a solution. The chief of protocol's decision is not binding but is generally accepted lest some guest take offense and blame the hostess.

In recent years husbands of ambassadors have created new problems to perplex protocol chiefs. Frequently a vigorous female ambassador will insist that her husband be seated above ministers. However, ministers represent sovereign states. Husbands represent something less. Husbands of ambassadors present other anomalies. When Winthrop Aldrich was American ambassador in London rumors spread that Mrs. Henry Luce, then in Rome, was to replace him. Meeting Mr. Luce in New York, Mrs. Aldrich is reported to have said to him: "Henry, I hear you are after my job."

The Rules of Vienna are fairly easy to apply when it comes to arranging ambassadors Indian file in a cortege. But how do you seat them around a square or rectangular table or on a reviewing stand? Universal protocol rules have largely solved the table problem but the rules for placing ambassadors on reviewing stands are less uniform. If there are only two to place, the order generally accepted is 2-1 (the senior on the right). With three, the order is generally 3-1-2 (senior in the center). With four, usage splits. The British claim 4-3-2-1; but other authorities argue it should be 4-3-1-2. With five, it becomes complicated: 5-3-1-2-4. However, even these rules have their exceptions: for example, in Scandinavia and Turkey and in certain religious ceremonies in Catholic countries, the left-hand place is the place of honor.

The rules of protocol are often based on plain common sense. For instance, at a formal banquet on which side of the table should the hostess sit? Since she is the last to enter the dining room, any parking lot attendant could tell you she should sit on the side nearest the door.

A newly arrived ambassador has his first taste of protocol when he prepares to present his letter of credence to the chief of state of the host government. This is not the prime minister but the sovereign or president or, as in Russia, the chairman of the ruling council. He

will already have been met informally at the station or airport by the chief of protocol and will have sent the foreign minister a carbon copy of his letter of credence and of any speech he feels moved to make on the occasion.

On the morning set for the presentation the new ambassador, if he is an American, puts on his tails with a black waistcoat and white tie for reasons we shall discuss presently. His staff, including his military attachés in their dress uniforms, foregather in his parlor. At the appointed hour the chief of protocol of the host government arrives either in a state limousine or, in Madrid, for example, in a state carriage drawn by six horses for an ambassador but by only two for a minister. Usually extra coaches or cars are sent to take the ambassador's staff. At the palace, provided the country is a monarchy, he is greeted by the foreign minister and the court chamberlain and eventually taken to the throne room, where he bows once on entering, once when he is halfway across the room, and a third time as he stops before the King. He then hands him the letters and does or does not make a speech. Ordinarily the chief of state will carry on a few minutes of desultory chatter the length of which is severely prescribed lest he talk longer to one ambassador than to the next. At a signal the ambassador brings forward his staff and presents them individually and then, in royal ceremonies, makes his exit walking backwards at least part of the way. For those not accustomed to it, walking backwards can be the most awkward part of the ceremony. The King of Afghanistan requires an ambassador to take only three symbolic steps backwards, and then he may walk out like an ordinary human being.

The ambassador and his party are then escorted back to the embassy in the coaches or Cadillacs. There he can take off his wing collar and, if he wants to impress his new staff, break out some champagne.

Now begins what is probably the most burdensome of all diplomatic functions: the making of calls. Every new ambassador must personally call on every other ambassador in the capital and receive the first calls of all ministers, except the representatives of countries his government does not recognize. Each call must be returned in person. Since there are often sixty or seventy ambassadors to call on, the calls often last no more than ten minutes during which there is scarcely time to discover what one's colleague looks like.

The custom of calls is probably one of the most anachronistic aspects of diplomatic protocol. When there were only a few embassies

in a capital, when mails were slow and business was conducted leisurely, the call had a useful function in permitting an ambassador to
get to know his colleagues and form at least a first impression of their
personalities. Today it is an empty ritual which only consumes precious
time.

In many capitals the calling routine is extended to members of
the diplomatic staff. Even third secretaries are required on occasion to
call not on ambassadors but upon their wives, this being the ceremonial manner of getting on the ambassadress's invitation list.

The calling card is an equally anachronistic auxiliary of the formal
call. Before coming to a new post every ambassador and every secretary of embassy should be informed by his embassy how many calling
cards he should have engraved. (Since protocol secretaries in embassies
are invariably among the most snobbish of human beings, they almost
instinctively run their thumbs over every card they receive to make
sure it is engraved and not printed.)

The calling-card routine requires that every new arrival, including
the least important member of the diplomatic staff, send his cards to
every diplomatic member of every other embassy and legation.
Ordinarily this is done automatically by the embassy's protocol secretary, who simply stuffs the required number of the newcomer's cards
into an envelope and adds one card from the ambassador signifying
that he is presenting (by messenger) his newest secretary. Thereupon
the receiving embassy protocol secretary stuffs the required number of
cards in another envelope and sends it back. The land-office business
thus created for engraving companies has occasionally tempted secretaries to establish a calling-card clearinghouse, whereby the cards are
returned to the owner for use on another occasion.

Calling-card lore is replete with quaint symbolic signs. A card with
a dog-eared corner means that it was delivered in person by the owner
and ranks above the unbent card in social if not in reissuance value.
The letters "p.p.c.," "p.r.," "p.f.," and "p.c." penned in the lower left
corner signify "pour prendre conger" (to take leave)—sent when the
diplomat is leaving a post—or "pour remercier" (to thank)—sent
after enjoying a colleague's hospitality—or "pour feliciter" (to congratulate) sent on national holidays and similar occasions—or "pour
condoler" (to condole)—sent after a national or personal bereave-
ment.

Diplomats had hardly been invented before host governments dis-

covered they could be bribed to great advantage. Simultaneously the home governments discovered the same phenomenon. As a result it early became taboo for ambassadors to receive valuable gifts. Thereupon host governments began to resort to conferring valuable decorations as a form of bribe. Home governments retaliated by forbidding ambassadors to accept decorations without special permission. When two of her ambassadors violated these instructions, Queen Elizabeth I sent them both to jail.

The United States government today is particularly strict about refusing to let its diplomats receive decorations. The Constitution itself specifically forbids government officials to accept presents, titles, or decorations from foreign governments. This can cause embarrassment, especially when a foreign sovereign at a public ceremony unexpectedly pins a medal on an American diplomat's coat. In the past on such occasions the State Department agreed to take the medal in question and hold it in storage until the recipient had resigned or retired. Nowadays, however, this graceful escape is closed and the recipient of an honor must send it back by return messenger. Special exceptions have, however, been authorized by Congress in exceptional circumstances involving allied governments in time of war.

An exception to the rule is also permitted in the case of small token gifts of no great value. In some countries, for example, it is the custom for guests to send flowers or small trinkets to a host after a formal party. These need not be returned. They do, however, pose a problem for diplomats and their wives who must scour the local market for suitable trinkets.

American business corporations have recently discovered what diplomats have known for many centuries—that wives are valuable auxiliaries. The Venetians, who were the first to establish permanent embassies, were initially skeptical on the subject of wives and required ambassadors to leave them at home—to avoid indiscretions. But they were required to take their own cooks—to avoid poisoners. When Ambassador Bullitt recruited his embassy to reopen diplomatic relations with the Soviets in 1933 he stuck to the old Venetian rule and with few exceptions took with him only bachelors as junior officers. However, as the Venetians doubtless discovered, the romantic attachments and resulting complications of the bachelors soon outmatched

any indiscretions wives might have committed and today the recruiting policy for the Moscow Embassy is quite the reverse—preferably no bachelors.

Although the State Department has not gone as far as American businessmen in subjecting wives to intelligence, psychiatric, and social tests, it does take a good look at the spouses before the neophyte diplomat completes his probationary period. But this rule does not apply to wives of politically appointed ambassadors.

Before World War I the German government considered the social distinction of the ambassador's wife so important that when it wanted to name a certain Count von Hatzfeldt as ambassador to London, he was informed that before he could be appointed he would have to divorce his American commoner wife of Jewish extraction. Hatzfeldt refused, but eventually agreed to a legal separation for the duration of his assignment.

The social life of a diplomatic colony is carefully circumscribed by international and local protocol rules. Often the smaller and more primitive the host's country the more jealously are the rules observed. Even at the most informal parties the host will violate protocol in arranging the "placement" or seating order at his table at his own risk. Many a diplomat from a small country, finding himself improperly seated, has sent for his hat and coat and gone home.

The fact that the seating arrangement puts together people with no interests or even language in common makes no difference. During my year and a half in Kabul, my protocol rank followed the Iranian chargé d'affaires' and night after night I found myself seated beside his fat and jolly wife who could speak nothing but Persian. My knowledge of that language soon showed a marked improvement.

Local protocol often prescribes whom you may and may not invite to dinner. Sometimes the chief of state does not allow diplomats to invite him to dinner lest he be forced to spend his life on a round of diplomatic banquets. In some capitals diplomatic secretaries are not supposed to invite ambassadors to formal dinners.

When Ambassador Davies was in Moscow he wanted to give a dinner in honor of the newly arrived Italian Ambassador Rosso. He was much put out when told that he could not invite any other ambassador since all of them outranked Rosso and therefore automatically were entitled to the place of honor.

DIPLOMAT

The forms of diplomatic entertainment, contrary to general belief, vary little from those in other walks of life. They include everything from the crowded cocktail party to the stiff "white tie" ball or reception where ancient aristocrats, their chests agleam with miniature decorations and their shirt fronts gaudy with bejeweled orders, dodder about gulping champagne.

Graham H. Stuart, in his authoritative *American Diplomatic and Consular Practice,* warns against "extravagant opulence" in diplomatic entertainment and cites as an example a Spring Festival given by Ambassador Bullitt in Moscow. In fairness to the ambassador it must be said that the arrangements for the festival were made in his absence by me as my first effort as a diplomatic impresario. It was never repeated. But in self-defense it might be added that at the Spring Festival there were no comedian waiters who intentionally spilled soup down the necks of indignant diplomatic guests as they did at a gala performance given by Ambassador Dawes in London. The worst that happened in Moscow was that a baby bear forgot himself on the gaudy tunic of a Soviet general, not by prearrangement.

Mr. Stuart warns also against "parsimonious frugality." After serving some years with Mr. Bullitt in the thirties I was transferred to Berlin under William Dodd, a professor of history whom Roosevelt had recruited as ambassador. At the first embassy reception I attended in Berlin Ambassador Dodd, taking his youngest vice-consul aside and with an air of admonition not unmixed with pride, confided that one could give a reception for two hundred people with only one bottle of gin if one was careful. The punch he served bore unmistakable evidence of the ambassador's carefulness.

At that time, when peoples were choosing sides between the dictators and the democratic world, it was sufficient to attend one of the glittering receptions of the Italian ambassador, arranged with impeccable taste by his wife Countess Atolico, and compare it to Ambassador Dodd's frugality to know who was setting the pace for the diplomats of the smaller uncommitted nations represented in Berlin. Dodd's frugality, in part due to his own lack of private means, demonstrated his and his compatriots' contempt for Nazi Germany, but it also contributed to the picture Hitler was attempting to paint of a miserly Uncle Sam indifferent to the good opinion or even to the fate of Europe.

When Dodd was eventually withdrawn his place was taken by Alexander Kirk as chargé d'affaires. Being a wealthy man, Kirk reversed Dodd's policy and entertained extensively. Each Sunday he invited several hundred people to a buffet luncheon. At that time, to save his food resources, Hitler had decreed that Sunday luncheons for Germans should consist of a single, simple dish. Kirk's lunches therefore became popular among not only his colleagues but German high officials as well, most of whom had standing invitations to come each week. On one occasion when Kirk was suddenly called to Paris for consultation on a Saturday afternoon he instructed his deputy, then George Kennan, to cancel the weekly luncheon. Upon his return from Paris he called in Kennan and thanked him, but remarked that he had forgotten to notify two people of the cancellation—his chef and the Japanese ambassador.

Parsimony can take many forms. One American ambassador used to serve cheap local wines from bottles bearing the labels of famous Rhine or Burgundy vineyards. Once when entertaining a visiting foreigner known to most of the guests as a great authority on Rhine wines, the ambassador served a particularly ordinary native product in a Rhine wine bottle. As the distinguished guest took a sip and carefully rolled the liquid around his tongue, the other guests watched in awkward silence. Then the guest put down his glass and bowed to the ambassador. "Most unusual," he commented and ostentatiously reached for his water glass.

The same ambassador also invariably saved the place cards of his more frequent guests, including his staff. His daughter was charged with cleaning them up after each meal with an India-rubber eraser. As the cards grew grayer the ambassador's staff grew more indignant until they adopted the expedient of surreptitiously dunking their place cards in the red wine. No amount of rubbing could take out the stain and the cards were finally replaced.

The main occasion for entertaining is invariably an ambassador's national holiday—the Fourth of July for the Americans, the King's or Queen's Birthday for the British, Bastille Day for the French, and so on. A generation ago it was more or less obligatory for diplomats to call on their colleagues on the national day and "sign the book"— a guest book prominently displayed in the embassy front hall—after which they were free to go home. Even today in royal courts it is the

practice to put out the book on festive occasions—the marriage of a member of the royal family, the coming of age of an heir, or the birth of a prince—whereupon the diplomatic corps is notified that their signatures are awaited.

But nowadays, instead of putting out the book on national days, one usually gives a reception complete with cocktails and hors d'oeuvres. Though essentially a national holiday reception is to receive the congratulations of one's colleagues, in the period between the wars it became customary for the American community in a foreign capital to expect the ambassador to entertain all his compatriots at a giant reception. The result was that gradually the Fourth of July became the occasion not to receive colleagues' congratulations but to alleviate the homesickness of the American colony. In Paris the Fourth of July became a monstrous free-loading operation to which even tourists temporarily in France flocked with or without invitation and often the number of guests reached several thousand.

Not to be outdone, American ambassadors in smaller capitals tried to emulate their Paris colleague by making their receptions as big as possible. An American ambassador in Prague once advertised his reception in the local papers, inviting "all Americans and friends of America." His staff was somewhat startled when a popular bargirl well known for the lavish manner in which she bestowed her affections on lonely foreigners appeared at the Fourth of July in a flashy low-cut dress and a huge picture hat. Asked by an acquaintance what she was doing at the embassy on the Fourth of July, she replied archly that she was the best friend of a lot more Americans in town than one might guess.

The Fourth of July is by no means the only occasion for diplomatic entertainment. As air travel has grown so has the number of important officials visiting foreign lands. Congressmen, prominent editors, assistant secretaries of departments, to say nothing of the secretary of state himself, all require luncheons or dinners or even business breakfasts. During his two years as ambassador in Paris David Bruce once complained that he'd had exactly one meal with his family—and that was a breakfast.

Then there are the parties one must give to repay one's colleagues for social obligations. Even when there are no visiting firemen to entertain, one's colleagues can force even the most retiring diplomat

into throwing parties. In Moscow, between the wars, few officials came from abroad requiring entertainment, since the Soviets were frugal with visas and neither Moscow's business nor her pleasure attracted foreign firemen. Bored embassy wives made up for the lack by constantly giving dinners, dances, receptions, and cocktail parties, each one of which created a dozen more obligations on her guests to return the hospitality. Thus the breeding of social events became as prolific and incestuous as that of rabbits.

As Moscow between the wars demonstrated, a bored diplomatic colony is bad public relations. To avoid a bad name among diplomats, a host government will often go to great lengths to keep its guest ambassadors and their wives amused. Though the ambassadors of the larger countries are ordinarily kept busier than they care to be, other embassies are less put upon. Furthermore, their wives, including Americans, relieved of most of the household chores by adequate staffs of servants, often find time hanging heavy. Consequently, the host governments, if they are properly advised by their protocol chiefs, will make great efforts to organize entertainment. Gala performances at the theater or opera, concerts, and art exhibits are the commonest ways of keeping diplomatic colonies out of the mischief arising from idleness.

Other forms are wine-tasting expeditions to famous cellars, boat trips on famous rivers, and the oldest form of diplomatic entertainment—hunting stags, wild boar, pheasant, or other game. (Strangely enough, diplomatic fishing parties have never caught on. Perhaps it is because diplomats are usually too gregarious or garrulous to enjoy standing silent and alone by a trout stream.)

A generation ago the ability to shoot a gun was as important for the diplomat as being able to waltz. But today standards are lower and a diplomatic shoot is often regarded by experienced hunters as one of the more dangerous pastimes. I have spent the better part of several diplomatic shoots flat on my face in a ditch while bullets whistled above me. On one occasion at a state shoot in Germany I was "contained" behind the thick trunk of an oak by a colleague with a rifle on the next stand until I discreetly waved a white handkerchief on the end of a stick. My neighbor subsequently explained that he had seen something move and thought it was a stag hiding from him behind the tree.

DIPLOMAT

Even the Soviets have not been able to remove all the traditional sport from diplomacy and will if pressed provide shooting for diplomats—at a fee. Under Socialism, they explain, one must pay for one's pleasures. Only when Communism has been fully established will everything be free. In capitalist countries the dogma is ignored and all state shoots for diplomats are on the cuff.

Since World War II, however, the Communist lust for respectability has grown, and shooting preserves and deer parks have once again come into their own as marks of distinction. A few years ago at a reception given by Marshal Tito for Mr. Khrushchev on the broad terrace of the White Palace outside Belgrade, guests were startled when, at the end of dinner, Tito leaped on a chair and clapped his hands. Suddenly several huge spotlights lit up the palace park beyond and a magnificently crowned stag blinked bewildered into the glare while the Eastern guests roared approval. A few months later Khrushchev, not to be outdone, was escorting some American diplomats around his estate outside Moscow. Approaching a grove of trees, he put two fingers in his mouth and let out a piercing whistle, whereupon an entire herd of stags leaped from behind a thicket and galloped off across the lawn.

Before the men's fashion market moved from Paris to London, where it was decreed that men should wear only the dullest clothing, the male of the human species, including the diplomats, delighted in appearing just as gorgeously attired as their brethren in the bird world. Since then on ordinary occasions only the military have been permitted to display their sartorial vanity.

Court dress was obligatory in all capitals and the smaller the capital the gaudier the costumes were supposed to be. Even today for gala occasions many countries provide a ceremonial uniform for their diplomats.

However, when the United States came on the world scene, young, self-conscious and imbued with its mission to propagate the republican ideology, it resented not only the pomp and pageantry with which royal courts surrounded themselves but also the "nonsense and flummery" of court dress.

Benjamin Franklin, we have noted, made his first appearance at the court of Versailles dressed in an old coat, his balding head wigless, and supporting himself on a crooked crabapple cane. He soon dis-

covered, however, that if he was to make any contribution to the preservation of the then frail American Republic he had better conform to local usage rather than combine an attack on European sartorial habits with the business of making allies for his country. He thereupon devised for himself what he described as a modest but elegant court uniform. Subsequent American envoys followed his example.

In 1817 the State Department prescribed as diplomatic court dress a blue, silk-lined coat, a cape embroidered with gold, white knee breeches with gold buckles, white silk stockings with gilt shoe buckles, a three-cornered hat "not so large as those used by the French nor so small as those of the English," a black cockade with an eagle attached, and a sword.

This remained the uniform until the Age of Jackson, when the Common Man decreed that the coat should be black. In 1853 Secretary of State Marcy issued instructions that American diplomats should show their devotion to republican institutions by discarding the three-cornered hat, sword, and knee breeches and appear in court "in the simple dress of an American citizen," which included long pants—then worn chiefly by workers and waiters.

Marcy's idea commended itself to a number of American diplomats struggling under the financial burden of maintaining the more elaborate wardrobe. However, when they tried out the idea they met with varying success if for no other reason than that monarchs disliked having their throne rooms used as fashion shows for dangerous republican propaganda.

The Swiss Republic welcomed the idea warmly. The Swedish King, however, told the American minister that he would receive him on business in any costume he wanted to wear but that when he appeared at court he would wear court costume or not come at all.

James Buchanan, the future President but then minister in London, had the most difficult time of all with Mr. Marcy's innovation. He started cautiously by sounding out Queen Victoria's master of ceremonies, Sir Edward Cust, a crabbed old general. Sir Edward curtly suggested that Buchanan either wear court dress to court or absent himself. He went so far as to say that, though the Queen was above such matters, "the people of England would consider it presumption" for him not to wear court dress. Buchanan retorted testily that he did

not care whether he ever appeared at court or not. When he was subsequently invited to the opening of Parliament with an invitation reading "in full court dress" he simply stayed away. This was immediately picked up by the London press, including the *Times* which printed "an indiscreet and rather offensive remark."

Apparently Queen Victoria had more sense and tact than her master of ceremonies and sought to work out a compromise with the American minister. She sent word that if he should wear a small sword to distinguish himself from the court servants it would be all right with her. Buchanan did so and was greeted by the Queen with "an arch but benevolent smile." Thus the problem of appearing at the British court in "the simple dress of an American citizen" was settled for nearly a century until it was broached again by the singular attitude of Ambassador Charles G. Dawes. When asked whether he would wear the usual knee breeches at court occasions Dawes told the questioner, "You can go plumb to hell." The London protocol authorities and court officials humored Dawes with considerable understanding not only in the matter of dress but in his other peculiar manners.

Current regulations, backed by a federal law, require American diplomats to wear on formal occasions a tail coat and white tie and, instead of the normal white one, a black vest such as is worn by waiters in pretentious restaurants. In fact, except for the white napkin on the left forearm, there is often nothing to distinguish the waiters from the American diplomats, a circumstance that has given rise to confusion. On one occasion a testy old American minister was asked by a lady at a diplomatic reception whether he was the butler. "No," he answered angrily. "Are you the chambermaid?"

When Ambassador Choate was serving in London and attended a reception in the prescribed uniform he was approached as he was leaving by another guest resplendent in court uniform. "Call me a cab," the guest demanded imperiously.

"You are a cab, sir," Choate promptly replied. Then he added: "At least you had the courtesy not to ask me to call you a hansom cab."

The history of Soviet diplomatic costumes provides an interesting parallel to the American but has a slightly different ending. Immediately after the October Revolution the Bolsheviks were suffering from the same inferiority complex and sense of mission that the Americans had demonstrated after the Revolution of 1776. Their diplomats were

required to appear in the simple dress of a Soviet citizen—a business suit, though dungarees would have been more logical. Furthermore, they were not called "ambassadors" but simply "plenipotentiaries," to avoid the stigma of bourgeois flummery. However, the unfortunate "plenpots," as the title was abbreviated, soon discovered that under the Rules of Vienna they thus lost their rank as ambassadors. Thereupon the Kremlin dropped its devotion to the common man and named its diplomats "ambassadors" as everyone else did but continued to refer to them for many years in their home press as "plenpots."

Toward the end of the thirties Stalin abandoned even these pretensions and formally renamed his envoys "ambassadors" both openly and privately. He also devised for them a most elaborate costume which closely resembled the full-dress Soviet military uniform except that crossed quill pens replaced the crossed swords or guns.

Nevertheless, in Moscow the Kremlin leaders continued to appear at official receptions in their business suits even when formal or informal (black tie) wear was prescribed for foreign guests. Thereupon several foreign ambassadors decided collectively that if their hosts were not going to bother to change for dinner they would not either, and appeared in business suits. The Communists were visibly miffed.

Since the October Revolution is only forty-odd years old it is too early to say whether the next generation of Bolsheviks will raid the Kremlin museum, where the old royal robes are still preserved, to add color to their diplomatic receptions.

XXI

Mr. Ambassador: 1

SOME three hundred years ago the Duke of Tuscany complained to a Venetian official that the Venetian ambassador in Florence was stupid. The official said he was not surprised since there were many fools in Venice. "We have fools in Florence too," the duke replied, "but we take care not to export them."

Diplomacy, according to Callières, is so important that the fate of even the greatest state depends on the skill of its diplomats, whose qualifications both natural and acquired cannot be examined with too great care. What are these qualifications?

When Sir Henry Wotton, three hundred years ago, said that "an ambassador is an honest man sent abroad to lie for his country," he was promptly fired by King James I. Others who have parroted the aphorism more recently have been punished less severely for not knowing their business.

Whatever the qualifications of a modern diplomat, the art of deceit is certainly not one of them. Moral integrity, according to a leading French diplomat, Jules Cambon, is the essential quality of an ambassador: "He must be a man of the strictest honor if the government to which he is accredited and his own government are to place explicit confidence in his statements."

It might appear superfluous to stress this question of honesty were it not for the peculiar temptations of an ambassador, cloaked in his immunities and free from supervision, to be dishonest and the many

occasions on which ambassadors have succumbed to them.

Dishonesty can take many forms. One ambassador whom I served regularly swindled his clerks out of a substantial percentage of their salaries whenever he exchanged their money for them. On one occasion he handed me a bill from a local contractor for $90, together with $30 in cash to pay it. "And I don't want the natives to think I'm a kike either," he admonished.

However, intellectual dishonesty is more common among ambassadors than petty swindling. A European ambassador during the evacuation of Moscow watched from the window of the diplomats' train as it wandered across the farm lands of Russia where unharvested wheat, potatoes, and cabbage were rotting and frozen. But when he arrived in Kuibyshev he reported to his government that the countryside seemed to him prosperous and well supplied with food. In his anxiety to prove to himself that the Russians could withstand the German attack he had seriously misled his own government. Within months the United States found it necessary to send Russia shiploads of food to replace the imaginary crops the ambassador had seen on his departure from Moscow.

Earlier an American ambassador in Eastern Europe had been informed by a reliable German source that the Germans were about to invade his host's country. He was persuaded by his wife not to inform Washington lest it order the evacuation of the women of the embassy and leave him to the mercies of an adventurous woman correspondent then in the capital.

Less blatant but occasionally no less dangerous is the temptation to color one's reports of conversations in a way that will reflect greater brilliance on the reporter's part than is warranted. For example, the dispatch writer may report a dazzling *bon mot* that occurred to him only after the conversation he is describing. "Never report what you said," an old career diplomat once warned me, "and you'll never get in trouble."

Nicolson warns against a more common form of moral inaccuracy, that of quibbling: "All too often diplomatists are so afraid of being accused of lack of judgement that they avoid expressing any judgement at all. In evading these responsibilities they are omitting to perform one of their most desirable duties."

Frequently a government will instruct its ambassador to tell his

host government unpleasant truths which will displease it and therefore make his own position more difficult and detract from his popularity. Thus he will be tempted to soften his government's harsh words and give a false impression of its attitude.

Frequently the inexperienced diplomat, consciously or unconsciously, assumes the role of advocate for his host's country vis-à-vis his own. Anxious to be loved, he himself falls in love with his hosts. The result is that his dispatches take on the color of a lawyer's brief rather than a dispassionate objective report. Occasionally the opposite temptation arises when his love is rebuffed and he takes every occasion to condemn his host unfairly.

Localitis—the belief that one's post is the navel of world affairs —is a frequent cause of coloring one's attitude. During the years before the war a colleague serving in a series of small posts in Central America wrote me regularly that his present post was the most important in which he had ever served. His enthusiasms merely amused me until during my service in Kabul I found myself convinced that the world's political axis revolved around the mountains of the Hindu Kush.

Combined with an unavoidable unfamiliarity with conditions elsewhere, localitis frequently puts a severe strain on an ambassador called upon to carry out a policy that is contrary to his honest convictions, based on his limited knowledge. So long as he remains ambassador, however, he is bound by his oath of office to follow his orders.

A distinguished American ambassador, Hugh Wilson, has described the dilemma as that of an attorney vis-à-vis his client. He must do his best to persuade his client of his view, but if he fails and the client follows a course against the attorney's conscience he must withdraw. In 1958 the American ambassador in Indonesia was instructed to carry out a policy with which he so deeply disagreed that he requested a transfer and was sent as ambassador to Prague.

In addition to absolute honesty in relation to one's own government and to one's host's, the wise diplomat will be equally forthright toward his diplomatic colleagues. This does not mean that he will always tell them everything he knows but that he will never deliberately lie or mislead them. Temptations to do so are frequent in diplomatic life, where no two ambassadors represent identical interests.

Though a false statement can occasionally produce a short-run

advantage, truth will inevitably overtake it and the lying ambassador will eventually find his reputation for reliability ruined not only with victims of his lie but among the entire freemasonry of diplomacy. A reputation for trickiness will follow a diplomat around the globe as tenaciously as the dossiers prepared by his diplomatic colleagues pursue him from post to post.

In diplomacy as elsewhere no question is indiscreet, though the answer well may be. However, in professional diplomatic circles questions on delicate subjects are by convention considered "indiscreet." A hundred fifty years ago Lord Malmesbury advised a young diplomat: "If, as frequently happens, an indiscreet question which seems to require a distinct answer, is put to you abruptly by an artful minister, parry it either by treating it as an indiscreet question or get rid of it by a grave and serious look; but on no account contradict the assertion flatly if it be true, or admit it as true if false."

Despite the strictures of the authorities on diplomacy from Callières to Cambon, it would be fatuous to deny that deceit occasionally is resorted to by diplomats of small caliber. Few ambassadors measure up to the standards of Callières and their recourse to deception is a good measure of their imperfection or, as he puts it, "the smallness of their minds."

Except for a brief period during the twilight of the Romanov regime, honesty has played no significant role in Byzantine diplomacy as practiced by the czarist or the Soviet Russians. Soviet diplomats in their negotiations neither proffer nor expect honesty. Nor do they find it demeaning to be caught out in deliberate lies, as illustrated by the case of Simyon Tsarapkin in Seoul. It is largely because of this difference in diplomatic method that negotiations between Byzantine and Western diplomats are often so fruitless. Until the former learn, as the latter learned centuries ago, that probity facilitates negotiation while dishonesty paralyzes it, diplomatic dealings between the two schools will continue to suffer.

Except for probity, no natural qualification is so important to the diplomat as political sense—what the Germans call *Fingerspitzenge-fuehl*. Asked what quality he sought most in new recruits for the Foreign Service, Deputy Under-Secretary of State Loy Henderson recently replied, rubbing the ends of his fingers together: "Political sensitivity—without it a Ph.D. is useless. With it a high school student

is invaluable." Harder to define than to identify, it is the ability to sense the significance of the political forces playing on a given question and correctly to measure the resultant reaction.

Political sense is not like the instinctive knack of an old-fashioned weather prophet for seeing in a single sign—the wind direction, an aching bone, or the flight of a hoopoe—that it will rain tomorrow. Nor is it the intuitive power of a Hitler to see in a crowd's reactions the possibilities of a course of action. It is more like the ability of a talented meteorologist to recognize and then synthesize all available data into a prediction of the course and strength of a storm or of a skilled diagnostician to identify a disease. Yet it is more than a skill in weighing ponderables. It is a gift for dealing in abstract political phenomena, like the natural gift for music, mathematics, or linguistics present in some people and absent in others.

Political sense, however, does not assure adequate solutions for political problems any more than a correct diagnosis assures a cure. But it does guarantee that a policy maker is not operating in the dark.

The material on which the politically sensitive observer works is as varied as the forms of political expression. It may be the tone of an editorial, the results of a by-election or the reaction of a cab driver to a rise in the gasoline price. Anyone can observe any of these phenomena and report it accurately. But it requires political sense to distill from it what political meaning it may contain and to detect from a combination of observations trends of opinion or subtle shifts in policies.

The best known advice to diplomats is Talleyrand's "Et surtout pas trop de zèle"—"And above all don't get excited." In another chapter I have alluded to the diplomatic goat-getter and the necessity for keeping one's temper.

There is another aspect of Talleyrand's "zèle" that is equally important, especially for the American who by nature tends to be enthusiastic, unorthodox, and attracted to gimmicks. In the explosive atmosphere of the atomic age, hastily contrived, untested, or novel initiatives are liable to provoke dangerous reactions from the startled governments on whom they are tried. Surprise may be essential in war, but in diplomacy it has no place and can, indeed, produce catastrophic countermeasures.

244

By the same token, when one's adversary is a diplomat of the Byzantine school, where good faith and Western orthodoxy play no role, the Western diplomat must be both cautious and unexcitable lest his moral indignation, when struck a foul blow, provoke an ill-considered and rash retort.

Diplomats stationed behind the Iron Curtain, where daily provocations are routine, must constantly keep in mind that the international relations entrusted to their care have roots too profound and conflicts too ponderous to be susceptible of fundamental change by brash or ill-considered actions on their part. In the thirties it was risky and probably unwise to close the Panama Canal to Soviet ships because of a quarrel over a customs inspector. Today it would be folly to shoot at such flies with sixteen-inch guns.

The sensitivity and impressionability of newly established governments in other areas of the globe likewise call for calm and caution from the diplomat, even at the risk of being called stuffy. In a recent best seller, *The Ugly American,* the authors condemn a professional diplomat for rejecting the services of a twentieth-century minnesinger on a red motorcycle to win an election against Communists and of an amateur American astrologer to win the friendship of a local potentate. In real life when the professional diplomat is replaced by the gimmick-minded amateur diplomacy tends to become a circus with Uncle Sam cast in the role of the clown.

While affability and good nature, both outstanding American characteristics, are generally recognized as invaluable to the diplomat, they must be tempered with dignity. The picture of his government that the professional diplomat seeks to convey is one not only of friendship but of strength. In choosing its friends and allies, Cardinal Richelieu once said, a state should be governed not by sentimental attachments but by the respect the candidate commands because of his power.

Tolerance also is an indispensable trait of the good diplomat. Lord Malmesbury, writing in the seventeenth century, advised the young aspirant to leave his national prejudices at home and avoid taking offense at customs foreign to the British tradition. "Nothing goes to conciliate so much," he said, "as this sacrifice of your national prejudice to theirs." He was not suggesting that the British diplomat discard his bowler for a turban or even wear a burnoose rather than a tuxedo

at dinner but that he tolerate the idea that a turban or a burnoose may not be inferior to the Savile Row product.

For the modern American diplomat it is becoming increasingly difficult to display this virtue. At home in America tolerance is often hard pressed by conformism and in our relations with our neighbors we tend to adopt a similar attitude expressed in the slogan "Selling the American way of life."

In *The Ugly American* the authors have with considerable justification criticized the isolation in which American diplomats live in their gadget-equipped ghettos. One wonders, however, whether this is entirely the fault of the diplomat or whether it does not reflect the parochial narrowness of Washington bureaucrats and legislators.

All writers on the Ideal Diplomat have dwelt at length on the virtue of discretion. "Secrecy," says Callières, "is the very soul of diplomacy," and the ability to guard secrets is basic for the diplomat.

The first place where secrets are guarded is in the chancellery safe. When Sir Knatchbull-Hugessen, the British ambassador in Ankara during World War II, left the keys to his safe in his trousers pocket, it was an invitation to his astute valet, known as Cicero, to filch and sell his secrets to the Germans. Needless to say, this lapse on the part of a popular and able diplomat made him the laughing stock of the profession. In this era of total diplomacy, physical security is daily threatened by new devices and methods which the modern diplomat must constantly guard against.

Secrets, however, can be filched from the head as well as the safe. "The warmth of wine will often lead to the discovery of important secrets," says Callières, and until recent times an indispensable qualification for a diplomat in the hard-drinking northern capitals of Europe was a strong head. Even today the garrulous ambassador is a favorite dinner guest, particularly if he possesses valuable secrets.

The gambling diplomat, while he may be discreet with his colleagues, is a favorite target for blackmailers. In 1938 a Scandinavian diplomat was tried by his government and convicted of selling secrets to the Poles to pay his gambling debts.

Women are, of course, a classic source of indiscretion. Lord Malmesbury specifically warns against what he calls "attachments." "If the other party concerned should happen to be sincere it absorbs too much

time," he says. "If insincere it leaves you at the mercy of a profligate and probably interested character."

The warning was not based on any puritanical or moral grounds. In fact it was Lord Malmesbury, then Sir James Harris, who attempted to seduce Catherine the Great in her St. Petersburg boudoir. What he objected to was "engaging one's heart"—not flirtation or even seduction.

An American code clerk with whom I shared quarters for a brief time early in my career made a regular habit of engaging his heart to young ladies. In London during World War II he lost it to a Russian émigré who, he thought, was working for a movement to restore the czarist regime in Russia, a cause also close to his heart. To help her along he showed her a number of secret cables exchanged between Roosevelt and Churchill. The girl's cause, however, turned out to be Hitler's, and when Scotland Yard caught up with him my friend was sent to prison for seven years.

A more discreet bachelor ambassador whom I knew well was famous for the beautiful "nieces" who were constantly visiting him. When eventually one turned up whose pulchritude was well below his standards, his colleagues were forced to the conclusion that she really was a niece.

Courage is one of the attributes Callières insists a diplomat should have and he cites the case of a French ambassador who failed to draw his sword and challenge the Emperor Charles V to a duel when the Emperor insulted his master, Francis I of France. Francis angrily fired his nondueling envoy and vowed never to appoint another ambassador who was not an accomplished and enthusiastic swordsman.

Today another type of courage is required of diplomats. It is not sufficient to exhibit physical bravery, as Ambassador Winant did in London when he wandered through the streets during the blitz helping the victims and encouraging the fire fighters. Often a diplomat must draw heavily on his moral stamina to report and defend views unpopular at home. During the McCarthy era American diplomats abroad had to have considerable bravery to take stands unpopular with the senator and his friends.

Birth, breeding, and looks were once important criteria in selecting diplomats; one writer cites the mother of the Empress Catherine of Russia, who advised Frederick the Great to select as ambassador to

St. Petersburg a young man with a good complexion. Considering Catherine's habits, one wonders whether her mother was not pimping for her. Today wealth is still useful to amateurs seeking ambassadorial posts, though breeding and looks are no longer essential. However, as Callières acidly observed, a government can supply a brilliant but poor ambassador with money but it cannot equip a rich but stupid one with brains.

Wit, while often an asset in diplomacy, can, if not properly controlled, raise havoc with a diplomat's career. Between the wars a young career officer serving under Minister John Flournoy Montgomery, who had made his fortune in the dairy business, suggested a little too loudly that his chief's motto should be "All I have I owe to udders." The young man was demoted and transferred.

Many years later an ambassador who allegedly coined the phrase "Dull, duller, Dulles" soon found himself in a secondary post in Asia.

In 1959, when Mrs. Clare Boothe Luce implied that Senator Wayne Morse's judgment was affected when he was kicked in the head by a horse, she found it expedient to resign as ambassador to Brazil.

A catalogue of the basic virtues deemed necessary for an ambassador could, and sometimes has, filled several volumes. However, in addition to his natural qualifications, the would-be diplomat needs a long and arduous training before he can qualify for a post. Most authorities insist that no government should employ a diplomat until he has served an adequate apprenticeship.

The training should begin at home with a study of history. The trainee should learn economics and geography. The politics and personalities of the principal courts are considered essential study matter for the novice. In countries with parliamentary government, the rules of parliamentary procedure should also be learned. In other countries, a century ago, the diplomatic student was expected to familiarize himself with the genealogies of the reigning houses. Today the genealogies could be replaced by a careful study of the history, programs, and leading figures of the various political parties.

Once his homework has been done, Callières advised, the would-be diplomat should travel extensively, not as a tourist but as a student of political science, to meet the leading political figures and learn the characteristics of the political systems that govern foreign countries. Unless one traveled, he warned, one would never learn that the insti-

tutions and customs of foreign countries are often fundamentally different from one's own. Hence one would be tempted to make analogies that would be both superficial and misleading.

Languages have always been important to diplomacy. Even before World War I, when French was the diplomatic lingua franca, diplomats were expected to know German, Spanish, and Italian. Callières thought Latin essential to a finished diplomat. Though the last is scarcely useful today, it is even more important to know at least the basic languages and, if possible, one or two of the widely used but less common tongues such as Arabic or Russian.

It is not essential for a diplomat to be a perfect linguist. It is usually sufficient if he knows enough to carry on a political discussion and to read the daily press. Too great familiarity with a foreign tongue often, as Bismarck noted, provokes suspicion. A German speaking English with a Carolinian drawl or a Russian with a Brooklyn twang gives the impression of operating under a disguise.

XXII

Mr. Ambassador: 2

NATIONS, it has frequently been observed, are judged by their representatives abroad. For this if for no other reasons governments should take special pains in selecting their envoys. In the seventeenth century ambassadors were often selected from one of three professions: the church, the military, and the law. Today the first is seldom a source of recruits except for the Vatican. Though generals and lawyers are frequently appointed to diplomatic posts, most authorities agree that neither group is well suited to diplomacy.

Although on rare occasions brilliant generals have become excellent ambassadors, most have been failures. The military career has indeed little in common with diplomacy, and not only because one is directed toward war and the other toward peace. The headquarters atmosphere with its stress on procedures, channels of command, and external discipline is totally different from that of the chancellery, where individual methods are employed, informal relationships exist, and rank plays a lesser role.

There is an even greater difference in the subject matter of the military career and that of diplomacy. The one deals with weapons, logistics and organization; the other deals with political concepts, the written word, and personal relations.

A diplomatic friend, after reading in the papers of the appointment of a series of generals and admirals to diplomatic posts, asked facetiously: "Do you suppose that one day they will appoint Ambas-

sador Smith to take command of the Sixth Fleet or Counselor of Embassy Jones to head the 45th Jet Fighter Squadron?"

Although it is commonly supposed that a legal career is an advantage for diplomats and though many lawyers have been appointed to embassies, law in some respects is even less suited as training for a diplomatic career than the military profession. In fact Nicolson maintains that "the worst kind of diplomatists are missionaries, fanatics and lawyers." "The training of a lawyer," says Callières, "breeds habits and dispositions of mind which are not favorable to the practice of diplomacy. The occupation of a lawyer," he adds, "which is to split hairs about nothing is not a good preparation for the treatment of grave public affairs in the region of diplomacy."

Whether or not splitting hairs over nothing is the basis of a legal career, the superficial similarities between the law and diplomacy are perhaps one reason for their incompatibility. The lawyer, like the diplomat, deals in debate and compromise. A knowledge of law is essential to the diplomat, an ability to negotiate is essential to the lawyer, and a knowledge of human nature is essential to both.

But when the lawyer turns to international problems these similarities lead him to the false conclusion that diplomacy is a form of law. His whole training has accustomed him to presuppose a court where right is distinguished from wrong, legal from illegal, and where there are police and jails to enforce decisions. Moral as well as legal concepts govern his thinking.

When the lawyer faces a problem he attempts to solve it by legal agreements in which every contingency is foreseen and every detail is strictly defined. He seeks to regulate affairs by hard and fast formulas within a completely ordered system.

None of these concepts apply to international affairs. Even international law, which covers only a tiny part of the field of diplomacy, has few sanctions. The World Court can regulate but a fraction of the daily disputes and differences which occupy diplomats because sovereign states refuse to submit to a higher sovereignty despite idealistic proposals that they should do so.

The traditions, customs, and histories of different countries, areas and religions, on which their moral as well as their legal concepts are based, vary greatly. In Western countries Christian morality and principles prevail. In Arab lands the ethical rules of the Koran are the

basis of law. In the East Buddhist ethics dominate. In England only a judge may condemn to death. In Germany not even a judge has the power of pronouncing death but in Eastern lands a killer's life is at the disposal of his victim's family.

Nowhere is the difference more marked than between Western and Byzantine concepts of justice. In the Soviet Union a war to establish or defend a Communist dictatorship is a "just" war, a lie to the same purpose is a white lie, and what the West considers truth is often a bourgeois falsehood.

Diplomacy mediates not between right and wrong but between conflicting interests. It seeks to compromise not between legal equities but between national aspirations. Among nations, despite the efforts of statesmen since Grotius, no ordered system with a unified process of law enforcement exists. Furthermore, a nation's interests, aspirations, and the power to satisfy them vary from year to year, indeed from day to day. What yesterday was satisfactory may tomorrow be intolerable and unenforceable.

When the Western Allies relinquished their sovereign rights over Western Germany they sought to regulate the new relationship by the so-called "Germany Treaty." Owing largely to the preponderance of lawyers in the negotiations, particularly on the American side, a contract was drawn up that tried to foresee every contingency and provide by legal agreement for solutions to problems that until then had rested with the victorious powers as a result of the war. The abolition of cartels, the guarantees of democratic government, the punishment of war criminals, and a thousand other details were negotiated by a host of lawyers and legal experts as though a system of law existed into which the agreements might fit.

When after months of intense negotiation an agreement was reached, the chief German negotiator, State Secretary Hallstein, himself a brilliant professor of law, bursting with pride asked an Allied diplomat who had not participated in the negotiations what he thought of the treaty. The diplomat replied bluntly: "It is not a treaty at all. It reminds me of the fine print on the back of my fire insurance policy."

The diplomat's judgment was more than vindicated within months. By granting Western Germany her sovereignty, the treaty fundamentally altered the power relationship of the signatories. The limitations that it sought to impose upon the Germans became meaningless

because the power to enforce them no longer existed. Those obligations the German government assumed which corresponded with her national interests remained in force. The rest, in a matter of a few years, vanished all but unnoticed. All that remained were a few general principles, implicit but not explicit in the treaty, which reflected the realities of the new relationship created with the re-establishment of German sovereignty.

To the church, the military, and the law the twentieth century has added a fourth potential reservoir of ambassadors—business. It is widely believed, particularly in America, that diplomatic negotiations are essentially business deals and that the best negotiator is therefore a shrewd Yankee horse trader operating under the cover of a pair of striped pants. As a result, a number of successful businessmen without diplomatic experience have found themselves pantless and shirtless at the end of a negotiation with experienced diplomats.

However, diplomatic negotiations differ fundamentally from commercial or business dealings. In the first place, business, like the law, is conducted within the framework of a regulated system with self-enforcing powers. Business to a large extent is regulated by the laws of contracts. Even international business deals generally provide for arbitration in the courts of one or the other contracting party. Diplomacy has been defined as "commerce in mutual benefits" or the harmonizing of interests. Only as long as mutual benefits accrue or harmony prevails is there any real assurance that the agreements will be fulfilled.

The businessman who has concluded a "deal," whether to buy a factory or sell a shipload of coffee beans, knowing that the contract is binding, can often scarcely wait to announce his triumph to his stockholders and assure his associates of the profit he has made. The diplomat, however, never proclaims a diplomatic success. On the contrary, he will endeavor to advertise the benefits he has sacrificed to the other party.

In the second place, unlike the average businessman, the diplomat cannot pick and choose his associates. He must deal with the political power that rules. Nor can he ever be sure when power relationships will change and the government he rebuffed yesterday must be wooed as an ally today. Only the amateur or the Byzantine diplomat slams doors. The professional may say "perhaps" or "tomorrow" but he never

253

says "no," whether to a treaty of alliance or a request for a loan to build a dam.

Thirdly, unlike the businessman's, a diplomat's negotiation is never finished. A treaty may be signed and sealed but it is seldom irrevocably delivered. So long as it remains in force it is subject to modification, renegotiation, or denunciation. For example, the United States may find it advisable to establish airbases in Spain. Delicate feelers are first put out by the ambassador in Madrid. If the Spanish government responds favorably, formal negotiations are begun. Long discussions and haggling follow on sites, payment for and final disposition of the fields, the labor terms and material costs to build them, and legal jurisdiction over the American airmen who will eventually man them.

Even when the treaty has been signed and ratified, the diplomat's job has scarcely begun. Differences of interpretation of the most precisely drafted text will arise. Unexpected obstacles will develop as construction crews go to work, equipment is imported, and finally the crews and their families move into their strange environment and start to adjust themselves to local customs and laws. Each of these problems must be ironed out in endless negotiations. Meantime the mutual benefits accruing to the Spanish and American governments will fluctuate with new political or economic conditions and the development of new weapons.

The North Atlantic Treaty Organization, now ten years old, is practically in a perpetual state of renegotiation. Scarcely a week passes without discussions between the diplomats stationed at NATO headquarters to smooth out difficulties, modify impractical commitments, or even occasionally to prevent the entire edifice from collapsing because of conflicting interests between the partners, whether Turkey and Greece or England and the United States.

If churchmen, soldiers, lawyers, and businessmen make poor diplomats, Callières maintained, dilettantes make the worst of all. Men of small minds, he said, should content themselves with jobs at home where their errors may be easily repaired; for errors abroad are too often irreparable. Acknowledging that there is always a temptation to use ambassadorships to pay old debts or to quiet petty blackmailers, he warned that the public interest must be supreme and that government officials should steel themselves against the pressure of political friends or relatives seeking diplomatic posts. Those who become am-

bassadors for the prestige it affords are like the ass in the fable who mistook as meant for himself the homage paid the statue of the goddess he was carrying on his back.

Despite these and many other warnings from other statesmen, the export of fools in the guise of diplomats has continued to the present day and has frequently elicited complaints like the Duke of Tuscany's.

Such complaints are generally made discreetly and are carefully kept from the press. Some time ago, the Canadian prime minister is said to have complained that Canada had suffered her share of American dilettantes and hacks as ambassadors and pleaded that it be sent a professional diplomat. The President then sent a distinguished career officer.

After World War II the government of Luxembourg, having been host to a series of political party favorites as American ministers, let it be known in Washington that its patience was exhausted. If the next appointee was not a career official, it intimated, it would refuse to receive him. The United States again acceded.

The chief of one European state once complained to me that only two of the last six American ambassadors to his country had done a satisfactory job. The two he named were the only professionals among the six.

Other governments have grown accustomed to nonprofessional American diplomats, tolerating them as part of the American system of conducting diplomacy. However, as Nicolson points out, the United States has suffered much from political appointments under the "spoils system." "The capitals of Europe and Latin America," he says, "echoed with the indiscretions of these amateur diplomatists and much damage was done to all concerned . . . by politicians whose intelligence and conduct were not consonant with the dignity of the United States."

Nevertheless, the spoils system continues to dispose of many diplomatic posts. Today only four of the fourteen American ambassadors in important Western European posts are professionals. Because many non-European posts, especially in out-of-the-way places, do not attract office seekers, the percentage of professionals on a global basis is somewhat higher. Even so, about half our embassies are still headed by amateurs whose only training has been as successful bankers, salesmen, or race-horse breeders. Not all have been failures. Indeed some have revealed the rare talents of a born diplomat.

DIPLOMAT

It is popularly supposed that ambassadorships are bought by rich men with social ambitions or socially ambitious wives. This is only partly true. Aside from the professionals appointed from the career service, many ambassadors are selected by the President or the secretary of state because he genuinely believes that they possess the attributes of a good ambassador. They are good mixers. They make friends easily. They are conciliatory and have pleasing personalities or they have some special tie with a particular country that will make them popular there.

President Roosevelt, who, according to John Gunther, shopped about for ambassadors like a housewife shopping for potatoes, selected Professor William Dodd as ambassador to Germany because he was a specialist in German history and a fanatical enemy of Nazism. Dodd was a great scholar but a disastrous diplomat. President Eisenhower appointed an ambassador to Southeast Asia because he knew the country well from the frequent big-game shooting expeditions he had made there.

Nevertheless, money plays a prominent role in the distribution of diplomatic prizes. By making a substantial contribution to a political party, office seekers can enhance their chances for a diplomatic post, particularly if they or their backers can discover something in their background that passes for a diplomatic qualification: they have traveled abroad or know a lot of foreigners or are accomplished hostesses.

An old friend of mine who had served for many years in the Foreign Service found promotion slow and his chances of getting an embassy by way of the career ladder slight. Thereupon he resigned from the service and made a substantial contribution to the Republican party. Within months he had a good embassy.

In the roaring twenties a wealthy playboy was left a large fortune by his father, together with precise instructions about its disposition. One provision instructed him to make a heavy contribution to the Republican party. However, the elections of 1932 were in the offing and some of the playboy's Democratic friends persuaded him that the Republicans did not have a chance. His father, they argued, would have been just as pleased to back Franklin Roosevelt. He agreed and after the election found himself heading one of the choicest embassies in Europe.

Contributions to parties need not be monetary. Editors who put

their papers behind a political candidate can often count on an embassy for themselves or some member of their families. A lawyer may help a leading candidate to clear up a messy lawsuit and get an appointment to Sweden. Even mediocre journalists, by writing stories favorable to a candidate, can get a job as ambassador.

Exile to an embassy overseas has long been a way of sidetracking political opponents. Hitler thus got rid of former Chancellor Luther by sending him as ambassador to Washington. Chancellor Adenauer rid himself of a rival in his party by sending him as ambassador to London. More recently the head of Iraq's revolutionary government, after condemning a rival to death, offered to reprieve him if he would go as ambassador to Germany. The condemned man refused!

Some years ago a novice congressman from New York, having displeased his local party bosses, was offered by them either the embassy in New Zealand or the embassy in Portugal if he would step down and not run for re-election. Doubting their ability to dispose of embassies in this cavalier fashion, he made inquiries in the State Department and to his amazement learned that both posts had been put at their disposal. Nevertheless, he rejected the offer and is still a prominent member of Congress.

The national committees of both major parties supervise the disposition of political appointments to embassies through an informal system whereby the party in power maintains within the State Department and on the department's payroll a small group whose function it is to watch over the disposition of such patronage as becomes available within the department or the diplomatic service. They keep an eye out for possible openings for loyal party followers, check appointments with the patronage bosses of the state from which a candidate comes, and from time to time clean out the political appointees who have expended their patronage claims or dun them for further contributions.

Patronage bookkeeping is very informal, a circumstance that occasionally leads to misunderstanding and even bitter recriminations. An old friend of mine, a political incumbent of an embassy, was approached by his national committee chairman with the suggestion that he increase his annual contribution to the party or resign. The ambassador was well off, so he gladly upped his donation and settled back for another term in his pleasant embassy. However, the national

chairman was suddenly replaced and the new man, searching for a vacancy for a prominent politician in need of a job, reneged on his predecessor's assurances and my friend found himself an ex-ambassador. Unfortunately, there is no court of equity where patronage claims can be adjusted, so he built himself a house on the Riviera and has lived there happily ever after.

Since public opinion polls are not perfect and elections are notoriously unpredictable, eager office seekers occasionally contribute to both major parties. This practice is considered unethical by some politicians and is frowned upon by patronage bosses. However, since the contributor usually uses his wife's name for one contribution and his own for the other, it is not always easy to check.

Listening on the embassy radio to the returns coming in on the Willkie-Roosevelt campaign, I was astonished to hear my boss, a Democratic appointee, cheering the early lead established by Willkie. Blandly he announced that he had switched allegiance to the Republicans and had backed their candidate heavily. When Roosevelt caught up and eventually passed Willkie, however, the ambassador was equally unconcerned. His wife, he announced unabashed, had maintained her loyalty to the Democrats with an equally substantial contribution. The ambassador survived two more elections and eventually died "in harness."

Although embassies are usually much sought after, it occasionally happens that a deserving party follower prefers his rewards in the form of a judgeship or a post office nearer to home. In the thirties a Texas claimant to party favors was asked whether he would like to be minister to a Baltic capital.

"Minister?" he asked incredulously. "Hell, I've never even been in a pulpit let alone ordained." Nevertheless, he was induced to accept the post, where his lack of religious qualifications became all too apparent when he finally departed.

During the same period a patronage dispenser in Washington telephoned a deserving office seeker in South Dakota to offer him an embassy in Eastern Europe. Unfortunately, the man had a namesake in the same town and the call went to the wrong person. Not until the latter was on his way to his new embassy was the error discovered.

Before the establishment of the career service in 1924, all embassy officials were expected to submit their resignations when the presidency

changed hands. After that, career officers below chief of mission were considered permanent. In fact, several career ambassadors, assuming that they too were exempt, failed to submit their resignations. However, they were quickly put right by the White House and since then after every election all chiefs of mission whether career or political appointees submit their resignations.

Partly as a consequence of this practice, professional diplomats who have risen to ambassadorial rank often find their careers suddenly terminated when their resignations are accepted by a party in power in need of patronage posts. Since there is no way for a career diplomat to remain an ambassador for more than a limited period without an embassy, he must thereafter retire. Legislation to create a reserve pool of ambassadors who can retain their employment for several years is, in fact, one of the pressing needs of the Foreign Service today.

After every election the political patronage staff within the State Department sits down with the professional personnel director to divide the spoils. It has become a political tradition for presidential candidates to pledge their support of the career principle and to promise not to replace career ambassadors. However, in view of the automatic resignation procedure, it is relatively easy to circumvent such pre-election pledges.

Whenever a new party comes to power it is customary to demonstrate statistically that the number of professional diplomatic incumbents has been increased or at least not decreased. This statistical game is fairly simple to play no matter what inroads the patronage committee has made on the embassies, since the number of embassies has in recent years steadily increased with the creation of new independent states, many of which political office seekers do not consider desirable.

The most desirable diplomatic posts are generally those in Europe, especially London, Paris, Rome, and Madrid. The so-called "commuting embassies," Ottawa, Mexico City, and Havana, whence an incumbent can easily commute to his office in New York for the transaction of his personal business, also are highly in demand. Where climatic conditions are good outside Europe or where there is a special interest for an office seeker one also occasionally finds political appointees.

One office seeker with a large family in comfortable circumstances not long ago sought for and got an embassy in a far-off primitive post.

Asked by a friend why he wanted to give up his comfortable existence in Delaware for a squalid Asian city, he replied blandly, "My psychiatrist recommended it." Apparently the remedy for whatever mental disease ailed him was a success, for after serving several years there he applied for and got another embassy.

Not infrequently it becomes necessary to dismiss an ambassador to make room for an important politician who has lost an election or has been ousted from his job for other reasons. When the prospective victim is a political appointee it is relatively simple for a national committeeman or departmental patronage official to write him that the party deems its obligations to him fulfilled. Even this formality is not always observed. In 1958 an ambassador in Scandinavia read in the local morning paper that Washington had appointed a successor to him. Angrily he cabled for confirmation and shortly received it together with an urgent request for his resignation.

If the prospective victim is a career appointee, on the other hand, the procedure is more delicate. An old professional friend of mine with many years of service was happily serving out the last year or two before retirement in a not particularly pleasant post when suddenly a courier delivered an urgent letter from the State Department. It stated that it had been reconsidering his allegedly long-expressed wish for early retirement and reluctantly had decided to accept his resignation as ambassador. Since his successor, a New York lawyer, was planning to leave for his new post within a few days, it was suggested that he leave his embassy within the week. Sadly and bitterly the old diplomat wired his resignation, packed hurriedly, and retired on a substantially lower pension than he would have received had he been allowed to serve out his full career.

Diplomatic procedure demands that before a new ambassador is appointed the receiving government be asked if he is acceptable. However, American national committees have often found this procedure superfluous. When Robert Butler, the retiring finance director of the Democratic National Committee, was selected as ambassador to Australia, not even the State Department was aware of the appointment until it was publicly acclaimed at a banquet in honor of the appointee. Accustomed to being ignored in such matters, the department said nothing but the Australian government made it clear that it found

the American way of conducting diplomatic business both highhanded and discourteous.

Although the Senate under the Constitution is empowered to pass on all diplomatic appointments, its responsibility has until recently been fulfilled with perfunctory regularity. Only on the rarest occasions has an appointment aroused such animosity that the appointee has withdrawn. When, for example, Edward J. Flynn, the retiring chairman of the Democratic National Committee, was turned out to grass as minister to Australia in 1943, the public reaction against him was such that he was persuaded to request that his nomination be withdrawn.

Although, as we have noted, authorities on diplomacy have laid great stress on the prior training of an ambassador, the State Department has found it necessary to compress a political ambassador's briefing on the country to which he is assigned to a few weeks or even days. Largely because of the shortage of time, it frequently happens that an ambassador is not even able to pronounce the name of the country to say nothing of the name of its highest official, as Ambassador Gluck found to his sorrow. One ambassador assigned to Yugoslavia boasted to his friends that he was on his way to Czechoslavia and constantly confused the Masaryks with the Karageorgeviches.

Once arrived at his new post, even a professional ambassador expects to spend weeks if not months familiarizing himself with conditions and making the acquaintance of the host country's officials. For the political appointee a special and often costly routine has been established. As counselor or deputy chief of mission, an experienced professional will ordinarily be assigned to him. In addition, a junior professional officer is frequently designated as personal assistant to keep the ambassador informed of diplomatic usage and to reduce his diplomatic gaffs to a minimum. Against the weeks it takes a professional to work himself into a new post, it is an old axiom among career diplomats that an amateur often requires years.

It would be unjust to ascribe to pure cynicism this haphazard way of manning the key foxholes in the outer perimeter of our national defense. Whereas provincial party bosses and parochial national committeemen may deliberately overlook national interests, the political leaders in whose name the appointments are made are frequently

sincerely persuaded that the appointees foisted upon them actually possess qualifications popularly associated with "diplomacy"—affability, social grace, or Yankee shrewdness.

Furthermore, it is widely believed that the long-distance telephone and the cable have reduced the role of a diplomat to that of a Western Union messenger boy and that the risk of the irreparable damage, of which Callières warned, has been eliminated. Disregarded is the warning of Secretary of State Charles Evans Hughes. "It is perfectly idle," he said testily, "to believe that we can get along without diplomatic representatives. . . . We cannot rely on direct messages. We need the man in personal contact with other men in transacting the business of their government." The leading French diplomat Jusserand was even more explicit. "Experience has already shown and will more and more show," he said, "that no invention, no telephone, no airplane, no wireless will ever replace the knowledge of a country and the understanding of a people's disposition."

Few statesmen or diplomatic authorities have argued that diplomatic posts should be filled exclusively from the trained career service. Callières urged that men of letters be enlisted. Others have warned against the incestuous habits of mind that a closed professional service inevitably induces.

Every political generation produces a half dozen or more individuals capable of making a distinguished contribution to diplomacy without going through the long and arduous training of the professional service. If they are familiar with government practices and particularly foreign problems and have demonstrated their political sense, their appointment to diplomatic posts not only puts their talents to valuable use but also serves to refresh, invigorate, and inspire the career personnel. In recent years David Bruce, John Sherman Cooper, Chester Bowles, and Douglas Dillon have rendered outstanding service to the country in diplomatic posts. Great Britain, too, has frequently brought new blood into its career service through such men as Sir Oliver Franks.

Politicians have argued earnestly that the present method has for over a century adequately served our political system, providing the essential means for financing costly campaigns. For centuries, they point out, other countries also staffed their entire civil service by the same method. Indeed, up to the Crimean War the British Army was officered almost exclusively by the sale of commissions.

One of the most vigorous defendants of the present system, Mrs. Clare Boothe Luce, who has herself served as ambassadress, has pointed out that despite occasional lapses the United States has not done too badly with it. "In 181 years of our diplomatic history," she has said, "America has not yet made the irrevocable diplomatic blunder."

Could Lord Raglan, the British commander in the Crimea, have put the case for his officers more strongly as the Light Brigade charged into the valley of Death?

XXIII

The U. S. Foreign Service

A FEW years ago, on a visit to Germany, Senator Bourke Hickenlooper asked an American diplomat his reaction to a Congressional investigation of the Foreign Service then in progress.

Congressional investigations, the diplomat replied, reminded him of the German game laws. These, he explained, strictly prescribed the seasons of the year, the times of day, and even the types of weapon with which every form of game from stags to rabbits could be hunted in Germany.

"There is only one exception," the diplomat went on. "You can shoot at any season and at any hour with any weapon you like at wild pigs. It seems to me," he concluded wistfully, "that the Foreign Service are the wild pigs of Capitol Hill."

The hunting of the permanent officials of the State Department is nothing new. Thomas Paine, the forerunner of the first secretary of state, was dismissed on security grounds for leaking secrets to the public. James Lovell, Paine's successor in charge of foreign relations, was considered by Congress "of such eccentricities and temper as to lead at times to doubts of his sanity."

Yet not all diplomats have had so poor a reputation. Indeed many of them during the Revolution enjoyed at least as much prestige as the generals, and their successes in winning allies among the governments of Europe were hailed with as much enthusiasm as military victories.

During the first two generations of the Republic's life diplomatic

experience was considered an important if not essential prerequisite to high office. As I pointed out in an earlier chapter, until the election of William Henry Harrison, all our presidents with the exception of Washington and Jackson had served either as secretary of state or as a minister, and several had served in both capacities.

During the interlude that followed Jackson, as we have noted, diplomacy and diplomats enjoyed a sixty-year vacation. But ever since Wilson's failure at the Versailles Conference demonstrated the need for a professional service, the question of how to select, train, and organize a career service capable of handling twentieth-century diplomatic problems has continuously perplexed both Congress and the public.

Although these problems are more complex, extend over a far greater range of subjects, and require a much larger service then in the past, the principal tasks of the diplomat and the manner in which they are solved have not fundamentally changed, nor have the basic rules governing his selection, training, and management.

Ten centuries ago Liudprand was brought up, carefully schooled, and thereafter apprenticed to his father and his uncle, both ambassadors, before his patron, Emperor Otto, considered him competent to take over a diplomatic mission. In the intervening centuries, as already noted, the aspiring diplomat was expected to ground himself thoroughly in the basic subjects of history, economics, linguistics, and even science and then to travel abroad to study the political institutions and social customs of foreigners. Only after a probationary period was he finally considered sufficiently trained to become a full-fledged diplomat.

These principles were broadly followed in carrying out the Rogers Act, which in 1924 created the first American professional diplomatic service. Candidates were accepted at the bottom only and by means of stiff competitive examinations, lasting several days, in history, economics, mathematics, law, and one or two foreign languages. While previous foreign travel was not required, those who passed the written examinations were again orally examined to determine by personal interview whether they possessed the personality and adaptability necessary for living and working in foreign countries.

The system worked admirably and within a few years the rich young socialites who had staffed many of our embassies were replaced by able young men determined to make diplomacy their life profession.

Though they attracted little attention at home, the new generation of diplomats were soon winning recognition among their foreign colleagues as astute and able professionals.

With remarkable foresight, as early as the late twenties, the State Department was sending some of the ablest among them abroad to study, sometimes for four years, the languages, histories, and social problems of what twenty years later were to become the most critical areas: Russia, the Far East, and the Arab lands. Several of these early specialists later became the experts on whom we have relied in these countries since World War II—George F. Kennan and Charles E. Bohlen in the Russian field, Raymond Hare, now ambassador in Cairo, in the Arab field. The Far Eastern specialists, though invaluable during the crucial war years, later succumbed to the Congressional purges which followed the Communist take-over in China.

Other young officers, after demonstrating special qualifications during service in the field, were sent to universities for postgraduate work in economics and finance. But the great majority of the new recruits were assigned to general diplomatic and consular work, carrying on such limited negotiations as the isolationist policies then prevailing required, protecting American economic and political interests, and above all, keeping the State Department informed of the complex political maneuvers that were to culminate in World War II.

Despite the renovations accomplished by the Rogers Act, a bit of the old flavor of socialite diplomacy was carried over with the senior diplomats incorporated into the new service. The Ivy League colleges for some time continued to provide the majority of candidates. Expensive tutoring schools flourished to prepare those who could afford them for the stiff competitive exams. In the oral examinations the elder diplomats continued to judge the candidates largely on their "appearance, manner and adaptability."

To these older diplomats "appearance" sometimes meant a well-cut suit from Savile Row or Brooks Brothers. "Manners" meant in part graceful agility with a teacup as taught by the masters' wives at the best Eastern boarding schools. "Adaptability" meant, among other things, the ability to mingle inconspicuously in any society including the "best" Continental salons.

Because of their upbringing and early associations, these older diplomats had become adept in the social amenities. They knew their

French wines and Scotch whiskeys, their brandies and their ports. Frequently they had joined their diplomatic colleagues on fashionable hunting parties at the estates of Europe's old aristocracy or on the Scottish moors.

In Washington, too, they had followed the pattern set by the old society known as the Cliff Dwellers. As soon as they had been admitted to the service they had bought houses in Georgetown, joined the Metropolitan Club, and spent their weekends at country estates in Virginia or on the Eastern Shore. One of them, a rich young bachelor from the West, not only acquired a large house but hired an interior decorator from New York to furnish it. A less well-to-do colleague, invited to inspect the finished product, looked about the flamboyant entrance hall and announced to his young host, "I'll buy a bottle of champagne but I won't go upstairs."

Though many of the old service members were socialites, a considerable number were expert diplomats as well. C. Pinckney Tuck, Theodore Marriner, Alexander Kirk and Jay Pierpont Moffat were not the last of the snobs but the mentors of the first of the new class of professionals and among the most skilled and polished of the diplomats to whom the country is deeply indebted. However, a little of their "European" manner was transmitted to the new service in its earlier days and raised the eyebrows of Congressional visitors, foreign correspondents, and traveling private citizens.

Since the Foreign Service had specifically been removed from the spoils system, it was considered almost bad form to have too close associations with congressmen lest one be accused of currying political favor to further one's career. Publicity, too, was shunned. Even as late as 1936 a junior diplomat, offered a berth on the maiden voyage of the airship *Hindenburg*, was warned by the Foreign Service personnel chief to keep his name off the published passenger list.

Yet the service suffered from weaknesses that only later became apparent. The administrative heads of the service in Washington comprised a small, tightly knit group accustomed to old-fashioned administrative methods with a high degree of paternal supervision. At the top stood Wilbur J. Carr, who had run the consular service since its establishment in 1906 and had taken over the administration of the combined service in 1924. The personnel director under him knew almost every officer personally and administered discipline, supervised

promotions, and determined assignments not on the basis of impersonal standards or fixed rules but largely as he himself saw fit.

Acutely aware of the suspicion of Congress, the administrators in Washington sought to avoid conflict for the new service by submitting only the most modest budget requests, with the result that, though one could live on one's salary in many posts, it was a tight squeeze. Little or no provision was made to reimburse struggling young diplomats for the costs of essential official entertainment or even of studying foreign languages. Indeed, because of the shortage of personnel, it was generally strictly forbidden to study the local language during office hours. Embassies, too, were poorly equipped physically, and housing was often deplorable.

Despite these defects, for the small prewar staff of six or seven hundred diplomats the system functioned well enough and continued to attract able young men. The Ivy League monopoly was gradually broken as college students in other areas became aware of this new Foreign Service career. When Franklin Roosevelt became President he made it abundantly clear that American diplomats who stuffed their handkerchiefs up their shirtcuffs were not looked upon with favor. Examining boards modified their standards of "appearance, manners and adaptability" so that the "men with the hoe," as they were sometimes called, stood as good a chance as the suave candidates from fashionable Eastern schools.

By 1934 candidates began to be rejected because they were too European. One, who had passed his written examinations with high marks, was turned down because his manners were too Continental, and he was advised by the oral examiners to spend a year working on a Western ranch to get more Americanized. After having fulfilled this advice, he appeared for the second time, was again rejected and told to work for a year in a filling station. Finally at the third try he was accepted and is today an outstanding senior diplomat.

Successful candidates in the written and oral exams were commissioned as "unclassified" officers and sent to the field for a probationary service which lasted approximately a year. Theoretically those who did not live up to expectations in that period were dropped without further ado. In practice, however, less than a dozen failed to survive the probation in the first twenty years of the Foreign Service.

At their probationary posts, generally a consulate, they were assigned

for a few months at a time to each of the various sections or desks: visas, passports, commercial reporting, administration and coding, seaman and welfare sections. After about a year of training the probationers were recalled to Washington in groups of twenty or more.

For three months they then attended the Foreign Service School in a dank gloomy room in the basement of the old State Department. There they listened to lectures on the whys and wherefores of the complicated consular and administrative procedures they had learned in the field. They visited the various bureaus of the department, worked in the code room, watched the operation of the geographic desks where diplomatic instructions to embassies were prepared, and also visited and were briefed by other government agencies, such as the Departments of Commerce and Agriculture, which had special interest in their future work as diplomats.

Toward the end of their school term the student diplomats were asked to submit three preferences for their first permanent post. On the last day of school the director of personnel appeared in person to read out their assignments. It was always a tense moment in their careers, for many imagined that their first assignment would determine their entire future. Assignment to an obscure consulate, they felt, meant eternal stagnation in consular posts. A busy embassy, on the other hand, would give them, they thought, a quick opportunity to demonstrate their diplomatic talents and would mark the beginning of a dazzling career.

The actual assignments seldom corresponded to their expressed preferences, but they had already been warned of that. After they had learned their fates, they were taken in a group to call on the secretary of state, who gave them a collective word of encouragement and an individual handshake. For some, like myself, it would be their only glimpse of their chief in their entire careers. From then on they would daily write dispatches and cables directed to the Secretary and frequently receive instructions in his name but perhaps never would they see him again.

Finally, the handshaking over, they would assemble on the south steps of the old State Building for their class photograph with the director of the school and sometimes, if he could spare the time, with the chief of personnel. Years later these photographs would be a vivid yardstick of their relative progress. This face would have dropped from

sight. That one would appear periodically in the *New York Times*. And the owner's? If he had pushed ahead, the photograph would hang prominently in his office. If he had fallen behind, it would be hidden away in the den at home.

Despite their inadequate salaries, stunted staffs, lack of recognition from the Hill, and the inherent weaknesses of Wilbur Carr's paternalistic administrative system, the morale of the service in the prewar years was high. Intensely proud of having qualified for the most selective service in the government, the members jealously defended the two principles on which it was founded: entrance at the bottom by competitive examination and promotion on merit.

Though they knew they would never be as rich as others who had selected careers in private enterprise, they had the great satisfaction of working for the biggest boss of all. Having pledged themselves to serve anywhere in the world, they knew that, though occasionally life in a pleasant embassy would be plush, more often than not it would be uncomfortable, unhealthy, and even dangerous for themselves and their families.

Among themselves they complained of their hardships and small salaries, their ill-equipped offices and inadequate housing, especially during the depression years when their salaries were severely cut, and for several years recruiting was interrupted with fatal results. But secretly they usually enjoyed their martyrdom. Like members of a little mendicant religious order, they derived an almost masochistic pleasure from the ill-treatment they suffered at the hands of Congress and the public.

When war struck in 1941 and recruiting once more ceased, there were about eight hundred officers in the service. About a quarter had come in prior to 1924. About a hundred had been amalgamated into the service from the foreign services briefly maintained by the Departments of Agriculture and Commerce. The rest, some five hundred, had entered at the bottom through the front door of competitive examinations.

Since Congress had failed to provide funds for recruitment during the economic depression of the early thirties there was, however, a yawning gap of four years in which no one was taken into the Service.

The absence of these age groups was especially apparent when war came a few years later.

By then Wilbur Carr and his team had retired but their successors had carried on their paternal administration without elaborate personnel procedures or trained administrators. The officers themselves often argued, a little lamely, that they had entered the service to perform the diplomatic and consular functions of government not to be mere administrators, and whenever they could they had passed the administrative chores of the service to the noncareer clerks who, still less adequately paid and less rigorously selected, were untrained for the job.

Against this structure, the gigantic problems of total war diplomacy broke with devastating effect. Significantly, it was not a Foreign Service officer but an outsider temporarily called into the department who first recognized the inadequacies of the system for the tasks before it. Lawrence Duggan, a Latin-American expert, quickly realized that the embassies' staffs would never be able to cope with the problems of ferreting out Axis agents, preventing trade with Axis countries, assuring the availability of South America's raw materials for the United States war industries, and a thousand other jobs that the war effort demanded.

Since the Foreign Service officials were adamantly opposed to taking into their ranks outsiders who had not gone through the competitive procedure, Duggan proposed the recruitment for the "duration" only of an Auxiliary Foreign Service who would not be required to meet the stiff educational, age, and other standards which guarded the front door of the regular service.

Soon the Auxiliary Service equaled in size the regular Foreign Service. At first its members were often regarded with suspicion and not a little contempt by the regulars. But, staggering under their wartime burdens, the regulars were in no position to reject the help of the newcomers, who eventually found themselves welcomed by the overworked embassy staffs.

But even the Auxiliary Service was an inadequate remedy. As the wartime agencies in Washington expanded and demanded more and more services, the embassies were swamped. The agencies first complained bitterly of the poor service they were getting and eventually sent their own representatives abroad to handle their requirements.

These newcomers were even less warmly welcomed than the auxiliaries. Most of them were untrained in diplomatic procedures and many showed little comprehension of foreign mentalities or the way in which servants of different governments do business with each other.

Bypassing the embassies, they swarmed into foreign government offices and tried to do business with them as they would with American firms or government departments at home. The result was often not only confusion but open resentment on the part of the foreigners, whose ruffled feathers the regular American diplomats then had to smooth back into place.

On their part, the representatives abroad of the wartime agencies often considered their colleagues in the Foreign Service timid, stuffy, and downright incompetent. Doubtless some Foreign Service officers were all three of these things when faced with urgent wartime needs which they had never before in their careers encountered. Long trained to pursue a passive diplomacy of noninvolvement, some were unable to adapt themselves to the need for deals, agreements, and commitments deeply involving American interests which the total war required and which the newcomers of the wartime agencies were demanding.

On the other hand, the majority of career officers quickly recognized the need for the new policy of involvement in international affairs but insisted that it be pursued by the established procedures of international diplomacy. They therefore objected strenuously to the hasty improvisations and imprecisions of the deals the wartime agencies and their representatives were making behind their backs.

Early in the war a Lend-Lease Mission arrived in Moscow to negotiate an agreement on wartime aid to Russia. After several sessions in the Kremlin with Stalin, the Marshal dictated what he understood to be the schedule of deliveries and the conditions for them. This was translated by the Soviet Foreign Office into English and suddenly produced in treaty form at a huge Kremlin banquet, ready for signature by the three Allies.

An American Embassy official attached to the mission as chief interpreter and secretary vigorously objected to signature, pointing out that the English version was not only ungrammatical but frequently inaccurate. For example, one provision called for the delivery of several

272

hundred jeeps several months before the date of the agreement came into force. The Lend-Lease representatives equally vigorously objected to the stuffy formalism of the diplomat and insisted on going ahead. "The escape clause releasing the United States from obligations in case of unforeseen obstacles," they explained, "will take care of the inaccuracies. Besides, our primary purpose is to win Stalin's confidence. If we begin by nit-picking his document it will only arouse his suspicions."

The diplomat stood his ground, pointing out that the embassy and not the Lend-Lease Mission would be held responsible by the Soviets for carrying out the agreement. If even before the treaty was signed we did not intend to fulfill some of its provisions, the Soviets could easily impugn American good faith.

In the end the diplomat won the argument. Signature of the treaty was postponed till the next day, and all night he worked with a staff of experts and translators until a new, more precise version was ready for signing.

Such disputes were not confined to Moscow; they arose in every embassy around the globe and often wound up on President Roosevelt's desk for adjudication. Not a great admirer of the Foreign Service, Roosevelt frequently sided with the wartime agencies. But occasionally Cordell Hull, whom he not only liked but respected, insisted on the maintenance of the prerogatives of the State Department and Roosevelt gave in.

The end of the war brought no relief for the Foreign Service. On the contrary, its problems were greatly increased. Many of the tasks that had arisen during the war remained alive while the agencies that had performed them were disbanded. The OWI, OSS, Lend-Lease, and half a dozen other wartime boards and commissions left a large legacy of work: propaganda, information, and financial settlements. Furthermore, the agencies left huge staffs to be taken care of. With the war's end many of these returned to their old professions but many others, sometimes not the most competent, had found their wartime experience in government to their liking and decided to stay on. Where were they to be put? How were they to be integrated into the regular government establishment? What was to happen to the Auxiliary Foreign Service?

Unfortunately, the State Department had still acquired no adequate

administrative machinery for planning and supervising the recruitment and training of the staffs to perform the jobs it had inherited from the wartime agencies, let alone the jobs performed by the Auxiliary Foreign Service.

The members of the service, still strongly defending the principles on which the career had been founded—entrance at the bottom by competitive examination and promotion only on merit—insisted that these principles be applied to expand the service to the size necessary to handle its problems. But it was too obvious that such procedures would not provide the necessary trained manpower for at least a decade. Furthermore, congressional appropriation committees acting in the name of economy regularly cut the Foreign Service's budget requests to enlist new officers, with disastrous results to the recruiting program.

As the urgency grew, Congress finally reconsidered its attitude and authorized the immediate enrollment in the upper grades of 250 new Foreign Service officers from the Army and the Auxiliary Service. But the Foreign Service was so jealous of its career principles that, even though its need for more hands was desperate, only 165 of the 250 authorized were recruited.

Eventually the patience not only of Congress but of the political heads of the State Department itself was exhausted and a group of so-called professional administrators was brought in to put the necessary reforms into effect.

When the old career officers looked at these new administrators they did not at first realize what they were up against. Measured against the austere paternalists like Wilbur Carr the newcomers seemed like bumptious young interlopers—certainly not to be taken seriously. "They seem to forget," one Foreign Service officer said loud enough to be heard by the new men, "that they are essentially valets. Instead of pressing our pants they are trying to wear them." Tactless though the remark may have been, it was not unjustified. The newcomers, many of them graduates of schools of government administration, were unfamiliar with the objectives, problems, and methods of diplomacy. Yet, instead of confining their efforts to administrative problems, they rashly injected themselves into the substantive work of diplomacy. Furthermore, they established their own criteria for selecting, promoting, and transferring Foreign Service personnel, employing princi-

ples that might apply to domestic organizations but hardly to a diplomatic service.

The new administrators, unlike the old Foreign Service officers, made no pretense of shyness or aloofness in their relations with Congress, with whom they cultivated powerful friendships. By parroting old prejudices about cooky pushers and striped pants they found many allies on the Hill in their struggle against the "clique" of career officers. Exploiting the public dismay aroused by the discovery that several wartime employees of the State Department had apparently been Soviet agents, they made the most of their administrative security powers to harry and eventually rout the career officials from all authority over their own service.

Ruthless persecutions often resulted in needless resignations or dismissals and occasionally even in suicides; in addition, the recruitment of new officers was again interrupted. As in 1933 and in the war years, this failure to provide new young officers was a final fatal blow to the service established by the Rogers Act.

In the end the brave little mendicant band suddenly found itself wandering leaderless and aimless through the postwar Washington maze. Defeated, angry and sullen, some career officials resigned and the rest withdrew into their shells. Eventually the crude, roughshod methods of McCarthy and the "valets" aroused the resentment of the press and the public, and little by little their powers were curbed.

But the main problem of how to expand the service and how to recruit the additional staff remained unsolved. Thereupon a series of outside commissions made surveys and drew up plans for a new expanded Foreign Service. These surveyors and planners consisted largely of leading politicians, industrialists, bankers and educators, and even young college graduates. But they all had one thing in common. With the exception of Herbert Hoover, none had any knowledge of or experience with professional diplomacy.

Plan after plan was approved and ordered into effect. New charts were made. Officers were shifted from box to box and desk to desk. New classifications were established and Foreign Service officers found themselves one day Class III, the next Class IV, and the following day Class II. But still the basic problem of expansion was postponed until in 1954 the problem was put into the hands of the secretary of state's Committee on Personnel, generally known as the Wriston Committee

from its guiding spirit Dr. Henry M. Wriston, then president of Brown University.

The committee included a retired professional ambassador and one former Foreign Service officer, but Dr. Wriston, its energetic chairman, dominated its proceedings and drafted its final report. By this time there was strong public pressure to abolish the troublesome Foreign Service altogether and amalgamate it with the Civil Service. The efforts of the professionals were, therefore, directed not so much at planning a better Foreign Service as at salvaging whatever they could of the professional corps of diplomats.

Within three months the committee made its report and this time Secretary of State Dulles ordered the service to implement it without further delay or procrastination. The report pointed out that public confidence in the Foreign Service had been shaken. This was a classic understatement. Doubtless the reports of Red infiltration into the State Department had increased misgivings about the American diplomatic effort but, as we have already observed, the public had never really understood the functions of the Foreign Service and had regarded it with indifference bordering on contempt.

With respect to the problem of expansion, the Wriston Committee recommended a crash program to amalgamate into the service all jobs in the State Department "where their official functions coverage"— that is, practically all political, economic, consular, and administrative positions that handled jobs similar to those in embassies abroad. In addition the senior clerical staff was to be merged with the officer staff. Within two years, the report advocated, the service should be increased from twelve hundred to four thousand by this means.

Furthermore, to compensate for the repeated interruptions in recruiting it recommended that each year five hundred new officers be brought into the service at the bottom. To facilitate this increase, Dr. Wriston suggested simplifying and liberalizing the examination procedure, that is, making it easier, and modifying the previous emphasis on language qualifications. To offset this liberalization, the committee recommended that the Foreign Service Institute—the successor to the old Foreign Service School—be strengthened and that facilities for "in-service training" be augmented. Broader recruiting methods, including nationwide competitive scholarships, were likewise urged to "assure a more faithful mirroring of American life."

Finally, the report recommended that the Foreign Service follow the example of American industrial organizations in encouraging specialization among its members and recruiting specialists in various fields who would concentrate on specific problems or specific areas of diplomacy, such as economic or Far Eastern affairs, from the start of their careers. Later they would broaden their activities to become "generalists" in the diplomatic field.

Under the direction of a distinguished New York stockbroker, Charles Saltzman, the program was put into effect. Some years earlier Saltzman had sought my advice about whether he should enlist in the Foreign Service and had been advised not to do so on the ground that he had no diplomatic experience or background. Now he was placed in the position of reforming this very service.

Though Saltzman was a man of great integrity, good will and ability, the Wriston recommendations failed to restore the collapsed service morale or to achieve the essential reforms contemplated. Not only veteran diplomats but even junior officers continued to resign and applications for entry fell to a minimum.

Under the crash program about fourteen hundred State Department officials were transferred from the Civil Service rolls to the Foreign Service. This aspect of the Wriston reforms brought considerable hardship to many old civil servants whose previous terms of employment had not, as had that of members of the Foreign Service, included service at any overseas post at the will of the department. Firmly settled in their Washington homes, where they had lived all their lives, they were suddenly uprooted and ordered abroad. Some resigned. Some wangled transfers to other departments. Others reluctantly packed up, went overseas, and did their best to adapt themselves to the voluntary exile of the diplomatic service—some successfully.

A number of these department officials were specialists in various fields on whom the department had relied heavily in its dealings with technical government agencies which had interests abroad. At few embassies was their special knowledge put to the fullest use and the Foreign Service officers sent home to replace them seldom had the technical qualifications to fill their jobs.

Eventually an experienced Foreign Service officer, Loy W. Henderson, was appointed administrative chief, thus at last handing back to the Foreign Service responsibility for its own affairs. Henderson was

still on the job as this was written five years later. Under his direction many of the professional administrators and amateurs who had moved into the department after the war were eliminated and the key administrative posts of the service were returned to career officers with diplomatic experience.

Under Henderson, despite the sacrifice of the specialists, at least the problem of essential expansion was solved. However, the annual recruiting of five hundred junior officers was never even approached, seldom averaging more than a quarter of that figure despite a considerable relaxation of standards and a simplified examination system which used modern testing devices instead of the old-fashioned written exams.

The earlier examinations had included lengthy comprehensive tests of the candidates' knowledge of history, economics, mathematics, English, and law. They had taken several days to administer and sometimes months to evaluate. Though they had provided a thorough measure of the candidates' basic knowledge and education, they had been, in the opinion of Dr. Wriston, a university president, too cumbersome and "expensive."

The new tests recommended by Dr. Wriston and devised by the Princeton Testing Service consist of multiple-choice questions whereby the candidate is required to write no more than his own name. The rest of the examination is spent in putting X's in squares. Candidates who have passed it successfully complain that it fails to test their hardly acquired knowledge in the subjects that qualified authorities have for centuries prescribed for aspiring diplomats. An inarticulate engineer, they complain, stands as good a chance of passing as a man who has spent years training himself not only in the basic disciplines but in the art of self-expression—a fundamental requirement of diplomacy.

Older diplomats confronted with the new recruits have complained that they frequently lack the basic education which a polished professional requires. (One is reminded of the complaints of leading scientists of the lack of qualifications of science students in American universities today.)

However, as Dr. Wriston points out, the new form of testing has the advantage of quick and cheap administration. By means of machines, the new examination papers can be processed in a matter of

minutes while the older examinations took trained academicians days to grade.

Despite the badly needed administrative improvement achieved by the Wriston reform, professional diplomats still entertain grave doubts that the concepts on which the new type of foreign service is based are entirely sound. They are even skeptical that the new service can win the confidence of either Congress or the public, which, as Dr. Wriston correctly pointed out, is essential to a strong diplomatic service.

Both in its composition and in its recommendations the Wriston Committee provided evidence of a less than complete comprehension of the true role of diplomacy. Like almost all other commissions, teams and survey groups named to reorganize the Foreign Service, the majority of its members were recruited from circles having little or nothing in common with the diplomatic profession. One suspects that the senior political officials appointing these groups themselves regard diplomacy not as a profession but as an occupation, qualification for which requires no special knowledge, training, or experience.

There is further evidence that the drafters of the Wriston Report spent more time studying the precedents provided by industrial organizations, banks, and universities than those provided by diplomacy itself over the past two thousand years.

"The Foreign Service Officer Corps" says one passage of the report, "has developed on the nineteenth century [*sic!*] theory or philosophy that diplomacy is fundamentally a field for 'generalists,' political specialists with a generalized knowledge about practically everything likely to have any connection with the conduct of foreign affairs. . . . The hard fact is," the report avers, "that in diplomacy as in other areas of collective endeavor, the 'generalist' theory has been out-moded by events." The development of "generalists" for top management posts it continues, "has been all but abandoned by large scale private enterprise—first by business, not much later by banks and finally by universities. . . . Prevailing management practice today emphasizes the development of an individual around his specialty, with the generalism coming later as he approaches full maturity."

Quite aside from the doubts often expressed that a chemistry professor makes the best college president, the notion that the problems of diplomacy are comparable to those of large-scale private enterprise

business, banks, or universities seems to be based on unfamiliarity with what diplomacy is all about. The most superficial study of the profession would reveal that the so-called "nineteenth century theory or philosophy" is at least a thousand years old. Though the past twenty years have seen profound advances in technology, communications, and international intercourse, it does not necessarily follow that these events have suddenly outmoded practices that have existed for nine centuries during which progress was comparable at least in extent if not in speed to that of the past twenty years.

The manner in which the Foreign Service Institute and the facilities for "in-service training" have been expanded provide further evidence that the basic principles of diplomacy are not yet wholly understood. At the Wriston Committee's recommendation the director of the Institute in which candidates are to be taught diplomacy is a distinguished educator—not an experienced diplomat. His permanent teaching staff includes not one professional career officer. As a student of the institute once described it to me, the faculty regards professional diplomats as underprivileged adults whose only salvation lies in at least a modicum of progressive education.

Because of the inadequacy of language studies in American colleges and universities, the language training conducted by the institute is a valuable contribution to American diplomacy. It is open to question, however, whether languages are not more quickly learned by study not in a Washington institution but in a school or college in the country where the language is spoken and where the student, living in a native family, is constantly subjected to hearing and speaking it.

However, the institute's initial orientation course is regarded by many of its students as a thorough waste of time and the so-called advanced courses as even less useful.

Senior diplomats in the Foreign Service today doubt the contribution to a diplomat's training of the courses that form the bulk of the institute's activity, including such subjects as "reading rate improvement" and "conference leadership"—described in the institute's catalogue as "effective arrangement and management of conferences, planning agendas, incentives to participation, crystallizing and recording results."

The mirth which such courses provoke among professional diplomats gives way to resentment when the institute expends some of its

$5 million budget to improve senior American diplomats with courses in social psychology, cultural anthropology, and conceptual methods of analysis. Since the days of Callières, they believe, the professional diplomat has been trained by a thorough grounding in the basic disciplines of history, economics, and languages followed by active experience. They fear that the educationalists' efforts to produce better diplomats will be as costly and unsuccessful as the "life adjustment" courses designed to produce better high school students.

However, professional diplomats welcome the practice of sending younger diplomats to outstanding universities to study the languages and politico-economic conditions of a critical area—provided no better way of obtaining the experience and knowledge is available in the area itself and provided it is not regarded as the only way to acquire the label of "specialist" or "expert."

In the late fifties, working with me in the U. S. political Liaison Office in Bonn, was a young Foreign Service officer who was in daily if not hourly contact with leading officials, members of Parliament, editors, and commentators. In fluent German he discussed with them every political or economic facet of the critical German problem.

One day he came to me and asked to be nominated for a course on Germany being given at Harvard University to which young diplomats were then being sent. Asked how he imagined that any such course could compare with the opportunity he had to study the problem at first hand he answered that he did not believe it would but, since he wanted to specialize on German affairs, it would be necessary for his record to study the German problem on the banks of the River Charles rather than on the Rhine. His application was approved by the State Department and he left Bonn to spend a year in Cambridge.

One final misconception about the diplomat's job shared by Congressmen and the public is that the chief function of an American diplomat is to be a model of the average American. As Congressman Leo W. O'Brien picturesquely put it, there should be a "massive transfusion of Main Street into the arteries of the foreign service."

The Wriston report reflects the same view. The Foreign Service Corps must become "more broadly representative of American life," and to this end it recommends a recruiting system to "draw upon young Americans from all states and from all walks of life" by setting up quotas for each state in accordance with its population. To achieve

this aim is one of the reasons given for lowering the entrance requirements of the service, which heretofore had aimed at recruiting not the representative average but the best.

Though representation is an important function of diplomacy, it is only one of many and certainly not the most important. Its purpose, as Benjamin Franklin discovered, is not to depict the average American or provide a parade of regional American types, the result of which inevitably would be that the embassy in New Delhi would draw, say, the typical cowboy, Tokyo the typical Southerner, and Rio the typical Yankee. The real purpose is to represent the best available, be he from Seattle or Fort Lauderdale, from Main Street or the Main Line.

While it is most desirable that the American diplomat act like an American and not like a "European expatriate," to use Franklin Roosevelt's phrase, it is equally important that he be qualified in other respects to observe, to negotiate, and to protect American interests. For one thing we can be sure of, when he is pitted against a Soviet diplomat across the green baize, Moscow will have selected as his adversary not the best worker or best peasant in Omsk or Tomsk but the roughest, toughest, shrewdest, and ablest Mr. Tsarapkin from whatever oblast or walk of life he comes.

In recent decades sociologists have noted with misgiving a growing prejudice in the United States against elites and a preference for the conforming average. Fortunately this has not always been the case. The drafters of the Constitution certainly had an elite in mind when they created the United States Senate. The Corps of Cadets at West Point, the Midshipmen at Annapolis, and the Marine Corps have always regarded themselves as elites. In World War II the Commandos with their careful selection, special training, and special equipment were publicly acclaimed as an elite.

When the Soviet Sputnik started its travels, American scientists suddenly emerged from their ill-paid and ill-regarded obscurity and were hailed as an elite. To cope successfully with the critical problems of the cold war the United States requires no less of an elite in its Foreign Service. This in turn requires a basic comprehension of the diplomatic profession and a readiness to accord its practitioners the same recognition accorded the soldier, the scientist, or the surgeon.

NOTES AND ACKNOWLEDGMENTS

Chapters I–III. The activities of the American Embassy in Beirut are derived largely from personal observations on the spot during the last month of the crisis. I am, however, greatly indebted to the staff of the embassy, particularly the ambassador, the counselor and the members of the "Command Post," for the background information they furnished me on events during the earlier phases and for the opportunity to accompany some of the patrols into the hinterland.

Chapter IV. For the history of Western diplomacy I am largely indebted to Sir Harold Nicolson's *The Evolution of the Diplomatic Method* (New York: Macmillan, 1954), *Diplomacy* (New York: Harcourt, 1939), and *Peacemaking* (New York: Houghton Mifflin, 1933). I have also made use of Sir Ernest Satow's *Guide to Diplomatic Practice* (New York: Longmans, 1957) and to Graham H. Stuart's *American Diplomatic and Consular Practice* (New York: Appleton, 1952).

Chapter V. The account of Luitprand's mission is taken from the German translation of the Latin original, in the Munich State Library. The observations of Emir Abdur Rahman are quoted from *The Life of Abdur Rahman, Amir of Afghanistan* (London, 1910). E. V. Tarle's observations on "bourgeois" diplomacy are quoted from *Istoriya Diplomatiya*, edited by V. P. Potemkin (Moscow-Leningrad, 1945). Descriptions of Byzantine diplomatic practice are taken from *Byzantine Civilisation*, by Steven Runciman (London: Longmans, 1933).

Chapter VI. For the early history of American diplomacy I have made use of *The State Department of the United States*, published by the U.S. Government Printing Office in 1898. On the Versailles negotiations I am especially indebted to Nicolson's *Peacemaking 1919*. I have also used George F. Kennan's *American Diplomacy 1900–1950* (Chicago University Press, 1951) for material on American diplomatic methods in the past two generations. On the Constitutional problem of the supervision of foreign affairs I have used Robert A. Dahl's *Congress and Foreign Policy* (New York: Harcourt Brace, 1950) and *American Foreign Policy and*

NOTES AND ACKNOWLEDGMENTS

the Separation of Powers by Daniel S. Cheever and H. Field Haviland, Jr. (Harvard University Press, 1952).

Chapter VII. My principal source for the historic methods of diplomacy is François de Callières's *On the Manner of Negotiating with Princes,* translated by A. F. Whyte (New York: Houghton Mifflin, 1919). I have also referred to Cordell Hull's *Memoirs* (New York: Macmillan, 1950) and to Nicolson's and Kennan's works cited above.

Chapter VIII. In addition to Callières, materials on the mechanics of negotiation are taken largely from Satow and Stuart, cited above.

Chapter IX. Much material on conference diplomacy is taken from Nicolson's works cited above, especially *Peacemaking 1919* and *Diplomacy.* My quotations from Ambassador Henry Cabot Lodge are taken from the *Hearings before the Subcommittee of the Committee on Appropriations United States Senate, Eighty-fifth Congress, First Session.*

Chapter X. The quotation from Hugh Gibson is taken from *Hugh Gibson 1883–1954* (New York: Belgian American Educational Foundation, Inc., 1956).

Chapter XI. Stuart's *American Diplomatic and Consular Practice* has been used in describing some of the functions of a consul.

Chapter XII. The story of Herbert O. Yardley has been taken from Yardley's *The American Black Chamber* (Indianapolis: Bobbs-Merrill Co., 1931). I have also used *On Active Service in Peace and War* by Henry L. Stimson and McGeorge Bundy (New York: Harper, 1947).

Chapter XIII. I am grateful to *The Leatherneck, Magazine of the Marines,* for material on training marines for embassy duty. Also used was *The American Ambassador* (Dept. of State Publication, Washington: U.S. Government Printing Office, 1957).

Chapters XIV–XV. For materials on the origin of the OSS and the CIA, I am indebted to Sherman Kent's *Strategic Intelligence* (Princeton University Press, 1949). For the description of national estimates and national intelligence surveys I have made use of Harry Howe Ransome's *Central Intelligence and National Security* (Harvard University Press, 1958). I have also quoted from *Memoirs* by Harry Truman (New York: Doubleday, 1955–56).

NOTES AND ACKNOWLEDGMENTS

Chapters XVI–XVII. The quotations from George V. Allen are taken from a speech before the Zonta International Convention, June 26, 1958, and from *Propaganda in a Goldfish Bowl,* also by Mr. Allen.

Chapters XVIII–XIX. My principal sources on diplomatic privileges and immunities are the works of Satow and Stuart cited above. The book *The Truth about American Diplomats,* by Annabella Bukar, was published as *Pravda ob Amerikanskikh Diplomatakh* (Moscow: Literaturnoi Gazety, 1949).

Chapter XX. In addition to the standard works by Callières, Nicolson, Satow and Stuart cited above I am indebted to Richard B. McCornack's "The Diplomatic Costume Revolution" published in the *Foreign Service Journal,* May, 1958.

Chapters XXI–XXII. In addition to the works already cited, Jules Cambon's *The Diplomatist* and Jusserand's *School of Ambassadors* (New York: Putnam, 1925) contain much valuable information on the selection and training of diplomats. The quotation from Mrs. Clare Booth Luce is taken from "The Ambassadorial Issue: Professionals or Amateurs?" published in *Foreign Affairs,* October, 1957.

Chapter XXIII. Material on the early history of the State Department is taken from *The Department of State of the United States* (Washington: U.S. Government Printing Office, 1898). On recent reforms of the Foreign Service I have made use of material in *Toward a Stronger Foreign Service* (the so-called "Wriston Report") (Washington: Department of State Publication No. 5458, 1954); *The Quarterly Projection of Courses of the Foreign Service Institute* of the Department of State; *The Reorganization of the American Foreign Service* by Charles E. Saltzman (Department of State Bulletin, September 27, 1954); and *The State Department and the Foreign Service,* by Zara S. Steiner (Center of International Studies, Princeton University, 1958).

For most of the anecdotes and examples in this book I am indebted to my former colleagues in the Foreign Service and the Department of State.

Finally, I am most grateful for the suggestions and corrections made by a number of ambassadors and members of the Foreign Service to whom I submitted the original manuscript but who, at their own request, shall remain nameless.

C. W. T.

Index

A, B and C codes, U.S., 145
Abdur Rahman, 57–58
Abyssinia, 61
Adams, John Quincy, 64, 154
Adenauer, Konrad, 180–181, 257
administrative section, embassy, 158–159
advertising experts, 194–196, 198–199
Afghan Army, 169
Afghanistan, 158, 168–169, 215; King of, 228; Russian diplomacy in, 57
aggressors, Tarle's description of, 61–62
Aide-Mémoire, 99
Air Force, U.S., 197
airplane, effect of on diplomatic life, 47
Alaska, purchase of, 68
Aldrich, Winthrop, 227
"alert status," 7, 9
Allen, George Venable, 195, 199
allies, choosing of, 46
Alternat, signature procedure, 104
ambassador, acceptability of, to receiving government, 260–261; assassinations of, 202; businessman as, 253; calls by, 228–229; churchmen as, 251–252, 254; dealings with opposition forces, 13; dismissal of, 216–217; distinguished from consul, 130; first rule for (Callières), 87; form of address for, 122–123, 212; gossip and spying required of, 45; Hull's four requirements of, 81; involuntary "retiring" of, 260; lawlessness in, 216; nonprofessional, 26; personal assistant to, 124; political party favorites as, 255; press relations and, 192; qualifications for, 240–249; rank of in protocol, 32, 226–227; recall of, 215–216; recruiting of, 250–257; "single-chief and single-policy" of, 46–47; "specialists" among, 266; staff duties of, 125–126; training of, 248–249;

use of "secret" classification by, 175–176; women as, 227; *see also* diplomat; diplomatic immunity
"ambassador extraordinary," 122
"ambassador plenipotentiary," 122
American Black Chamber, The, 144
American children, problem of, overseas, 27
American citizens, evacuation of, 10
American Diplomacy, 68
American diplomacy, congressional elections and, 80; delays and waste time in, 79; four tasks of (Hull), 81; history of, 64–80, 263–265; "elite" corps in, 282; impatience in, 96; "Main Street" in, 281; passive role of, following World War II, 75–76
American diplomat, chief function of, 281; *see also* diplomat
American Diplomatic and Consular Practice, 232
American Embassies: Beirut, 21–22; London, 115; Madrid, 222; Paris, 222; Rome, 222; Moscow, 94, 207
American Foreign Service, 166, 220, 223, 264–282; American way of life and, 281; Auxiliary Service and, 271–272; Congressional investigation of, 264; "elite corps" in, 282
American loans, 76
American nationals, round-up of, in Lebanon, 22–23
American popularity, 183
American Red Cross, 85
American Revolution, 184, 238, 264
American tourists, demand for "entertainment" from, 221–222
American types, regional, 282
Anglo-Russian Convention of 1907, 57
Ankara, Turkey, 246
Antheil, Henry, 156
anti-Americanism, in Lebanon revolt, 11–12

287

INDEX

Foreign Service Institute, 276, 280

Foreign Service Journal, 87, 149

Foreign Service Officers Corps, 279

Foreign Service Regulations, 72

Foreign Service School, 269

Fourth of July, celebration of, abroad, 233–234

Fowler's Modern English Usage, 128

France, long association with Middle East, 14

Francis I, France, 247

Franco-German War, 149

Franklin, Benjamin, 64, 164, 195, 236–237, 282

Franks, Sir Oliver, 262

Frederick the Great, 61, 247

French diplomacy, 83

French language, in diplomacy, 102

French Revolution, 61, 184

frugality, dangers of, 232–233

Fulbright Program, 192

G-2, 166–167

Gallatin, Albert, 205

Gamarra, Don Estevan de, 163, 166

gambling, 246

Garfield, James R., 204

garrulousness, 246

"generalists," development of, 279

generals, as ambassadors, 250

Gênet, Citizen, 219

Geneva Conference, 1958, 106

German code, breaking of, 142

German diplomacy, 83

German Finance Office, 92

German Foreign Office, 206

German-Japanese alliance, 153

"German Treaty," 252

Germany, attack on Soviet Union by, 94, 203; occupation of, 75

Gibson, Hugh, 113, 202

gifts, protocol in, 230

goat-getting, Molotov's technique in, 95–96; U.S. success in, 97–98

Goebbels, Paul, 134, 185

Gold Bug, The, 140

grammar, in diplomatic cables and reports, 127–128

Gray Code, U.S., 150

Great Britain, as ally of Afghanistan, 58; career service appointments in, 262; paramount position in Middle East, 14; *see also* British (*adj.*)

Greek city states, failure of, 80

Greek civil war, 78–79

Greek diplomacy, 38–40

Grotius, Hugo, 45–46, 50, 226

Gruenther, Gen. Alfred M., 100

Guizot, François, 102

Gunther, John, 256

Gusev, Soviet ambassador, 100

Hadd, Lt. Col., 33–35

Haiti, 1937 massacres in, 4

Hamilton, Alexander, 65

Hare, Raymond, 266

Harjes et Cie, 166

Harriman, Averell, 188–189

Harriman, Kathleen, 189

Harris, Sir James, 183, 247

Harrison, William Henry, 265

Harvard University, 281

Hatzfeldt, Count von, 231

Hawthorne, Nathaniel, 131

H-bomb, 38

Helen of Troy, 38

Hemingway, Ernest, 197

Henderson, Loy W., 128, 243, 277–278

Herodotus, 130

Herwarth, "Jonny" von, 84

Hickenlooper, Bourke, 264

Hillstein, Secretary, 252

History of Diplomacy (U.S.S.R.), 60

Hitler, Adolf, 42, 61–62, 120, 166, 170–171, 178, 185, 211, 217, 232–233, 244, 257

Holloway, Adm. James, 34–35

Holy Roman Empire, 43, 46

Homer, 38, 87

honesty, as "best policy," 47–48

honor, honesty and, 240–241

Hoover, Herbert, 275

Hoover, J. Edgar, 58, 198

Hopkins, Harry, 88

horsetrading, 253

House, Col. Edward M., 69, 140

Hughes, Charles Evans, 262

Hull, Cordell, 73, 81, 273

Humanité, L', 186

Hungarian revolt of 1953, 50, 199, 208

hunting, as diplomatic sport, 235–236

INDEX

identic notes, 99
Ignatiev, S. D., 179
immigration law, 136–137
immunity, diplomatic, *see* diplomatic immunity
impatience, danger of, 96
indiscretion, 243
infiltration, Syrian, in Lebanon revolt, 11, 24
information, methods of extracting, 177
informers, 18th-century, 164
in-service training facilities, 280
intellectual dishonesty, 241–244
intelligence, diplomatic, 173–182; strategic, 161–172
intelligence agent, diplomat's relations with, 176
intelligence "experts," 181–182
intelligence survey, national, 174
internal affairs, chancellery and, 124
internal conflicts, exploiting of, 62
international conferences, after World War II, 106
International Co-operation Administration, 159
international diplomacy, Communist history and, 62; *see also* diplomacy; Soviet diplomacy
international law, diplomatic rights and, 93; father of, 46; lawyers vs. ambassadors in, 251
international love, 183
international propaganda, U.S. efforts in, 187–189; *see also* propaganda
international trade, diplomacy and, 47
interpreters, need for, 102–103
Iraq, 8; Soviet Union ties with, 62
Iron Curtain diplomacy, 245; *see also* Soviet diplomacy
Irwin, Frank, 158
isolationism, U.S., 66; end of, 73; following Versailles, 71
Italian codes, "sale" of, 146
Italian diplomacy, 43–44, 83
Italian Embassy, Washington, 206
Italy-Yugoslavia postwar claims, 96
Ivy League monopoly, 266, 268
Izvestia, 179

Kabul, Afghanistan, 158, 168–169, 185, 231, 242

Kadar, Janos, 208
Karami, rebel leader, 19
Keblinger, Wilbur, 90–94
Kelley, Robert F., 87
Kennan, George F., 68, 82, 233, 266; dismissal of, by Soviet Union, 218
Kennedy Memorial Hospital, 6
Kherson, Crimea, 50
Khrushchev, Nikita, 62, 82, 179, 182, 236; offensive letter to Eisenhower, 100
Kirk, Alexander, 233, 267
Knatchbull-Hugessen, Sir, 246
Koniev, Marshal Ivan S., 103–104
Koran, 251–252
Korean independence, 97
Korean War, 50
Kremlinology, 178–179
Krivitsky, W. G., 59

languages, knowledge of, 249
language studies, inadequacy of, in U.S., 280
Latvia, 211
Lawrence, T. E., 14
laws, observance of, by diplomat, 214
lawyer, as ambassador, 251
League of Nations, 46, 110; rejection of, by U.S. Senate, 69
Lebanese Army, 16; "precarious" mental state of, 33; retiring of, in Marine landings, 35
Lebanon, British occupation of, 14; "Christian counterrevolution" in, 37; independence of, 14; "massive infiltration" from Syria charged, 24; number of Americans in, 22; political factions in, 3; revolt in, 11–33; *see also* Beirut
legal career, advantages of, in diplomatic service, 251
legation, defined, 122
Lend-Lease Mission to Moscow, 272–273
Lenin, Nicolai, 60–62
Leopold III, Belgium, 4
letters, diplomatic, 99
liquor, importing of, 210
Litvinov, Maxim, 55, 73, 87–88, 184, 209, 211

INDEX

Liudprand, Italian historian, 50–56, 85, 201, 265
lobbying, vs. diplomacy, in United Nations, 112
"localitis," 242
Lodge, Henry Cabot, 112
London, American Embassy in, 82, 115
London Economic Conference, 73, 155
London Foreign Ministers Council, 96
London *Times*, 218
Louis II, Frankish king, 50
Louis XI, France, 43
Louis XIV, 62, 70
Louis XVI, 164
Lovell, James, 264
Luce, Clare Boothe, 218, 227, 248, 263
Luce, Henry, 227
Luxembourg, 255
lying, 242–243

MacArthur, Gen. Douglas, 87
McCarthy, Joseph R., 275
Machiavelli, Niccolò, 43, 45, 58, 62, 66, 73
Machiavellianism, myth of, 69, 71
MacLean, Mrs. Ned, 120
Maclean, Sir Fitzroy, 84
Madrid, American Embassy in, 119, 222
Mahomet III, Turkey, 56
Main Street, essence of, in American Foreign Service, 281–282
Malay Peninsula, 68
Malenkov, Georgi, 179
Malik, Dr. Charles, 8, 24
Malmesbury, Lord William of, 243, 245–247
Manchester Guardian, 11
Mao Tse-tung, 172
Marcy, William Learned, 237
Marine Corps, U.S., 27, 30, 282; as couriers in World War I, 154; diplomatic standards for, 121; as embassy guards, 119–120, 148; "invading army" aspect altered, 34; landing of, in Beirut, 29; number of, in diplomatic posts, 121
marriages, witnessing of, 132
Marriner, Theodore, 267; assassination of, 74
Marshall, Gen. George C., 87, 96, 178
Marx, Karl, 184, 195

Matson Lines, 166
Mazarin, Jules Cardinal, 95
medals and decorations, 230
Medieval Europe, diplomacy in, 43, 50
memoir, 99
Menshikov, Aleksandr D., 86
men's minds, battle for, 183–200; *see also* propaganda
Methodius, 49
methods and mechanics, of diplomacy, 81–112
Metropolitan Club, Washington, D.C., 267
Metternich, Clemens Lothar von, 98, 112
Mexico, oil disputes in, 101
Michael, king of Rumania, 62
microphones, in totalitarian diplomacy, 147
Middle Ages, diplomacy in, 43, 50
Middle East, British and French hegemony in, 14
Migone, Bartolomeo, 84
Mikoyan, Anastas, 86
military advisors, domination of foreign policy by, 75
military attachés, 166, 228; *see also* attachés
military career, diplomacy and, 250
military-diplomatic relations, 32
military intelligence, 166–167; Central Intelligence Authority and, 173; reform of, after Pearl Harbor, 168
Mindszenty, Joseph Cardinal, 208
minister, defined, 122
mixed relations, 102
Moffat, Jay Pierpont, 267
Molotov, Vyacheslav M., 61, 84–85, 95, 97
money, as diplomatic qualification, 67, 256–257
Montgomery, Field Marshal Sir Bernard Law, 120
Montgomery, John Flournoy, 248
moral integrity, 240
Morgan, John Pierpont, 115, 166
Morocco Crisis, 62
Morocco, Sultan of, 115
Morrow, Dwight, 101
Morse, Wayne, 248
Moscow, American Embassy in, 73, 94,

207; American military attaché in, 167; first American Embassy in Soviet Union, 55; Lend-Lease Mission to, 272–273; night clubs in, 120
Moscow Ballet, 180; intelligence and, 163
Moslems, Beirut, 6, 11; looting and murder by, 27
most-favored-nation treatment, 93
Munich, American Embassy in, 116
murder, "diplomacy" through, 43
Murphy, Robert, 36
Mussolini, Benito, 61, 120, 185, 206

NATO, see North Atlantic Treaty Organization
Naguib, Maj. Gen. Mohammed, 4
Nagy, Imre, 59
Napoleon I, 62, 167
Napoleon III, 61
Nasser, Gamal Abdel, 3–4, 8, 14, 24, 62
National City Bank, 166
national holidays, celebration of, 233–234
national interests, Richelieu's principle of, 46
nationalism, rise of, 47, 193
national prejudices, sacrifice of, 245
national security, 106
National Security Council, 174
National War College, Washington, D.C., 32
Navy Department, U.S., 74
Nazi radio network, 185
Nazis, spying techniques of, 146–148
negotiations, mechanics of, 98–101
nepotism, precaution against, 123
New Diplomacy, 45–46
New York Times, 4, 189, 218, 238, 270
Nicephorus II, Byzantine emperor, 52–56, 85
Nicholas II, Russia, 61
Nicolson, Sir Harold, 38, 46–47, 49, 69, 72, 82, 95, 109, 111, 241, 255
night clubs, closing of, 20; in Moscow, 120
Nixon, Richard M., 81
North Atlantic Treaty Organization, 58, 254; attempted sabotage of, 62

note, diplomatic, 99; rejection of, 100
note verbal, diplomatic, 99
nuclear explosions, detection of, 106
Nuri as-Said, assassination of, 28

OSS, see Office of Strategic Services
OWI, see Office of War Information
O'Brien, Leo W., 281
October Revolution, see Bolshevik Revolution
Odeen, Sgt. Bill, 120
Office of Facts and Figures, 186
Office of Strategic Services, 168–173, 177–178, 273; liquidation of, 176
Office of War Information, 186–187, 194, 273
oil pipelines, 20
Old World diplomacy, 76; American contrast to, 64; see also European diplomacy
On the Manner of Negotiating with Princes, 47
Open Door Policy, China, 68
opium smuggling, 42
opposition, embassy "friendship" with, 13
oral negotiation, 101
Oriental diplomacy, 41–42; see also Byzantine diplomacy; Soviet diplomacy
Ottawa Conference, 75
Otto I, Holy Roman Empire, 51
Otto II, Emperor, 51, 55, 265
Oumansky, Ambassador, 94

Paine, Thomas, 264
Palais Rose Conference, Paris, 107
pamphlet-dropping, British, 187
Panama, 1932 revolution in, 4
"panic button" incident, Beirut, 16–17
papal nuncio, 226
Papen, Franz von, 217
Parallel Notes, 99
Paris, American embassy in, 115, 222; Soviet Embassy, 208
parliamentary diplomacy, 82, 110–112; see also United Nations
parliamentary proceedings, 108
parsimony, 232–233
party favorites, as ambassadors, 255

passports, "handing" of, 216; registration of, 132
patience, diplomat's need for, 95–96
patronage, 256–259
peace, as function of diplomacy, 60
"Peace in the World" slogan, Soviet Union, 61
"peace-loving friendship," 58
Pearl Harbor, attack on, 73, 168, 174, 186
personal assistant, role of, 124
"personal diplomacy," 36; advantages and disadvantages of, 108–110; vs. conference, 105
persona non grata, 218–219; declaration of, 216
"Pertinax," commentator, 186
Petchenegs, nomadic people, 50
Peter the Great, 219
picketing, of embassies, 206–207
Pinkerton, Allan, 165
place cards, saving of, 233
"plenipotentiary," Communist, 239
Poe, Edgar Allan, 140
Poland, delay in aid to, 79
Polish government-in-exile, 59, 62
Polish minister, murder of, 202
political appointments, 256–261; supervision of, 257
political asylum, in embassy, 207–208
political science, beginnings of, 45
political sense and sensitivity, 243–244
political warfare, 169
"politicos," 26
popularity, Americans' passion for, 183
postwar diplomacy, 76
Potsdam Conference, 96
pouch, diplomatic, 99, 126, 154; black market and, 212
pouched report, 126–127
Pravda, 85, 95, 179–180, 190
President, U.S., vs. Congress, 66
press, immunity from attacks in, 202–203
press relations, propaganda and, 192, 196–197
Prince, The, 43
Princeton Testing Service, 278
probationary period, 268–269
propaganda, aggression and, 61; diplomacy and, 183–200; foreign

policy and, 199; limitations of, 200; public relations and, 193–196; "selling" in, 195–196
propaganda films, 193–194
protocol, 224–239; chief of, 227, 235; in conference diplomacy, 108; origins of, 224; *see also* calling cards; banquets
protocol officer, 123
psychological warfare, 186–187
public opinion, diplomacy and, 98; foreign policy and, 46; propaganda and, 192–193
public opinion polls, 258
public relations, 194–196, 198–199; "bored" diplomatic colony and, 235
publicity, shunning of, 267

Quaroni, Pietro, 185
quibbling, 241

Radio Bari, 185
radio broadcasting, totalitarian diplomacy and, 185
Radio Moscow, 187
radiotelephone, diplomatic relations and, 81, 126
radio transmitter vs. bombers, 199; illegal, 152
Raffalovich, Arturo, 186
Raglan, Baron Fitzroy James, 263
railroads, mobilization and, 164
Rakovsky, Christian Georgeyevich, 184
Razin, Stenka, 86
Realpolitik, 70
receptionist, embassy, 121
reciprocity, 93
Repin, Ilya Yefimovich, 56
report, supplanting of dispatch by, 127
reports, courage in making, 163
representation, diplomat's striving for, 183
République, La, 186
retaliation, reciprocity and, 93
rich, diplomats chosen from among, 67, 256–257
Richelieu, Cardinal, 46, 50, 245
"right of chapel," 209
Rogers Act of 1924, 72, 265, 275
Roman diplomacy, 40
Rome, American embassy in, 121, 222

INDEX

INDEX

RUSSIA TODAY:

What Can We Learn from It?

OTHER BOOKS BY SHERWOOD EDDY

INDIA AWAKENING

THE NEW ERA IN ASIA

THE STUDENTS OF ASIA

SUFFERING AND THE WAR

WITH OUR SOLDIERS IN FRANCE

EVERYBODY'S WORLD

FACING THE CRISIS

THE NEW WORLD OF LABOR

NEW CHALLENGES TO FAITH

RELIGION AND SOCIAL JUSTICE

SEX AND YOUTH

THE CHALLENGE OF RUSSIA

THE CHALLENGE OF THE EAST

THE WORLD'S DANGER ZONE

THE CHALLENGE OF EUROPE

RUSSIA TODAY

What Can We Learn from It?

▼

By *George* SHERWOOD EDDY

FARRAR & RINEHART

INCORPORATED

PUBLISHERS   NEW YORK

CONTENTS

PART I

THE WARNING OF RUSSIA'S EVILS

CHAPTER

PART II

POSSIBLE CONTRIBUTIONS TO HUMAN WELFARE

RUSSIA TODAY:

What Can We Learn from It?

FOREWORD

During the past summer I was asked to deliver the sixth in the series of the Merttens' Lectures in England upon the subject chosen by the Committee, *The Russian Experiment: What Can We Learn From It?* It may be somewhat galling for the Anglo-Saxon to admit that he has anything to learn from such a source. Soviet Russia, on the one hand, striving desperately to make good in her self-appointed task, is still in the midst of her great experiment. We, on the other hand, hope that we are nearing the end of the great world depression. That depression, like the World War before it, has revealed seams of weakness in our economic and social order which we are seeking to understand and to correct.

We need not look to Soviet Russia as a model or perfect example in anything. We ourselves are consciously far from perfect. But we may learn from a competitor, or even from an enemy in war time, as we did during the last World War. It would have been absurd for the Allies at the beginning of the World War to say that they had nothing to learn from the Germans, when their ships were being sunk at an alarming rate, and their armies driven back in the trenches by superior artillery. The situation could not be met by mere propaganda against German atrocities. They had to change their methods and to do it in time. This is not to suggest that Soviet Russia is an enemy comparable to Germany in war time, but we should take a view as realistic as the Russians of the class war which they believe is already a reality. We may learn much from another country, whether by way of warning or of suggestion, from its failures as well as from its successes. We surely have much to learn from both in the case of the Soviet Union.

I have just returned from my tenth visit to Russia. As my work leads me to cross Europe each year I shuttle back and forth between these two contrasted systems of individ-

ualism and collectivism, of capitalism and communism. Russia is almost as unlike the rest of the world as the planet Mars must be. Despite its glaring evils and manifest shortcomings it is the most amazing, the most disturbing, yet in some respects the most fascinating country in the world.

In the western world we have been cursed with *unemployment and overproduction*—some thirty millions having been left without work during long periods of the depression, unable to buy the goods which they themselves have produced. In Soviet Russia there is *no unemployment but most serious under-production*. They will not be able for years if not decades to come to overtake the demand for home consumption in this colossal Republic with its population of over 165,000,000, which stretches for almost six thousand miles over nearly one-sixth of the habitable globe. The growing demands of its population for a rising standard of living are increasing even more rapidly than its numerical strength which is adding ten thousand a day to its numbers, or about as many as all the rest of Europe combined. Here is the largest country in the world, with vast undeveloped resources, trying the boldest experiment in history. Here on a huge scale they are trying to build a new world, a new humanity. For the first time in history a whole section of mankind is being suddenly and radically changed in conformity to a new ideal, with the attempt to create a new environment, a new psychology, a new economic, political and social order, reconstructed from its very foundations. Russia is a land of limitless contradictions whose high ideal ends are often defeated or postponed by its ruthless use of means.

My latest visit to Russia confirmed and deepened my conviction regarding the four chief evils of the Soviet system, the last three of which are so serious, so enduring and so of the very essence of Communism itself that they would make it quite impossible for me ever to accept it. These evils are a paralyzing and ineffective bureaucracy, the essential denial of liberty, the danger of violence and compulsion especially in a seemingly interminable "continuing revolution," and finally a

narrow and exclusive dogmatic basis, as illustrated by the dogmatic atheism and anti-religious zeal required of every orthodox
Communist or Party member. These evils are described in
Part I of the present volume. They are, however, more briefly
treated because I have already covered them in my previous
book, *The Challenge of Russia,* and because we have not so
much to learn from these evils as from Soviet Russia's possible
contributions to human welfare which follow in Part II.

At first sight these evils are so serious that one is tempted
to wonder if any good thing can come out of a system which
contains such essential defects. But wider experience suggests
that all social systems and all countries are mixtures of good
and evil. If one were to judge conditions in America from
the Russian press reports he would conclude that there could
be no good in a land of lynching, of gangsters, of slums and
of unemployment, which offers to its unfortunate masses so
little security of life. As a matter of fact, however, the Soviet
Union knows that it, too, has much to learn and it is calling
in American and European experts by hundreds and even thousands to acquire all that it can find adaptable from the competing system of capitalism. We should have the advantage
of Anglo-Saxon tolerance, of our traditional liberalism, and
of our spirit of self-criticism to make us willing to learn from
a competitor and even from a country that may count us
among its class enemies.

I frankly state my own attitude to Russia so that the reader
may be on his guard against any possibilities of bias in the
following pages. When I was a student in the chemical laboratory I came to have a great respect for sulphuric acid as
a chemical reagent. I knew that in its pure form or in certain
explosive compounds it had death-dealing properties, but that
in other combinations there was no more valuable reagent in
the laboratory. I have somewhat the same realistic fear and
respect for Soviet Russia.

In the closing chapter on *The Interpretation of History,* I
have expressed the belief that the five great achievements of
the human race must all find adequate realization in the social

order of the future. It must include the contribution of Greek culture, of Hebrew moral and spiritual insight, of Roman law and order, of scientific technique, and of social organization. These essentials must be provided, not as in past centuries for an aristocratic favored few, or privileged owners of the means of production, whether individuals or nations, but socialized and shared with all. What the Greeks called "the good life" must include all the five elements of man's inheritance. If any social order persistently denies intellectual culture, spiritual freedom, law and order, scientific discovery, or social justice, it cannot endure. For many millenniums favored portions of mankind have had access to culture, religion and law, and for a century and a half to modern science. But never for the masses of the poor has social justice been provided, whether under slavery, serfdom or capitalism—charity often, but never equal justice. At last one nation has stood for this missing link of human experience for the workers. It has lost much of the first two of the five essential elements above mentioned. It has leveled down life to a drear and drab uniformity where few free men would care to live. With such a fundamental denial of intellectual liberty and spiritual freedom in a dictatorship which is a cruel tyranny to all whom it chooses to consider its enemies, it cannot in its present form possibly provide a full and satisfying social order which will include the above five essentials.

In the West while we have claimed to a considerable extent a measure of the first four elements of our human heritage, we are almost living in the stone age in certain predatory relations of our social life. We have lacked in socialization and distribution. After centuries of our religion and education, our scientific achievements in the production of wealth, and our boasted liberty and democracy in government, we have signally failed to provide basic economic justice for all. That is the immediate imperative in the present crisis in world affairs. No culture, religion, order or science can take its place. In the dialectic conflict of the capitalist and Communist orders, between our individualism and their collectivism, mankind may yet arrive at a synthesis which shall include both liberty and

justice and which may embrace all of the five elements of our common human inheritance. In the meantime, with Soviet tyranny or Anglo-Saxon injustice, can either say that it has nothing to learn from the other?

Russia is practically the only country in the world that was ever wholly free to sweep away its dead past and audaciously attempt to build, here and now, an entirely new social order. The Russians are the only people ever privileged to try the experiment of creating their ideal in flesh and blood, not under the hectic opportunism of an individual dictator, but based upon a considered and complete philosophy of life, as bold as Plato's Republic, or Sir Thomas More's Utopia, or a Kingdom of Man on earth, in the form of a classless society where no one may exploit his neighbor or use him merely for his own profit, but where those who toil by hand or brain must labor, all for each and each for all. Whatever inevitable shortcomings or failures there may be—and they are legion—and whatever crudeness or cruelty may characterize their methods, such a unique experiment should be instructive both in its failures and successes. America especially is in the midst of a very bold plan for a "new deal" and anything that may be learned about how *not* to do, or how to do, certain things without economic disaster may save her much in costly experience.

Without, as I have said, holding up Soviet Russia as a model in any regard, we may find it stimulating and suggestive in certain matters such as the following: its ideal of social justice and of social planning; its aim of a classless society which supersedes race and color prejudice; its new penology and humane treatment of criminals; its remarkable care of children, its method of challenging and inspiring youth to service and sacrifice; its new motivations and incentives that supersede the profit motive; its method of eliminating unemployment and its definite plan for housing and slum clearance; its revolution of collective agriculture; the rational, experimental basis of its new morality; the value of a unified philosophy of life; the light thrown upon the problem of religion for Russia and the world; and finally an interpretation of history which

may recognize the significance of the Russian experiment and of the signs of the times in which we are living today.

The outstanding fact observable during our visit in 1933 was that, in contrast to the last year when we found the country in the midst of the gravest economic crisis since the great famine, on this visit they were reaping the largest crop ever known in all their history. Conditions bordering upon famine, where many had died of hunger in the Ukraine and the South, were soon relieved by this bumper harvest.

Our party, consisting of about twenty persons, while passing through the villages heard rumors of the village of Gavrilovka where all the men but one were said to have died of starvation. We went at once to investigate and track down this rumor.[1] We divided in four parties with four interpreters of our own choosing and visited simultaneously the Registry Office of births and deaths, the cemetery, the village priest, the local soviet, the judge, the schoolmaster and every individual peasant we met. We found that out of 1100 families three individuals had died of typhus. They had immediately closed the school and the church, inoculated the entire population and stamped out the epidemic without developing another case. We could not discover a single death from hunger or starvation, though many had felt the bitter pinch of want. It was another instance of the ease with which wild rumors spread concerning Russia.

On every side there was evidence of the building of roads, factories and new industrial cities and the increased production of tractors and machinery. In some matters, such as cleanliness, sanitation, and the primitive use of force, Russia is far behind the more advanced and civilized countries of Europe, as it has been ever since the Tartar invasion put the clock back

---

[1] The writer was in Russia twice in Czarist days and eight times during the present régime. Each year he takes a party confined to educators, editors, and men engaged in public speaking and writing, to study conditions in the principal countries of Europe. In Russia we have had the privilege of choosing our interpreters, bringing them from America if desired, of freely interviewing friends or foes of the Soviet régime and of going practically everywhere without question. We have never been refused admission to any part of the Soviet Union.

for two centuries. Yet in other respects, such as in social organization, it seems almost a century in advance of the rest of the world.

My thanks are due to several friends for critically reading portions of the manuscript, the names of some of whom, however, as being considered friendly or unfriendly to the Soviet régime, it would not be a kindness to mention. Since my last visit to Russia I have tried to immerse myself in the literature of that country. In certain portions of the manuscript my debt will be quite evident to such writers as Professor Sidney Hook in his *Toward the Understanding of Karl Marx,* to Professor John Macmurray of University College, London, to Professor Berdyaev of Paris, and to the suggestive series of articles by Sidney Webb, now Lord Passfield, published in *Current History.*

My thanks are due to the Dean of Canterbury for providing a haven of refuge as an ideal place for writing in the garden of the deanery beside the great cathedral and for his Preface to the present volume.

I write both as a realist and as a critic of the U.S.S.R. and of the U.S.A. I am not blind to the serious defects of the Soviet Union, but the title of this lectureship limits me to what we can learn from it. I am proud of my own country and would not for any inducement take up my residence in Soviet Russia. But loyalty to America compels me to point out unsparingly the evils from which we as a nation suffer, and to suggest possible lessons which may be learned from Soviet Russia, even though they may be much worse than we are at many points. Now that the United States has recognized Soviet Russia, following Great Britain and the European nations, there is need of a fresh study of the Soviet Union. Recognition may have a bearing upon recovery, trade, prosperity and the peace of the world.

The *Merttens' Peace Lectures,* of which this volume constitutes the sixth in the series, were founded in 1926 by Frederick Merttens of Rugby, England. The five preceding volumes which were published by the Hogarth Press, London, were as follows:

1927 *Justice Among Nations,* by Horace G. Alexander
1928 *War and Human Value,* by Francis E. Pollard
1929 *Danger Zones of Europe,* by John S. Stephens
1930 *Britain and America,* by John W. Graham
1931 *The Race Problem in Africa,* by Charles Roden
      Buxton, M.P.

The Deanery, Canterbury, England,
  October 9, 1933.

PREFACE

Dr. Sherwood Eddy has a thousand contacts in two hemispheres. North, South, East and West he travels, observes, speaks and is consulted. I doubt if the man lives who has a wider range. Very early he came in touch with the East; working for fifteen years in India. For twenty-six years he has been moving in and out of China; I could name a score of Chinese cities where his name is honoured, and a dozen where a thousand students would assemble to hear him speak. Very astonishing would be the list of high Chinese officials who have owed to him their earliest youthful visions.

Nor is Dr. Eddy a whit less familiar with Europe. Every year he visits England, Germany, France, Poland, Austria and Russia, concentrating especially upon countries with a problem, and bringing with him from the United States so distinguished a group of thinkers, writers and publicists, that he can readily command the audience of the most important citizens in every land, whether it be the primate or premier of England, von Papen of Germany, or Masaryk of Czecho-Slovakia. Russia he knows peculiarly well.

If, then, we are seeking information on the "Russian Experiment"—and who among thoughtful men is not?—we shall find in Dr. Eddy several of the qualifications we need. He is a citizen of the world, able to view Russia in a world perspective. He can see Russia of today in the setting of her past from actual experience; can compare post and pre-war Russia. He has, in a word, standards of measurement denied to most of us and they equip him to adjudge the growth or the decay of the Russian Communist organism.

He can see two sides of a movement and balance the good against the bad. He has a mind of his own and the courage of his convictions. His speech in Berlin in the summer of this

past year was witness to that. To tell a German audience of today, not only of the Nazi elements which gave him hope, but of those which he and the whole world deplores, calls for a candour which all admire and few possess.

It is with the same candour that he speaks to and writes of Russia. For this is a book as vigorous in its indictment as it is generous in its praise. And the indictment is the more convincing for its obvious fairness. The writer has no axe to grind, and with a straight spear he tilts at oppression, religious persecution, denial of free speech, and the brutality which refuses human rights to enemies, or even to critics of the Soviet system.

All that and more there is which makes Communism, as Russia practices it today, an impossible creed for Dr. Eddy. But he never allows these things to hinder acknowledgment of Russia's astonishing achievements nor praise of her nobler accomplishments. For noble accomplishments indeed there are, and some of her activities, such for example as her treatment of criminals are so Christian in their spirit as to seem wellnigh incredible, at least to us who have never dared to practice this particular type of Christianity.

Dr. Eddy believes that we could do these things, and do them in our own and a better way, and without their terrible accompaniments. Very profitably we may enquire where the present rulers of Russia learned that righteous passion which constrains them to seek for every child the best, which makes them succour motherhood in childbirth, raise women to complete equality with men, treat crime in a redemptive way, remove the colour bar which separates the races, and regulate their personal lives with singular austerity as men who would minister and not be ministered to.

Lenin, Stalin and Trotsky grew up in no moral vacuum. It is these higher elements which give us hope. Insistence upon them is Russia's contribution to the religion she believes that she opposes root and branch. Practice and insistence alike serve as a challenge and stimulation to us. Assuredly we may cherish the hope that they are preparing the ground for a renaissance of religion on Russian soil. The moral elements will

persist and bear their fruit; the blatant brutalities slowly spend their force, as fear for the stability of the new order grows progressively less.

Seated more firmly in the saddle with each passing year, Russia can afford by degrees to relax and then to expand and add to those new elements of morality which she possesses, the religion which she needs. We on our part, setting our own house in order, and learning from her what she has in her power to teach, may ourselves come to possess a nobler religion. Thus in mutual enrichment we shall draw the nearer.

HEWLETT JOHNSON, *Dean of Canterbury.*

PART I

THE WARNING OF RUSSIA'S EVILS

CHAPTER I

Upon visiting Russia this past year I was first of all impressed by the paralyzing bureaucracy of the system. There are two conflicting elements that are the cause of this evil. It is the result of a centralized government plan in conflict with a democratic worker's control. The official, manager, or technician is caught between two fires: the Gosplan, or State Planning Commission, and the G.P.U., or State Political Police. The former compels him to take responsibility, but the latter sometimes interferes with him in the execution of his task and is often ready to punish him if he does not succeed.

Bureaucracy seems also to be a combination of the red tape of the inflexible system, which does not as yet sufficiently locate responsibility nor develop official initiative, coupled with the defects of character of the casual Russian peasant. The peasant of the old order was noted for his fatalism, shiftlessness, dishonesty and sloth. Considering the human material it is not surprising if this undisciplined peasant or proletarian worker cannot at once grasp and execute the intricacies of the most elaborate series of plans the world has ever seen, nor master the new complicated machinery placed in his hands. It proves to be much easier to build factories than to operate them, or to draw up a plan on paper than it is to carry it out in practice.

It was a fine democratic saying of Lenin that "every cook, every common laborer should be drawn into the conduct of the government." It was in keeping with Marx's romantic idealization of the proletariat as the chosen, messianic class which was to deliver humanity. But it is not so easy in practice. Just before Lenin's death he united the Central Control Commission of the Communist Party with the Workers' and Peasants' Control Commission, known as the R.K.I., which was

3

to enable the masses to check the government. It has a staff of three hundred but it mobilizes thousands of volunteer assistants who furnish information to the government and turn over the worst cases for punishment by the G.P.U. In 1929, after a split in the Party and the finding of sabotage among engineers and administrators, a general "cleansing" was called for to weed out the unfit, first from the Party and then from all government offices and institutions. During this same year the Electric Works in Moscow adopted as its charge the Commissariat of Finance. "About 3,000 workers participated with the R.K.I. in the cleansing of the nation's financial centre. As a result 300 officials were removed as aliens to the workers' state and three bureaus were eliminated as unnecessary. . . . Labor headquarters at Moscow reports that over five million workers have taken part in meetings for cleansing government machinery, that the unions have already nominated twenty-five thousand workers for government posts." That has a fine, democratic and almost romantic sound. But realistically let us suppose an army of husky workers and coal-heavers, or a body like the bonus army descending upon Washington to clean out all incompetent, or "highbrow," or bourgeois officials. Undoubtedly they would do some good and much harm. They would probably plentifully throw monkey wrenches into the already complicated government machinery. They would remove a lot of senators, congressmen and cabinet members and put a number of well-meaning manual workers in their places. But how well would these departments be running when the next "cleansing" came a few years later? There would probably be the same paralyzing bureaucracy that there is in Soviet Russia today.

Two things, however, are incontrovertible; one that the older peasant is inefficient and the other that the workers in general and youth in particular are learning as rapidly as could be expected, or as is humanly possible under the circumstances. Yet almost everywhere there is still much waste and heart-breaking delay. A visitor notices this immediately upon arrival at his hotel. You state your name and find it unrecognizably transliterated into Russian upon a stray piece of paper

and placed with other slips or sheets of various sizes. A friend, inquiring for you a few hours later, may be informed that there is no such person in the hotel.

When you ask for your bill you are referred by the clerk to another person and then to a third. The last one may suggest that as you are not leaving today there is no hurry. Everything possible is postponed to the proverbial "tomorrow," but when tomorrow comes it is still left undone. After insistent demand a different clerk now begins a search for the incomplete record. On an ancient oriental abacus of wooden beads strung upon wires the account is calculated. Then the operation is repeated to check it. Finally it is copied on paper. If now you offer to pay either in dollars, pounds or roubles, they may not have the exact change for any one of them, so you may either accept short change or again postpone the settlement. If your time is short at a hotel, shop, or ticket office you finally may be driven to leave for the time being in desperation with the goods unpurchased or the account unsettled.

While their glowing hope of ultimate triumph, when the state will "wither away" and be no longer needed, gilds the future, almost every major objective is to be attained in just five years. Confident predictions are made. They are to "build socialism," "to catch up with and to surpass the capitalist countries" in material standards. Yet at the end of the given five year period they are short of almost all commodities and are decades behind Europe and America in material standards. If the Soviet Union has prodigal supplies of anything it is of oil, yet we found long queues waiting outside the stores in Moscow for much needed supplies of kerosene because of a badly organized system of distribution and transportation which at times almost breaks down under the strain of their wellnigh impossible plans. Meat, fats, sugar, shoes, clothing, tobacco, matches, cigarette paper—almost all such supplies have been rationed for years, or supplied in quantities utterly inadequate, or at prices often prohibitive.

Years ago I found an American in Soviet Russia manufacturing efficiently excellent lead pencils and stationery supplies, but his concession was purchased and taken over by the govern-

ment. Today the supply of all writing materials is utterly inadequate. Any Russian or foreigner in the country is glad to get a good pencil while the majority of school children cannot hope to possess them. The same is true of almost all other commodities and consumption goods.

You may enter Woolworth's in New York or London, or Wertheim's department store in Berlin, and find that practically everything in the store would be counted a priceless luxury to friends in Russia where the government has been bending all its energies in the production of the iron and steel of heavy industry. Paper, ink, pens, fountain pens or pencils, writing materials, soap, toilet paper, elastics, pins, needles, buttons, hooks and eyes, collar buttons, shoe laces, stockings, socks, handkerchiefs—almost everything on the shelves is either almost unobtainable in Russia, or is so crude, or supplied in such small quantities or at such high prices, that it is practically prohibitive for most.

Before me as I write is the *Summary of the Fulfilment of the First Five Year Plan* published by the State Planning Commission. It is a statesmanlike document of titanic achievement in great things. There is no mention, however, of a multitude of seemingly little things and also of some important essentials in which the Plan was not such a great success. At the close of the first Five Year Plan prices were far higher than the Plan called for. Money wages under a mild inflation were higher but real wages and the standard of living were far lower than anticipated, while consumption goods and necessities of all kinds were far more scarce than the Plan had promised.[1]

It is sheer inefficiency which still requires waiting queues at the Torgsin stores for foreigners, at post offices, etc., though the pathetic "bread lines" of Moscow have been greatly re-

---

[1] In the original schedule of the first Five Year Plan the cost of living was to be reduced by 14 per cent. Urban workers were expected to consume 27 per cent more meat, 72 per cent more eggs, 55 per cent more milk, while country peasants were to increase their consumption by almost as great a percentage. None of these were ever fulfilled yet they are not mentioned in the above glowing report which concentrates attention chiefly on construction in heavy industry and mechanized agriculture.

duced. A stamp to send a letter to California over eight thousand miles away costs 15 kopeks, but to send a letter to the suburbs of Moscow eight miles away costs even more, 20 kopeks. It would be an exaggeration to say that it takes almost as long to send it, but the service is still disgracefully slow. They may put the sign of the slow-moving tortoise on a given post office to seek to shame it into more speed and efficiency but it will take a long time to transform the peasant whose vocabulary for centuries has centered in "tomorrow" and "it does not matter." Nothing mattered in the old days of Czarist fatalism and semi-serfdom, but everything is at stake in the tempo and efficiency of their new planned economy.

We have spoken of the paralyzing inefficiency of a bureaucracy which does not adequately locate responsibility in the individual nor develop official initiative. The administrative system is still cumbersome and inflexible. Without the partial automatic adjustment of the free play of the market under a looser individualism, everything must be included in the plan. This refers too many details back to the center which tends to wear out the pivotal officials. Dyerjinsky's last speech before his death protested against the immobile and unwieldy bureaucratism of the state machinery where every detail must pass through a score of hands or half a dozen departments, until "no one is finally answerable for anything."

The brilliant Rykov at the fifteenth Party Congress also complained of this inefficient bureaucracy. He quotes the protest of a manager interfered with in his duties by nine separate control commissions and committees of inspection. He says: "My time is wasted on reports, conferences, negotiations. The trade union organisations formed three factory councils, three organisations for discussing production and three commissions for setting up standards and settling disputes. When am I to find time for my work?" Finally this manager was hailed before the secret police by "a childish whim of an official of the G.P.U. who wished to show that he was a person of authority." Rykov concludes: "This whole system of revision and control combined with a lack of personal responsibility is hardly

calculated to ensure successful work. Our system is still centralized to a degree based on mistrust of every minor link of the chain." Rykov himself has now been demoted and removed, together with almost every member of the right or left deviation from the orthodox Party line of the central bureaucracy which is always infallibly right.

In August, 1930, a number of men in Russia were shot for hoarding silver change. A month later forty-eight specialists of the meat packing industry were publicly reported as executed in connection with a food plot, and many others lost their lives who were not reported. The following month a larger number were tried in connection with an alleged worldwide conspiracy. More recently there was the execution of thirty-five officials of the Department of Agriculture. This was followed by the arrest and trial of British and Soviet engineers of the Metropolitan Vickers firm. Whether all these and many other accused men in Russia were guilty or innocent it must be recognized that a terror not only terrorizes but it paralyzes. If an engineer in Russia makes a mistake, if his bridge, or dam, or factory does not succeed, he is frequently accused of deliberate sabotage and counter-revolutionary activity. Fear soon takes hold upon others. Each hesitates to take responsibility. Each passes on the decision to an official higher up, if possible to the foreign engineer. In the meantime an American employer or engineer would make a hundred decisions or innovations with a fair percentage of mistakes without fear of punishment. The loose individualism of uncontrolled *laissez faire* capitalism tends to anarchy. The planned economy of an over-centralized collectivism tends to tyranny and bureaucracy. Each has its own dangers and shortcomings.

Another instance of the sometimes disastrous effects of bureaucracy occurred last autumn when writers and newspaper correspondents were refused permission to enter the worst parts of the Ukraine and the North Caucasus, where alleged famine conditions had prevailed. There had undoubtedly been much suffering and many deaths in these districts. But a record harvest had supplied grain enough for all regions and to spare. Some higher body or individual had decided that the corre-

spondents were not to be allowed to visit these worst regions. The officials gave out the childish reason that these five or ten men would be in the way and impede the work of the harvesters. Accordingly, the rumor was broadcast by much of the press over Europe and America that terrible famine conditions still prevailed, when actually they had ended with a prodigious harvest. Someone or some group in control had blundered and a paralyzing and inefficient bureaucracy had only itself to blame for this damaging rumor. Such costly mistakes are frequently made in many departments under this system.

Time mentions a recent incident which is typical and revealing of the fatal effect of this bureaucracy under the dictatorship.[1] A man in workman's clothes, who happened to be Daniel Sulimov, Chairman of the Council of Peoples' Commissars, the Premier of Russia proper, took his place recently in a waiting queue outside a State store in Moscow. After an hour's shuffling forward he was given a sticky handful of some noisome substance when he asked for soap. When he requested the surly clerk for change he was told there was none in the store. Upon asking for wrapping paper the clerk jeered: "Afraid you'll get your hands soiled?" When he demanded the manager he was told that he was "upstairs somewhere." After being referred from place to place he was finally told that the manager was out. Suddenly he grew angry and thundered "I want the manager of Store 134, and I want him quickly. I am Sulimov." When at last the alarmed manager came the Premier is said to have hurled his package on the floor and roared: "Do you call this soap?" An investigation had shown that it had been made from garbage and that the fats assigned for soap had been diverted and sold for profit by certain officials.

In Tammany Hall or under a recent Mayor of Chicago such graft would not even be news, but in Russia it is punishable with death. Such things are happening every day in the Soviet Union. It is not so often graft as bureaucracy. It will take more than orders thundered from the Kremlin or a few executions to stop it. It may take a long time but it will be done.

---

[1] *Time,* September 11, 1933, p. 20.

Imagine trying to work a Five Year Plan with Israelites fresh from the bondage of Egypt, or the Negro newly released from slavery in America. It is a testimony both to the Plan and to the Russian people that, with heartbreaking delays and many failures, slowly but surely their economic projects are being carried out. Bureaucracy is a persistent but not a permanent evil.

Bureaucracy falls like a blight upon initiative everywhere. Its chief source is the over-centralized power of the State and Party. The dictatorship, far from relaxing, ever tightens its grip. Instead of withering away the state becomes ever more autocratic. Stalin recently said: "The attrition of the state will come not by weakening the government's power but by strengthening it to the very limit."

The Kremlin should determine general policies and let local authorities apply and work them out. Instead, it constantly interferes in details to try and direct almost every move in distant provinces. Robbing local officials of initiative, inculcating a dread of failure where each seeks to play safe, the "bureaucratic octopus" extends its cold tentacles to the most distant points to grasp almost every act or phase of life. It reaches out to demand constant reforms and interferes everywhere, with little intelligent appreciation or sympathy for the human—or inhuman—consequences of the dictatorship.

For this is the nature of bureaucracy, as it was in old Czarist Russia. It results in prolific paper reports to satisfy Moscow, concerning quantity rather than quality, with lowered productivity and often sullen resentment on the part of the peasants. True to Lenin's dictum that "great problems in the lives of nations are solved *only by force*," any means are justifiable if they promise quick though ruthless results. But the consequences are often dismally disappointing, partly due to Lenin's false theory, partly to the petty official bureaucrat, and the rest to the inherent defects of a deadening bureaucracy.

Efficient non-Party experts or elected officials are constantly replaced by politically loyal Party members who are frequently ill-prepared, unqualified bunglers. This is not for graft yet it closely resembles in effect the inefficient spoils system of other

lands. Almost everywhere, in every department and district, the U.S.S.R. is suffering from this paralysis of excessive bureaucracy. Some day Stalin and the Kremlin will have to tackle and reform this fatal system at the center and source, before they seek to reform everything and everybody in Russia, always laying the blame upon others for the failures of the central bureaucracy.

Stalin acknowledged and sought to correct this defect of bureaucracy in the third of his famous six points in his speech of June 23, 1931, when he said: "We must put an end to depersonalization, improve industrial organization, and locate the responsibility of each worker for a definite piece of work. We must stop the careless attitude toward equipment and the frequent breakdowns of machinery." But it will take years and even decades to correct this evil of bureaucracy which remains as one of the major deficiencies of the Soviet system.

The Denial of Liberty

There is in the Soviet Union today an undoubted denial of liberty. The government does not pretend or profess to provide for this "bourgeois prejudice" of liberty or formal democracy. It is a frank dictatorship. Although in aim it seeks to be democratic so far as the working class is concerned, for all others it takes the form sometimes of a tyranny and sometimes of a terror. It denies at one sweep freedom of speech, of the press, of assembly, or association. One and only one political party is allowed. That dominates the government, which in turn absolutely controls the press, the radio, and all means of communication. There is a universal censorship of all publicity and of all news, and the complete suppression of any organized opposition to the dictatorship or its program. For all opponents of the régime or for all members of the Communist Party who do not conform to the "Party line" as determined by the group in power, there is no civil or political liberty as we understand it in the West, and no organized opposition is tolerated after a decision is arrived at by the higher legislative organs of the Party. While the whole régime al-

ways seeks the material welfare of the laboring class collectively, there is no necessary respect for individual life or liberty, for the individual has no rights against the state which it is bound to respect. He has no Declaration of Independence nor Bill of Rights which entitles him to life, liberty and the pursuit of happiness. He has no protection of *habeas corpus* against ancient tyranny or an ubiquitous secret police.

On the tenth anniversary of the founding of the Fascist State in Italy it was claimed that there were already seventeen countries where parliamentary government or formal democracy had broken down, or where some form of dictatorship had been installed. If, as we believe, fascism is the last stage of decaying capitalism, we are likely to witness a further extension of such dictatorships, whether fascist or communist, in this period of transition in history. Even most liberty-loving Anglo-Saxons are forced to admit that dictatorships are a necessary evil at certain periods of history. We would prefer the dictatorship of a Cromwell, in spite of its ruthless cruelty in Ireland, to the rule of the dissolute Stuarts with their pretension of the divine right of kings. But if dictatorships are at times a *necessary* evil they are none the less an evil.

We are compelled to ask two questions concerning any such dictatorship, regarding the ends it seeks and the means it uses. Are the ends sought for the undeniable social welfare of all, or at least for the majority of the population, so that they justify an inevitably rigorous use of means? And are the means used as humane as possible, or are they gratuitously cruel, ruthless or even barbarous? For instance, no avowed humanitarian ends for the favored class of workers can justify the persecution of other whole classes of a population who are now underprivileged and without impartial justice as the workers once were. And no ruthless and continued persecution of all whom a state chooses to regard as its enemies is likely to validate itself before the conscience of mankind.

As we in the West do not profess to provide perfect liberty for all, Soviet Russia on the other hand does not completely deny it. Many believe that at the present time *Anglo-Saxon*

countries give a greater measure of political and religious liberty, while the Soviet Union gives more freedom in the economic and moral sphere. There is also less paternal authority and more self-government in the field of education, in the treatment of alien nationalities within their own borders, and in the reclamation of criminals in Russia than in the West. If we make an exception of their treatment of their supposed enemies, this claim is probably true. We shall examine in a later chapter the spheres where they are supposed to give a greater measure of freedom.

All liberties in Russia are only class liberties, though the privileged class is now the majority, not the minority. They believe that individual rights can have no validity until all exploiting classes are destroyed. The most significant of all liberties in Russia is economic, the provision of security of life which banishes the haunting fear of unemployment and helpless dependence upon some irresponsible individual who may possess a monopoly of the means of production.

The middle class and the proletarians hold different conceptions of liberty. Liberals think of themselves as individuals with rights, while masses of workers are naturally collectivists and necessarily emphasize social control. Liberals of necessity emphasize personal liberty, reverence for personality, the rights of property and personal obligations of good will and benevolence. The proletarian centers in group loyalty, solidarity and social welfare. Each point of view is legitimate. If the worker in Russia is in agreement with the system, within its rigid limits he is free and feels free. If he is not in agreement— may heaven help him! Though there is no heaven allowed and no help on earth for him if he is counted an enemy or an outcast. Many workers and peasants are reckoned as enemies. The "proletariat" is a theoretical term defining those workers who adhere to the Communist doctrine. Liberty and justice are reserved for this theoretical proletariat.

It is when we pass to the political and religious realm in

Russia that we most feel the rigor of the dictatorship. Marx held that all history proved that capitalism was based upon force and that it would finally defend its property rights against human rights by all necessary use of violence. He therefore insisted that the only hope for the proletariat was a violent revolution followed by an iron dictatorship. "From the first hour of victory the workers must level their distrust against their former allies—by execution, imprisonment, forced labor, control of the press—Revolution is war and war is founded on terror."[1]

The dictatorship, beginning with the political sphere, widens out to the control of almost all of life—the government, industry, forcibly collectivized agriculture, all trade and commerce, the propagandist education of the young, what every teacher must teach and every pupil must learn, the press, the radio—all that the people are publicly told from birth to death, the dictatorship seeks to control. While this dictatorship widens to almost the whole of life the principle of "centralism" narrows the monopoly of power to the few. The whole proletariat must be led by the determined minority of the small Communist Party. This in turn must be centered in a central executive and a plenum of that executive. Since there are at least two factions striving to dominate these bodies one or the other must be excluded and no right or left "deviation" from the party line can be permitted. Finally the inner control narrows down to ten members of the inner Political Bureau, each of whom must be in harmony with the General Secretary who places his own loyal followers in all key positions of authority. Any astute politician, whether in Italy, Russia or elsewhere, can make sure of the support of the final executive and legislative organs of the Party and the Government. A dictatorship like a war makes the state everything and the individual nothing.

---

[1] Marx wrote in 1875: "Only in Communist society when the resistance of the capitalists has finally broken down—only then does the State disappear and one can speak of freedom. Only then will be possible and will be realized a really full democracy." Lenin declared the dictatorship to be in a new sense democratic, for the proletariat and the poor, and in a new sense dictatorial, against the bourgeoisie.

Then a small group or an individual may control the all-powerful state and all the individuals in it.

A decade and a half after the Revolution, when the Soviet Union claims to be, and probably is, the most secure government in Europe, when there is no possible alternative to it and no sign of effective revolt against it, there is nevertheless a continuing and at times even growing severity toward whole elements of the population. Tens of thousands of peasants have just been dislodged from their homes and transplanted bodily, two, three and even five thousand miles away. Thousands of peasants have been mobilized for timber cutting in the cold Archangel district. A whole canal was recently dug in the North by prison labor.[1] Something like twenty-five thousand are held in concentration camps. Whole Cossack communities, the poor as well as the prosperous, have been uprooted from their homes in the Caucasus by the beautiful Black Sea and exiled "to work near the Arctic Circle." Could one imagine an American government shipping in freight cars whole communities of say 46,000 citizens from Florida to Alaska because they had not obeyed the dictatorship in Washington with regard to their orange crop? This year also Stalin and Molotov signed the decree regarding the "fixed farm produce tax." Those who do not fulfil their quota "will be treated as criminals."

A rigorous system of passports, or citizen's registration, has been instituted for dwellers in the larger cities in order to remove the pressure of the surplus village population upon the undeveloped urban centers. Hundreds of thousands who had once been producing food had drifted into the congested cities. Deportations from Leningrad began to assume the proportions of a wholesale exodus. A vast campaign to speed up the production of lumber in the northern regions involved the conscription of peasants in these sections. Large numbers of Party

---

[1] The Stalin Canal from the White Sea to the Baltic was dug during nineteen months by 200,000 criminals and political prisoners. As a reward for digging this canal the sentences of 59,516 prisoners were reduced and 12,484 were set free as "completely corrected."

members and 15,000 Young Communists were ordered into the forests to supervise the work of the conscripted peasants. "Stalin's March" is to double the present rate of cutting timber in these regions. Ruthless measures seem to multiply. Thousands have been exiled in lumbering, mining or distant agricultural regions in the pioneering stage, as part of a big colonization movement. All other citizens have had their lives and habits strictly regimented. Sunday as a day of rest is abolished. A seven day week is suddenly changed, first to a five then to a six day week. Any opposition to these sweeping changes is counted as counter-revolutionary sedition. Worst of all has been the government's attitude towards and treatment of all whom they choose to regard as their enemies. Some are traditionally opposed to the Communists but many would become loyal supporters of the régime if they were allowed to do so. Had the authorities shown half the sagacity, the tolerance, the generosity to all other classes of the population that they have to criminals they would have been rewarded with a like loyal and generous response, but the dictatorship has been adamant. Political opponents need expect no quarter. Whether it be Trotsky, Kamanev or Zinoviev on the left; or Rykov, Bukharin or Tomsky on the right, no one who differs from Stalin's Party line may expect any mercy.

If Trotsky and the "left deviation" think the pace of collectivization and the liquidation of the kulaks should be faster, and if they agitate against Party decisions secured by the group in power, they are counted traitors, the most hated men on earth, hounded into exile or banishment. Then, when a much faster tempo is adopted than even Trotsky had advocated, which places the majority of the population under a tremendous strain for years, and when the "right deviation" dare to express the conviction that the pace is now too hectic and that the workers will break under it, they also are evicted, or demoted, until they come with humiliating public confession of their sins, with complete subservience to the group in power. Roger Baldwin says, "Estimates run from 5,000 exiles of the old bourgeois classes and 1,000 Socialists and anarchists to ten

or fifteen times that number: 60,000 to 75,000." Whatever the number may be, it is far less than in Czarist times.[1]

Trotsky and several hundred were banished or sent abroad and thousands of his followers were imprisoned or sent into exile. Many of the most important political prisoners are kept in the famous Butirky prison, while the Solovietsky Islands near the Polar circle are both a prison and a place of exile with a capacity of many thousands. Such a policy means that men like the brilliant Christian Rakovsky and Sosnovsky, the friend of Lenin, are excluded, while wooden, unimaginative, plodding workers like Molotov are placed in positions of power for their loyalty to the dictator.

On the whole not only members of the old classes of privilege but their children have been often cruelly treated or handicapped, unless the children publicly renounce and repudiate their parents. The euphonious phrase, "liquidation of the kulaks," covered a merciless policy. Many of them were, as their name implied, "fists," closed to grasp or to strike. Many were exploiters and money-lenders. But large numbers of them were merely hard-working, prosperous peasants who had succeeded by greater intelligence or industry in acquiring a little property and a cow or two. The Communists were doubtless right in determining that at all costs the evils of capitalism should not dominate Russia and her peasantry. They dread and hate the curse of it more than all the plagues and pestilences of the earth combined into one. They would gladly die rather than see it return to Russia. But their thinking is always class thinking, mass thinking, hard and fast and often ruthless. The individual was nothing. The prosperous peasants were counted kulaks, therefore enemies. They must be exterminated, or more euphemistically, "liquidated." It would take whole libraries to record the tragedies, the injustices, the suffering in thousands of cases. But they will never be known. A whole class has been simply wiped out—a few shot, many

[1] During 1908 alone, "no less than 70,000 were banished for political offences and 782 executed, while the persons in exile numbered no less than 180,000." *Liberty Under the Soviet*, p. 220.

dispossessed, transported, or exiled. The most fortunate had all their possessions confiscated and were permitted to begin life again in poverty near their own homes or, more frequently, at a distance.

Justified though it may have been from the Communist standpoint, the complete "liquidation of the kulaks as a class" meant the suffering of five million relatively prosperous farmers, many of whom were treated with incredible cruelty. The few who were shot or committed suicide were more obviously tragic, but the subjection of whole disfranchised classes to economic pressure, that amounted at times almost to slow starvation, was even more serious.

In 1929 began the trek of German colonists from all over Russia to Moscow, where they asked to be permitted to leave the Soviet Union. Thousands came from Siberia, the Ukraine, and the German Republic on the Volga, declaring that they would not return to such conditions of tyranny and want. President Hindenburg of Germany subscribed his pittance to help meet the need of these poor sufferers. A few were permitted to leave but most were forcibly driven back to their homes.

The Soviets' treatment of the intellectuals or intelligentsia has been another blot upon their record. These were the writers, the leaders, even the revolutionaries of the old Russia from the days of the Decembrist Revolution in 1825. This was the class that produced Lenin and most of the brilliant leaders of their own October Revolution. Yet when the now privileged proletariat came into power the factory population became at times an instrument of vengeance and persecution of the intellectual and white collar class, whose position was only a little better than the penalized, disfranchised or declassed elements. The Soviets often flattered the proletariat and handicapped or despised the intellectuals. A whole class held under suspicion was made to suffer for a few who were seditious or counter-revolutionary. One professor complained that the Soviets divide society "into two classes: those who eat, namely the workers, and those who starve, the bourgeoisie." Because another professor had taught that the "natural sciences cannot explain

the mystery of life" and that materialism is not a complete philosophy of life, he and his colleagues were ordered to be disciplined and watched. For the mere holding of opinions that are counted unorthodox there has been practically a medieval inquisition instituted in the Soviet Union. Stalin, in the fifth of his famous six points, acknowledges that the Soviets must change their policy toward the intellectuals and experts.[1] But this tardy acknowledgment has been slow and inadequate in its effect.

Another aspect of Communist tyranny and the denial of liberty is the refusal to allow any of the vast majority to leave the Soviet Union. Although a few more have recently been granted passports upon the payment of a high fee which is for most of them quite prohibitive, it cannot be denied that hitherto not one per cent of the population has been granted passports or allowed to leave the country. Only a few trusted technical students and agents for trade are permitted to go abroad. A place where one is forced to stay and not allowed to leave becomes for one who resents it a prison house. That is exactly what Russia is today for multitudes. Our group this past year met one loyal member of the Communist Party who would like to get permission to go abroad for his wife's health. But this is refused him. He can get another wife if necessary, but her health or life is not a sufficient reason for him to be allowed to leave Russia.

Such an incident is like an open window through which we may view conditions in Russia under a stern dictatorship. If few are allowed to leave Russia, if passports would be granted to less than one per cent of the population, if even a member of the Communist Party who is a shock brigader is not permitted to leave the country even to save his wife's life, can we

---

[1] On June 29, 1931, Stalin said: "We must change our policy toward the old technical intelligentsia. Now, when these intellectuals are turning toward the Soviet government, and are no longer infested with the wrecking disease, our attitude must be one of conciliation and solicitude. 'Expert-baiting' is a disgraceful phenomenon. We began by smashing and utterly defeating the capitalist elements in town and country. But there is now a new attitude on the part of the old bourgeois intelligentsia, so we must also change our attitude to one of co-operation."

put ourselves in the place of this man in imagination and ask how many free men would be willing to live under such a dictatorship.

Since the decree of August 7, 1932, for "the protection of the property of state enterprises, collective farms, and coopera- tive societies and the strengthening of socialized property," many have been shot or imprisoned for theft or damage to public property in order to teach them this lesson: "He who raises his arm against socialistic public property—be it in a factory, a railway line, a collective farm, an eating establish- ment—commits a grievous crime against the state. No mercy can be shown to the foes of the people and of the Soviet order."

In the *Komsomolskaya Pravda* of August 6, 1933 we read: "Punishment immediately followed crime. Karavaieff had not had time to stretch out his hand to pluck a flower from the bush covered with lovely fragrant flowers when a threatening voice sounded behind him:

"What are you doing, citizen?"

Karavieff's arm dropped. He turned round and faced a policeman.

"I only . . . wanted to pluck a flower. I am on my way home after evening work, and the flowers smell so good."

"They smell . . . But do you know, citizen, of what your act smells? The garden is a public one."

"Well, what of it?"

"You are guilty of spoiling public property. Come with me, citizen."

Karavaieff was arrested. Soon he was brought before the court and sentenced to several years imprisonment for breaking the law of August 7, 1932, regarding the protection of socialistic property.

"This is not an imaginary case. It took place in Kazakstan and was related to me by our collaborator, the procurator of the U.S.S.R., Akouloff. We know of very many cases when the law of August 7 has been perverted. The railway tribunal of the southwestern line sentenced to some ten years imprison- ment an old cooperative workman for appropriating supplies because he received some petroleum and a pair of slippers for

ready money. And at the same time a shepherd in one of the Machine and Tractor Stations of the Middle Volga was caught red handed in stealing cattle, was arrested, and then set free without any punishment, and reinstated in his former post. In some cases we see a misguided, useless application made of the law of August 7, in others a criminal leniency and absence of class wakefulness.

"According to the data received from the procurators, out of the 486 cases brought before the tribunal in the course of a year concerning thefts in the Sheep Breeding Trust only 66 cases have been investigated. The political section of the Tchembar Machine and Tractor Stations informs us that in the People's Court there are over 1,000 and in the police court over 4,000 cases of theft not investigated.

"The procurators of the U.S.S.R. will struggle in merciless manner against all such demobilizing tendencies and against the weakening of class wakefulness. "The aim of the procurators and the tribunals," said Comrade Akouloff, "is to strengthen the struggle against all plunderers of socialistic property, not only insisting on a speedy investigation of every single case liable to the law of August 7, but also in a widespread mobilization of public opinion, so as to create a 'moral atmosphere' which would make it impossible for our foes and the spoliators of public property to exist."

Such laws may be necessary to prevent theft and the neglect of public property, but when they are multiplied they come to constitute a terror for numbers of the population. A dictatorship of violence and compulsion becomes a stern reality.

In Manchuria and North China alone there were over a hundred thousand of these poor refugees who had fled over the border. I am not now referring to members of the White armies who naturally sought to escape, but to simple peasants, many of whom believed that they would be denied freedom of conscience in the new collective farms and who wished to preserve their lives and liberties. I have referred in a previous volume to individual peasants whom I interviewed in Manchuria who had escaped over the border. One young man was imprisoned for his refusal to join what he regarded as an anti-

religious collective. He and his friends, 149 persons in all, tried to cross the ice on the Amur River at night. Only nineteen of them escaped, four of them being wounded. The rest were shot or captured and taken back to be shot.

If in the United States a single Negro is lynched the Communist cries to heaven in righteous indignation, and rightly so. But in lands where liberty is at least an ideal, men may freely leave the country in peace. Under a dictatorship where the state has all power and the individual who in conviction differs from it has no rights whatever, there is no moral wrong in shooting down over a hundred men in cold blood. The only crime is theirs in trying to escape. But such a policy is as short-sighted as it is barbarous. It is natural that the Soviet Union should wish to retain every individual worker as an economic unit, and every penny or kopek of value. It is not to be wondered at that they do not wish their enemies, the "White" Russians, to go to other lands carrying their lurid and often exaggerated reports of persecution of the disfranchised. They do not see, however, that though they may hide anything from their own carefully guarded and propagandized population, they cannot control the press and platform in other lands, and that such acts of cruelty are always broadcast and do more damage than would a living refugee. After all why do so many wish to flee from a country except to escape its tyranny?

This denial of liberty is of the very essence of the Russian dictatorship and does not commend itself to free men. Yet William Z. Foster, Communist candidate for President in the United States in the last election, tells us frankly what we may expect if they ever gain power here: "Under the dictatorship, capitalist parties—Republican, Democratic, Progressive, Socialist, etc.—will be liquidated, the Communist Party functioning alone as the party of the toiling masses. . . . What stupidity it would be for the victorious workers, whose aim it is to liquidate all classes, to permit these counter-revolutionary elements to organize themselves into political parties and thus enable them to sabotage the new régime, to fight for the re-

establishment of their system of robbing the workers and generally to act as a barrier to the progress of the new society. . . . Religious schools will be abolished and organized religious training for minors prohibited.   Freedom will be established for anti-religious propaganda. . . . God will be banished from the laboratories as well as from the schools."

Here is the second evil in a system which for many of us is made morally impossible by its gratuitously ruthless denial of liberty.

CHAPTER II

Fundamental and practically permanent in the system of Communism is the element of violence, of force, of compulsion. This is all the more serious in a "continuing revolution" which is to be perpetuated until the last enemy is dead or utterly crushed. The Communist can no more assure his final utopia when the state will "wither away," when all citizens will be spontaneously cooperative and benevolent and will live happily ever afterwards, than can the fundamentalist promise his millennium or his future heaven in lieu of providing justice on earth here and now.

A ruthless dictatorship of force was necessary to Marx's whole system. His avowed object was the revolutionary overthrow of the existing order. Engels' highest praise beside his grave in Highgate Cemetery was: "Before all else Marx was a revolutionist." He himself had written: "There is only one means—revolutionary terrorism." Thus closes the *Communist Manifesto* in 1848: "Communists scorn to hide their views and aims. They openly declare that their purpose can only be achieved by the forcible overthrow of the whole existent social order. Let the ruling classes tremble at the prospect of a Communist revolution." [1]

When the time is ripe the Comintern or Communist Inter-

---

[1] It is unnecessary to multiply quotations upon the element of force and violence in Communism. Lenin writes: "Scientifically defined, a dictatorship is an authority based directly on force, an authority which is absolutely unrestricted by any laws or regulations. . . . The dictatorship means power, unlimited power, based on force and not on law." Joseph Stalin's *Leninism*, pp. 22, 28.

national, directed from Moscow, calls for the violent over-throw of the whole existing social order and the complete destruction of each state, if possible by a minimum of bloodshed, but if required by all necessary use of violent destruction. Once having seized power there is the constant temptation of every dictatorship not only to perpetuate itself but to ever tighten its hold by greater ruthlessness. Every enemy without or within the Party must be crushed. This creates a new ruling class that practically dictates, and a large inert mass that is dictated to. Not only the avarice of wealth but power corrupts. As Henry Adams said, "power is poison." Einstein adds his credo from experience: "I am convinced that degeneracy follows every autocratic system of violence, for violence inevitably attracts moral inferiors. Time has proved that illustrious tyrants are succeeded by scoundrels. For this reason I have always been passionately opposed to such régimes as exist in Russia and Italy today." [1]

The danger in the Communists thus committing themselves to the unlimited use of force and violence is evident. They must begin by precipitating a class war, by making the workers class conscious, and kindling in their hearts the flames of hatred. Hatred is essentially destructive. It has murder at its heart. They must enter the field of trade union activity, patiently built up for over a century, and endeavor to capture for their creed of violence, or else split wide open with bitter division, every local trade union and every national labor movement in the world. Both in theory and practice the Communist Party must resort to tactics that are sometimes brutal and vulgar. Hatred, lying, falsehood, misrepresentation, brawling, and violence must be freely used and are used. If they are not, Moscow pours forth the vials of its wrath and the contempt of the Comintern upon this chicken-livered cowardly Party in any country which is not living up to Lenin's Twenty-one Points. [2]

---

[1] *Living Philosophies,* p. 5. This is in harmony with the experience of Lord Acton that "power corrupts and absolute power corrupts absolutely."

[2] Adopted by the second congress of the Communist International in 1920: "The revolution must be prepared for as civil war approaches in every country. . . . Communist agitation must be carried on in every trade union move-

All of the above ruthlessness assumes for the Communist a "successful" revolution. But there is no guarantee of success in this most hazardous of enterprises. Marx and Engels predicted that the revolution would first occur in the prepared and favorable countries of France and Germany, and Engels prophesied that European revolutions would occur by 1885.[1] Yet more than eighty-five years after the predictions of the *Communist Manifesto* a proletarian government has been set up in one country alone, and that under unexceptionably favorable circumstances. Even in favored Russia between 1917 and 1921 through war, revolution, famine and pestilence ten millions perished. For every successful revolution there are a score of revolts and unsuccessful uprisings. With a thinly populated agricultural people that could sustain themselves through years of civil war, Russia proved to be in many respects the most favorable country in the world for revolution. But in a highly industrialized country like England, Germany or the United States, with millions that could be isolated in cities cut off from food supplies, or in overcrowded, impoverished populations like those of China or Japan, the possibilities of slaughter and suffering in a continued civil war or Communist revolution and régime lie beyond the power of the human imagination to visualize. Bukharin admits that "in such countries, the civil war will inevitably assume a more savage form than in Russia." [2]

Communists may sweep aside the appeal to reason, the disciplines of liberty, the evolutionary, constitutional and educational institutions built up in the hard-won triumphs of civilization throughout the centuries. They may loose the forces of the volcano and the earthquake and the forest fire which will quickly sweep beyond all human control. Destruction is more easy and certain than construction. They must not ask us to

---

[1] Sidney Hook, *Toward the Understanding of Karl Marx*, p. 23.
[2] *The A. B. C. of Communism*, p. 133.

---

ment. . . . Each member must subordinate his entire activities to the interests of the revolution. . . . All decisions of the Comintern Congress and the Executive Committee are binding upon all parties," etc.

destroy the patient gains of a millennium for an irresponsible promise of utopia.

A class is more cruel than an individual, especially a long oppressed class. Deifying a class inflates it with egotism and vindictiveness. Its vengeance becomes destructive. Thus Trotsky writes: "As for us we were never concerned with the Kantian priestly vegetarian-Quaker prattle about the sacredness of human life! To make the individual sacred we must destroy the social order which crucifies him and this problem can only be solved by blood and iron." Thus class hatred or fanaticism "shuts the gates of mercy on mankind." It proposes the annihilation of one class to insure the supremacy of another.

When a few months ago in Moscow I asked a member of the Comintern if his organization existed to foment class war and, when the time was ripe, to overthrow one by one the governments in all countries, looking toward the consummation of world revolution, he frankly answered: "Certainly, it exists for no other purpose." One could not but appreciate his candor and courage and long life of sacrifice. But on the other hand Communists cannot blame us if we do not accept but rather repudiate with horror their proposed solution. To them violent revolution seems to be scientifically demonstrated as the only possible solution of our social problems. To us it seems an unproven dogma, which at its best is terrible, and at its worst is beyond the power of the human imagination to visualize.

As we have already observed, nowhere does the denial of liberty and the use of violence become more crucial than in the treatment of its class enemies and of those who try to escape from the clutches or stranglehold of the system. One might wonder why there should be such persecution or harshness under a government perhaps more firmly established in power than any in Europe, when there is no effective political revolt or opposition. Might we not expect a little more tolerance a decade and a half after the establishment of this régime?

The terrific pressure of the Five Year Plan often made not only heavy but impossible demands upon all classes in almost every industry. Fantastic goals were sometimes set in the grandiose Plan. When these were not fulfilled, the Government sometimes came down upon the scientific specialists, engineers, or technicians, especially the intelligentsia, with terrible vengeance even though some of them had pointed out that the goals set were impossible. They were accused of deliberate sabotage, of being "wreckers," class enemies, etc. No fault was ever admitted by the central government in its Plan.

Trials followed in rapid succession, some in open court but more in the secrecy of the G.P.U. There was the Shakhta trial, that of the Prompartia or Industrial Party, that of the Mensheviks, etc. In the Palchinsky trial apparently all the accused were shot. In "the trial of the 48," all were shot in one day as announced in the papers, and others were executed later in secret. In 1933 in the Ministry of Agriculture trial 35 others seem to have been shot. But much more serious than these spectacular trials were the cases of alleged "wreckage" and sabotage in the timber, chemical, textile, rubber, electric, glass and other industries, including the Putilov factory, the cooperative movement, the military-technical academy, etc., etc. The outside world has no means of knowing whether the accused were innocent or guilty. If these hundreds and even thousands were guilty as the government claimed, why were the intelligentsia and specialists so driven into opposition to intolerable conditions? If, as seems incontrovertible in hundreds of cases, numbers of the intelligentsia were in sympathy with the main purposes of the régime and were endeavoring to cooperate with it, why were so many of them unjustly accused? Why were they subjected to the inhuman and almost unbelievably cruel methods of the "third degree" of the G.P.U. which often exerted wellnigh diabolical pressure to force them falsely to sign statements of their own guilt?[1]

---

[1] The testimony of Vladimir Chernavin, in the *Slavonic Review* for July 1933, is a typical instance which may be multiplied by scores in Paris, London, Helsingfors or Riga from personal witnesses or written records. There are many more who dare not talk or have any intercourse with foreigners in Soviet Russia itself.

Many of these men, on the report of reliable members of the intelligentsia who have escaped, were left in unsanitary, verminous prisons and subjected to mental torture till they gave way. Some were shot, some sent to concentration camps, or into Siberian exile, and some to the dreaded Arctic Solovietsky island. Under the over-simplification of the Marxian formula most of these "class enemies" are accused of "counter-revolution" under Article 58 of the Criminal Code, which is widely interpreted. After long confinement, as one of them says, "dirty, ragged and covered with lice, a man begins to despise himself, and it is doubtless easier to break his will." The inadequate diet and unsanitary conditions often produce scurvy, boils and illness and undermine the prisoner's resistance. When he is offered the alternative of signing a "confession" of his guilt which has been prepared for him, or of being shot, the temptation of a lonely man to sign even a false statement is great, especially if he is shown the forged "confessions" of others implicated in the same case. If the man refuses to sign a confession which he knows to be false he may be told: "We are in no hurry. I will send you to your cell and call for you in six months. By that time there will only be a shadow left of you, and then you will sign anything I want." In one instance a prisoner was suddenly confronted with his wife with the appeal: "Spare your wife. Save yourself. Sign a sincere repentance and confession. I propose this to you for the last time. Otherwise you will be shot." The man refused to sign this confession which was false, so he was sent to a concentration camp for five years. Had he signed he might have been shot.[1]

There is no need to extend this painful narrative as there is little to learn from it. Confessedly and undeniably there is violence and compulsion at the heart of the Soviet system in the present and in any future that we can contemplate. However understandable it may be in Russia, which has never known good government, such violence after centuries of advance in rational and non-violent processes, is for us a reversal

[1] *Slavonic Review,* July 1933, p. 76.

to the primitive and barbarous. Whatever our own evils may be, it is worse than anything we have ever known in our history. It does not commend the system to any but dispossessed classes as a counsel of despair. The lesson is obvious that in lands that have achieved enormous production, far beyond that of Russia, some reasonable system of distribution and socialization should make such classes impossible.

CHAPTER III

DOGMATISM, ATHEISM AND ANTI-RELIGION

Most Communists believe their system to be strictly scientific. Marx is held to have completely demonstrated his positions and to have provided a foundation for his whole system by his strictly scientific theory of value and of surplus value. There is supposed to be no element of faith in the system, not even the apocalyptic or eschatological vision of the future when the state "withers away." It is claimed that all is demonstrated. But Communism is not only a philosophy, a tactic of revolution, and an economic theory; it also has its dogma. There must be some reason for the fact that almost everywhere there is an element of bigotry, or intolerance and of fanaticism implicit in it. It cannot win its way by moral suasion or rational appeal alone, but in practice a determined minority which has accepted the dogma must impose the system upon the majority by force.

I have elsewhere endeavored to point out that Marx, who, for all his giant intellect, was himself so intolerant and dogmatic, was never able to grasp the full significance of our complex world.[1] By an oversimplification, Marx forced all history into the arbitrary channels of two classes and their inevitable conflict. The complex of reality is reduced to stark black and white and men are thrown into two simple classes of robbers and robbed, exploiters and exploited. All possible experimental solutions are impatiently swept aside and one panacea is substituted for the whole world.

---

[1] Sherwood Eddy, *The Challenge of Russia*, p. 206. Marx's system was prevailingly scientific but his temperament, unlike that of Darwin, was dogmatic, like most of his followers today.

31

Professor Laski says of Marx: "After thirty years in London, he was still at the end a German stranger testing facts and constructing theories in terms quite alien from the circumstances around him. . . . Thus, while he wrote with superb profundity about the material environment of men's lives, he rarely penetrated into the inner substance of those lives. With such tracts of experience—religion for example—as were alien from his own knowledge he could neither sympathize nor understand. The seeming logic of his attitude is deceptive, for it in part rests upon a failure to test his own assumptions, and in part upon an abstract view of human nature with which the totality of facts is in direct contradiction. . . . Where Marx was wrong was in the belief that the catastrophe was, in itself, worthy of attainment. . . . He may have hated too strongly, he was jealous, and he was proud. . . . He was often wrong, he was rarely generous, he was always bitter." [1]

Marx, Lenin and Stalin are all examples of the incarnation of this element of dogmatism in the Communist system and of the price that has to be paid for it. They were all heroic but harsh, hard and destructive. Communism in its very nature is necessarily so.

One aspect of this dogmatism is found in their attitude to religion. While religionists are allowed to meet in their respective places of worship, no one can be a good Communist or a member of the Party who is not both in profession and practice a dogmatic atheist with anti-religious zeal. There is no place for the scientific, reverent agnostic like Charles Darwin. Communists in Russia repeatedly assure you with the "sumptuosity of security" that "every true scientist is an atheist." No one can be a member of the Communist Party if he is a believer in religion, if he ever attends church or takes any part in the rites of religion, or if he does not accept the position of dogmatic atheism.

It is true that the Constitution of the Soviet Union guarantees liberty of conscience and of worship. It is true also that

[1] Harold J. Laski's essay on *Karl Marx*, pp. 28, 48.

many churches are open and that their services have been un-interrupted since the Revolution.   Priests who are considered harmless in the Orthodox Church are permitted to conduct the mass or service of worship.   But though Communists keep the letter of the law, it is also true, as we shall find in a future chapter which deals with religion, that every prophetic voice is silenced in Russia, that every effective preacher or dynamic religious worker is either exiled, or banished, or placed under a ban of strict silence.   While the Constitution once guaranteed "freedom for religious and anti-religious propaganda," now only "freedom for religious confession and anti-religious propaganda is recognized for all citizens." [1]   All the wealth and weight of the government dictatorship of the U.S.S.R., all the strength of the Communist Party, all the fanatical zeal of the Union of Militant Godless, which claims five and a half million members, flooding Russia with their propaganda literature, their enthusiastic closing of churches, their often vulgar and blatant attacks upon the faith and worship of simple peasants, is thrown into the scale against the helpless believers. We shall postpone the full consideration of the subject of religion to a later chapter on *The Reformation of Religion*.

This element of dogmatism is in complete contradiction to Communist dialectic philosophy and is not truly Marxian. Whatever it is, dialectic is not dogmatic.   It implies constant progress through ever imperfect systems, by the necessary and valuable interpenetration of opposites, toward the goal of a pure and benevolent Communism, where all state control shall have ceased as unnecessary.   Such a consummation is not within horizons of a dogmatic dictatorship.   In this confessedly temporary transition which has hardly yet approached real Socialism, much less Communism, which is only a provisional thesis in a new series, it might have allowed or even welcomed the challenging antithesis of an interpretation like that of Trotsky, or of genuine moral and spiritual insight of religion at its best.   But not the slightest deviation is permitted.

---

[1] Redaction adopted by the Congress of Soviets in May 1929. *Izvestia*, May 22, 1929.

Dogmatism always implies finality. If a group has already discovered all essential, final truth in a complete philosophy of life, there need be no further search. Truth must now be imposed by a "determined minority" upon the unwilling majority who cannot or will not see it. Thus by William Z. Foster and his comrades in their future America "God will be banished from the laboratories as well as from the schools." It is only a dogmatic inversion of the inquisition which by all necessary use of violence or persecution will impose the final truth of right dogma as the only means of salvation for humanity. The dogma of final truth backed by the unlimited power of the dictatorship will dominate the laboratories and the schools. Scientists will be thrown into prisons or concentration camps or hounded over the world as emigrès and exiles without a country. Then the proletariat, reduced to a drab level of uniformity, will live happily ever afterward. Such is the dogmatic, "scientific" Utopia offered us by Communism.

Present Communist propaganda is untrue to its principle of dialectic advance. It has adapted a hard and fast Marxian fundamentalism which is a contradiction to Marxian theory. This un-Marxian fundamentalism and dogmatism values fixed ideas above things. Communists sometimes forget that the revolution of Marx has already taken place; they are not proceeding to build the order he foretold.

Nothing blinds men more than hatred. It often prevents men in Russia from thinking realistically. They see the whole capitalistic world according to their class formulæ. Capitalism is always the villain and Communism the hero. Capitalists and kulaks are always and everywhere base and hypocritical, the proletariat are virtuous or messianic. The city proletariat ruthlessly regiment life for the peasantry and force it into their own molds. They have little use for the home, so the peasant must have none. They scorn religion, so it must be denied the peasant. He must be forced wholesale into vast collectives and state farms, with the killing, imprisoning, banishing or "liquidating" of several million kulaks and prosperous and intelligent peasants, often at the hands of their jealous neighbors.

They boast that they won their "battle of the Marne" against

the peasants two years ago. But think of a war on their own peasantry, of bloody battles and killing and heartless crushing of the more intelligent farmers of a whole nation. Then when the battle is "won," when the cattle have been killed and the indignant, sullen peasantry will not cooperate, and famine or near famine results, not from lack of rainfall or any failure of nature but from their own ruthless plans, they find that an awful price has been paid for a mere experiment, ofttimes unsuccessful.

Many collectives and state farms are unwieldy and unworkable. Pledges have been broken with the peasantry by frequent changes made in policy. Costly blunders have been made for which the peasantry have paid dearly. Then next season a new plan must be railroaded through, or the steam-roller of the city shock brigades must sweep over the countryside with some new experiment or half-baked city plan, only to find that the city workers' heads were turned, dizzy from success, and plans must be reversed or changed again the next year. An unnumbered multitude lies dead after the last famine which was largely man-made and unnecessary. And multitudes more will perish from the bigotry and tyranny of a harsh regimented life leveled down to a drear and dead level by materialistic dogmatists. Whole libraries could be filled, but never will be, with the story of a peasantry suffering at the hands of a harsh and unfeeling, proletarian dictatorship which regards itself as a messianic class.

It was the decree of January 6, 1930, that quickened "the pace of collectivization" by the aid of "shock brigades" of industrial workers from the city, Party members and agents of the government. They resolved to deal a death blow to the developing capitalism of private enterprise and to "liquidate the kulaks as a class." It mattered not to them if there were prosperous individuals who were not exploiters but simply more enterprising, intelligent and successful peasants. There could be no exceptions when they were dealt with "as a class." There were plenty of jealous, or shiftless, or avaricious poor peasants who were prepared to complain bitterly of the successful peasant as a "fist" or exploiter. The government com-

plained that "the kulak let loose a wave of terror against the organizers of collective production, attempting to disorganize the collective farms through arson and looting." This was often true, but it was as nothing compared to the wave of terror which the government officials, the zealous shock brigaders and the ruthless Party members often launched against the kulaks, whether guilty or innocent. The individual was nothing; the class everything.

Broadly, the kulak class was undoubtedly capitalistic and menacing and had to go. The one thing which the leaders would rather die than permit was capitalism. Remembering their own suffering of a lifetime under its devastating conditions it is not strange that they took the methods they adopted to destroy it, root and branch.

The individual peasant had often been able to hide his grain and outwit the government by sabotage and evasion of his taxes. The collectives being more public could be more easily managed, and they enabled the government to standardize and socialize all processes and to control a monopoly of agricultural produce. The Communist Party suddenly cast a bomb into the midst of individual peasant agriculture that blasted and shattered it, and applied pressure often with such ruthless ferocity that it roused the hostility and resentment of the peasantry. Kulaks were cast from their homes, driven to some piece of waste land, deported to the wilds of Siberia, or the lumber camps of the North, as convict or forced labor. If they resisted or fought back they were promptly shot or arrested.

In the grandiose scheme of wholesale collectivization where Yakovlev, Commissar of Agriculture, had promised twice as much meat and milk as the country possessed at the beginning, everything went against them. There was the harshness and cruelty of the initial movement, the removal of the best brains and experience of the kulak class, the wholesale slaughter of cattle by a suspicious and rebellious peasantry, the bad rainfall and poor crops of 1931 and again in 1932, and finally, the blunders of inexperienced and over-zealous officials and Party members. These included the repeated changing of laws

DOGMATISM, ATHEISM, ANTI-RELIGION   37

and methods and the breaking of promises, with insensitive harshness to the sufferings of the outraged peasantry.

For instance, after promising in 1930 that their livestock would be exempt from socialization, the government proceeded to compel the members of collectives to turn over their animals to the community herds. In reply there was a second defiant slaughter of livestock. The Communist officials in the Ukraine exaggerated and falsified their figures on acreage and yield with the result that too heavy collections of grain were ordered from Moscow, and sometimes reimposed and collected a second time. In July, 1932, Molotov admitted that "in a good many districts and collective farms after they had fulfilled their quotas, new quotas were given" on the same crop.[1] The awful result was famine or near famine in the Ukraine, the North Caucasus, and other parts of the South the next year. Three officials were shot in the Ukraine for falsifying grain figures. It is estimated that a quarter of the cows, a third of the sheep, half of the pigs and ten per cent of the horses were slaughtered or perished for lack of fodder during this fierce campaign. As a result of this combination of official blunders, poor crops, lack of machinery, and mismanagement, followed by a dearth of food supplies and fodder, the peasants became discouraged and sullen. Sabotage followed in the working of the collectives. Out of revenge or apathy there was poor sowing and cultivation. The disastrous effects of this were felt by the people and in the grain collectives of the government. Thievery became common and was now punishable by death in some cases. The resistance of the Cossacks in the South led to wholesale deportation of whole communities.

[1] Molotov said: "In some cases this repeated itself three or four times. In the case of the Drabova district, where the leaders were tried for the abuses, the lines laid down by the Party were disregarded to an extraordinary degree. The slightest neglect of agricultural issues leads to most undesirable results." This is a mild understatement of the many deaths and deep resentment caused by such callousness and stupidity. Kaganovitch, Stalin's most brilliant lieutenant, arraigned the whole Communist Party of the Ukraine for mismanagement and ill treatment of the peasantry, saying: "The peasant joined the collective farm to obtain the advantages of large-scale farming, and if he does not obtain them he will feel badly, and will seek improvement for himself elsewhere."

For Rousseau's democratic myth of the sovereign people Marx substitutes the socialist myth of a messianic proletarian class. Marx was given to thinking in sharp antithesis of contrasted black and white, of universal and absolute character. This becomes rigid class thinking. The proletariat, atheism and virtue are one; the bourgeois, religion and greed are one. Selfishness and hypocrisy, religion and spirituality, for instance, are human traits. But to Marx selfishness, greed, hypocrisy, religion, are bourgeois or capitalistic traits as contrasted with proletarian virtues. The result is not only class thinking but mass cruelty to the kulaks, and class privilege for the proletariat.

Marx never grasped the full value of personality or of humanity as a whole. The class is always placed above humanity while the collectivity crushes personality. Materialism turns men into things. While Marx revolts against capitalism he carried its crass materialism over into his own economic system. His class dualism is a struggle between light and darkness; between the chosen class, which he substitutes for the remnant of his own chosen people, and the power of darkness. The demon of hate is never exorcised in his teaching.

Life in Russia, like the jerry-built, hasty mass structures they are rushing to completion all over the Soviet Union, is being regimented in the dreary barracks of a military system, in mass kitchens and in dirty dining-rooms, at the sacrifice of the priceless values of the home, of the whole world of free culture and thought achieved over the centuries. Class mentality and rigid materialistic orthodoxy smother, or crush, or asphyxiate the spiritual man. Free men are heavy of heart, silent and fearful in Russia. The proletarian mob rules and regulates with its crass materialism.

The social theorist de Man interprets Marx in the light of Adler's psychology. Marx upholds the proletariat's messianic vocation. This class reverses its inferiority complex and asserts its superiority. It makes up in arrogant egoism and imposes its former sufferings in venom upon all others conceived as class enemies. Revenge becomes a compensation for former humiliation.

In connection with the evils of the Soviet system I am compelled to speak of the unpleasant subject of the disreputable and repulsive methods which Communists feel called upon to employ in some countries. That is held to be right which furthers the Revolution, whether it be truth or falsehood, fairness or slander. All methods are lawful in warfare and they are at war with all the rest of the world. There must be no quarter for their class enemies. Since 1921 the Communist International has made efforts and overtures to secure a united front with the Socialists. But almost before any negotiations can be opened Communists in each country begin by pouring contempt and at times slander upon all Socialists and other more radical workers' organizations or parties. Their hatred of men like Ramsay MacDonald or Norman Thomas seems to know no bounds. They follow Lenin's description of the British Labor Party as "filthy froth on the surface of the world labor movement," or Rosa Luxemburg's designation of the German Social Democratic Party as a "stinking corpse."

The rôle of Norman Thomas, who is classed by them with ex-Mayor James J. Walker of New York City, is said to be "to assist fascism in placing its iron ring around the necks of the workers" who are warned against the "paralyzing pacifist poison of Thomas and the social fascists." "The Socialist Party is the third capitalist party and is allied with the gangsters and bosses." [1] Such tactics probably appeal to the mob, or men of a cerain type, but in the end they are self-defeating.

The Communist International controls the Communist parties in the various countries. It may arbitrarily remove any leadership which deviates or differs from its own and is not subservient to the shibboleths of the Moscow party lines. These national leaders often have to manufacture favorable reports of "growing radicalism" in each country. They sometimes do not understand national or local conditions, nor the problems of sectionalism in the United States, for instance. North, South or West are all one. There is no American nor

---

[1] See the New York *Daily Worker*, March 30, 1932, May 19 and June 7, 1933, or almost any current number.

British idiom. All conditions are judged by those in Russia
and slogans are bodily transferred without critical intelligence.
Imagine, for instance, as supposedly successful propaganda,
advocating setting up a Negro Republic in the Black Belt of
the South even before the anticipated workers' revolution in
America! Yet we are solemnly assured by the Communists
in New York that this is wise strategy, in harmony with American conditions, and that such propaganda is the autonomous
decision of the Communist Party in America.

They often begin to agitate, not upon strategic economic
problems, but by attacking all values, as for instance, in the
field of religion, by a harsh, dogmatic atheism. The dogma
and the propaganda are frequently unintelligent and inflexible,
not in the least adapted to conditions and realities in Anglo-
Saxon countries. They seem to learn no lesson from the small
vote polled by their Party in America, or of the fact that in
the last election in Great Britain, with an open safety valve
of the utmost freedom of speech, not a single Communist nor
avowed Fascist was elected to Parliament. Some of the most
radical labor workers, who are organizing the unemployed in
various states of America, report as follows: "If the Communists complain of the Socialists as the third capitalist party,
we could reply that the Communists are the second capitalist
party. Indeed the capitalists could well afford to hire them
for their stupid tactics in splitting or stultifying with venomous
hatred and division every labor movement which does not
swallow whole their harsh dogma and the demand for their
entire program of violence and propaganda, however out of
contact it may be with all reality."

There are those whose reactions to Russia are solely and
violently emotional. There are many who say: "If these things
are so, if the system in Russia embodies so much of evil it
must be wholly bad; we cannot possibly learn anything from
Russia and we will read no further." There are others whose
reaction is emotionally favorable. While they are hypercritical
concerning every evil in their own land, everything in Russia
is seen under a golden halo. They entirely lose their critical
faculty and all sense of realism in dealing with that country

because of the high idealism of its social aims. For my own part I shall attempt to pursue the middle course, calling a spade a spade, endeavoring objectively to recognize every virtue or vice, every good or evil, with dispassionate and unstinted praise or blame. Like any middle course it will inevitably receive the stones from both sides of the road.

The reactionary will be quite sure that all who have a good word to say for Russia are "supported by Moscow gold." The Communist will pour upon us his contempt and righteous indignation, and no copy of this book will be officially permitted in the Soviet Union. In spite of both I shall endeavor to tell the truth about Russia just as I see it, whether good or bad.

Before passing on to its possible positive contributions to human welfare, at the outset I wish to bring this indictment against the system in Soviet Russia. For its paralyzing bureaucracy, for its denial of liberty and its dictatorship that extends to almost all of life, which takes the form sometimes of a tyranny and sometimes of a terror; for its policy of world revolution by violence as the only panacea of social deliverance; and the relentless coercion of its continuing revolution, for the intolerance, bigotry and anti-religious persecution which spring from the harsh dogmatism of the system, we make our indictment. "Here, in sympathy at least, we are all in their crucible. Our civil liberties, our religious freedom, our tolerance, our liberalism, our whole complex of priceless values, which the coarse thumb and finger of a materialistic dogmatism fail to feel—nearly all we most value in life is at stake."

PART II

POSSIBLE CONTRIBUTIONS TO HUMAN WELFARE

PART II

POSSIBLE CONTRIBUTIONS TO HUMAN WELFARE

CHAPTER I

SOCIAL JUSTICE AND SOCIAL PLANNING

The central idea of the Soviet Union and Constitution is proletarian justice. By the abolition of functional private property no man may exploit his fellows or make a fortune from the toil of others. The state holds in trust for the workers all land, all means of production and credit for the use and profit of all on a basis of approximate equality. Russians, of course, do not claim that the present system is State Socialism, much less Communism, but modified State Capitalism. Their goal is complete socialization leading to Communism. They reject the conception of abstract or absolute justice for all classes as incompatible with the class struggle. "Justice" is held to assume "rights" under the capitalist class tension between exploiters and exploited. Under socialist society there may still be some demand for rights but in future Communism the tension will have disappeared and with it all conceptions or "rights," "justice," or "classes." There will then be true justice and liberty.

Thus in the end what we call justice will be secured for all. In the present imperfect transition each order represents a form of injustice. The West gives justice for the favored few owners and their more fortunate dependents; but it can guarantee neither assured employment, security of life, nor equal justice to the dependent workers. The Soviets provide justice for the mass of workers, and either retribution, or what we would call charity, for the former bourgeois minority. Their system has the advantage in providing for the majority, possibly nine-tenths of the population. Our Anglo-Saxon economic order has been based upon the principle of liberty, without always realizing that liberty for the strong means inequality

and injustice for the weak. The Soviet system is based upon the principle of what we call justice as an end, but through the means of the chosen class. It is easy for each to see the manifest defects in the system of the other. Certainly, if our contention in the first chapters has been true, the Soviets have much to learn in the matter of liberty and tolerance to make possible a richer life than their drab uniformity as yet provides. The more practical question for us will be what we have to learn in the matter of justice for our underprivileged masses and whether we will be willing to learn our lesson. The tendency of each system is to deny its own shortcomings.

A leading article in *Izvestia*,[1] the government organ, tells the world that: "The Soviet Government has never persecuted religion and religious organizations. On the contrary, as has frequently been confirmed by churchmen themselves, 'only in the U.S.S.R. does religion have actual and complete liberty.'" The hypocrisy here is as unconscious as in capitalist countries which insist that they have always given the workers equal justice and complete liberty. Each takes seriously its own virtues and the other's vices. In the minds of Communists it is not merely a question of which is theoretically the higher of two theories of abstract justice. It is rather the conviction that one system alone can provide equal justice, first for workers and ultimately for all. They believe that whatever the end in view, or the ideals professed, there can never be what we call social justice as long as the means of production are owned by one minority class and, therefore, that the conditions of life for the multitude are controlled by aliens in their own interest. No possessing class has ever given equal justice or privileges equal to their own to the non-possessing dependent class. The inevitable result is class strife, unemployment, suffering, injustice and final war or revolution.

For centuries Russia had suffered from an unjust tyranny of capitalism, imperialism and militarism under which, in the interests of the favored few, the masses of the people had been exploited, crushed and abandoned to poverty and illiteracy.

---

[1] *Izvestia*, January 4, 1931.

The means of production, and therefore the control of life itself, were in the hands of these few, with the result that society was sharply divided between rich and poor, and torn between the rising strife of classes, races and nations. The consequence was growing injustice and constantly recurring wars to redress the balance of this injustice. For a hundred years the struggle against the merciless tyranny of this system had been in vain. The warnings and pleadings of idealists like Tolstoy, the individual violence of the anarchists, and the influence of socially impotent religion, had not only failed to bring relief but had seemed instead to forge ever more firmly their chains of bondage. At last there appeared a system of philosophy and a technique of social change which not only promised relief in theory, but which created a body of leaders intelligent and ruthless enough to carry it out.

The heart of this system and the force of its appeal to both intellectuals and the masses was its ideal of ultimate justice. As between the ends of justice, liberty, peace, plenty, happiness, etc., justice is the highest and most rational objective for society at large. Liberty without justice or equality becomes license for the favored few. Peace without justice becomes stagnation, or tyranny over servile states or classes. Law and order, or the rights of property without justice, mean only the maintenance of inequality and of parasitic privilege. No system, no philosophy, no state, or church, or social order can permanently endure which does not both in theory and practice stand for fundamental justice.

The aim of the Communists was to confiscate all unearned wealth and all functional property. A man might have his personal property, such as a house, clothing, objects of art, a bicycle, an automobile, a radio, a bank account and government bonds. He might save his money, though there was now little opportunity or incentive to do so. All the privileges or security for himself or family for which he had once saved or hoarded were now *socially* provided for all who worked. No saving or seizing would enable him to own the raw materials, the machinery, business, or credit by which to make money or profit from his fellow men. The aim of proletarian

justice is not to provide charity but to abolish poverty and individual dependence by a social guarantee of livelihood. It proposes to practically equalize opportunity in material conditions and through the socialization of leisure and culture. All life and its privileges are to be shared.

The original theory of Communism was that the state should receive from each according to his ability and pay to each according to his need. But with the shiftless habits inherited from Czarism, in competition with the whole capitalist world, which was against them, the leaders were forced for a time to compromise and adopt some of the methods and incentives of capitalism. Thus in the second of his six points Stalin says: "We must put an end to the fluidity of labor, and its disastrous turnover of 30 or 40 per cent in half a year. We must introduce a more widely differentiated wage scale, providing a stimulus for advancement by piecework, and a higher reward for skilled labor. Marx and Lenin said that under Communism the difference between skilled and unskilled would disappear, but under our present conditions of socialism 'wages' must be paid according to labor performed and not according to need. In order to attach the workers to the factories we must improve living conditions. We demand labor discipline, intensity of effort, socialist competition, and shock-brigade methods." [1]

In the Soviet Union they seek approximate but not meticulous equality. They do not believe that all men are "born equal" or that they are equal in ability or in the value of their work, but the spread of inequality is less than in any other land. On the collective farm where we stayed this past summer the Chairman of the Soviet, or manager, together with the technicians, received less than three times the income of the cook in the kitchen. Wages in Moscow vary from about fifty to eight hundred roubles a month. The average is 1,432 roubles a year. The differences are functional, based upon ability or the quantity or quality of labor performed. They are not based upon inheritance or unearned income.

_____
[1] Stalin's speech at the Conference of the Leaders of Industry on June 23, 1931.

In England income varies in normal times from two shillings to a thousand pounds, or from fifty cents to five thousand dollars a day. The Viceroy of India receives over five thousand times the average income of India.[1] Henry Ford in good years received nearly forty thousand times as much as his individual workers.[2] In the estimation of the Russians this means not a system of justice but of privilege at one end of the scale, and of unemployment and poverty at the other. It is the very antithesis of justice.

In capitalist countries there is undeniably an ideal of material success and possession. There is liberty for the individual to amass an almost limitless fortune by speculation, manipulation of credit, or making money out of human labor, and by the monopoly of natural resources—water, gas, electric power, coal, minerals, the land, the dwellings of the poor—everything except the air men breathe. Upon these things chiefly the great fortunes of men have been built. They have seldom been founded upon invention and technical skill. Even a man like Henry Ford has "liberty" to amass a fortune of from one to two billion dollars, using men and machines for ten or twenty years and then scrapping his machines or laying off his men at a moment's notice without further obligation to either. If unemployed men march in peaceful procession to ask that he either give them work or meet his responsibility to them like other employers of the city, his private gunmen can shoot them down, kill some and wound others without interference.[3]

In the application of the ideal of what we call justice, more than in any other country in the world, the leaders of the Soviet Union share all that they have with the masses, at least all save power. They do not amass huge fortunes nor live in luxury. Instead of special privileges, which are few, the members of

---

[1] Mr. Gandhi wrote to the Viceroy: "Take your own salary. It is 21,000 rupees a month. . . . You are getting over five thousand times India's average income. The British Prime Minister is getting only ninety times Britain's average income. On bended knee I ask you to ponder over this phenomenon." *India and the Simon Report*, p. 180.

[2] *The New York World*, February 4, 1927.

[3] As on March 11, 1932.

the Party are loaded with heavy responsibilities. Their time, their money, their service, even much of their home life, must be sacrificed. In court, if guilty of any misdemeanor, the Party member is without excuse and is given the heaviest penalty or punishment.

This simplicity of life and requirement of heroic sacrifice is in keeping with the leaders who spent twenty years in prison, in poverty, in exile or in banishment. In the case of Marx in London: "For the first ten years, the family was hardly over the verge of starvation and he had to pawn his clothes for necessary expenses." His receipts as correspondent of the *New York Tribune* were a mere pittance and averaged less than a dollar a day. Lenin, with fortunes and palaces within his grasp, lived on less than two dollars a day in simplicity that bordered upon poverty. Stalin, after twenty years as a hunted conspirator, often hungry and for years in prison or in exile, formed the habits of long hours of work and the simple fare upon which he still lives. The leaders still try to maintain the austere revolutionary tradition. While engineers, especially foreigners, opera singers, and a few writers may make money and enjoy a higher income, the Party member must be limited to the bare essentials of the simple life. Upon him a "Party maximum" has been imposed. For years this was 225 roubles a month or about $3.75 a day. Most of the Party members received far less. But under the present inflation, where one "gold" rouble is worth some thirty paper roubles, and where the purchasing power of the rouble is worth only two or three cents, except in favored "closed" shops or kitchens or restaurants, this sum would hardly afford a bare living. There has been a tendency to abolish the "Party maximum" for men in certain favored positions such as technicians. But from their extra earnings the Party or government takes the greater part in excess taxes.

The rigor of the Communist's life is shown by the hours of strenuous service he has to give, his liability to be ordered off or transferred to any part of the U.S.S.R. on special duty, the periodic "cleansing" by which nominal or unworthy mem-

bers are weeded out, and by the budget of any member which shows his actual income and expenditures.

While we were in Russia this past summer the periodic cleansing of the Party was taking place. This occurs every few years and lasts for many months, often for several hours a day. One of the Communist leaders arrived from such a meeting for his interview with us a full hour late. No matter what the engagement he could not think of leaving the meeting which was protracted for five hours. Practically every member of the Party is placed as it were on trial for his faith, his works, his manner of life. Searching questions are asked of the man himself, of his fellow members, and of outsiders, concerning his orthodoxy, his zeal, his sacrifice. About ten per cent of the three and a half million members will be excluded during this cleansing. It would have been well for the Christian Church, not to mention political parties, if they had had such periodic cleansings to prune away the dead wood and keep them vital and in touch with reality.

Concerning the budgets of Communists I shall give two which I believe to be typical. "A" is a skilled worker, a Party member, a shock brigader. His wage is approximately 400 roubles a month. For obvious reasons I will not be too specific. Before the deflation of the dollar this would have been about $200 by the official government exchange. But with roubles selling freely on the "Black Bourse" or by individuals at forty to the dollar, the purchasing power of his wage is *very* little.[1]

Out of his 400 roubles a month this worker in Russia spends 16 roubles, or about 4 per cent, for rent. All rents are low for workers. Of his wages 10 per cent must be invested in the State loan under pressure. This is harder to escape than was the purchase of Liberty Bonds in war time. He pays 10 roubles in income tax, 8 to his trade union, 16 for dues to the

[1] Mr. W. H. Chamberlain observed while in America: "What is regarded as acute want in America might easily pass as a satisfactory standard of living in the Soviet Union. The food allotments which our unemployed receive in cities like Milwaukee, where relief work is well organized, are about equal to the normal rations of many employed workers in Russia." *Atlantic Monthly*, July 1933.

Party, 15 for cultural and social services. Upon his ration card he obtains 2 pounds of bread a day for himself and 1 pound for his wife. Bread costs him about 9 roubles a month, meat 3.50, sugar 4, grain 5. But upon these limited rationed amounts he cannot live, especially as his wife is ill. In the outside stores or in the open market prices are very high. Butter is 20 roubles a pound, bread 6 roubles a loaf, ham 35 roubles a kilo, milk 2.50 a litre, shoe repairing 11.33 per pair. Medicine and education for his children are free. The equivalent of about a third of his salary he receives in such social services. This worker is typical in the fact that he can save nothing and that his life is hard. As a loyal Party member he is a firm believer in the system, but his wife is sick and he can get no passport nor permit to leave Russia.

"B" is also a prominent and influential Party member. His salary and income are over 700 roubles a month. The tax he pays to the government is only 7 roubles a month. His rent also is small. Of his salary he must pay to the Party 3 per cent on the first 350 roubles, but upon all he receives above that he must pay also 20 per cent of the remainder. In all he pays about 100 roubles a month to the Party. To his trade union he must pay about half that amount. One and a half month's salary every ten months he must advance for Soviet loans or bonds. There are then a seemingly endless number of societies, appeals, obligations and causes to which he must subscribe. Already 250 roubles of his month's salary are required to meet his special obligations as a Party member. He is just able to live upon the remainder in some degree of comfort as a specially privileged member. But he can save practically nothing. Except for his free sixth day out in the country, his life is hard. All life is hard in this strenuous land. This man has made heavy sacrifices for his cause. Members of his family who fought in the White Armies perished during the civil war. But if he had lost them all, or if he sacrificed life itself, he would still believe unto death in his ideal of justice for the masses for whom he has been struggling as an intellectual ever since his student days. In this he is a typical embodiment of the ideal.

Social Planning

We shall consider in this section the value of planning both in Russia and in Anglo-Saxon countries. In sharp contrast during the world depression while production and trade fell disastrously and unemployment mounted to over thirty millions in the West, the Soviet Union entirely eliminated unemployment, doubled its industrial production and began the transformation of backward rural Russia into a modern mechanized, industrial state.

It is the firm belief of the Russians, though time only can prove it, that they have permanently eliminated the cyclical evil of forced unemployment and domestic crises. For at least a generation to come consumers' demands, with a rapidly rising standard of living, will be in excess of production. Continuous payment of prescribed wages automatically insures purchasing power and calculable effective demand. There are no wastes of idle machinery or labor force, none in competitive advertising, in an army of needless middle-men or in useless luxuries. The needed production of each necessity can be calculated and the whole unified mechanism of production, distribution and consumption, of industry and agriculture, of credit and home and foreign trade can be adjusted in one harmonious "plan of the whole." A planned economy has maximum production power both for men and machines, and needs less capital and plant when neither is idle. There is no idle class to support at the top or at the bottom of the social scale. Almost the whole adult population is engaged in productive work. The percentage of non-working elements such as the bourgeoisie, clergy and declassed or disfranchised elements was reduced from 5.1 per cent in 1926 to 1 per cent in 1931. There is almost no sabotage and no wastage from long strikes. While the U.S.A. is using its agricultural machinery a little over forty per cent of its capacity, the U.S.S.R. uses its machinery almost one hundred per cent. The chief advantage of the Soviet system is that it prevents the accumulation of profit and capital in the hands of the few.

Instead it turns wealth into the two channels of use and the production of new wealth without hoarding.

Russia has the double advantage of an open frontier with the rapid pioneering development of her vast resources, harnessed not to competitive individual enterprise, but to a coordinated plan. Unemployment they believe to be unnecessary in a planned system, granted sufficient intelligence, experience and social control. A planned economy can fully utilize without wasting its natural resources. In the oil fields the wells are properly spaced and economically worked, in contrast to the forest of wells crowded on both sides of a boundary line to tap a competitor's flow in California and other states. Congested private wealth in Russia is considered a hindrance to personal happiness and to social usefulness. Social wealth justly shared may be a boon to all.

Over the entire economic system of the U.S.S.R. is the Council of Labor and Defence which originally directed the Red armies in the field upon all fronts. Still very much like a General Staff directing and coordinating the armies of industry, agriculture and trade this Council is practically a Cabinet directing the whole economic life of the nation. It will be recalled that the turn toward Allied victory in the War came only when a General Staff was established to coordinate and direct all forces.

Under this Soviet Council the actual mechanism of planning is operated by the experts of the Gosplan, or State Planning Commission. This is an advisory body, not an executive authority. It has gradually built up the largest staff of trained statisticians and experts that ever existed, not for theoretical reports but for immediate, practical nation-wide use. It is the cortex, or brain center, of the toiling masses to coordinate their every activity and balance demand and production. Each September the "draft control figures" calculate the expected output of each branch of industry and agriculture. This plan is submitted and discussed, often the workers democratically proposing a "counter plan" to further increase output. Since the whole plan and plant and output is their own, and since

all the profits go toward increasing either their income or their capital, the workers most of all have their hearts in it.

After submission of the tentative plan to each enterprise, when revised and reconsidered, it passes the Cabinet of the Council of Labor and Defence and the Political Bureau. When finally sanctioned it is published as the law of the land. *The Plan couples long democratic discussion with highly centralized control, as of an army in the field; the practical experience of every laborer and manager, with the directing brain of the expert, with no thought of the profit or advantage of any one class but of the welfare of the whole practically equalitarian body.* This Plan is annually checked up by actual results and in the light of experience fresh control figures are issued each year.

The Five Year Plan once adopted, charted, visualized, detailed and placarded before each factory and individual workman, and proclaimed by all the popular and powerful propaganda agencies of the state, assumes almost mystic significance. It proposes to change the face of the landscape, build cities near the supply of raw materials, to rationalize, mechanize, industrialize the whole country, to "build socialism" and make the country self-sufficient and impregnable from a military point of view. It becomes one giant stride toward the building of a new social order and civilization. The nation dreams it, dramatizes it. Youth incorporates it in their plays and sports and dances; they shout its slogans in parades and processions. And finally, in spite of many faults and failings and postponements, the toiling peasants and workers at last incarnate it in the national life. Both in conception and achievement it is something new under the sun.

The Russians believe that national character depends upon environment and that it is almost infinitely adaptable. They have suddenly passed from the slowest to the fastest tempo in the world, though not without agony.[1] But they plan like

---

[1] Molotov is realistic when he admits: "In capitalist production there is a general anarchy, but in each separate industrial establishment there is a plan. In the Soviet Union, on the other hand, there is a general plan, but within many industrial establishments there is anarchy."—He puts his finger here upon the weakness of each system.

titans and believe that they can slowly change human nature within, and the landscape without. The latter they are certainly doing.

The whole scheme is a plan of the multitude as well as of the experts. Millions are engaged in drawing it up and in its execution. From start to finish they feel that they are not hands, nor cogs in a machine for private profit of alien possessors, but equal owners and operators. Gradually a new social acquisitiveness takes the place of the old industrial profit motive and competition. A new initiative is developed in the working multitude and a new interest that always comes with ownership. As industry is organized for use instead of profit gradually there is built up the habit of the will to serve, in place of the greed of gain. There is no appeal to the heroic. A change of plan based upon principle means a change of environment, which in turn modifies character. The whole process is logical, natural, scientific. It does not go against the grain of human nature but is based upon a sound psychological understanding of the human being.

Once the fear of insecurity is removed, once the dread of sickness, old age or unemployment is eliminated, the system has the same effect that it has upon the owner in other lands. The average employer in capitalist countries does not lie idle because of his security. He may play a bit more golf but probably he works harder than any of his men. So in Soviet Russia the risk is lifted from the shoulders of the individual and distributed mutually among all. The individual blows of fate—death, accident, illness, old age and unemployment—can be triumphantly borne under a scientifically shared risk, socially insured. The social ownership of his job and the right to work is now guaranteed to each. Fear and anxiety for his job, his health, his family and their future are now lifted to the broad shoulders of the new social order. Mutual dependence gives independence of fear and want. There is no longer excuse or incentive for profiteering or exploiting the needs of others. Habits of cooperation gradually replace those

of competition, as the jungle gives place to the civilized city. The impossibility of owning productive capital cuts the root of the profit motive and the human soil is cleared for a new growth.   The benefits of a planned economy are not merely material.   They extend to every realm of life.

Not to believe in a plan is not to believe in human reason. It is to believe that the law of the jungle and of raw nature "red in tooth and claw," are superior to planned intelligence. It is to hold that blind selfishness will produce better results than cooperative endeavor.   The plan must be judged, however, not by its ideals but by its fruits and concrete results.   Here for the first time in history 165,000,000 people were united in a single plan in one titanic endeavor.   They lived upon a dream and a ration of bread.   The bread was none too plentiful, but after one experiment they are ready for another.   Shall we pause to review, in brief outline, the broad accomplishments of the first Plan which lasted from October 1, 1928, to December 31, 1932, or four and a quarter years?

Did the First Five Year Plan Succeed?

The first Five Year Plan shook Russia like a blast of dynamite.   There was, it is true, a measure of failure, a postponement or shortcoming in certain important matters such as transportation, coal, metals and consumption goods.   Prices were higher, living standards and real wages were much lower than the Plan had called for, and quality was sacrificed to quantity.   Nevertheless, viewed broadly, the achievements of the shortened period of four and a quarter years were impressive and undeniable in most fields.

While the proportion of most other countries declined, the U.S.S.R.'s share of world trade increased and moved up from seventeenth place, which it occupied at the beginning of the Plan, to eleventh place at the end.   In 1928 Russia was a

backward agrarian country; in 1933 it was a reorganized industrial country.[1]

The fixed capital of the socialized sector of national economy more than doubled under the Plan, while the gross output of industrial production increased 218.5 per cent and was three-fold higher than the pre-war level. The machine building industry increased 4.4 times under the Plan and ten-fold over pre-war figures. In 1932, 10,000 harvesting combines were manufactured.[2]

During normal years, in good times, the United States has increased its industrial production about 4 per cent a year; the industrial increase in the U.S.S.R. during the Plan averaged 21.6 per cent per annum.[3] From 1920 to 1930 the average annual increase in the productivity of labor in the United States was 4.7 per cent; during the Plan in Russia it increased 41 per cent. The average annual wages of workers increased from 153 roubles in 1923, to 703 in 1928, and to 1432 roubles in 1932,

---

[1] In 1928 the share of industry represented only 48 per cent of the total production of industry and agriculture, while at the end of 1932 it represented 70 per cent. *Summary of the Fulfillment of the First Five Year Plan,* p. 11. This compares well with the output of industry in Germany of 80.3 per cent, and in the United States of 82.6 per cent in 1929.

[2] In 1928 the output of machines in the Soviet Union was only 7 per cent of the United States. By 1932 machine output was 56.9 per cent of the United States, 140 per cent of that of England, and 151 per cent of that of Germany. During the period of the Plan the output both of electrical engineering and agricultural machinery increased 5.5 fold, general engineering 4.4 fold, electric power 4 fold, iron and steel industries 3.5 fold, mining and lumber 2.5 fold, fuel industries 2.3 fold, the output of clothing 3.5 fold, and the food industry 2.2 fold. All this during the period of the world depression constituted a world's record. *Ibid.,* pp. 14, 59.

[3] The decline of industry in the West in contrast to its increase in Russia during the depression, reckoning 1928 as normal at 100, was as follows:

Countries	1932
The Capitalist World	67
U.S.A.	57
Great Britain	89
Germany	57
France	74
U.S.S.R.	218.5

Ibid., p. 18.

an increase in money wages of 103.6 per cent during the Plan.[1]

There was a fourfold increase in social insurance funds during the Plan and remarkable progress in cultural activity. Whereas in Czarist Russia in 1913 some 33 per cent of the population was literate, in 1932 the proportion was 90 per cent.

If we compare the indices of construction for three principal industrial countries during the depression they are as follows:[2]

Year	U.S.S.R. Capital Construction	U.S.A. Building Permits in 37 states	Germany General Index of Construction
1928	100	100	100
1932	357.4	20.8	37.6

It would be instructive to know how far this contrast was due to accidents of fortune, or how far to a planned economy in contrast to planless competition which regards depressions as inevitable results of a "natural" cycle.

Characteristically the Cooperative public catering services in the towns increased from 1500 to 15,982 establishments, including factory kitchens. The number of workers served in the cities by these catering establishments increased during the period of the Plan from 750,000 to 14.8 millions, serving 29 million dishes a day. The Soviets believe this has released millions of women who had been "oppressed, smothered, dulled and degraded by petty household cares." They are now engaged in productive work which they seem to prefer with their independent wages and equality of status.

Without burdening the reader with unnecessary statistics a general summary of the achievements of the first Five Year Plan may be condensed in a footnote.[3]

---

[1] There is, however, a controlled but substantial inflation which was no part of the Plan. Since the middle of 1930 the official index numbers of prices and wages are no longer published, unfortunately, and we cannot compute the real wages.

[2] Figures for U. S. A. are from the Federal Reserve Bulletin for March 1933.

[3] During the Plan in total industrial production in the world the U.S.S.R. has moved from fifth to second place, in the production of pig iron it rose

Planning in America and Britain

One has only to review the articles in the press and magazines during the last five years, the proceedings of the American Congress or of Parliament in Britain, and the bibliographies of the libraries to see the wide influence which the Russian system of planning has had in Anglo-Saxon countries both in the realm of theory and practice. The necessity of this was accentuated of course by the world depression which seemed to indicate that there were fatal defects and handicaps in a planless economy. This conclusion became the more glaring and unescapable when the one country alone which had a plan was advancing while all the others were receding or falling off in their whole economic life. The Russian Plan seemed to turn a searchlight upon our chaos. Wesley Mitchel in his study *Business Cycles* admitted that they were the accompaniment of capitalism. The question at once arose, *could capitalism plan?* Would a plan be a waste of good paper to decorate the archives of libraries, except in the exact measure of its social control? And would the independent American people in the land of *laissez faire* accept governmental interference in business? Could the billion "wild horses" of industry be harnessed for the service of mankind, and would the present owners permit it?

When the number of the unemployed finally rose to some

---

from third to second place, in coal from sixth to fourth place, in machine building from fourth to second place, in electric energy from eighth to third place.

The place now occupied by the U.S.S.R. in regard to the basic industries compared with 1913 and 1928 is as follows:

	1913	1928	1932 In World	1932 In Europe
Electric Power	15	10	6	4
Coal	6	6	4	3
Pig Iron	5	6	2	1
General Machine Building	4	4	2	1
Agricultural Machinery	—	4	1	1
Oil	2	3	2	1
Automobiles	—	12	6	4
Total Industrial Production	—	5	2	1

sixteen millions in America[1] and over thirty millions in the industrial nations of the West, a flood of suggestions and a whole literature on planning emerged, beginning with the writings of Lewis Lorwin of the Brookings Institution in 1928, and continuing up to the series of concrete plans proposed and inaugurated by President Roosevelt in 1933.[2]

Planning was now transformed from a Bolshevik heresy to an orthodoxy of capitalism in the effort to save itself. It was generally agreed by most of the writers that the philosophy of *laissez faire* had been fairly tried and had hopelessly failed: "We are at the end of an epoch, the epoch of free and unrestricted competition. Our system has failed. Six million (later sixteen million) unemployed prove it. We need a new system." [3]

It was pointed out that national planning was but an extension of the best engineering practice and had been successfully tested under the War Industries Board controlling 350 industries, fixing prices and determining production with a total staff of 1500 business men, economists, engineers and statisticians running the country. Only planning had won the war. "A tendency to reject peace-time planning on grounds of an-

---

[1] This included an estimated number of twelve millions out of work and four million youth who had been unable to find employment according to *The Business Week* and the *Bureau of Labor Statistics*. President Roosevelt in his broadcast of October 22, 1933, said: "Fair estimates showed twelve or thirteen millions unemployed last March."

[2] Among the official or semi-official plans suggested were those of President Hoover, *A Twenty-Year Plan for America,* Senator La Follette, Congressman Person, Henry Harriman, President of the Boston Chamber of Commerce, the National Chamber of Commerce, William Green and Matthew Woll of the American Federation of Labor, as well as numberless private individuals like Newton D. Baker, Charles A. Beard, Nicholas Murray Butler, Stuart Chase, J. M. Clark, Wallace Donham, E. C. Lindeman, Lewis Lorwin, H. S. Person of the Taylor Society, George Soule, author of *A Planned Society,* Gerard Swope, President of the General Electric Company, Owen D. Young, M. J. Tolley, with a plan for agriculture, and the "Brain Trust" of President Roosevelt.

[3] J. Russell Smith of Columbia. John Stuart Mill well said: "When society requires to be rebuilt, there is no use to rebuild it on the old plan." Charles A. Beard writes: "The challenge to capitalism and the effort to meet the challenge by a combination of individual liberty and initiative with collective planning, control and action, seem to mark a new phase in the intellectual and moral development of mankind."

tipathy against the Russian Revolution would be as silly as it would have been for our forefathers to discard democracy just because democracy in France was one of the achievements of the French Revolution." [1]

Gerard Swope urged that industry should be given a first chance to save itself. Organized industry should take the lead, production and consumption should be coordinated. He proposed the protection of employees by unemployment insurance, life and disability insurance, pensions, etc., in the interest of the efficiency of business itself. Owen D. Young pointed out that "we are forced to recognize that every advance in social organization requires the voluntary surrender of a certain amount of individual freedom by the majority and the ultimate coercion of the minority. If results are to be attained they call for surrender somewhere." [2]

Many of the plans proposed some kind of a National Economic Board, the stabilization of prices, the control of credit, finance and speculation, and a nationally organized labor market, with a nation-wide employment service such as exists in other advanced industrial countries. They urged the study of the Russian plan in order to apply some of its principles to our own economic system. An American plan must deal with sick industries suffering from chronic excess capacity and occasional over-production, and the persistence of inefficient, high-cost concerns. It must deal with serious technological unemployment, with business cycles and depressions, and finally it would be forced to face international trade, credit and war debts. Lewis Lorwin foresaw an ultimate non-political *World Planning Board*.

With all these suggestions, however, *industry could not or would not reform itself* and it was finally left to Mr. Roosevelt, while business was still sinking into ever deeper depths of depression which seemed to have no bottom, to devise and boldly to execute a series of plans for the recovery of industry

---

[1] George Soule, quoted by Hugo Haan in his *American Planning*, p. 41.
[2] New York Times, Sept. 17, 1931.

and agriculture. Meanwhile the more conservative British were busily suggesting various plans to save the failing industries of England.[1]

American industry had been left alone by government as it sank through almost four years of the depression, but it proved to be pathetically helpless. It warned the public of the terrible dangers of a planned economy. Economic life was said to be a self-regulating thing, relying upon the unconscious, automatic functioning of the markets. It was presided over by some sacred law. The only intelligence admitted must be that "of individuals or organizations seeking their own particular wages or their own particular profits, but not seeing with any great clearness the movements of the system as a whole." One central plan would be highly dangerous. For safety there must be a "multitude of conflicting special plans."[2] Perhaps

---

[1] Captain Harold Macmillan, himself a capitalist and a Conservative member of Parliament, suggested the following plan which would consolidate each industry under the great banks and trusts, in his memorandum *The State and Industry*, as follows:

A. "Representative National Councils for each industry or group of industries whose function would be to encourage and assist the efficient coordination of purchasing, production, marketing, and research, on lines which would enable the industry concerned to evolve towards the highest possible unity of policy and the necessary degree of centralization of control.

B. "The Councils to be given status by Government recognition of them as the authority with which it would deal on all matters affecting the interests which they represented.

C. "Provision to be made for the association of Labor with the discussions of these Councils in all matters affecting the welfare of the workers, with a view to avoiding strikes or lockouts.

D. "In the ten groups listed by the Board of Trade Journal for purposes of the Index of Production in manufacturing industries, it would be easy to transform existing national associations into the proposed industrial councils. By extending the scheme to the 24 groups listed by the Ministry of Labour Gazette the whole field of industry, commerce, and finance would be covered.

E. "A sub-parliament of industry elected from these Councils each sending two or three representatives. These representatives would be available for consultation by the Import Duties Advisory Committee in its efforts to reconcile the interests of producing and consuming industries where protective measures were under discussion."

[2] Benjamin M. Anderson, Jr., economist of the Chase National Bank, *A Planned Economy*, pp. 7-11. Even with all the banks closed and the steel industry working only 22 per cent of capacity, Mr. Albert H. Wiggin could only assure us: "We will always have economic cycles and periods of depression and prosperity."

Russia might plan, but America must face the future blind-folded and trust to luck, or providence, or the working of some mysterious and unknown law. We had brilliant examples of a plan for a single company or plant like the American Telephone and Telegraph Company in changing from manual to dial telephones, or the Ford Motor Works in its efficient mass production. Intelligence could operate here, but it was held to be highly destructive in the coordination of unified planning. In the limited experience of a succesful and rich nation with its recent frontier and present mass production it was not realized that to draw the line at the application of intelligence to the individual plant or company, was as illogical and as self-defeating as to advocate that each machine in a given plant should be owned and operated independently by an individual operator. Experience is a hard taskmaster and the logic of events and the breakdown of the old system was driving the country inexorably toward disaster or else effective planning under social control. Mr. Roosevelt within the framework of capitalism felt forced to launch upon a gigantic experiment just as Soviet Russia had been, with her back against the wall of the past failure of an obsolete system. Members of the old order in both cases whose special privileges have been lost or threatened will resent both experiments and prophesy their dire failure. But whether the plan in the U.S.S.R. or that in the U.S.A. succeeds or fails it must be recognized that as surely as we have left the ninetenth century for the twentieth, so certainly have we passed, at least for the time being and perhaps finally, from an era of individualistic, haphazard *laissez faire* to one of economic planning under social control, whether we call it a Five Year Plan, or use the euphemistic phrase of "the partnership of business and government," under a "new deal." Adapted to our own ends we are already beginning to learn our first lessons from Soviet Russia's planned economy.

The American people are now in the midst of one of the most momentous experiments ever undertaken by any nation. Undoubtedly it is the boldest and most far-reaching plan in industry, in agriculture and in the whole sweep of economic

life ever undertaken by any nation except Soviet Russia. We must also realize that we must either whole-heartedly give the experiment a fair trial or else refuse to give it. We cannot serve two masters, nor operate under two contradictory economic systems at once. We must take our choice between a planless and a planned system. Each has its advantages and disadvantages.

On the one hand is the possibility of an unplanned economy with its advantage of individual freedom and initiative, but with its danger of anarchy and chaos, increasing crises, depressions and colossal unemployment. This planless drifting, trusting to the natural law of supply and demand, seemed after a fair trial for nearly three and a half years, from October 29, 1929, to March 4, 1933, to have disastrously failed. After over 10,000 banks had failed and all the remaining banks in the country had been compelled to close their doors, we appeared to be on the verge of national bankruptcy. There seemed to be no way out of the depression under an unplanned economy.

On the other hand, if we take the path of a planned economy we must have a complete plan and go the whole way. Conceivably we might succeed under either economy, but with half a plan, half free and half controlled, no nation can succeed. Professor Rexford G. Tugwell, one of President Roosevelt's most trusted advisers, just a year before he himself began to participate in the plan, wrote these farsighted words regarding the undeniable difficulties in capitalist planning as follows: "It would be as unnatural for American businesses, which live by adventures in competition, to abdicate their privileges voluntarily, as it is to expect rival militarists to maintain peace, and for the same reason. . . . The deadliest and most subtle enemy of speculative profit-making which could be devised would be an implemented scheme for planning production. . . . Every depression period wearies us with insecurity; the majority of us seem all to be whipped at once; and what we long for temporarily is safety rather than adventure. Planning seems at first to offer this safety and so gains a good deal of unconsidered support. But when it is discovered that planning for production means planning for consumption too; that some-

thing more is involved than simple limitation of amounts which can be sold at any price producers temporarily happen to find best for themselves; that profits must be limited and their uses controlled; that what really is implied is something not unlike an integrated group of enterprises run for its consumers rather than for its owners—when all this gradually appears, there is likely to be a great changing of sides. . . . The essence of business is its free venture for profits in an unregulated economy. Planning implies guidance of capital uses; this would limit entrance into or expansion of operation. Planning also implies adjustment of production to consumption; and there is no way of accomplishing this except through a control of prices and of profit margins. . . . To take away from business its freedom of venture and of expansion, and to limit the profits it may acquire, is to destroy it as business and to make of it something else. . . . Little by little, however, *we may be driven the whole length of this road;* once the first step is taken, which we seem about to take, that road will begin to suggest itself as the way to a civilized industry. For it will become more and more clear, as thinking and discussion centers on industrial and economic rather than business problems, that *not very much is to be gained until the last step has been taken.*" [1]

---

[1] Rexford G. Tugwell, *Proceedings of the American Economic Association,* March, 1932, pp. 83, 88-89. Italics are ours.

CHAPTER II

A CLASSLESS SOCIETY

In contrast to Anglo-Saxon race and color prejudice and the economic exploitation and political disfranchisement of the Negro in parts of the United States, Soviet Russia has adopted as its goal a classless society without distinction of race, color or caste, and is pressing forward with determination toward its attainment. There is probably less race and color prejudice in the Soviet Union today than in any country in the world that has a mixture of races. And this is in a land of recent Jewish pogroms fomented by the Czarist church and state. If we can learn any lesson in this regard from Russia, we are forced to ask why, if the Communist and the Moslem can attain to such a measure of practical brotherhood and equal comradeship, the Anglo-Saxon nations should be so cursed with the malady of race prejudice?

The ideal of a classless society, involving complete racial equality, is a matter both of fundamental principle and of consistent practice in the Soviet Union. Their dominant aim is: "The abolition of exploitation of men by men, the entire abolition of the division of the people into classes, the supression of exploiters, the establishment of a socialist society." They purpose "to abolish all parasitic elements, free from enslavement millions of laborers in Asia and the exploited nations, obtain self-determination for oppressed nationalities and complete equality for all citizens regardless of race, color or nationality." They aim "to end the domination of capitalism, make war impossible, transform the whole world into a

cooperative commonwealth, and bring about real human freedom and brotherhood." [1]

In Soviet Russia the classless principle of racial equality is applied among the more than 180 nationalities, white, brown and yellow, who speak some 150 different languages and dialects. All the republics and nationalities are granted racial, linguistic, cultural and a measure of local political autonomy; but not economic independence. All, of course, must conform to the Marxian political program and the economic plans of the U.S.S.R. They have complete determination of their own language, literature, schools and culture. There has been a progressive elimination of racial, cultural and national hostilities which were rife under Czarist oppression and the former forced Russification of these conquered peoples. Apart from political enemies they have no minorities problem such as exists in Germany, Poland, or Italy.

The principle of human equality runs through the whole Soviet system. Every great revolution proclaims *liberty* for oppressed classes, centers in *equality* and aims at *fraternity*. This principle of racial equality is a powerful factor in challenging the imperialistic rule of the white race over some seven-eighths of the planet. For the first time since British rule, which now extends over a quarter of the globe, began govern-

---

[1] From the Manifesto on the *Third Moscow International*. The Constitution of the U.S.S.R. proclaims: "National freedom and equality and the fraternal collaboration of nations peacefully dwelling side by side. The attempts of the capitalist world to solve the problem of nationalities by combining the free development of peoples with the system of exploitation of man by man have proved fruitless. . . . It has become possible to abolish national oppression root and branch . . . to form one socialist family." In Part II of the Constitution the ten principal Republics "agree to unite into one federal state to be known as the Union of Soviet Socialist Republics." In Article 4: "Each Union Republic shall retain its right freely to secede from the Union." In the Constitution of the Russian Republic, or R.S.F.S.R.: "The right of all citizens to practice freely any religious belief or to engage in anti-religious propaganda remains inviolate." In Article 9: "The Republic regards labor as an obligation for all citizens." In Article 69: "The following persons may not vote or be elected: a. Any person who employs hired labor for profit; b. who lives on unearned income; c. private traders and middlemen; d. ministers of any religious denomination; e. agents of the former police force and members of the former reigning dynasty; f. any person of unsound mind; g. any person sentenced for crime."

ing colored peoples on the aristocratic principle, that principle is now challenged in the Orient by that of the proletariat with its equalizing, leveling principle. White rule has been established upon the basis of its claimed superiority in race, culture, wealth and power.[1] But that rule is now challenged to its very foundations not only by Soviet Russia but by almost the whole of the awakening continent of Asia and by the more advanced portions of Africa. The principle of racial equality will appeal powerfully to every oppressed, or conquered, or exploited people. Race prejudice thus becomes not only an ethical issue but a very practical problem for the imperialistic white race, especially for the dominant Anglo-Saxon.

No people has profited more by this classless principle than the Jews who for centuries had been subject to geographic, economic and religious discrimination. They were forbidden from favored areas and occupations and educational institutions. Most lived in residential "pales" and in poverty. They were chiefly middlemen and city people yet they were formerly forbidden to live in Leningrad or Moscow. Religious and economic prejudice against them was fomented by pogroms under the Czarist régime. While the Hitler revolution has persecuted the Jew, that in Russia has emancipated him. There are now nine teachers' colleges, five state theatres, forty newspapers, a complete school system and many agricultural colonies especially for Jews.[2] There is a hold-over of some Jewish prejudice from Czarist days among the older generation, but

---

[1] Lord Lawrence as Viceroy of India said: "We are here by our own moral superiority." Lord Shaftesbury claimed: "The natives of India know perfectly well that they are governed by a superior race." Lord Curzon informed India "that truth was rather a Western than an Oriental virtue and that craftiness and diplomatic wiles have in the East always been held in much repute." Since the rise of the Soviet Union foreign viceroys and imperialistic rulers no longer dare use such insulting language. The above quotations are from the author's *Challenge of the East,* pp. 56, 57.

[2] Of three million Jews in the U.S.S.R., over half a million are workers, chiefly in heavy industry, half a million are handicraft workers, a quarter of a million are peasants, and several hundred thousand are in government departments, education and the professions. Some 86,000 Jews were settled in their own agricultural colonies on eleven million acres of land. A fuller account of the Jewish problem will be found in Appendix II of this volume.

no government in the world is so determined to exterminate
it and no people are so rapidly responding to the new ideals.
Persecution of Jews, which is secretly encouraged in Germany,
is severely punished in Soviet Russia.   Peasants who beat a
Jew in one village were sent to jail for three years, and one
man was sent to prison for making an anti-semitic joke.   When
the old intelligentsia were largely eliminated, the Jews had the
best brains among those who remained.   Associated with Stalin,
as the most brilliant of the ten members of the inner Political
Bureau, is L. M. Kaganovitch who is a Jew.   So also are four
cabinet ministers, M. M. Litvinov in Foreign Affairs, Y. A.
Yakovlev in Agriculture, A. P. Rosengoltz in Foreign Trade,
and M. L. Rukhimovitch who has headed the Department of
Railways, now succeeded by A. A. Andreyev.

Communists consider race prejudice to be degrading and
they are particularly indignant at any manifestation of it.
When in 1930 two Americans objected to the presence of an
American Negro in a dining hall in Stalingrad and insulted
and then assaulted him, public opinion all over Russia was
aroused.   The Americans were first sentenced to two years
imprisonment, but the sentence was commuted to expulsion
from the U.S.S.R. for ten years on the grounds that "they had
been inoculated with race hatred by the capitalist system of
exploiting the lower races."

At any manifestation of racial or anti-Jewish feeling the
Communist Party, the Soviet Government, the labor unions,
the public schools, the youth movement and the press are
uncompromisingly against it, and the younger generation is
growing up with less race prejudice than in any other country.
When Negroes travel in Russia all hotels, resorts and homes
are as open to them as to white people.   The Russians do not
care whether a man is white or black, yellow or brown.   They
are particularly friendly to people of backward culture and of
other races.   Though there is not the slightest prejudice against
intermarriage, it is little practiced, and racial identity is preserved rather than destroyed.   The Russian word "comrade"
covers a more real equality than does the more romantic but
less real term "brotherhood" in the West.   Even in old Czarist

days the Russians got on better with Oriental races than did Anglo-Saxons. Today their doctrine of equality is making an increasingly powerful appeal to all conquered or exploited peoples in Asia.

Anglo-Saxon Race and Color Prejudice

As I have had to meet the people of many lands during the last forty years I find there are principally four peoples who suffer most from this disease of race and color prejudice. I never find it among Slavic peoples nor to any great extent among the Scandinavian or Latin races of Northern or Southern Europe. It does not exist among the peoples of Latin America or over most of Asia. It has taken its deepest hold among the Americans, the British, the Germans and among the high caste people of India in their treatment of the "untouchable" outcastes.

In the United States we practice segregation of the Negro as an inferior race. In the cities of a whole section of South Africa the Negro, by law, is forbidden the use of the sidewalks, but must walk with the cattle in the street just because he is an African upon his own continent and does not belong to the conquering race. If gold or diamonds or other wealth is found upon his lands he is quickly dispossessed. Democracy in South Africa by British and Boer alike has been based upon the exploitation of black labor, not by chattel slavery but in economic servitude.

In India, the Philippine Islands, and other Asiatic countries it is the assumed racial superiority of the Anglo-Saxon which never admits the man of a darker race as an equal, and which, like a suffocating atmosphere, encompasses the Oriental and produces in him an inferiority complex. "Subjection for a long time to a foreign yoke is one of the most potent causes of national deterioration." [1] This breeds increasing bitterness, racial strife and the determination to be free from the foreign yoke. When all non-violent methods seem to fail, as in the case of Gandhi and his followers, it makes a powerful case

---

[1] Sir John Seeley, *The Expansion of England*.

for the violence of the Communist. This is especially true in a country like China which tried in vain to abrogate the seventeen unjust and unequal treaties imposed upon her by foreign nations. Soviet Russia alone abrogated the advantageous imperialistic treaties which had formerly exploited China and treated her as a friend and equal. When, in 1923, Sun Yat Sen turned in vain to the United States, Britain and France for aid, only the Soviet Union gave him help. Portions of central China are being ruthlessly exploited by their own corrupt officials today while the neighboring Communist areas in the Chiangsi Province are being honestly administered in the interests of the poor. If a large area in central China should turn Communist and should be joined to the U.S.S.R., along with Outer Mongolia, the Soviet Union will have a still greater part of its area in the East. It will then make a much more intimate and immediate appeal to the races of Asia and Africa, especially where they are smarting with resentment under assumed racial superiority and economic exploitation. With the word Russia significantly omitted, the very title of the "Union of Soviet Socialist Republics" is deliberately designed for the inclusion of whole races, peoples or republics in the East— or in the West—if we are guilty of the folly or impotence of another World Massacre. We are entering upon a new epoch in history when it will be no longer possible for the white race permanently to hold the colored races in economic or political servitude. The very existence of the Soviet Union under a new classless and economic order, inter-racial, international and equal, will in time make such exploitation impossible.

In no country, unless it be South Africa, is the race problem more acute than in the United States. Lynching, while it affects directly but a small number, is the visible symptom and symbol of the underlying racial problem and prejudice which affects the whole Negro race and the white race as well. When in 1926 I challenged the leaders of the *Godless* society to a debate upon the subject of religion in Moscow, among some two hundred written questions which were handed up to be answered was this: "Please explain to us the relation between lynching and Christianity. We do not lynch people over here,

nor deny them justice because of their color or race, but we understand that you do lynch Negroes in Christian America. What is the relation of that practice to your religion?" In the most remote villages of Russia today Americans are frequently asked what they are going to do to the Scottsboro Negro boys, and why they lynch Negroes. When we asked the little children of five and six years of age in a nursery this summer who inhabited America, they said: "Negroes and bourgeoisie." In the reputed race and class conflict there those were the two groups with which they were most familiar.

We are indebted to a Southern white man, Mr. A. F. Raper, for the most objective and dispassionate account of this evil in his recently published *Tragedy of Lynching*. Mr. Raper shows that since 1889 there have been 3724 persons lynched in 41 years, of whom four-fifths were Negroes. Not one-sixth were even accused of rape. Of the tens of thousands of lynchers and onlookers only 49 persons have been indicted and four sentenced in forty years. Many of the mobs were ferocious after a man-hunt with bloodhounds. Many among them were church people, women, and children. The prevailing excuse to justify lynching was "to keep the Negro in his place." There was seldom any protest before or after the lynching from local organizations, churches or individuals. Mr. Raper states that the Negro is commonly robbed of education. In hundreds of counties from ten to twenty times as much is spent per capita for the education of the white child as for the Negro, and in some areas forty times as much. In seventeen Southern states, where there is a white population three times that of Negro, there are twenty-eight times as many high schools for whites as for Negroes.[1]

In the light of all the facts we must admit that one-tenth

---

[1] A. F. Raper, *The Tragedy of Lynching*, University of North Carolina Press. The annual average of the number lynched has recently fallen from 187.5 a year to 16.8. Of 21 lynched in 1930, two were certainly innocent of any crime and the guilt of eleven others was doubtful. In the seventeen Southern states where there is a total population of 9,009,096 Negroes and 28,546,689 whites, there are 205 state accredited high schools for Negroes and 5,828 for white students. *The Journal of Negro Education* and the *World Tomorrow*, Nov. 23, 1932, p. 499.

of the people of America live under a sense of insecurity, of
injustice and at times of jeopardy. The Scottsboro and
Decatur trials were championed by the International Labor
Defense which is a Communist organization. The left-wing
group insists that the color problem is a part of the Marxian
class war, and that the Negro can gain security and justice
only by enlisting on the side of social revolution. It is a
sobering thought to find that there are multitudes of professing
Christians who look with horror upon Communists, their
beliefs and methods of violence, and deeply resent their interference in the alleged right of the white man to keep the Negro
"in his place," whether by legal methods or by lynching as
he may see fit. As I crossed the continent of Asia on my last
trip, I found the American practice of lynching thrown in my
face by students in various countries. I read the story of the
latest lynching in the United States in the press in India and
China, and in a Japan daily I saw a photograph of the scene.
In an Italian paper there was a cartoon where Americans were
held up to scorn as the only people guilty of this savage
barbarity.

We must remember that the Negro and the Asiatic do not
bring their indictment against the personal kindness or benevolence of the individual of the white race. There is no race
more kindly—unless it be the Negro himself. Southern white
men, even more than those in the North, treat the Negro as
kindly, or almost as kindly, as most of the masters undoubtedly
treated their slaves.[1] It was not cruelty that made slavery
wrong. It was false in principle and an absolute denial of
human brotherhood. It is the same principle which is at stake
today in the almost universal exploitation, injustice and humiliation of all colored peoples wherever the white man goes. It
is this principle of essential spiritual equality and brotherhood
which is embodied in the ideal of a classless society in Soviet
Russia and denied in practice, save in a few exceptions, by the
Anglo-Saxon race and their "Christian" church members.

---

[1] Thomas Carlyle thus characterized the difference between the Northern
and Southern white man's attitude to the Negro. The Southerner said: "God
bless you, be a slave"; the Northerner: "God damn you, be free!"

If we question whether we have anything to learn from Russia in this regard, let us read seriously the calm and objective statement of a representative Negro which follows. It voices what practically every educated or enlightened Negro in the United States feels, and represents the view of a growing proportion of the white race. Negroes and Indians in South Africa or Kenya feel the same and the people of India agree completely with this statement in principle. In fact, almost all the colored or conquered peoples of the world could make this indictment against the Anglo-Saxon white race. If we really grasp its spiritual significance it is even more terrible than the record of lynching. Dr. W. E. Burghard Du Bois as an American Negro writes as follows:

"Let us consider the facts:

"We may begin with marriage. A Negro in this country may not, in twenty-six of the thirty-eight states, marry the person whom he wishes to marry, unless the partner is of Negro descent. A colored girl who is with a child by a white man in the south has no legal way of making her child legitimate, and in most southern states and many northern could get no standing in court. The Negro married couple may not live where they wish or in a home that they are able to buy. By law or custom, covenant or contract, or by mob violence, they are everywhere in the United States restricted in their right of domicile and for the most part must live in the worst parts of the city, and on the poorest land in the country; their sections receive from the local government the least attention and they are peculiarly exposed to crime and disease.

"Negroes are especially restricted in the chance to earn a living. If they are farmers in the south, the quality and situation of the land they can buy, their access to market, their freedom to plant and do business is seriously curtailed. They are often restricted and systematically cheated in the selling of their crop. They have little chance for the education of their children, they have no voice in their own government and taxation, and over wide areas in Louisiana, Mississippi, Alabama, and Georgia, Negro farm labor is held in actual peonage.

"In general, Negroes are 'segregated,' which means that their

normal social development in all lines is narrowed, curtailed, or stopped. They cannot develop as a part of the larger group because the developing and differentiating individual who by ability, education, wealth or character seeks to rise from the average level of weakness, ignorance, poverty, and delinquency of his group is clubbed back by the color bar and condemned to submersion or fruitless revolt.

"This is especially illustrated in the Negroes' efforts to earn a living. Their small capital, their inability to gain practical experience by contact, and their lack of credit dooms them from the start. Negroes forming one-tenth of the population own but 1/1140 per cent of the wealth. Their per capita wealth is $215 as compared with over $3,000 for the average American. They can command certainly not more than 1/10,000 of current bank credit. If they learn mechanical trades they are restricted by the unions, most of which either by actual legislation or by vote of local unions will not allow them to join. If they do not join the union, they only get a chance to work as scabs, in which case they are in danger of mob violence. Negroes must, therefore, compete mostly for unskilled and semi-skilled labor below the current rate of wages.

"In transportation, they can only work as common laborers and porters. In those southern states where eight of the twelve million Negroes live, there is not a single Negro member of the legislature, not a single Negro who holds a county office, not a single member of a city council and of the 1,700 southern cities and towns of 1,000 and more inhabitants, not fifty have a single Negro policeman. Negroes are thus taxed without representation.

"On the stage and in literature and art, the Negro has some opportunity, but his genius is limited by a public who will not endure any portrayal of a Negro save as a fun-maker, a moron, or criminal. There have been some few exceptions to this but they emphasize the rule.

"The Negro is forced into crime. His lawyers stand small opportunity in the courts. The Negro is arrested by an ignorant, prejudiced, and venal white policeman and his mere arrest

usually means conviction. His crime in the south is traded in so that many states actually make a surplus income by selling the work of criminals to private profiteers. The courts for years in the south have been made instruments for reducing the Negro to peonage and slavery.

"There were in 1926 in the United States 232,154 churches, of which 42,585 are confined to Negroes. This leaves 189,569 white churches. Of at least 175,000 of these, no Negro can be a member. There are 5,535 Y.M.C.A. and Y.W.C.A. organizations, of which 200 are for Negroes. No Negro can join at least 5,000 of the other associations.

"The opportunity of the Negro for education is limited. In the sixteen former slave states in 1930, over a million Negro children of school age were not in school a single day in the year; and half the Negro children are not in regular attendance. Southern Negro children, forming a third of the school population, received one-tenth of the school funds. In the south, the Negro cannot travel without the insult of separate and inferior cars, for which he pays the standard price. On many express trains he cannot travel at all.

"He lives under a stigma which is increased by deliberate propaganda. It is practically impossible for any Negro in the United States, no matter how small his heritage of Negro blood may be, to meet his fellow citizens on terms of social equality without being made the subject of all sorts of discriminations, embarrassments, and insults. There are innumerable exceptions, personal and geographical. Nevertheless, by and large, this is a true picture of the caste situation in the United States today.

"This, then, is the situation, and the question is, what are modern, educated people going to do about it, whether they are white or black?" [1]

Let us thoughtfully contrast the attitudes and practices in their relations to other races of Soviet Russia and the Anglo-Saxon peoples, of Communists on the one hand and Chris-

[1] Published in *The Christian*, April 29, 1933. In these excerpts the quotations are not continuous.

tians on the other. Then let us ask in common honesty: Which
is the more just, which is the more human, which is the more
Christian? Let us inquire: Which of the two is likely, in the
long run, to appeal to the non-white races and the subject peoples? Let us not forget that the citizens of Soviet Russia
have had but a decade and a half to try and apply their principles, while the West has had nineteen centuries. Outside of
Russia the white races have controlled seven-eighths of the
globe, while the Soviets have a little less than one-sixth. We
of the West are among the rich nations while Russia is still
poor. We claim the advantage of the Christian religion and
believe that Russia is handicapped by her anti-religion. If,
however, we compare the two at this single point of race relations, which has the better record, and which is morally superior? Which has the greater need to learn from the ideal of
a classless society of equal justice and comradeship?

CHAPTER III

THE TREATMENT OF CRIMINALS

In sharp contrast to their often merciless attitude toward political enemies is the Soviet Union's treatment of criminals, which is in many respects the most humane, the most scientific and the most successful of any in the world. It is typical of the whole penal system that they have abandoned the word "prison" and use instead *ispravdom,* meaning house of redemption.

With the exception of their treatment of their enemies the system is not punitive, penal or vindictive. It aims at being purely redemptive. The primary object is to reclaim the criminal and secondarily to protect society during his period of probation. Prisons are being superseded by reclamation colonies, farms, agricultural camps, psychopathic clinics, laboratories and the infliction of social discipline upon offenders, such as deductions from wages, which does not involve confinement. Such a system does not manufacture professional criminals embittered against society, but endeavors to create new men. This is one of the countless anomalies of a system commonly supposed to be founded upon violence and hatred. It is in marked contrast to the penal systems of some Western countries and to the old Czarist prisons which are so vividly described in Dostoievsky's own experience in his *House of the Dead,* which contains some of the most terrible passages in all literature.

Like all their other activities Soviet penology is a planned system grounded upon principle. The basic conception upon which the whole system is founded is that environment shapes the organism. Once they discover, eliminate and treat separately the mentally defective, they believe that if men go wrong

and form anti-social habits it is usually because of the poverty, slums, ignorance or neglect for which society rather than the unfortunate individual is responsible. Marx indignantly repudiated the popular slogan, "you can never change human nature." Instead he says, "the whole of history is nothing but the progressive transformation of human nature."[1] He held with Engels that the unfortunate and fatal divisions into classes between owners and dependents "are always the products of the modes of production and exchange." In their belief the abolition of the monopoly and private ownership of the means of production would cut the root of oppression, injustice and crime and lead, ultimately, to a classless society. Society must change the environment if it is to change the individual; psychological modifications will be produced by social ones; only a new society will create a new man.

Communists hold that there are three possible causes of crime—ignorance, economic pressure, physical or mental defect. They aim to remove ignorance by education. They are removing economic pressure by providing employment and, increasingly, an adequate wage for all. Physical or mental defect must be discovered by scientific tests and separately treated. Many of these defects can be corrected or removed. Communists believe that there is no such thing as a natural or an incorrigible criminal. Those who are counted such are made by society itself, by its unjust conditions or its unfavorable environment.

Based upon this foundation of a right environment there are certain principles which govern Russian penology and their institutions of correction which might be stated as follows:

---

[1] Marx would have endorsed the statement of Professor Hocking in his *Human Nature and Its Remaking:* "Human nature is undoubtedly the most plastic part of the living world, the most adaptable, the most educable. Of all animals, it is man in which heredity counts for least, and conscious building forces for most. Consider that his infancy is longest, his instincts least fixed, his brain most unfinished at birth, his powers of habit making and habit changing most marked, his susceptibility to social impressions keenest. . . . Nature now charters man to complete the work and make of himself what he will." He adds that the human creature must finish himself. "It is human nature to change itself. If it is to be changed at all it is only in ways that will leave it more completely satisfied." *Human Nature and Its Remaking*, pp. 15-20.

1. Trust in human nature in its normal response to a right environment and the belief that it can be re-instructed, re-conditioned and reclaimed.

2. Realistic trust in the individual criminal that will stimulate him, call out his best and in the end produce the desired response.

3. The healing quality of healthy occupation, especially of free, congenial, creative labor, adequately paid for and rewarded with the hope of the ultimate attainment of the good life.

4. The principle of self-government and self-discipline imposed by the democratic organization of the inmates themselves, who feel the reasonableness of the slight social penalties imposed upon them by their fellows for individual and social welfare.

5. A planned system of technical education to teach each man a useful trade and restore him as quickly as possible as a useful member of society.

6. The ideal of self-development and self-expression in a system of education and recreation through active participation in clubs, study classes, interest groups, bands, orchestras, dramatics, entertainments, and other forms of voluntary activity.

7. The provision of a normal environment within the institution, and contact as soon as it is merited with the outside world, with the maximum of freedom and healthy social intercourse, admission when earned to the trade unions, parole and vacations, consequent removal of an inferiority complex, of resentment, or of hopeless or sullen despair, and the restoration of favorable motivations.

8. The abolition of long, hopeless sentences and the provision as far as possible of normal home and even sex life. The offender can have an annual vacation of from two to four weeks, or he can have twelve monthly visits to his home. Family life is recognized as a great incentive to reformation. In advanced institutions permission is given to marry and make a

home if granted by the Commission elected by the inmates themselves.

9. Provision for immediate occupation and full restoration to society after his release without the handicap of "a criminal record."

10. Faith on the part of officials, inmates and the community in a system which works and which validates itself by its results.

Though these principles lie at the basis of their whole penology they find much fuller application in their more advanced institutions.[1] Sentences include reprimands, fines, probation, compulsory labor while left in freedom at one's regular work, and imprisonment. Terms of imprisonment are even shorter than in England and far shorter than in the United States. For sentences of one year or less the offender remains at home in his regular work under supervision and the control of his pay. Paying on the instalment plan in deduction from his wages impresses the prisoner. The maximum sentence for murder, for instance, is ten years.

Capital punishment is looked upon with aversion yet as a temporary, necessary evil to eliminate those who are incorrigible or confirmed enemies of the system. There have been many instances of public shootings which shock the sensibilities of the West. The average sentence is three years and under the "progressive system" the average offender can shorten his sentence by half. There are frequent amnesties and the government seeks to meet the prisoner halfway and to achieve the purpose of the sentence, which is the reclamation of the offender, in the shortest possible time. There is almost no limitation as to the amount of literature and correspondence allowed the prisoner or of visits from his friends.

---

[1] Their institutions include the houses of confinement, labor reformatories, labor colonies for those having a maximum sentence of five years, vocational isolators, transitional labor reformatories and reclamation colonies, hospitals for treatment of the physically and mentally abnormal, and real prisons for political prisoners, like the Butirky Prison and the Solovietsky Islands near the Polar circle. These members of the "enemy classes" are such as kulaks, manufacturers, Nepmen and profiteers, priests, pacifists, and political radicals who desire the overthrow of the present government.

The principles and practices of the new régime in Russia are embodied in new handbooks and literature. One handbook is entitled *What the Prison Personnel Should Know.*[1] There is a companion volume, *What Every Prisoner Should Know,* guarding the prisoner's right of complaint against unjust treatment by the administration or individual guards. No other country has given such freedom and status to its prisoners. The whole penal system strives to substitute science for force.

The more than a thousand prisons of Czarist days have been reduced to a little over two hundred. The 200,000 prisoners in 1914 have now been reduced to 80,000.[2] Except at times and in areas affected by food shortage there has been a considerable reduction of crime by the elimination of unemployment and the private ownership of the means of production. There has also been a decrease in sex crimes with the sharp reduction of prostitution looking toward its complete elimination. Other things being equal a social order founded upon social justice should produce less crime than one of *laissez faire.* Crimes of violence have decreased in Russia, together with attacks on persons and property. Drunkenness and theft are still common, also cases of "hooliganism" such as breaches of the peace and general disorderliness.

Each republic of the U.S.S.R. has a complete system of courts. Instead of a jury there is a permanent judge and two

---

[1] This handbook instructs the guards: "The Soviet Government cannot look upon the criminal as upon an enemy who is to be subdued or as upon a sinner who must be brought to a state of penitence by humiliating punishment. . . . The purpose of imprisonment is not to cause pain to the man but to re-educate him. . . . It has been repeatedly shown that men have been condemned as criminals in consequence of their neglected education, of their poor upbringing and of their hard and cheerless life. . . . Prison attendants should act as older brothers to such prisoners. . . . They should not employ coarse or insulting language but act with calmness, with restraint and impartiality. Prisoners should not be handcuffed or made to wear chains. They should not be deprived of food or thrown into solitary confinement. Corporal punishment in any form is forbidden and attendants violating this rule should at once be handed over to the authorities for trial." Quoted by Elias Tobenkin in *Stalin's Ladder,* pp. 242-244, 277.

[2] The last Czarist prison census gave the number as 183,000, but there was a marked increase of revolutionary disorder and imprisonment following this in 1914.

laymen as co-judges, while a higher court has three permanent judges. Mr. D. N. Pritt, K.C., of England, after visiting Russia, considers that on the whole the right of arrest is more limited than in England, that the simplicity of the procedure, the greater certainty of the law arising from the absence of a vast fungus of reported cases, and the freedom from all the hindrances that excessive wealth on one side or the other can place in the way of justice, all tend to make it less essential to employ an advocate; nevertheless, advocates are frequently employed. Mr. Pritt makes a list of suggestions and recommendations drawn from Russian procedure that might be applied to Europe. With regard to prisons he says: "Everything that Russia has recently done is what English reformers have preached for years with unflagging courage." [1]

Maxim Gorky describes a chain of fifty reclamation colonies, prison farms and reformatories. Personally I have visited several times, and visited again this past summer, the Rehabilitation Colony at Bolshevo in the beautiful pine woods two hours' motor ride out of Moscow. The Director is a member of the Red Army, his chief assistant is a friendly doctor, who showed us about the institution. It was founded a decade ago in 1924 by this doctor and his associates who brought here 18 boys who had formed criminal habits during the great famine. The doctor had no gun, no walls, fences or means of confinement for these boys. They were placed upon their honor under a voluntary system of self-government right out in the open country. The boys were told that they could leave if they wished but if they wanted to become men these older comrades would help them. I noticed as we walked about that the boys affectionately called the doctor "Uncle." The whole atmosphere was so friendly and informal that it was hard to realize that we were in a "penal" institution. Most of the inmates have been convicted several times of theft and other crimes, many were once hardened thieves or criminals, though most of them are only from eighteen to twenty-six years of age.

---

[1] *Twelve Studies in Soviet Russia*, Gallancz, 1933, p. 175.

Over a period of ten years the 18 original inmates have increased to 2,032. There are still no walls, fences or armed guards. The doctor and boys laughed when I asked him if he were armed. There are five older officials who act as friendly advisors in this self-governing colony or commune. There are also eighteen teachers or technical instructors in various trades, together with elected voluntary helpers.

At the time of entrance there is a physical and mental examination to discover and treat defectives. After a short period of probation of about two months to learn the ways of the place the inmates are permitted leave in Moscow for a day and a night three times a month. After a year they are allowed a month's holiday at home.

They have a large farm, trade schools, machine shops, manufacturing departments of textiles, clothing, carpentry, plumbing, electricity, metal work, sports goods, the making of excellent tennis rackets, skates, skis, footballs, boxing gloves, etc. A town and community are being built up around the colony where the men may settle permanently if they choose at the expiration of their sentences. Apart from new buildings the community is almost self-supporting. Each boy or man is allowed to choose some congenial or useful form of labor. All are paid wages according to their skill, with an average wage of over one hundred roubles a month. The directors and some of the instructors receive over four hundred roubles. After three years the worker is admitted to the trade union and restored to full citizenship. He may then have the coveted honor of entering the Communist Party.

The inmates are free to leave if they wish, and of these wild, undisciplined young criminals in the early months of their residence about 16 per cent do leave. But many return and ask to be taken back. Of those who enter the trade unions only five or six have ever left during all these years.

The community is entirely self-governing under its own discipline. They elect several commissions in charge of various departments and a Conflict Commission is composed of the chairmen of other commissions. The Conflict Commission decides upon disciplinary measures and penalties for infringe-

ment of rules. Serious cases are referred to the democratic general assembly of the members of the commune.

The members have their own personal effects, their savings bank and bank accounts, receiving interest at six per cent and making loans to members at two per cent. They have their own cooperative store and a multiplicity of organizations, interest groups and circles. Over 500 belong to these circles. They have five bands and orchestras, a glee club, a dramatic club where many of the actors share the same dormitory, voluntary educational classes, sports clubs and numerous entertainments.

There are some 200 girls and women included in the community. The members are permitted to cultivate the friendship or love of members of the opposite sex within the institution, in their own home towns or in a neighboring village. Anyone may marry if he obtains the consent of their own elected Commission, choosing a partner either from the commune or from outside. Some four hundred have married and there are now about five hundred children in the colony.

While we conferred in the rustic summerhouse we asked if we might question the inmates. We were allowed to do so freely either in the presence of the doctor or officials, alone, or in groups as we walked about the place or entered individual homes. All were equal comrades and there seemed to be almost no distinction between officials or inmates. Each was quite free in the presence of the other. It was a classless community. I recorded brief notes at random regarding several of the inmates we met casually: "A" was 28 years of age. From the age of thirteen he had been a thief for nine years. He had been convicted or sentenced six times for his crimes. He has now been admitted to the trade union and the Communist Party. He received 300 roubles a month in wages. Was he free to leave? Certainly, but why should he wish to? This was the commune that had made him an honest man. It had trusted him, it had given him hope, it had taught him to work and to love it. Now he wanted to stay and teach others who had gone astray as he had done.

"B" has been in the colony for a year and a half. He, too, had been a thief for eight or nine years. He had been con-

victed eight times. He was finally sent here from a prison camp. He has not yet been admitted to the trade union. He plays the clarinet in the orchestra, he is a member of an interest group, he is a "shock brigade" worker. What help had he received here? First of all, the commune had taught him to work and to form steady habits. He could not steal now for that would make him a class enemy. He is happy, living a life of hope and useful service.

"C" is 35 years of age and has been here for six years. Formerly he had been a criminal for seven years. Now he is the leader of one of the orchestras which is working just now on Beethoven's Fifth Symphony. Two of their members have been sent to study in the great Conservatory of Music in Moscow. Soon they will return, one to become the trained leader of a band, the other of an orchestra. This man became so enthusiastic about his music that we quite forgot to ask him about his wages. They did not seem significant to him or to us.

"D" is 28 years of age. He was a thief from the age of eleven and has been here nine years, though his sentence was completed some years ago. He is now an instructor earning 300 roubles a month. He is married and took us proudly to his home for which he pays a rent of 22 roubles. It was neat and clean, with lace curtains at the windows, and attractive with flowers and plants. Here was a radio which he had bought, his bicycle, and other prized possessions. His boy was out playing tennis on the courts below the window. His wife earns 120 roubles and they save money every month. What help had the commune been to him? He replied: "I came here practically naked. See me now! I have been a member of the trade union for four years and also belong to the Party. I have a happy home. My wife was a peasant girl. I now have a clean record and I can face the world. I would be sorry if I had to leave. We are all one big family here. I am as free as the air."

"E" is the head of the shoe factory. He is obviously a man of commanding ability. His life story would make a thrilling novel. He was formerly a brigand or desperado, a highway robber and safe-cracker. After one of his desperate

crimes he was sentenced to death. He was finally sent here as a last resort as it seemed a pity to execute so bold and brilliant a man. He is now one of the most steady, dependable and able leaders in the institution. No one would dream that he had ever been a criminal himself. He is looked up to with admiration and affection by the younger members, not as a "big shot" but as a social leader.

"F" is an attractive and beautiful girl. She was formerly the head of the pickpockets of Moscow. Now she is a useful citizen, a constructive member of the commune, who is finding her satisfaction, not in anti-social activity, but as a happy member of a truly cooperative society.

When I left this healthy, happy community, out in the open sunshine and surrounded by beautiful pine woods, I somehow had the feeling that I had been worshipping in some great cathedral built not of stone and stained glass but of a new humanity actually being reclaimed in this Rehabilitation Colony of Bolshevo.

Crime in England

Turning from Russia to England one is impressed by the rapidity of the advance and sweeping reforms effected in penology in the Soviet Union within ten or twelve years as compared to the slow centuries required for reforms in the British penal system, while Britain in turn is decades if not generations in advance of conditions in the United States. Though slow, Great Britain's record of advance in the humane treatment of crime is remarkable as compared to our own.

In sixteenth century England thousands of peasants who were driven homeless from the land without work were treated as "vagabonds" and "sturdy beggars," for which they could be whipped "till the body was bloody," branded, and finally, for a third offense of idleness, hanged. For a long period every Lord of the Manor or large landowner could have his own gallows for hanging whom he pleased. Not till 1790 was the law repealed by which women were burned at the stake. Blackstone has listed 160 offenses which were punishable with

death.   Property was sacred, personality was cheap.   The brutal ferocity of the criminal laws was no deterrent from crime but served to further brutalize the population.   In England, during the reign of Henry VIII, there were about seventy thousand hangings.   During an equal period today in the United States there are about forty-five hundred, while in England itself there are now almost none.

Every village in England formerly possessed its pillory, stocks and whipping post.   London was called the city of the gallows, as one entered under a line of gibbets hung with rotting corpses.   The Hammonds record a committee of one member of the House of Commons, with a clerks' boy, arranging for the penalty of hanging for any peasants who should chance to object to an enclosing Bill which was designed forcibly to take from them the common land.   "This resolution was unanimously agreed to."

At the executions thousands of spectators gathered at the foot of the gallows to pass the time in drinking before enjoying the brutal spectacle.   After the hanging the body of a prisoner guilty of treason was publicly "castrated, disembowelled, and quartered." [1]   Romilly's humane bills were defeated with scorn by the House of Lords when he objected to the law "which requires the tearing out of the heart and bowels from the body of a human being while he is yet alive and burning them in his sight."

Sidney and Beatrice Webb have described *English Prisons Under Local Government*.   From 1700 to 1773 the prisons were indescribably bad.   In some: "The stench and nastiness are so nauseous . . . that no person enters there without the risk of his health and life."   A medical man testified: "Vagrants and disorderly women of the very lowest and most wretched class of human beings, almost naked, with only a few filthy rags, almost alive and in motion with vermin, their bodies rotting with . . . scorbutic and venereal ulcers . . . are drove in shoals to the gaols. . . .   There thirty and sometimes

---

[1] Margaret Wilson, *The Crime of Punishment*, pp. 172-180.   Mr. Lytton Strachey in *Elizabeth and Essex* describes such an execution in June, 1594; Thackeray describes a similar spectacle during his day in 1840.

forty of these unhappy wretches are crowded or crammed together in one ward where in the dark they bruise and beat each other. . . . In the morning the different wards . . . are more like the Black Hole in Calcutta than places of confinement in a Christian country." [1]

A quarter of the prisoners died during confinement. The jailers tortured their victims for the purpose of bribery and extortion, encouraged drunkenness and vice. "Every capital prison was a public house," and many were brothels kept under the protection of the law.

In 1777 John Howard exposed the prisons of England as indescribably filthy and breeding centers of disease and crime. Many who escaped the gallows died of slow torture or came out emaciated and diseased. " 'Tis reckoned there are about sixty thousand miserable debtors perishing in the prisons of England and Wales, where hundreds die weekly of want and infectious disease." [2]

In 1800 the punishments of England were more savage than those of Europe or America. Beccaria challenged the use of torture, the rack and the thumbscrew. Howard exposed the prisons as places of disease, filth and death. Then England reduced the indiscriminate death penalty, banishment, transportation and solitary confinement. Next they abolished long sentences in overcrowded, unsanitary prisons. In 1878 the Government took over the 113 local jails and instituted reforms. Before 1900 they had closed all but 56 and since 1914 a score of others have been abolished. They now have, including those used for juvenile offenders, only 36 prisons in all England and Wales. Reduction of long sentences and

---

[1] Sidney and Beatrice Webb, *English Prisons Under Local Government,* pp. 19-23. See also *English Prisons Today,* Report of the Prison System Enquiry Committee by Stephen Hbhouse and A. Fenner Brockway.

[2] In his opening paragraph Howard, upon first visiting the prisons of England, describes men "expiring on the floors, in loathsome cells, of pestilential fevers, and confluent smallpox . . . covered with rags; almost famished. . . . Many prisons have no water. . . . Debtors and felons, men and women, the young beginner and the old offender" were herded together by day and sometimes at night. Howard found far better conditions in Holland, while in Russia at that time they were most inhuman.

the introduction of more humane treatment, with an unarmed police force, have left half the cells empty.[1] "It has not been imprisonment but the *disuse* of imprisonment that has contributed to make England the law-abiding nation of the world."

At the climax of her lawlessness England was spending millions on her prisons and almost nothing on a bribed police force.[2] Now she spends little on prisons and much on her justly world-famous police force, while the United States is building costly prisons and providing no adequate state and federal police force. Up to the age of 16 offenders in England are not even sent to a reformatory but to a school under the control of the Home Office. Beyond that age they are sent to the half dozen enlightened Borstal institutions where the gates remain open and the boys go freely from their rooms to the workshops in their football clothes. Matches are played on Saturday half holidays.

Characteristic of Anglo-Saxon individualism there is a fine corps of 600 experienced voluntary workers who regularly visit the English prisons for interviews, classes, lectures and the cultivation of friendships. Following the work of John Howard, Elizabeth Fry and Thomas Wright, the Aid Society begins work at the time of the prisoner's admission and is ready to seek employment and rehabilitation for him upon his discharge. So successful has been the system that nine-tenths of the inmates never have to return. In support of their policy of leniency there is no case of a reprieved murderer ever having committed another similar crime. Britain now assimilates her discharged prisoners and does not ship them abroad as for-

[1] Margaret Wilson, *The Crime of Punishment,* pp. 253-256, Jonathan Cape, Publisher. Since 1878 the prison population has been reduced to half. Only 2.2 per cent of the sentences exceed one year; 53.1 per cent do not exceed one month; only .3 per cent exceed five years. On the last year reported there were no life sentences. *The Crime of Punishment* is particularly valuable for American readers.

[2] Millbank Prison alone cost some two and a half million dollars, though it is not on a par with the new federal prison Lewisburg, Pa. In 1928 England spent less than four millions of dollars on her prisons, while she spent over thirty millions on her police. Illinois spent millions on the new prison at Joliet, but long sentences still overcrowd nearly all American prisons, new and old. *Ibid,* 301-313.

merly. In 1930 there was no execution and not a single life sentence; only 40 were tried for murder in England and Wales. With a population of forty millions all England and Wales have fewer murders than several cities in the United States. In 1932 only 186 deaths were attributed to homicide, including murders, manslaughter, infanticide, etc.

After such a brilliant advance in penology it is to be hoped that England will soon abolish imprisonment for debt. Of 64,046 offenses in 1930, 58,500 were concerned with property. There is a noticeable increase in crime during times of unemployment. This is natural in a land where until recently one-tenth of the people possessed nine-tenths of the wealth and the remaining nine-tenths of the people had but one-tenth of its material goods.

Crime in the United States

The American people may well look with envy upon both Soviet Russia and England in their success in dealing with crime. America has recently witnessed an alarming increase of crime with gangs collecting tribute and issuing death warrants. Crime commissions follow crime waves but the public has remained apathetic. Louis McHenry Howe, the able confidential secretary to President Roosevelt, points out how interstate and city gangs grow bolder and terrorize our cities with machine guns while boy bandits are freely permitted to go armed. This would be unthinkable in England or Russia.

As I write, the news comes of a friend in Los Angeles who was just robbed in his automobile standing by the sidewalk in a city of over a million people. The bandit had successfully held up three cars within a couple of hours. Because my friend's lady companion nervously spilled part of the contents of her purse in handing it over my friend was shot in the neck by the bandit while the lady was shot through both eyes and wantonly blinded for life. Yet America permits without protest free private traffic in arms, as an international menace, and the arming of her gangsters, criminals and reckless youths, who are provided concrete instruction in methods of crime by our moving pictures. Profiteering of arms manufacturers in

New Haven and other cities continues. In some cities the machine guns taken from criminals are sold at public auction as if to invite criminals to arm.

In England no man may carry firearms without a license.[1] It is most hopeful that Mr. Roosevelt, where all other recent Presidents have been so helpless, has turned his attention to the crime which has caused the United States to be known as the most lawless country in the world. Mr. Dern, the Secretary of War, referred to "the 400,000 professional criminals in this country who may be described as constituting the 'Scarlet Army of the United States,' numbering three times as many as the soldiers of the Regular Army." The Department of Justice considered this an understatement since the Bureau of Investigation has on its files the names of 4,431,419 persons with criminal records. Each year in the United States 12,000 persons are murdered, 3,000 have been kidnapped, 100,000 assaulted and 50,000 robbed. Over 30,000 automobiles are stolen annually. Robbery is a hundred times as prevalent in Chicago as in London. England and Wales have less than 200 homicides a year while Chicago's record mounts to over 500 in some years.[2] Mark Prentiss says: "Today the greatest outstanding menace in America is crime."

An obvious obstacle to law enforcement is the connection between local police forces, powerful politicians and criminal

---

[1] English law prohibits the purchase, possession or carrying of firearms without a certificate from the chief of police. The illegal possession of firearms leads to fine and imprisonment and lengthens the sentence of a criminal. No pawnbroker may expose or own such weapons. The police keep a register of all dealers in firearms. In the United States profit-making in arms has been ably defended by the Senator from Connecticut and every effort to suppress the manufacture of machine guns has so far failed, though Mr. Howe says "a man who buys a machine gun buys it for the purpose of murder and no other purpose." He adds: "The reduction of crime, so far as I know, has never been made a real issue by any candidate for public office. There was nothing about it in either party platform in the last election." *The Herald Tribune Magazine,* Feb. 12, 1933.

[2] If we take the number of murders per 100,000 of the population, in Norway and in England and Wales it is only .8, in New York City 6.4, in Chicago 17.5, in Nashville 36, in Jacksonville 58.8, in Memphis 70, per 100,000. Chicago had 222 homicides in 1918, 389 in 1923, 509 in 1924, as against 154 in all England and Wales. Frederick L. Hoffman, *The Homicide Problem,* pp. 97-105.

elements. As Mr. Medalie, Federal District Attorney for New York, says: "The gangs are part of the machinery for municipal control, and not until politics are divorced from municipal affairs shall we get rid of gangsters." The people of Russia and of England can never understand why Americans permit shameless records like those of Tammany Hall to continue in their great cities.

Some of the states in America are also very backward. California has over five hundred times the proportion of long-term criminals that England has, with Mooney and Billings among them, despite the Wickersham Report and the condemnation of world public opinion. California has fifteen times as much punishment as Connecticut, but not as much as Georgia which has the unenviable record of making a profit of $3,269,-098.70 in four years from the labor of its 2,800 imprisoned lawbreakers with their excessive terms.[1]

A perusal of the fourteen volumes of the Wickersham Reports makes mournful reading. Here we find that "the criminal is the end result of a long series of social causes." Poor housing conditions, great poverty and dependence, inadequate open air play facilities, unemployment and lack of economic security are obvious causes. To change these conditions would, of course, invade the sacred precincts of private profit and "the American system." The Commission holds that "responsibility for crime rests upon society." As Victor Hugo said: "Society stands in the docket with every criminal." That, too, is the doctrine of Soviet Russia, but we do not, like Russia, apply a logical remedy. The Wickersham Commission quotes the R. G. Dun Agency as to our increase in wealth, industry, commerce and banking: "Each step in this swift progress . . . has been followed by a marked increase in the number of criminals." [2] The Commission also finds that the police do not apprehend more than twenty per cent of the individuals who commit felonies, and adds the oft-quoted statement of the late

---

[1] *The Crime of Punishment*, p. 293.
[2] *National Commission on Law Observance and Enforcement*, Vol. XIII, pp. 115, 119.

President Taft: "The administration of the criminal law in this country is a disgrace to our civilization." [1]

In their Report on Penal Institutions the Commission notes that in a year nearly 400,000 pass through the gates of 3,000 institutions, including chain gangs. This is in striking contrast to the 17,000 confined in the 36 prisons of England and Wales. The United States spends for the upkeep of her penal institutions thirty million dollars a year, or $350 for each inmate. The buildings cost over 100 millions. We spend 247 millions a year for law enforcement in large cities, and $3,900,000 a year for armored cars in our class war with criminals. Our mails are defrauded to the extent of 68 millions a year and private insurance against crime costs us another 106 millions. But the Commission is unable even to estimate the total cost of crime, immediate or ultimate.

The Commission finds our prisons overcrowded, many of them with the obsolete cell block system. There is insufficient work and many are maintained in idleness. The percentage of prisoners employed in productive labor declined from 75 in 1885 to 61 in 1923. The chief reasons are poor management, the inertia of government officials and overcrowding, as the result of long sentences and the increase of crime. Many of the guards are underpaid and unqualified. The Commission finds that prisoners let out on the lease system are often cruelly treated by private contractors. Around every corner of our penal system and every tier of obsolete cells leers the inhumanity of our profit-making economic order.

In many institutions the Commission finds "the present sanitary and health conditions are inadequate." The tubercular, insane, feeble minded, drug addicts and venereally diseased are often not isolated from the others. The Commission says: "We conclude that the present prison system is antiquated and inefficient. It does not reform the criminal. It does not protect society. There is reason to believe that it contributes to the increase of crime by hardening the prisoner. . . . The present system of prison discipline is traditional, antiquated,

---

[1] *Ibid.*

unintelligent and not infrequently cruel and inhuman. . . .
There is no national plan." [1]

I sailed for Europe last June fresh from a visit to the new
federal prison Lewisburg, Pa., where I addressed the prisoners.
Outside it was a grim fortress, inside a palace in stone and
steel. It obviously cost millions to erect. Undoubtedly it is
the finest prison building in the world. The highest human
ingenuity went into its construction "to prevent escape at all
hazards." Beside the armed keepers lay the Great Danes,
larger and more menacing than bloodhounds.

As I spoke, the contrast between this prison and the friendly
reclamation colony at Bolshevo, which I have described earlier
in this chapter, and the two systems of treatment of crime, was
vividly in my mind. It was a Sunday service and I was expected to take a text from the Christian gospel. The words
stuck in my throat. I was ashamed to tell these men before
me about the Russian colony and the Russian system. They
were inmates in a "Christian" country of a system efficient in
stone and steel but inhuman and pagan to its last stone.

The problem of crime in the United States is becoming yet
more acute during the depression. While the proofs of this
chapter are being corrected I have reached Seattle, where the
Chief of Detectives is compelled to warn "people of prosperous
appearance to keep off the streets at night if they want to avoid
being slugged and robbed. . . . They should take precautions
to avoid bandits." A gangland war is on in Detroit. Mary
Roberts Rinehart fears that "we are facing government by
gangsters and control by the underworld." [2] She believes that
we are meeting with sluggish apathy the growth of crime
during the last fifteen years in this country. More than two
hundred and fifty rackets now prey upon business, collecting
some twenty-five million dollars a year from shippers and dock

---

[1] *Ibid,* Vol. IX, pp. 170-171. Warden Lewis E. Lawes of Sing Sing Prison,
reviewing the Wickersham Reports, says: "Our prison system is futilely pur-
poseless and utterly ineffectual." "Prison leaves bitter memories." The
Warden says criminals cannot be reformed inside the walls without a new
deal outside. *New York Times Magazine,* August 16, 1931, p. 3.

[2] Mary Roberts Rinehart, *Can Women Stop Crime?* in *The Saturday Evening Post,* November 18, 1933.

operators, and, according to Senator Copeland, raising the cost of living in America by 20 per cent. In six years the population of our prisons has increased 50 per cent [1] while the cost of crime to the people is said to be three times the annual budget. Drug addicts alone are said to spend each year five times the cost of the Panama Canal. Under our present system all law-enforcement agencies are regarded as political plums.

One must make almost daily additions to this chapter of crime in America. In one column in the morning paper of November 29, 1933, is the record of three recent lynchings.[2] No one can defend the crimes nor the criminals nor our tardy and uncertain system of justice which late President Taft well called "a disgrace to civilization."

In defence of the two men lynched in California the head-lines announce: "Governor Rolph Will Protect Lynchers." While some citizens boast that they organized or took part in the lynching, the same Governor who keeps Tom Mooney in prison after seventeen years defends the lynchers by saying that "this is the best lesson California has given the country." He concludes: "It is little wonder that the people of the community in which the murdered man and his family resided arose in their wrath and took vengeance on Brooke Hart's slayers." In the meantime, the Rev. Henry H. Darlington, rector of the Church of the Heavenly Rest of New York, wires the Governor: "Congratulations on the stand you have taken." Judge Kyle of Kansas City telegraphs: "I congratulate you on your attitude toward lynching, and the people of California *for their noble example* in dealing with criminals."

In St. Joseph, Missouri, 7,000 persons stormed the county jail, dragged a Negro from his cell and hanged him. On that same day, in Princess Anne, Maryland, a mob disinterred the body of George Armwood, a Negro whom they had recently

---

[1] In 1932 there were 158,947 prisoners in 116 State and 12 Federal prisons. Of these only 82,276 were occupied in productive labor, with wages ranging from two to fifteen cents a day. Prisoners built 1,200 miles of roads valued at $15,000,000, one-third of which were in Georgia. This resembles the building of the White Sea-Baltic canal in Russia. The latter country, however, has never learned to make a profit out of its prisoners as has Georgia.

[2] *The Morning Oregonian,* November 29, 1933.

lynched, and hacked off his head. In Salisbury, Maryland, a "mob of more than 1,000 men stormed the state armory here today in an unsuccessful effort to free four men accused of participating in last month's lynching at Princess Anne. Cries of 'Lynch Governor Ritchie' could be heard."

Within twenty-four hours after they are released the stories of these lynchings will be in the press of Russia, India, China and Japan. In the last country, during a former visit, I saw upon the front page of their largest daily paper a photograph of a late lynching in the United States, as the one country in the world that descends to this measure of barbarism. Many in these countries will wonder whether the Governor of California is not placing himself upon the same plane as the criminals as he brazenly defends lynching and keeps innocent men in prison.

On a train a few weeks ago, while completing this book, I listened to two men in the next seat, both of whom had just been released from prison and who were almost dead drunk. One of them was very loud. After a twenty-two year sentence in a penitentiary in New York State he had just gained his liberty. He was telling his companion that he would repeat his crime, and do it all over again just as he had done in 1911. "Within twenty-four hours," he boasted, "I'll have a gun on my hip again, and believe me, I'll shoot quick this time." There is no country in the world, except the United States, where criminals may arm so freely, where there is a greater likelihood of their continuing in crime, or where there is a larger proportion of repeaters, for 48 per cent of our captured criminals are such.

We need a strong state police force in every one of our forty-eight states, with police and law enforcement taken out of politics. Criminals and boy bandits should be disarmed and registered. A thorough reform of our prisons and our whole penal system should be demanded. If Russia and Britain can become law-abiding countries the United States should be able to do likewise. Only when there is an awakening of public opinion on moral issues that lie beyond the profit and money-making which have hithertofore engrossed us, can we hope for

improvement in the prevention of crime and treatment of our criminals.

In the light of the whole situation have we anything to learn from Soviet Russia either in the matter of their penal system, or justice in the economic order that lies behind it? Many of my American friends are troubled by the question of whether Soviet Russia can endure without religion. I am also troubled as to whether we can endure with it. This we shall discuss in the chapter on *The Reformation of Religion*. If at this single point we contrast the criminal record and penal systems of the two countries, which is the more scientific, the more humane, the more Christian?

CHAPTER IV

THE CARE OF CHILDREN; YOUTH AND EDUCATION

One of the most brilliant achievements of the Soviet Union is in the sphere of childhood and in its attainment of free, compulsory, universal primary education. This is surprising to the newcomer in Russia who would perhaps have expected in a revolutionary government a concentration upon material things and a more Spartan rigor or even neglect in dealing with childhood. Instead, it is as if the Revolution had taken a little child and set him in the midst of the whole system, to occupy the first place of regard and almost of reverence. Children must be considered first in every law and plan. They must have the best milk, the most humane and scientific care, the chief consideration in everything. This is both instinctive and reflective. No people in the world have a greater natural wealth of affection for their children than the Russians, and no system gives more recognition to their importance. This is one evidence of the farsighted and enduring nature of the whole movement.

One looks upon the old and bearded peasants, stolid, stupid and superstitious, as most difficult and unpromising material for a new order. But the children, who are pliable, molten and glowing, run quickly into new social moulds. They blaze with hope and enthusiasm. They shake the rafters of the village nurseries or schools with their fiery songs. They carry home an overwhelming conviction and wield a strong influence upon their elders.

As nearly one-half the population of the Soviet Union is under twenty years of age there must be some eighty million children and youth in the crucible of this new order. The government begins to plan for them in prenatal care and in-

struction of mothers, through the home and crèche, the nursery, kindergarten and school.

Within a few years, in this vast unwieldy country, over five million children have been organized in pre-school institutions, over twenty-three millions in primary and secondary schools, and more than ten millions in the youth organizations of three ages. Throughout the financial depression Russia, alone among the nations, has continuously increased its expenditures for education, both in amount and in proportion. This supposedly materialistic land, even in the darkest days of civil war and famine, never parted with its treasures of art and archeology, or the crown jewels of the Czars, but its greatest treasure has always been regarded as childhood.

In the ubiquitous propaganda of the Soviet state parents and teachers are taught to respect the emerging personality of the child and to provide for his individual development. All violent or provocative discipline is forbidden. Russia's old *Domostroy* book advises the man freely to use the rod on wife or child to bring them to submission. Under the Soviet law to strike a child in the home or school is a criminal offense. In all my travels I have never seen more kindly or scientific treatment of children. Self-government is the aim of home and school from the very earliest age and in practically all organizations, even among criminals, which seems a surprising anomaly in a dictatorship. Their trust in the child, in human nature, in the common man and in the poorest class as the most promising human material, is significant.

This placing of large responsibility and power in the hands of youth has not been misguided. It has not produced an unruly and impudent class of "flaming youth." The child is taught the obligation to serve, if not at his mother's breast then at least with the first lessons of the kindergarten. This indoctrination of the child and his toys, games and songs are planned with as great care as his studies.[1] The five logs in

---

[1] One sees model toys made by teachers or pupils exhibited for the instruction of teachers and leaders in many such institutions as the Institute of Mother and Child in Moscow. One poster reads: "Games are not mere play but preparation for creative labor."

the campfire of their scouts symbolize the five continents, and nothing less than the workers and poor of all the world are held up as their field of sympathy and endeavor.   Their ideas of internationalism are, if possible, even more intense than the nationalism inculcated in the youth of Germany, Italy or Japan.

Perhaps the most remarkable development in the care of children is exemplified in their system of crèches and nurseries now organized throughout almost the whole of Russia in city and country, in factories and on farms.   These serve the double purpose of the release of mothers from the drudgery of the home for what is considered creative work, and the training of the children far more effectively than would be possible in their ignorant peasant homes.   In many respects the newly educated children are in advance of their illiterate parents and in a naïve way become their instructors.   The campaigns for literacy, sanitation, anti-alcohol, economic and political causes are carried into almost every home by the children.   The mothers visit the crèche periodically to nurse their children and while there they also come under the spirit of the place.   In the most distant nurseries, kindergartens and village schools, miles from any railway, I have found the whole spirit of the Revolution as one would find it in the Kremlin, and freer from red tape and bureaucracy.   The children are not taken from the home save in the daytime.   The Soviet Union has done away with private property but it will never abolish the family or the home.

The New Education

The achievements during the period of the first Five Year Plan were as far-reaching in the field of education as in industry or agriculture.   Universal obligatory education was first introduced from the ages of eight to eleven years.   Rapid progress is now being made in a plan for the development of universal education during a period of seven years of schooling.   During the second Plan they hope to introduce universal obligatory technical education for all youth up to the age of seventeen.   This will be in contrast to the system of compulsory education in England which only goes to the age of fourteen.

During the period of the first Plan the number receiving primary education was doubled, raising the enrollment from 11.2 to 23.1 millons. The U.S.S.R. now holds first place in the world in the number attending school. It is claimed that the number of children and adults in all educational institutions and extension classes has now reached the colossal total of fifty millions. Already the Plan has doubled the number of trained specialists as educators, engineers and doctors, raising the total from 493,000 at the beginning of the Plan to 973,000 at the close of it. The Soviets claim two and a half millions in their new class of intelligentsia.[1]

The broad achievements in the field of education from the beginning of the Plan in October, 1928, to the end of 1932, in four and a quarter years, are tabulated as follows:[2]

Educational Achievements During the Plan

	1928	1932	Percentage of Growth
In Universities and Higher Technical Schools	160,000	501,300	313
Students in Secondary Technical Schools	253,600	949,200	374
" " Factory Schools............	178,300	1,177,300	660
" " Workers' Colleges..........	49,200	444,400	903
" " Elementary Schools	9,870,000	18,754,000	190
" " Secondary Schools	1,409,000	4,359,000	309
" " Pre-School Institutions	308,000	5,232,000	1,698
Literacy Level, percentage of population 8-50 Yrs.............................	58.4	90	

[1] The U.S.S.R. claims to enroll half a million in universities and institutions of higher education compared to 159,300 in Germany; and 234,300 in higher technical education compared to 49,700 in England and 63,888 in the United States.

[2] *Fulfillment of the First Five Year Plan,* pp. 229, 296.

This compares very favorably with the enrollment in the last prosperous year in the United States as follows: In 1928, out of 30,887,167 children of school age, aged 5 to 17 inclusive, there were enrolled in public elementary schools and kindergartens 23,503,416; in secondary and normal schools, 4,321,361; in American universities and colleges, 868,793; in all institutions, public and private, 29,410,615. Of illiterates of voting age there were 5.2 per cent males and 5.4 per cent females. *Statistical Abstract of the United States,* 1931, p. 109. The United States Office of Education in 1928 showed that of 1,000 pupils entering the elementary schools, 974 reached the sixth grade, 855 the seventh, 768 the eighth, 610 proceeded to the high schools, 438 continued to the second year, 321 to the third year, 268 to the fourth year, and 260 completed the course; 160 went on to college, and of these, 50 graduated.

Some of their statistics based upon local reports are perhaps over-enthusiastic and must be taken with a grain of salt, though on the whole they try to make them scientifically reliable. While I was interviewing an official in the department of education this summer I asked him the percentage of enrollment under their system of compulsory primary education for the whole U.S.S.R. He claimed it was 100 per cent. I refused to record or take seriously such a romantic and unscientific statement. It was the experience of Germany, the most highly educated nation after a hundred years of effort, that no country could ever reach perfection. The official I am referring to was not the head of the department and simply did not know his facts.

The Russians are the first to confess that much of their education is still of poor quality. There is a dearth of trained teachers, textbooks, equipment and buildings. Yet there has been a widespread application of modern methods in their educational system which is almost being created *de novo*. Their whole system is the most utilitarian, materialistic, experimental and socialized of any in the world.

Beginning with the latest "complex" method of education, they often swept away the traditional curriculum, substituting this development of the project method. They would study life in the home, the village, the farm, the factory, the seasons of the year, etc. The unsatisfactory results of this casual education were resented in a bluntly worded resolution of the Communist Party Central Committee which demanded "fully literate pupils, properly mastering such basic subjects as physics, chemistry, mathematics, the Russian language, geography, etc." Accordingly, the systematic study of subjects for accurate knowledge is being reintroduced instead of, or along with, the study of the "complex" as a cross section of life itself. The schools must turn out not merely political agitators but trained workers and constructive leaders.

Lenin was the pioneer in education as in all else. In 1920 he had said: "In an illiterate country it is impossible to build a Communist state." The result has been a class war upon

illiteracy, ignorance and superstition equal to that carried on against capitalist industry and agriculture. Through their school system, adult education and campaign against illiteracy the government was able to announce that the number able to read and write had been raised from 33 per cent in 1913 to 90 per cent at the end of 1932.[1]

Plato and Aristotle believed that the educational system of any community should be determined by the character of the political state. The Soviet Union is the first complete modern embodiment of that doctrine. The whole system is designed for the creation of the Soviet citizen and state.

Russian educators believe that the educational systems of capitalist countries train their children for an atomistic organization of society which perpetuates by the competitive spirit, individual selfishness and exploitation of the weak by the strong. The ambition of "success" is stimulated to equip oneself by education to join the ranks of the strong and to become rich by exploiting human labor. In theory at least, the way is open in America "from log cabin to White House" or Wall Street for the favored few to get on in the competitive race. Indeed the chance is promised for all in the words of Herbert Hoover: "The first ideal of our democracy is to maintain a state where each individual shall have an equality of opportunity to take that position in the community to which his intelligence, ability and ambition entitle him." Such a statement ignores the poverty, slums and unemployment which handicap so many.

The Russians believe that this idea of the "freedom" of the individual in practise encourages the exploitation of the helpless and that the state becomes the rule of the propertied class. They hold that all education is consciously or unconsciously for the *status quo,* or the political ends of the class or party in power. In the United States "Americanization" programs for foreigners and patriotic ceremonies connected with the flag are for the ends of the capitalist state as it now is, while

---

[1] *The First Five Year Plan,* pp. 32, 296.

in Russia the whole educational system is devised to destroy the old classes and build the new classless society of the future.

The bulk of the population constitutes an aristocracy of labor, directed by the Communist Party. Education is frankly propaganda and propaganda is education. If you already have the truth you do not need to think to discover it. You have only to teach it, impose it and govern by it. I have heard intelligent Russian students vehemently defend the practical infallibility of Marx. Education is not a search for truth but the teaching and application of fundamentalist Marxism. Education, however, rather than the police force is the principal means of building the new man and the new society. "So-called academic freedom is bourgeois humbug."

Every pupil is indoctrinated and every citizen must accept the fundamental principles of socialization, the abolition of private property, the dictatorship of the proletariat under the guidance of the Communist Party, and the class struggle in Russia as the pioneer, and, finally, throughout the world to establish a classless society. All the awakened ones must not seek advancement for themselves but become militant revolutionaries to aspire to enter the Party, the shock brigades, the organizations of leadership to build the new world. It is collective mass education at the antipodes from *laissez faire* individualism.

In the West education is chiefly considered as a short period of preparation for real living, confined to the school or college. In Russia it seeks to embrace the whole of life. "Education is life and life is education." [1] From the home, the nursery, the kindergarten with its militant songs, from the school, the workshop, the youth organizations, the trade unions, the press, the radio and cinema, the countless museums, social centers and excursions to the factories and collective farms with their Red Corners, evening classes and endless meetings—all the creative processes of life are harnessed in one educational plan under the direction of the Communist Party and the control

---

[1] For an excellent account see A. P. Pinkevitch, *The New Education in the Soviet Republic,* and I. L. Kandel, *Comparative Education,* pp. 69-76, 172-187.

of the government. If you accept it, as the vast majority do, it becomes to them a glorious crusade; if you do not, the system becomes an instrument of torture in a prison house. Capitalistic education prepares its pupils to enter a competitive steeplechase or hurdle race with its glittering prizes for the winners; but there is no social purpose that can integrate, fuse and draw all into one burning unit, where the individual is lost in a consuming cause, as in the World War, or in the continuing Revolution of the Soviet Union.

The impression a visitor to a Russian school or college receives is that they are different from anything he has ever seen. From the earliest ages there is political indoctrination by instruction and by stirring proletarian and anti-capitalist songs which always include the toilers of the world in their call to a fervid crusade. The students, boys and girls alike, and from the lowest to the highest, are class conscious proletarians. They are keen and enthusiastic, with an earnest purpose and a thirst for knowledge that is perhaps unique in the world. Any flagging of interest is fanned to flame by shock brigades of Komsomol or Party members who urge the students on to ever greater endeavors, longer hours of study and more efficiency. Every institution has an intense political atmosphere as a Revolutionary center with a world horizon. Russian education is never nationalistic but always international in scope. Whether the course be technical, medical or law, primary or University, there is instruction with almost religious fervor and dogma in Marxism, Leninism, Darwinism, dialectic materialism and revolutionary technique. Every institution has its Red Corner and all are expected to take part in "social" activities. Examinations have been abolished and promotion depends upon the professor and the student self-governing organizations.

One of the fundamental principles of Soviet education is "conditioning" the pupil in a certain direction beginning with crèches and nurseries for infants. From the cradle to the grave one system of truth is taught to the whole population of Russia: "Only after rigorous indoctrination can the individual be trusted to be free. . . . For the present the Soviet

system of administration seeks to define for the individual the truth which is to make him free."

The official representative of the Department of Education frankly told us that there were four principles that lay at the basis of Communist education in the Soviet Union today: 1. Soviet education must be scientific and teach the basic elements of the sciences. 2. It must relate scientific education everywhere to practical life and social work. 3. It must not be narrowly nationalistic and "patriotic," but everywhere international, in the Communist sense, and anti-religious, *i.e.,* anti-superstitious and anti-reactionary, always for the secular workers' state, and against the capitalistic Church-State. 4. It must include physical training, hygiene, and athletics to produce "iron muscles and steel nerves."

Soviet education is all founded upon labor which is conceived as the central axis of the entire school. "All teaching is unified through one central synthetic scheme of colossal importance—*human labor.*" From the age of fourteen, for several hours a day during several months of the year every student is engaged in the workshop which is found in every well-equipped school. For boys or girls, students of law or medicine, work is the basis of their education. Every brain worker is educated also as a toiler with the hands. All his life he feels himself to be one of the working class because he is one. It is an aristocracy of labor for all save a few disfranchised outcastes or suspected old intelligentsia, many of whom would now gladly become one with the workers if they were allowed to do so. The classless society is already rapidly forming. Two generations of such education should make all Russia into a single class, an educated proletariat.[1]

---

[1] The means used in its system of education are well adapted to the ends it seeks. A liberal like John Stuart Mill, suspicious of all state education, would hold in horror its means and ends alike: "A general state education is a mere contrivance for moulding people to be exactly like one another; and as the mould in which it casts them is that which pleases the predominant power in the government, whether this be a monarch, a priesthood, an aristocracy, or the majority of the existing generation, in proportion as it is efficient and successful, it establishes despotism over the mind, leading by natural tendency to one over the body." *Essay on Liberty,* 1859.

The Cultural Revolution

The cultural revolution is the extension of the plan of education to the population as a whole. It includes not only literacy and the importing of general and technical knowledge, but the diffusion of culture to a primitive people and the development of their esthetic life in literature, art, music, the drama, etc. The Russians have been uncultured and crude in social amenities but have large capacity for artistic development.

Culture is developed through their social centers, Houses of Culture and a network of agencies extending throughout the Union. The young Komsomols are a vital force in organizing "cultural raids" in literacy classes and technical instruction. The labor unions also take a large share of responsibility in the broad educational program.

The women of Russia, now largely set free from the drudgery of the kitchen, are supplying the need for Red nurses, organizers of kindergartens, nurseries, playgrounds, communal dining rooms, libraries and clubs. They provide their quota of judges on the bench, officials taking the chair at meetings, and more than their share in the development of the cultural life. There are also camps, institutions for homeless children, "forest schools," sanitaria for consumptive children and a variety of such social institutions scattered over Russia.

As one sees the new painting, the new sculpture, the new architecture, and especially the revolutionary theatre and music of Russia, he sees a vast possible development in the esthetic sphere, all the more, perhaps, as religion is being eliminated from the life of the new generation. There are those who believe that Russia will eventually become the most extensive market for art in the world. This will be powerfully stimulated by the attitude of the government to the cultural revolution.

One of the principal channels of the cultural revolution is carried on by means of the press, periodicals and books. The newspaper circulation has increased among this newly literate population over that in Czarist days from 2.7 million in 1913, to 36 million copies of 6,500 newspapers in 1933. The circu-

lation of books has risen to 53,800 new titles a year. This vast volume of literature is issued in 90 languages within the U.S.S.R.[1]

In the daily press, workers correspondents are encouraged and developed in the factories, villages and in the Red Army until there are now two million of these. At the head of the list they place Maxim Gorky as "the first shock writer in literature." Children are already being selected and trained as future correspondents. There were over 8,000 in 1932. There are also thousands of workers and peasants in journalist shock brigades. The Red Army is a powerful cultural force and its discharged men become leaders in agricultural and cultural reconstruction.

The government provides in its plan for the whole supply of literature. This is organized in many centers but not a book is printed in Russia for private profit. Its more than 50,000 books and pamphlets a year have a circulation of 900,-000,000 copies. Sidney Webb estimates the total issues of the press and all literature as greater than that in the United States, Great Britain and Germany combined. And this in a country which was two-thirds illiterate twenty years ago! The population seems famished for literature, although the publication of papers and magazines is nine-fold greater than in 1913. The government cannot keep pace with the voracious demand as all this campaign is carried on in ninety languages, several of which have only recently been reduced to writing by the Soviets. Over 600,000,000 copies of pamphlets were sold last year by the State Publishing House of Moscow, some six or seven copies for every adult and youth in the entire population. School textbooks must now be supplied for over twenty-five million students and pupils, together with literature for the 10,000 professors and lecturers and 500,000 teachers in the U.S.S.R. All this constitutes a veritable Renaissance, in a

---

[1] A network of 46,000 reading rooms and 1,500 houses of socialist culture provide literature free. For statistics in this chapter see *The Fulfillment of the First Five Year Plan,* pp. 228-238. and articles by Sidney Webb in *Current History,* 1932 and 1933.

proletarian population as eager for learning as any academic or privileged group in all past history.

There is, naturally, a censorship. Considerable scope is allowed within a rigid framework, save in the realm of economics and politics. Of course every civilized country has some censorship, whether official or of public opinion; but that in Russia does not as yet encourage the possibilities of the creative imagination in spontaneity, variety, and scope. At least pornographic and libellous literature is not permitted. One sees no sex appeal such as one finds openly on the news-stands of New York, London or Paris. Such an emphasis as Russia is making upon education, culture, literature, discussion, democratic public meetings and "self criticism" does not seem to indicate that the leaders will be hostile to *eventual* liberty. Real tyranny dares not educate.

A New Youth Movement

Whatever else the Revolution may be, it is a Renaissance of youth. As one faces this new type of deadly serious "flaming youth" he is constrained to ask: If Soviet Russia can challenge and inspire its youth to heroic daring, titanic achievement and sacrificial service, why cannot the Anglo-Saxon and capitalist countries do so? If we say that it is because of the war spirit, why is it that from one decade to another they seem to be able to maintain this psychology of war with all its heroic sacrifice and strenuous endeavor? How is it that the goal in sight and life itself can be made to seem so worthwhile that they do not count the cost of life or death in the quest?

Russia is today a land of youth and dominated by the spirit of youth. Probably a hundred million of the 165,000,000 of the population were born since 1910 and are under 25 years of age. The bulk of these have never known any other than the present order. They have been conditioned and moulded by the whole designed, educational process of the Revolution. They have grown up in this atmosphere of mental uniformity. It is not merely a fiction to maintain the spirit of war. They

have never known normal life since 1914, two decades ago. They have fought successively in the World War, when they mobilized fifteen million men, the Civil War against the invading foreigners and White Armies, then against the bourgeois class in the industrial revolution, when it was long an open question as to who would win, then against the "wicked" class of kulaks in the villages, and now, since there are few class enemies to lift their heads within Russia itself, their eyes are turned toward the great foreign capitalist nations, feeling themselves to be the faithful defenders of a beleaguered fortress hemmed in by five-sixths of the jealous world. There are enough incidents and trials played up by the unified Russian press to justify the most vigilant defense against an anticipated invasion and to require military science as a compulsory subject for both sexes. It is a moving scene to see 50,000 Pioneers in a great stadium asked by the orator through the loud speaker: "Pioneers, are you ready?" and to hear them answer in unison: "We are ready!"

And this development has been during a period when the bulk of Anglo-Saxon students were concerned with finding jobs and making a bare living, not with building a new social order or changing the world according to any known pattern or plan. A plan or philosophy of life was the last thing that most of them had, whether individual or social. The danger in the Russian character, on the other hand, is that they plunge headlong into novelties and fresh causes, but have hitherto lacked the prosaic and plodding Anglo-Saxon character of patient endurance. They undertake more than they can finish and fight on too many fronts at once. But even in this they are beginning to learn by experience.

There is considerable overlapping and interpenetration in the organizations of youth in the U.S.S.R. in the three stages. The Young Octobrists include children all the way from 6 to 14; the Pioneers take the children from 10 to 17; the Komsomols, or Union of Communist Youth, take the now seasoned youth from 14 to 23. The fortunate, selected ones are counted worthy to enter the Communist Party at 18, and naturally influence and train the Komsomols, as they in turn guide and

inspire the younger organizations, though each is autonomous. There are some three and a half million members of the Party at the beginning of 1934, and over ten million youth in the three organizations strenuously preparing themselves for leadership in what they conceive to be their moral crusade for world deliverance.

These more than thirteen millions have been conditioned and largely weaned from the conscious desire for personal acquisitiveness. They have been taught to look upon wealth as a sign not of success but of failure, not as a measuring rod of honor and achievement but of disgrace. They have been made socially minded by every ideal held up before them since their birth. In a school to say that a little boy's father is a capitalist or profiteer is a more terrible thing than to say that his mother is a woman of the street. A prostitute is looked upon with pity, as a wreck from a capitalist civilization, but a profiteer is regarded with burning indignation. While the youth of other lands in recent years have been talking of depression or decline, with a feeling of frustration, or futility, or pessimism, the youth of Russia in their plain clothes have the buoyant spirit of Garibaldi and his thousand—nothing to offer for the moment but rags, but a world to win. Russian youth is too old for its years. It feels the weight of responsibility for the country, for the world, for the future. It takes itself seriously, often too seriously. But this has been its chief moral corrective.

The students feel themselves on the firing line of an economic "front." All their spare time is demanded of Party or Komsomol members for strenuous service. They lead city workers to the country or descend as often unwelcome "shock brigaders" upon some factory. They edit "Wall Newspapers," organize excursions, lead literacy or government loan campaigns. All their activities knit them into the life of the workers and peasants.

Youth and Education in the West

No system of education could stand in sharper contrast to the regimented, collective mass education of Soviet Russia

than does the English. Its privileged universities of Oxford and Cambridge were founded nearly eight hundred years ago. Owing to the long abstention of the state from the provision of education at public expense, and to the historic, haphazard growth of private and religious education and the unwillingness of the government to disturb already established vested interests, the result is a strange conglomerate.

Only in 1861 the government began to take an interest in secondary education. The extension of the suffrage led as late as 1870 to the Elementary Education Act, which was the first movement toward a system of national education. Finally, in 1902, the attempt was made to reduce the wide variety of schools to some system. As late as 1900, almost a century after France and Germany had laid the foundation of a public system of secondary education, the English Court of Appeal virtually decided that there was no Public Authority in England with legal power to establish and maintain secondary schools.

H. J. Laski says: "We are the only people in the modern world whose system of education is deliberately built on class distinctions. That initial choice has largely confined the positions of command in society to the children of the economically privileged classes. . . . Its result has been the inevitable one, so clearly foreseen half a century ago by Matthew Arnold, that there is no real community of spirit and culture between the different classes of this country. The environment of the class which governs is so alien from that of the class dependent upon it that they seem, to any careful observer, to live in different worlds." [1]

In England compulsory education begins very early and continues up to the age of fourteen. For the vast majority all education ends here. In striking contrast to conditions in Russia, R. H. Tawney points out: "Ninety per cent of the 2,500,000 young persons between fourteen and eighteen are receiving no kind of education." [2] Some 650,000 of them

[1] H. J. Laski, *Democracy in Crisis,* p. 220.
[2] R. H. Tawney, *Secondary Education for All,* p. 15, George Allen and Unwin, Ltd. In 1919-20, 11,134 children in England and Wales were refused

reach the age of fourteen and leave the primary schools each year. Most of them will have no adequate opportunity in life save as hewers of wood and carriers of water or in white collar clerkships. A hand-to-mouth, piecemeal education means a piecemeal social order. Mr. Tawney and others have made an impassioned plea for a completely reconstructed plan which would provide secondary education for the majority of children from eleven to sixteen years of age, yet two million children in England are clamoring for secondary education in vain. Mr. Tawney maintains that a nation is sterilizing itself if all that it demands of the majority is orderliness, docility, and a capacity to understand orders and obey them. One class is then free while another belongs to a servile state dependent upon "their betters." Soviet Russia will disturb the conscience of the world in this regard.

While quantitatively England is strangely backward, the quality of education in the United States leaves much to be desired. In American universities and colleges are 868,793 students, in Soviet Russia some 500,000, in the English universities 32,500.[1] In secondary education, high schools, etc., the United States has enrolled 5,000,000 youth from 12 to 18 years of age; in Soviet Russia there are 4,359,000. In England and Wales there are but 570,187 of all ages, and even from this number it would be necessary to deduct many from 7 to 11 years of age who are really primary students. When I remarked to an English lecturer who annually visits the United States, "Is it not a disgrace that nine-tenths of your children never go beyond primary education?" he replied, "Yes, but when I see the products of your high shools with their stereotyped mass education, I do not think that our children are missing much."

If we compare the percentage of children of secondary or high school age enrolled in educational institutions in the various countries we find the following: United States 27.2;

---

[1] *Year Book of Education*, 1932, p. 178.

admission to secondary schools because there were no free places available for them.

Scotland 9.1; Japan 8.4; Philippine Islands 7.9; England and Wales 3.9.[1] Soviet Russia claims to hold second place in this list. Sidney Webb makes the statement that the Soviet Union is spending more per capita upon the education of its children than is Great Britain. We may compare the percentage of the national budget expended for the army and for education in certain large countries for which we have the data as follows:[2]

Country	Army	Education
England	4.5	6.4
France	12.9	6.0
Italy	12.8	6.6

In the unified budget of the U.S.S.R. they are spending 1.63 billion roubles, or 5.4 per cent, for education. For administration and defense combined they spend 1.84 billion roubles, or only 6.1 per cent of the budget.[3] This is a far smaller proportion, of course, than is spent in England or in the United States. Raymond B. Fosdick says: "In the United States the expenditure attributable to war, service of war debts, war pensions and current cost of armaments, constitute 80 per cent of the total Federal budget. In Great Britain this expenditure is 77 per cent of the budget; in France it is slightly less. 'While other nations have felt that they were forced to prepare for war,' said Mr. Coolidge, 'our situation has been such that we have always been preparing for peace.' "[4]

With all their faults, as one reviews the achievements of Soviet Russia in the care of children, in education, in general culture and art, in the organized youth movement and in their ability to challenge and inspire the rising generation to service and sacrifice, all but the most cynical or prejudiced among us must admit that we have much to learn from them, not in copying their system but in transforming our own.

[1] Paul Munroe, *A Survey of Education.*

[2] I. L. Kaplan, *Comparative Education,* p. 207. The figures for the U.S.A. cannot be given, as the greater proportion of the cost of education is borne by the several states rather than by the Federal Government.

[3] *The Five Year Plan,* p. 29. Of its budget the U.S.S.R. spends 39.4 per cent on industry, 17 per cent on agriculture, 12.8 on transport and communication, 5.4 on education, and 6.1 on administration and defense.

[4] Raymond B. Fosdick, *Atlantic Monthly,* August, 1931.

CHAPTER V

NEW MOTIVES AND INCENTIVES

It was the basic conviction of the Marxian and Russian leaders, who had been fighting against capitalism for more than half a century, that the root evil of the whole system was the private ownership of the means of production which automatically divided the people into antagonistic classes of privileged owners and helpless dependents. The powerful profit motive was operative for the owners, but the workers, divorced from the means of production, who were the tools of gain for others, were afforded neither any share in the profit themselves nor security of life.[1] Once the Russian leaders had destroyed the old system, root and branch, what motives and incentives might be utilized to impel the workers not only to compete with but to surpass the capitalist world?

Under the old order a growing number of workers who had nothing to sell but their labor power were driven into open hostility by a system which could not provide them with regular work and made them feel that they were under "wage-slavery" for the enrichment of others. The whole system of the largest reward for the least work, like chattel slavery before it, encouraged shirking and the regarding of work as an evil

---

[1] Professor Taussig of Harvard says: "Under the existing social organization, every man, whatever his bent, is constantly under the sway of the narrower self-regarding motives. The whole structure of private property is built on the foundation of a striving for one's own. Inventors, poets, painters, business men all alike are in the folds of a system which compels them to exercise their powers for their own advantage." *Inventors and Money Makers,* pp. 21-23, 52. Professor Rexford Tugwell adds: "If profits are so important to our system, why do we allow them to be used in such ways as not only to destroy the source of future earnings, but to create unemployment and hardship amongst millions?" *American Economic Review,* March, 1932.

instead of a common social obligation for the equal welfare of all. Thus capitalism offered motivation, reward and development for the few, but left the latent potentialities of the great mass undiscovered. Mr. Laidler points out that Napoleon and Nelson were poor as subordinate officers but became distinguished commanders.[1] It was the conviction of Marx that many a worker carried a marshal's baton in his tool kit but that it would never be discovered so long as he had no share in the ownership of the means of production nor any hope of reaping the full reward of his labor.

Some advocates of the old order maintain that owner and worker alike in the competitive scramble must be driven by fear of disaster. The Soviets, on the other hand, believe that under a planned economy if the worker is relieved of fear of unemployment, sickness and helpless old age, it will have the same beneficial effect upon him that it has upon the employer in other lands. They believe, with the early Christians, that the love of money is the root, if not of all evil, at least of a whole brood of anti-social consequences. The sweeping away of all privately owned productive capital and functional property at one stroke cuts the root of the unhealthy profit motive and leaves the ground free for a more healthy growth of socialized values. With a host of parasitic middlemen eliminated, all the workers are left free for creative work. With the saving of the enormous waste of competitive advertising in the selling of the product, with no idle plant, labor or capital, with no waste in the production of useless luxuries, in what Ruskin called "illth" in contradistinction to true wealth, with an adequate plan for distribution and consumption as well as for production, and above all, in the aim of basic justice for all who toil, where labor feels it is sharing in the entire surplus value which it creates, the workers tend to do their best under a system that wins their confidence and loyalty. Where the workers with new solidarity feel that they are working for themselves, they have the same successful motivation that the owners had in the early days of the capitalist system. The

[1] H. W. Laidler, *Incentives Under Capitalism,* p. 48.

workers now become capitalists, not individually but as a class, without the evil effects of the old system.[1]

While Marx and the Soviet leaders admitted the enormous productive power of capitalism as a necessary stage of development and an advance over all previous stages, they believe that they are now well rid of a whole brood of evils which had increased under a system of *laissez faire,* rugged and ruthless individualism, with their orthodox dogmas of "the economic man," "the iron law of wages," "the law of supply and demand," and the "dismal science" of outworn economics, with its inevitable injustice, irrational planlessness, falsity and failure. They believe that just as Japan and Germany created a new national psychology through their controlled educational system, that Communists could create a whole new social order based upon a new philosophy of life, with higher and healthier motivations.[2]

In the creation of their new system the Soviet leaders believed that *laissez faire* economics from the time of the Manchester School were false in holding that men would only do their best work with the opportunity for unlimited personal profit, and that the motive of competitive selfishness would benevolently work out for the good of all. On the other hand they do not rely so much upon appeals to individual unselfishness and nobility of character as they do in the creating of a more healthy and scientific environment where the interests of the individual and of society become practically identical. They do not plan first to change human nature, but the social situation, so that a whole network of healthy motives can enable both the individual and society to function more effectively than the old capitalist profit motive which had commercialized and debased almost all human relations.

Beginning with the lower and more individual incentives, and rising to higher and more social ones, we may distinguish some

---

[1] No book makes this so plain as Professor Harry Ward's *In Place of Profit.*

[2] Marx says: "With us it is not a matter of reforming private property, but of abolishing it; not of hushing up the class antagonisms, but of abolishing the classes; not of ameliorating the existing society, but of establishing a new one." *Address to the Communist League.*

twelve motivations which are chiefly operative in Soviet Russia today, as follows:

1. *Self-interest.*—The Soviet leaders do not hesitate to appeal to the self-interest of the worker in a way that is subjectively closely akin to the old profit motive. Objectively, the difference is not in the motive but in the system where the self-interest of the individual is enlisted not for monopolistic private gain but for the common good, where self-interest and social-interest are almost identical. In offering the worker more pay for skilled labor or piece work, this adds to the production and profit of the whole community in which the worker will have his full share. In doing this the leaders are realistic rather than idealistic. They recognize that the habits of the worker have been warped by the old system under which he has worked. They know that they are not creating an ideal Utopia in a vacuum, but building socialism in the midst of a hostile capitalist world which has already opposed them by intervention, invasion, a hunger blockade, adverse competition and propaganda.

They deliberately appeal to the worker's instinct of self-preservation. They are not at all afraid to take a leaf out of the book of capitalism if they can use it temporarily to hasten the realization of their own system. Stalin suggested in one of his famous six points on June 23, 1931: "We must introduce a more widely differentiated wage scale, providing a stimulus for advancement by piece work and a high reward for skilled labor."

These methods include opportunities for adult education to improve the workers' status and wage, group bonus schemes, prizes and medals, the winning for one's factory of an improved social center, lunch rooms, entertainment hall, a day nursery for the children, etc. In every advance the worker knows that he is helping himself and his cause at the same time. When I was in Russia a decade ago in 1923 the average wage for the U.S.S.R. was only 25 cents a day, or $6.41 a month, which was less than 15 roubles a month or 180 roubles a year. This year the average annual wage was 1,432 roubles.

Real wages had also advanced, though not as much as the money wage. The work day had been shortened from 9.9 hours in 1913 to 7 hours in 1933. The output per worker had increased 2.8 times since 1913 and 61 per cent during the Five Year Plan.[1]

2. *Moral indignation, hatred and fear* were powerful motivations, especially in the early, destructive stages of the Revolution. There was an outraged sense of justice that burned in the heart of Marx and in all the early revolutionaries. This, of course, was often dangerous and destructive. Fear is also a common human motivation, especially in Russia today. Fear of invasion by the capitalist world is constantly played upon by the leaders and the press to unite the population in loyal defense. The former Allied intervention and hunger blockade, with the famine and pestilence that followed, are still vividly remembered in Russia. This was one of the component motivations in the Five Year Plan. Fear, as we have seen, is also a negative and paralyzing motive which leads many technicians to avoid the responsibility of decisions lest they be accused of sabotage in case of failure. This is always a handicap under any dictatorship which feels itself forced to use ruthless methods.

3. *Pugnacity, the fighting spirit and the class war* are all invoked in the cause of the "continuing revolution." They develop a high steam pressure of feeling against injustice. New revolutionary ardor has often been known to lift masses of humanity upon a wave of enthusiasm. This is usually destructive and short lived and passes when they undertake the more patient and arduous work of construction which follows. In Russia they have been able in a remarkable way to harness this fighting spirit to the creative, constructive and peaceful work which succeeded the dramatic stage of destruction. The

[1] Stalin has been receiving 300 roubles a month and men under him from 700 to 800 roubles. Judge Gary received in 1917 $425,000; Sir Henri Deterding, head of the Royal Dutch Shell Company, $5,000,000 in 1930; Mr. George W. Hill, President of the American Tobacco Company, $2,000,000 the same year; George Gordon Crawford, President of the Jones and Laughlin Company, regularly received $350,000 a year. H. W. Laidler, *Incentives Under Capitalism*, p. 7.

whole Five Year Plan was such a constructive undertaking. It was the industrial rather than the military elements of this plan which most appealed to the people. The factory worker is taught that he is "a soldier on duty" and is carrying on the fight for socialism against the capitalist world. He is a shock brigader taking part in the industrial and cultural attack. Military metaphors are freely and successfully used. They are thus far able to keep up the sacrificial spirit of the World War in peace time, with its heroism and daring.

4. *The will to power, the stimulation of a sense of personal dignity and of self-importance* tend to remove the inferiority complex from the workers and to make them feel that they are the messianic class which is to deliver the world. Whether it be true or not, it gives the workers a status, a sense of mission and belief in their own indomitable power that motivates them for tremendous undertakings. A messianic consciousness has played an important part in many critical periods of history. No "chosen people" ever took themselves more seriously than do the Communists. As Mr. J. A. Hobson says: "The sense of doing important and interesting things has a high personal value which can be enhanced by fame and honor." If you believe that you are saving the world and that there is no other way of deliverance, any sacrifice or suffering seems justified. Power has frequently been a more effective incentive than profit, and power the workers of Russia have. Similar to the power of the aristocracy in England or the plutocracy in America, the worker's chance for promotion and the exercise of leadership is infinitely greater in the Communist than in the capitalist world. Here the struggle for power has replaced the struggle for wealth.

5. *The creative instinct* is another powerful motivation. The desire to find satisfaction in excellence of performance, the impulse to create something which many could approve or enjoy was more powerful in early handicrafts and during the Renaissance than after the machine swept this away under the system of mass production. In Russia the spirit of youth

predominates.   Precedents, conventions, restraints, traditions have been brushed aside.   They feel that almost everything they do makes a record for "the first time in history."   It is a moving experience to hear fifty thousand youth shouting in perfect unison as I did in Moscow: "We are changing the world! We are changing the world! We are changing the world!"   It is always stimulating to be living in a creative epoch in history when to be young is "very heaven."   It is very different if youth feels that it is living near the end of a decaying order with a sense of frustration or cynicism as in many lands today.   In Russia all the parasitic pursuits and privileges of inherited wealth or titles have been destroyed and the ground cleared for creative construction.

All this gives a new dignity to labor which neither slavery, feudalism nor capitalism could give.   In the "Declaration of the Rights of the Toilers" [1] the Constitution of the Russian Republic "recognizes labor as the duty of all citizens and pro-claims the principle 'He who does not work neither shall he eat.'"   They may or may not have recognized that they were quoting from Saint Paul.   The right to vote is enjoyed only by those who perform "labor that is productive and useful to society."   The profiteer, the idle rich, the stock gambler, the speculator, the man who is out for "easy money," and all parasitic elements which exist in other countries are classed with the criminal and the gangster.   In a creative society money ceases to be a measuring rod of success or power.   "Making good" no longer means making money.   Human values have more chance in a world not governed by finance; and Mammon is classed with Moloch.

6. *Social acquisitiveness* gradually takes the place of personal acquisition as a new social order replaces the old artificial, competitive, atomic individualism.   The principle "every man for himself" has made money for the monopolist but it has not created the great epochs of history.   Nothing is more natural than the sharing of food.   A young man sacrificing for his

---

[1] As adopted July 10, 1918.

wife and children finds a motivation in the family more power-ful than the independent bachelor. The Soviets are learning that the family circle may be widened for the toiler to include his country, his class and the workers of the world; that social acquisitiveness is far more valuable and effective than anti-social individual acquisitiveness. Some day they may learn that any exclusive class, however large, is relatively narrow; and that all humanity is a nobler whole than any section of it, even if it be the disinherited. But in the meantime they have made a great advance over selfish individualism when the individual already feels the glow of self-identification with a consuming cause.

Communists would no more think of commercializing for private profit the necessities of their fellow men for housing, water, gas, electric power, transportation, telegraphs, tele-phones, radio, moving pictures, or financial credit than they would try to profiteer out of fresh air, or sunshine, or the educational system. They have found greater efficiency and lower costs in public rather than private ownership and opera-tion of electric power, for instance, just as has the Province of Ontario in Canada in contrast to the profiteering of the capitalistic utilities in the States.

7. *Social competition and the sporting instinct* is appealed to constantly and effectively. This seems to be already almost as powerful and far less anti-social than cut-throat individual competition. William James maintained that rivalry did nine-tenths of the world's work. All the competition engendered in college athletics and school sports is utilized in Soviet social-ist competition. Self-seeking gives place to social serving as in all true team play. Lenin saw this as early as 1918 when he wrote on "How to Organize Competition" as follows: "Only now has the possibility for wide and really mass display of enterprise, competition and bold initiative been created. Every factory from which the capitalist has been ejected, every village from which the landowner exploiter has been smoked out, is now a field in which the working man can reveal himself, straighten himself and feel that he is a man."

The Soviet system coordinates the egoistic and altruistic incentives under a scheme of ownership where a man necessarily works for others when he works for himself, and where all share almost equally in the profits. In one aspect the whole Five Year Plan was a supreme achievement in socialist competition. They throw into competition worker with worker, group with group, factory with factory. They compete with their past record, with the goal of the Plan, with the capitalist world. All this competition is powerfully organized by the propaganda department of the Party to educate the masses by the preparation of slogans, posters, exhibits, literature, the cinema and the radio.

8. *The appeal to the heroic, the dramatic, and to social approval and disapproval* are used as incentives.

In capitalist countries money is power in business, politics and the press. In Russia all success is harnessed to service not profit. This changes the whole atmosphere of the factory, the farm and the school. It will entirely change the character of the moving picture, the radio and the press. In time it alters the psychology of the people as well. There is a transvaluation of ethical values. All exploitation is held to be dishonorable. All using of men as means to another's profit, as pawns in a game, or cogs in a machine, or "hands" in a private enterprise become immoral. Every organization in the Soviet Union from the kindergartens and the youth organizations upward becomes imbued with this spirit. From birth to maturity no other ideal is ever held up before young or old.

As the visitor passes down the Hall of Fame in any Russian city or park he sees statues and tablets not to generals, admirals or politicians, but to the heroes of industry who have led the way to the success of the Five Year Plan. As Stalin truly said: "Here in the U.S.S.R. the most desirable course which earns social approval is the possibility of becoming a hero of labor, a hero of the shock movement, surrounded with the glamor of the respect of the millions of toilers."

Social approval and disapproval are much more powerful in a close-knit communal society than under a competitive indi-

vidualism. All suffer if there are individual slackers and all
share in socially successful leadership. Public opinion in disapproval or approval is powerfully brought to bear upon each.
The dramatic instinct of the Russian and his power to visualize
is brought to bear to stimulate the ambition of the workers and
expose their shortcomings. A large proportion of the factory
population is in attendance at evening technical classes to
improve their skill and their individual and social usefulness.
Society is proving to be more powerful than the isolated and
competitive individual.

9. *Mutual aid and cooperation.*—Prince Kropotkin, who was
imprisoned by the Czar, traced the evolution of the mutual aid
principle from its origins in the animal kingdom, developing
in the higher ranges of life, while the brute struggle for life
dominates in the lower ranges. The whole development of
the cooperative movement bears witness to this principle. We
are all familiar with the forty-eight flannel weavers of Roch-
dale, England, who founded their little cooperative in 1848
which is now doing a business of more than a billion dollars
a year and includes in its membership and among its patrons
nearly a third of the families of Great Britain. They have
commanded able leadership like that of William Maxwell,
President for twenty-seven years of the Scottish Wholesale
Society, who never received more than $1800 a year, for a
society whose sales during his administration mounted to
$40,000,000 a year. These cooperative societies throughout
the world grew until they enrolled over 70,000,000 members
whose families numbered some 200,000,000 or nearly one-ninth
of the population of the world. But today Soviet Russia alone
has over 70,000,000 members of cooperative societies. She
may prove to the world that cooperation is more effective than
competition, and mutual aid more potent than the motive of
self-interest. The capitalist world is geared to the incentive
of self-interest so that often a man must choose between self-
regarding motives or starvation. The Soviet Union is building a social environment geared to the higher social motives of

cooperation and mutual aid.   The question is which motives are fittest to survive.

10. *Humanitarian and higher ethical ends* are increasingly utilized as incentives in Soviet Russia.   Their faith in human nature and especially in the common man that he will respond favorably to a favorable environment is validating itself in results.   Although Marx undoubtedly idealized the proletariat as a messianic "remnant," a class that was to deliver the world, his faith in the workers has been rewarded by a vast development of their unsuspected potentialities.   We have already seen in their redemption of criminals how these higher motives work in practice.   The Soviets do not parade these ideals.   They say very little about them.   They imagine that they are always scientific, as indeed they usually are.   Such achievements are not only sound in their science, their psychology and their underlying philosophy, but in their humanitarian and ethical motivation as well.   Sometimes both they and we are better than our narrow creeds.   Some day the Russian East may rise above the narrow confines of class war, and the West of selfish profit, to the service and building of a common humanity.   In the meantime we doubtless err in being too individualistic and they too exclusively social in their emphasis.   We are building a richer, fuller human personality and they a juster social order. Each has something to learn from the other.

11. *The motive of hope, of triumphant optimism, of almost fatalistic conviction in an eschatological future* is potent in Russia.

Repeatedly in history some chosen people has believed itself called to some great destiny which was to change history. Greece, Judea, Rome, modern imperialisms, various religious faiths and social systems have believed in such a destiny.   The Moslem with his sword, foreordained for victory on earth or paradise in heaven, swept over the world for centuries.   Missionaries of various faiths have altered the channels of history in many lands.

It may have been more than accidental that Marx himself

belonged to the chosen people whose bondsmen out of Egypt believed that they were destined to inherit the promised land and whose prophets, even when they foretold doom or captivity, firmly believed in the ultimate rule of righteousness on the earth.

Marx's almost fatalistic faith in the triumph of the proletariat and of the cause of human justice seemed to himself to be an obvious scientific demonstration but it was an undemonstrable and almost religious faith. There was an unconscious element of wishful thinking in his psychology, and his view of the proletariat is not realistic but an idealization. But within the bounds of the possible, faith tends to create the thing it seeks. Marx's faith was never quietistic. Others had interpreted history, he and his followers were going to change it. Nothing was impossible to them. However great his idealization of the proletariat, however unjustified his vision of the state "withering away" after the violent habits and methods of a ruthless dictatorship, and whatever the source of his beliefs, conscious or unconscious, he had the same essential faith in the ultimate triumph of truth, goodness and beauty, of justice and liberty, as Plato or the prophets of Israel. Such a faith often becomes creative and builds its dream on the solid earth of reality. For myself, while I see no adequate sign of the tyranny of the proletariat lessening, I must admit that in general the optimistic faith and hope of the Communists is tending to actualize and validate itself.

12. *Religious emotion, almost fanatical faith, sacrifice, missionary zeal,* and international world-wide objectives which are closely akin to their eschatological hope, are dynamic incentives in Russia today. As to whether or not Communism may be considered a religion we shall discuss in the chapter on *The Problem of Religion.* Certainly after their unfortunate association with the only type of religion they knew, Communists themselves indignantly repudiate the term. For every discredited word in our vocabulary Communists have used or coined another. Words like "love," "brotherhood," "religion" seem to them to savor of hypocrisy. When so many religions

instead of demanding and providing social justice have been prevailingly in alliance with the worst economic evils of the *status quo,* and have been reactionary and anti-social, it is not strange that Communists draw the conclusions they do.

We must go deeper than our conventional vocabulary. Upon this journey and while writing this book good people have repeatedly asked me whether Russia or any nation could survive without religion. The implication of these good people is that we have religion and Russia has not; that we are a Christian and the Soviet Union is an atheist nation. Such a sweeping generalization in both cases is quite untrue. We have not wearied of reiterating the evils of the Soviet system in this book. But we maintain that in many respects we have much to learn from Russia. Take, for instance, the questions of their insistence upon basic economic justice for all workers, their handling of unemployment, the absence of race prejudice and their treatment of criminals.

The final question is not which motives are higher in the light of ethical ideals but how do they work, and what are their fruits? Professor Harry Ward spent a year in Russia recently studying these motivations to ask "whether the building of Socialism was developing incentives which promised more for the continuing of human society than those which are manifestly failing in the capitalist world." He found in Russia a going concern which was economically succeeding especially in this field of motivations. He thinks: "It is doubtful if there has ever in history been such an organized conscious attempt as this to change the customs and habits of a people, certainly not since the great days of the Roman Church." In Russia where motives are anticipated ends, the very bigness of the end modifies all ordinary pursuits and methods. Immediate needs can be controlled in the light of long time values. Actually where private property in land and all means of production has practically ceased to exist; and where it is virtually impossible to make a private fortune, human service is taking the place of private profit upon such a scale that it is something new under the sun.

CHAPTER VI

ELIMINATING UNEMPLOYMENT AND SLUM CLEARANCE

During the period of the first Five Year Plan in capitalist countries the numbers of employed, their wages and standard of living had been steadily reduced, owing to the world depression, while the condition of the workers in the Soviet Union had been improved. The latter have long had a more complete system of social insurance and of social services than any workers in the world. Although there is a serious turnover in labor the Soviet Union is the only industrial country in the world which has completely eliminated unemployment. As unemployment has ceased for two years insurance for this purpose was withdrawn. During the four and a quarter years of the first Plan the number of workers in the U.S.S.R. was practically doubled, being raised from 11.59 millions to 22.8 millions, which was 44.7 per cent greater than the number called for in the Plan. Yet even this enormous increase, coupled with rapid mechanization, did not supply workers enough.[1]

---

[1] There are indeed too many employed as unskilled workers where fewer men could perform the same work much better in America or Britain. Hearing of better conditions in food or housing, workers move on to other factories or cities. Stalin complains: "We must put an end to the fluidity of labor, and its disastrous turnover of 30 or 40 per cent in half a year." In 1928 the Labor Exchange registered 1.3 million unemployed, in 1929 1.6 millions. Instead of fifty million roubles annually spent in unemployment benefits during these years, twice that sum was provided the next year for training new industrial workers, as the unemployment benefits were encouraging the migration of the Russian workers. The number of women workers in the national economy more than doubled during the period of the Plan, and is now 31.5 per cent of the entire number engaged in non-agricultural work. The Plan measurably fulfilled the objectives adopted by the Fifth Congress of Soviets, which were: "The rise in the technical equipment of labor, the labor enthusiasm of the masses of the people, the strengthening of enthusiastic

Sidney Webb and almost every other important economist who has visited the Soviet Union in recent times bears witness that for two years the Russians have known no involuntary unemployment and have no apprehension of it in the future. The nearly 10,000 managers of state works are "striving desperately to enroll additional men." Upon the notice boards of every government employment agency the large numbers wanted in each department of labor are published.

From 1920 to 1927 estimated unemployment in the United States ranged from 1,500,000 to 2,315,000. In 1932 it was about 10,000,000. In 1933 it rose at one time to about 16,000,000 on a given day, including the unemployed, the partly employed and the youth who had never been able to find work. Even when full allowance is made for the exaggerations of technocracy, the growth of technological unemployment coupled with increasing mechanization and rationalization is undeniable. While habitually paying too much in profits to the owners for investment in increasing production and over-production, with equal consistency industry has paid too little in wages, with the result that the purchasing power of labor, employed and unemployed, has been chronically or periodically inadequate. During prosperity from 1926 to 1929, while dividends and interest payments by corporations increased by approximately 73 per cent, wage payments in manufacturing remained practically stationary in the United States. By September, 1932, wages in industry had fallen to only 38 per cent of what they had been from 1926 to 1929, yet dividends and interest payments for the first nine months of 1932 were 64 per cent above those of 1926.

There has often been a lag in theory to account for the practice of recurring crises and depressions of disastrously increasing intensity. The titanic effort of the whole nation, with industry and government cooperating, has as yet only partly taken up the slack of unemployment in America. Unem-

and conscious socialist discipline, better organization of economic management, the determined struggle against bureaucracy, the widest possible development of self-criticism, the widest possible development of socialist competition." *The Fulfillment of the First Five Year Plan,* p. 181.

ployment, overproduction and recurring crises seem to remain the permanent problems of our system.

If we contrast the situation in Soviet Russia during the same period of world depression, which has been a heavy drain and handicap upon their own national economy, there seem to be certain conditions or elements in combination which many of our own economists believe will permanently eliminate from Soviet Russia these three evils—unemployment, over-production and resulting depressions. As we have seen, their economy combines vast undeveloped domestic resources, the world's largest and richest remaining open frontier, a rising standard of living, a calculable effective demand in steadily increasing purchasing power, and the elimination of the competitive wastes of advertising, of uneconomic luxuries, of injurious products and of squandered natural resources. All these are united in one intelligent and adequately controlled plan, or series of plans, which need never result in over-production or unemployment so long as they are controlled by intelligence and corrected by experience. In a word, they have a complete plan and we have not. They have no unemployment and we have much.

In connection with the question of employment we may consider working conditions for Russian labor. It will be long before the backward Russians can overtake the West, but at least they are now making more rapid economic and cultural progress than any other nation. Conditions for the Russian worker are steadily improving. His real wages are still low but he has many advantages. First of all, he has, and feels that he has, *security*. Even though the tempo is fierce, and a heavy proportion of the national income is laid aside for social capital and increase of plant, even though the individual must sacrifice in the present for the sake of the communal future, the worker feels he owns and shares and has behind him all the resources—land, labor and capital—of the largest country on earth. He has faith in the system which he believes promises less for the profiteer and more for the laborer, less for privilege and more in equal justice than any competing economy. He feels he is not the hand or tool or helpless wage dependent of an individual capitalist, or heartless corporation,

but that he is at once an owner-director-worker of the largest single economic unit ever in existence.

The detailed advantages of his life are considerable. His rent is low and seldom exceeds ten per cent of his wage. Without charge he has the service of a public health department, which means free medical attendance for all his family, including medical care, hospital, drugs, convalescent and rest homes and provision for vacation with full pay. All necessary education is provided free, from pre-school nurseries through university or technical school for his children, and night classes for continual technical and self-improvement for himself. His wife has the opportunity for work with full wages. For eight weeks before and eight weeks after childbirth, she receives free obstetric service and aid in the rearing of her children, in a country which has the largest system of nurseries in the world.

The worker has attained a new dignity and status. Three-fourths of the workers, or more than eighteen million of them, are united in trade unions in 1934. Instead of being fighting organizations to win rights from a class of owners with opposing interests, the unions have developed into creative and constructive administrative organs to increase output, lessen cost of production, administer the workers' own welfare organizations and social services and to adjust local personal grievances.

The forty-six great industrial unions unite all the workers by hand or brain in each industry. Each is built up in a great hierarchy, from the local democratic shop meeting and the factory council of about a dozen members to the highly organized national union, and finally the U.S.S.R. Trade Union Congress which unites them all. The worker normally contributes 2 per cent of his earnings to the union and usually takes full part in its constant discussions which involve criticism of the work of the plant and of the management.

Most of the workers are now on a piecework basis, which nearly all prefer because it provides higher wages for the workers and increased production. The Central Council of the workers' Trade Unions together with the workers who are

on the Presidium of the government's Supreme Council for National Economy agree upon a minimum wage, which is usually a bare living, and upon a wage scale rising to three or four times the minimum for skilled work. Sometimes from half to nine-tenths of the workers in a factory attend free evening classes to improve their skill, their production and their earning power as well as their cultural life. A large proportion also voluntarily enlist in "shock brigades" to speed up production and solve the problems of the backward plants. The production of every plant as listed by the Plan is under constant scrutiny.

Strikes are theoretically permissible but the reason for them is largely eliminated with the passing of the profit motive and of the conflicting interests of owners and wage dependents. Workers as owners and consumers negotiate with workers as producers to determine what proportion of the local or national income shall go into communal capital and what into wages. The "Triangle" of a representative of the management, the trade union and the Communist Party forms a local committee to hear every dispute which if not adjusted may be referred to higher bodies in a complete mechanism for the settlement of all differences by arbitration. All parties belong to the same class, all are workers, producers, consumers, owners. There is no bitterness, friction or waste in a conflict of interests between classes. They have more than a nominal or fictitious "freedom of contract." They have essential basic economic equality and identity of interests.

When the writer saw Lord Lothian in Moscow he felt that this gigantic experiment was the greatest thing of its kind on our planet and that it should not be compared to the destructive French Revolution but rather to a Renaissance and Reformation combined as a great emancipation of mankind.[1]

If Soviet Russia has the most complete workers' social services in the world, if nearly a score of advanced industrial countries have some effective form of social insurance, especially for unemployment, should the richest country in the world

---

[1] *Current History* for January, 1933, p. 399.

remain the most backward at this point? Should plans for unemployment insurance, despite Mr. Roosevelt's platform and promises and endeavors, be so defeated or postponed in state after state? If Russia could insure her unemployed, when she had them, why cannot the United States do so? If Russia can eliminate unemployment altogether, apart from a too rapid turnover, can we? And if not, why not?

Housing and Slum Clearance

The housing plans of the Soviet Union include the destruction of all unsanitary slum areas and, ultimately, the adequate housing of all the workers in the U.S.S.R. at reasonable rentals. This usually approximates about ten per cent of the individual salary. Already the government is constructing upon a large scale dormitories for workers and entirely new socialist cities near the recently developed centers of electric power and of raw materials. They are still, however, lacking in experience, in skilled technicians, in workers and in building materials. Consequently, much of this building is as yet far from satisfactory. Housing is still their weakest point.

In Czarist times the homes of the poor, whether in city or country, were unsanitary, overcrowded and filthy. Recurring famines and decimation from disease were reminiscent of the Middle Ages in other more advanced countries. Women were old and worn out before the age of fifty, while the infant death-rate was scandalous.

Cities like Moscow are still the most overcrowded in the world. Built to accommodate a little over a million, with a flood of peasants pouring in from the country to seek the higher wages and other perquisites of the favored industrial workers, Moscow now suddenly has to house three millions. Under a system that was straining every nerve to double and treble the construction of factories and production in heavy industry no possible plan could suddenly provide adequate housing for such a population. Even so their building program though qualitatively poor has been quantitatively vast.

In the new schemes for town planning the industries are

to form the heart or pivotal center around which the life of the community is to be built. According to the plans all uneconomic factories and, where possible, the slum dwellings, are to be pulled down. Each large factory or group of factories is to be a self-contained unit around which satellite communities are to be built in three separate zones—industrial, social and agricultural. Even the factories are supposed to be laid out along model lines, with wide roads and with provision ultimately for gardens. With the workers' dwellings are grouped the communal laundries, schools, hospitals and social centers. In theory nine square metres of space, or about ten feet square, are allowed for each person, but in actual practise where the chief concern is speed, seven or less are often realized.

In these town-planning schemes the consulting engineers have often been American and the architects German. In design the architecture, like the painting, sculpture, music and literature of Soviet Russia, feels the influence of the Revolution in its ideology. Quite naturally they have chosen the functional style which is practical rather than aesthetic. There is a square and drab sameness about the early construction that makes the houses like factories or hospital blocks. Engineers rather than architects have had their way. Working with an acute shortage of almost everything the standard of construction has been very low. The plumbing has often been bad, the carpentry rough, the electric installation poor.

Dnieperstroy is an honorable exception among their new socialist cities, but in others, like Magnetogorsk, their grandiose projects for a model town have been sadly unrealized. Many possess five-story red brick box houses which resemble barracks and will soon be condemned tenements giving place to more permanent and more comfortable structures.[1]

---

[1] The report of the director in charge of the socialist city of Magnetogorsk, on May 11, 1933, complained: "Many buildings show cracks in walls and foundations. Work on several buildings had to be stopped because of the complete unfitness of the work which had been done; some of these have already been demolished." The engineer, Kozmenko, writing in *Trud*, observes: "Architecturally the construction of entire sections of the new cities, as well as of individual houses, is extremely monotonous. No streets or sidewalks are laid out. The territory around the houses is choked with refuse and dirt. Often entire blocks of houses have neither light nor water."

The most hopeful part of their new construction is found in the social centers, in the parks, libraries, theatres, amusement halls and "red corners." They will learn only by experience. Quantity will in time give place to quality in their emphasis. The awakened criticism of the workers in these new quarters and the turnover in work where conditions are the worst will bring improvement. In the meantime they have at least a plan and will in time achieve it.

For the possibilities of such socialist cities under a planned economy we may turn to the example of Vienna. Their goal has almost been achieved within twelve years in spite of great poverty and economic handicaps. In 1921 the city planned to construct 70,000 lodgings before 1934. At the beginning of 1933 65,000 dwellings, homes or apartments had been completed. The city officials have attained an enviable reputation for honesty and efficiency with a maximum salary of $350 a month. No case of graft has been known in a decade and a half, or since the war. One-fifth of the city's budget is devoted to health and social welfare, about one-tenth being set apart for housing. Some of the great courts like the George Washington Apartments accommodate as many as eight thousand people, while individual garden homes in the suburbs afford more privacy for those who prefer it. The architecture is simple but artistic. The apartments are constructed with a view to a maximum of fresh air and sunshine, with playgrounds, community centers, libraries, lecture halls, facilities for family laundry and often swimming pools for the children. The rents of apartments range from $1.50 a month to $7.00. Seventy municipal baths accommodate over 200,000 persons a day. There are thirty socialized parks and 100 model kindergartens. Vienna, with its remarkable system of housing, of education and of public health, is almost a model city. The water supply, the coal, gas, tramways and almost all electric power and light plants are owned by the city and operated economically and efficiently. The same is true in many of the cities of Germany. Such cities, including even the crude beginnings in Soviet Russia, are a standing reproach to some countries in the West where housing for private profit is still

used as a means of exploiting the workers through exorbitant rents. Such a system would be considered robbery in Russia.

Within the last few years Great Britain has made a real beginning in tackling its housing problem. Since the war some two million homes have been built, about three-fifths of them with State assistance. England in ten years should be in sight of solving its housing problem.

When some forty years ago Charles Booth made his study of *The Life and Labor of the People,* followed by Rowntree's studies of housing in York, the slums of England were among the most noisome and inhuman in the world. When the Labor Party was in office, under the Greenwood Act in 1930 a new beginning was made and some eight thousand houses were constructed. At the Labor Party Conference at Hastings in 1933 a comprehensive national program was submitted on *Housing and Slums.* They proposed to attack the present accumulated shortage of a million houses by a colossal and continuous drive to tear down miles of slum streets, beginning with the construction of 250,000 new houses a year in addition to private building. The Minister of Health would have "Munition Act powers."

The Conservative Minister of Health, Sir Hilton Young, in April, 1933, sent out a circular requesting all cities and local authorities to submit five-year programs for the abolition of slums and the construction of new housing. Some fifty cities and towns sent in their plans well before the allotted date in September. Nottingham, which proposes to clear 75 areas in five years, and Cardiff are already within sight of ridding themselves of slums altogether. Congested cities, however, like Liverpool and Glasgow, Leeds and Bradford, cannot hope to solve their problems within five years. A small city like Chester, with only 40,000 population, has decided to remove 1,500 houses. Sheffield has already cleared thirty unhealthy areas since the war and now proposes to demolish or rebuild 14,433 houses that are unfit for habitation.

The public opinion of Britain is beginning to be quickened concerning the slums as their "damning inheritance": "They make impossible the birthright that we profess to uphold for

every citizen in body and soul. We drag their children out for 'education' and thrust them back again into slum-mindedness. We spend money on public health and tolerate dwellings that undermine it every hour."

John Galsworthy recalls how the people of Seville in Spain in 1401 resolved: "Let us build a church so great that those who come after us may think us mad to have attempted it." Galsworthy continues: "We used to have the manor house with half a dozen hovels in its support. Now we have twenty miles of handsome residences with 120 miles of back streets redolent of dullness, dirt and discontent. The proportions are still unchanged, and the purple patches of our great towns are too often as rouge on the cheeks of a corpse. Let us fantastically conceive the civic authorities of London solemnly resolving: 'We will remake of London a city so beautiful to dwell in, that those who come after us shall think us mad to have attempted it'—to remake of London a stainless city, full of baths and flowers and singing birds."

The conscience of England is stirring over its slums. But what shall we say of the United States? Cleveland, almost alone, had the inception of a program for slum elimination. It plans to rebuild the Negro section and Mayor Miller has placed the President, Executive Secretary and Social Welfare Chairman of the Federated Churches upon his housing committee. In one or two other cities a feeble beginning has been made and occasionally a philanthropic individual has attempted a model block, or apartment, or enterprise. There are now real possibilities for the beginning of "a new deal" in this regard in the provision of the N.R.A. for housing and even slum clearance.

New York, the richest city in the world, has had over 600,000 persons living in its inexcusable slums. A terrible painting by the Mexican artist, Diego Rivera, which now hangs in the Museum of Modern Art, reveals this cancer. The strata of our industrial civilization is shown in three successive tiers. Above, rise the highest skyscrapers in the world. That is all most of us see. In the second tier below, one sees a verminous "flop house" with its rows of sleeping humanity, where the unem-

ployed, the refuse, the dregs of our selfish civilization are stranded. In the lowest tier is revealed one of the bank vaults filled with its huge store of sterile gold and located close to the slums, the flop houses, the haunts of the gangsters and the criminals.

Diego Rivera sees below the surface. He knows how the proletariat lives. Practically all the cities in the United States, even the small towns, have their slums, or poor quarters, or hovels, or shacks, breeding centers of crime or anti-social tendencies. Yet few church people or "respectable" citizens even know of their existence or have any conscience in the matter, much less a plan to grapple with the evil. Have we anything to learn even from backward Russia with regard to a plan for every city for housing and slum clearance?

CHAPTER VII

THE REVOLUTION IN AGRICULTURE

When we inquire what we may learn from Russia in agriculture the answer must be, up to the present, almost nothing; ultimately, very much indeed. The Soviet Union is now in the midst of the greatest revolution ever known in agriculture. Backward agriculture and the dislocation of the relation between the city and the country has been a perennial problem since the decay of the Roman Empire. For four and a quarter years the Soviets tried not only to transform a primitive agricultural country into a modern industrial state, but to collectivize, mechanize and socialize its agriculture among a hundred million peasants scattered over one-sixth of the surface of the habitable globe. That, of course, was impossible, but that "impossible" was almost accomplished, and the back of the rural problem was actually broken. The Soviets have fought their "battle of the Marne" with the peasants—and won. Russia will never retreat from collectivization.

Until two years ago there was the menace of over twenty million individualistic, potentially capitalistic, land-hungry peasants, who had a deep antipathy toward socialism and might some day defeat or overthrow their Union of Soviet Socialist Republics. After the industrial workers, the peasants will now become the most socialized class. Whatever its over-hasty and faulty execution, this will probably yet become one of the great achievements of history. But we must examine the ruthlessness, the blunders, the human suffering and even starvation, that occurred during the transition.

Originally the first Plan anticipated collectivizing less than one-fifth of the cultivated area. Actually four-fifths of the land and two-thirds of the peasants were collectivized, or

thrown into the "socialized sector" that embraced the state and collective farms. In four and a quarter years the portion of the total sown area in the collectives was raised from 1.2 per cent to 68 per cent, that of collective and state farms combined from 2.7 per cent to 78 per cent of the sown area, while the percentage sown by individual farmers fell from 97.3 to 22 per cent.[1]

For this vast undertaking of socialized agriculture during the first Plan 53,000 agronomists, organizers and directors were supplied, while 57,700 additional students were enrolled in agricultural colleges. As an illustration, the production of cotton was doubled and the textile industry greatly extended during the Plan.

The Peasantry Old and New

To grasp the full significance of the revolution which is taking place in the Soviet Union we must view it against the background of Russian history. Two centuries of Tartar rule had left Russia the most backward country in Europe. The serfs had been reduced almost to slavery and could be sold even apart from the land. Repeated peasant uprisings testified to their desperate misery. As late as 1861 eleven million serfs

---

[1] The first Plan called for 17.5 per cent of the sown area to be in the socialized sector; its realization was instead 78 per cent. In 1928 there were 24.5 million individual farms with an average of 4.5 hectares, or about ten acres each. At the end of 1932, or the beginning of 1933, there were 14.7 million households gathered into 210,000 collective farms embracing 61.5 per cent of all peasant holdings and 75.6 per cent of the sown area. The government had established 2,115 tractor stations to supply mechanization and 98,207 tractors, a ninefold increase during the period of the Plan. The socialized sector of state and collective farms now supplies 84.2 per cent of the marketable grain and 83 per cent of the cotton. The average sown area of the state farms had increased fourfold, to 2,303 hectares, or about 5,700 acres; while the collective farms averaged 434 hectares, or about 1,080 acres. Of the collectives, 91.7 per cent were artels which usually had joint ownership and use of land, horses, implements, and livestock; 4.7 per cent were mere cooperative organizations for joint tillage without joint ownership; and 3.6 per cent were advanced communes without private property save personal possessions, where they shared almost everything including dining-rooms, dormitories, their educational and cultural life. *The First Five Year Plan*, pp. 20, 145-166, 285.

of the Czar and the state, with an equal number belonging to private owners, were nominally freed. But they were given the worst land, the heaviest burden of taxes, and bitter poverty became their lot. This resulted in "a servile mentality—truckling humility and beastly cruelty, treachery and avarice, hypocrisy, cowardice and superstition."

The kulak embodied the peasants' land-hunger, with an acquisitive desire to own and add to holdings, hire labor and grow rich. He was the natural enemy of the new Communist State, as were the twenty-seven million peasants with private holdings, with their superstition, their suspicion and their aversion to all change and to all government, after four centuries of Czarist oppression. In the meantime the kulaks were growing richer, and however poor the peasantry, the system of private capitalism was being built up among the majority of the population who resisted government taxes, grain collections or even suggestions of new methods in agriculture. The same leaders who had overthrown capitalism and established militant Communism in the cities now carried the Revolution and the class war into the villages.

Russian agriculture was in an even worse state than that of the rest of the world. The machine age, under the control of finance, had created the economic war between industry and agriculture, had cut the roots of healthy rural life and led to the deterioration of agriculture. The Soviet leaders resolved by extending the Revolution to the peasants to socialize agriculture, bridge the gulf between the city and the country, unite and coordinate industry and agriculture and by the union of culture and toil create one vast classless socialist community. It was a task far more titanic and difficult than the overthrow of Czarism or the setting up of the Communist Republic.

We might trace three stages in the development of the collective farms: the spontaneous growth during the experimental stage, the rapid, coercive collectivization of most of the land by a violent campaign in 1930, and now the steady increase and natural growth that follows upon the experience of greater

efficiency, larger yield and more privileges shared by the members of the collectives.

We must take a realistic view of the chronic food problem of Soviet Russia which no single harvest can solve. The broad fact remains, fifteen years after the inauguration of the régime and five years after the beginning of its planned economy, that there is still a stringency of food after years of rationing. There must be some reason for this, especially in a country so rich in natural resources. Sugar, for instance, has until recently been rationed to about one pound a month.

As we have seen, the terrific pressure of the Five Year Plan forcibly collectivized an often unwilling peasantry and "liquidated" and lost the most intelligent five per cent of the peasantry as kulaks who, whatever their political faults, had the best brains and experience in rural Russia. The Plan forced up exports, made rigorous grain collections and left the herded peasantry in the collective discontented, with an inadequate supply of industrial goods. The transportation system has been overstrained and inadequate. In 1930 there were some fifty-seven derailments due to rail breakages compared to only three in Germany. The inefficiency of the railways was in striking contrast to the systems in North America or Great Britain.

The crop of 1930 was 80 million tons. The figures of 1931 and 1932 were significantly not published but were probably less than this, though the Plan had called for 100 millions in 1932. The 150,000 tractors in the 2,000 central tractor stations were frequently breaking down despite the political department connected with each station as a kind of intelligence and police force. After five years of the Plan there was still a dangerously low productivity per capita for the fifteen and a half million families in the 200,000 collectives. The state exactions of grain doubled between 1928 and 1931. The food supply in the North Caucasus, the Ukraine and Kazakstan was lower in 1932 than at any time since 1922. No matter what the statistics on paper of any one harvest may be all of these facts must be taken together realistically as indicating a hitherto

chronic problem of food and of a low per capita yield in agriculture.

Stalin early saw that a mistake had been made in forcible collectivization. Within two months of his decree for rapid collectivization he warned his followers of "dizziness from success," that the movement against the middle peasants must be henceforth voluntary and not repressive. Blame was placed as usual upon local officials rather than upon the center.

Covering a period of some three years their "battle with the peasants" was fought and won. Not all their difficulties and problems had been surmounted but the worst was now over. The leaders and the peasantry had both made fatal mistakes and both had learned costly lessons. But collectivization had come to stay. The great harvest of 1933 set its seal of success upon the Plan as a whole. Some 2,000 tractor stations have been strategically placed. All the loyal forces of the country in the Party, the trade unions, the youth movement and even the Red Army, have been mobilized to heal the breach between officials and peasants, city and country, industry and agriculture. And they are now slowly and painfully succeeding.

For illustration, our party visited the A M O automobile and munitions factory in Moscow. This factory has undertaken special care and responsibility for certain state farms on the Lower Volga. They have sent to the farms over 100 of their best city workers together with six trucks and much machinery. The factory workers organized 26 crèches and nurseries to care for the children of the mothers during the sowing campaign. The Komsomol members of the factory made 500 cots for these crèches out of scrapped metal. They provided a special automobile for a travelling cinema, equipped the farms with radios and telephones and organized a farm paper. In return the peasants are eager to supply their comrades in the city with farm products. Thus a very practical cooperation is established between city and country which goes beyond anything achieved in this line even in Denmark after a generation.

In the campaign of 1930, out of 70,000 industrial workers who volunteered, 25,000 of the ablest were chosen to help

organize the mass movement on the collective farms. When one unit of 200 workers started from Moscow for the Caucasus a demonstration of 30,000 saw them off with great enthusiasm. The workers realized that their food problem was in the villages, and the peasants knew that their machinery, clothing and supplies must come from the cities. Both were consciously striving for the success of the workers' and peasants' federated republics. The Komsomol members in the cities go in brigades into the country at the time of seed sowing and harvest. The students in the universities and technical schools spend their summers in the collectives or on state farms, while the children of the peasantry go to the cities for their education with the industrial workers. The young actors of the School of Theatre Art in Moscow spend their summers on the farms giving plays, organizing games, songs and dances, and lead in the cultural life of the villages. Every professional student in law or medicine, as an essential element of his education, takes part in manual work in industry or agriculture during the winter, and in the summer the soldiers of the Red Army work in the fields with the peasants. All are workers in a workers' republic. A community of interest is developing between city and country which is new in the world.

Collectivization will gradually transform the Russian peasantry. The old individual farmer's conservatism, primitive methods and resultant poverty have been almost swept away from four-fifths of the land. His ancient fragmentation of the land in narrow and scattered strips, his primitive plough, his sickle and hand flail have given way to broad undivided fields, increasingly cultivated and reaped by modern machinery. Hitherto the peasants' methods of cultivation had been almost unchanged for a thousand years. The individual peasant, fearful of hunger and famine, would take no risks, adopt no new methods. But now in the periodic conferences and public meetings of the collectives, the proposals of the agricultural experts are hailed with enthusiasm and adopted after full discussion, often by unanimous vote. Newly educated youths or younger men are in the lead and are elected to positions of responsibility. The lessons in cooperation and education for

a new peasantry learned in the course of a generation in little Denmark are being crowded into a decade in giant Russia. Denmark stood for quality, the Soviet Union stands for quantity. The former voluntarily and gradually achieved a national success. The latter is more forcibly and suddenly carrying through a huge undertaking that will eventually be of far-reaching international significance.

Ten years ago I saw on some waste land in Moscow a great fair or Agricultural and Industrial Exhibition which attempted to bring together from all over the U.S.S.R. the industrial workers and peasants and to visualize and interpret the problems of each to the other. On that same waste land today stands the permanent Park of Culture and Rest, with an attendance on a free day of from 100,000 to 300,000. A large proportion of the workers present are young peasants who have poured into the city from the country. This park is made a training ground for workers, and similar parks on a more modest scale are being established in all cities and in many of the towns. The social centers, the theatre, radio, cinema and sports are being carried out into the country; and rural life is being mechanized, socialized and culturalized. Thus they are rapidly building a classless society, more equal, more comradely and more united than any other in the world. The declassed, disfranchised, non-working urban population has now been reduced from 5.1 to 1 per cent.

"Peace, land and bread" were the demand of the workers' and peasants' revolution and the offer of the Communists in 1917. With farsighted statesmanship Lenin united in one system the interests of proletariat and peasant as Marx had done before him. By one of its earliest decrees, November 7, 1917, the Soviet government nationalized the soil and forever abolished private property in land, which henceforth was to be held in trust by the state for the people. The land-hungry peasants who took possession at first regarded the land as their own. Henceforth the Revolution was theirs. But they were slow in learning the lesson that the land was theirs not for private profit but for social use. The peasant is now to become an educated, voting member of a collective, with a rising stand-

ard of living, a rich cultural life and with almost all the advantages of the city brought to the once distant farms. It took a revolution as violent in the country as in the city to transform him from an individualist into a collectivist, from a desperately poor but potential capitalist into a potential Communist. He is still poor, but if he belongs to the younger generation he is a new man, almost as far removed from Czarist serfdom as from the ice age and the mammoths.

Life In Peasant Russia

Our most interesting time in Russia this past summer was spent out in the villages where three-quarters of the population live. We walked for several days through village after village, questioning every peasant we met. They spoke quite freely of their troubles, and sometimes with great indignation, if they chanced to be from among the old, inefficient individual peasants who are still standing out against the government and all its plans. If the government is anathema to these older peasants, they are certainly the chief problem of the new régime. The marvel is that so much has been accomplished with them and in spite of them. Among these individual peasants the average farm has now become less than nine acres. Their grain had been reaped when we visited them and they were threshing it with the old-fashioned flail of two sticks tied together with a thong.

In the villages we found three different levels of life, and it could be noted almost at a glance to which level each group belonged. On the lowest level were the individual farms. Here were chiefly old, backward, superstitious peasants, averse not only to the new collectives but to all progress or change of method. We could be sure that in these homes the family still slept on the broad brick stove, that there was no sign of new life, and that in a corner, as the symbol of the old Church and the old order, an ikon would be found. These peasants always voiced complaints. They were disgruntled and out of joint. All about them the tides of progress were sweeping on and leaving them stranded. At least they were not afraid

to speak out, to shout or roar their complaints. Whatever might be said of the city, the Revolution opened the peasant's mouth and gave *him* freedom of speech. He dares to protest to officials, the local soviet, or any passerby. He tells the whole world of his troubles.

On a distinctly higher level are the newly organized collective farms. Here were signs of life in the village. Here instead of the little nine-acre strips the broad unfenced fields stretched away, with the harvested grain standing in shocks, as far as the eye could see. The harvest was abundant and undeniable. Here in the collectives we saw the first signs of new machinery, tractors and threshing machines with enormous straw stacks, though the supply of machinery was still inadequate. Here also we observed more whitewash and cleanliness in the homes. New ideas in agriculture, sanitation, education and culture were taking root. The occupants of the homes slept in beds. Here and there we found a clock and other evidences of a sense of time. There was a new cooperative spirit; they were working in larger companies with more hope and energy and enterprise. There were the beginnings, too, of a new cultural life, a larger and better school, a new social center, with periodic motion pictures of educational value interpreting the Revolution to the peasant and instructing while amusing him. The radio was bringing the message from the great city, the speeches of officials, instructions for the farmer, or music and diversion. The children were bringing home new songs, new ideas and new methods.

Posters and charts of the Five Year Plan held aloft the new goals or achievements. There were others against alcohol and sundry evils, or for the mother in the care of children and the home. Newspapers and pamphlets were blowing a gale of new ideas through the mind of the younger generation. We listened to the songs and watched the joyous dancing of the young people in the evening, sensing the cultural life and recreation that is such an essential part of the whole great movement.

As we journeyed through the villages we found, on the highest level of all, the communes where everything is shared.

Typical of these was the Lenin Commune where we had stayed before for three days, and we returned now as to old friends to see how they were faring. The Commune was founded ten years ago by some fifty peasants who had left Russia in despair, emigrated to America, and had made money there as industrial workers. After the Revolution, believing that there might be a chance for a new life in their homeland, they pooled their earnings and with a combined capital of some $30,000 they purchased machinery and supplies and returned to Soviet Russia. They were given the land from the Obolensky estate, which had been sadly mismanaged in Czarist days. The absentee landlord had lived in luxury in Moscow or in his villa in Italy while the peasants on the estate, underpaid and living in wretchedness, were forced to render tribute with every possible penny that could be wrung from them.

When we arrived at the railway station to visit the Lenin Commune we were met, not by the farmers' haywagons, but by a powerful motor truck of Russian make which took aboard our whole party. We slept on benches covered with blankets in their entertainment hall, or out under the open sky in the great straw stacks a hundred feet long, which were rising daily beside their busy threshing machines. We shared the rich farm table of good bread made from their own flour, butter, milk and cream, cheese, meat, delicious soup, vegetables and fruit. Potatoes, tomatoes and cherries, from their own model orchards, were abundant. The fare was better to a foreigner's taste than that received in any hotel in Moscow.

We found the workers intelligent and friendly; one could no longer call them "peasants." They were quite unlike the simple villagers on the remaining individual farms nearby. A score or two talked in English with us freely and intimately. They had learned this during their years in America. Several, especially among the younger ones, would like to return to the relative plenty and the higher material standard of living in the United States. But the majority considered this a retreat to the fleshpots of capitalism. Instead they must press on through the wilderness to take possession of their promised land.

On the first night in the Commune, after a tiring day walking through the surrounding villages, we questioned the members, their elected soviet, or committee of management, and the youth of the Commune, about their economic, social and political life. On the second night of our stay they requested a meeting where they could question us about conditions in America: How many unemployed had we? What were we doing for them? What prospect had we of eliminating unemployment as they had already done? What means were we taking to get out of the depression? What was Mr. Roosevelt going to do about the bankers? Had Mr. Morgan made his money legitimately in Wall Street? Were we going to confiscate the ill-gotten gains of our bankers or permit their further profiteering? What was the present condition of our agriculture and industry? How far were we victimized by a capitalist press? Could we by loyal, evolutionary methods build a new social order in America without revolution? Etc., etc.

There were other questions which they were too considerate or too polite to ask of us as guests, but which were in the backs of their minds or on the tips of their tongues. These they asked individually or in groups whenever they were free and felt they could be frank: "Why do you lynch Negroes in America and why do you refuse them economic justice and equal treatment? What are you going to do with the Negroes in the Scottsboro trial? What did you do to Sacco and Vanzetti; to Mooney and Billings? Why does your capitalist system result in great wealth for a few and in unemployment, poverty and slums for so many? Why are you the helpless victims of recurring cyclical depressions which Marx said would culminate in the final disintegration and collapse of capitalism? Are you giving equal justice to all, or can you ever do so under the conditions of capitalism? Why are the capitalist countries so unfriendly to the Soviet Union and will they invade our country or again attempt intervention?" Etc., etc.

We had one meeting to question the whole Commune, another with the Komsomols, in from the fields at the noon hour, and

others with groups and individuals. Before me as I write is a transcript of accounts from their books. The membership of the Commune has grown in a decade from 59 to 586. They have 1,654 hectares, or some 4,000 acres of land, with their own flour mill, foundry, sawmill, orchards, dairy, cheese factory, etc. They have a capital investment of 972,168 roubles. They have had good crops of wheat, rye, oats, vegetables and sunflower seeds, averaging per capita from one and a half to twice those of the individual peasants about them. After their sales for the year they have 89 horses, 450 cattle, 700 sheep and 879 pigs.

The Commune pays no tax to the government but instead is required to sell to it about one-quarter of the grain at a nominal price, very much lower than can be obtained in the open market. They are still short of needed machinery and asked if we could get them a tractor or truck from America. Each year they have added to their plant, capital account and individual income. They have personal accounts to their credit, but they are not large. Save for the increase of plant and capital account they make little but their living, though with a steadily rising standard. There is neither the necessity, the possibility nor the desire for personal profit and acquisition. They have developed social security and social acquisition rather than individual, but their social life is rich indeed.

The nurseries, kindergarten and schools were a delight to see. We took motion pictures of the children and Komsomols in their singing and dancing. The dancing of the young people to music on the green in the moonlight every evening was a sheer joy to watch. It was less boisterous than at one of our Western cornhuskings, but far more graceful and beautiful. In the dance, the drama and music perhaps no peasants or farm folk in the world excel them. And their recreation is on a higher plane altogether than the sophisticated dancing or jazz in the cities of America. The young folks seem less developed individually than those of equal age among farm communities in either the United States or England, but in their social life they are far more serious, enthusiastic, hopeful and cooperative. The farm boy of the West often wants to go to the city

to seek his fortune. These Russian youths, on the successful farms, are an enthusiastic social unit and feel they are building a new world. It is not just a new country but a new social order for the workers of the world for which they are consciously striving.

The Communars have their library, in Russian and English, their reading room with periodicals and papers, their radio and educational cinema. In the evenings during the winter they all study from five to ten P.M. and have their folk schools as in Denmark. The moral life of the young people combines a large measure of personal freedom with rather strict self-discipline imposed by the Komsomols. Practically all of their marriages are registered, as compared to about half in the city. Vodka is forbidden in the Commune. It can only be obtained individually in the distant city.

The members are organized in a democratic self-governing body with almost complete autonomy, with little interference from Moscow or the district center. They elect their soviet or committee of management of five members every three years. The Communist cell nominates three and the general meeting elects two other members. Of the 586 members in the Commune, 135 are members of the Party and the Komsomol. They include all the best members. There is not such rigorous discipline, such inexorable cleansings, such sacrificial service or honor connected with the Party as in the city, but it furnishes the leadership and the ideals for the whole body.

As I watched the daily lives of these people—and some of them are almost old friends of several years standing—it seemed to me that on the whole they as Russians were better off here than they would be in America, either as farmers or as foreign industrial workers. They receive less wages in money, to be sure, and lack many material conveniences of the mechanized farm of the West, even though they have their own electric light plant, tractors, threshers, radio, cinema and modern laundry and shower baths, but their social life is richer and freer and more cooperative than it would be in Anglo-Saxon countries. As we in the West have learned to live individually, they are learning to live collectively. We live by

competition, they by cooperation. We have developed the individual, they are building a new social order. Each has much to learn from the other.

In the country we found less dogma and anti-religious zeal and more tolerance than in the city. With the surrounding peasants on the individual farms who had their ikons still hanging in their huts, religion was a subject of interest or of deep concern. Not so with the young Communists. Up to the present at least they have been more than occupied in building a serious, moral, secular social order. They may find the need of other values with the growth of a wider tolerance and freedom in the future. On the whole, however, their life is on a distinctly higher plane than that of the superstitious, individual peasants about them.

The situation in agriculture, both in America and in Europe, would indicate that there were lessons to be learned from Denmark, from Russia and elsewhere. In Denmark a generation ago the backward peasants were mostly ignorant tenants. Today nearly nine-tenths of them own their own farms. They have built up their remarkable system of cooperative societies and of education to improve their material and cultural life. In the United States, so recently the land of the open frontier, the farmers had been losing their farms until almost half had become tenant farmers. The return from crops and livestock had fallen to one-quarter the 1920 price, while the farmer was paying 6 per cent more for commodities for living and operating expenses than before the World War. He was crushed between the upper millstone of a precipitous fall in income and the nether millstone of debt and fixed charges, often contracted when prices were from two to five times higher. The ratio of debt to the total value of mortgaged farms had risen to about 50 per cent.

At the inauguration of Mr. Roosevelt, who was the first President seriously to tackle the problems of the farmer, the farm mortgage debt exceeded eight billion dollars. It had risen from $3,320,000,000 in 1910 to its peak of $9,468,-000,000 in 1928. That amount was somewhat reduced, partly

by foreclosures.   As the wave of foreclosures increased it was met by near-riots on the part of the embittered farmers.

It was in this desperate situation that President Roosevelt launched his bold plan for the relief of the farmer.   We are still in the initial stages of that great experiment and it is too early to pass judgment upon it.   At least the administration has a plan and a very daring one.   Doubtless we and the Russians will both learn by experience, both from our failures as well as our successes.

CHAPTER VIII

THE NEW MORALITY

A new morality is the natural product of the new social order which the Soviets are seeking to build. It is founded chiefly upon experience as interpreted by reason. It has swept away Czarist legal and moral codes which were in the interests of man as against woman and of the propertied class as against the proletariat. It believes in no eternal principles, no sweeping moral absolutes of an unchanging, universal, authoritative ethic, no external supernatural or ecclesiastical authority. It recognizes that the *mores* or customs of each stage of human development were crystallized into the legal and moral codes of the time and then perpetuated in later periods with divine or human sanction long after changed conditions demanded a revision of an inflexible system.

The customs of the primitive tribe registered in the emotional responses and habits of the individual became his conscience. In every primitive agricultural period codes similar to the Ten Commandments were evolved, whether under divine or human sanction. Law or duty in feudal society was based upon the ownership of land, in capitalist society upon the rights of private property, in Communist society upon the welfare of the proletariat or working mass. In the new Soviet morality all that aids the revolutionary ideal and the formation of the just classless society of the future is right, all that hinders it is wrong. Its touchstone is in the future rather than in the past.

In every age morality changes with experience. The morality of one epoch becomes the immorality of another. At one period the burning of witches was a virtue and the lending of money at interest was a vice. Individual thrift and profit-

making is a Puritan virtue but a Communist vice. Almost every practice has been at some time counted right and at another wrong. In each age consciously or unconsciously the class in power makes the laws and influences standards of conduct. Morality, whether in Russia or the West, thus becomes more or less class morality until the classless society of the future is reached.

Marx, Engels and Lenin all recognized this relativity of morals and the changing standards of a class morality, but also by their willingness to bear ostracism and grinding poverty, their refusal to compromise with truth as they saw it, and their heroic sacrifice for the society of the future they showed their own moral principles.[1]

After the mass murder and brutalization of the war there was an outbreak of lawlessness, dissipation and juvenile crime in many countries, but nowhere more than in Russia. But there is a corrective, an unescapable discipline in all life that brings its own nemesis. This time of licentiousness, of venereal disease, of boys and girls in their teens becoming parents, of reckless abortion and of ruined health brought its inevitable social consequences which hindered the Revolution and the building of the new order. Soviet Russia had to learn again some of the first principles of morality in the hard school of experience.

These things brought their penalty also in the heart of young Russia, in the disintegration of personality. This bore fruit in public opinion in the new literature and in the standards of the youth movement. For a long time the most popular novel among youth was *The First Girl in the Kom-*

---

[1] Marx writes: "The proletariat regards its courage, self-confidence, independence, and sense of personal dignity as more necessary than its daily bread." Engels said in 1878: "The three classes which go to make up modern society, the feudal aristocracy, the bourgeoisie, and the proletariat, each has its own code of morals. From this we may conclude that men, consciously or unconsciously, create their moral outlooks in the last resort out of the conditions of everyday practical experience, the conditions upon which they depend as a class, *i. e.,* out of the economic conditions of production and exchange." *Communist Manifesto,* with Notes by W. Ryazanoff, p. 174.

somol. It recounts the experience of many others in the story of the girl Sanya, the leader of the Komsomol. She is a kind of crusading Joan of Arc in the economic and political regeneration of her country. When later she surrenders her chastity first to one and another and then to many, her sacrificial revolutionary life becomes debased. When several young men who have contracted disease from her are about to thrash her in public she is shot dead by her best friend to save her and the Komsomol from disgrace. Such a story and such a repeated experience taught its own lesson in experience as interpreted by reason.

Against such dissipation and its anti-social results Lenin protested: "Licentiousness in sexual life is bourgeois, is a symptom of degeneracy." [1] The Youth organizations increasingly took a strong stand as in their central organ the *Komsomol Pravda*: "For the time being the commune considers sexual relationships and a licentious sexual life to be inadmissible. In its opinion the sexual question can be correctly decided in only one way: steadfast and lasting marriage founded on love. Marriage of this kind can result only from reciprocal friendship, psychical agreement, and the community of interests between the girl and the young man. Marriage without love, based on 'reciprocal favors' and frivolous and casual sexual relationships, which are bound to lead to various ugly consequences, are vigorously opposed by the commune."

Such a conclusion based solely on the experience of Russian youth itself finds countless parallels in Puritan and Victorian literature. Indeed there is a stern almost Puritan element in Soviet morality though it is coupled with personal liberty and the absence of convention and external restraints.

The new morality seeks to give the utmost freedom to the

---

[1] He continues: "A great part of youth is vehemently striving to 'revise the bourgeois point of view and morality' in the matter of sex. . . . Does the normal man, in normal circumstances, lie down in the muddy street and drink out of a puddle? Or even out of a glass the rim of which has been smeared by many lips? But the social side is more important than everything else. . . . The Revolution requires concentration and enhanced energy, from the masses, from the individual. It will not tolerate an orgiastic state of affairs such as is normal for d'Annunzio's decadent heroes." Lenin to Clara Zetkin in 1920.

individual consistent with social welfare. It is "a striking mixture or balance between liberty and discipline, personal enjoyment and social responsibility, utter frankness and utter disdain of abuses." Every act must be judged in the light of its consequences. What is the effect upon the woman, upon the child, upon the man, the home, and more especially upon the goal of the new classless society? The new morality is against individualism, but not against the individual. The welfare of the whole, of the mass, always comes first. Probably only gradually and out of deep experience will the Soviets learn reverence for personality and full respect for the individual. At the moment Russia is more occupied with society and the West with the individual. Neither has learned the full coordination of individualism and collectivism. We balance egoism against altruism, but Russia's dialectic of "the interpenetration of opposites" should in time lead her eventually to a more harmonious experience.

The new morality recognizes no external moral order but out of its own experience evolves such abiding values as social justice, freedom of self-development for all, solidarity, cooperation, the sacrifice of the individual for society and of present gratification for future welfare.

It takes no supernatural revelation nor prohibition legislation for the new youth to see the ravages of drunkenness, which are probably worse in Russia, as a holdover from the old order, than in any other country. The young Pioneers march with their school band and banners to the factories or place posters in the workshops: "We your children call upon you to give up drinking, to help us to shut drink shops and to use them as cultural institutions, pioneers clubs, reading rooms, etc." The government appears to join in the campaign but really leads with effective posters, moving pictures and the education of public opinion. The whole youth movement, however, feels that it has real moral autonomy. While allowing a maximum of individual freedom in morals there is such constant social pressure in the demand for the attainment of their strenuous social goals that it forms a corrective to indi-

vidual license and self-gratification. Every act is judged by its social consequences.

All this does not imply that young Russia has solved its problems or that its standards would be counted morally satisfactory if judged by those of the Victorian era. It does mean, however, that they bear no resemblance to the individual dissipation of "flaming youth" in the disintegration of an old social order, which on the material side offer only future goals of individual profit seeking and money making, and in the present of pleasure seeking. There is still the imminent danger in Russia that the individual may be lost in the mass, that spiritual ends may be submerged in the material, and moral character sacrificed to the sensuous. Russia may be still in the primary standards in the school of experience. But she is studying in a great school. In the meantime the chief influence for the new morality comes not from social convention or penalties, nor from the restraints of the older generation, nor any external religious sanctions, but from the self-governing authority of the youth movement itself and from the discipline of its periodic cleansings. They have at least disproved the conventional assumption that without religion there would be no moral restraints, or that conduct in the present is dependent upon the anticipation of future rewards and penalties.

Our New Morality

Standards of conduct will inevitably differ between Russia and the West. Under their collectivism the Russians naturally emphasize the factor of social obligation and control; while we in our individualistic order tend to stress more personal considerations. Ethical conduct in all lands and epochs is regulated either by custom, authority, instinct, reason or experience. The standards of Czarist Russia were chiefly fixed by custom based upon authority. The new morality of Soviet Russia has swept away custom and authority, and, as we have seen, substituted the standard of experience, social and individual, as interpreted by reason.

Have we any other standard? What makes a thing right or wrong for us? Is it the dictum of some authoritative person, a passage from some sacred book, the custom or convention of society about us, the voice of reason or conscience within us, or the result of our experience, collective or individual?

Our word morality is of course derived from the Latin *mores,* meaning custom, and our word ethics from the Greek word of the same meaning. It was the custom or convention of the tribe that determined for the individual what was right or wrong. Morality became then, as now, the regulation of natural instincts in the interests of social welfare. The individual in the tribe had only an external standard and his "conscience" was the voice of the tribe registered in his emotional responses and habits. The individual was at the mercy of the tribe.

Morality always begins as custom; it gradually hardens into law, and only later it rises to the plane of individual reason and reflection. Man always tends to assign objectivity to his subjective experience. But to this day the moral ideas of the multitude, whether in Russia or the West, are derived chiefly from the authority of others and are only an echo of social or religious sanctions. Our morality has its origin in primitive custom or in the trial and error of earlier experience. The *mores* often embody our racial experience and, on the whole, make for survival. But they are usually derived from conditions of an earlier epoch, now codified and static, but often no longer applicable to present conditions. Thus any body of law like the Mosaic code, arising in an early pastoral and agricultural society, tends to harden with repression and to impede growth. It became yet more inflexible when based upon divine sanctions. Not only the Sabbath and the law, but morals also are made for man, not man for morals. As Rudolf Eucken says: "Whereas man was once held responsible before the bar of morality, now morality has to justify itself before man; the old time judge now stands in the dock."

Are our moral standards today based upon authority or experience? The child which has almost no experience to guide it, nor a mind developed to interpret the same, must depend

upon the authority of its parent or elders. The tendency, however, is always to perpetuate such tutelage unnecessarily, to
lay down external rules of conduct for the child instead of
letting it think for itself and learn self-government from the
earliest possible age as in Soviet Russia. As the normal person
reaches the age of discretion, group morality, custom and
authority should become growingly autonomous, personal and
reflective. Many adults remain in a state of dependence under
some system of control which claims practical infallibility.
They fall back upon an external authority of the party line
or an infallible church and distrust private judgment. Religious and social systems may be divided into those of authority
and those of freedom, where either social control is the dominant factor or private judgment. Suppose one becomes a
religious follower of Christ on the one hand, or a Party member and follower of Karl Marx on the other. The acceptance
of either must be upon the testimony and under the influence
of others, or else as an individual act of faith or personal
decision based upon one's own study and experience. If the
teaching of either system powerfully appeals to one the tendency is to attribute universality and practical infallibility to
the entire body of teaching, or to the person or organization
which declares or embodies it. But even then there is a wide
difference of interpretation between various schools of thought
and sectarian divisions.[1]

There is no ultimate test of such a system as a whole, or of
each precept or doctrine it contains, save social and individual
experience as interpreted by reason. Few individuals, however, whether in the Communist Party or the Christian Church,
ever subject either the system as a whole or any element of
it to this test. For the mass and the multitude authority is
always external; morality is tribal or class custom, and conscience is still the voice of the tribe. All unconsciously Roman
Catholicism largely embodies the past collectivist authority of

---

[1] No "luxury of sectarianism" is permitted by Stalin's stern socialist party
line in Moscow, but there are fifteen divisions or competing groups of Communists and Socialists in New York City all more or less impotent, and of
course many more religious denominations.

feudalism; Puritan Protestant morals are often those of individualist industrialism and capitalism, while those of Russia are the class morality of the proletariat under the present socialized means of production. The Russians believe that universal ethics can only be realized in a classless society. All our moral codes have been unconsciously conditioned by the class, the tribe or the area in which men lived. Everywhere we are under the aegis of relativity. Moral relativism has been very widely the experience of youth, especially since the World War, which shook or shattered many of the old sanctions.

As Pascal says: "There is nothing just or unjust which does not change its quality with a change of climate." Moral codes differ "East of Suez" or west of it, and between the possessing class which emphasizes the rights of property and the propertyless which defend the rights of the person. The codes of each class or epoch are made by the privileged class in power whether capitalist or Communist. But neither has permanent or absolute sanction. As Macaulay in his essay on Machiavelli says: "Every age and every nation has certain characteristic vices (and virtues). . . . Succeeding generations change the fashion of their morals with the fashion of their hats." No precept or principle has been held "always, everywhere by all men."

Every crime has been held at times as a virtue. Murder became sacred when practiced by the *Thugs* of India in providing bloody sacrifices for their gods, and by certain of the Nazis of Germany, not as offerings for Thor or Woden, but, to use the Kaiser's phrase, for "the good old German God" of tribal, chauvinistic nationalism. Adultery, as well as murder, has been incorporated frequently in the erotic worship of a thousand temples.

The unthinking fundamentalist Christian is like the Communist in that each admits the sphere of relativity only up to the threshold of his own castle Absolute. The religious emotion of either, though it is an invaluable driving dynamic and a charged dynamo of motivation, leads him to think that his system is practically infallible and his morality absolute.

Lenin, for instance, who would have scorned such an absolute in theory, is never able to find any flaw in Marx or Engels. The stern discipline of life, however, drives one into relativity; but we shall find that a yet deeper experience leads one to the recovery of a moral imperative.

It may seem sacrilegious for the believer to question his sacred traditions and he need not do so as long as he remains a moral or intellectual minor. The Ten Commandments, for instance, seem sacred and inviolable. As a matter of fact, similar codes were evolved in human experience by many pastoral and agricultural peoples from the time of Hammurabi.

We need not go so far on the Commandments as Bernard Shaw, who maintains that: "The whole ten are unsuited and inadequate to modern needs, as they say not a word against those forms of robbery, legalized by the robbers, which have uprooted the moral foundations of our society and will condemn it to slow social decay if we are not wakened up as Russia has been by a crashing collapse." He finds in the moral and religious encyclopedia of the Bible fresh fountains of truth, but that religionists seldom "throw out the dirty water of the past" of lower moral standards and conceptions like that of the God of Noah after the flood. The deity is pictured as having just destroyed man and beast from the earth but was appeased in his wrath by the odor of animal sacrifice. Shaw sees in this: "The atrocious ritual of human sacrifice to propitiate a murderous tribal deity, who was, for example, induced to spare the human race from destruction in a second deluge by the pleasure given him by the smell of burning flesh."[1]

We may examine moral custom and obligation upon different levels of experience. Upon the surface there seems to be an endless change in the content of moral codes and in concrete, ethical customs relative to each civilization; there is apparent moral relativity everywhere, past or present, in systems social or religious. But if we look deeper there appear certain attitudes or principles of morality underlying and under-

---

[1] *The Adventures of the Black Girl in Her Search for God,* pp. 65–69. Cf. Genesis VIII: 21.

girding the various epochs of history, such as courage, loyalty and unselfishness. Leaders in every age might have said, equally with Karl Marx, regarding the chosen people, or any class, or the ultimate classless society that it counted "its courage, self-confidence, independence and sense of personal dignity as more necessary than its daily bread."

Deeper still, seen in long perspective, there appear, as in every other sphere in life, progressive standards evolving in history as the individual and society develop. Evolving moral standards tend to become more inward and less external, as inner impulsion takes the place of outward compulsion, more rational and less governed by instinct and appetite, more experimental and autonomous and less authoritarian, more complex, difficult and demanding, more personal and human, more social and cooperative, and finally there seems to be an apparent advance toward progressive harmony, wholeness and unity in racial experience.

But deepest of all we come upon a moral imperative in the sense of obligation to be completely loyal to the highest we can discover. Loyalty or treason to the cause is a matter of life or death to the Communist, to the Christian, to the rational humanist, to every man. Codes and their contents, rules, precepts and practices will differ, but man may still stand in awe of the moral order within and of the starry heavens above him.

The smallness of man's mind and the limits of his experience force him dialectically to shuttle back and forth between two poles of thought and experience. He must include the subjective and objective factors, the individual and society. Truth is often found where the subjective and objective factors meet, where the individual and social combine, where personal judgment and experience critically confirm the social experience. It may include "the inner light" and social control, reason and the authority of the gathered experience of the race.

When one first realizes the relativity of all moral codes and standards he may be tempted, as they were for a time in Russia after the war, to have his fling in a self-centered life of dissipation, to drink from "the mud-puddles" which Lenin condemned. But experience is a stern taskmaster and our con-

duct does not differ as much as our creeds and our codes. If one examines the advancing moral standards from those we have cited under the sanctions of a "jealous" God down to the present time, he will find, without exception, that the *content* of all codes and standards is always relative. Yet the final ground of moral obligation is absolute.

Morality is a spirit rather than rules. If Mohammed lays down the law that a man may have four wives but not more, it chains his system to medieval Arabia rather than adapts it to the advancing ages of culture. The purpose of religion is not authoritatively to teach morals and lay down prohibitive absolutes, but rather to inspire and motivate, to seek true ends and values. There are no final, universal, absolute rules of conduct.

We have found that the content of developing moral codes, whether social or religious, is always relative. But life habitually presents itself as a series of alternative choices, as between immediate gratification and ultimate life-realization, between the selfish and the social, between a lower and a higher. Apparently some things aid and some injure life; some make for happiness and human well-being and others for human misery; some enhance life individually and socially while others lead to the disintegration and degradation of personality and society. We may count that right which enhances life as a whole, which makes it finer in quality, richer and more abundant, individually and collectively. On the other hand we may count that wrong which injures or destroys life, my own, my neighbor's or that of society, present or future.[1]

We may weigh these alternatives in the light of our imperfect moral codes. But, in the best light that we know, once alternatives present themselves to us as right or wrong, a lower or a higher, while the content of our code is relative, *there is an absolute obligation laid upon us.* We must choose what seems to us the right rather than the relative wrong, the

---

[1] See the author's *Sex and Youth,* Chapter III. Compare also H. Richard Niebuhr's *Moral Relativism and the Christian Ethic,* and W. R. Sorley's *The Moral Life.*

good rather than the evil, the higher rather than the lower, the social rather than the selfish. For the Communist or the Christian there is a moral obligation laid upon each to follow his highest insights. A man owes it to himself to build the finest character that he knows, in a growing harmony of experience, of all reason, impulse and emotion. He owes it to his fellow men, as a social individual, to build a better world, looking toward the end of a new social order and a classless society. If he is in a rational universe not only of matter but of mind, where he believes not only in appearance but in Reality, he owes loyalty to the true, the good, and the beautiful. Groping amid all the conflicts and evils of his little life he may discover the absolute within the relative.

Capitalist and Communist Moral Codes

Marx maintained that "the ruling ideas have been the ideas of the ruling class." This is equally true today whether in capitalist or in Communist countries. In the former, individual rights, especially of the strong under *laissez faire* economics, and the sacredness of private property are maintained as moral laws, whether in day school or Sunday school, in the press or courts of law. They are successfully engraved in the inner "conscience" of the individual who is quite unaware of their class origin.

In Communist society the ideas of the new messianic proletariat, the long-suffering class now in power, shapes the moral code in the interests of this chosen people, the mass. That is counted right which makes for the present and future well-being of the working class which accepts the Marxian code. All who do not accept this code, whether members of the abhorred bourgeois class and their children, or political enemies who do not accept orthodox proletarian "truth," such as members of a right or left deviation from the straight and narrow moral path determined by the small clique in power, are enemies to be destroyed or crushed if they cannot be quickly disciplined and brought to repentance. They are considered literally to have no more rights than vermin in a human dwelling. They

have no right which must be respected, even to life itself, much less to liberty or the pursuit of happiness.

In morality and religion, as well as in economics and politics, the Communist and non-Communist are living in two different worlds. Non-Communist morality in Western lands is, as we have seen, prevailingly individualistic. It centers in the sacredness of personality and of property. The *mores* or social customs, crystallized in moral and legal codes, which are still largely Puritan in their prohibitions and proprieties, place chief emphasis upon individual character and "public morality" for the preservation of the present social order.

Into the complex of the prevailing Western conceptions of right and wrong various elements enter. The judgments of the past persist in such influences as of the Ten Commandments of the pastoral Hebrew tribes, New Testament standards, Puritan asceticism, and capitalistic property rights of the present social order.

In the new Soviet Union all these, together with the standards and ideas of the Czarist state and church, are violently swept away. The dead hand of the past is amputated at one stroke. As we have seen, social welfare rather than individual character becomes the touchstone of conduct. The well-being of the ruling proletarian class of the Soviet Union and of the workers of the world not yet emancipated becomes the standard of conduct.

Resembling proletarian justice we have proletarian morality. Similar to the sacredness of private property in the West, where in Feudal England the Lord of the Manor had his private gallows and could hang offenders for the sin of poaching, so now public proletarian property becomes sacred. If men steal from the common harvest of the collective or state farm, or injure socialized property, by the law of August 7, 1932 they may be shot or imprisoned. The theft of bourgeois property is a light offense, and the murder of an individual, unless it is a political crime, receives a maximum penalty of eight or ten years in prison. But poaching upon the preserve of the collective, or stealing a dollar's worth of grain, if it is socialized property, may merit the death penalty. As capitalist property

was once considered more sacred than the human life of the poor, so now public property becomes more sacred than personality in Soviet Russia.

Under this system of class morality there is a very dim and undeveloped conception of individual personality, of the family, and of the ideal of humanity as a whole. The chosen class is above them all. It becomes the absolute norm for all. Their treatment of their political enemies, in the light of our ideals of personality, the family, and of humanity, seem to us ruthless and barbarous. They reveal their crude and primitive class level and norm. They can no more plead an alibi by promising more humane treatment in the ideal classless society of the future, than can the capitalist West in its hope of a better world beyond, or of a just social order in the optimistic promise of an evolutionary Utopia which is yet to come. Here and now Soviet Russia is as inexcusably cruel to its class enemies as is capitalism.

One difference, however, must always be remembered—in the West it is the minority of owners who hold the whiphand over their dependents, who are in the majority, while in the Soviet Union the ruling class, or proletariat, is in the majority, while their enemies are in the minority. Both are wrong in principle, but that of the West is the greater and more inexcusable wrong. We must always remember, however, that neither moral standard is absolute. Each is relative to the conditions of its social order.

The new morality of Soviet Russia is as yet only a class morality with all its egotism, selfishness and cruelty. It has never yet even faintly realized the higher possibilities of individual personality, of the family at its best, and of a complete humanity. We do not mean by a complete humanity that easy expectation of a classless society, after it shall have exterminated all its fancied enemies, and reduced to a drab, dead level all life leveled down to a coarse and crude materialistic standard. Rather, we mean a humanity which tolerates and includes political opponents and all enemies in the dialectic progress occasioned by the healthy conflict of ideas, parties and minorities, all of which will make their contribution to the final synthesis

and symphony of life.   If this is true, we shall find much that is suggestive in a new morality based upon experience as interpreted by reason, while they will have much to learn in reverence for personality, the hitherto undreamed possibilities of the family, and of a whole undivided humanity, which is a larger concept than any class, even the proletariat.

Communist ethics demands the subjection of the individual to the well-being of the proletariat for the building of the socialist state, as a means to the classless society of the future Communist world.   It derives its sanction from the absolute social control of the Party majority.   Its goal is social welfare. The individual personality is not yet differentiated, valued, freed or assured of development.   Collectivism suppresses individuality save as the individual is a unit in conformity and submission to the social whole.   The individual is lost in the mass. Class ethics which now prevails in Russia is conceived as a means to ultimate social ethics.

In Western ethics the *ideal* is the fullest development of every human personality through the cooperative effort of the community, ever-widening in intent to the creation of a worldwide brotherhood.   Hitherto the first and chief emphasis has been placed upon the individual, not upon the community. Cooperation and social responsibility have been weakened or destroyed by unshared class privilege and power.   Capitalism, nationalism and imperialism contradict and destroy our moral standards.   In ideal we desire the welfare of all, but we are paralyzed by natural selfishness in an individualistic, competitive, class economic system which develops personality only in the favored few at the cost of others, and which destroys brotherhood or comradeship in an inherently unethical system. The economic system thus dominates ethical standards and politics.   Profit-seeking economics destroys moral ideals or makes them appear a scandalous hypocrisy.   Without justice, true morality becomes impossible.   The basic economic order must be moralized or else it makes impossible any new morality. Thus Soviet Russia exposes us if we separate theory and practice, the ideal and the actual, and forces us to test our morality by its fruits and its economic causes and results.

Clean Moving Pictures

Russia takes her art seriously.   Like everything else it has a purpose and a plan.   The Russians conceive the theatre, cinema and radio not as an avenue for money making, or even primarily for entertainment, but "a school for human behavior," for "idealogical education," for inculcating ideas and ideals in the impressionable minds of youths and adults.   They would no more contemplate the prostitution of the cinema for the enrichment of a few profiteers than they would that of their school system.   In the West we think of the moving picture industry for profit, or exploitation, for entertainment or excitement.   In the Soviet Union it is a great educational force to build the new social order.

Acting is a well-paid, secure, responsible and respectable profession without scandal.   There is no hero-worship of stars, but rather the exaltation of ideas.   Art becomes the servant of life not the panderer or prostitute of pleasure.   The leaders deprecate mere "frothy entertainment."   Up to April 23, 1932, when they dissolved the censorship of the *Rapp,* or Proletarian Writers' Society, the danger was that the cinema would be too moralizing and dull.   It was often over-serious and educational. Yet the people were deeply appreciative of it even at its worst. It was an escape from the drab monotony of their toil and their cheerless homes.   In technique the Soviet film is not yet equal to the American, but Russians are so superior in dramatic ability and artistic appreciation that there is bound to be a unique development in this branch of art and education.

Over 100 million people visited the theatres, operas and cinemas in 1932.   Two thirds of the films produced by the Soviet moving picture organization are educational and informative, for use chiefly in workers' and village clubs.   They are no more concerned for profit in the cinema than in the school system, the medical service, or the housing of the people. Thirty thousand village teachers have been in training as cinema operators.   A few American films by Harold Lloyd, Douglas Fairbanks or Charlie Chaplin are used in Russia for

sheer amusement, but nine-tenths of the American pictures would be excluded as too demoralizing, or as inculcating false ideals regarding wealth, luxury, drinking, sex and crime. The Russians are very realistic and naturalistic in the sphere of sex but it is never used as a suggestive lure in art, the cinema or the press. Folk dancing is encouraged but jazz is scorned as "the music of decaying capitalism," and the fox trot as inculcating "a degenerate and false sexuality."

Drink is an evil to be fought and the cinema and the organized youth movement are united and unanimous against it. Crime, divorce scandals, or sex escapades do not occupy the stage or the press to pander to excitement or amusement. The press, the stage and art are for *use* to educate and to mold youth and age in the new idealism. Think of the effect upon Russian youth if from infancy to maturity they never have, according to their standard, a false ideal portrayed or subtly inculcated.

The hero of the cinema is not a two-gun wild-west adventurer, a successful gangster, a profiteer, a luxurious parasite, a seducer, nor a selfish individualist out for his own pleasure or profit. He is always the social leader, often of the Edison type, who builds a railway, heals disease, drains the swamps, lifts the level of well-being and happiness of the whole community. And in the end the spotlight falls not upon the hero as such, nor upon the film star, but upon the cause, the idea, the Revolution, the new social order. One sees portrayed a new creative epoch in human history.

One receives nothing less than a shock to return from the clean, dramatic, educational films of Soviet Russia to the often demoralizing American pictures that pour forth from Hollywood. All thoughtful people in Russia and America recognize that the moving picture is one of the most powerful creative forces, whether for good or evil, in shaping the minds of impressionable childhood and youth. The Motion Picture Producers and Distributors of America claimed in prosperous times a weekly attendance of 115 million. A four-year study of the effects of the films on American minds in the making was initiated by the Motion Picture Research Council, and executed by the Payne Fund, under the direction of a group

of psychologists and sociologists. This has resulted in a considerable quantity of literature and magazine writing.[1]

The average exposure of the child at the movies is about two hours, or about twice the exposure of the child in the Sunday school. Practically all children stay to the end and many sit through the program two or three times. As to the subjects of the films Professor Dale of Ohio State University found that crime, sex and love were the subjects of 82 per cent of all feature films. The shift in recent years has been away from love stories to sex and crime pictures.

As to the character of the American films, the investigation showed that of 500 features produced in 1930, 137 had crime as their major theme, 44 were primarily devoted to war, horror and mystery, and 70 centered in sex. Over 50 per cent of the average child's mental stimulus consisted in sex, or crime, or violence.[2] Many of the criminals are romantically attractive, only half receive any legal punishment, many go scot free and remain in the imaginations of youth as envied heroes. In a mid-western community practically without race consciousness, race prejudice had grown like a weed after showing the anti-Negro film, *The Birth of a Nation*. A child of eight had nightmares for a month after seeing *Tarzan of the Apes*. Some 78 per cent of all films contain liquor situations, which are much more effective than advertisements. The weekly *Time*, after listing a dozen female film stars, said they had "all in recent pictures attractively performed functions ranging from noble prostitution to carefree concupiscence."

Most of the films are shown against an attractive back-

---

[1] We are all indebted to such papers as the *Christian Century* and the *Survey*, and to such books as Henry James Forman's *Our Movie-Made Children*. Nine other valuable research volumes have followed, published by the Macmillan Company. The Payne Research Committee estimated a total possible audience in America of 105 millions, a national weekly attendance of 77 millions, of whom 36 per cent were children and adolescents. A child thus sits in every third seat and there is an average of a movie a week for each child or adult in the United States.

[2] In 115 recent pictures 406 crimes were committed; in 35 pictures there were 54 murders; in 26 films were 17 holdups and 21 kidnappings. Of murders, the heroes committed 13, the villains 30, and others 11.

ground of luxury, and the investigation showed that the desire to make easy money had stimulated one-fifth of the boys even in a good neighborhood. Professor Blumer reports: "The good is infrequent and fleeting, the bad suggesting easy money, incitement to crime and glorification of crime, is constant, cumulative and to some children almost irresistible."

One boy convicted of crime said: "As I became older the luxuries of life showed in the movies made me want to possess them." Among a group of truants and boys who had gone wrong, 55 per cent said that the pictures of gangsters had stimulated them to desire to follow their example. One boy of eighteen convicted of robbery and rape said: "I would see in a picture the 'Big Shot' come into a cabaret. Everyone would greet him with a smile. The girls would all crowd around him. . . . When I would see pictures like this I would go wild and say that some day I would be a 'Big Shot'." [1] Of 110 young men in prison, 49 per cent said that the movies had created in them the desire to carry a gun and 28 per cent a desire to pull off a hold-up.

Of the goals of life held up before children in American films only 9 per cent could be classed as social. In Russia over 90 per cent are such. In order of frequency Dr. Dale lists the following goals in 115 pictures analyzed: Winning another's love, marriage for love, professional success, revenge, crime for gain, illicit love, thrills or excitement, . . . concealment of guilt, marriage for money, etc. Such are the goals which are being taught—and attained. We are reaping in our national life just what we sow in our films. There are in consequence annually more murders, homicides and holdups in a single city like Chicago than in the whole of England and Wales, or than in almost all the cities of Russia combined.

---

[1] *The Survey Graphic,* May, 1933, quotes Professor Blumer, listing thirty-one valuable scenes of training in burglary which young fellows in prison testified had helped them in their criminal careers. One youth said: "Movies have shown me the way of stealing automobiles, the charge for which I am now serving sentence." Another: "I learned from the movies the scientific way of pulling jobs, to leave no finger-prints or tell-tale marks." A third: "I learned something from *The Gateway to Hell.* It is a gangster picture. It shows how to drown out shots from a gun by backfiring a car."

The American film organized for profit is a moral menace not only in the United States but to the youth in other lands. Lord Irwin, when Viceroy, protested against their demoralization in India, and they are a curse to China. Fortunately all save a few are banned from Russia where the cinema and the organized youth movement together make the chief demand for the inculcation of a high idealism.

It is not for a moment denied that there are commercial and political reasons for excluding many American films from the Soviet Union. But quite apart from these, on moral grounds alone, most American films are considered to give false views of life that are demoralizing to Russian youth. What concerns us much more is the question as to how far they are demoralizing to American youth. Any one who is familiar with the moving pictures of the two countries must admit that on ethical grounds and in the matter of inculcating a high idealism, the Russian films are upon a superior plane.

Mr. Will Hays, as President of the Motion Picture Producers and Distributors of America, in his report for 1932 claims a weekly world audience of 250,000,000. The influence and power of these films, for good or evil, can hardly be exaggerated. Mr. Hays admits that "the proof of everything in our business lies in the product." It is just this product that makes the better portion of the American public indignant.

We do not deny that Mr. Hays' organization has achieved some results, nor that he has succeeded in the first two objects of the Association. It has fostered "the common interests of those engaged in the motion picture industry." Apart from the depression, it has paid enormous profits to the profiteers as narrated by William Fox.[1]

Again, Mr. Hays says: "The function of motion pictures is

[1] *Upton Sinclair Presents William Fox.* Mr. Fox complains that he was plundered of considerably more than $100,000,000 of the just profits of his company. If the statements are libelous, they should be disproved in court. "The men who had hung him up and skinned him" left poor Mr. Fox with a paltry "part of his skin—$15,000,000 in actual cash, $3,000,000 in notes from Clarke, and the promise of a check from Fox Film to the amount of $41,666.66 per month for five years"—together with invaluable patents worth tens of millions.

to *entertain* . . . first of all, pictures must entertain." This, they certainly have done.

The Report on the *Public Relations of the Motion Picture Industry* [1] admits that "the Hays organization has entertained some laudable purposes" but "there is a disappointing disparity between promise and fullfilment." The wholesale merchandizing of block booking and blind booking continues. The report condemns "persons responsibly placed who receive honoraria from the industry." One leader, for instance, occupying one of the most important positions in the Protestant world was receiving $1,800 a year by private arrangement as an "advisor."

Many voluntary workers throughout the country have undoubtedly been trying to improve the films. After twelve years of trial, however, during which Mr. Hays has professed to be trying to reform this demoralizing industry, we must judge him and the motion picture business, not by their professions but by their practice. The Report of the Federal Council shows why the cooperation of better people has not been won: "Confidence is lacking. There is no adequate basis in confidence for full and hearty cooperation with the industry." Just as truly as Mr. Roosevelt broadly has won the confidence of the country, Mr. Hays and the motion picture industry have as signally failed to win it.

They have shown that they can produce good pictures when they care to do so. The basic fact remains that here is a vast and powerful industry, apparently chiefly concerned for its own profits, which is producing all too often a volume of demoralizing films. Does the profit motive furnish an adequate basis for morals in this, or in other industries, or in banking? How far do our economics underlie our morality, our ideas and institutions? Does anyone doubt that if Mr. Roosevelt and the government took over the business from the profiteers in Hollywood and New York that we should have as clean moving pictures as Soviet Russia? Which is more important, the character of our youth and the crime of our cities, or the profits of Hollywood?

---

[1] *Report by the Department of Research and Education of the Federal Council of Churches*, 1931, 105 East 22nd Street, New York, pp. 144-150.

CHAPTER IX

A UNIFIED PHILOSOPHY OF LIFE

Russia has achieved what has hitherto been known only at rare periods in history, the experience of almost a whole people living under a unified philosophy of life. All life is focussed in a central purpose. It is directed to a single high end and energized by such powerful and glowing motivation that life seems to have supreme significance. It releases a flood of joyous and strenuous activity. The new philosophy has the advantage of seeming to be simple, clear, understandable, all-embracing and practical. We shall later examine critically what appear to be the defects of this over-simplified system.

Some philosophies have existed as a dream in the mind of a man, or of an esoteric group, or they have been discussed in academic grooves, or recorded in the archives of classic libraries. But this philosophy is being incarnated in the life of a nation covering nearly one-sixth of the earth. Never was any other system so swiftly and completely embodied in the life of mankind. Man individually and socially needs a philosophy or a working faith. The life of the animal is one of blind instinct, it is set in fixed grooves and habits. But insofar as man is lifted above the brute and does not live a mere hand-to-mouth animal existence, he lives unconsciously by some belief, or way of life, however crude or superstitious, that is capable of rational statement. If we take philosophy at its simplest as the attempt to understand the meaning of experience, it is evident that man ought to try to comprehend the significance of his own life. As he advances in experimentation and conscious reflection he may finally ask, with Royce, where he can find a cause, or way of life, that is rational, supreme, compelling, all-embracing and fit to centralize life.

What are the real values in life and can they be harmonized and integrated in a single purpose, embodied in a unified personality and achieved in society?

There have been favored periods in the past, creative epochs, when men achieved such a unified philosophy of life. There were such periods in early Greece. Even in the wide diversity of various schools of thought many were united in some way of life that seemed supremely worth while. Again, in certain periods of German philosophy life was rationalized and meaningful. In some early religious movements, as in Buddhism and Christianity, when they were in the nascent state, when tides of new life and experience demanded expression and interpretation in thought, life was unified and made whole. In the Middle Ages, whatever their defects, men were united under a single philosophy.

The modern world has lost such a philosophy. The World War destroyed the faith of the nineteenth century. It was a rude awakening to stark and sordid realities. Life was shattered, disintegrated, dissipated. Faith had given place to cynicism, and hope to despair. Yet it was in just this period of shell-shock, disillusion and pessimism after the war and in the post-war depression that a large section of mankind achieved again what had seemed forever impossible, a unified philosophy of life. It was a way thought out by Karl Marx, a student of Hegel, an heir of the classic philosophy of Greece and Germany, thinking and writing as an exile in the British Museum in London, and later applied by the son of a petty Russian nobleman, Lenin. No philosophy ever played a more violent or dynamic part in history, or so sharply divided our modern world. We will do well to try to understand it.

Before Marx there had been much scattered thought, strong emotion and sporadic action on behalf of various socialistic theories. But Marx gathered up all the vague revolt and desire of the oppressed toilers and gave them what appeared to be a clear philosophy, a program of action, and such a relationship to cosmic forces that it seemed that the very stars in their courses were fighting for them for certain victory.

This philosophy seemed to explain their past and to give rational justification for their foreordained future. Every great revolution has had some philosophy behind it, but no other ever had such an effective weapon, like a shining sword of thought. It unites the ultimates of philosophy with practical economics, applied science, dynamic sociology and social psychology, coupled with an almost religious emotion and future prophecy, that has the appearance not of faith but of scientific certainty. The hope of a glorious future nerves the faithful for immediate social action. For union with the infinite is substituted unity with the social whole. Preparation for a future life is replaced by sacrifice for a future generation. Their philosophy holds to a rational principle in the universe, an ethical progress in history, and a personal and social dynamic for almost impossible achievement in the transforming both of the material environment and of human nature.

There are possible spiritual implications for the future in this as yet truncated philosophy which must and will be worked out in less strenuous times, but for the present the whole system is concrete and compelling. Labor is dignified and intellectualized by its vision of purpose and goal. Everything that they can envisage in life is to be shared by all. As its goal is in the future the system is not static but requires continual progress and endless achievement. Unified by a rational plan it need never degenerate in rotting luxury, or hopeless poverty, or individual hedonism. The ever-progressive good life must be achieved for all. They have a world to win. And their philosophy gives them such a living faith that their leaders in the past through decades of prison and poverty and exile were sure of ultimate triumph. Whatever its limitations or defects such a philosophy is certainly effective.

As surely as Soviet Russia has become united, we of the West have witnessed a philosophic decadence and disintegration. Where feudalism once united the world, capitalism has divided it by the competitive anarchy of a loose individualism. Not organized society but the insecure individual is now the unit, where every man is for himself. The economics of profit conflict with the aims of culture. The gain of the few is

pitted against the welfare of the many. This whole *laissez faire* philosophy of life breeds competitive strife between individuals, classes, races and nations. It is rife with inner contradictions and conflicts and actually results in a succession of crises, depressions and wars, which have now almost inevitably become world wars.

This decadence and division is witnessed in our institutions and in our literature on both sides of the Atlantic. Our most effective literature is frequently that of despair, cynicism or protest. Though almost none of the writers agree as to what they want they nearly all unite in condemning the present disintegrating order.

On the English side Aldous Huxley is characteristic of the present decadence in contrast to the moral fiber and evolutionary hope of his Victorian forbear, Thomas Huxley. His *Brave New World* is terrifying and devastating as it depicts his vision of our materialistic future. Human life is conveniently bred in the test-tubes and beakers of laboratories, as in incubators, and it is scientifically conditioned and moulded at will. Life is "nasty, brutish and short," lived in a moral cesspool that has long passed beyond all distinctions of good and evil. Men swear "by our Ford" or "in the year of our Ford." However amusing, or contemptuous, or cynical such writing may be, it offers no possible philosophy for creative achievement or high living for youth. It is decadent.

The spirit of the age is characteristically expressed in an American volume of *Living Philosophies* which contains the intimate credos of more than a score of writers on both sides of the Atlantic.[1] In one of the opening essays John Dewey says: "The chief intellectual characteristic of the present age is its despair of any constructive philosophy—not just in its technical meaning, but in the sense of any integrated outlook

---

[1] *Living Philosophies,* Simon and Schuster, New York, 1931. A series of intimate credos by Albert Einstein, Sir James Jeans, Theodore Dreiser, James Truslow Adams, Sir Arthur Keith, Beatrice Webb, Fridtjof Nansen, R. A. Millikan, Hiliare Belloc, George Jean Nathan, Bertrand Russell, John Dewey, H. G. Wells, H. L. Mencken, Julia Peterkin, Irving Babbitt, Joseph Wood Krutch, Lewis Mumford, Hu Shih, J. B. S. Haldane, Irwin Edman, and Dean Inge.

and attitude. . . . The result is disillusionment." Theodore
Dreiser writes: "I find life to be a complete illusion or mirage
. . . in the wholly inexplicable world . . . . The best I can
say is that I have not the faintest notion of what it is all about,
unless it is for self-satisfaction. . . . I catch no meaning from
all I have seen, and pass quite as I came, confused and dis-
mayed." Irving Babbitt says: "Unless there is a reaffirmation
of the truths of the inner life in some form—religious or humanistic—civilization is threatened at its base." James Truslow Adams writes: "We are now floundering in a morass. . . .
The present situation cries aloud for some code. . . . We are
bewildered."

George Jean Nathan takes a position that would be regarded
with contempt in Russia when he says: "In hedonism I believe
above all other beliefs. To me pleasure and my own personal
happiness—only infrequently collaborating with that of others
—are all I deem worth a hoot. . . . I have all I can do to
look out for my own happiness and welfare." Mr. H. L.
Mencken states his credo of cynicism and Mr. Bertrand Russell
writes again as formerly on "the firm foundation of unyielding
despair. . . . Brief and powerless is man's life; on him and
all his race the slow sure doom falls pitiless and dark." It is,
however, Joseph Wood Krutch in his credo and more fully in
his *Modern Temper* who is typical of our decadent modern
philosophy and of its results. He writes: "If one turns to the
smarter of these novelists—Mr. Aldous Huxley, Mr. Ernest
Hemingway—one will discover in their tragic farces the picture of a society which is at bottom in despair because . . . it
has lost the sense of any ultimate importance inherent in the
experience which preoccupies it. . . . To Huxley and Hemingway love is at times only a sort of obscene joke . . . de-
baucheries born of nothing except a sense of the emptiness of
life . . . in this generally devaluated world." Mr. Krutch
further says: "A color has faded from our palette, a whole
range of effects has dropped out of our symphony. . . . We
are carried one step nearer to that state in which existence is
seen as a vast emptiness. . . . We have grown used to a Godless universe, but we are not yet accustomed to one which

is loveless as well, and only when we have so become shall we realize what atheism really means." [1]

These typical credos of our age are unconscious expressions of a decaying economic order. Karl Marx, with all his inadequacies, shows why that order, filled as it is with inner contradiction and strife, is doomed, and why we are nearing the end of an epoch. Though never taking the time to formulate a comprehensive system of philosophy, he at least outlined a new theory and way of life which was destined to be the creative instrument of a new epoch. We are struck by the contrast of the impatience and gloom of the modern temper of the age and of our lost philosophy, as contrasted with the faith and hope and titanic creative energy of Soviet Russia. It is our belief that whatever we may conceive to be the defect of the Marxian system that would make it impossible of acceptance for most of us, we have need as individuals and as a society to understand and evaluate this system, and insofar as we find it inadequate to endeavor to achieve again for ourselves a unified philosophy of life. If we are not satisfied with the philosophy of Marx have we a better one of our own? In the meantime, without taking anything for granted, we must first try to state as simply and clearly as we can the most important elements of Marx's system.

The Philosophy of Karl Marx

Marx's teaching resolves itself into three principal elements: a philosophy of history, an economic theory, and a practical program for the realization of a new social order.

We may sum up these three principal positions as follows:

1. His philosophic method, *the dialectic process,* maintains that evolution in nature, history and the human mind is through the conflict and resolving of opposing forces. His philosophy of history, in its *materialist or economic interpretation,* holds that the principal influence which shapes human progress is the method of economic production in each period.

---

[1] Joseph Wood Krutch, *The Modern Temper,* pp. 113, 303.

2. His *labor theories of value* and of *surplus value* endeavor
to show that the workers who create value receive less than
they produce, under a system where the owners of the means
of production appropriate the surplus.

3. His theory of social development is that the *conflict of
classes* is the driving force of history, which leads, through
the inner contradiction of an economic system, to its ripening
and decline, to the end of one epoch and the birth of the next.

His practical program is through the organization of labor
unions, the waging of the class war, and setting up at the
appropriate time, upon the breakdown of the old order, under
the dictatorship of the proletariat, the new Socialist State,
which is ultimately to bring in the final, classless society of
Communism.   Each of these we shall briefly examine before
proceeding to a criticism and evaluation of the system.[1]

1. *Dialectic Materialism—The Economic Interpretation of History*

Hegel had borrowed the term *dialectic* from the Greeks, who
had employed the word as denoting the art of discussion by
discourse and rejoinder, the search for truth by the bringing
out of contradictions and antitheses in the open conflict of
opposing views.[2]

According to Hegel, not only all matter and mind but the
entire universe is in motion in the evolutionary process.   The
dialectic process, of progress realized through conflict, appears
in nature, in history and in the human mind.   In the logical
statement of this process we have first a positive assertion of

[1] I am indebted throughout this chapter not only to the writings of Marx,
which I shall quote, but to the interpretive works of Doctor A. D. Lindsay,
the Master of Balliol, in his *Karl Marx's Capital;* Professor Sidney Hook's
Toward the Understanding of Karl Marx; the writings of my friend Max
Beer; Professor Harold Laski's *Communism* and his essay on *Karl Marx;*
the Ryazanoff edition of the *Communist Manifesto,* and other works.

[2] As illustrated in the writings of Plato: "Dialectic is the process of thinking by which the dramatic conflict of ideas is resolved by definition, differentiation, and re-definition, until one ultimate, luminously self-evident insight
is reached in which the original conflict of ideas is harmonized."   Sidney
Hook, *Toward the Understanding of Marx,* p. 77.

something; then the contradiction, the antagonistic element, or negation; and finally the negation of the negation, or the reconciliation of these two opposites in a higher unity. Thus there is a thesis, a challenging antithesis, and then the inter-penetration of these opposites till they are resolved in a higher synthesis. Somewhat arbitrarily Hegel forces all the movement of nature, of history and of the human mind into the mold of his dialectic, or progress by conflict and the reconciliation of opposites.

No concrete illustration does full justice to the dialectic process which is not mechanical and repetitive. We might think of a pendulum swinging to the two extremes at two successive moments, carrying the hour hand of progress along the face of time, advanced equally by the backward as by the forward swing. We might suggest two poles of an electric current, the positive and the negative, as the constructive and destructive, the evolutionary and revolutionary process of progress, both necessary. We might think of an ascending spiral as we pass around a complete circle, never to return to the same point but to rise ever to a higher level, which becomes the starting point of a new ascent.

But we can better conceive of a discussion of two parties, each seeking, not to defeat the opponent, but with full recognition of the limited value in the partial thesis and antithesis, to discover a new position which will conserve the element of truth in each and combine them in a fresh creative synthesis. This will offer no dogmatic finality of absolute truth but the fresh starting point of further progress through the challenge and resolution of contending forces, in endless progress through conflict.

Hegel saw all nature and history as one majestic process of development propelled by the Idea, the Eternal Thinking Process, the Absolute or Divine mind, in creation, negation and recreation. Marx accepts his dialectic formula and method but in place of the abstract and mystical Idea he substitutes economic forces as the dynamic of change. In place of Hegel's idealism he substitutes his own materialism. Instead of making the material world as the mere vestment of the reality of the

something; then the contradiction, the antagonistic element, or negation; and finally the negation of the negation, or the reconciliation of these two opposites in a higher unity. Thus there is a thesis, a challenging antithesis, and then the interpenetration of these opposites till they are resolved in a higher synthesis. Somewhat arbitrarily Hegel forces all the movement of nature, of history and of the human mind into the mold of his dialectic, or progress by conflict and the reconciliation of opposites.

No concrete illustration does full justice to the dialectic process which is not mechanical and repetitive. We might think of a pendulum swinging to the two extremes at two successive moments, carrying the hour hand of progress along the face of time, advanced equally by the backward as by the forward swing. We might suggest two poles of an electric current, the positive and the negative, as the constructive and destructive, the evolutionary and revolutionary process of progress, both necessary. We might think of an ascending spiral as we pass around a complete circle, never to return to the same point but to rise ever to a higher level, which becomes the starting point of a new ascent.

But we can better conceive of a discussion of two parties, each seeking, not to defeat the opponent, but with full recognition of the limited value in the partial thesis and antithesis, to discover a new position which will conserve the element of truth in each and combine them in a fresh creative synthesis. This will offer no dogmatic finality of absolute truth but the fresh starting point of further progress through the challenge and resolution of contending forces, in endless progress through conflict.

Hegel saw all nature and history as one majestic process of development propelled by the Idea, the Eternal Thinking Process, the Absolute or Divine mind, in creation, negation and recreation. Marx accepts his dialectic formula and method but in place of the abstract and mystical Idea he substitutes economic forces as the dynamic of change. In place of Hegel's idealism he substitutes his own materialism. Instead of making the material world as the mere vestment of the reality of the

2. His *labor theories of value* and of *surplus value* endeavor to show that the workers who create value receive less than they produce, under a system where the owners of the means of production appropriate the surplus.

3. His theory of social development is that the *conflict of classes* is the driving force of history, which leads, through the inner contradiction of an economic system, to its ripening and decline, to the end of one epoch and the birth of the next.

His practical program is through the organization of labor unions, the waging of the class war, and setting up at the appropriate time, upon the breakdown of the old order, under *the dictatorship of the proletariat,* the new Socialist State, which is ultimately to bring in the final, classless society of Communism. Each of these we shall briefly examine before proceeding to a criticism and evaluation of the system.[1]

1. *Dialectic Materialism—The Economic Interpretation of History*

Hegel had borrowed the term *dialectic* from the Greeks, who had employed the word as denoting the art of discussion by discourse and rejoinder, the search for truth by the bringing out of contradictions and antitheses in the open conflict of opposing views.[2]

According to Hegel, not only all matter and mind but the entire universe is in motion in the evolutionary process. The dialectic process, of progress realized through conflict, appears in nature, in history and in the human mind. In the logical statement of this process we have first a positive assertion of

---

[1] I am indebted throughout this chapter not only to the writings of Marx, which I shall quote, but to the interpretive works of Doctor A. D. Lindsay, the Master of Balliol, in his *Karl Marx's Capital;* Professor Sidney Hook's *Toward the Understanding of Karl Marx;* the writings of my friend Max Beer; Professor Harold Laski's *Communism* and his essay on *Karl Marx;* the Ryazanoff edition of the *Communist Manifesto,* and other works.

[2] As illustrated in the writings of Plato: "Dialectic is the process of thinking by which the dramatic conflict of ideas is resolved by definition, differentiation, and re-definition, until one ultimate, luminously self-evident insight is reached in which the original conflict of ideas is harmonized." Sidney Hook, *Toward the Understanding of Marx,* p. 77.

A UNIFIED PHILOSOPHY OF LIFE 183

2. His *labor theories of value* and of *surplus value* endeavor to show that the workers who create value receive less than they produce, under a system where the owners of the means of production appropriate the surplus.

3. His theory of social development is that the *conflict of classes* is the driving force of history, which leads, through the inner contradiction of an economic system, to its ripening and decline, to the end of one epoch and the birth of the next.

His practical program is through the organization of labor unions, the waging of the class war, and setting up at the appropriate time, upon the breakdown of the old order, under *the dictatorship of the proletariat,* the new Socialist State, which is ultimately to bring in the final, classless society of Communism. Each of these we shall briefly examine before proceeding to a criticism and evaluation of the system.[1]

1. *Dialectic Materialism—The Economic Interpretation of History*

Hegel had borrowed the term *dialectic* from the Greeks, who had employed the word as denoting the art of discussion by discourse and rejoinder, the search for truth by the bringing out of contradictions and antitheses in the open conflict of opposing views.[2]

According to Hegel, not only all matter and mind but the entire universe is in motion in the evolutionary process. The dialectic process, of progress realized through conflict, appears in nature, in history and in the human mind. In the logical statement of this process we have first a positive assertion of

[1] I am indebted throughout this chapter not only to the writings of Marx, which I shall quote, but to the interpretive works of Doctor A. D. Lindsay, the Master of Balliol, in his *Karl Marx's Capital;* Professor Sidney Hook's *Toward the Understanding of Karl Marx;* the writings of my friend Max Beer; Professor Harold Laski's *Communism* and his essay on *Karl Marx;* the Ryazanoff edition of the *Communist Manifesto,* and other works.

[2] As illustrated in the writings of Plato: "Dialectic is the process of thinking by which the dramatic conflict of ideas is resolved by definition, differentiation, and re-definition, until one ultimate, luminously self-evident insight is reached in which the original conflict of ideas is harmonized." Sidney Hook, *Toward the Understanding of Marx,* p. 77.

something; then the contradiction, the antagonistic element, or negation; and finally the negation of the negation, or the reconciliation of these two opposites in a higher unity. Thus there is a thesis, a challenging antithesis, and then the interpenetration of these opposites till they are resolved in a higher synthesis. Somewhat arbitrarily Hegel forces all the movement of nature, of history and of the human mind into the mold of his dialectic, or progress by conflict and the reconciliation of opposites.

No concrete illustration does full justice to the dialectic process which is not mechanical and repetitive. We might think of a pendulum swinging to the two extremes at two successive moments, carrying the hour hand of progress along the face of time, advanced equally by the backward as by the forward swing. We might suggest two poles of an electric current, the positive and the negative, as the constructive and destructive, the evolutionary and revolutionary process of progress, both necessary. We might think of an ascending spiral as we pass around a complete circle, never to return to the same point but to rise ever to a higher level, which becomes the starting point of a new ascent.

But we can better conceive of a discussion of two parties, each seeking, not to defeat the opponent, but with full recognition of the limited value in the partial thesis and antithesis, to discover a new position which will conserve the element of truth in each and combine them in a fresh creative synthesis. This will offer no dogmatic finality of absolute truth but the fresh starting point of further progress through the challenge and resolution of contending forces, in endless progress through conflict.

Hegel saw all nature and history as one majestic process of development propelled by the Idea, the Eternal Thinking Process, the Absolute or Divine mind, in creation, negation and recreation. Marx accepts his dialectic formula and method but in place of the abstract and mystical Idea he substitutes economic forces as the dynamic of change. In place of Hegel's idealism he substitutes his own materialism. Instead of making the material world as the mere vestment of the reality of the

something; then the contradiction, the antagonistic element, or negation; and finally the negation of the negation, or the reconciliation of these two opposites in a higher unity. Thus there is a thesis, a challenging antithesis, and then the interpenetration of these opposites till they are resolved in a higher synthesis. Somewhat arbitrarily Hegel forces all the movement of nature, of history and of the human mind into the mold of his dialectic, or progress by conflict and the reconciliation of opposites.

No concrete illustration does full justice to the dialectic process which is not mechanical and repetitive. We might think of a pendulum swinging to the two extremes at two successive moments, carrying the hour hand of progress along the face of time, advanced equally by the backward as by the forward swing. We might suggest two poles of an electric current, the positive and the negative, as the constructive and destructive, the evolutionary and revolutionary process of progress, both necessary. We might think of an ascending spiral as we pass around a complete circle, never to return to the same point but to rise ever to a higher level, which becomes the starting point of a new ascent.

But we can better conceive of a discussion of two parties, each seeking, not to defeat the opponent, but with full recognition of the limited value in the partial thesis and antithesis, to discover a new position which will conserve the element of truth in each and combine them in a fresh creative synthesis. This will offer no dogmatic finality of absolute truth but the fresh starting point of further progress through the challenge and resolution of contending forces, in endless progress through conflict.

Hegel saw all nature and history as one majestic process of development propelled by the Idea, the Eternal Thinking Process, the Absolute or Divine mind, in creation, negation and recreation. Marx accepts his dialectic formula and method but in place of the abstract and mystical Idea he substitutes economic forces as the dynamic of change. In place of Hegel's idealism he substitutes his own materialism. Instead of making the material world as the mere vestment of the reality of the

2. His *labor theories of value* and of *surplus value* endeavor to show that the workers who create value receive less than they produce, under a system where the owners of the means of production appropriate the surplus.

3. His theory of social development is that the *conflict of classes* is the driving force of history, which leads, through the inner contradiction of an economic system, to its ripening and decline, to the end of one epoch and the birth of the next.

His practical program is through the organization of labor unions, the waging of the class war, and setting up at the appropriate time, upon the breakdown of the old order, under *the dictatorship of the proletariat,* the new Socialist State, which is ultimately to bring in the final, classless society of Communism. Each of these we shall briefly examine before proceeding to a criticism and evaluation of the system.[1]

1. Dialectic Materialism—The Economic Interpretation of History

Hegel had borrowed the term *dialectic* from the Greeks, who had employed the word as denoting the art of discussion by discourse and rejoinder, the search for truth by the bringing out of contradictions and antitheses in the open conflict of opposing views.[2]

According to Hegel, not only all matter and mind but the entire universe is in motion in the evolutionary process. The dialectic process, of progress realized through conflict, appears in nature, in history and in the human mind. In the logical statement of this process we have first a positive assertion of

---

[1] I am indebted throughout this chapter not only to the writings of Marx, which I shall quote, but to the interpretive works of Doctor A. D. Lindsay, the Master of Balliol, in his *Karl Marx's Capital;* Professor Sidney Hook's *Toward the Understanding of Karl Marx;* the writings of my friend Max Beer; Professor Harold Laski's *Communism* and his essay on *Karl Marx;* the Ryazanoff edition of the *Communist Manifesto,* and other works.

[2] As illustrated in the writings of Plato: "Dialectic is the process of thinking by which the dramatic conflict of ideas is resolved by definition, differentiation, and re-definition, until one ultimate, luminously self-evident insight is reached in which the original conflict of ideas is harmonized." Sidney Hook, *Toward the Understanding of Marx,* p. 77.

Idea, he places the material world as the basic reality and man's ideas as "the material world reflected by the human mind and translated into terms of thought." He believed he had thus taken Hegel's dialectic and "turned it right side up." Thus inverted it becomes Marx's materialist conception of history or economic determinism.

Marx follows Hegel in trying to show that social change is produced by the interaction of nature, society and human intelligence. For illustration, the objective conditions, natural and social, provide the positive *thesis;* the human needs and purposes provoked by these conditions furnish the answering *antithesis;* these interpenetrating provoke a course of action as a *synthesis,* which leads to a social advance.[1]

Marx in his economic determinism, or the materialist interpretation of history, does not hold that man is only actuated by material motives. His studies had convinced him, however, that the *chief* factor in social change was not geographic environment, nor the ideas of an age, but economic conditions, especially the method of production of the time. If, for instance, in different periods you have slave labor, then the feudal windmill, and later the industrial steam mill or factory, these will not only affect the lives of the owners and workers but also the institutions of the period and finally its ideas.[2] Thus the key to the development of society is economic struggle and the means of production of any period create their own type of economic structure and division of society into classes, as between masters and slaves, lords and serfs, owners and wage dependents. In his materialist conception of history Marx was combining two schools of thought, the Hegelian conception of collective historical development and the classical English individualist economics; the one philosophical and the

---

[1] *Ibid,* p. 84.

[2] Marx says: "The sum total of these relations of production constitutes the economic structure of society—the real foundation on which rise legal and political superstructures and to which correspond definite forms of social consciousness. The mode of production in material life determines the general character of the social, political, and spiritual processes of life." *Critique of Political Economy,* p. 11.

other economic. His system thus allows for the interaction of culture, including politics, and economics. But the predominant cause of the changes and developments under capitalism in the last century and a half were the methods of production introduced by the industrial revolution.[1]

For Hegel, all history is but the development of the idea of freedom. Marx also sought ultimate freedom when economic determinism should be overcome in the establishment of a classless society. Economic forces dominate society only until society takes the control of economic forces. In the meantime each class is governed by self-interest. While rare individuals may sacrifice their economic interests for the welfare of society, classes as such never do so. "In every epoch," says Marx, "the ruling ideas have been the ideas of the ruling class." These are today exercised through the control of the press, the cinema, the radio, the school, the church, industry and government. The owners of the means of production dominate each epoch, whether they be the workers in Soviet Russia or the capitalists in America. Marx was not trying to fix the chains of a system of economic determinism upon the workers, but rather the opposite. He offered them a method of understanding and of *making* history. Man could change his environment and himself, for he was meant for freedom.

In our experience we distinguish between things and ideas. Which of the two is primary? Hegel, Marx's leader, as an idealist held that thought is primary and action secondary, that ideas of things are more important than things themselves. Thought is the judge of life. Things and the material world are only the appearance of the idea. A true philosophy would then be the supreme need, to apprehend the universe—which is an idea. This results in the tendency "to substitute ideas for

---

[1] Marx did not teach a rigid mechanistic determinism but opposed it. Engels, after his death, says: "Marx and I are partly responsible for the fact that the younger men have sometimes laid more stress on the economic side than it deserves. In meeting the attack of our opponents it was necessary for us to emphasize the dominant principle, denied by them, and we did not always have the time, place or opportunity to let the other factors concerned in the mutual action and reaction get their deserts."

things, to take refuge from reality in imagination, to live in make-believe."

Marx, as a realist, held that things are prior to ideas, action is more important than thought, and practice more important than theory. The brutal economic facts of life determine its thoughts. Man must seek freedom for his spirit by the control of economic necessity, especially of the means of production for his material life. There must be no escape in a dream world, even of great thoughts like those of Plato and Hegel. *Theory and practice are one.* All theory must then seek to validate itself in action. No belief can be demonstrated by abstract argument. Knowledge is no longer an end in itself. A true philosophy is only an instrument for creating the good life for all. This is what it means to be a true realist. We must change the brutal external facts of life, remake man's environment and then man's own nature. This is the dialectic march of progress through the interpenetration of opposites.[1]

2. *Value and Surplus Value*

Marx was a great sociologist rather than a modern scientific economist. He may be ranked as the first great economic historian, or as the last of the school of classical economists. These included Adam Smith, 1723–1790, Ricardo, 1772–1823, and Marx, 1818–1883. These early economists sought to find a theory of value to account for the variation in prices. The first two found value to be the result of "natural law" and therefore presumably just. Marx accepted Ricardo's theory that labor was the basis of all commercial values but dropped his idea of natural law and revolutionized his classical economics.

Political economy arose as the apologetic of a social order and it is often so to this day. Ricardo was the apologist for the bourgeois and Marx for labor. The early classical economists believed that as the economic order was ruled by natural law it was in stable equilibrium. Marx showed that the system

---

[1] Professor John Macmurray of University College, London, makes the clearest statement of this position in his *Philosophy of Communism*.

was full of inner contradictions, in unstable equilibrium. He challenged the liberals' claim that liberty, equality and fraternity were provided by the system and showed that these were not realized by the helpless workers. The system meant freedom for the capitalist and exploitation for labor.

Marx in his labor theory of value sought a universal principle of social valuation, or "real cost," to which varying price relations could be referred. He made the unit and cause of value an hour of socially necessary labor, of a given degree of intensity and skill, applied according to the normal technique of an industry. Commodities should exchange in proportion to the socially necessary labor hours required for their production.

The owner of the means of production bought the labor power of the worker. This was a mere commodity that had to be quickly sold at whatever was offered if the worker was not to starve. Under "freedom of contract" and *laissez faire* individualist economics the worker thus became primarily a commodity rather than a member of society entitled like the employer to a just reward. Wages were as low as possible and gravitated to the cost of maintaining the laborer. Labor produced more than it was paid and the balance was taken by the owner for his profit. In a given number of hours labor created enough value to earn its wage. The balance of its time went to the creation of "surplus value" which formed the reservoir from which profit, interest and rent were drawn by the owners of the means of production.

Profit was the exploitation of the value of labor and its product. It was not the result of a natural law but the special privilege of a private system of ownership. Value, profit, wealth, were social products but they were not socially shared. They were chiefly appropriated by the few fortunate owners of the land, raw materials and machines. The fault was not that of the individual employer but of the system; just as the "good" slave owner was not to blame for the evils of slavery, but the system itself. Marx does not look upon slavery, feudalism and capitalism primarily as moral wrongs but as necessary historical epochs. The mission of capitalism was to open

up and multiply the forces of production, to create abundant material wealth for all. Its function was production not distribution. Adequate distribution was impossible where a few owned all the means of living, for each class always seeks first its own interests. The owners would make the profit but would never distribute it. This was human nature. One cannot ask men arbitrarily to change their nature, rather it is the outworn system of private monopolistic ownership which must be changed. To expect to change human nature, without changing the environment, would be like asking water to run uphill. It would be as fruitless as to ask slave owners to be more generous to their slaves. Even if they were it would not touch the real problem, which was of ownership. As long as one man is left in the keeping of another, at the mercy of another, injustice is certain.

An undue proportion of surplus value was bound to go to the monopolist owners. This wealth the few could not possibly consume nor spend upon themselves. They were forced to invest it as capital for the production of more wealth, in ever-growing production and over-production. Labor would always receive too little in wages to purchase this increasing over-production. This would inevitably create a series of crises of depression and unemployment of ever-growing intensity until finally the system would break down because of its inherent contradictions. Thus, as truly as slavery and feudalism before it, and for the same reason, capitalism was doomed.

Under this system the ever-multiplying forces of production and the progressive limitations upon consumption lead to anti-social consequences. When many are hungry and cold, commodities are deliberately destroyed to raise prices. There is a growing concentration of wealth and power for the few and growing discontent for the many. It is idle to tell the unemployed and the exploited wrecks of the system that skilled workers have privileges and luxuries which princes did not enjoy in former times. There is not increasing misery and an absolute decline in the workers' standard of living. Relatively, however, labor never receives an adequate share of the value in the creation of which it is the chief factor.

Marx says: "Profit and not use is the leading motive of capitalist production. Capitalism is shaken to its very foundation if we make use and enjoyment and not profiteering the leading motive of production."[1]

For a time the system is maintained by the extension of capitalism to imperialism. The raw materials and labor power of the backward or helpless people are exploited in the colonies and conquered areas of the capitalist nation. But this only multiplies the contradictions and injustices of the system. Greater crises, *world* depressions and *world* war are the inevitable results of this class system of strife when projected upon an imperialist scale.

Based upon the exploitation of labor, which is despoiled of the surplus value which it creates, Marx tries to show that there is a necessary and irreconcilable antagonism between master and man, owner and wage worker, when he says: "Accumulation of wealth at one pole is, therefore, at the same time accumulation of misery, agonized toil, slavery, ignorance, brutality, mental degradation; at the opposite pole, that is, the class which produces its own product in the form of capital."

After centuries of the teaching of benevolent idealism, of more generous charity, or of the optimistic hope of evolutionary liberalism that the conditions of labor will be improved and that the employers in due time will give the workers all that they deserve, the followers of Marx are still able to point to the brutal facts of wealth unshared side by side with poverty unrelieved, because of the divorce of the masses from the ownership of the instruments of production. They are able to show that their economic helplessness results inevitably in the denial of equality in personal freedom, in justice, in education, in health, in privilege of all kinds and in political power. As truly as when Marx made the indictment in 1848 natural resources are still being wantonly wasted and human beings exploited. It is still true and more glaringly apparent than when he wrote, that crises of growing intensity occur with world depressions, and that the economic system culminates

---

[1] *Capital*, II, p. 136.

in periodic wars that have now become world wars. All this is confirmed in many volumes of modern literature, as in the *Decay of Capitalist Civilization,* by Sidney Webb, now Lord Passfield.

Marx in his *Capital* thus describes the ripening and fall of capitalism: "As soon as this process of transformation has sufficiently decomposed the old society from top to bottom, as soon as the laborers are turned into proletarians . . . then the further socialization . . . takes a new form. That which is now to be expropriated is no longer the laborer working for himself, but the capitalist exploiting many laborers. This expropriation is accomplished by the action of the immanent laws of capitalist production itself, by the centralization of capital. One capitalist always kills many. Along with the constant diminishing number of the magnates of capital, who usurp and monopolize all advantages of this process of transformation, grows the mass of misery, oppression, slavery, degradation, exploitation; but with this too grows the revolt of the working class, a class always increasing in numbers, and disciplined, united, organized by the very mechanism of the process of capitalist production itself. The monopoly of capital becomes a fetter upon the mode of production, which has sprung up and flourished along with and under it. Centralization of the means of production and socialization of labor at last reach a point where they become incompatible with their capitalist integument. This integument is burst asunder. The knell of capitalist private property sounds. The expropriators are expropriated." [1]

Marx's theory was one of natural right; it was the application to economics of the principle of human equality. He did discover that value was a social product; that labor was not a mere commodity; that it was being exploited and that such an unjust system could not and need not continue. He shows that a few own the bulk of the earth, its raw materials, factories, banks, instruments of production, and means of living, and grow rich by a system which compels the majority

---

[1] *Capital,* I, pp. 836, 837.

to work for them for a bare living wage. Is the system just? Must it continue? No! Marx shows the masses a way out. It is a way, he tells them, grounded in science and in natural law. It is bound to win, for the very stars in their courses are fighting for them. By some mystic and incomprehensible "dialectic process," by a supposedly scientific theory of value and of surplus value it is all being worked out for them. They do not need to understand it. They must believe that they are being exploited and join in the crusade for their own emancipation.

They accordingly believe that they see in Russia the first fulfillment of Marx's prophecy. They see for themselves economic crises and world depressions of growing intensity. They hear of wars and rumors of wars for capitalist imperialism. Finally they hear the prophetic promise of deliverance and of a new social order. What competing offer can the *status quo* of capitalism make? Is it any wonder that in spite of its ponderous economic theory, despite its glaring defects and inconsistencies, the burning heart of the message of Marx has gone straight to the heart of labor in many lands?

3. Class Conflict and a Program of Action

Marx sees the world growingly divided by private property into conflicting classes of possessors and dispossessed, and the driving force of history as the struggle between these two classes. He does not desire or create these classes but finds them already in existence. He and Engels describe many primitive communal societies with the common ownership of land in Russia, among the Teutonic tribes and "everywhere from India to Ireland." But with the rise of private property society becomes divided between master and slave, then lord and serf, and later industrial capitalist and wage worker. Marx holds that their interests are sharply antagonistic and irreconcilable. The employers will buy labor power as cheaply as they can, labor will sell for as high a wage as possible; but the wage worker is in a poor position to bargain, as he must work or starve. This gives an enormous advantage to the

owner of the means of production for the control of almost all of life.[1]

Society is made up of persons in relation; human relationships are what matter. Society is divided into two classes, those who will not starve if they don't work and those who will starve if they don't work. It is always in process of change and this change makes history. All men must first seek bread, to provide for their economic needs. The means of production are steadily improving by technical skill. This change in production changes the relations of men.

The two classes of owners and dependents struggle for the control of the means of production, or for their economic security. This control over nature and machines gives control over the lives of men. This struggle to control the means of production, this change and process is the driving force of history. The sociological principle, or dialectic, of progress through conflict, is the cause of change. Such is Marx's philosophy.

Marx makes the sweeping assertion in the opening of the *Manifesto* that: "The history of all human society, past and present, has been the history of class struggles. . . . More and more society is splitting into two great hostile camps, into two great and directly contraposed classes: bourgeois and proletariat." [2]

While there have been endless disputes as to the meaning of Marx's abstruse philosophy and "dialectic," the heart of his whole system was the class struggle leading to revolution. Man's business was to make history, which he defines as "the activity of man in pursuit of his ends." Marx says: "Hitherto, philosophers have but variously *interpreted* the world; it is

---

[1] "The modern State authority is nothing more than a committee for the administration of the consolidated affairs of the bourgeois class as a whole." *Manifesto*, p. 28.

[2] The *Manifesto* continues: "Freeman and slave, patrician and plebeian, baron and serf, guild-burgess and journeyman—in a word, oppressor and oppressed—stood in sharp opposition to each other. They carried on perpetual warfare, sometimes masked, sometimes open and acknowledged; a warfare that invariably ended, either in a revolutionary change in the whole structure of society, or else in the common ruin of the contending classes."

now their business to *change* it." He also says: "By acting on the external world and changing it, man changes his own nature." As Professor Hook points out Marx's philosophy is one of social *action;* it is a theory of social revolution. He furnishes "the fighting philosophy of the great mass movement." His method is the clue to his abstruse and seemingly contradictory doctrines. All his works were programs of action. As Engels said at his funeral in Highgate Cemetery: "Before all else Marx was a revolutionist." [1]

In the view of Marx, derived from Hegel's philosophy of the conflict of opposites, the class struggle is the vital factor in producing social change. It is the locomotive of progress. For instance, feudal society in its trade and commerce produced a commercial class, which, as an outcast "third estate," became antagonistic to the ruling class of feudal landowners, and in struggling for its rights led to the destruction of feudalism and the building up of a more advanced capitalist society. Capitalism was a mighty achievement and was itself the result of class struggle. In the same way the now outcast proletariat,[2] or fourth estate, is driven to struggle for its rights as each of the now privileged classes has in turn done before it.

Marx was a fighter and such a man can best be understood by the things he fights against. For four and a half decades he fought against an unjust economic order and its defenders of privilege, against the philosophical idealists who were not realistic, against mechanistic materialists and fatalists who did not leave room for man's freedom under mechanistic deter-

---

[1] "What, then, must we ask, is distinctive of Marx's thought, if it is neither his problems, his purposes, nor his conclusions? The answer suggested here is that what is characteristic of Marx's thought is the *dialectical method* by which he undertook to solve these problems and attain his purposes." As Lenin wrote: "Our theory is not a dogma but a manual of action, said Marx and Engels." Sidney Hook, *Toward the Understanding of Karl Marx,* pp. 9, 70, 71.

[2] In ancient Rome the *proletarius* was the poorest class of the population, whose sole wealth consisted in its offspring, *proles.* Marx uses the word as denoting one whose only means of living is the sale of his labor power. The class war in Rome was carried on not by the slaves but between the free rich and the free poor. "The Roman proletariat lived at the expense of society, whereas modern society lives at the expense of the proletariat."

minism, against romantic and Utopian socialists and religionists who would not effectively organize to bring in a new epoch,
and against selfish individualists and atomists who did not see
the necessity of a class movement.[1]

Competition is the war of all against all, where even the
workers compete with one another. The class struggle in the
thought of Marx was a war to end war. In the Marxian
dialectic, or conflict of opposing forces, the capitalist class
furnishes the positive or conservative thesis, the proletariat
is the negative or destructive antithesis, which must finally
triumph by abolishing itself and its opposite of private property. This leads to the final synthesis "a synthetic unity of
itself and its contrary" in the establishing of a new social
order where the means of production will be owned and operated in common. When the conflict becomes acute between
the material development of production, with all the evils of
the machine age, and the social form of the discontented and
unemployed proletariat the time is ripe for the leap from evolution to revolution.

Marx held that the working of the same inexorable laws of

---

[1] Professor Hook thus enumerates the opposing positions which he attacked: "Against the idealism of Bruno Bauer and his Young Hegelian associates, Marx presents the arguments for materialism. Against the passive
materialism of Feuerbach, Marx defends the principles of activity and reciprocity which were central to Hegel's dialectic. Against the fatalism of both
absolute idealism and 'vulgar' mechanism, Marx proclaims that human beings
make their own history. . . . To the *wahre Sozialisten* who sought to initiate
a movement of social reform on the basis of absolute ethical principles like
'social love' or justice, Marx declares that every realistic social movement
must be a class movement. To simon-pure trade unionists struggling for 'a
fair day's wage for a fair day's work' he insists that every class struggle is
a political struggle. . . . Against the classical school of economics . . . he
urges that economic categories are transitory. Against the historical school
of economics he vindicates the necessity of analysing the structure of political
economy independently of speculative fancies about its origin. As opposed
to the anarchist ideal of complete decentralization, he defends the principle
of authority. To the Lasallean cult of the state, he counters with the idea
of its ultimate disappearance. He was as critical of petty bourgeois opportunism of the right as he was contemptuous of the ultra-left sectarianism of
Most and Bakunin. The critics who made so much of Marx's contradictory
positions never made an attempt to find a point of view from which these
alleged contradictions turned out to be applications of the same principles and
purposes to different historical situations." *Ibid*, p. 66.

dialectic conflict which had overthrown slavery and feudalism would, with scientific certainty, bring about the disintegration of capitalism and the rise of socialism. There were various causes for this, all of which he enumerates in the *Manifesto* in the excerpts which will be found in Appendix 1. These causes of the disintegration of capitalism include:

1. *The Concentration of Wealth and Production.*—Ever larger trusts and corporations will combine with growing centralization in industry, commerce, transportation and banking. Agriculture, however, has not yet followed his course save in Soviet Russia.

2. *The Absorption of the Middle Class.*—The *petit bourgeois* and small shopkeepers in Marx's view will be driven to the wall. A few will rise to the ranks of the capitalists and found trusts and chain stores. More will sink as wage workers, or into the proletariat. "The Industrial revolution acted as a cream separator dividing the middle class milk into the capitalist cream and the proletarian skim milk." [1] As Marx foretold, there has been "the accumulation of wealth at one pole of society" and of poverty at the other. . . . There has been, as he prophesied, a vast concentration of wealth and a growth of a proletariat. He could not have foreseen, however, the creation of a new white-collar middle class, nor the diffusion of ownership in modern corporations coupled with concentration of production and control.

3. *The Growth of Unemployment.*—As Marx prophesied, there has been a growth of a vast "reserve army" of the unemployed to further weaken the position of labor. Even prior to the world depression the percentage of unemployment in Europe was higher than before the war. During that depression the army of the unemployed rose to over thirty millions in Europe and America. Only Soviet Russia was able to eliminate unemployment upon the Marxian plan.

---

[1] See the excellent statement by Professor Paul Douglas in the *World Tomorrow*, March 15, 1933, p. 257.

4. *The Increasing Misery of the Workers.*—Marx says: "In proportion as capital accumulates, the condition of the worker, *be his wages high or low,* necessarily grows worse." The pressure of unemployment forces down wages.[1] Marx holds that increasing misery would be the outcome of *unmodified* capitalism. But we have had *controlled* capitalism, modified by the social control of government, of legislation, of trade unions and of a plan. The condition of the workers has, of course, not grown absolutely worse, for real wages have risen since Marx wrote. But have they risen as rapidly as profits and interest, especially before the depression from 1922 to 1929?

5. *The Increasing Severity of Crises.*—Marx believed that crises would occur because too much capital and surplus value would be invested in overproduction and too little would be paid as wages to furnish purchasing power. Surplus stocks would close plants, increase unemployment, and create depressions. The contradiction between the expanding power of capitalist production and labor's limited consumption would become more intense and growing crises would result.[2] Recurring wars would follow as a result of the present economic order and world imperialism. The World War and world depression seem to have borne witness to the fulfillment of this prediction.

6. *The Rise of a Militant Working Class.*—Marx believed that as the working class increased in numbers and as its condition became worse in recurring depressions, it would become more class conscious and unite for its own protection and the achievement of its destiny. Class

---

[1] *Capital,* I, p. 714.

[2] Engels says: "Crises such as these have been wont to occur every five years." And again: "During the whole century . . . at intervals of from five to seven years a similar crisis has occurred, bringing in its train intolerable wretchedness of the workers." While writing *Capital,* Marx thought such cycles between prosperity and slump embraced periods covering ten or eleven years. The League of Nations economic experts estimate that in recent decades they have occurred on an average of every four and a quarter years. *Manifesto,* Ryazanoff edition, p. 98.

conflict cannot be resolved without changing the whole
structure of society. The state as the agency of the
interests of the dominant class will always cultivate the
propaganda that the state is above all classes and that
all are one, with identical or harmonious interests.
Every legal code and educational system will declare
this. Strikes will be broken by the force of the government which always stands in defence of the *status quo*.
But in the end the workers will learn that only through
class struggle can they attain their rights. And they
will achieve them. Such were the teachings and predictions of Marx regarding the class struggle.

Though Marx does not so minutely subdivide them, under
the dialectic of conflict, history is to pass through the following
epochs: 1. Primitive Communism; 2. Slavery, the antique
economy; 3. Feudal Serfdom; 4. the Capitalist Wage System;
5. Transitional State Capitalism; 6. State Socialism; 7. Pure
Communism. Marx is chiefly concerned with Slavery, Feudalism, Capitalism and Socialism.

Whatever mistakes we may find in the positions of Marx,
they certainly served to remove the inferiority complex of
masses of workers. Some of his prophecies have been fulfilled
in the disintegration of the capitalist system. There is no
contradiction to this trend in the experience of fascist countries
under dictatorship, if fascism be understood as the last phase
of decaying capitalism, or the last struggle of the middle class
in the effort to save itself. Soviet Russia seems to furnish
an example of the working of the Marxian system even in the
first and hardest decade and a half of its existence. There we
witness the progressive elimination of national, racial, cultural,
and even class distinctions insofar as property is concerned,
in what seems to be a growingly classless society.

The words "class war" and "revolution" have an ugly sound
to patriots in any "land of the free." They do not object to
a war of independence to establish their country, a civil war
to preserve it, a World War to make it safe for democracy.
These are the fruits of patriotism. But any revolt of the workers is counted sheer sedition. Such are the traditions of a class,

conditioned to glorify war and abhor revolution. There is nothing more sacred about a nation than the wider humanity of which it is but a part, nor more sacrosanct in a territorial than in a functional community. The propertied class and their white-collar dependents will stand loyal to the nation which gives title to their possessions, while many of the dispossessed will believe that their loyalty is due to their class and to the workers of the world. As long as there are classes of possessors and dispossessed, or what Disraeli called "two nations," the rich and the poor, so long there will be discontent and class conflict. *Class strife is, indeed, a present fact and no honest realism can ignore it.* There is no possible ultimate solution save to abolish these classes by providing equal justice for all, either by evolution or revolution. History reiterates that if the possessing class will not give it, the dispossessed will take it; just as the capitalist class themselves wrested power from their feudal superiors. There was nothing more sacred in their former struggle than in that of the workers today.

Revolutions are almost inevitably destructive. They occur only when evolutionary progress to justice is blocked by the class in possession and power, when the hard crust of the *status quo* restrains the molten lava of discontent until the volcano of revolution bursts into eruption. Nearly always the possessing class is blinded by its own self-interest and class ethics of property "rights," so that it cannot see in time the injustice of the system which seems hallowed by custom and tradition. This class fondly believes that trouble is due to agitators, that if people would only be quiet and not "rock the boat," the present unjust system could be indefinitely perpetuated. They do not see that class conflict is already here and must be faced, and that they themselves, rather than agitators, have inevitably created it.

The Revolution

In classical theory the state had existed to secure the interests of society as a whole. In prevailing practice, however, under the class divisions created by private property, not the

well-being of the masses but of the privileged classes became the chief concern of the governing class. Criminal law was often more severe upon offenses against property than against the person. The amended American Constitution guarantees the Negro freedom and the franchise, and the worker equal rights with the capitalist. But in certain areas the Negro dare not vote and the force of the state in its troops and police is habitually called out to defend the property of the employer rather than the rights of striking workers.

The state is necessarily the embodiment of force and force habitually upholds the *status quo*. "The state is a special organized public power of coercion which exists to enforce the decisions of any group or class that controls the government." But force is also the method of revolution. Those in revolt believe they are driven to use it because it will be employed against them if they do not.

According to the Marxian formula, as the advance guard of the working class, a Communist Party must be organized with centralized power, under iron discipline, with a single mind and will. The sole purpose of this party must be to prepare for and direct the coming revolution which Marx sees as the only solution of the class struggle. No class has ever been known to surrender its special privileges and share them equally with the dispossessed, unless it was forced to do so. With the anticipated growing disintegration of capitalism, chronic unemployment, the failure of the mechanism of credit and the private banks, the breakdown of the machinery of production, distribution or exchange, there will be strategic crises. Organized labor is urged to lead the class-conscious struggle with strikes, riots and mass demonstrations. With the touchstone of the dialectic the party must know when the psychological moment comes to seize all the key positions, political and economic, and the state itself.[1]

---

[1] It was Lenin who almost alone realized when the hour had struck for revolution in St. Petersburg. In the Smolny Institute, where he lived and directed the Soviets of workers, peasants and soldiers, is exhibited the time-table of the crucial day when all the strategic centers of Czarist control were seized. Lenin writes: "The fundamental law of revolution . . . is as follows. . . . Only when the masses do not want the old régime, and when the

Once the state has been seized the workers are bidden to establish a dictatorship of the proletariat under the direction of the vanguard of the Communist Party. The Party then seeks to make the revolution permanent and continuing until all the members of the ruling and possessing classes are deprived of power. "Political force must derive its ethical sanction from some positive social function." Marx considered a dictatorship of the proletariat as better than the present dictatorship of the bourgeoisie, for in a class society economic justice and social equality were impossible. It seemed to Marx that as the present order was established by force, is founded in force and will never yield its monopoly of privilege to any reformist evolutionary procedure, there was no other way than to meet organized force with force, as did the American Colonies in 1776. If living today, he would suggest that any half-hearted hesitation in any necessary use of force would only result in the establishing of a fascist tyranny as in Italy and Germany and as in the case of the French Commune in 1871. He would point out the moral and intellectual renaissance that followed the French Revolution and the creative energy released by the great upheaval in Russia. Indeed, the whole Russian Revolution is almost the complete embodiment of all his principles and programs insofar as they could be applied up to this stage. It was the belief of Marx, as it is of all Communists today, that the costs of a short violent revolution are far less than the appalling death rate from chronic slums, poverty, unemployment, malnutrition and recurring wars. Therefore they believe that their ultimate purpose is not to destroy, but to save the life that our unjust order is already wantonly destroying.

It is interesting to note that Marx thought in 1872 that the United States and England might prove exceptions and that the workers in these countries might win justice without the necessity of a violent revolution. In his speech to the working men at Amsterdam he said: "Some day the workers must con-

---

rulers are unable to govern as of old, then only can the revolution succeed. This truth may be expressed in other words: Revolution is impossible without an all-national crisis, affecting both the exploited and exploiters."

quer political supremacy. . . . Of course, I must not be supposed to imply that the means to this end will be everywhere the same. . . . There are certain countries, such as the United States and England, in which the workers may hope to secure their ends by peaceful means." [1]

The dictatorship of the proletariat was regarded as a necessary evil during the transition from a capitalist to a Communist society. It is not part of Communism but quite inconsistent with it. The appearance of a Communist society would abolish all dictatorship, but the indefinite continuation of the present dictatorship in Russia postpones even the distant approach of real Communism.

The state, which was originally organized as an instrument of class dominance, is supposed in time to disappear under a classless society. After a temporary dictatorship, whose sole object was to build a socialist society as quickly as possible, they would then achieve their ideal of "production according to one's capacities, and distribution according to one's needs." Rigid state socialism is expected to end in Communism. People will have learned right habits and the government will be a mere organ for the administration of production. The political state will then "wither away." [2]

Marxian Parties and Conflicts

The followers of Marx, during and after his lifetime, like those of every other great philosopher or religious leader, divided into various competing schools of thought and action,

---

[1] Speech at Amsterdam, 1872, in the *History of the First International*, quoted by Sidney Hook, *Toward the Understanding of Karl Marx*, p. 291. It is only fair to say that Lenin believed that though it might be possible to avoid revolution in these lands *at that time* it is true no longer, and practically all Communists would agree with him today.

[2] Marx says: "Then there will no longer be any political power, in the strict sense of the term, seeing that political power is the official expression of the conflicts within bourgeois society." Engels says: "In one domain after another, the intervention of a state authority in social relations becomes superfluous, and therefore spontaneously ceases to occur. The government of persons is replaced by the administration of things and by the management of the processes of production. The state is not abolished, it withers away." Marx, *Misere de la Philosophie*, p. 243. Engels, *Anti-Duhring*, p. 103.

each of which claimed to be carrying out the real purpose of the master. Each was able to maintain its own position by quoting certain proof-texts and passages and emphasizing congenial doctrines. Of these there were four principal movements or schools of thought.

1. "Orthodox" Marxists, of whom Karl Kautsky of Germany was the leader, turned Marx's philosophy of social revolution and his program of immediate action into an evolutionary science of respectable social development, which began to compromise with reformist, and then nationalistic, and later even militaristic and imperialistic practices. As the German Social Democratic Party grew powerful, with three million voters and a strong representation in the Reichstag, and later gaining the backing of nearly ten million tradeunionists, with property valued at ninety million marks, they ceased to be a compact revolutionary body and gradually became the party of opposition with prospects of winning control of the state by parliamentary methods. They increasingly emphasized gradual social reform as a successful benevolent organization and respectable political party.

Marxism now became an "objective science" of social development for the understanding of history rather than the making of it. There was a comfortable creed of "inevitability" of "processes at work in the order of things" which accepted the orthodoxy of correct belief in lieu of revolutionary action. In the end the Social Democratic Party became the chief support, with the Catholic Center Party, of the Weimar Constitution and Republic. They accepted the plums of office but they were weakened by compromise and corruption. They entered the World War to the goosestep of Hohenzollern imperialism instead of holding to Marx's moral cause of the oppressed workers. Orthodoxy in social democratic Germany, and later under the Soviet dictatorship, became the nemesis and paralyzing blight upon Marx's free revolutionary dialectic.

2. The German revisionists under Bernstein swung still farther to the right from Marx's philosophy of radical revolution. Bernstein, who was the student of Engels and the teacher of Kautsky, accepted certain ethical and political doctrines of

Kant of a social order that ought to be. Revisionist socialism became a kind of religion and a moral code which must win its way by peaceful persuasion not violence. It blunted the clear-cut class struggle to a movement for reform for a vague and general humanity. Bernstein dropped much of the Marxian phraseology, substituting "a democratic, socialistic party of reform." He criticized the accuracy of Marx's analyses which were not being fulfilled, as in the case of the non-disappearance of the middle class. By dulling the edge of their class consciousness the workers were prepared to enter the World War as national "patriots," thus betraying their international revolutionary class cause. Kautsky admitted that he and Bernstein were Siamese twins in party affairs. Revisionism had reduced Marxism to a liberal philosophy of social reform in direct contradiction to the *Communist Manifesto*.

3. The Syndicalist heresy developed in France as a critical reaction to Marx, accepting some of his doctrines but repudiating others. In France the influence of Blanqui, Proudhon, and the anarchist, Bakunin, were powerful. The trade unions, suspicious of political parliamentarism and the ambitious careers of their former Socialist leaders who had deserted them, lined up solely on the economic front and adopted the general strike as almost their sole weapon. This was an isolated, ineffectual instrument which could terrorize but not construct. Sorel, who later influenced Mussolini, attempted to revise Marxism, ignoring or repudiating its political program but retaining and emphasizing its revolutionary violence. Sorel had a strong anti-intellectualist, anti-cultural, iconoclastic element in his system which repudiated all pacifism and the evolutionary orthodoxy of Kautsky, rejected both state socialism on the right and anarchism on the left, but tried to build a loose movement of revolutionary syndicalism without any political party and without the dialectic continuity of Marx's much more practical program of organization and action. Like the I.W.W. of America, with its slogan of "no party," the movement, naturally, went to pieces, as Marx's writings clearly foretold that it must.

4. It was Lenin in Russia and Rosa Luxemburg in Germany

who challenged and repudiated the three foregoing diversions of Marx and recalled the movement to its original revolutionary purpose. They held that reform and compromise would never bring the socialist state nor would it come automatically by evolutionary progress. Lenin's aim was the realization and promotion of the whole dialectical social process culminating at the right moment in the seizure of the political power of the state. The goal was the conquest of power, the means was the class struggle, reforms were mere byproducts, never ends in themselves, and at times even dangerous as seductive palliatives and opiates.

While Kautsky and "orthodox" Marxism led logically to the founding of the short-lived German Republic, Lenin and revolutionary Communism led to the founding of the U.S.S.R. dictatorship. Lenin was the reformer who recalled the followers of Marx from the by-paths of compromise with the German Social Democratic movement and the Kerensky Russian Republic to the original goal and method of the class struggle.

Lenin advanced in the application of Marx's dialectic to the phase of worldwide imperialism which had developed from the simpler nationalistic capitalism of Marx's own day. Marx was the giant intellect and social philosopher, Lenin the greatest practical revolutionary who ever lived. It has been the part of Stalin to guide the Russian dictatorship as a shrewd politician through the series of five year plans which seek to build socialism and prepare for future Communism. On the whole, although without Trotsky's brilliance, he is the best man in Soviet Russia to guide the continuing revolution in the building of socialism. In spite of its forced and cruel haste, collectivization has given Stalin the third place in Soviet Russian history following Marx and Lenin. He is fearless, ruthless, shrewd, distinterested and genuinely concerned for his cause, as were Marx and Lenin before him.

What Can We Learn From Karl Marx?

In the preceding statement of the teachings of Marx, in the effort to clarify and simplify for the beginner, there has

undoubtedly been an over-simplification of his system, which itself over-simplifies the complexities of life. In our effort to evaluate the system we must not be led astray either by a mere difference in vocabulary or by our own bias. We must recognize the initial prejudice with which most of us approach the system. Many of us belong, or hope to belong, to the economically privileged, or to the comfortable middle class dependent upon them. We know little and therefore care inadequately how the other half of humanity lives, which belongs to the poor, the unemployed, the economically disinherited. We do not realize how largely our whole view of life is economically determined by our social environment and the views of the class to which we belong. We see the slow gains in social conditions, in political liberties, in the economic status of organized labor, and believe that everything will come right of itself if only men will be patient and reasonable. But we must remember that by the renunciation of a great sacrifice Marx had placed himself among that other half of humanity and that he speaks for them. Whether they know anything about his abstruse philosophy or not, his general position increasingly represents the attitude of the dispossessed masses of the world.

Broadly, the economic order is following the path which Marx predicted. And there is always Soviet Russia standing as the spokesman and warning to represent his point of view and challenge the rest of the world. After five thousand years, the heirs of those who built the pyramids beneath the whip, the helots of Greece, the slaves of Rome, the serfs of the Middle Ages and the victims of the industrial revolution, have been made class-conscious and taught that they also are destined for emancipation and even sovereignty. They are proving that they themselves can rule in one considerable section of the world. But it must be remembered that five thousand years of the history of privileged classes has never given them their heritage. And after nineteen centuries the religion which claims to be the most social in its teachings has not even demanded, much less achieved, social justice for them.

Not many philosophers recognize the subjective coloring of

their ideas as does Bertrand Russell when he says: "My outlook on the world is, like other people's, the product partly
of circumstance and partly of temperament." Hegel was able
to deduce, from his seemingly objective process of thought,
the German people, Protestantism and the Prussian state as
the highest manifestations of the Idea in history. Thus the
state is to him "the march of God on earth." Marx likewise,
unconscious of wishful thinking, was able to find a system
that contained all of his desires and a universe that was cooperating with him. He imagined that he had discovered by
strictly scientific processes the laws which made the ultimate
victory of the proletariat practically demonstrable. There was
a holdover of animism, or theology, or quasi-religious faith
in his system which he did not recognize. Nevertheless it
gave an unconquerable faith to the workers like that of the
warriors of Mohammed, which promised them victory or
paradise. Engels, under the spell of Hegel's spiritual idealism,
at the age of twenty-two had written: "That everlasting struggle and movement of peoples and heroes, above which in the
eternal world soars the Idea, only to swoop down into the
thick of the fight and become the actual, self-conscious soul—
there you have the source of every salvation and redemption,
there the Kingdom in which everyone of us ought to struggle."
He and Marx later repudiated the vocabulary of this philosophy and theology; but, however illogically, as a religious faith
in the ultimate triumph of their cause of proletarian justice it
remained with them. Theirs was a materialism touched with
idealism and fired by it. Their prophetic vision was a secu-
larized version of the oft-repeated apocalyptic vision of a
redeemed society for the disinherited classes. It was not
wholly a scientific demonstration but partly an unrecognized
religious hope. It was drawn from Hegel, and much of
Hegel's thought was derived unconsciously from religion. As
a result there is a great deal of religion and idealism in Russia
today not recognized under a complete change of vocabulary
and of ideas.

From the point of view, let us say, of one of the Friends
or Quakers as an attendant of the Merttens' Lectures, or from

the standpoint of a modern liberal, how may we fairly evaluate the teachings of Marx?

A complete, a final, a perfect system of philosophy has never been the achievement of mortal man. Yet there have been truths and values as well as serious limitations in all the really great systems. If we take the philosophy of Plato, of Aristotle, of Kant, of Hegel, or of Marx, each is like the bed of Procrustes. We have to amputate the extremities of the complex facts of the body of human experience to make it fit into any one of these systems, certainly into that of Marx.

Let us begin with Marx's dialectic process and his economic interpretation of history. To Hegel the dialectic meant the process through which reason, by the reconcilement of opposites, advances in self-development to the perfection of absolute Spirit. To Marx the dialectic furnished chiefly the interpretation of the conflict of opposing classes in the social order which led to their emancipation.[1] To both it meant progress through conflict. To Hegel it was primarily a philosophic concept, to Marx a social dynamic. To Hegel, as to Plato, it meant the sublime contemplation of an other-worldly, spiritual Idea. Marx, with his feet on the earth, was passionately concerned with the material conditions which could emancipate the toiling helots of history. Hegel was lost in metaphysical communion with the Absolute. Marx was consumed in the liberation of humanity. Hegel attempted to write a *philosophy* of history, Marx essayed to change it. It would have been much simpler and more in harmony with his own materialism, as opposed to Hegel's abstract idealism, if Marx and his followers could have taken a simple functional view of intelligence, regarding thought as primarily purposive, as an instrument of action, instead of being bound by a cumbersome dialectic in thought.

There was some real value but also a heavy incubus in Marx's Hegelian presuppositions and abstract vocabulary which few of his followers really understood. They could never prove that this dialectic conflict of opposites was a law

---

[1] Engels defines the dialectic as "nothing more than the science of the universal laws of motion and evolution in nature, human society, and thought."

of nature or of thought. They could never demonstrate that the planets in their courses were formed or sustained by this law, nor that their own process of thought was by a conflict of opposites. Apart from the class conflict they could neither prove this dialectic nor anything by it.

But it was another matter when they turned from this mysterious and abstract logic to purposive thought and action in the reconstruction of the social and economic order. Here it seemed to explain, to create, to justify and to fulfil the class struggle for liberation. Their cumbersome metaphysic and psychology did not greatly interfere with their flexible, revolutionary social realism. They were primarily not metaphysical philosophers but prophets of action. And here their system seemed actually to work. It apparently succeeded like success. It *seemed* to give them a mysterious philosopher's stone which unlocked the secrets of nature, the meaning of history and the hidden depths of human thought. It combined the attraction of the mystic and the magic with the hard realism of seemingly demonstrable science. It appeared to provide, ready made, a science, a philosophy, and almost a religion to the disinherited class.

Even a modern Friend need find nothing necessarily incompatible with his own view in the dialectic interpretation of history. The conception of opposites clashing, interpenetrating and mutually fructifying one another has had a long and valued history. Heraclitus had proposed this principle of interpenetration some five hundred years B.C. Plato, a century later in his Phaedo, had given it careful analysis and criticism. Professor Hocking has emphasized the "principle of alternation" in our own day, as have countless others.

Neither need our Friend be unduly alarmed at the harsh sound of "dialectic materialism" if he remembers Marx's fight for freedom against the mechanism, determinism and fatalism of much of the self-sufficient science of his day.[1] Certain aspects of the economic interpretation of history may

---

[1] Professor Hook says: "Materialism in this regard means, then, nothing but a denial of *original* creation."

be as readily assimilated today as was the similar thought of Aristotle by the early church and during the Renaissance. If we remember that Marx and Engels did not deny that there were other contributory elements, we ourselves cannot fail to admit that a major factor, and many of us would say that the *principal* determinant of social change, is the economic environment, especially the changes in the modes of production of a given age. We cannot deny that the largely monopolistic ownership of the means of production by the property owning class on the one hand, and the economic dependence of the vast army of wage workers and the unemployed on the other, not only affect but mold and determine the institutions, the laws, the economic and political organization of society, the ideas of men and the history of our time.

We would not oppose but supplement this economic view by an emphasis upon the element of the *moral* determination of history. It is when the economic forces represent moral realities that they become overwhelming. The economic plight of the workers makes an ethical demand upon the conscience. As Professor Flint says: "The welfare of society is dependent upon a practical recognition of moral principles—the laws of morality are conditions of the progress, and even of the existence of society." A world which starves in the midst of plenty, which enriches a few and pauperizes many in spite of over-production, which divides and destroys mankind by greed and strife and war, needs the challenge both of realistic economics and of idealistic morals. To Marx and the prophets the two are one. If we have been deaf to the message of "Moses and the prophets" it is not strange that we resent the denunciation of Marx. But if we do, the very stones of hard reality cry out against us.

We must, however, supplement the much-needed Marxian social and collective emphasis with a higher view of the sacredness of the person and the rights of the individual. We should make room for the creative principle in history of the individual person. This we have learned from other sources. Extreme individualism, however, had over-reached itself and needed the corrective of some such social emphasis as that of Marx.

Individualism and collectivism are two poles in a true dialectic which should lead to the destruction only of the unhealthy extremes of each in isolation, and to the synthesis of both in a new society.   The chaos of *laissez faire* individualism and the tyranny of the corporative fascist state, or dictator, must both give way to a planned and cooperative society.   Soviet Russia represents one dialectic pole, one moment in the great evolutionary process of history toward a new social order in which we all believe.

Marx's ideas of value and of surplus value need not present great difficulties unless we are asked to accept them as final or infallible economic theories.   If we were more sure of a satisfactory alternative theory of value of our own we should be more ready to criticize the seemingly manifest inadequacies of Marx's almost classical economics which are no longer in vogue and which are the most vulnerable part of his system. His *Capital* is in part a cumbersome combination of ponderous German philosophy and out-of-date classical economics, neither of which is wholly defensible.   He deals with the supply of labor and capital but neglects the important element of demand. As the Master of Balliol says: "A theory of value which says practically nothing about demand is a theory of value which says practically nothing about valuing."

There is, however, very obvious need of the corrective of the unsound atomistic individualism of our capitalist order by a more close knit social system.   Our boasted "rugged individualism" proved to be a rope of sand when it came to lifting our country or the world out of the depths of the economic depression, without economic planning and social control.   The World War and the depression have proved the final failure and inadequacy of *laissez faire* individualism.   Any return to it, or to a fascist financial dictatorship, would only mark the beginning of the end and hasten the fulfilment of Marx's prophecy.

The demand of Marx for justice had been made by the prophets for centuries.   Because it was still unheeded he had to thunder forth the message anew.   He did more, however, than repeat a verbal demand.   He almost "turned the world

upside down." According to the record of the ancient prophets their message went often unheeded by a stiff-necked people. Plato's idealistic dream hardly touched the earth, though it fructified in later thought. Sir Thomas More's Utopia was never established nor taken very seriously. But Marx has thrown the whole world upon the defensive. He embodied his philosophy in organization during his lifetime and within a generation it was incorporated in nearly one-sixth of the planet. It is now disturbing the other five-sixths, whether we approve of his methods or not. Can it be denied that from the time of Socrates and Plato, and of Amos and Isaiah, no man ever made such an *effective* demand for economic change or so compelled the world to take him seriously? Though not more terrible than Amos, it is in the tones of the prophet that he closes the *Manifesto* as he thunders: "Let the ruling classes tremble at a Communist revolution. The proletarians have nothing to lose but their chains. They have a world to win. Working men of all countries, unite!"

To understand Marx himself will be much more efficacious than to consider secondhand descriptions of him. His own words in the *Manifesto* are incorporated in the first Appendix of this volume and give the clearest idea of his teaching.

To deny that labor deserves a larger part and a just part of the vast surplus it has created seems to take a position equal in moral blindness and hypocrisy to the Scribes and Pharisees of another day. The privileged world may hate Marx for his exposure, but the burden of proof rests upon us to offer some effective alternative that is non-violent. We can stone a prophet but we cannot destroy an idea. We cannot crucify it. Marx demands justice for the workers of the world—no less—from the surplus of value and "over-production" which our corrupt, decaying economic order has produced but has not distributed.

When it comes to the class struggle our Quaker friend will naturally have more hesitation than with Marx's interpretation of history or his economic theory. But even here it must be remembered that Christianity, although non-violent, was established by a founder who was executed as a daring revolutionary. He was the first revolutionary of the modern era under

which we still date our letters. The founders of this religion when it was in the nascent state, as Communism has still the good fortune to be, were opposed as having "turned the world upside down."   This revolutionary body, persecuted, outcast and abhorred, existed as a communal society.[1]

It is true that in ancient history and up to the present there have been frequent periods of class struggles from the time of Moses, Lycurgus and Solon.   It is also true that in all such periods the majority of the respectable and privileged states-men, writers, philosophers and poets have been on the side of the old and decaying order of privilege.   But it is a sweeping exaggeration to say that "all human history has been the history of class struggles."   It can only appear so to one who sees red and looks for nothing else in the record.   Marx follows Hegel in the belief that there are historic periods of slow evolution which culminate in a leap of revolution to a new order or a higher synthesis.[2]

Revolutions can never be created merely by a few agitators but are brought about by the suppression of social wants by outworn institutions.   It must also be admitted that liberalism, after a long innings, has not recreated society nor witnessed the fulfilment of its optimistic dream by happy and harmonious evolution.   It is today losing many of its followers, who are going over, some to the ranks of reaction and some to radical-ism.   This tends even further to sharpen the increasing conflict. Not only the early church but renewed and authentic Christian-

---

[1] "Not one of them considered anything his personal property, they shared all they had with one another.   There was not a needy person among them, for those who owned land or houses would sell them. . . . It was then dis-tributed according to each individual's need." Acts IV : 32. Moffatt's trans-lation.

[2] In Engle's preface to the German edition of the *Manifesto* of 1883 he states Marx's fundamental proposition which forms the nucleus of the *Mani-festo* as follows : "In every historical epoch, the prevailing mode of economic production and exchange . . . form the basis on which is built up the political and intellectual history of that epoch; consequently the whole history of man-kind has been a history of class struggles. . . . Now-a-days a stage has been reached where the exploited and oppressed class, the proletariat, cannot attain its emancipation from the sway of the exploiting and ruling class without at the same time, and once for all, emancipating society at large from all ex-ploitation, oppression, class distinctions and class struggles."

ity has frequently generated revolutionary movements. Its own founder warned his true followers that they would be persecuted even to death and pronounced his woes upon the lukewarm and compromising of whom the world would speak well.

A genuine Quaker or pacifist as a "maker of peace" may consistently challenge Marx's program of violence. But the patrioteer or the religionist who is ready to rush into war and to compel all others to do so, whatever their convictions, cannot fairly object to Marx's similar use of force. The last World War left, of combatants and non-combatants, 26,000,000 dead. The Marxist October Revolution did not sacrifice 2,600 in the actual fighting of a revolution which was almost bloodless, until during the counter revolution there was an attempt to kill Lenin and to restore the Czarist order. Wherein was a war holy which slew in its Moloch sacrifice twenty-six millions, and a revolution for social justice and a new social order of a classless society abhorrent which sacrificed less than twenty-six hundred lives? It is not the Quaker or the pacifist who most holds up his hands in horror at the Marxian class struggle and revolution but the war makers and followers of capitalism, nationalism, imperialism and militarism.

We need not pause long upon the apocalyptic element either in Communism or Christianity. One looks forward when the state, no longer needed, will "wither away" and all will live happily ever afterward. There will then be left no criminals, no classes, no selfish individuals nor groups. No faction will desire to rule or impose its will upon the rest; no thirst for power nor greed for private gain or wealth will remain.

These happy atheist fundamentalists, loyal to their Party line, having preached and practiced hatred till their last enemy is exterminated or "liquidated," will now dwell in love, though they of course repudiate the vocabulary of such sentimental idealism. Having prepared their people by the most inexorable tyranny that will not allow "the luxury of any sectionalism" or the slightest deviation to the right or the left from the orthodox line determined by the group in power, the dictators will now unanimously and eagerly surrender all power. And this beatific eschatology is supposed to be demonstrated by the inexora-

ble logic of their mysterious dialectic and to require no faith for its firm acceptance!

The fundamentalist religionist also looks forward to a millenial reign in Jerusalem. This also is to be a reign of love after blood has flowed in the streets up to the bridles of the horses.[1]

But it is unkind to point out the inconsistencies of either of these apocalyptic pictures. The fundamentalists of both systems do not always see that both stand upon the same basis of undemonstrable religious faith and hope, and rest upon the authority of the original writers. The fabled visitant from Mars, uninitiated but impartial, who has already had so many duties to perform upon our troubled planet, might have some difficulty in believing that comradely cooperation would be the logical fruit of destruction, or that the complete withering away of power would be the culmination of its limitless exercise. He might also not appreciate the "love" of a system which flows in blood up to the bridles of the horses. It might seem to the Martian that the latter system was even more blood-thirsty than a painless process of withering away, where all are to do good spontaneously by moral suasion alone, from the heart of their changed natures. But then what could one expect of a mere Martian, who was uninitiated and had not the requisite faith to become an unquestioning fundamentalist in either system? In the meantime our liberal Quaker friend, who was never an orthodox fundamentalist, with his inner light of reason and conscience will have to interpret human experience as best he can, and critically discriminate between what seems to him the truth and error of the Marxian system.

If we take the system of Marx as a whole we can neither accept it all nor reject it all uncritically. We have already pointed out some of the defects of the system. Also on the negative side are the vast omissions of this hard and fast "complete" philosophy of life. Many of us feel toward materialistic Marxism what Wordsworth, as one of the romantic poets,

---

[1] Revelation XIV:20.

felt in the early struggle of the nineteenth century: "What moved him was moral repulsion. He felt that *something had been left out,* and that what had been left out comprised everything that was most important. . . . Wordsworth alleges against science its absorption in abstractions. His consistent theme is that the important facts of nature elude the scientific method. Berkeley, Wordsworth, Shelley, are representative of the intuitive refusal seriously to accept the abstract materialism of science. . . . The romantic reaction was a protest on behalf of value."[1]

This is just what many of us feel today as to Marxism, *something has been left out.* Religionists, humanists, liberals of various schools of thought will not be appealed to by the drab monotony of the materialistic mass life of Russia. Even after long struggle when they may have gained material abundance they will become more than ever aware that they cannot live by bread alone.

Behind our experience of things and ideas, behind or within the ordered universe, what is the nature of ultimate reality? It may be conceived as mechanical, as organic or as superorganic. Mechanically conceived, the universe may be considered as a heartless machine, and man an automaton of fate, all his actions like the cogs of a machine bound by a rigid determinism. A man may then use his fellows as instruments for making money in a heartless and sordid materialism. No man more than Marx repudiated such mechanistic determinism or more demanded freedom from slavery to things and machines.

Or, second, reality may be conceived, with Hegel and Marx, as an organic process. Hegel conceives it idealistically as the self-realization of the Idea in history. Marx, in his dialectical materialism, takes up the mechanical relationships into his wider organic interpretation. But there is a third form of relationship that is superorganic, of which friendship would be a type. Such personal relationships are not merely mechanical, or organic, they are not in the dialectic process of becoming something else. So long as life lasts they abide.

---

[1] A. N. Whitehead, *Science and the Modern World,* Chapter V.

Such social life is not of the nature of the mechanics of the machine, nor of a biological organism. It moves on a higher plane of reality and experience. Personal reality is super-organic.

Now the ultimate reality of the universe may be conceived as a determined machine, or a mere organic process, or in terms that are superorganic and personal. When Herbert Spencer says that we are everywhere in the presence of an infinite and eternal energy from which all things proceed, we may ask whether that energy is like matter or like mind, is it like the lowest or the highest that are known? Is it merely mechanical, and the universe a heartless machine? Is it organic, and the universe a vast cosmic process? Or is there intelligence and purpose at the heart of it?

If the latter, man's will to progress will express itself in the field of ideas as the demand for freedom. In the field of action it will express itself with demand for justice in human rela-tionships. He will refuse to separate theory and practice, faith and works. He will not merely seek adaptation to environment but to adapt nature to the purposes of developing man, building as a titan. He will see that the economic interpretation of history applies only within limits. He recognizes the mechan-ical level in the physical world, the organic level in the bio-logical sphere, but he lives also on the higher spiritual and personal level of the superorganic, in a world of values of the true, and the good, and the beautiful. He is fundamentally a realist with his feet on the earth. But he holds also to the ideal which he strives to realize, by a legitimate faith—though as undemonstrable as that on the two lower planes of the me-chanical and organic—in Reality as superorganic. He may believe that the stars in their courses are fighting, not for him or his little credo, but for the ultimate realization of a larger and ever-progressive good, which shall embrace the good life for all. His faith in the future is as sure—and as irrational—as that of Marx, but it is larger. While none of the three can prove his position, and while abstract demonstration is as im-possible as it is fruitless, at least he need not be ashamed of his larger faith and hope, nor does he feel that love as an ideal,

however debased or betrayed in the past, need abandon the field to destructive hate.

Professor Macmurray suggests that the revolution did not come as Marx expected in an advanced industrial country but in semi-feudal Russia. It seems to work under feudal conditions and appeals more to the Far East than to industrial Europe. Marx was not infallible in his thought. The thesis of Communism produced its own negation in the antithesis of Fascism. Both are crass economic systems of the mechanism of state. The interpenetration of opposites may lead to the dialectical development of free and genuine socialism, in a synthesis of a really classless society, without the class tyranny of either Russian Communism or bourgeois capitalism. Communism which maintains a class dictatorship involving servitude and denying the spiritual and the superorganic cannot be the final term or synthesis of life.

Marxism on the one hand and Christianity and all idealism on the other differ most sharply in their basic outlook as to the structure of reality. To the Marxist the material world forms almost the whole of reality. A vast range of values in the spiritual and intellectual life are ignored or denied.[1] Communism may be complete as a social system but not as a satisfying philosophy.

We can make use of some of the unique values of the Marxian system, to implement our idealisms by Marx's rugged realism in the insistent demand for social justice and a new social order. From whatever source it may be derived that demand imperatively needs to be made today. And, broadly

---

[1] As we have seen, their psychology is defective. Lenin fanatically accepts every word of Engels that sensation is "a copy, photograph and reflection of a reality existing independently of it." It is but the "mirror-reflections of things." Thought is derivative and has no adequate creative power; ideas have no significant history. Yet, as Professor Hook points out, "Their own ideas have had a history in the last seventy-five years much more significant than any changes in the mode of production that have taken place." The word "dialectical" is a magic symbol rather than a clearly defined concept, and cause, law, history and many other terms are not critically defined and analyzed. Their insistence upon the Hegelian triad leads to "a slavish fidelity to words."

speaking, it is not being effectively made at present by idealists or religionists. The washed-out, pale tincture of sentimental idealism and mere exhortations to love and brotherhood have proved more of a subjective salve to the conscience, an excuse, or alibi, or substitute for action, than a stern demand for action here and now.

A very few in England and in Russia count themselves "Christian Communists." It will, however, be a thankless and lonely position. The conventional majority of the religious community will shun them as dangerous radicals, while most orthodox Marxists will despise and ridicule them.

Both the idealism of religion and the realism of the Communists have much in common at their best. The individual Communist is absorbed in the social purpose for which he lives in daily sacrifice. The present flaming zeal and strenuous service of the Communists of Russia is probably greater than in any religious body in the world today, and it comes nearer to the common life and is more concerned with actual human needs and conditions.

Marx wrote to Ruge in 1843 : "The struggle against religion is therefore indirectly the struggle against the world whose spiritual aroma religion is. . . . The abolition of religion as the *illusory* happiness of the people is the demand for its *real* happiness. The demand to surrender illusions about its conditions is a *demand to surrender the conditions which need illusions.*"

In just so far as religion depends upon illusions and unrealities and identifies itself with the "rights" and special privileges of the few, rather than with the wrongs of the many, it will write its own doom. If it does not press the "demand to surrender the conditions which need illusions" it will be left to the forces of anti-religion to do so. The time was when Christianity fought against the world. Is it now to become, along with big business, its chief defender? Czarism and the Russian Church furnished only one among many illustrations of the depths to which organized religion can sink when it loses at once its spiritual source and its social passion.

The followers of an executed revolutionary who was cruci-
fied should not fail to note this rude reminder of a sacrificial
social movement which finally became anti-religious only when
religion had become anti-social. We need to learn here, not
from Marx but one greater than he, that originally this faith
was not an opiate, but was a revolutionary message which
inevitably demanded social justice, as did Communism. Both
have in common the call to build a new social order at the cost
of revolutionary sacrifice. The one is non-violent, the other
was driven to violence because so many were impotent and
unfaithful to their trust. Both have a great ideal. The task
is almost too great for all combined. Neither the Communist
sixth nor the capitalist five-sixths of the world have as yet
attained anything to boast of in actual accomplishment. Russia
is still too poor and the West too disgracefully rich in unshared
wealth and undistributed overproduction. In the meantime,
where organized institutional religion has been unfaithful to
its trust, it will have much to learn from this section of humanity that has once again found a unified and consistent
philosophy of life.

With Professor Macmurray many believe that in the dialectic
process Communism, in its present form of a dictatorship of
a materialistic economic state as a challenging thesis, provokes
its antithesis of Fascism, also under the form of the dictatorship of an economic state. Certainly both Mussolini and Hitler
have tried to justify the tyranny of their dictatorships as a
deliverance from what they declare to be the boundless evil
of Communism. If Communism and Fascism be considered
as two opposing terms in the dialectic process of history, neither
dictatorship could be considered as the final stage, but both
would require a higher synthesis, presumably of some form
of socialism, which would reconcile this conflict of opposites.
This synthesis would have to include liberty and justice, the
welfare of the one and of the many, the initiative of a healthy
individualism with the social control of collectivism. It would
have to eliminate the evils of the tyranny both of the Soviet
and the Fascist dictatorships.

Marx, despite his own critical realism, seems to cast an

hypnotic spell over many of his followers of practical infallibility. We must never lose our own critical faculty in dealing
with Marx, nor be blind to the glaring errors and omissions
of his system.

There was an evident flaw in his interpretation of the dialectic
which would have required the revolution to take place first
in a highly industrialized country like Germany, not in a backward, semi-feudal land such as Czarist Russia. World revolution was supposed to follow the Russian revolution, but after
more than sixteen years there is less sign of it than ever.
Even today Communism is not immediately threatening the
advanced industrial countries such as Great Britain, America
and France, nor Fascist Italy, nor Germany, but the semi-feudal,
industrially backward countries of the Orient, especially China.

But if we deal with Marx critically it must also be with equal
fairness. Many professors of economics or sociology in America and Britain point out the flaws in Marx's theories of value
and of surplus value, and his predictions which have not come
true, such as the disappearance of the middle class, and then
sweep Marx aside as if they had disproved his whole system.
The proceeding is as easy as it is unfair. Marx's theory of
value was not original but based upon the classical economists,
Adam Smith and Ricardo, who are treated with respect. Even
if Marx was wholly in error on these disputed points they do
not really touch the heart of his system.

Speaking for myself, I find Marx a challenge and a stimulus.
I can accept his realism and the position that thought and
action, theory and practice, must be one. Theory cannot be
verified in the armchair of the philosopher; it can only be
validated in human history. I can accept the dialectic as the
best interpretation of organic processes in the universe. As
to the economic interpretation of history, I believe that the
chief factor which conditions human life in the institutions,
organization and ideas of each age are the material conditions
of life, especially the method of production and the technological changes which accentuate the struggle to possess these
all-important means of life, whether by private owners or the
workers themselves.

In the matter of surplus value, while I am not much concerned with either the classical or modern theories of value, I agree with Marx that the private owners always receive too much and labor habitually too little of this surplus value, and that to just that extent the latter are being defrauded. I do not believe that the system which has habitually and inevitably done this is fit to survive or that it can or will survive.

I regard the classes automatically created by the private possession of the means of production as an undeniable fact and the class conflict as occasioned by it as equally undeniable. Whether class conflict will develop into the mass destruction of class war will depend upon the sagacity of the possessing class and their political representatives. I must strive, as well as the Marxian, for a classless society in a new social order.

At two fundamental points I must challenge Marx and part company with him: 1. I do not believe that violent revolution is a dogmatic necessity, nor an historical certainty as the result of the dialectic process. I sympathize with the workers in their age-long struggle and join with them in it, but as a pacifist I will take no part either in a capitalistic world war nor in a violent revolution or civil war. We may weigh the probabilities or improbabilities of drifting into either one or the other, but I will take no destructive part in either. The basic motivation of my philosophy of life is not hatred but love, however much that word, as every other in the language, may be debased; and my method is not destruction but creative construction.

2. As to the nature of Reality, I do not believe it to be mechanistic, nor organic, but superorganic. When I see not a chaotic multiverse but an ordered universe, when I see personality, intelligence and purpose in the solid fact of the universe as it is, I find it easier to believe that there is intelligence and purpose in the cause as well as in the effect, than I do to believe in a universe of chance or a mechanistic universe of mere matter and force. Even if the universe were "self existent," existence is rooted in intelligence and purpose.

Of the five achievements of humanity mentioned in the last chapter—culture, law and order, moral and spiritual insight, scientific achievement and social justice—for me the spiritual

is central, pivotal, creative. I cannot accept the hard materialism of Marx nor its harsh, inhuman results, as in the hatred
and destruction of the class war, or the drear and drab stand-
ardized existence to which life is leveled down under the present
Soviet dictatorship.

Marx is for me personally and in human history like a powerful reagent in the chemical laboratory. He is like the necessary
charge of dynamite in the blasting of an oil well to release its
flow. His burning passion for social justice kindles a like
indignation in me. He implements for me in the practical program for the building of a new social order the purer and
clearer motivation which I get from a greater than Marx. But
I am forced to admit that this element of justice, implicit or
explicit in our broader and more humane program of religion,
humanism, or liberalism, was never taken seriously by any adequate number, nor made effective in history until Marx blasted
the encrusted strata of custom and tradition of our social order
and set free the deeper original flow in our lives.

I cannot accept the shattered and cynical credos of the West
mentioned at the beginning of this chapter and which are largely
the almost inevitable result of our unjust economic order.
Neither can I accept and swallow whole the over-simplified
materialistic philosophy of Marx. I believe, however, that there
is value, and a tremendous dynamic in a unified philosophy of
life and that Soviet Russia is experiencing the dynamic of such
a unified philosophy, but also paying the price of its materialistic
over-simplification. I believe that individually we can have, and
that socially we must win again, a unified philosophy which is
all but impossible under our present unjust and chaotic order.

CHAPTER X

Religion is a problem in Russia and in the modern world today. As we have already seen, the Constitution of the R.S.-F.S.R., or Russia proper, guarantees to all freedom of conscience and of worship.[1] It is the aim of the Communist Party and of the Soviet Government to keep at least the letter of this law, to permit the remaining religious edifices to be open upon their day of worship, but by a materialistic system of secular education, by the activities of their voluntary atheistic missionary society, the *Union of Militant Godless,* and by the cooperation of other agencies such as the aggressively organized youth movement, to root out the last vestiges of religion from the human heart, especially from the minds of youth. If the elders among the stubborn peasantry still cling to this "superstition" they are to be left to die off if they cannot be converted by their "enlightened" godless youth.

To understand the Soviets' honest dread and hatred of religion as a soporific "opiate" as Marx called it, or a positive "poison" of reactionary, anti-social superstition as Lenin and Stalin considered it, we have to recall the history of religion as they knew it in Russia. From the establishment of Christianity by the official conversion of Vladimir of Kiev in 988 A.D. and from the time when Peter the Great and all succeeding Czars had forcibly made themselves the autocratic heads

---

[1] Article 5 formerly read: "In order to provide the workers actual freedom of conscience the church is separated from the state and the school from the church, while freedom for religious and anti-religious propaganda is recognized for all citizens." This has been significantly revised to read: "Freedom for religious confession (or worship) and anti-religious propaganda is recognized for all citizens." The believer may only worship, while the whole establishment of government, education and the full tide of propaganda and activity of the Union of Militant Godless is enlisted to uproot religion.

both of church and state, Russia had developed a religious type of aesthetic mysticism.   Along with much genuine piety of peasants and the lower clergy, the character of the religious life of Czarist Russia was pietistic, individualistic, other worldly and prevailingly reactionary and anti-social.   It lacked both moral fiber and social vision.   It stood for charity not justice, reaction rather than reform.   The life of many of the monasteries and among the higher clergy was a scandal and the miracle-working mummies of the "incorruptible" bodies of the saints were a symbol of the official degradation of the church.

At the head of the whole system was a feeble minded moron, the Czar; over him was a neurotic, hysterical Czarina; and in his temporary influence over them both a human beast, Rasputin, called the "holy devil," who spent his nights in drunken orgies and his days in political plotting among officials of the state, church and army.

Far more serious and deadly than the scandals and immoralities of such an individual beast was the identification of the church, not with the needs and sufferings of the masses in their neglected ignorance and poverty, but with the worst evils of the time in superstition and anti-social reaction.   It is hardly to be wondered at that the revolutionary leaders concluded that religion was not a mere harmless superstition but a positive evil, far more deadly than drink or prostitution.

I must confess that this description does not do full justice to the elements of value in religion in Russia.   The practical Anglo-Saxon almost inevitably underestimates the significance of Greek Orthodox religion.   In fairness it must be said that there was a large amount of active social, educational and spiritual work done by the church in Czarist Russia all of which is forbidden by the Soviet government, which now permits to the church only the formal services of worship.   Some true religion was found among all classes, including even the aristocracy.   Rasputin, though a degenerate and renegade Christian, a scoundrel such as has appeared in many countries, was not typical of the system.   But whatever can be said of the

personal piety and saintliness of many individuals in the system, religion in Russia was on the whole a powerful reactionary and anti-social force.[1] In using the word "reformation" in connection with the Russian church I do not mean to imply that a cleansing, or renewal, or revival of religion in the Soviet Union will ever take the form of the Protestant Reformation.

We cannot lay the whole blame of the Communists' attitude toward religion upon the faults of the Greek Church, as we are sometimes tempted to do. That attitude was early determined by Marx and Engels who, so far as is known, never saw a Greek priest and had no direct knowledge of the activities of the church in Russia. Communists deny the existence of religion in a "normal" or Communist state. Lunacharsky said: "It is a weed to be pulled out by the roots." The Communists do not fundamentally distinguish between good and bad religion, true or false. They frankly aim to destroy *all* religion in time by their process of education and propaganda.

One reason why Russian Communists so persecute religion is that their own system is an intolerant and persecuting kind of rival religion. Their faith is a social dynamic in a country that had never known real religious freedom. From the time of Peter the Great in 1729 until 1905 it was a punishable crime for an Orthodox Church member to leave the church. The Old Believers and other sects were persecuted.

A Communist pamphlet issued in Moscow in 1932 gives a further answer to the cause of the persecution of religion in Soviet Russia in brief as follows:

1. "Religion hinders the cultural development of the workers, for all religion is the opposite of science.
2. It harms our economic life.
3. It supports bourgeois traditions and sanctifies property-owning egoism.

---

[1] For an appreciation of the elements of value see G. Fedotoff's *The Russian Church Since the Revolution*. The system in Czarist Russia was a continuation of the monistic philosophy in which church and state were a unit. The Czar was the head of the system in which state and religious functions were intertwined or identical. Rasputin was not a monk, nor was he ordained to any rank in the church.

4. It diverts from the construction of socialism, teaching that the better life is beyond the grave.
5. It is used by kulaks and our class enemies as a cloak, or weapon against us.
6. The clergy of all countries are helping the capitalists in their struggle against the workers."

The government organ, *Izvestia,* tells the world that: "The Soviet Government has never persecuted religion and religious organizations. On the contrary it has frequently been confirmed by churchmen themselves: 'Only in the U.S.S.R. does religion have actual and complete liberty.'" [1]   Four days after making this claim religious propaganda was forbidden. The magazine, *Bezbojnik,* or the *Godless,* concludes: "Now any activity of propaganda on the part of religious or church people . . . falls under the action of criminal and civil laws. . . . Religious propaganda is not permitted." It is silenced before the blast and broadside of powerful atheistic propaganda. It is now a criminal offense.

Unfortunately the statement of *Izvestia* that religion has complete liberty in Russia is not in accordance with the facts published in the historical review in *Fifteen Years of Godlessness in the U.S.S.R.* [2]

The first days of the October Revolution, from November 7, 1917, did not affect the church, but in January, 1918, came the decree of separation of church and state and church and school. Of the three active factors in the struggle between atheism and religion, the Party, the Soviet Government and the masses, the third was proverbially religious. It became the task of the first two to root out religion from the masses.

In 1918 began a campaign to close shrines, chapels in schools, private churches, etc., and some 2,000 of such were soon reported closed. The year 1919 saw the confiscation of the property of the monasteries and the closing of all church and theological schools. The year 1920, during the civil war, witnessed the murder or death of a number of bishops and priests.

---

[1] *Izvestia,* May 22, 1929.
[2] State Anti-Religious Publishing House, Moscow, 1932.

In 1922 the government decree directed the removal of church treasures and valuables and the first issues of *The Godless* magazine appeared. Protests against religious persecution were made by the Pope, the Archbishops of Canterbury and York and the Free Churches of Great Britain.[1]

In 1925 the first Congress of the Union of the Godless was held. During that year the Metropolitan Peter was arrested and exiled. He is still in Siberia. The next year his successor, the present Metropolitan, was arrested and released. In 1929 the new law restricted religious activities and altered the Constitution, prohibiting all religious activities save that of worship and clearing the field for effective anti-religious propaganda. The Children's Anti-religious Movement and the first Godless Shock Brigades in industry were organized.

In 1930, following arrests, trials, exile and some executions of clergy and laymen by local authorities, and the excesses which accompanied the forced collectivization of agriculture, a Day of Prayer for Russia was called by the Archbishop of Canterbury. Several days later a Party decree prohibited the further use of administrative government measures against religion. After 1930 the Party turned away from blasphemy, open persecution, and the coarse methods of a frontal attack upon religion to education, economic compulsion and anti-religious propaganda to overcome religion.

---

[1] During this year, 1922, the policy of the government in effect was as follows: 1. Permit the church services, but divide and disorganize the church. 2. Discredit the bishops and clergy. 3. Organize within the church, both by terror and bribery, a network of its own informers and spies. 4. Make growingly difficult or impossible the legal and material position of the clergy and hinder the communication between bishops and dioceses and parishes. 5. Hinder the religious education of youth and strengthen anti-religious education. 6. By legal restrictions and taxation starve out the richer and poorer churches. 7. By arrest, exile, or silencing deprive the churches of the most energetic, talented and effective pastors, preachers and organizers. 8. Prohibit all religious propaganda, by sermons, through the press, etc. Diminish the number of churches, close the most revered shrines and principal cathedrals, using them as anti-religious museums, or demolish them to make way for government buildings. 9. Stimulate every possible form of anti-religious education, propaganda and activity. By propaganda rather than by the frontal attack of open persecution make war on religion to the death.

In 1932 a campaign to suppress religion on collective farms was conducted, many peasants tried to escape from the Soviet Union to avoid joining these farms, and some of them were shot at the border. Then came the closing of many sectarian and free churches which had become so effective that the *Komsomol Pravda* stated that there were "up to two million youth in their Christian organizations."

A broadside of propaganda was organized by the voluntary Godless organizations with magazines, papers, pamphlets, lectures, anti-religious plays and films, traveling museums, a songbook, etc., etc. They report: "The Godless children had great influence in their families, in dormitories and in apartment houses . . . *leading to the conversion of entire households!*"

Taken together in its totality the policy of the Communists unites legal permission for public worship with active, or subtle, or economic persecution. The statement that "only in the U.S.S.R. does religion have actual and complete liberty" means either complete ignorance or sheer hypocrisy. Yaroslavsky, the President of the Union of Militant Godless, and with Stalin a member of the inner Political Bureau, after fifteen years of anti-religious activity called for "a Godless 1933." By every method and slogan and effort religion must be "liquidated" at the earliest possible moment.

After a decade and a half of anti-religious propaganda, in August, 1932, Yaroslavsky thus estimated the religious and anti-religious forces in the Soviet Union: "At the present moment the Union of Militant Godless counts five and a half million members. . . . In the Trade Unions over 40 per cent are godless, in Moscow unions as much as 80 per cent. . . . This means 10 million persons . . . and not less than 10 million godless among the tens of millions on the collective farms." He recently said: "If we are to estimate the entire number of believers in our country at 100 million, and this means more than half of the entire population, I would say that less than half the total number of children are believers."

Yaroslavsky continued: "The religious organization in Russia is still very enormous. In our country there are tens of

thousands of churches, tens of thousands of priests with enormous experience. . . . We must not content ourselves with the idea that religion is finished in Russia . . . that it will die of itself. This is not true! . . . The Leningrad Soviet discovered that 77 per cent of the farmers still have ikons in their homes . . . only 18 per cent consider religion harmful. In the Belozersk district 90 per cent of the collective farmers have ikons; 30 per cent consider religion harmful but still maintain ikons 'just in case.' . . . Every individual farmer keeps his ikons, and 82 per cent consider religion a good thing. Only 7 per cent think it harmful and 10 per cent put us off by saying they do not know. . . . The enemy is still firmly rooted and has a willing audience among tens of millions of toilers." [1]

Men such as Yaroslavsky and many leaders in the Union of Militant Godless are of transparent honesty and earnestness of character. They sincerely believe religion to be a positive evil and menace. The religious emotions which operate in other countries are canalized into social channels in Russia, or find expression in the voluntary missionary activity of the Union of Militant Godless. They complain, however, of the indifference of the majority to their anti-religious program, which has never proved a popular cause, and they meet the silent, stubborn opposition of many peasants who cling to religion with tenacity.

Up to January, 1934, more than three-quarters of the churches in the cities have been closed but over half of those in the country are still open for worship, which has been conducted continuously in spite of the Revolution in 1917. The services are still the most beautiful of any in the world in aesthetic mysticism but there is as yet no effective spiritual reformation evident to the casual observer in the churches. Religion in all its history has never had to meet so intelligent and implacable a foe. The present condition and future prospects of religion in Soviet Russia present a problem. As Yaroslavsky warns the forces of anti-religion that they must not underestimate the strength of organized religion in Russia,

---

[1] Yaroslavsky's speech, reported in the *Bezbojnik,* April 17, 1933.

the same principle holds with regard to the attitude of religionists toward their opponents. However mistaken or fanatical they may be, we must give them credit for sincerity and earnestness in their honest opposition to religion as they have known it.[1]

Count Witte, the best of the Czar's later statesmen, wrote: "In my opinion the greatest danger confronting Russia is the degeneration of the official Orthodox Church and the extinction of the living religious spirit of the people. . . . No body politic can exist without higher spiritual ideals. These can only sway the masses if they are simple, lofty, and accessible to everyone; in a word, if they bear the imprint of the divine. Without religion the masses turn into herds of intelligent beasts. Our Church has unfortunately long since become a dead bureaucratic institution. We have less faith than any other nation. Japan has defeated us because she believes in her God incomparably more than we do in ours." [2]

The Communists could not seek to destroy religion, which occupied so large a part of Russian life, without trying to put something which seemed to them better in its place. It is a disputed point as to how far Communism itself is to be considered as a religion. The answer will depend upon the definition of the word. Northern Buddhism, for instance, is a polytheistic religion, while orthodox Southern Buddhism is atheistic, yet the latter is none the less a religion. Upon a broad definition Communism has many of the qualities and aspects of a religion, though Communists themselves repudiate and abhor the very word.

Here is a system which has its dogma and its creed, its orthodoxy and heresy, its "cleansing" and discipline. It has a sacred literature and a personal founder, who is revered though never worshipped. It offers a salvation that is social

[1] Lenin wrote: "'Religion is the opium of the people,' this saying of Marx is the corner-stone of the entire world outlook of Marxism in the question of religion. Marxism regards all religions and churches of today, all and every religious organization, always as the organs of bourgeois reaction, which serve to protect the exploitation and deception of the working class."
[2] Quoted by S. K. Ratcliffe, *Russian Communism as a Religion*, Yale Review, December 1931.

rather than individual. For ikons in the corner of each home it substitutes the picture of Lenin. It has its missionary zeal, its heroic sacrifice, its element of prophecy and faith, its emotional fanaticism, its own substitute for confirmation, marriage and burial. It has a world field and a horizon of universalism. It has its persecution and martyrdom, its panacea for the world's ills and its unproven religious hope of a glorious future. Communism is primarily a system that is economic, social and political, based upon a narrow but almost complete philosophy of life. While realistic and eminently practical, in certain aspects it may be considered as a dogmatic, fanatical religion of atheistic humanism.[1]

The present hierarchy of the Communist Party is under as rigid a discipline and surveillance as ever were the Dominican or Jesuit orders. They have practically to take the vows of poverty and obedience, though the Party has no interest in their chastity unless it has anti-social consequences. Marxian economics are made the canon of orthodoxy. Children and youth are indoctrinated in Marx and Lenin with religious fervor. The dogma is practically infallible. The writings of Marx and Lenin form the Old and New Testaments of Communism. Communists constitute a kind of secular priesthood. Oppression and terror are not for the faithful but for the enemies of the truth. They do not deify the machine nor worship it as a moneymaker to enslave man, but utilize it for his release from bondage.

The youth of Russia have never known any other system and look with horror on the capitalist world as described by their own press. Mrs. Cecil Chesterton wrote: "I knew as I saw those strong and eager faces that it is the Russian youth who feed the flame of Communism. To them the Soviet is an inspiration and an ecstasy, comparable only to the fierce

---

[1] If religion be defined as a sense of the absolute, or as the whole man seeking the whole of life, or as the effort to integrate life and relate it to its source and ends, upon any such broad definition Communism may be considered as a religion without God. However the Russians themselves may repudiate the term religion, it is significant that a large number of writers consider Communism as a form of religion.

ardor of a religious cause, for which they proudly live and would gladly die."

Lenin is not worshipped but he is a symbol, an example, and the embodiment of the proletarian ideal. It is a moving sight to visit the tomb of Lenin and see the long queue of several thousand youth waiting in the Red Square until the doors open each afternoon at five o'clock. The tomb is of dark red marble, much more impressive than that of Napoleon, Washington or Lincoln, and it is probably visited by as many as visit all the last three combined.

The embalmed body lies there under a glass case with a Red soldier standing at attention at the head, and another at the foot. With his short stubby reddish hair about his almost bald head he is dressed in a plain workingman's blouse. The figure is very lifelike, as if he had just fallen asleep. There is silent admiration but no sign of superstitious veneration in the youthful devotees. There is no sense of death but an impression of life and of a living cause in the scene. Every eye is fastened upon the face of their leader. To them he was one who had spent twenty years in prison, in poverty and in exile. After his brother was shot by the Czar's police he had moved for years, fearless in constant danger of death. When he had fortunes and palaces in his grasp he had lived the simple life on two dollars a day. The suit on his back is the uniform of the impoverished proletariat. You see these youth file round this body with every eye fastened on his face to rekindle the flame of devotion to their cause, that they also may be willing, as he was in his day, to spend two decades, or a lifetime if need be, in prison, or poverty, or exile, in fearless and selfless service for their cause.

Just after midnight, above the tomb of Lenin, the chimes of the great Kremlin ring out over the sleeping city of Moscow the anthem of the *Internationale:* "Arise, ye prisoners of starvation. . . ." In the background, within the great church in the Kremlin, the dead Czars of the past are buried with all the memories of that long era of human injustice under the divine right of kings.

As one hears these chimes or views the ranks of youth filing

past the body of Lenin it is evident that he is for them, as is the *Internationale,* the symbol of a great principle. Youth seeks to rekindle the same passion for justice which burned in the heart of Lenin as in that of Marx before him. It is this which is voiced in the anthem which has for them the solemn religious character of a hymn, when fifty thousand sing it in unison and with deep feeling in the great stadium of Moscow. It is this ideal which is at the heart of all that is best in the whole movement of Soviet Russia: *"Arise, ye prisoners of starvation."*

There is an undeniable dynamic and heroic appeal in this fierce, secular, social religion. Actually it is able to challenge and inspire youth and call them to heroic service and sacrifice as religion in the West is unable to do for its youth. The difference is not so much in the two forms of religion as in the social order with which each is associated. Linked to an unjust and decaying economic order of profit and exploitation, which offers its glittering prizes to the strong and ruthless, religion finds it difficult to call men to heroic service within this order just as it did under the system of slavery. In the building of a new order based upon justice the system can call youth to its banner for sacrifice, battle and death in Soviet Russia.

Religion presents a problem in Soviet Russia to the Soviets, to its own followers and to the world. How was it that a religion of such high personal and social idealism in its origin could have become so identified with an autocratic state and a corrupt social order? How did it become not only a personal solace to the faithful but so habitually anti-social that it finally came to be regarded as an opiate and even a poison? After nearly ten centuries of trial, how could it have become so impotent and debased that the Communists deliberately determined to destroy it as a boundless evil and a menace to a just social order?

To answer this question of the problem of religion in Russia we must view it in a wider context and ask why organized religion in other lands, which often began as a radical revolt with definitely social implications, has become so prevailingly conservative and at times reactionary and anti-social.

Religion in the West

Two streams have flowed from organized religion in general and from Christianity in particular, the one social, the other individualistic and at times anti-social. In its origins religion has been often social and at times even communal in form. We find the common ownership of pasture lands and other possessions among the pre-Hebrew Asiatic tribes. The Exodus was a form of migrant communism. The Essenes who were contemporaries of Christ lived a communal life. The early Christian community had "all things common" in a society of spiritual, voluntary communism. The idea of common sharing was symbolized in its worship, the agape and the eucharist. Jesus of Nazareth pronounced his blessings upon the poor and his woes upon the rich, who would find it as difficult to enter upon his way of life as a camel the eye of a needle. His followers were forbidden to lay up treasure on earth in congested private property and wealth, but were to share all that they possessed, and to go out like the good Samaritan to bind up the wounds of despoiled and robbed humanity.

Aversion to wealth, ideas of the simple life of sharing and even of voluntary communism remained in the church for centuries.[1] Communes of monastic orders arose in protest against worldly accumulation, they multiplied and some continue in existence to this day. Throughout the centuries, wherever its original message was re-discovered and proclaimed,

---

[1] From 70 to 110 A. D. wealth bore a stigma: "Thou shalt have all things common with thy neighbor and not call them thy *private property*," says the Epistle of Barnabas. From 110 to 180 A. D. Justin and Tertullian still maintain: "We have everything in common except our wives." In the fourth century Augustine holds that "private property has no right in nature" and Chrysostom says of the rich: "They are truly as robbers, who, standing in the public highways, despoil the passers-by." For more than twelve centuries groups maintained voluntary poverty and sometimes the communal life. Wycliffe in the fourteenth century says: "Not our theory of the community of goods, but the possession of the unrighteous involves theft." Several hundred such quotations could be given from the early days of Christianity which show the same denunciation of greed and of private wealth which is made by Communists today.

Christianity maintained an essentially equalitarian doctrine of universal human brotherhood.

There was a potent stream of influence that flowed from the ideas of early Christianity of reverence for personality or the sanctity of human life, universal brotherhood, and the religious principle of love, which was translatable into the rational concept of social justice. Like all coins which are worn thin and counterfeited, the greatest word in the human language, "love," has been often debased. If it means for the individual self-realization through self-sacrifice, and for society the full sharing of life, it implies and becomes equivalent in one aspect to social justice.

As Mr. Lecky shows, these dynamic principles of early Christianity in their social effects overcame paganism, bestowed the priceless boons of the humanitarian spirit and directed civilization for a thousand years. It would take volumes to describe their influence upon individual moral character, the redemption of childhood, the uplift of womanhood, the dignity of manhood, the sanctity of the home, the impetus to education, the stimulation of science, the fructification of the ideas of political liberty and democracy, the ministry of philanthropy, the motivation of social passion and the world outreach and sharing of this multiform inheritance of a common humanity. All this, and more, has constituted a stream of social influence which has flowed from organized religion. If this were all we should not have to consider in this chapter the problem of religion, or the reformation of religion. It would be merely an individual and social dynamic.

But, unfortunately, organized religion has had, not only in Russia but in the world, its anti-social side as well. There is no lesson that needs more to be learned from Russia than this negative one of the social failure of organized religion. There we may see impartially and objectively in the Soviet Union what is too common, too subtle, too close to us to be realized in our own life.

Why was it that from the time of Constantine, and even before his time, Christianity became growingly identified with

the evils of paralyzing asceticism, the system of slavery, of war, the inquisition, feudal serfdom, injustice and the inequality of wealth, the industrial revolution and, probably the most serious of all, with the whole system of modern capitalism?

Beginning as a religion of peace Christianity became during and after the reign of Constantine a religion of war, and for sixteen centuries the church has been entangled in the war system. Whereas the early Christians always left the army, after 416 A.D. only Christians were allowed to serve in it. Mr. Lecky speaks of "the gradual fusion of the military spirit with Christianity" and maintains that with the exception of Islam no other religion has done so much to produce war.

For fifteen centuries the church was entangled in the system of slavery. It would have disappeared centuries before had it not been for the support of the churches. It was left undisturbed until the economic forces transformed it into the serfdom of the Middle Ages. Long after Great Britain had freed all the slaves in her Empire and compensated the owners without bloodshed, the institution lasted in America until 1861 and only ended with a fratricidal war. Out of the common sentiment of southern Christianity the Southern Presbyterian Church declared, even after that date, its "deep conviction of the divine appointment of domestic servitude" and of the "peculiar mission of the Southern church to conserve the institution of slavery." [1] To this day the Roman Catholic Church has never categorically repudiated slavery.

From 1095 to 1291 the church was occupied in the butchery of the Crusades and, for several centuries, in the tortures of the Inquisition during which a reign of terror prevailed. This was followed by violence on the part of Protestants. The Roman Catholics list two hundred and fifty-three martyrs in England at the hands of the Protestants from 1535 to 1681.

---

[1] Dr. Leonard Bacon, *History of American Christianity,* p. 346, quoted by Kirby Page in *Jesus or Christianity.* Mr. Lecky says: "Slavery was distinctly and formally recognized by Christianity and no religion ever labored more to encourage a habit of docility and passive obedience." *A History of European Morals,* Vol. II, p. 66.

J. L. and Barbara Hammond have told us of the exploitation of men, women, and children during the industrial revolution in England. Canon Raven reminds us that: "In the whole eighteenth century no great church and, save Methodism, no great religious movement breaks the very low level of English Christianity." [1] Wilberforce, who labored to free the African Negro, opposed every attempt to free the white slaves of British industry. The great Christian Socialist Charles Kingsley and Frederick Dennison Maurice were persecuted. Kingsley said that in his day the Bible was turned into "a mere constable's handbook—an *opium-dose* for keeping beasts of burden patient." Maurice was hounded from his post. The church as a whole was not interested in social justice, but rather anti-social in its sympathies. The result was that *social reform did not follow Maurice but Marx.* It was forced to the path of violence. Organized religion up to 1848 had not espoused the cause of labor. Non-violence had almost abandoned the field. Religious people still defended their liberties but as Carlyle said: "Liberty, when it becomes liberty to die by starvation, is not so divine."

All the national churches of Europe have opposed the hard-won advance of political and economic democracy. All execrated the French and Russian revolutions and resisted their good influences. The church fought against Italian unity and the establishment of republics and popular education in a score of lands. It is easier to recognize the fatal record organized religion has made in the past and the tragic mistake it made in Czarist Russia than it is to realize its entangling alliance with the evil of capitalism today and the problem for religion which this creates. This alliance bids fair to be even more fatal than its former entanglement with the systems of war and slavery.

On its social side religion is founded on reverence for personality, equal brotherhood, and love, or justice, as implying

---

[1] Canon C. E. Raven, *Christian Socialism,* pp. 7–14.

practically equal sharing with all. Our present economic order is founded upon the profit motive, monopolistic ownership and consequent class inequality, injustice and strife. Here is a fatal contradiction. The whole western world has become conformed to the ethical presuppositions of capitalism. It is the atmosphere it breathes. Calvin's ethics gave a powerful impetus to capitalism. The ending of opposition to usury, the thrift and acquisition of Protestants enabled them to amass the greater part of the wealth of the world. Capitalism has affected all our economic, political, ethical, educational and ecclesiastical life. Although the issues today are more blurred and obscured, there is at bottom as clear an issue and contradiction between Christianity and capitalism in the West as there was between Christianity and Czarism in Russia.[1]

Now that it is too late we see the mistake which organized religion made in being compromised and bound up with these historic evils of the past in the ancient world and in Russia. Man's tendency is always to side with his selfish economic interests rather than his religious ideals. But he cannot serve two masters. He must either seek first and serve a just society, or acquiesce in the ethics of capitalism as he previously did in war, slavery and feudalism. Compromise between two masters leads to hypocrisy, which is nearly always unconscious. Men are as honestly convinced of the justice and inevitability of capitalism today as they were of slavery and the other evils of the past. When religion is bound up with the old order it must either break away and lead in reform, or else suffer and be dragged down with the decaying order.

Capitalism, which holds and hides such mass injustice, leads to hypocrisy. It hides behind the face of justice in its apparently legal and lawful methods. It passes its laws, controls its

---

[1] Both systems became unjust and anti-Christian. The capitalist economist, Mr. J. M. Keynes, writes: "Modern capitalism is absolutely irreligious, without internal union, without much public spirit, often, though not always, a mere congeries of possessors and pursuers." Few or many benevolent business men no more radically alter the system than the many Christian owners altered the character of slavery as a system.

press, calls out its army, police, national guard, or gunmen to protect its private property and monopoly. It appears lawful and the workers who vainly demand justice seem to be lawless. Capitalism thus adds hypocrisy to its greed, injustice and exploitation, though this hypocrisy, however glaring and obvious to others, is quite unconscious to those who are blinded by their own self-interest.

The alliance with and dependence upon capitalism by organized religion is one of the dominant facts of our time. Multitudes are still unconscious of it. Max Weber of Germany in *The Protestant Ethic and the Spirit of Capitalism*, R. A. Tawney of England in *Religion and the Rise of Capitalism*, and now Georgia Harkness in *John Calvin: the Man and His Ethics*, have shown how Puritan thrift and Calvinist ethics gave a powerful impetus to capitalism and how Protestants have become the capitalists of the world. John Wesley long ago foresaw this problem and danger for religion when he wrote: "Religion must necessarily produce both industry and frugality, and these cannot but produce riches. But as riches increase so will pride, anger and love of the world in all its branches. Is there any way to prevent this—this continual decay of pure religion? We ought not to prevent people from being diligent and frugal; *we must exhort all Christians to gain all they can, and to save all they can; that is, in effect to grow rich.*" Wesley himself remained poor by giving all and sharing all with the needy. But when the first enthusiasm passed, Wesley's converts of the second and third generations continued to gain and to save but not adequately to give. Protestants in time became rich and their interests, as Marx clearly pointed out, were with the system that had made and gave title to their wealth rather than the contradictory principles of their religion, whose first concern was for human personality and society, for individual character and the building of a new social order.

While religionists were temporizing and compromising Marx saw the contradiction and hypocrisy of the old economic order as clearly as the Jewish prophet, Amos, had seen it twenty-six centuries before. But the religious men of both

periods were unconsciously blinded by their economic interests. Religionists were as abhorrent of the last call to social justice as they had been of the first; they were as bitter in their denunciation of Marx as they had been of Amos.

Those who are identified with the present economic order, whether religious people or secular, do not often recognize that their abhorrence and often violent emotional reaction to Soviet Russia is at bottom their fear and hatred of this new economic system which demands equal justice instead of special privilege. They do not realize how long spiritual communism and equal sharing was a part of their own religion, nor how the ideas of justice and equality in Soviet Russia today are much nearer to the early principles both of Judaism and Christianity than to modern capitalism, which is more akin in principle to pagan Rome or Babylon. In the sixteenth century children in Ireland were baptized with their right arms held above the water so as not to affect their participation in future warfare. Much of our modern life is as contradictory to religious principles as war or slavery.

Marx is looked upon with horror by many religious people. In the Old Testament the Persian Cyrus, though a pagan idolater, was regarded as an unconscious instrument of divine providence.[1] The chosen people, the religious nation, had betrayed its trust. Failure and captivity followed. It was necessary to use some other instrument to recall them from captivity and restore them to their inheritance and their original high calling.

Marx was dealing with the eternal problem of human suffering. It is evident in all his writings that the iron had entered his very soul. It was suffering that he wanted to remove and the entire philosophy and program of Marx and Lenin was

---

[1] In Isaiah XLV: 1–5, Cyrus, all unconscious of any such purpose, is called God's anointed, his Messiah, the instrument of his purpose: "I girded thee though thou hast not known me." His significance is not measured by his consciousness of mission, nor by the orthodoxy of his religious beliefs, but by his fulfilment of function for human welfare.

aimed at that object. He may have been unconsciously influenced by Calvinist theology and Jewish messianism. He had an idea of a chosen people, a suffering people, a chosen class. He thought he could remove the suffering of the great mass of people; with his materialist philosophy he sees the complete elimination of those who cause the suffering. Freedom was to be achieved by the elimination of the elements that oppress, the exploiters and the religious element. But the solution must be found by a synthesis of the conflicting elements in the individual, and between the individual and the collective.

As we approach the probable end of an epoch, the ripening and decay of an economic order, have we reached a similar crisis? Not only the church but the four sources to which we might have looked for a possible solution of the problems of our social order have all in turn failed to meet the situation—industry, government, education, and organized religion.

Business and industry in America could not put their own house in order and after four years of disjointed effort during the depression they could not agree upon any plan to save themselves. Governments in Europe and America had also failed to act decisively and effectively. The boldest action was finally taken by President Roosevelt. Much is at stake in his plan beyond the immediate and apparent issues. Every loyal citizen who can see beyond his own selfish and party interests and who does not believe in Communist violence as the best solution should not only wish him success but loyally strive to make the plan succeed. Short of violent revolution no more daring plan could have been launched with any hope of success. If the plan fails it is one more and perhaps the last failure of a non-violent plan. Even if the plan succeeds, while we shall have made a long stride forward, we shall still have controlled capitalism. The banks, for instance, while somewhat safeguarded, are still left with their monopolistic profits for the few, and the powerful weapon of credit, unsocialized, in private hands.

If business and governments have failed to resolve the contradictions of our social order, has education succeeded? It

has been the theory of most modern educators and sociologists that our chief lack is intelligence; that if we can only educate men it will presumably make them benevolent and almost automatically solve our social problems. But has education succeeded in this? At the moment of writing, outside my window are the privileged boys of a school for higher education thirteen hundred years old. Yet after thirteen centuries of aristocratic education, as we have already seen, nine-tenths of the youth of this age have no secondary education provided for them in England while the privileged one-tenth have been for the most part too largely identified with the economic interests of their class to solve the social problem. In democratic America, likewise, we have found that the ideals of a generation are shaped more by their material conditions than by what they are taught in school, and that flag-waving patriotism for the *status quo* has been much more potent than the ideal of equal justice for all.

The institutions of organized religion have had longer than those of education to confront and grapple with the social problem. If it was impossible to serve two masters, which have they served? Is it true that instead of demanding radical change they have all too often become entangled in or identified with the social evils of each age? Have the churches demanded that their followers declare a clear break with the evils of these systems or have they only asked that they should be *"Christian"* warriors, slave owners, feudal landlords, masters of the industrial revolution, and now Christian business men?

Has their prevailing strategy been in terms of philanthropy and charity or of the organizing of a just society? The very suggestion of the latter seems today academic, unreal and foreign to our tradition. For fifteen centuries we have taken for granted class divisions and inequality in such violent forms as slavery, or wealth and poverty, tolerated up to the very threshold of the other world.

As in the case of education it has been assumed by the churches that if they could only gather the masses into their membership, preach a message with a tincture of the Sermon

on the Mount, or the principle of "love," it would make men benevolent. But has this been the result? A small measure of individual responsibility has been inculcated rather than social obligation. Have the churches demanded or effected radical social change more than business, government or education?

In the meantime the present order or epoch, as in the case of slavery or serfdom before it, ripens toward its end. Capitalists and their supporters are largely in the ranks of organized religion, especially of Protestantism, while the workers are for the most part outside the churches. We are witnessing the dangerous anomaly of the followers of religion defending special privilege and those of anti-religion demanding proletarian justice. We are presented with the same alternative that they were in Czarist Russia over again. Now that it is too late, we see the fatal error of organized religion in Russia but not in America and England.

Religion, as we have seen, became gradually and unconsciously bound up with the evils of the social order of its time and the existing *status quo*. We repeat that what was originally a religion of peace became that of the warring world powers with amassed wealth and armed to the teeth. Indeed, it is one of the most amazing paradoxes of history that these warring tribes and nations, and these capitalistic and imperialistic peoples, should have adopted such a spiritual and sternly social religion which so challenges and condemns their characteristic traits and evils. Despite the high ideals of its founder and its precepts and principles, after nineteen centuries organized religion has failed not only to Christianize its material environment, but even to demand a new social order of equal justice and the sharing of the good life for all.

Now is the judgment of this world and of our economic order. We are left without excuse. We can no longer find an alibi nor ask for nineteen centuries more of charity and amelioration to point out that the world is slowly getting better. Undoubtedly it is in some ways, but it is not because the forces of organized religion are leavening society or are solving its

economic problems.   They stand as impotent before the ethical bankruptcy of the economic order as they did before the World Massacre of 1914-1918.   If they object to the violent methods of Marx are they effectively applying non-violent methods of their own?   Apart from their discredited prophets, it is not only that the forces of organized religion do not solve the economic and social problem of their day.   For the most part they do not even see it.   Or they realize it too late.

We need today a prophet of relentless realism, a prophet of disillusion to strip us bare of our unconscious hypocrisy.   Indeed he has come already but unheeded like the rest.   Apart from its unfortunate and unguarded statement concerning our "illusions," etc., *Moral Man and Immoral Society* [1] remains an unanswered challenge.

Here is the problem of religion today.   Russia did not solve it.   We are not solving it.   If we have no way of deliverance, Marx claims that he has.   If we have a better way, and I for one believe we have, let us recover it and apply it in time. If the moral prophets of Israel fail, a Cyrus of force is at hand.   If the prophets cannot lead the church out of its economic Babylonian captivity of capitalism then some other instrument must do so.

---

[1] Reinhold Niebuhr, *Moral Man and Immoral Society,* The World Tomorrow, 52 Vanderbilt Avenue, New York.   Middleton Murray says: "It is a book which may well prove to be as epoch-making as *The Social Contract,* or the *Communist Manifesto*."

CHAPTER XI

Hegel, in his philosophy of history, finds in all evolution the development of the idea of freedom. Marx, in his dialectic of the strife of opposing forces, finds in every period the class struggle leading toward a resolution of the contending forces in the fresh synthesis of a new epoch. Man's pilgrimage is supposed to rise like an ascending spiral toward its culmination, in the classless society of the future.

We must be content with a more modest examination of human progress in the past to find its possible promise and meaning for the future. As in the view of Hegel and Marx nothing can be understood in isolation "in its bare immediacy" without seeing it in all its relations, so we cannot comprehend the present experiment in Russia and its far-reaching significance without viewing it in a wider context.

In the dead level of primitive society, whether brutal, savage or barbarian, we find prevailingly the rule of force, usually under autocratic forms. All life is fettered by custom or convention with little opportunity for experimentation to explore the potentialities of life. There is no legally secured justice or liberty for the individual.

In Ur, in the valleys of the Euphrates and the Nile, in Northern India and China, we find the beginnings of a culture and of a civilization that were later to be developed in other lands and finally to become the heritage of mankind.

As we review the history of the last three thousand years there seem to have been five creative epochs, five movements or achievements of the human spirit which chiefly have shaped the life of mankind. These were: the flowering of the Greek mind in free thought and life; the achievement of the Hebrew

spirit in the moral and spiritual interpretation of life; the development of Roman law, order and organization; the Scientific movement in its growing understanding of the laws of nature and the mastery of man's environment by the machine in material production to supply human need; and, finally, the Social movement with its ideal of equal justice for all realized in the socialization of all life. Let us examine these five movements a little more in detail before asking how we may interpret their history in quest of its possible meaning.

1. *The Flowering of the Greek Mind in Free Thought and Life.* After tracing the dead level of fettered and conventional life in other lands, we are almost bewildered by the splendor of the versatile achievement of the Greeks in almost every realm of life. In philosophic speculation on the source of life and the nature of reality, in psychological analysis of the human personality with its determination "know thyself," in æsthetic creation of forms of beauty in sculpture and architecture, in the tragedy of the drama, in an indescribable wealth of literature, in pre-scientific analysis and the charting of the fields of human knowledge, the free Greeks as daring voyagers explored the potentialities of human life. They formed the imperishable ideals of truth, goodness and beauty, as they sought to understand reality, to discover the ethical principles of the good life, and to harmonize their life within and without, in tune with nature and the infinite. The Greeks were pioneers in the development of western culture to which other races in the East and in the West have made their invaluable and permanent contributions.

But, Greek civilization, while it has enriched all the cosmopolitan life of the world since its day, was short lived and had in it the seeds of decay. The Greek, who sought to know himself in thought, never gained the moral mastery over himself as did the Hebrew. Plato records the excesses and dissipation of life which led to the demoralization and even the final extinction of the free Greeks. They never attained to Roman order, organization, unity or permanence. Their failure to recognize the sacredness of the human person, or the spiritual equality and unity of collective life, never shared the

aristocratic privileges of the free, nor lifted the slave from his arbitrary subjection. Glorious, but incomplete, Greek civilization was not destined to survive, but it had shown for all time the value of free thought as the permanent heritage of the human spirit.

2. *The Achievement of the Hebrew Spirit in Moral and Spiritual Insight.* Parallel to the flowering of Hellenic thought, through a thousand years of history, the prophetic experience of the leaders of this most virile and enduring race achieved a unified view of life with moral and spiritual meaning and purpose. Amid a surrounding sea of superstition, polytheism and idolatry, often with their logical accompaniment of erotic worship and moral decay, this isolated people maintained its ethical advance. For the Hebrew the ground of Reality was one, and life had a single high purpose. It was integrated in an ethical monotheism, but there was a polarity of relationships in its duty to God and man.

The active virtues of the Greeks—courage, temperance, wisdom and justice—were supplemented also by the passive virtues, all culminating in the active principle of love, implying the full sharing of life. Man's social goal was to be consummated in a new social order, conceived as a Kingdom of God on earth. The single purpose of life was to seek this social goal through the love of God and man.

But, an exclusive preoccupation with religion ignored as secular or profane a whole world of humanistic life and thought which led to Jewish and later Puritan narrowness or bigotry. The early prophetic moral and spiritual insights hardened into pharisaic legalism whose limitations became embodied in the isolated Jewish race, or in abstract Gentile theologies. Finally early spiritual insights were engulfed in worldly materialism. As Hegel shows, the idea gives birth to the institution, then the institution tends to destroy the idea.

3. *Roman Law and Order.* In the eternal antithesis between liberty and order, the rights of the one and of the many, Greece supplied the former and Rome the latter. The Romans' capacity for organization and the formulation of law, their practical statesmanship and political sagacity, their tolerance and capacity

for compromise built up the first enduring world empire. A mixture of good and evil, Rome reverted too largely to primitive force and autocratic rule. It was, however, an advance in providing a framework for civilization, and it was instrumental in unifying and preparing the world for a better order.

But, it lacked the Hellenic freedom and culture, the Hebraic moral discipline and the sound economic base of a just society. It lost its early democracy and simplicity and degenerated to a class society divided between the exploiting rich and the exploited poor, first in the domestic regions of their decaying agriculture, and then to the last outreach of their expanding imperialism. The social order became economically unsound and morally corrupt with inner contradictions and class conflict. The collapse of the Empire left the world without a center of unity, and the weakening of the monopoly of the unifying Church of the Middle Ages left the shattered world to sink into a seeming chaos of competing nationalisms. But certain hardy racial stocks like the Italian, the Teutonic and Anglo-Saxon produced the leaders who later became the pioneers and adventurers still in quest of the grail of a new society.

4. *The Scientific Movement.* The unity of the world had been shattered by the fall of Rome and its light lost in the dark ages. The Renaissance, however, had recovered the heritage of Greek thought and the Reformation rediscovered the spirit of early religion. Man was again set on the quest of truth, goodness and beauty. In the search for truth many devout believers like Roger Bacon, and later Kepler and Newton, took part in the new scientific movement. The discovery of the scientific method of experiment, the acquisition of the scientific spirit, the achievements of pure and applied science gave man a growing knowledge of the laws of nature and the ability to construct the machine in order to harness its energies for boundless production to meet all the wants of his material life. It made each man the potential master of a host of slaves of energy. The titanic production of scientific technology has placed within man's grasp the permanent abolition of poverty and the provision of material plenty.

But, when science was isolated from the humanities or largely

monopolized by a small class which owned its machines and operated them for private profit, it produced the horrors of the Industrial Revolution, smoking cities with their blighting slums, poverty, unemployment and a whole brood of kindred evils. Scientifically man had advanced to the nineteenth century but socially he was living almost in the stone age. Technology had mastered the problem of production, but man in his collective life had hardly scratched the surface of the graver problems of distribution, consumption, credit and the socialization of all life.

5. *The Social Movement.* Up to the beginning of the twentieth century wide areas of life had realized one or more of the four preceding achievements of man but often in isolation. Industry, commerce and imperialism had made the world one neighborhood in an inter-related and interdependent community, but neither religion nor social organization had made it a brotherhood or a cooperative fellowship. Instead, it was divided into competing classes, races and nations in endless strife, issuing periodically in overt war. This in a world community had now assumed the proportions of *world* war.

Even if it could appropriate its inheritance of the preceding four epochs or movements the competitive world with its vast wealth unshared still lacked one thing—socialization. The social message of the new epoch was not unique but an effective social movement was. The prophet Amos twenty-six hundred years before had thundered his bold denunciations against economic exploitation, coupled with the threat of the downfall and destruction of the unjust nation of Northern Israel, which had perished as he prophesied.

Almost an unbroken line of prophets and Utopian idealists from the time of Amos and Plato had in turn denounced the old and visioned the new and just social order. But their message had gone for the most part unheeded. Conditions in the industrial revolution a century ago, and even today among the urban unemployed, are often worse than in the time of Amos. Twenty-six centuries of prophecy, nineteen centuries of religion and centuries of education[1] had neither provided social justice

---

[1] The school for higher education outside my window as I write was founded thirteen centuries ago, in Canterbury.

nor even culminated in the *demand* for it.   The processes of evolution had waited long and in vain.

In 1848 a German student, descended from a long line of Jewish rabbis, burned his three volumes of original poems, turned his back upon his classical and legal studies, sacrificed his academic career, and went out into the wilderness with the disinherited proletariat, as Moses had done centuries before. This man now began to make the age-long demand for social justice effective.   He proclaimed his dialectic of conflict, his interpretation of history, his economic theory of surplus value for the exploited workers.   He was naturally impatient after so many centuries of delay, but finally he called for a program of action and attempted to unite into a brotherhood for its achievement the first international organization of workers.

A demand which had gone largely unheeded for some twenty-six centuries now became clamant and concrete.   Economic crises and war followed, as this stern social prophet had foretold, and within a few years of his death, over a sixth part of the earth's surface, a new order, conceived in a desire to socialize all life and introduce a classless, equalitarian society, was set up under a government of workers and peasants.

But, of the five achievements of the human spirit which we have noted, the Russian experiment seeks to incorporate only the last three.   Its tyranny has more than Roman law and order, it almost worships science and the machine, and its central passion is social justice.   Yet it is as remarkable for what it omits as for what it includes.   Greek thought and freedom it scorns as bourgeois prejudice.   Religion it seeks to destroy. It is cursed by a paralysis of bureaucracy, the coercion of violence, the dogmatism of atheism and an anti-religious inquisition.

Is such a one-sided tyranny fit to be the final form of society or likely in isolation to usher in a complete or satisfying social order?   Can any society which deliberately excludes any of humanity's fivefold inheritance of liberty, spiritual insight, law and order, scientific achievement, and the complete socialization of life expect to do so?

Herein is the significance of the Russian experiment and we should let no prejudice blind us to it.   It is true that it is crude,

one-sided, coercive. It is true that like ancient Rome it is partly a reversion to primitive force and autocracy. But here for the first time on this relatively young planet, after thousands of years of struggle and strife, there has been set up the first approximate realization of equal social justice for the masses in any large community or area on earth. Indeed, it is the first country even to proclaim the equalitarian ideal, with the abolition of private property and monopolistic privilege which has prevailingly characterized human society for ten thousand years.

Was Marx, then, in the succession of the prophets? What is a prophet? Is he a man who is infallible, who makes no mistakes, who has a balanced knowledge of all truth? Or is he rather one who, at the psychological moment, foretells some great truth which meets the deep need or evil of an epoch, and foretells the doom of those who reject and the lot of those who accept the truth? We have already pointed out the inadequacies, the defects, the errors of many of his doctrines, of the violent means he advocated and the unloveliness of some sides of his character. But can it be denied that, more than Amos or Isaiah, more than Plato, Sir Thomas More, Robert Owen, the Utopians, the reformers, this man made a greater demand for social justice, and more to make it effective in the earth, more to challenge the age-long evil of exploitation and to introduce a new social order, than any other? Is he also among the prophets? He himself would be the first to deny it. We stone the prophets and crucify the saviors of humanity when they are with us. It is only long after that we recognize them.

On the extreme left wing of social experimentation we have the Soviet Union seeking to embody the idea of justice. On the right we have the Anglo-Saxon countries seven centuries after winning their Magna Carta of freedom. From the time of Socrates, some twenty-three centuries ago, through Cromwell, Rousseau and Jefferson, through the English, French and American revolutions, we have made an attempt to realize man's deathless demand for liberty. We have claimed to provide liberty, but there is little justice—unless slums and poverty in

the midst of plenty and waste be justice.   Soviet Russia has sought justice but denied liberty.

Here are two one-sided extremes or antitheses.   Surely mankind needs both liberty and justice; he cannot do with less.   We can neither accept the easy promise of the Soviets of the tyranny of the state "withering away," nor the promise of justice in a world beyond, or in an indefinite future.   In the meantime, while our life is so imperfect, we must recognize the significance and the imperative importance of a social order that attempts to preserve liberty, and also of one which provides justice for the masses which were so long neglected.   Indeed the fifth and last attainment of socialization is the point of humanity's greatest weakness today.

In man's long economic pilgrimage he has already passed through various phases or epochs.   The primitive stage, slavery, feudalism and capitalism have in turn succeeded one another.   At the moment we have on the right a number of countries in various phases of fascism, which we have interpreted as the last phase of disintegrating capitalism.   On the left, Russia is in a temporary or transitional stage of state capitalism under a dictatorship that is rapidly "building socialism."   In between, President Roosevelt is trying his experiment in controlled capitalism under a plan that already embodies many socialistic elements.   All these experiments have to be corrected by experience. It will be impossible to maintain a permanent tyranny in any land.   The world is in a state of flux and rapid transition.   Consciously or unconsciously, willingly or unwillingly, it will be forced toward an already dangerously delayed and desperately needed socialization of all life, and the sharing or abolition of all special privilege.

We are standing near the close of an epoch; we are on the threshold of a new era.   It will be well if we can read the signs of the times and take warning in season.   We may still have time to choose whether we shall go forward by rapid, unimpeded evolution, or whether reaction will try to dam up the rapidly rising waters of discontent until they burst into revolution.   It is the belief of most Anglo-Saxons that Britain and

America, at least, may choose the better part and make the great transition of the sharing and socialization of life by non-violent means.

Can Capitalism Survive?

Our interpretation of history is not that of Marx, of inevitable class war leading toward the dictatorship of the long oppressed masses, who are conceived as a messianic class of deliverance. Communists have proved at least as ruthless to their enemies as capitalists ever were, and as unwilling to end their monopoly of power. We admit that there will be inevitable class struggle as long as there are classes of privileged and underprivileged, exploiters and exploited, owners and owned. Whether the class struggle, which is already an undeniable fact, shall become a class war of blood and iron, of hatred and destruction, of starving cities, famine and pestilence, will depend upon the class of owners in power. Will this class share its privileges in time, and will it give full justice to the workers, not merely as a sop or pittance wrung from the owners of the means of production in their unwilling greed, but satisfying and equal justice?

If it is true that in capitalism and Communism we now have in the world two contrasted and challenging social orders, it ought to give us a valuable point of reference for the evaluation and criticism of each system from the standpoint of the other. One of the most disturbing but useful lessons which may be learned from the Soviet experiment is the possibility of an objective criticism and evaluation of our own economic system of capitalism.

By capitalism we mean the private ownership of the means of production, not primarily for use but for the profit and power of the owners. Private ownership includes all the means of life such as the raw materials, the industries, banks and credit, which rest in relatively few private hands, under a system of competition and individual initiative with a minimum of government interference. At the other extreme, the Soviet system represents state ownership and control of all means of production,

distribution and exchange, under a dictatorship exercised on behalf of the working class. Socialism, of the prevailing Anglo-Saxon variety, midway between, commonly aims at the gradual socialization of the principal means of production, by consent rather than by compulsion, by constitutional, parliamentary action, through constructive, evolutionary processes, rather than by sudden, violent revolution.

In the opening chapters we have already discussed the evils of Communism. In the light of the Russian experiment what are the defects of our own system of capitalism?

In attempting an appraisal of the system we must recognize the immense advance of capitalism over all preceding systems, the wealth it has produced for America and the capitalist countries, and the high standard of living it has provided for employed skilled workers and the middle class. It has magnificently succeeded in production under advanced technology to such an extent that it has brought us within sight of the banishing of poverty from the earth. It can provide abundantly for the material wants of the entire population if we can but solve the problem of equitable distribution, of the purchasing power of the workers, and of adequate consumption. We must remember, also, that whatever the defects of the system, we did not individually create it and that we do not attempt to place the blame upon individuals who are all suffering, though not equally, under its disabilities and injustices.

Among the evils of the capitalist system we may note the following effects upon the two classes, owners and dependents, which it automatically creates:

1. *Private ownership and a proletarian army of dependents.*— The private ownership of the means of production creates a class of relatively few owners and ever-increasing concentration of wealth, power and privilege in their hands, with resultant control over economic and political life, over the press, and to a considerable extent in the field of education, and even of organized religion.

On the other side, at the negative pole, the system leaves the vast majority of the workers, sometimes employed and some-

times unemployed, together with a growing army of white collar dependents, divorced from the means of production and from the control of the sources of their own life. Deny it or disguise it as we may, here are two classes separated by the cleavage of private property, with a deep and fundamental conflict of interests, with unequal privileges, without equal justice, divided between owners who are strong and dependents who are weak. Unless the latter can be drugged temporarily by an opiate, here are the makings of class conflict.

2. *Surplus profit for the owners with recurring under-consumption, growing crises and depressions for the workers.*— As the owners operate under the profit motive in normal years the system yields them more in profit than they can either consume or economically invest, and less in wages to the workers than they need to purchase the goods they have produced. The owners are forced to reinvest their surplus of profit and their increasing wealth in more production, which, in time, develops into over-production. There comes automatically to be an excess of producers' capital and a deficiency of consumers' capital for purchasing power. This produces a crisis of over-production and under-consumption, followed by a depression where increasingly workers are laid off as unemployed. This operates in a vicious circle to further decrease purchasing power and increase the effects of the depression.

The economic experts of the League of Nations find that such a cycle of over-production, crisis and depression has occurred on an average of every four and a quarter years. Such crises recur with ever-increasing intensity and severity. They result in idle workers, idle plant and idle capital. At the moment of writing, after four years of depression in the United States, the rate of interest on ninety-day notes has fallen to one-tenth of one per cent because of idle capital.

In *A Picture of America* we see dramatically visualized by the camera the depressions which occur periodically in the United States. Side by side are the tallest skyscrapers in the world, the mightiest industries, overflowing farms, the most prodigal natural resources and gushing oil wells—and the longest breadlines

in the world. This book records nearly a score of similar depressions in the last century, since 1837, with clippings and excerpts from the press which repeat the same helpless reports of over-production and unemployment, without evidence of having learned any lesson or of discovering any way to avert these periodic and devastating disasters under the present system. The pendulum of over-production and unemployment swings with fatal regularity to mark the cycles of our present planless system.[1]

3. *Unequal wealth and "security" for the few: unemployment, poverty and insecurity for the many.*—With a virgin continent to exploit, the few who came into monopolistic ownership of its natural resources amassed huge fortunes. The wealth of the United States rose from 7 billions in 1850 to 400 billions in 1926, according to the claim of the late President Coolidge.[2] The banks had deposits of 28 billion dollars; life insurance totalled 108 billions; and the savings of the American people reached the sum of 56 billion dollars by 1930.[3]

But how was this vast wealth divided between the owners and dependents? Ogden Mills, then Under Secretary of the Treasury, made the statement: "For the income year 1925, .29 of one per cent of the population (or less than a third of one per cent) pay over 95 per cent of the individual income tax; 17 per cent pay less than 5 per cent of the tax, and the remaining 82 per cent pay no income tax."[4] In 1929, 513 multimillionaires paid income tax on individual incomes of over a million dollars a year, while 1,032,554 owners of the means of production reported incomes of from $5,000 to $1,000,000 a year. During the last decade Americans spent from six to ten billion dollars a year on luxuries, according to the *Business Week*. The 2,000 millionaires living on Park Avenue in New York

[1] *A Picture of America,* Simon & Schuster, New York.
[2] Address at Kansas City, November 11, 1926, and Report of Federal Trade Commission, 1926, p. 2. According to the *Statistical Abstract of the United States,* 1932, the official estimates of national wealth in billions of dollars was as follows: 1850, 7 billions; 1900, 88 billions; 1922, 320 billions; 1923, 339 billions; 1929, $361,800,000,000.
[3] Throughout this section I have drawn freely upon the excellent material gathered by Kirby Page in his recently published *Individualism and Socialism.*
[4] Ogden Mills, in *The Literary Digest,* April 16, 1927.

City, in 1929 spent an average of $84,000 per year per family. One rich man in New York City possessed more money than all the six hundred thousand dwellers in the slums and more than a million of the families of the poor combined. In 1929, 93 per cent of the receipts from the Federal income tax came from the 3 per cent of rich taxpayers. Only four adults in a hundred possessed enough income to pay any tax at all.

A large proportion of the great fortunes of America were amassed through monopoly, by anti-social and unscrupulous means. These fortunes were made through individual control of the nation's natural resources of oil, coal and minerals, appropriation of the unearned increment due to the rise in land values, speculation and manipulation of the stock and grain markets, government privileges in land grants, franchises and high tariffs, exploitation of the workers through low wages and long hours, and by the inheritance of unearned wealth gained by these means.[1] A genuine "self-made" millionaire, who has not exploited labor or used any of these monopolistic and anti-social means of acquiring wealth, can hardly be found. Later we shall examine men of the Henry Ford type.

Many American fortunes were amassed by exploiting the public domain of 2,186,862 square miles, or 1,309,591,680 acres. A large proportion of this fell into the clutches of speculators. Professor Ripley of Harvard University estimates that the total land grants to the railroads of 242,000 square miles constituted a territory larger than Germany and France, or nearly four times the area of New England. According to Professor Ripley, government grants and profits from the sale of land grants covered practically the entire cost of constructing all American railways up to 1870.

---

[1] Stuart Chase, *A New Deal,* lists some of the anti-social means of "how men grow rich" as follows: Artificial monopoly and the raising of prices, as by the Mellon monopoly of the world's aluminum deposits; patent secret processes; selling credit to the needy; the manufacture of useless products; false advertising; the manipulation of dubious stocks and bonds; speculation in securities; cornering the market; parasitic industries; graft in politics; graft in business; blind over-production in competitive industry, etc., all resulting in ill-gotten gain for the few and waste, ruin, unemployment and poverty for the many.

Out of franchises and monopolistic grants from governments and municipalities to operate street cars, elevated railways, subways, gas and electricity in New York, Chicago, Philadelphia, Pittsburgh and a hundred smaller cities, a group of seven men made swollen fortunes—Yerkes, Widener, Elkins, Dolan, Whitney, Ryan, and later, Insull.[1] These and similar fortunes were often connected with monopoly, speculation, or crooked municipal politics. Andrew D. White declared: "With few exceptions the city governments of the United States are the worst in Christendom—the most expensive, the most inefficient, and the most corrupt."

We would have to add the fortunes from public loot as when, under President Harding, Secretary Fall was bribed by Harry F. Sinclair and Edward F. Doheny to lease government oil lands at Teapot Dome and Elk Hills. The same rugged individualists who freely used the government for special privilege in making their fortunes now cry to heaven in righteous indignation if anyone like Franklin D. Roosevelt places restrictions upon their liberty to plunder the public.

The Supreme Court of the United States has upheld the inviolability and sacredness of private property against the rights and needs of the people, regardless of the methods by which these fortunes were secured, whether by means honest or dishonest, social or anti-social; whether the millionaire "may have made his fortune dealing in slaves" or looting the municipal or federal government or the public domain.[2]

More than a decade ago our country had "three billion slaves of energy resources," and according to the United States Department of the Interior we now have "the equivalent of sixty slaves for every man, woman and child in the United States." But for whom are these slaves of energy working? Do they serve the unemployed, the dwellers in the slums, the farmer, the masses, or chiefly the few owners of the means of production and of life? Under capitalism the dice are loaded for the capitalist.

---

[1] Burton K. Hendrick, *The Age of Big Business*, pp. 121-124, 147, 148.
[2] *Ibid*, p. 110. Decision of Supreme Court in 1894.

According to Stuart Chase, the man-power of 20 million out of our 40 million adult workers in the United States is being wasted. President Arthur Morgan of Antioch College estimates that "we squander 94 per cent of our productive capacity." [1] President Hoover's committee of the Federated American Engineering Societies, in their report on *Waste in Industry,* showed that from 50 to 81 per cent of the waste in various industries is due to the inefficiency of management.

The colossal squandering of our natural resources in coal, water power, oil, natural gas and timber, great as they have been, is less than the even greater waste in our system of planless production and distribution. Prodigal waste is an inevitable concomitant of monopolistic capitalism. It is evident that this system of private ownership has not furnished security nor ended unemployment for the dependent masses. But has it provided security even for the favored few privileged owners themselves? Business failures in the United States from 1915 to 1932 have increased from 22,156 to 31,822 a year, with aggregate liabilities rising to approximately a billion dollars annually.[2] The average life-span of a factory is now only seven years.

Of course the vast bulk of the burden of insecurity and want falls not upon the owners but upon the dependent classes. The average wages of men employed in manufacturing throughout the United States in 1932 was only $18.18, while women averaged $13 a week and farmers less than $10 a week income. Miss Frances Perkins, before she became United States Secretary of Labor, reported wages in Pennsylvania as low as $3 for a 51 hour week. Mr. John T. Flynn in the *Forum,* in 1933, after analyzing wages in various trades, concludes: "The simple yet alarming truth is that our whole system of wages is crumbling." Even before the depression: "From two-thirds to three-fourths of the women workers . . . in industrial occupations generally work at wages of less than $8 a week, one-

[1] Henry Demarest Lloyd, *Lords of Industry,* p. 334.
[2] *Statistical Abstract of the United States,* 1932, p. 175.

fifth earn less than $4." [1]   Even in 1927, 18.5 per cent of the citizens, or 22 millions of them, were living either upon a bare subsistence level or in poverty. [2]

Thus capitalism has produced throughout the last century, in good times and in bad, congested wealth unshared, side by side with poverty and want unrelieved.   Yet all the while it tries to deny even the existence of classes and the class struggle. Many toil in poverty or walk the streets vainly looking for work while others grow rich by manipulation.

For the first three years of the depression dividends and interest payments were maintained at a surprisingly high figure while wages paid to the workers fell disastrously.   Taking the year 1926 as the normal standard at 100, the relative amounts paid in dividends to the owners, and in wages to the dependents is significant of the whole capitalist system, as follows: [3]

Year	Total Dividend and Interest Payments by All American Corporations	Relative Amounts (1926 100)	Relative Amounts of Wage Payments by Mfg. Establishments (1926 100)
1926	$4,391,000,000	100	100
1930	8,578,000,000	196	80
1931	8,228,000,000	187	60
1932 (9 months)	5,413,000,000	164	38 (Sept.)

Up to September, 1932, wages in industry were only 38 per cent of 1926 and 1929, yet dividends and interest payments for the first nine months of 1932 were 64 per cent above those of 1926.

The heaviest burden of insecurity falls upon the poor in unemployment.   At the low point of the depression the unemployed in America were variously estimated at from 12 to 17 millions.   The conservative Wall Street *Financial Chronicle* says on March 4, 1933: "Today the industrial machinery of the country is almost at a complete standstill, with an army of between 15,000,000 and 16,000,000 unemployed."   The *Busi-*

---

[1] Commission on Industrial Relations appointed by Woodrow Wilson in 1915.

[2] George Soule, *A Planned Society,* p. 236.

[3] Prof. Paul Douglas, of the University of Chicago, *Real Wages in the United States,* 1890–1926, p. 124.

ness Week in November, 1932, estimated the number of unemployed at 15,252,000. Unemployment is chronic under capitalism though it has been eliminated in Soviet Russia. From 1890 to 1925, under capitalism, the months of prosperity totalled fifteen years, and of depression ten years.[1]

Professor A. A. Berle, Jr., one of President Roosevelt's intimate advisers, estimates that on March 4, 1933, at the time of the President's inauguration, "one-fourth of the population was practically on the street and that half of the population was living at a bare subsistence level, with wreckage behind and not even hope ahead." [2]   At the present time the Children's Bureau of the U. S. Department of Labor finds that "one-fifth of all pre-school children and school children in the United States are showing the effects of poor nutrition, of inadequate housing, and in many cases the effect of the anxiety and sense of insecurity that prevails wherever there is no work." [3]

By May, 1933, after private charity had broken down, 28 metropolitan cities were spending $29,533,827, or an average of a million dollars a city per month, less than one dollar in fourteen of this coming from private charity.[4]   The richest country in the world was still unwilling to provide a sound system of unemployment insurance to which labor could make its self-respecting contribution, as in a score of industrially advanced countries, but was willing to give charity or relief where it could not provide employment.   The *Chicago Tribune* thus resents this charity: "The recipients of unemployment relief are objects of charity.   They are on the country.   It was their duty to support themselves and their families and in addition to help support the common government.   For one reason or another they have failed to make the grade. . . . The (relief) money has been given not because the victims of the hurricane have a right to it. . . . The assumption in the minds of the spokesmen was that they are entitled to support by right and to levy the taxes which support them in idleness.   It is a false

---

[1] *New York Times,* July 16, 1923.

[2] *Scribner's Magazine,* September, 1933, pp. 129, 130.

[3] Release of July 28, 1933.

[4] *United States News,* July 1–8, 1933.

assumption, and if allowed to go unchallenged it will place a premium on incompetence, laziness and shiftlessness." [1]

This typical capitalist paper has almost daily bitterly attacked Mr. Roosevelt's strenuous effort to save the tottering system of private capitalism by the President's invading of the precincts of privilege and power and the sacred rights of private wealth however amassed. It would be difficult to find in Bourbon literature before the French Revolution or in the Czarist press before the Russian Revolution anything more blind, selfish, reactionary or dangerous than such utterances. If the rich have the sacred right to their fortunes however made, and if the unemployed, for whom the capitalist system cannot provide honest work, have no right to the "charity" or relief of the system, how long will they suffer its monstrous injustice? Here at least Soviet Russia should teach us a lesson.

4. *Capitalism provides palaces, country houses and summer resorts for the rich: city slums, foreclosed mortgages, lost farms and homes for the poor.*—Typical of these palaces and resorts for the rich were those built by Mrs. William K. Vanderbilt, later Mrs. O. H. P. Belmont. After spending $3,000,-000 on her New York house, modelled after the Château de Blois, and $8,000,000 for her Marble Hall at Newport, she was ready to give the most costly balls and entertainments to further her social aims. After marrying her daughter unhappily to the Duke of Marlborough, divorcing her husband and marrying O. H. P. Belmont, she was ready to achieve her further impetuous ambitions by using her vast wealth and prestige as a leverage and a plaything.[2]

Meanwhile there were two-thirds of a million wretched people crowded into the slums of her city and over a hundred thousand darkened tenement rooms that never saw one ray of direct sunlight all the year round. It is, of course, not suggested that it was the fault of the irresponsible and socially ambitious Mrs. Vanderbilt that these slums existed. No doubt she gave her pittances to charity as generously and as conspic-

---

[1] *Chicago Tribune,* November 9, 1932.
[2] *Time,* February 6. 1933, p. 18.

uously as any. It was the *system* that gave monopolistic ownership in railways, the vital means of production, and land values which included the homes of the poor, to the few to play with or squander on their personal whims, instead of providing for the life of the masses. It is the *system* which is now being revealed in its stark injustice and inefficiency and against which we make our indictment.

When millions of people moved into New York City and gave value to the Astor lots and farms, the Astor family quickly amassed a fortune of over a hundred million dollars for themselves. In rents alone they sometimes "collected twenty-five to thirty million dollars a year." [1] While one family amassed this wealth from values created by the people, over 600,000 were living in slums with no share in the values they had produced, exploited by the rich in the rents of their miserable homes. It was the people who made these great fortunes in land, but it was the owners and not the people who enjoyed the wealth thus created.

The absentee private ownership of land, houses and mortgages in congested fortunes meant that every period of depression like the last would impoverish many of the owners of homes and farms who were in debt and give the power of foreclosure to the absentee capitalists. In Hartford, for instance, out of forty insurance companies one alone had foreclosed and taken over two thousand farms early in the depression. The farmers were steadily losing their farms and the homeowners their homes at the time of Mr. Roosevelt's inauguration. It remains to be seen how far this great experiment can save these endangered farms and homes and yet retain a system which tends to concentrate the ownership of all the essential things of life in relatively few private hands. We have nothing whatever against an Astor or a Vanderbilt. They are just as good and as important as any dweller in the slums, but they are no more so. Those who have come into close contact with the radical farmers of the West, now on the defensive, and with other revolting classes begin to see the handwriting on

---

[1] Burton K. Hendrick, in *The Age of Business*.

the wall, which slowly dooms the system now overripe and rotten. It is not the farms and homes of America which ultimately will be lost through foreclosure but the system itself which is now foredoomed.

5. *The power of credit, manipulation and "easy money" for the few: the growth of crime, racketeering and lawlessness among the poor who are now also seeking "easy money."*— Past all controversy, under a system of banking in America which was highly insecure, there had been an enormous concentration of wealth and the power of credit in the hands of relatively few men. We may take the Morgan firm, not as the worst but as among the best in the American banking world. No firm of bankers has had a better individual leadership. Mr. Thomas W. Lamont of J. P. Morgan & Company says: "No civilized country of modern times has suffered so cruelly from unscientific and inefficient currency and banking systems as has the United States in the last hundred and fifty years. Within that period the country has gone through a long series of banking collapses, due largely to like causes and bringing the American community prodigious losses." [1]

As indicating concentration of wealth some 200 big companies and corporations control 49.2 per cent, or practically half of all the non-banking corporate wealth of America, while twenty of the great banks concentrate more wealth and power than ten thousand smaller banks. Approximately 2,000 individuals out of a population of one hundred and twenty-five millions control and direct half of American industry. There has been some decentralization of ownership but a growing consolidation of control of wealth, banking and industry, in this country. [2]

The investigation by the Senate Committee in May and June, 1933, revealed that 24 partners of J. P. Morgan & Com-

---

[1] *Ibid,* p. 172. Mr. Pierre Jay, formerly Chairman of the Board of the Federal Reserve Bank of New York, writes of these bank failures: "The vast majority of them were due to mismanagement reflected principally in overlending, in exploitation by officers and directors and in some disregard of legal restrictions."

[2] *Ibid,* p. 127.

pany are directors of 89 other corporations, which possess assets of over 20 billion dollars, or about a billion dollars for every Morgan partner. The Morgan firm alone has brought out over six billion dollars in securities and financing since the war. The Morgan utility empire covers 36 states and sells over half the electric light and power in the United States. Their fixed capital of fifteen billion dollars is five times the federal government's annual budget and more than one-third the country's estimated annual income. The Senate inquiry showed that this firm made a profit of nearly ten million dollars in securities in 1930 and 1931, yet the bank's partners paid only $48,000 in Federal income taxes. They admitted that they paid none whatever in 1931 or 1932, while thousands of relatively poor men were paying such taxes. They were able to distribute a gratuity of $5,130,760 among their influential friends and the membership of the New York Chamber of Commerce, and to let a few favored individuals have Alleghany stock at $20 a share while it was selling to the general public at $35 a share.[1]

If the Morgan firm was the best, we need not recall the record of the worst of the private bankers. The same daily paper that records the disgraceful disclosures of the banking operations of the former head of America's largest bank with shameless speculation with depositors' money, gambling pools and tax evasions, narrates the death from suicide of workers living on the relief of public charity. One crazed father, out of work for a year, attacked his whole family with an axe as they slept, killing two and leaving the four remaining victims unconscious, after committing suicide himself. Another makes his mute appeal for the silent men in the capitalist breadlines and on behalf of the millions of jobless men in the following narrative: "Red tape was blamed for the suicide of Baggio Castiglione. Unemployed for two years, he went to a home relief bureau November 2nd. He waited in line six hours without breakfast, it was said, to sign a transfer application. Nervous and exhausted, he then walked two miles uptown to

---

[1] *New York Times,* May 26, 1933, and *New York World Telegram,* June 5, 1933.

an emergency work bureau, where after waiting two hours, he was told he would have to go back to the relief bureau and sign his name. He went back, authorities were told, and stood in line until almost nightfall. Then he went home and got into bed, refusing to move. The next day he arose and hanged himself."[1]

Thus we have side by side in almost every daily paper the record of rich bankers and speculators like the money changers in the temple, and the death by starvation or violence of the desperate poor. The signs of the times at the close of this epoch of capitalism are as clear as they were at the end of the Bourbon or Romanov epoch just before the French and Russian revolutions. But we are blinded by the same vested interests and ideas as they were. We are moral men in an immoral society, in an unjust and growingly impossible social order.

According to the Controller of the Currency, "during the past twelve years 10,484 banks with deposit liabilities of $4,882,-481,000 have failed in this country." Today millions of dollars belonging to innocent depositors are still locked up in closed banks, and millions are being hoarded in this country as the result of fear occasioned by bank failures. While in 1932 the unsound banks of America had only enough resources to cover their liabilities and while "the equity of their stockholders was almost zero," yet "the fiscal year 1932 established a new record in banking profits." [2]

It cannot be denied that the whole capitalist banking and financial system, with all its speculation, has added to the record of *Graft in Business* as narrated by John T. Flynn. In fourteen years Kreuger, the Swedish match king, collected over 750 million dollars from investors and lost half a billion dollars of the people's money. When the two billion dollar Insull bubble burst, after years of crooked accounting which had begun long before the depression, the public was defrauded of nearly $700,000,000, or almost as much as by Kreuger. James M. Beck testified before the House of Representatives: "The

---

[1] Associated Press report of November 13, 1933.

[2] Kirby Page, *Individualism and Socialism*. Many of the facts in this chapter are drawn from this source.

corporate life in this country is rotten to the core. . . . The losses have been in billions." [1] No wonder that Mr. Roosevelt at his inauguration thus testified against the bankers: "Practices of unscrupulous money changers stand indicted in the court of public opinion, rejected by the hearts and minds of men."

Graft in business leads to increased political corruption until Judge Samuel Seabury of New York is forced to conclude: "When you have a bad system of law plus corrupt administrators, you reach the lowest form of government known to man." [2] In seeking "easy money" big business is followed by corrupt politicians and in time by gangsters, racketeers and criminals. Their activities in America have been surveyed by the Wickersham Commission, which has been quoted at length in the chapter on *The Treatment of Criminals*. We thus have a concentration of wealth at one pole of the system of capitalism, and of crime, lawlessness and disorder at the other. Is it not evident that such a system of injustice is in unstable equilibrium?

6. *Competitive capitalism creates class conflict and recurring wars: the capitalist system is inevitably a war system.*—It is not surprising that such a system of owners and dependents, of wealth and poverty, of unequal privilege and injustice should automatically produce strife. A growingly educated working class, as it suffers from the periodic unemployment of the system and sees the march of privilege and privation side by side, will not forever tamely submit to these conditions. This is accentuated when capitalism and its evils come into glaring contrast with the Soviet system, which provides complete social insurance, the elimination of unemployment and gives the workers themselves the virtual ownership and control of all industry and the full sharing of the surplus values which they create. Undeniably capitalism has resulted in industrial warfare. Professor Sumner H. Schlichter, of the Harvard School

---

[1] *Ibid,* p. 99.
[2] *New York Times,* January 5, 1933.

of Business Administration, says: "Had we deliberately planned an industrial system which would create intense conflict between capital and labor, we could scarcely have devised one which would have achieved this result more completely than the existing economic order."   John R. Commons admits that since 1877 the system "has frequently resulted in civil war." [1]

As capitalism becomes international, as it pushes out to capture world markets and takes possession of the raw materials of backward countries, it develops into the phase of imperialism.   It then subjugates not only classes of dependents at home but whole peoples and races abroad.   It now extends in conquering empires over the globe until over half of Asia and all but one-twentieth of Africa have been brought under its sway.   But the awakening of these once backward peoples and "the revolt of Asia" foment revolution and threaten the system with war.

Competitive capitalism thus produces inevitable strife between classes, races and nations.   It actually results in periodic wars which have now become world wars.   The last World War was caused in part by economic competition between Germany and Great Britain.   The present menace of Germany to world peace has its basis in unjust and impossible economic conditions to which the capitalist Allied powers have subjected Germany as a practically servile state, after having broken the Fourteen Points which were offered as a basis for the armistice, and their promise made to Germany of disarmament.   Competitive capitalism thus moves in a vicious circle of class strife and war.

Dr. Harry Emerson Fosdick says: "Can capitalism so adjust itself to this new world, so move out from its old individualism dominated by the profit motive into a cooperative epoch of social planning and social control that it can become the servant of the welfare of all the people? If it can, it can survive. If it cannot, our children will have some form of Communism thrust upon them. Be sure of that."

[1] Sumner H. Schlichter, *Modern Economic Society,* p. 64, and *Senate Document No. 415,* p. 183.

Secretary Ickes, speaking in Philadelphia, said that the old *laissez faire* "rugged individualism" would now be a museum piece, and that the United States in repudiating the old capitalism had turned its back "definitely and finally upon an era that history will appraise as at once sordid, ruthless and glorious." He continued: "After all, we are not in the world to work like galley slaves for long hours at toilsome tasks in order to accumulate in the hands of two per cent of the population eighty per cent of the wealth of the country." [1]

We repeat that we are not blind to the many achievements of capitalism, especially in the field of production, but when we survey the whole system it does not seem fitted to survive in the form we have known it. Capitalism has placed a debt burden upon the people of America which cannot be borne. The 134 billion dollars of long-term debts in this country yield, even at four per cent interest, $5,360,000,000 annually, chiefly to the same owners who collect profit and rent. [2]

In dealing with the present economic order of capitalism it may be instructive to recall our relationship to the former system of slavery. That system affected not only some ten thousand owners and a million slaves, but lowered the standard of living for the poor whites of the South. Unconsciously it affected every member of the white and of the black races. It dragged more than one of the early presidents of the United States into adultery, until finally the wife of President Madison indignantly protested against this demoralizing system which was affecting the life of the home.

Yet the population as a whole was, as it were, asphyxiated by a system which was poisoning the very air it breathed. When William Lloyd Garrison declared that slavery must go, and stood for the complete abolition of the whole system by revolutionary though non-violent means, every church in Boston and New England closed its doors against him. He was mobbed in Boston and several other cities and a price was

---

[1] Secretary of the Interior Ickes speaking to the Board of Trade in Philadelphia, November 3, 1933.

[2] *Ibid*, p. 166. *The Internal Debts of the United States,* edited by Evans Clark, The Twentieth Century Fund.

placed upon his head in two states. If the churches after eighteen centuries, reading from their open Bibles, could not even see that slavery was wrong, is it not presumably highly probable that they would be as blind to the evils of the economic system of the present? Not only are their livelihood, their habits of life and thought, all bound up with the system of capitalism, but their ideas and attitudes and relationships have been largely derived from it.

These two economic systems of slavery and capitalism are not wholly dissimilar. Slavery intensively, in its complete domination of the individual slave, was worse than capitalism. But while rural slavery affected primarily a million slaves, urban capitalism affects more widely the whole population. If we include the death rate in the slums, the 26 million combatants and non-combatants killed in the last war, the 30 millions who have been unemployed during the depression and the insecurity of life for multitudes, the total impact of urban capitalism upon the whole population, except for the favored two per cent that Mr. Ickes mentions, is more widespread and devastating than that of slavery. Except for the individual slave, the evils of urban capitalism as a whole, if we include its concomitant of war, are worse than those of rural slavery.

Slavery at least furnished security for the slave. There was more security for the slave, for the serf and for the farmer's mule than there is today for the farmer himself who has lost his farm or for the unemployed worker on the streets of our great cities. Taken as a whole, and "glorious" as were some of its achievements, the old competitive capitalism has failed economically, it has failed internationally under the phase of imperialism, and it has failed morally. We repeat that the old system of rugged individualism and competitive capitalism is doomed. It is as doomed as slavery and for the same reason. There is a holdover of certain effects and elements of slavery and feudalism in the present system of capitalism, just as there are inevitable capitalistic elements that still persist in Soviet Russia.

In the United States, for instance, there are areas which are still feudal preserves, as in some of the mining regions of

Kentucky and West Virginia, and in Dearborn, Michigan, under the hitherto feudal control of Henry Ford. In the former there are regions where a few rich men or corporations like those of the Mellons, the Morgans and the United States Steel Corporation largely own the coal beneath the soil, the surface of the land, sometimes the church buildings, schools and the homes of the workers, who can often be turned out at a few days' notice as the victims of "yellow dog" contracts, if there is any disturbance of the conditions of almost absolute feudal control. Most of the churches have been identified in their interests and sympathies not with the workers but with the owners who contribute largely to their support and dominate the press, the courts, the legislation, the state and local governments through the ownership of the means of production in these regions.

My own private secretary, a devout theological student, under the burden of this situation went into the South to see if he could win any of the religious leaders and church people to sympathy with the cause of the workers. He utterly failed to do so. Although he could not agree with their economic theories and tactics, he was forced to admit that almost the only people who were suffering and sacrificing for the workers, ready to lose their liberty and their lives for them, were the Communists. The officials of the state government ordered him to leave the region. When he refused to go they debated whether they would "take him for a ride" and put a bullet through him, as had already been done to others, or throw him in jail. They followed the latter course and left him in jail until he agreed to leave the state. The Constitution did not control these areas just as it did not control similar areas in feudal England.

Many of the mines of these regions were not paying the operators during the depression. The bishop of the diocese of Kentucky in the starvation-ridden coal fields of human misery was bitter in his condemnation not of those responsible for the economic exploitation of the region, but of the social workers guilty of "gratuitous impertinence" in coming in from

the outside with "foreign agitators" to let the world know of the misery of the Kentucky hills. The good bishop and most of the other church leaders, of course conscientiously and all unconsciously, took their stand just where the ecclesiastical forces did in Czarist Russia, and in the time of Constantine, and possibly even in the time of the Scribes and Pharisees. Once again the Church was found on the economically strong side, but the morally wrong side of the economic issue of the day.

We do not question the *bona fides* of men who are still honestly living in feudal areas or times. We do not question the good faith of former President Herbert Hoover when he says: "I emerge an individualist—an unashamed individualist. . . . We dare not abandon self-interest as a motive force." [1] We do not even question the sincere conviction of another American business man, William Kixmiller, when, even in 1933, he says: "The solution literally is Bigger and Better Capitalism. . . . Chicago is the most progressive city in the world because politically it is the worst. . . . Capitalism fits the biological nature of mankind" [2]—just as slavery once did.

We do not question the good faith of Henry Ford any more than we do of any feudal lord in old England who had his private gallows. Mr. Ford says "that every man should take care of himself and be responsible to himself is the foundation of American life." Many point to Mr. Ford as one who has amassed a fortune by methods which have at the same time benefited the whole community, not by speculation or monopoly, but by sheer mechanical, financial and executive genius. As he is undeniably a typical capitalist we must examine his methods a little more in detail. He began three decades ago in 1903 with a paid-up capital of $28,000 and a nominal capitalization of $100,000. In 1924 Hornblower and Weeks offered to pay a billion dollars for the company but the offer was refused. In 1927 the business was estimated as worth from a billion and a half to two billion dollars. Ford's

---

[1] Herbert Hoover, *Individualism*, pp. 7–10, 17, 66.
[2] William Kixmiller, *Can Business Build a Great Age?* pp. 85, 249, 301, 302.

income was then estimated by the *New York World* as nearly two hundred dollars a minute, $11,415 an hour, $273,976 a day, or about $80,000,000 a year.[1]   Working at $6 a day for fifty years it would require 11,500 workers to earn a billion dollars.   Mr. John S. Gray, who invested $10,500 in the Ford business at the beginning, received in dividends and principal $36,605,075 in sixteen years, or 21,700 per cent annually on the money he had invested.[2]   His profits were negligible, however, compared to Mr. Ford's.

For three decades Mr. Ford has claimed the absolute right to scrap his machines or lay off his men at a moment's notice without further obligation to them.   When I went to Detroit to attend the Student-Faculty Conference some two years ago one of Mr. Ford's 60,000 employees came to see me, complained of the treatment he had received, and wrote me the following statement of his case: "After working for this man for nearly twenty years, hard and faithfully, with no fault found in my work, I am left today, after a score of years of faithful service, $800 in debt, owing five months' rent, served with notice of eviction by my landlord, and with nothing with which to face the future.   Here I am at the moment laid off for a number of weeks in enforced idleness.   When we go back to work, this man's skillful publicity agent will inform the world that he is employing sixty or seventy thousand men.   It will omit to mention the fact that weeks ago we were laid off with no provision whatever.   When I last had work it was three days a week, before that it was four days a week.   I am now earning $24 a week.   This would have been less than $1500 a year as one of the poorer paid half of American working men, simply because I could not get regular work from this man.   And this has been true for a number of years.

"Is it just, when these vast values were socially created, when we all worked together to produce this result, that one man should make a fortune estimated at two billion dollars, with an income in good times of over $270,000 a day or eighty mil-

---

[1] *New York World,* February 4, 1927, and *The World Tomorrow,* October, 1927.

[2] Kirby Page, *Individualism and Socialism,* p. 166.

lion dollars a year? Is it right that, speeding up production under these high pressure methods, where we have to do ten hours' work a day in eight hours or less, paid only for eight hours, that we are left unprovided for, with no responsibility on his part whether we are employed or unemployed, whether we live or starve? Is not this typical of the whole system of monarchic and competitive capitalism? Is it just, is it right, is it human? How long will the workers be contented with this? For myself, the one purpose of my remaining years is to open the eyes of the workers to see their unfair, precarious and degraded position, living from hand to mouth, working to amass vast fortunes for the few irresponsible capitalists, many of whom own no responsibility to these multitudes who toil for them to make their wealth."

Henry Ford seems to have been an irresponsible kind of Jekyll-Hyde, with almost a dual personality, sometimes generous, sometimes ruthless. Though he claimed that any individual or group could make their own complaints, on principle and in practice he indignantly denied labor's right of collective bargaining. During the depression when other employers were giving hundreds of thousands of dollars for the relief of the unemployed workers of Detroit, Mr. Ford would not admit his own responsibility for the unemployed and claimed immunity in his feudal suburb of Dearborn.

In order to give publicity to their wretched condition the workers decided upon a peaceful demonstration, to march to Ford's River Rouge plant and ask him either to give his former workers employment or else contribute his share to unemployment relief as the other employers of Detroit were doing. On the evening of March 11th at 7:30 P.M. the procession, entirely unarmed, marched to Ford's plant to make their appeal. They thus state the result of their plea: "Four workers lie dead while scores are wounded as a result of bestial, coldblooded and deliberate massacre of the Ford Hunger March. This massacre is Ford's answer to the demand for jobs or relief of the unarmed, unemployed Ford workers. . . . The sudden and murderous attack of Ford's police left the workers no choice. . . . Grimly and heroically defending themselves against tear-

gas, clubs and pistols with nothing but bare fists and stones, the aroused and angry workers drove the Dearborn cops before them in an inglorious retreat. At Gate No. 4 firehoses were brought into play and a number of workers were shot, some of them fatally. . . . When the workers were leaving the Ford plant, a murderous machinegun fire was poured out upon the unprotected backs of the unarmed, unemployed men, women and youth. . . . Join the mass funeral Saturday, 2 P.M., at the Workers Home."

And all this is in a plant that has made more boasts of high wages than any in the world, and that has most embodied the mechanical, financial and executive genius of the age. Mr. Ford can truly say that his workers have their own autos and radios and conveniences that kings did not possess in feudal times. But he and many other employers should realize that we are no longer living in feudal times and that the workers will not much longer accept such feudal conditions. These men do not realize that even if the N.R.A. and the New Deal should fail they cannot return to "the good old times" of *laissez faire* capitalism, for the same reason that Russia will never return to Czarism. If the attempt is made by a fascist dictatorship of big business and every non-violent plan fails, there will be nothing left but the Russian method of violence. Among the many lessons that may be learned from the Russian experiment none is more obvious or more final than this.

We repeat that we are today nearing the end of an epoch. We are standing on the threshold of a new era. We are already in the midst of the greatest transition of all history, in the midst of what at the moment of writing is still non-violent revolution. We cannot put the clock back permanently. Progress will surely come, early or late, by unhindered evolution or by revolution. The new social order must include both justice and liberty. It must embrace, or make room for, the five great achievements of the human race—culture, moral and spiritual insight, law and order, scientific achievement, and, last but not least,—that which has hitherto been the missing link of human experience—socialization, social justice, the sharing of the good life for *all*.

APPENDIX I

Karl Marx (1818–1883) was born at Treves in Rhenish Prussia. His ancestors on both sides were Jewish rabbis but he himself remained anti-semitic in sympathy. In the University of Berlin Marx threw himself with tremendous intensity into the study of the classics in Latin and Greek, philosophy, law, history, literature and art. He later burned three volumes of his original poems which recorded the strenuous nature of his search for truth and his dawning social passion, as in his lines:

> *"Ne'er can I perform in calmness*
> *What has seized my soul with might,*
> *But must strive and struggle onward*
> *In a ceaseless, restless fight."*

In his philosophical struggle he turned his back upon the abstract idealism of Kant and Fichte and was taken captive by his great master Hegel and his dialectic method. His association with Feuerbach turned him to materialistic realism but he forever retained Hegel's method of interpreting life and history. He married the beautiful and gifted daughter of a Prussian official, Jenny von Westphalen, a descendant on her mother's side of the Earl of Argyle, and she became the faithful companion of his labors in poverty and hardship.

In his passionate search for truth he sacrificed the ambition of his father that he should become a successful lawyer, and the hope of a professor's chair in the University of Bonn. He turned temporarily to journalism and literary work in Germany and France. His association with Friedrich Engels, the son of a rich German manufacturer who owned a cotton mill near Manchester, led to a life-long friendship and cooperation between these kindred spirits. Marx finally settled in London, where for thirty-four years he pursued his studies and writing in the British Museum.

Marx and Engels had founded a German workers' society and

277

joined the League of the Just which became later the Communist League. At its second congress in London in 1847 Marx and Engels were commissioned to draw up a statement of the basis of the organization. This appeared in 1848 as the *Communist Manifesto* which gave a philosophy and a program of action to the gathering movement, as Rousseau's *Social Contract* had to the French Revolution.

For his first ten years in London as correspondent of the *New York Tribune,* Marx had at times to pawn his clothes and "was hardly over the verge of starvation." While Darwin was devoting twenty years to his hypothesis of Evolution, Marx worked for three decades, often sixteen hours a day, on his social system. What Darwin did for biology Marx did for sociology. Each was the leader of a movement which became a great historic watershed.

Marx became the leading spirit in the First International, organized in 1864. In 1867 appeared the first ponderous volume of his *Capital.* After the last decade of struggle against pain and disease, studying higher mathematics and the Russian language in his periods of recreation, he died peacefully in 1883.

The First International was organized as the International Working Men's Association. Its ten years of troubled existence were ended by the division between the Socialists led by Marx, and the Anarchists led by Bakunin, "the apostle of universal destruction." Fifteen years later, in 1889, the Second International was founded as a loose organization of the World's Labor and Socialist Parties. The World War destroyed the unity of all such international workers' organizations. In 1919 the Third International was organized uniting the Communist Parties of all nations under a controlling central organ in Moscow. This is the Comintern, or Communist International.

As to the title of the *Communist Manifesto,* Engels wrote in the preface: "Socialism was, in 1847, a middle-class movement, Communism a working-class movement. Socialism was, on the Continent at least, 'respectable'; Communism was the very opposite. And as our notion, from the very beginning, was that 'the emancipation of the working class must be the act of the working class itself,' there could be no doubt as to which of the two names we must take. Moreover, we have, ever since, been far from repudiating it.

"The *Manifesto* being our joint production, I consider myself

bound to state that the fundamental proposition which forms its nucleus, belongs to Marx. That proposition is: that in every historical epoch, the prevailing mode of economic production and exchange, and the social organization necessarily following from it, form the basis upon which is built up, and from which alone can be explained, the political and intellectual history of that epoch; that consequently the whole history of mankind (since the dissolution of primitive tribal society, holding land in common ownership) has been a history of class struggles, contests between exploiting and exploited, ruling and oppressed classes; that the history of these class struggles forms a series of evolution in which now-a-days a stage has been reached where the exploited and oppressed class—the proletariat—cannot attain its emancipation from the sway of the exploiting and ruling class—the bourgeoisie—without, at the same time, and once and for all, emancipating society at large from all exploitation, oppression, class-distinction and class struggles.

"This proposition which, in my opinion, is destined to do for history what Darwin's theory has done for biology, we, both of us, had been gradually approaching for some years before 1845."

In the following pages the *Manifesto* is quoted almost in full in all its vital parts which apply to conditions today. As a potent historical document that is furnishing not only the philosophy but the program of action for increasing numbers of men within and without Russia, it needs to be understood whether by those who agree or who disagree with it.

MANIFESTO OF THE COMMUNIST PARTY

By Karl Marx and Friedrich Engels

A spectre is haunting Europe—the spectre of Communism. All the powers of old Europe have entered into a holy alliance to exorcise this spectre; Pope and Czar, Metternich and Guizot, French Radicals and German police-spies.

Where is the party in opposition that has not been decried as communistic by its opponents in power? Where the Opposition that has not hurled back the branding reproach of Communism, against the more advanced opposition parties, as well as against its reactionary adversaries?

Two things result from this fact.

I. Communism is already acknowledged by all European Powers to be itself a Power.

II. It is high time that Communists should openly, in the face of the whole world, publish their views, their aims, their tendencies, and meet this nursery tale of the Spectre of Communism with a Manifesto of the party itself.

To this end, Communists of various nationalities have assembled in London, and sketched the following Manifesto, to be published in the English, French, German, Italian, Flemish and Danish languages.

I

Bourgeois and Proletarians [1]

The history of all hitherto existing society is the history of class struggles.[2]

Freeman and slave, patrician and plebeian, lord and serf, guild-master and journeyman, in a word, oppressor and oppressed, stood in constant opposition to one another, carried on an uninterrupted, now hidden, now open fight, a fight that each time ended, either in a revolutionary re-constitution of society at large, or in the common ruin of the contending classes.

The modern bourgeois Society that has sprouted from the ruins of feudal society, has not done away with class antagonisms. It has but established new classes, new conditions of oppression, new forms of struggle in place of the old ones.

---

[1] Footnotes by Engels: By bourgeoisie is meant the class of modern Capitalists, owners of the means of social production and employers of wage-labor. By proletariat, the class of modern wage-laborers who, having no means of production of their own, are reduced to selling their labor-power in order to live.

[2] That is, all written history. In 1847, the pre-history of society, the social organization existing previous to recorded history, was all but unknown. Since then, Haxthausen discovered common ownership of land in Russia, Maurer proved it to be the social foundation from which all Teutonic races started in history, and by and by village communities were found to be, or to have been, the primitive form of society everywhere from India to Ireland. The inner organization of this primitive Communistic society was laid bare, in its typical form, by Morgan's crowning discovery of the true nature of the gens and its relation to the tribe. With the dissolution of these primeval communities society begins to be differentiated into separate and finally antagonistic classes. I have attempted to retrace this process of dissolution in "The Origin of the Family, Private Property and the State." (Chicago, Charles H. Kerr & Co.)

Our epoch, the epoch of the bourgeoisie, possesses, however, this distinctive feature; it has simplified the class antagonisms. Society as a whole is more and more splitting up into two great hostile camps, into two great classes directly facing each other: Bourgeoisie and Proletariat.

The discovery of America, the rounding of the Cape, opened up fresh ground for the rising bourgeoisie. The East-Indian and Chinese markets, the colonization of America, trade with the colonies, the increase in the means of exchange and in commodities generally, gave to commerce, to navigation, to industry, an impulse never before known, and thereby, to the revolutionary element in the tottering feudal society, a rapid development.

The feudal system of industry, under which industrial production was monopolized by closed guilds, now no longer sufficed for the growing wants of the new markets. The manufacturing system took its place. Steam and machinery revolutionized industrial production. The place of manufacture was taken by the giant, Modern Industry, the place of the industrial middle-class, by industrial millionaires, the leaders of whole industrial armies, the modern bourgeois.

Modern industry has established the world-market, for which the discovery of America paved the way. This market has given an immense development to commerce, to navigation, to communication by land. This development has, in its turn, reacted on the extension of industry; and in proportion as industry, commerce, navigation, railways extended, in the same proportion the bourgeoisie developed, increased its capital, and pushed into the background every class handed down from the Middle Ages.

We see, therefore, how the modern bourgeoisie is itself the product of a long course of development, of a series of revolutions in the modes of production and of exchange. Each step in the development of the bourgeoisie was accompanied by a corresponding political advance of that class. An oppressed class under the sway of the feudal nobility, an armed and self-governing association in the mediæval commune, serving either the semi-feudal or the absolute monarchy as a counterpoise against the nobility, and, in fact, corner stone of the great monarchies in general, the bourgeoisie has at last, since the establishment of Modern Industry and of the world-market, conquered for itself, in the modern representative State, exclusive political sway. The executive of the

modern State is but a committee for managing the common affairs of the whole bourgeoisie.

The bourgeoisie, historically, has played a most revolutionary part. The bourgeoisie, wherever it has got the upper hand, has put an end to all feudal, patriarchal, idyllic relations. It has pitilessly torn asunder the motley feudal ties that bound man to his "natural superiors," and has left remaining no other nexus between man and man than naked self-interest, than callous "cash payment." It has drowned the most heavenly ecstasies of religious fervor, of chivalrous enthusiasm, of philistine sentimentalism, in the icy water of egotistical calculation. It has resolved personal worth into exchange value, and in place of the numberless indefeasible chartered freedoms, has set up that single, unconscionable freedom—Free Trade. In one word, for exploitation, veiled by religious and political illusions, it has substituted naked, shameless, direct, brutal exploitation.

The bourgeoisie has stripped of its halo every occupation hitherto honored and looked up to with reverent awe. It has converted the physician, the lawyer, the priest, the poet, the man of science, into its paid wage-laborers. The bourgeoisie has torn away from the family its sentimental veil, and has reduced the family relation to a mere money relation. It has been the first to show what man's activity can bring about. It has accomplished wonders far surpassing Egyptian pyramids, Roman aqueducts, and Gothic cathedrals; it has conducted expeditions that put in the shade all former Exoduses of nations and crusades.

The bourgeoisie cannot exist without constantly revolutionizing the instruments of production, and thereby the relations of production, and with them the whole relations of society. Constant revolutionizing of production, uninterrupted disturbance of all social conditions, everlasting uncertainty and agitation distinguish the bourgeois epoch from all earlier ones. All fixed, fast-frozen relations, with their train of ancient and venerable prejudices and opinions, are swept away, all new-formed ones become antiquated before they can ossify. All that is solid melts into air, all that is holy is profaned, and man is at last compelled to face with sober senses, his real conditions of life, and his relations with his kind.

The need of a constantly expanding market for its products chases the bourgeoisie over the whole surface of the globe. It must nestle everywhere, settle everywhere, establish connections everywhere.

The bourgeoisie has through its exploitation of the world-market given a cosmopolitan character to production and consumption in every country. All old-established national industries have been destroyed or are daily being destroyed. They are dislodged by new industries, whose introduction becomes a life and death question for all civilized nations, by industries that no longer work up indigenous raw material, but raw material drawn from the remotest zones; industries whose products are consumed, not only at home, but in every quarter of the globe. In place of the old wants, satisfied by the productions of the country, we find new wants, requiring for their satisfaction the products of distant lands and climes. In place of the old local and national seclusion and self-sufficiency, we have intercourse in every direction, universal inter-dependence of nations. And as in material, so also in intellectual production. The intellectual creations of individual nations become common property. National one-sidedness and narrow-mindedness become more and more impossible, and from the numerous national and local literatures there arises a world-literature.

The bourgeoisie, by the rapid improvement of all instruments of production, by the immensely facilitated means of communication, draws all, even the most barbarian, nations into civilization. The cheap prices of its commodities are the heavy artillery with which it batters down all Chinese walls, with which it forces the barbarians' intensely obstinate hatred of foreigners to capitulate. It compels all nations, on pain of extinction, to adopt the bourgeois mode of production; it compels them to introduce what it calls civilization into their midst, i.e., to become bourgeois themselves. In a word, it creates a world after its own image.

The bourgeoisie has subjected the country to the rule of the towns. It has created enormous cities, has greatly increased the urban population as compared with the rural, and has thus rescued a considerable part of the population from the idiocy of rural life. Just as it has made the country dependent on the towns, so it has made barbarian and semi-barbarian countries dependent on the civilized ones, nations of peasants on nations of bourgeois, the East on the West.

It has agglomerated population, centralized means of production, and has concentrated property in a few hands. The necessary consequence of this was political centralization. Independent, or but loosely connected provinces, with separate interests, laws, gov-

ernments, and systems of taxation, became lumped together in one
nation, with one government, one code of laws, one national class-
interest, one frontier and one customs-tariff.

The bourgeoisie, during its rule of scarce one hundred years, has
created more massive and more colossal productive forces than have
all preceding generations together. Subjection of Nature's forces
to man, machinery, application of chemistry to industry and agriculture, steam-navigation, railways, electric telegraphs, clearing of
whole continents for cultivation, canalization of rivers, whole populations conjured out of the ground—what earlier century had even
a presentiment that such productive forces slumbered in the lap
of social labor?

We see then: the means of production and of exchange on whose
foundation the bourgeoisie built itself up, were generated in feudal
society. At a certain stage in the development of these means of
production and of exchange, the conditions under which feudal
society produced and exchanged, the feudal organization of agriculture and manufacturing industry, in one word, the feudal relations
of property became no longer compatible with the already developed productive forces; they became so many fetters. They had
to burst asunder; they were burst asunder.

Into their places stepped free competition, accompanied by a
social and political constitution adapted to it, and by the economical
and political sway of the bourgeois class.

A similar movement is going on before our own eyes. Modern
bourgeois society with its relations of production, of exchange and
of property, a society that has conjured up such gigantic means of
production and of exchange, is like the sorcerer, who is no longer
able to control the powers of the nether world whom he has called
up by his spells. For many a decade past the history of industry
and commerce is but the history of the revolt of modern productive forces against modern conditions of production, against the
property relations that are the conditions for the existence of the
bourgeoisie and of its rule. It is enough to mention the commercial
crises that by their periodical return put on its trial, each time more
threateningly, the existence of the entire bourgeois society. In these
crises a great part not only of the existing products, but also of
the previously created productive forces, are periodically destroyed.
In these crises there breaks out an epidemic that, in all earlier epochs,
would have seemed an absurdity—the epidemic of over-production.
Society suddenly finds itself put back into a state of momentary

barbarism; it appears as if a famine, a universal war of devastation, had cut off the supply of every means of subsistence; industry and commerce seem to be destroyed; and why? Because there is too much civilization, too much means of subsistence, too much industry, too much commerce. The productive forces at the disposal of society no longer tend to further the development of the conditions of bourgeois property; on the contrary, they have become too powerful for these conditions, by which they are fettered, and so soon as they overcome these fetters, they bring disorder into the whole of bourgeois society, endanger the existence of bourgeois property. The conditions of bourgeois society are too narrow to comprise the wealth created by them. And how does the bourgeoisie get over these crises? On the one hand by enforced destruction of a mass of productive forces; on the other, by the conquest of new markets, and by the more thorough exploitation of the old ones. That is to say, by paving the way for more extensive and more destructive crises, and by diminishing the means whereby crises are prevented.

The weapons with which the bourgeoisie felled feudalism to the ground are now turned against the bourgeoisie itself. But not only has the bourgeoisie forged the weapons that bring death to itself; it has also called into existence the men who are to wield those weapons—the modern working-class—the proletarians.

In proportion as the bourgeoisie, i.e., capital, is developed, in the same proportion is the proletariat, the modern working-class, developed, a class of laborers, who live only so long as they find work, and who find work only so long as their labor increases capital. These laborers, who must sell themselves piecemeal, are a commodity, like every other article of commerce, and are consequently exposed to all the vicissitudes of competition, to all the fluctuations of the market.

Owing to the extensive use of machinery and to division of labor, the work of the proletarians has lost all individual character, and, consequently, all charm for the workman. He becomes an appendage of the machine, and it is only the most simple, most monotonous, and most easily acquired knack that is required of him. Hence, the cost of production of a workman is restricted, almost entirely, to the means of subsistence that he requires for his maintenance, and for the propagation of his race. But the price of a commodity, and also of labor, is equal to its cost of production. In proportion, therefore, as the repulsiveness of the work increases, the wage de-

creases. Nay more, in proportion as the use of machinery and division of labor increases, in the same proportion the burden of toil also increases, whether by prolongation of the working hours, by increase of the work enacted in a given time, or by increased speed of the machinery, etc.

Modern industry has converted the little workshop of the patriarchal master into the great factory of the industrial capitalist. Masses of laborers, crowded into the factories, are organized like soldiers. As privates of the industrial army they are placed under the command of a perfect hierarchy of officers and sergeants. Not only are they the slaves of the bourgeois class, and of the bourgeois State, they are daily and hourly enslaved by the machine, by the over-looker, and, above all, by the individual bourgeois manufacturer himself. The more openly this despotism proclaims gain to be its end and aim, the more petty, the more hateful and the more embittering it is.

The less the skill and exertion or strength implied in manual labor, in other words, the more modern industry becomes developed, the more is the labor of men superseded by that of women. Differences of age and sex have no longer any distinctive social validity for the working class. All are instruments of labor, more or less expensive to use, according to their age and sex.

No sooner is the exploitation of the laborer by the manufacturer so far at an end, that he receives his wages in cash, than he is set upon by the other portions of the bourgeoisie, the landlord, the shopkeeper, the pawnbroker, etc.

The lower strata of the middle class—the small tradespeople, shopkeepers, and retired tradesmen generally, the handicraftsmen and peasants—all these sink gradually into the proletariat, partly because their diminutive capital does not suffice for the scale on which Modern Industry is carried on, and is swamped in the competition with the large capitalists, partly because their specialized skill is rendered worthless by new methods of production. Thus the proletariat is recruited from all classes of the population.

The proletariat goes through various stages of development. With its birth begins the struggle with the bourgeoisie. At first the contest is carried on by individual laborers, then by the workpeople of a factory, then by the operatives of one trade.

But with the development of industry the proletariat not only increases in number, it becomes concentrated in greater masses, its strength grows, and it feels that strength more. The various in-

terests and conditions of life within the ranks of the proletariat are more and more equalized, in proportion as machinery obliterates all distinctions of labor, and nearly everywhere reduces wages to the same low level. The growing competition among the bourgeois, and the resulting commercial crises, make the wages of the workers ever more fluctuating. The unceasing improvement of machinery, ever more rapidly developing, makes their livelihood more and more precarious; the collisions between individual workmen and individual bourgeois take more and more the character of collisions between two classes. Thereupon the workers begin to form combinations, Trades' Unions, against the bourgeois; they club together in order to keep up the rate of wages; they found permanent associations in order to make provision beforehand for these occasional revolts. Here and there the contest breaks out into riots.

Now and then the workers are victorious, but only for a time. The real fruit of their battles lies, not in the immediate result, but in the ever expanding union of the workers. But every class struggle is a political struggle. And that union, to attain which the burghers of the Middle Ages, with their miserable highways, required centuries, the modern proletarians, thanks to railways, achieve in a few years.

This organization of the proletarians into a class, and consequently into a political party, is continually being upset again by the competition between the workers themselves. But it ever rises up again, stronger, firmer, mightier. It compels legislative recognition of particular interests of the workers, by taking advantage of the divisions among the bourgeoisie itself. Thus the ten-hour bill in England was carried.

Finally, in times when the class-struggle nears the decisive hour, the process of dissolution going on within the ruling class, in fact, within the whole range of old society, assumes such a violent, glaring character, that a small section of the ruling class cuts itself adrift, and joins the revolutionary class, the class that holds the future in its hands. Just as, therefore, at an earlier period, a section of the nobility went over to the bourgeoisie, so now a portion of the bourgeoisie goes over to the proletariat, and in particular, a portion of the bourgeois ideologists, who have raised themselves to the level of comprehending theoretically the historical movements as a whole.

Of all the classes that stand face to face with the bourgeoisie today, the proletariat alone is a really revolutionary class. The

other classes decay and finally disappear in the face of modern industry; the proletariat is its special and essential product.

The lower middle-class, the small manufacturer, the shopkeeper, the artisan, the peasant, all these fight against the bourgeoisie, to save from extinction their existence as fractions of the middle class. They are, therefore, not revolutionary, but conservative. Nay more, they are reactionary, for they try to roll back the wheel of history.

The "dangerous class," the social scum, that passively rotting mass thrown off by the lowest layers of old society, may, here and there, be swept into the movement by a proletarian revolution; its conditions of life, however, prepare it far more for the part of a bribed tool of reactionary intrigue.

The proletarian is without property; his relation to his wife and children has no longer anything in common with the bourgeois family-relations; modern industrial labor, modern subjection to capital, the same in England as in France, in America as in Germany, has stripped him of every trace of national character. Law, morality, religion, are to him so many bourgeois prejudices, behind which lurk in ambush just as many bourgeois interests.

All the preceding classes that got the upper hand, sought to fortify their already acquired status by subjecting society at large to their conditions of appropriation. The proletarians cannot become masters of the productive forces of society, except by abolishing their own previous mode of appropriation, and thereby also every other previous mode of appropriation. They have nothing of their own to secure and to fortify; their mission is to destroy all previous securities for, and insurances of, individual property.

All previous historical movements were movements of minorities, or in the interest of minorities. The proletarian movement is the self-conscious, independent movement of the immense majority, in the interest of the immense majority. The proletariat, the lowest stratum of our present society, cannot stir, cannot raise itself up, without the whole superincumbent strata of official society being sprung into the air.

Though not in substance, yet in form, the struggle of the proletariat with the bourgeoisie is at first a national struggle. The proletariat of each country must, of course, first of all settle matters with its own bourgeoisie.

In depicting the most general phases of the development of the proletariat, we traced the more or less veiled civil war, raging within existing society, up to the point where that war breaks out into

open revolution, and where the violent overthrow of the bourgeoisie lays the foundation for the sway of the proletariat.

Hitherto, every form of society has been based, as we have already seen, on the antagonism of oppressing and oppressed classes. But in order to oppress a class, certain conditions must be assured to it under which it can, at least, continue its slavish existence. The serf, in the period of serfdom, raised himself to membership in the commune, just as the petty bourgeois, under the yoke of feudal absolutism, managed to develop into a bourgeois. The modern laborer, on the contrary, instead of rising with the progress of industry, sinks deeper and deeper below the conditions of existence of his own class. He becomes a pauper, and pauperism develops more rapidly than population and wealth. And here it becomes evident that the bourgeoisie is unfit any longer to be the ruling class in society, and to impose its conditions of existence upon society as an over-riding law. It is unfit to rule, because it is incompetent to assure an existence to its slave within his slavery, because it cannot help letting him sink into such a state that it has to feed him, instead of being fed by him. Society can no longer live under this bourgeoisie, in other words, its existence is no longer compatible with society.

The essential condition for the existence, and for the sway of the bourgeois class, is the formation and augmentation of capital; the condition for capital is wage-labor. Wage-labor rests exclusively on competition between the laborers. The advance of industry, whose involuntary promotor is the bourgeoisie, replaces the isolation of the laborers, due to competition, by their involuntary combination, due to association. The development of Modern Industry, therefore, cuts from under its feet the very foundation on which the bourgeoisie produces and appropriates products. What the bourgeoisie therefore produces, above all, are its own gravediggers. Its fall and the victory of the proletariat are equally inevitable.

II

Proletarians and Communists

In what relation do the Communists stand to the proletarians as a whole? The Communists do not form a separate party opposed to other working-class parties. They have no interests separate and apart from those of the proletariat as a whole. They do not

set up any sectarian principles of their own, by which to shape and mould the proletarian movement.

The Communists are distinguished from the other working class parties by this only: 1. In the national struggles of the proletarians of the different countries, they point out and bring to the front the common interests of the entire proletariat independently of all nationality. 2. In the various stages of development which the struggle of the working class against the bourgeoisie has to pass through, they always and everywhere represent the interests of the movement as a whole.

The Communists, therefore, are on the one hand, practically, the most advanced and resolute section of the working class parties of every country, that section which pushes forward all others; on the other hand, theoretically, they have over the great mass of the proletariat the advantage of clearly understanding the line of march, the conditions, and the ultimate general results of the proletarian movement.

The immediate aim of the Communists is the same as that of all the other proletarian parties; formation of the proletariat into a class, overthrow of the bourgeois supremacy, a conquest of political power by the proletariat. The theoretical conclusions of the Communists are in no way based on ideas or principles that have been invented, or discovered, by this or that would-be universal reformer.

They merely express, in general terms, actual relations springing from an existing class struggle, from a historical movement going on under our very eyes. The abolition of existing property relations is not at all a distinctive feature of Communism.

All property relations in the past have continually been subject to historical change consequent upon the change in historical conditions.

The French Revolution, for example, abolished feudal property in favor of bourgeois property. The distinguishing feature of Communism is not the abolition of property generally, but the abolition of bourgeois property. But modern bourgeois private property is the final and most complete expression of the system of producing and appropriating products, that is based on class antagonism, on the exploitation of the many by the few. In this sense, the theory of the Communists may be summed up in the single sentence: Abolition of private property.

We Communists have been reproached with the desire of abolishing the right of personally acquiring property as the fruit of a

man's own labor, which property is alleged to be the ground work of all personal freedom, activity and independence.

Hard-won, self-acquired, self-earned property! Do you mean the property of the petty artisan and of the small peasant, a form of property that preceded the bourgeois form? There is no need to abolish that; the development of industry has to a great extent already destroyed it, and is still destroying it daily.

Or do you mean modern bourgeois private property? But does wage-labor create any property for the laborer? Not a bit. It creates capital, i.e., that kind of property which exploits wage-labor, and which cannot increase except upon condition of getting a new supply of wage-labor for fresh exploitation. Property, in its present form, is based on the antagonism of capital and wage-labor. Let us examine both sides of this antagonism.

To be a capitalist is to have not only a purely personal, but a social status in production. Capital is a collective product, and only by the united action of many members, nay, in the last resort, only by the united action of all members of society, can it be set in motion.

Capital is, therefore, not a personal, it is a social power. When, therefore, capital is converted into common property, into the property of all members of society, personal property is not thereby transformed into social property. It is only the social character of the property that is changed. It loses its class-character.

Let us now take wage-labor.

The average price of wage-labor is the minimum wage, i.e., that quantum of the means of subsistence, which is absolutely requisite to keep the laborer in bare existence as a laborer. What, therefore, the wage-laborer appropriates by means of his labor merely suffices to prolong and reproduce a bare existence. We by no means intend to abolish this personal appropriation of the products of labor, an appropriation that is made for the maintenance and reproduction of human life, and that leaves no surplus wherewith to command the labor of others. All that we want to do away with is the miserable character of this appropriation, under which the laborer lives merely to increase capital, and is allowed to live only in so far as the interest of the ruling class requires it.

In bourgeois society, living labor is but a means to increase accumulated labor. In Communist society, accumulated labor is but a means to widen, to enrich, to promote the existence of the laborer.

In bourgeois society, therefore, the past dominates the present; in Communist society, the present dominates the past. In bourgeois society capital is independent and has individuality, while the living person is dependent and has no individuality.

And the abolition of this state of things is called by the bourgeois, abolition of individuality and freedom! And rightly so. The abolition of bourgeois individuality, bourgeois independence, and bourgeos freedom is undoubtedly aimed at.

By freedom is meant, under the present bourgeois conditions of production, free trade, free selling and buying.

But if selling and buying disappears, free selling and buying disappears also. This talk about free selling and buying, and all the other "brave words" of our bourgeoisie about freedom in general, have a meaning, if any, only in contrast with restricted selling and buying, with the fettered traders of the Middle Ages, but have no meaning when opposed to the Communistic abolition of buying and selling, of the bourgeois conditions of production, and of the bourgeoisie itself.

You are horrified at our intending to do away with private property. But in your existing society, private property is already done away with for nine-tenths of the population; its existence for the few is solely due to its non-existence in the hands of those nine-tenths. You reproach us, therefore, with intending to do away with a form of property, the necessary condition for whose existence is the non-existence of any property for the immense majority of society.

In one word, you reproach us with intending to do away with your property. Precisely so; that is just what we intend. From the moment when labor can no longer be converted into capital, money, or rent, into a social power capable of being monopolized, i.e., from the moment when individual property can no longer be transformed into bourgeois property, into capital, from that moment, you say, individuality vanishes.

You must, therefore, confess that by "individual" you mean no other person than the bourgeois, than the middle-class owner of property. This person must, indeed, be swept out of the way, and made impossible.

Communism deprives no man of the power to appropriate the products of society: all that it does is to deprive him of the power to subjugate the labor of others by means of such appropriation.

It has been objected, that upon the abolition of private property all work will cease, and universal laziness will overtake us. According to this, bourgeois society ought long ago to have gone to the dogs through sheer idleness; for those of its members who work, acquire nothing, and those who acquire anything, do not work. The whole of this objection is but another expression of the tautology: that there can no longer be any wage-labor when there is no longer any capital.

All objections urged against the Communistic mode of producing and appropriating material products have, in the same way, been urged against the Communistic modes of producing and appropriating intellectual products. Just as, to the bourgeois, the disappearance of class property is the disappearance of production itself, so the disappearance of class culture is to him identical with the disappearance of all culture. That culture, the loss of which he laments, is, for the enormous majority, a mere training to act as a machine.

But don't wrangle with us so long as you apply, to our intended abolition of bourgeois property, the standard of your bourgeois notions of freedom, culture, law, etc. Your very ideas are but the outgrowth of the conditions of your bourgeois production and bourgeois property, just as your jurisprudence is but the will of your class made into a law for all, a will, whose essential character and direction are determined by the economic conditions of existence of your class.

The selfish misconception that induces you to transform into eternal laws of nature and of reason, the social forms springing from your present mode of production and form of property— historical relations that rise and disappear in the progress of production—this misconception you share with every ruling class that has preceded you. What you see clearly in the case of ancient property, what you admit in the case of feudal property, you are of course forbidden to admit in the case of your own bourgeois form of property.

Abolition of the family! Even the most radical flare up at this infamous proposal of the Communists. On what foundation is the present family, the bourgeois family, based? On capital, on private gain. In its completely developed form this family exists only among the bourgeoisie. But this state of things finds its complement in the practical absence of the family among the proletarians, and in public prostitution.

The bourgeois family will vanish as a matter of course when its complement vanishes, and both will vanish with the vanishing of capital. Do you charge us with wanting to stop the exploitation of children by their parents? To this crime we plead guilty.

But, you will say, we destroy the most hallowed of relations, when we replace home education by social. And your education! Is not that also social, and determined by the social conditions under which you educate, by the intervention, direct or indirect, of society by means of schools, etc.? The Communists have not invented the intervention of society in education; they do but seek to alter the character of that intervention, and to rescue education from the influence of the ruling class.

The bourgeois clap-trap about the family and education, about the hallowed co-relation of parent and child, becomes all the more disgusting, the more, by the action of Modern Industry, all family ties among the proletarians are torn asunder, and their children transformed into simple articles of commerce and instruments of labor.

But you Communists would introduce community of women, screams the whole bourgeoisie in chorus. The bourgeois sees in his wife a mere instrument of production. He hears that the instruments of production are to be exploited in common, and, naturally, can come to no other conclusion, than that the lot of being common to all will likewise fall to the women.

He has not even a suspicion that the real point aimed at is to do away with the status of women as mere instruments of production. For the rest, nothing is more ridiculous than the virtuous indignation of our bourgeois at the community of women which, they pretend, is to be openly and officially established by the Communists.

The Communists are further reproached with desiring to abolish countries and nationalities. The working men have no country. We cannot take from them what they have not got. Since the proletariat must first of all acquire political supremacy, must rise to be the leading class of the nation, must constitute itself the nation, it is, so far, itself national, though not in the bourgeois sense of the word. National differences, and antagonisms between peoples, are daily more and more vanishing.

In proportion as the exploitation of one individual by another is put an end to, the exploitation of one nation by another will also be put an end to. In proportion as the antagonism between

classes within the nation vanishes, the hostility of one nation to another will come to an end.

The charges against Communism made from a religious, a philosophical, and generally, from an ideological standpoint, are not deserving of serious examination.

Does it require deep intuition to comprehend that man's ideas, views, and conceptions, in one word, man's consciousness, changes with every change in the conditions of his material existence, in his social relations and in his social life?

What else does the history of ideas prove, than that intellectual production changes in character in proportion as material production is changed? The ruling ideas of each age have ever been the ideas of its ruling class.

When people speak of ideas that revolutionize society, they do but express the fact, that within the old society, the elements of a new one have been created, and that the dissolution of the old ideas keeps even pace with the dissolution of the old conditions of existence.

When the ancient world was in its last throes, the ancient religions were overcome by Christianity. When Christian ideas succumbed in the 18th century to rationalist ideas, feudal society fought its death-battle with the then revolutionary bourgeoisie. The ideas of religious liberty and freedom of conscience merely gave expression to the sway of free competition within the domain of knowledge.

"Undoubtedly," it will be said, "religious, moral, philosophical and juridical ideas have been modified in the course of historical development. But religion, morality, philosophy, political science, and law constantly survived this change."

"There are besides, eternal truths, such as Freedom, Justice, etc., that are common to all states of society. But Communism abolishes eternal truths, it abolishes all religion, and all morality, instead of constituting them on a new basis; it therefore acts in contradiction to all past historical experience."

What does this accusation reduce itself to? The history of all past society has consisted in the development of class antagonisms, antagonisms that assumed different forms at different epochs.

But whatever form they may have taken, one fact is common to all past ages, viz., the exploration of one part of society by the other. No wonder, then, that the social consciousness of past ages, despite all the multiplicity and variety it displays, moves within certain

common forms, or general ideas, which cannot completely vanish except with the total disappearance of class antagonisms.

The Communist revolution is the most radical rupture with traditional property-relations; no wonder that its development involves the most radical rupture with traditional ideas.

But let us have done with the bourgeois objections to Communism.

We have seen above, that the first step in the revolution by the working class is to raise the proletariat to the position of ruling class, to win the battle of democracy.

The proletariat will use its political supremacy, to wrest, by degrees, all capital from the bourgeoisie, to centralize all instruments of production in the hands of the State, i.e., of the proletariat organized as the ruling class; and to increase the total of productive forces as rapidly as possible.

Of course, in the beginning, this cannot be effected except by means of despotic inroads on the rights of property, and on the conditions of bourgeois production; by means of measures, therefore, which appear economically insufficient and untenable, but which, in the course of the movement, outstrip themselves, necessitate further inroads upon the old social order, and are unavoidable as a means of entirely revolutionizing the mode of production.

These measures will of course be different in different countries.

Nevertheless in the most advanced countries the following will be pretty generally applicable:

1. Abolition of property in land and application of all rents of land to public purposes.

2. A heavy progressive or graduated income tax.

3. Abolition of all right of inheritance.

4. Confiscation of the property of all emigrants and rebels.

5. Centralization of credit in the hands of the State, by means of a national bank with State capital and an exclusive monopoly.

6. Centralization of the means of communication and transport in the hands of the State.

7. Extension of factories and instruments of production owned by the State; the bringing into cultivation of waste lands, and the improvement of the soil generally in accordance with a common plan.

8. Equal liability of all to labor. Establishment of industrial armies, especially for agriculture.

9. Combination of agriculture with manufacturing industries; gradual abolition of the distinction between town and country, by a more equable distribution of population over the country.

10. Free education for all children in public schools. Abolition of children's factory labor in its present form. Combination of education with industrial production, etc., etc.

When, in the course of development, class distinctions have disappeared, and all production has been concentrated in the hands of a vast association of the whole nation, the public power will lose its political character. Political power, properly so called, is merely the organized power of one class for oppressing another. If the proletariat during its contest with the bourgeoisie is compelled, by the force of circumstances, to organize itself as a class, if, by means of a revolution, it makes itself the ruling class, and, as such, sweeps away by force the old conditions of production, then it will, along with these conditions, have swept away the conditions for the existence of class antagonisms, and of classes generally, and will thereby have abolished its own supremacy as a class.

In place of the old bourgeois society, with its classes and class antagonisms, we shall have an association, in which the free development of each is the condition for the free development of all.

(A section on Socialist and Communist literature is here omitted.)

Conservative or Bourgeois Socialism

A part of the bourgeoisie is desirous of redressing social grievances, in order to secure the continued existence of bourgeois society.

To this section belong economists, philanthropists, humanitarians, improvers of the condition of the work class, organizers of charity, members of societies for the prevention of cruelty to animals, temperance fanatics, hole and corner reformers of every imaginable kind. This form of Socialism has, moreover, been worked out into complete systems.

We may cite Proudhon's "Philosophie de la Misère" as an example of this form. The socialistic bourgeois want all the advantages of modern social conditions without the struggles and dangers necessarily resulting therefrom. They desire the existing state of society minus its revolutionary and disintegrating elements. They wish for a bourgeoisie without a proletariat. The

bourgeoisie naturally conceives the world in which it is supreme to be the best.

A second and more practical, but less systematic, form of this socialism sought to depreciate every revolutionary movement in the eyes of the working class, by showing that no mere political reform, but only a change in the material conditions of existence, in economical relations, could be of any advantage to them. By changes in the material conditions of existence, this form of Socialism, however, by no means understands abolition of the bourgeois relations of production, an abolition that can be effected only by a revolution.

Critical-Utopian Socialism and Communism

We do not here refer to that literature which, in every great modern revolution, has always given voice to the demands of the proletariat: such as the writings of Babeuf and others.

The Socialist and Communist systems properly so-called, those of St. Simon, Fourier, Owen and others, spring into existence in the early undeveloped period, described above, of the struggle between proletariat and bourgeoisie.

In the formation of their plans they are conscious of caring chiefly for the interests of the working-class, as being the most suffering class. Only from the point of view of being the most suffering class does the proletariat exist for them.

The undeveloped state of the class struggle, as well as their own surroundings, causes Socialists of this kind to consider themselves far superior to all class antagonisms. They want to improve the condition of every member of society, even that of the most favored. Hence, they habitually appeal to society at large, without distinction of class; nay, by preference, to the ruling class. For how can people, when once they understand their system, fail to see in it the best possible plan of the best possible state of society?

Hence, they reject all political, and especially all revolutionary action; they wish to attain their ends by peaceful means, and endeavor, by small experiments, necessarily doomed to failure, and by the force of example, to pave the way for the new social Gospel.

These proposals, therefore, are of a purely Utopian character. The significance of Critical-Utopian Socialism and Communism

bears an inverse relation to historical development. In proportion as the modern class struggle develops and takes definite shape, this fantastic standing apart from the contest, these fantastic attacks on it lose all practical value and all theoretical justification. Therefore, although the originators of these systems were, in many respects, revolutionary, their disciples have, in every case, formed mere reactionary sects. They hold fast by the original views of their masters, in opposition to the progressive historical development of the proletariat. They, therefore, endeavor, and that consistently, to deaden the class struggle and to reconcile the class antagonisms.

They, therefore, violently oppose all political action on the part of the working class; such action, according to them, can only result from blind unbelief in the new Gospel.

The Owenites in England, and the Fourierists in France, respectively, oppose the Chartists and the "Reformistes."

Position of the Communists in Relation to the Various Existing Opposition Parties

The Communists fight for the attainment of the immediate aims, for the enforcement of the momentary interests of the working class; but in the movement of the present, they also represent and take care of the future of that movement.

But they never cease, for a single instant, to instill into the working class the clearest possible recognition of the hostile antagonism between bourgeoisie and proletariat.

The Communists turn their attention chiefly to Germany, because that country is on the eve of a bourgeois revolution, that is bound to be carried out under more advanced conditions of European civilization, and with a more developed proletariat, than that of England was in the seventeenth, and of France in the eighteenth century, and because the bourgeois revolution in Germany will be but the prelude to an immediately following proletarian revolution.

In short, the Communists everywhere support every revolutionary movement against the existing social and political order of things.

In all these movements they bring to the front, as the leading question in each, the property question, no matter what its degree of development at the time.

Finally, they labor everywhere for the union and agreement of the democratic parties of all countries.

The Communists disdain to conceal their views and aims. They openly declare that their ends can be attained only by the forcible overthrow of all existing social conditions. Let the ruling classes tremble at a Communistic revolution. The proletarians have nothing to lose but their chains. They have a world to win.

Working men of all countries, unite!

APPENDIX II

THE JEWISH PROBLEM: THE CAUSE OF ANTI-SEMITISM

While Soviet Russia is building up a classless society more free from race prejudice than any country in the world, we have been witnessing such medieval and savage persecution of the Jews under Hitler's movement of National Socialism in Germany, and such a recrudescence of anti-semitism in other lands that it raises the whole question as to why the Jews are persecuted and what can be done to bring about better relations.

The most pronounced manifestation of this hostility at the moment is, of course, found in Nazi propaganda, where they make the long-persecuted Jew the convenient scapegoat for many of the woes of the German people. Their boasted Aryan and Teutonic superiority seems to be a defense reaction from an inferiority complex. It is strange if these superior Nordic and Aryan German people, constituting over ninety-nine per cent of the population, could not successfully compete with the one per cent who are Jews. This small fraction had produced, out of all proportion to its numbers, many of the best minds and most brilliant leaders of Germany for more than two centuries, from men like the great philosopher, Moses Mendelssohn, in the eighteenth century, to Einstein, of our own day.

While I was in Germany recently I learned of the distinguished philanthropists, Maurice Oppenheim and his wife, who were donors of buildings to Frankfort University, and who, at the climax of a series of insults, indignities and persecutions, went quietly away and committed suicide at the age of eighty-four. At the same time I learned of a boy of twelve whose parents are seeking to prevent his committing suicide. One of his parents is Jewish and the boy is so spat upon and insulted by other children that he sees no hope in life in that land.

I found textbooks which are instilling hatred of the Jews into the hearts of the children of Germany. I heard Josef Goebbels speak with such flaming hatred of the Jew as "the father of lies"

that it might have led logically to pogroms. The Nazis boldly declare their policy of "the humane extermination of the Jews." National Socialists can no more deny or defend such prejudice and barbarities than can Americans their treatment of the Negro.

Persecution of the Jews was, of course, common in ancient and medieval Europe from the time of the destruction of Jerusalem till they were scattered as a homeless people in the ghettos of Europe and subjected to pogroms and massacres. But what is the cause of Jewish prejudice and persecution?

Some sixteen million Jews [1] scattered around the world today are descended from the best racial stock of the Southern Kingdom of Judea, centering in Jerusalem. From the Babylonian Captivity in the sixth century B.C., and more completely from the final destruction of Jerusalem in 70 A.D., scattered Israel of the dispersion has been a people without a homeland. Like every other race the Jews are a product of their environment. They are the resultant of a complex of forces which includes a hardy racial stock, the influence of the highest ancient religion of ethical monotheism, coupled with the reaction of centuries of persecution. As an educated people they are nearly two millenniums older than the European races. In the various countries during the Middle Ages they were among the few who could read, write and keep accounts. In spite of their native ability and experience, prejudice and persecution excluded them from most professions and forced them to concentrate upon certain lucrative but unpopular callings, such as money lending, tax collecting, and finance. They were excluded from the trades by the guilds, which were religious bodies. The Church which forbade usury to Christians did not prevent the Jews from taking interest and amassing fortunes. They grew rich as did the later Puritans.

Five centuries of bitter persecution which robbed them, impoverished them and hounded them over Europe from country to country, began with the first Crusade in the eleventh century and continued until after the Spanish Inquisition. Volumes have been filled with the almost unbelievable record of the persecution of this

---

[1] Of the 14,900,000 Jews in the world in 1914, some two-thirds were in Eastern and Southeastern Europe, including 7,000,000 in Russia. Of the remaining third, two-thirds or about 3,000,000 were in the United States, with 600,000 in Germany and some 500,000 in the British Empire. The 16,000,000 Jews in the world's population of some 2,000,000,000 today make up only one in 125 of the whole population.

unfortunate people. Their fierce struggle for existence under continued persecution, that would have extinguished a less hardy race, has made them *different*, a peculiar people. They have refused to be assimilated to pagan and Gentile cultures, but have persistently preserved their own. Only the American Negroes, the Armenians and the untouchable outcastes of India have been so persecuted.

Most writers are agreed that there are three principal sources or elements of Jewish prejudice today: the religious, the economic and the combined political and racial.[1] During the Middle Ages the principal source of anti-semitism was in the intolerance and bigotry of the medieval Church, often led by the clergy. After the sixteenth century the economic element became stronger. The Jew became the middleman, between the noble and the peasant. Kings and nobles in order to secure money for the Crusades turned to the Jew, first to borrow his money and then in jealousy to strip and banish him. Yet the towns that received the Jew, like London, Hamburg and Bremen, prospered, and the countries that expelled him, like Spain, often declined. Not a citizen, with many duties but few rights, the Jew was driven through his very insecurity to quick profits and to aggressive competition, but despite this fierce struggle he survived. It sharpened his wits but made him unpopular. A leading Jew in Russia recently told the writer that to hope to enter the university in Czarist days he had to be the best boy in the class. Working night and day developed the faculties of this boy. The same thing happened to his race under persecution.

When the Polish noblemen were given the privileged monopoly of alcohol in 1496, they farmed it out to the Jew. This enriched the Jew but led finally to the Polish massacres of 1648. The same fate awaited him in other countries. The monopoly of alcohol and bootlegged liquor, the exploiting of the backward peasantry in Eastern Europe, later profiteering and high finance, the monopolistic privileges resulting from great wealth, the control of the press, the theatre, the moving picture industry and other amusements, all in turn have made the Jew wealthy but unpopular.

To early religious prejudice and economic jealousy were added the political and racial antagonisms of the nineteenth century. Men first exclude the Jew, and then find him foreign or hostile to them. It was the Exile that produced the Jew's zeal for the Law, and

---

[1] For the best account that has been written for Gentiles see James W. Parkes' *The Jew and His Neighbor,* Student Movement Press, 58 Bloomsbury St., London.

persecution which developed the strong qualities which have made him survive. But all that makes the Jews a peculiar people tends to isolate them.

Jews had been expelled from England as early as 1290. The possibilities of complete expulsion from country after country in Central Europe lay always before the Hebrew people until the eighteenth century, and in Russia until the World War. Even Poland, which had once been their refuge, became one of their most bitter persecutors. The results of this persecution and prejudice have lingered long and abide to this day in many quarters. Not until 1870 was every position, except that of sovereign, open to the Jews, even in liberal England. In Germany they were excluded from the Cabinet until 1919.[1]

The liberal and democratic movements of the modern world have given the Jew the measure of freedom which he now enjoys. From the French Revolution and its demand for equality, to the Russian Revolution and its destruction of privilege, the Jew has won partial emancipation. From the democratic, liberal and radical movements of the nineteenth century, with the rise first of the middle classes and finally of the masses, the Jew has been released from the bondage and oppression of the medieval world.

Jewish prejudice remains as a blot upon the modern world. Centuries of struggle and suffering have left the Jew what he is today. An unfriendly environment often brings out his worst qualities. All ancient governments were to him dictatorships. He was excluded from churches and guilds, by state and society. The Russian Pale and the narrow ghetto of the European slums have sometimes left a "ghetto of ideas," or a narrow ghetto of character.

The training and inheritance of the Jew has given him the highest average intelligence of any race in the world. The *British Journal of Psychology* made an investigation of the intelligence of children in the public schools in England in 1927 and found that "Jewish children were conspicuously superior to all other classes." An investigation conducted by Columbia University during the follow-

---

[1] The partial emancipation of the Jews in England in 1655 was followed by complete emancipation in 1753 but again withdrawn. Parliamentary rights were accorded in 1858 and complete liberty in 1870. Emancipation followed in France in 1791; in Holland, 1796; in Hamburg and Bremen, 1811; in Prussia, 1848; in Spain, 1858; in Italy, 1859; in Switzerland, 1866; in the German Empire, 1870; in Soviet Russia, 1917; in Poland, 1919. See Israel Cohen, *Jewish Life in Modern Times*, p. 117, quoted from *The Jew and His Neighbor*, p. 126.

ing year led to a similar conclusion. When Professor Terman selected the one thousand most gifted boys and girls from the public schools of California he found twice as many Jewish children, in proportion to their numbers, as any others. In financial ability the Jew habitually excels. His very superiority and even conceit are largely the defense mechanism developed by a long-continued inferiority complex.

Broadly the civilization of the modern world is derived chiefly from the two sources of Hellenism and Hebraism. From the one we inherit our richest culture, from the other our deepest character. Nothing can ever repay our debt to Greece or Judea.

While the Jewish people differ almost as widely as Gentiles, and while we admit the danger of oversimplification, the total situation has produced broadly two types of Jews. Individuals of one type are the finest people in the world. We are reminded of Amos or Isaiah by some of them. Many of the outstanding leaders of the world today are numbered among them.

But there is another type of modern Jew who is aggressive, materialistic, offensive and vulgar. One is tempted to flee far from such people whether they are Jews or Gentiles. And that is just what many people do. One winsome young rabbi informs me that if he is on a vacation for pleasure he tries to avoid this type of his own people which he recognizes as far from uncommon. As a result he often turns to Gentiles for companionship.

The problem of relationships between Jews and Gentiles is by no means simple or one-sided. And Jewish prejudice remains to a humiliating degree among the majority of Gentiles in both Europe and America. It presents a problem both to the Jew and to the Gentile. The latter is probably chiefly to blame if we take a long look at the past over centuries of persecution. But it will take the best efforts of both races working in growing understanding and cooperation if we are to solve the problem.

On the one hand the Jew himself must make his choice between assimilation and Jewish nationalism. If he chooses the former, intermarriage frequently results and his race as a distinct entity tends to be absorbed and lost. If he chooses the latter he retains his own competing culture which makes him more or less an alien, not only unconventional and non-conformist, but sometimes seemingly unpatriotic, disloyal or hostile. In Soviet Russia today where the Jew is chiefly choosing assimilation, about twenty per cent of the marriages are already mixed, and it looks there as if the Jew

might in time be absorbed. The race that gave ethical monotheism to the world is today producing the largest proportion of dogmatic atheists in connection with Communism. In ethical responsibility and social passion, on an average the Jew is in advance of the Gentile, and the synagogue of the church, but not in the field of religion.

The Gentile has also to face his side of the problem. For centuries he has persecuted the Jews. Whatever his qualities, he, largely, has made the Jew what he is. One of the most humiliating of his failings, one of the most obvious defects of the Gentile, is his race prejudice. Individually, each must strive to stamp out the last remnants of this poison as he would the lingering after-effects of some dread disease. No man is truly noble, and no man is fully human who suffers from the curse and blight of race prejudice. It is a despicable and degrading thing. There are certain broad aspects of anti-semitism as a social problem in which both communities must cooperate in fighting. Here also one must frankly realize that there are two sides to the problem.

The persecution of the Jews in Germany has accentuated anti-semitic prejudice in some quarters in Europe and America, and has made the whole problem of Jewish racial prejudice more acute. At the same time the suffering of this long-persecuted race has powerfully appealed to the liberal and better elements of our population. This time of German persecution as a medieval reversion, coinciding with the advance of Soviet Russia toward a classless society which is rising above race prejudice, furnishes an occasion when justice for the Jews may become a moral cause based upon principle similar to the abolition of slavery, the prevention of war, or any other major reform. It is a call to all who feel deeply the solidarity of one common humanity to rid themselves forever of this blight, this disease of racial prejudice and persecution, and to unite in every feasible and right use of means for the relief of this people.

We must recognize that the Hitler movement is fomenting anti-semitism all over the world. This is the third attempt to establish such a movement in America. The first was by the vicious campaign of falsehood carried on by Henry Ford's *Dearborn Independent* with its wild tales of ritual murders, of a Great Conspiracy of Jewish financiers for the conquest of the world, and the use of the forgeries of the *Protocols of the Wise Men of Zion* by the renegade Russian *agent provocateur* Sergei Nilus. It is difficult

to realize the credulity and superstition of some of our people as when Representative McFadden of Pennsylvania can accuse both Presidents Hoover and Roosevelt of being tools of such a conspiracy in America.

The second wave of anti-semitism came with the formation of the *Ku Klux Klan* against Negroes, Catholics and Jews. Weakened by graft and corruption within, and condemned by public opinion, the movement came to an end with a period of national prosperity. It is in hard times, as at present in Germany, that men seek some scapegoat and release from their own frustration and inferiority complex.

The present depression and the entrance of scores of Nazi agents for propaganda into the United States[1] furnish the occasion of a third movement for anti-semitism in America. The Industrial Defence Association in New England, the Khaki Shirts of America, and the Silver Shirts are among the organizations now seeking to foment anti-Jewish hatred and race prejudice. It is not the Jews only who are threatened by such base movements; it is our common humanity.

The organizers of at least one of the above organizations get half the enrolment fee for each new member. It is a lucrative occupation as in the case of the former *Ku Klux Klan*. They are even now widely circulating the long-discredited *Protocols of the Wise Men of Zion* in America. This forgery was produced by Nilus under the auspices of the Russian Black Hundreds which sought to save the tottering throne of the Czar by diverting public attention by Jewish pogroms. The *Protocols* were written by this former monk Nilus to depict a conspiracy by Jews against the governments of the world, and thousands of Jews were murdered in Czarist Russia on the basis of these forgeries. President Theodore Roosevelt attempted to deliver a protest petition against these to the Czar which the latter refused to receive.

Later, ex-President William Howard Taft after an exhaustive study showed the documents to be fraudulent and forged. Two members of the Black Hundred induced Henry Ford to sponsor their publication in America. When Mr. Ford discovered that he had been duped by this scurrilous forgery he discontinued the *Dearborn Independent*.

---

[1] See John Smertenko, "Hitlerism Comes to America," *Harpers*, November, 1933.

Today the Nazis of Germany and the above-mentioned organizations are again trying to prey upon the ignorance, the credulity and the superstition of the public by their vicious propaganda of racial hatred. The false stories which are even now being circulated almost remind one of the medieval superstition which circulated charges against Jews for a conspiracy with the lepers of the world, for poisoning the wells and causing the Black Death. The present methods of Hitler, his agents and the American organizers of anti-semitism are centuries old in laying the blame for the ills of humanity upon this long-suffering vicarious people. Such methods make no appeal in an intelligent country like Great Britain nor in Soviet Russia where they are endeavoring to stamp out the last remnants of the poisonous and cancerous growth of race hatred.

INDEX

309